"Here's to the future."

They downed the whiskey at the same time and she'd bent to reach for the water when a mouse darted across the coffee table, brushing against her hand in the journey from one end to the other. It bounded off the edge like it had a tiny parachute on its back, scampered across her bare foot, and did a couple of circles around the Christmas tree until it got its bearing and dashed off toward the kitchen.

Carlene tried to walk on air but she had no wings. She jumped up on the coffee table with both feet and all four legs went out from under it. She was falling forward, hoping she didn't break a bone, when suddenly strong arms were around her, and her feet were dangling several inches off the floor.

All those old feelings she thought she'd buried swirled to the surface. Jace's heavy eyelashes fluttered down to rest on his cheekbones and her tongue darted out to moisten her lips. The kiss started out soft and tender, barely grazing her mouth; then it deepened into more, sending waves of desire through her body. Then just as quickly as it started, it was over and he set her on the floor.

High Praise for Carolyn Brown

"Brown always gives the reader emotion, eternal love, and all the excitement you can handle."

—Fresh Fiction

TOUGHEST COWBOY IN TEXAS

"One of the best feel-good reads I've had the pleasure of reading yet this year! It tugged on your heartstrings and had you cheering for true love."

—Once Upon an Alpha

"Top Pick! A beautiful second-chance love story that has humor, HOT cowboys, and an amazing HEA."

—Harlequin Junkie

"Terrific...an emotional star-crossed-lovers tale with tangible depths and an attitude that's relatable to real life."

—RT Book Reviews

"The *Toughest Cowboy in Texas* is a delightful, fast-paced novel full of dynamic and lively characters and, more important, white-hot romance!"

—Romance Reviews Today

WICKED COWBOY CHARM

"A nice blend of warmth, down-home goodness, humor, and romance. Lively, flirty banter and genuine, down-to-earth characters are the highlights of this engaging story...The flirty banter between Deke and Josie is amusing and heart-warming, and the chemistry between them sizzles."

—*RT Book Reviews*

MERRY COWBOY CHRISTMAS

"Top Pick! Carolyn Brown writes about everyday things that happen to all of us and she does it with panache, class, empathy, and humor. 4½ stars."

—*Night Owl Reviews*

"A captivating cast of characters fills the pages of this sweet and funny novel."

—*Publishers Weekly*

"Brown's modern storytelling and fun-filled plot will engage readers and wrap them up in this sweet, Southern holiday romance."

—*RT Book Reviews*

HOT COWBOY NIGHTS

"Humorous storytelling, snappy dialogue, and colorful characters are the highlights of this story."

—*RT Book Reviews*

"Carolyn Brown manages to create a romance that's steamy, light, and fun, while also a relationship with substance and heart...a character-driven delight for romance fans."

—*Fresh Fiction*

WILD COWBOY WAYS

"With an irresistibly charismatic cowboy at the center of this story, Brown's latest is a sexy, fun read...The genuine, electric chemistry between Allie and Blake jumps off the page."

—*RT Book Reviews*

"A breathtaking romance filled with soul-sizzling passion and a heart-stealing plot. A five-star hit!"

—*Romancing the Book*

"Heartwarming and funny...*Wild Cowboy Ways* will pull you in and won't let you go until the end. I loved this book and recommend it to everyone. 5 stars."

—*Book Junkiez*

"A perfect read to just curl up with. The book is light, sweet, and just the right amount of humor and emotions to keep you reading along. Carolyn Brown will get you falling in love with the characters before you can blink...It made me feel like I was watching a classic Hallmark movie. *swoon*"

—*Once Upon an Alpha*

Also by Carolyn Brown

The Happy, Texas series

Long, Tall Cowboy Christmas
Toughest Cowboy in Texas

The Lucky Penny Ranch series

Wild Cowboy Ways
Hot Cowboy Nights
Merry Cowboy Christmas
Wicked Cowboy Charm

Luckiest Cowboy of All

A Happy, Texas Novel

Carolyn Brown

FOREVER

New York   Boston

Copyright © 2018 by Carolyn Brown
Preview of *Cowboy Bold* copyright © 2018 by Carolyn Brown
Hometown Cowboy copyright © 2017 by Sara Richardson
Compilation copyright © 2018 by Hachette Book Group, Inc.
Cover design by Elizabeth Stokes
Cover copyright © 2018 by Hachette Book Group, Inc.

Forever
Hachette Book Group
1290 Avenue of the Americas, New York, NY 10104
forever-romance.com
twitter.com/foreverromance

First Edition: January 2018

Forever is an imprint of Grand Central Publishing. The Forever name and logo are trademarks of Hachette Book Group, Inc.

The publisher is not responsible for websites (or their content) that are not owned by the publisher.

The Hachette Speakers Bureau provides a wide range of authors for speaking events. To find out more, go to www.hachettespeakersbureau.com or call (866) 376-6591.

ISBNs: 978-1-4555-9750-5 (mass market), 978-1-4555-9749-9 (ebook)

Printed in the United States of America

OPM

10 9 8 7 6 5 4 3 2 1

ATTENTION CORPORATIONS AND ORGANIZATIONS:

Most Hachette Book Group books are available at quantity discounts with bulk purchase for educational, business, or sales promotional use. For information, please call or write:

Special Markets Department, Hachette Book Group
1290 Avenue of the Americas, New York, NY 10104
Telephone: 1-800-222-6747 Fax: 1-800-477-5925

*Dedicated to my awesome team
at Forever...
My editor, Leah Hultenschmidt, for all the
fantastic support; Melanie Gold for everything in
the managing editorial department; Elizabeth
Stokes, who keeps turning out amazing covers;
Estelle Hallick for all her work in publicity; Jodi
Rosoff and Danielle Egnozzi for all the marketing
support; and Bob Levine, Raylan Davis, and Gina
Wynn in the sales department, who do such a
wonderful job making sure readers can find my
books in so many stores. You are all totally
fantabulous.*

Dear Reader,

It hardly seems possible that the Happy, Texas series is coming to an end with *Luckiest Cowboy of All*. Seems like only yesterday that we were anxiously awaiting the launch of the debut book, *Toughest Cowboy in Texas*. And then it was on the shelves and everyone wanted to know if Kasey and Jace were going to get their stories told. Thank all of you for that and for your support through the whole series.

But all good things must come to an end, or so I'm told, and this is the last of the Dawson cowboys for now. Who knows about later? They could pop up in a future book because, after all, Texas ranchers do know each other. It's not easy for me to tell characters who've been like family to me for over a year goodbye. Shhh...don't tell anyone, but they even wake me up at night to talk to me about the next scenes in the story. But the time has come to move on.

Before we do, I would like to say thank you to a few people. A book begins as an idea and goes through a process not unlike refining gold. Words cannot begin to thank my editor, Leah Hultenschmidt, who helps me take something that looks like common rocks and turn it into gold. She brings out a side of my writing that I had no idea was even there, and I appreciate her so much for it! Also to my whole Forever team—I'm grateful for each and every one of you!

I would also like to thank my agent, Erin Niumata, and Folio Literary Management. Erin and I have been working together so long that we feel like family. We joke that we've been together longer than some Hollywood marriages.

And a big hug to Mr. B. I couldn't make it through my hectic schedule without his support. He's always ready to drive me wherever I need to go so that I can sit in the passenger seat and take notes or eat takeout three nights in a row so I can meet a deadline. He's a keeper for sure.

And a big thank-you to Sara Richardson for permitting us to give you her book, *Hometown Cowboy*, as a double treat with Jace and Carlene's story. Two cowboys for the price of one—you can't beat a deal like that.

Although one door closes as we say good-bye to the Dawsons, another one opens as we say hello to the Maguires! Cade Maguire kicks off the Longhorn Canyon Ranch series in May with *Cowboy Bold*...so keep your cowboy hats right handy!

Happy reading to you all. Enjoy Jace and Carlene's story as they work hard to overcome the past and dive right into the present.

Until next time,
Carolyn Brown

Contents

Luckiest Cowboy of All

Carolyn Brown

Chapter One

Sometimes it's too late to do what you should've done years ago. Aunt Rosalie had said that so many times that it should have been in a book of famous quotes.

"I get the message loud and clear," Carlene whispered around a lump the size of an orange in her throat.

"You okay, Mama?" Her daughter, Tilly, ran from the porch out to the minivan. "Here, let me take that box. I can carry it inside."

Carlene shifted the box of stuffed toys into Tilly's hands and picked up a heavier one to carry inside the little two-bedroom frame house. With its peeling paint and hanging rain gutters, it looked like the last wilted rose of summer right now, but come spring she'd put a coat of fresh white paint on it, maybe plant some bright-colored flowers around the porch, and it would look better then.

As she headed from her bright red minivan to the porch, a bitter cold north wind whipped her long blond hair into her face, reminding her that spring was a long way off. Tilly opened the door for her and then closed it behind her.

"I made you a cup of tea."

"Thanks, baby girl." Carlene smiled. "Did you make one for yourself?"

"I made me some hot chocolate," Tilly said. "I liked our house in Florida better than this one."

"Why?" Carlene pulled a wooden rocking chair closer to the coffee table and picked up the mug of steaming chamomile tea. It was too hot to drink, but it warmed her hands. Tomorrow, when she and Tilly made a grocery store run to Amarillo, she'd have to remember to buy gloves for both of them.

"This place smells funny," Tilly said.

"We'll light some candles this afternoon and air it out on the first day we get some nice weather. When we're settled, we'll start giving it a face-lift. You'll be surprised what new paint and a little fixin' up will do."

"And we'll get rid of that dead Christmas tree." Tilly glanced at the brown pine tree in the corner. "That's disgusting."

Carlene's eyes went to the sad tree in the corner of the living room. Aunt Rosalie loved her live tree and always put it up the day after Thanksgiving, so by now it had been there almost six weeks. There was no telling how long it had been without water—no wonder it was brown and brittle.

"Of course," Carlene said. "If you want, you could start to unpack what's in your room and I'll get those last three boxes out of the van while my tea cools."

"Okay." Tilly carried her cup of hot chocolate to the bedroom.

With five moves in her eight years, Tilly was a pro at moving. Carlene had no doubt she was back there in her room organizing her stuffed animals and books everywhere there was a flat surface. But Tilly was in the third grade and it was time for them both to put down roots. So when Aunt Rosalie passed away and Carlene inherited the house and then immediately got a job offer to teach, she saw it as a sign that could not be ignored and came back to the town that she should never have left.

Carlene leaned her head back on the rocking chair. It had been ten years since she'd been in the house. In those days Aunt Rosalie bragged that she'd never met a speck of dust she couldn't conquer. There were now cobwebs in the corners and dust on everything. It would take days, possibly weeks, to get the house whipped into shape.

"That's tomorrow's work. Today's is getting Aunt Rosalie's stuff sorted through to make room for ours. Happy New Year to us." She raised her cup of tea and then set it on the table.

Carlene drew her jacket closer around her chest and headed back out for the rest of the boxes. "Thank you, Aunt Rosalie, for leaving me everything in your will. At least I have a place to live and don't have to pay rent."

As she stepped off the porch, she heard tires on the gravel road. Since this house was the only one on a short dead-end road, she was pretty sure the visitor would be pulling into her driveway any second. She tucked her hair behind her ears and shivered.

Shading her eyes against the bright winter sun, she watched a big black crew cab truck come to a stop right beside her minivan. Cowboy boots were the first thing that appeared when the door opened and then a very familiar figure followed.

Jace Dawson tipped back his hat and waved. In a few long strides he was close enough that she caught a whiff of Stetson aftershave—a scent that still created a stir in her hormones every time she smelled it.

Happy, Texas, had a population of less than seven hundred, so it was a given that she'd run into Jace someday, probably sooner rather than later, but the first day she was there, before she could even get unpacked, meant that the gossip vines had not died in the past decade.

"Carlene, I heard you were coming back to town. Here, let me help you get those into the house." He picked up all three of the remaining boxes and headed off toward the porch. "So you're going to be the new fifth-grade teacher, Mama tells me."

"That's right."

He filled out those Wranglers even better than he had in high school and had maybe even grown another inch or two.

"I'm real sorry about Miz Rosalie. She was a pillar in this town and the church. It's hard to believe that she's gone," he said.

"Thank you. It came as a shock to us too." She was amazed that her voice sounded normal, considering the way her pulse had shot up at the sight of him.

"Been a long time," he said. "Where you been all these years?"

She opened the door for him and he set the boxes in the middle of the living room floor. "Here and there. Moved around a lot. California, then Georgia and Oklahoma, back to Florida and then here."

"You plannin' on livin' here? Mind if I sit down?"

"When did we get to be so formal? Of course you can sit." She kicked off her shoes, padded barefoot across the cold hardwood floor, and sat on the sofa with her knees drawn up to her chin and her arms wrapped around them.

Avoiding the sofa, Jace sat on a wooden rocking chair.

He removed his black cowboy hat and laid it on the coffee table between him and Carlene, then raked his fingers through his dark brown hair. Carlene remembered that gesture well. Along with tapping his foot, it was what he did when he was nervous. She checked and sure enough, his cowboy boot was doing double time on the floor.

"So you went to college?" he asked. "Where?"

"California." She could hear Tilly humming in her room and hoped she stayed there until he was gone.

"And you're comin' from Florida, right?"

"That's right," she said. "Can I get you something to drink? I've got root beer and apple juice. Haven't been to the store."

"No, I'm good." His hand went toward his hair again. "I missed you when you left."

"We were just kids, right out of high school, Jace." She let her eyes drift from his chin upward, determined not to look at his eyes, but she failed.

His gray eyes locked with hers across the room and he took a deep breath. "You promised you'd stay in touch. We dated our whole senior year. What happened?"

"Life happened. Time and distance takes its toll."

Tilly had stopped humming and was talking to her stuffed toys, asking them if they liked the new house. Then her voice dropped to a whisper and Carlene couldn't hear her anymore.

"Come on, Carlene. Give me a little more than that. We were in love. You were going to text or call every night, and then you were gone and I never heard from you again," Jace said.

"Were we in love, Jace? Or were we just hormonal teenagers?"

"I thought we were in love," he said.

She shrugged. The lump in her throat kept her from answering.

"Okay, then." He inhaled and let it out slowly. "Look, I don't know how to tell you this...I'm real sorry to have to say it, but I bought this place from Rosalie last year. She was planning to move into a nursing home and said she needed the money." He removed his hat and laid it on the coffee table.

"No!" Carlene sank down onto the other end of the sofa and felt the color drain from her face. "She didn't...she wouldn't...she said..."

"I can bring the deed to show you. You goin' to be all right? I'm so sorry about this misunderstanding." His eyes were filled with true remorse.

"Sell it back to me." Carlene met his eyes across the short distance separating them. "I have enough savings for a down payment, and we can get a loan at the bank for the rest."

Jace inhaled deeply and let it out very slowly. "You can see for yourself, it's not real fit for livin'. Even so, I'd sell it to you and help remodel if I could, but it's all been deeded over to the rodeo association." Another deep breath. "Demolition is scheduled for February fifteenth. The contractors are starting the new buildings right after that."

"Dammit!" Carlene stretched her legs out, dropped her head into her hands, and covered her eyes. Surely this was a mistake. Aunt Rosalie would have told her if she'd sold the house. The lawyer who handled her affairs didn't say a word about it when he called to tell them that she'd passed away.

Jace had always had one of those faces that couldn't hide what he was thinking and it was plain that he was not lying to her. Still, surely to God if Aunt Rosalie had sold the property, she would have told Carlene. They talked every single Sunday evening from eight to eight-thirty and she always said that her greatest wish was to die in the same house where she'd been born. That her roots were in the place and it would make her life come full circle.

"The papers and the letter the lawyer sent are in that box. I'm going to dig them out right now. She must've gotten senile at ninety-five because she would've told me," Carlene whispered, still finding it hard to believe.

She left the sofa and ripped the tape from the top of the box marked IMPORTANT PAPERS. She pulled a big brown accordion file from the box and flipped through the tabs until she found the one she wanted. Removing a manila envelope from it, she shook out the letter from the lawyer saying that she'd inherited Rosalie's personal belongings and had even sent a key to the house so she could "get what she wanted out of it."

"I have the deed, the papers that the rodeo folks signed, and everything in a folder at home. I'll be glad to bring them over to you," Jace said.

"See, here's her handwritten will, dated two years ago, giving me everything that she owns." Carlene held it up.

"I bought the place a year ago," Jace said. "And I turned it over to the rodeo the next day with the understanding that we couldn't start to build until Rosalie had passed or she went to a nursing home."

She turned up the envelope and shook it but nothing else fell out. She opened it wide and for the first time saw another little folded piece of paper at the bottom. Another fierce shake didn't bring it out, so she ripped the side away and carefully removed the letter. With dread in her heart, she read it out loud:

My dear Carlene,

The lawyer says I don't need to redo my will. It does leave all my possessions to you, but I should tell you that I've sold the house to Jace Dawson. Do what you want with the money. I just didn't want you to be burdened with selling this place. It needs lots of work and should be torn down, but I was born here and it's my wish to die here. My memories are all tied up in this place. Jace donated the land to the rodeo association. That's a good thing and it makes me happy.

Love, Aunt Rosalie

"Well, now what?" She laid the letter aside and threw her hands up in defeat.

"Now, you can live here until the wreckers come if you want. There's not much rental property in town that's fit for you to live in but there are a couple of places for sale if you're plannin' to stay."

"I'd thought this would be my last move," she said. "I'm ready to put down roots and I always liked this small town."

"We'll find you a place, I promise." He reached out as if to touch her but dropped his hand in his lap. "You've got my word on it. I should be going unless you've got more boxes to carry in."

"No, that's all of them. My house and land are going to be part of the rodeo grounds. I can't wrap my mind around that." She had decided to move to Happy so that Tilly could grow up in Aunt Rosalie's house.

"Upside is that it gets real noisy around this area when there's a rodeo or bull riding going on," he said.

"You still ride?"

"Sometimes. Bulls. But saddle broncs are my specialty. I never was any good at bareback broncs," he answered.

"Dammit, Jace."

"What?"

"Nothing."

"Hey, I remember that look in those pretty brown eyes and you're mad as a wet hen after a wild Texas tornado," he said. "Spit it out."

"I'm mad about this house," she said through clenched teeth. It wasn't a lie. She was furious that she couldn't even buy it back from Jace. Understanding the whys and wherefores didn't make it a bit easier to accept. "I thought the place was mine. I was already figuring out ways to remodel it."

"Honey, it'd take more than paint and new curtains to make this place livable. The plumbing and wiring would all have to be replaced and the worst thing is that the foundation is termite infested and barely hanging on by the rusted nails. If it don't fall down around your ears in six weeks, you'll be lucky."

She got up and stomped around the boxes, out into the kitchen and back to the living room to the window, where she stared out at the two vehicles sitting side by side. "There's no way you can ask the rodeo people to sell it back to me?"

"Sorry." He shook his head as he stood. "I should be going now, Carlene. But like I said, it's no problem for you to stay here until the day before the wreckin' crew arrives. And if I can help you move or help find a place or anything, call me."

"Thank you," she said.

His heart was still as big and kind as it had been in high school. He'd been witty and charming as a friend and had

been an amazing boyfriend. Once they'd discovered sex together, they could barely keep their hands to themselves.
But it had been that sweetness about his heart that had
drawn her to him from the beginning and made her long for
him years afterward.

She turned around and stepped on a few bits of dead needles from the dried up Christmas tree in the corner. "Ouch!"

"Let me help you." He knelt beside her and gently removed the dried debris from her foot.

His touch sent delicious shivers all the way to her
scalp, just like it had when they'd dated in high school. If
he reached up and traced her jawline with his forefinger
like he did in those days, she'd be ready to drag him off to
the hayloft.

"There now." He rose to his feet. "Want me to help you
get rid of this thing? I can haul it out of here as it stands."

"No thanks. I'll want to keep several of her ornaments,
so I'll take care of it later."

He headed for the door and stopped in the middle of
the floor. "Mama says you still go by Varner. You ever get
married?"

She shook her head. "You?"

"I'm still holding on as the most eligible bachelor in the
panhandle."

"With that much power, surely you could sweet-talk the
rodeo folks into selling me this house," she said.

"Can't do it, Carlene," he said.

"Hey, look what I found." Tilly burst into the living
room, but stopped short at the sight of Jace. "Who are you?"

Her hair was all tucked up under a stocking cap with the
Florida Gators logo on the front, and big green sunglasses
covered half her face.

"I'm Jace Dawson. And you are?" He stuck out his hand.

She shook his hand. "I'm Tilly Rose Varner. Look what else I found." She turned around to face Carlene and held out an official stuffed alligator from the Florida football team. "I haven't seen him in a whole year. I guess Aunt Bee packed him for me."

"She probably found him under your bed," Carlene said. "Surely you aren't finished unpacking all those boxes."

"Nope, but I'm hungry. I'm going to make a peanut butter and jelly sandwich. You want one?" She laid the stuffed animal on the sofa and started toward the kitchen.

"Your little sister or niece?" Jace asked Carlene.

"No, I'm her daughter," Tilly giggled as she whipped off the stocking hat and a cascade of curly red hair fell to her shoulders.

An icy chill chased up Jace's backbone. "How old are you, Tilly Rose Varner?"

"I'll be nine on February twenty-fourth." She removed the oversized sunglasses and looked up at him with gray eyes sprinkled with gold flecks. Eyes that were exactly like his.

Suddenly, there was not a single doubt in his mind that Jace Dawson was staring at his daughter.

Chapter Two

Jace had trouble looking away from Tilly but when he did, Carlene was shaking her head. He was totally speechless as his gaze shifted from the petite blond girl he'd known in high school to the red-haired little girl not five feet in front of him. When he found his voice, the only word that came out was Carlene's name and that was barely a raspy whisper.

"Later," she mouthed.

He barely nodded. "Well, I really have to go now. If you need me to help with anything"—Jace put a lot of emphasis on *anything*—"my number is still the same, and if you've forgotten it or anything else…" He picked a pen out of a cup on an end table and grabbed her hand. Touching her skin for the second time that morning jacked up his pulse a few beats. He wrote his number on the palm of her hand and then blew on it to dry the ink. "I'll be expecting your call real soon."

"Sure thing," she said.

Jace stepped out onto the porch and pulled his jacket tightly around his broad chest on his way back to the truck. When he got inside, he slammed the door and slapped the steering wheel. He'd known since Christmas that Carlene was coming back to Happy to teach fifth grade. His mother, Valerie Dawson, was on the school board and everyone in town knew she'd been hired.

Despite her windblown hair, dark circles under her eyes, and looking like a bag lady in baggy sweats, Carlene was still the most beautiful woman he'd ever seen. She was a little curvier than she'd been in high school but that would come with having a baby—his baby—that she didn't bother to tell him about. Full, kissable lips were still the same as well as that thick blond hair that floated on her shoulders in big waves even if it did look like it did after a night in the bed of his truck.

A vision of her the morning after their graduation materialized as he started the truck engine and backed out of the driveway. He'd awakened in the hayloft to find her wearing his shirt and looking out across the fields toward the sunrise. That night had been the only time they had taken a chance on sex with no protection. It was crazy but they both wanted to see what it was like with no barriers and he'd planned to pull out before that final moment. Just one time of complete and utter abandonment because they were so much in love—or he thought they were at the time. He shook his head and replaced the visual with the one of that little girl looking up at him with those stunning gray eyes and long lashes.

His big hands shook as he started the truck engine and drove back toward town. He pulled over in front of the bank and parked because he couldn't focus on anything, not even the yellow line in the middle of the road. Using his fingers and counting at least eight times to be sure he was right, he knew beyond even a faint shadow of a doubt that Tilly Rose was born exactly, to the day, nine months after that night he and Carlene had laughed at the idea that one time could never get them into trouble.

"And she didn't even tell me." His hands clenched into fists. "I've got a daughter and she never let me know? Does that little girl even know?"

He pulled out his phone and dialed Rosalie's landline. Carlene answered on the fifth ring.

"She belongs to me, doesn't she?" he asked bluntly.

"She's mine and always has been."

"Does she know about me?"

"She knows that we dated in high school. That's what I told her when she asked after you left," Carlene said.

Jace threw his hat into the backseat and nervously raked his hands through his hair. "We need to talk about this, Carlene."

"I suppose we do," she sighed. "I knew when I came back here to live that we'd have to address it, but can I at least get unpacked and settled first?"

"No, I want to talk about it today," he said.

There's one thing about an old landline with a corded phone—when a person hangs up, it's with a bang. With ears still ringing and his mind going in circles, he tossed his cell phone onto the passenger seat and drove home to Prairie Rose, where he found his brother Brody in the kitchen making a fresh pot of coffee.

"I hear that you didn't waste any time going over to Rosalie's to see Carlene. It's gettin' colder and colder out there. Wouldn't be surprised if we get another snow or two before spring." He turned around to face Jace. "Good Lord, brother. What's happened?"

Jace slumped down in a kitchen chair and laid his head on the table. "Carlene didn't know that I bought that place. She had all these dreams of fixing it up and living there."

Brody poured two cups of coffee and joined his brother at the table. "So what are you going to do? That land has been promised to the rodeo association for over a year."

Jace ignored the coffee and went to the liquor cabinet in the dining room, poured a double shot of Jack Daniel's, and carried it to the table. Rather than sipping it, he threw it back like a cowboy who'd bellied up to the bar in an old Western movie.

"I told her that she could live there until the wreckers came and that I'd help her find another place. I was thinking about that cute little brick house about two blocks from the school, but property is the least of my concerns right now."

"What in the devil happened over there? It must be bad to have you drinkin' at this time of the day," Brody said.

"Bad or good is a matter of opinion," Jace said.

"Spit it out," Brody said. "Did you just figure out that you still have feelin's for her and she's married or something?"

"Sayin' it out loud ain't easy." Jace rubbed his chin and shook his head.

"I remember Carlene being a smart girl in high school. Is she still as pretty as she was back then?" Brody asked.

"She's beautiful," Jace said hoarsely. "Even in baggy gray sweats and her hair all windblown and no makeup, she's still gorgeous."

"But? I think I hear a *but*," Brody said. "Stop dancin' around it, Jace. Did your little cowboy heart skip a beat when you saw her?"

He took a sip of his coffee. "Yep."

"Maybe you'll get a second chance like I did with Lila."

Jace sighed. "She lied to me. I guess it was a lie, anyway. Do sins of omission count the same as a lie?"

"About what?" Brody asked. "Just tell me what in the hell is going on."

Jace hardly knew where to start or how to say the words. "You know we stayed in touch for a week or so after she left, and then she cut me completely out of everything. No phone calls or emails—nothing." There was a long pause before he went on. "I tried. Honest to God, I tried. I really liked her a lot. I even asked her aunt Rosalie about her. It was the week before I went to college. I remember it because you and Granny had a little party for me at the church fellowship hall and I asked Rosalie if she had Carlene's new number."

"And?" Brody asked.

"She told me that sometimes it's too late to do what you should have been doin' all along. Never did figure it out until today," Jace said.

"And what did you figure out today?" Brody asked.

"I have a daughter."

Brody set the coffee mug down with a thud and stared at Jace as if he'd grown a third eye right in the middle of his forehead. "You have a what?"

Although Brody was a little taller than Jace, there was no doubt that they were brothers. They had the same chiseled jawline, the same dark hair and swagger. The only difference was that Brody had inherited the clear blue Dawson eyes and Jace's were gray with little yellow flecks like the gold in peppermint schnapps. Just exactly like the eyes of a little girl who'd looked up at him when she whipped off that hat and sunglasses.

"Wait until you see her," Jace whispered. "She has my eyes. It don't take a genius to know, Brody. She didn't even tell me."

"Are you sure? Maybe Carlene has a red-haired ancestor," Brody whispered.

"There's no doubt. Her age matches up exactly to that one night…" Jace trailed off, heat rising in his cheeks. "We didn't use protection that one night and with that red hair, she's got the same Dawson genes as Kasey and little Emma."

"What the hell are you goin' to do?" Brody asked.

"The first thing is talk to Carlene as soon as possible. I didn't want to bring it up right there in front of the little girl. After that, I don't know," he answered. "What would you do? How on earth does a man start to be a father to an eight-year-old girl?"

Brody chuckled.

Jace pushed back the chair and began to pace around the room. "This isn't funny in any sense of the word."

"You been moanin' ever since Kasey moved back here with her kids that you wished you had children. Looks like you got your wish," Brody said. "I can't wait to get home and tell Lila."

Jace groaned. "What am I going to do, Brody?"

"You'll figure it out. I sure enough did."

"This is different. You were always in love with Lila."

"You sure enough moped around after she left and have brought her name up enough that I kind of thought you were in love with her," Brody said.

"I got over it," Jace replied. "You never did get over Lila."

"Nope, I didn't and I don't really think that you completely got closure when it comes to Carlene, either. This will make you start up things again or end it for good."

Jace put his hands on the back of a kitchen chair. "Sharing a child means it will never be completely over, now, doesn't it?"

"You can both be good parents without being together. Folks do that all the time in this day and age," Brody said as he pulled his phone from his hip pocket. "Got a text from Lila. The news is out that Carlene is at Rosalie's place, so she's on her way over there to welcome her back to town. If what you say is true, I won't have to tell her anything."

"I swear it gave me chills to look at that little girl and I'm still trying to process the whole thing."

"Talk to Carlene in person, not on the phone," Brody said.

"No worry about that," Jace said with a jerky nod. "My ear is still ringing from when she hung up on me last time."

*　　*　　*

Carlene was still in shock and stunned practically speechless for several minutes after she'd slammed the phone down in Jace's ear. He had no right to demand that she talk to him that very day. Hell's bells. She'd just gotten into town and found out that the house she thought she'd owned was about to be demolished. She had to be on the job on Wednesday and she had to find another place to live, get banking done, and all kinds of things—and he wanted to talk.

Hey, back up. If you were in his shoes, how would you be reacting right now? There was Aunt Rosalie in her head and it wasn't a bit difficult to imagine her with her hands on her hips and her eyes drawn into mere slits.

"I'd give him time to catch his breath first if the roles were reversed," Carlene argued, and then whipped around to make sure Tilly hadn't heard her. She eased down into an old wooden chair with rockers worn so smooth that the chair would hardly even move back and forth. She shivered when the north wind rattled the glass in the window behind her.

Maybe it was because she was sitting in Aunt Rosalie's favorite chair, but there was that sassy voice loud and clear in her head again. *Catch his breath, nothin'. You're lucky he didn't drop dead of a heart attack.*

"I thought I was over it, but I'm still angry, and I've got a right to be. I'm angry at you because you didn't even have a funeral so we could have closure and because you didn't tell me you were selling the house. And I'm mad at Jace because he still affects me the same way he did when we were in high school and I thought I was over him," she confessed.

She stood up and moved through the living room and kitchen. The house would be gone soon and memories would be all she had of the little place. She'd stayed with Aunt Rosalie more than she'd stayed home those two years they'd lived in Happy—the best years of her life. She ran a hand over the chrome kitchen table set where she'd gotten her homework done and ate many meals. There were always cookies or brownies or something for an after-school snack and the sounds of Aunt Rosalie bustling around with her dust rag making sure everything was shiny.

Tears flooded her eyes and ran down her cheeks. Aunt Rosalie had been her stability those years. Her mother was in Amarillo working every single day and her dad—well, he was gone all the time with his military position. They'd planned to move to Amarillo when her father got transferred there, but Aunt Rosalie talked them into renting a place in Happy so she could help watch over Carlene. Not that she needed babysitting. After all, she'd been sixteen, but Rosalie thought she might get into trouble if she was left alone all day and half the night.

"Boy, was she right, but it didn't take living in Amarillo to do that," she muttered as she looked out the kitchen window at the dormant pecan tree. That's where she and Jace shared their first kiss and where he carved a heart with their initials into the bark. Would they cut it down when they tore down the house?

She grabbed a kitchen towel and wiped away the tears. "Okay, so he deserves answers but not today. I've got too much to deal with for that."

"You okay, Mama? Sure you don't want a sandwich?" Tilly asked as she headed toward the refrigerator.

"I'm fine, sweetheart. I'll eat something in a little while." The thought of any kind of food, even chocolate, turned her stomach.

"Then I'll wait until we can eat together." Tilly got out a juice box and carried it back to her room.

She should be taking care of Tilly's needs, not the other way around. She was so engrossed in being mad and feeling guilty over not even thinking about Tilly's lunch, and all the memories surrounding her, that she didn't even hear the car outside. When someone rapped on the door, it startled her so badly that she jumped up and got a head rush. It took a moment for things to stop spinning but when she did get across the room, she found Lila Harris standing on the porch with a bag in each hand.

She threw open the door and the old-fashioned screen door and motioned Lila inside the house. "Lila Harris, I swear you haven't changed a bit."

"Hey, Carlene." Lila smiled. "I'd hug you but my hands are full. I came to welcome you back to Happy and I thought you might want some food."

Carlene followed her to the kitchen. "Thank you so much. Come in and please ignore the mess. Tilly and I'll be workin' all day getting things put away. And hopefully by tomorrow evening we'll have that horrible dried-up Christmas tree out of here."

"I don't envy you the job of taking those ornaments off those prickly branches. Don't let me slow you down. We can visit while you work. I'll just put this in the fridge for you. I brought milk, bread, and containers of black-eyed peas, collard greens, and smoked ribs for your lunch and a quart of vegetable beef soup for supper. Oh, and a chunk of chocolate cake." Lila shook her head at the brown Christmas tree. "Rosalie always did love a real tree. I remember coming here when we were in high school during the holidays for a Sunday school party. Man, she made good snickerdoodles."

"Yes, she did." Carlene dried her eyes again with the towel and tossed it on the cabinet. "I remember that party, but I'd forgotten that we need peas and greens for the traditional New Year's dinner, so a double thank you, Lila," she said. "Tilly and I will sure enjoy that. We need all the luck we can get."

"Tilly?"

"My daughter. She's in third grade. I'm sure she'll come out of her room when she hears us talkin'," Carlene answered.

"Didn't know you had a daughter, or I'd have tucked in cookies," Lila said as she got things put away. "I'm going to clean out this fridge for you. Everything in here is probably out of date."

"Thanks, that'd be great. Except for the juice boxes. Tilly and I just put them in there a little while ago. Aunt Rosalie told me that you'd moved back to Happy and married Brody." Carlene pulled the tape from another box—the one holding her books for the classroom. "We really will enjoy the home-cooked food, Lila. We were talkin' about havin' to go into Tulia this afternoon for a few things."

Lila raised her voice from behind the refrigerator door. "I

haven't kept in touch at all but I do have some good memories of us hanging out with the other kids at Henry's old barn. Did you hear that old Henry's nephew came back to town and is engaged to my sister-in-law, Kasey? They're planning a spring wedding."

"Aunt Rosalie mentioned that the last time we talked." Carlene swallowed twice before the lump in her throat disappeared. She hadn't even cried when the lawyer called to tell her that her aunt was gone and her body had already been taken away to be donated to science but now that she was back in Happy and in Rosalie's house, everything set off her emotions.

When the trash can was full, Lila took the whole bag out to the Dumpster and then came back in through the back door. "Can I help any other way?"

"No, that's enough. Thank you so much."

Lila joined Carlene in the living room, pulling the rocking chair across the floor to be closer. "Rosalie did things her way. Not even Hope crossed her, and Hope's been the queen bee of this place for as long as I can remember."

"That's the gospel truth. I talked to her one Sunday like always and the next Saturday I get a phone call saying she's passed and everything is over. I hate that there's not even a funeral." Carlene's voice broke.

Lila was a head taller than Carlene and she bent to wrap her up in a hug. "Have you even had a chance to grieve yet?"

"Not really, but it hit me when I walked through the kitchen. So many memories," Carlene answered, not willing to admit that a lot of them had to do with Jace. "That's what funerals and family dinners are for, to remember and then to let them go. We didn't get any of that."

Lila leaned back in the chair and sighed. "All that didn't

help much when my dad died, or at least I didn't think so, but looking back, maybe it did bring closure. Why don't we ask the preacher if the congregation could sing a couple of her favorite songs on Sunday and then we could go to the ranch for dinner? It wouldn't be a funeral or a memorial but it might help you finalize it in your mind."

"I'd like that a lot," Carlene said. "Thank you so much."

Lila wore her dark hair a little longer these days, but she still had that soft Texas twang to her voice and twinkling brown eyes. Carlene was always jealous of Lila's hair but even more of her height. She always reminded Carlene of a runway model in her tight jeans and form-fitting shirts. Back when they were all teenagers, they'd never had a dull Friday or Saturday night when Lila had been in the crowd.

"Hey, no problem. Granny Hope has been in a funk because Rosalie didn't let them have a funeral. It'll be good for her to have a little memorial too," Lila said.

Carlene sighed and went back to work. "I loved this place when I was a kid. I used to think that was the good Carlene and the bad one was when we'd all get together and go out to Henry's old barn after Aunt Rosalie and I baked goodies all day."

"You got that right." Lila smiled. "But we were just a bunch of bored kids who were just lookin' for a good time in a small town."

"Rosalie did things her way. I bet she was a force when she was young—maybe a lot like you." Carlene pointed at Lila.

"Oh, come on now. I remember that you were pretty sassy yourself."

Carlene finished unpacking a box and carried it over to the other side of the room. "Before I forget, congratulations on your marriage. You and Brody always did have eyes for each other, but I figured when you left it was forever and ever, amen."

"I didn't come back to Happy to stay, but..." Lila shrugged.

"Well, I'm here to stay until they take me to the Happy cemetery when I'm past ninety-five years old. I want Tilly to have a permanent place to call home. We moved around so much when I was growin' up that I never had roots and never felt like I belonged anywhere until we came here. Tilly has been shifted around to four different states already. It's time to put down roots. Livin' in Happy was the longest my family was in one place. I don't want that for her."

"I lived here my whole life until I graduated from high school. Leaving was the next to the hardest thing I ever did."

"What was the hardest?" Carlene asked.

"Comin' back and facin' Brody."

Carlene's head bobbed a couple of times in agreement. "And how did that first meeting with him go?"

"He came into the café and we flirted," Lila said with a twinkle in her eyes. "Think you and Jace will do any flirting when you see him?"

"I did see him. He came by earlier today, but I don't think there was much flirting involved and most likely won't ever be."

She wasn't going to admit that just seeing him had made her feel like she was that sassy teenager again who'd been late for curfew too many times when she was out at Henry's old barn on Saturday nights with all the kids in the area.

"How'd he know I was here anyway?" Carlene asked. "It was after dark when Tilly and I got into town last night and we're the only house on a dead-end road."

"This is Happy. Never forget the strength of gossip." Lila

laughed. "Fred was over at the rodeo grounds and called Jace."

"Jace told me about the plans the rodeo association has for the land," she said. "Did you know that Aunt Rosalie was born in this house and lived right here her whole life and well, it seemed like..." Carlene wiped away another tear making its way down her cheek.

Lila reached out and laid a hand on her shoulder. "It seemed like she'd live forever, right?"

Carlene blinked back tears.

"If you need a friend, I'm here," Lila said softly.

"Mama, I got my box of toys all put away on the bookcase in my room—" Tilly stopped as she realized her mom was with someone. "Hello, I'm Tilly Rose Varner." She crossed the room and stuck out her hand.

Lila shook hands with her and introduced herself with only a faint gasp.

"Dawson, huh," Tilly said. "Are you married to Jace? He came by earlier."

"No, I'm married to his brother, Brody." Lila stared, blinked, and then blinked several times. "Your name again?"

"Tilly. Rose. Varner," Tilly said with a pause between each name and then turned to Carlene. "Mama, it's goin' to take me years to figure out everyone in this town and you said everyone knew everybody. Can I drag that box back to my room and get the last of my stuffed animals out of it?"

"Of course you can," Carlene answered.

Tilly grabbed hold of the lightweight box and dragged it down the short hallway to her bedroom.

"Sweet Jesus!" Lila let all the air out of her lungs in a whoosh.

"That obvious, huh?" Carlene frowned.

Lila slowly shook her head. "That word doesn't even begin to cover it. She looks exactly like Kasey except for the eyes. Those are Jace's without a doubt."

"When she was born, my mother took one look at her and threatened to come back here and shoot one of the Dawson brothers. I begged her to let it go because it was as much my fault as his. I didn't want to ruin his life. Lord, we were only eighteen and he wasn't ready to be a father. If it hadn't been for my sister, Belinda, I don't know that I could have managed the responsibility of being a mother. And Tilly doesn't know. I'm hoping to break it to her in easy baby steps."

"Why did you come back here? Everyone is going to know the minute they see those eyes," Lila said.

"Stability for Tilly. She would have found out someday anyway, so I figured it might as well be now. And I needed a job. My school downsized and I've been doin' sub work in all the area schools for the past four months. Besides, it was time for Tilly and me to get out on our own and, like I said before, put down roots."

"When are you tellin' her?" Lila whispered.

"I want her to have a few days to settle into another new school first," Carlene answered. "Hopefully next weekend."

"And Jace?"

"He knew the minute he saw her," Carlene said.

"Well, I sure don't envy you this next week, but like I said, if you need to talk, just give me a call. And we'll plan on that dinner Sunday to remember Rosalie. She did love to sing and to come out to the ranch for dinner."

"She sure did. I'll bring snickerdoodles in her memory." Carlene didn't want her to go. Just having another woman there, one who understood the way things were in Happy, was comforting but she couldn't think of a single reason to make her stay.

Lila reached out her hand. "I should be going now and let you get back to work. Give me your phone and I'll put my number in it."

Without a moment's hesitation, Carlene picked up her phone from the end table and handed it to Lila. "Thanks again for everything, but most of all for the visit."

"Call me anytime you want to talk. Sometimes a woman just needs a friend. Kasey was here for me when I needed one, so I'm paying it forward. Besides, I remember that you were real good at keepin' secrets, so I probably owe you big-time."

"Had to be. Mama would have sent me to a convent if she'd known what we were doin' back then." Carlene smiled.

Chapter Three

Evidently folks were out and about early that Tuesday morning because the parking lot at the Happy Café was full. Jace pulled in beside the trucks belonging to Fred and Paul and started inside the café but when he saw the red van with a Florida tag, loaded full of boxes, he stopped in his tracks and walked around it twice. Either Carlene was leaving town or else she'd already found a place to move into.

He didn't know if he was relieved or disappointed. What if he never really got to know his daughter?

Glancing toward the café, he could see Fred and Paul in one window and Lila carrying a coffeepot around to each booth and table. Then he looked to his left and there was Tilly, the morning sun sparkling in her red hair every time she wiggled. Carlene smiled across the table at her antics and they both sipped glasses of chocolate milk. She'd always liked chocolate—candy, milk shakes, cookies, and ice cream. He licked his lips and could almost taste her kisses after she'd finished a hot fudge sundae.

He kicked a rock, sending it flying across the parking lot, where it then hit the café porch. Dammit! Whoever said that a person never forgot their first love was a genius because the day before had proven that Jace had never completely moved past Carlene.

He pushed inside the café, waved at Fred and Paul, and glanced at Carlene and Tilly. He went straight for the counter and sat down at the bar. Without even asking, Lila poured a cup of coffee and set it before him.

"What brings you to town this morning?" she asked.

His hands trembled when he picked up the cup. "I had a meeting with the rodeo folks to discuss the new project. You workin' all day or just through the lunch rush?"

"Molly had a doctor's appointment. She'll be back before noon. So." She leaned forward on the counter. "What're you goin' to do about Tilly Rose Varner?"

He set the coffee down and lowered his voice to a whisper. "I don't know yet. What's with all the boxes in their van? Did they already find another place?"

Lila lightly touched his arm. "You two need to talk and not in a public place like this. Paul and Fred already raised eyebrows when they saw that little girl, so you can bet that your mama is goin' to know all about her in the next half hour."

He glanced over his shoulder and caught Carlene's gaze. She didn't look any too happy about him being in the café, but it wasn't like he had a choice of a dozen restaurants in the little town of Happy. He looked back down at his coffee cup. If only it was a magic potion that could make this all disappear.

He could hear his father now: *Things will never, ever be*

the same. You've got a daughter and whether she's part of your life on a daily basis or in name only, it can't be undone.

"Just tell me where she's moving to, so I'll at least know where to go to talk to her," Jace whispered.

Lila shook her head. "That's not for me to tell. It's for you to ask. This is between you two, not the whole town of Happy. But you can bet the ranch that the phone lines will be hot as soon as those two old guys get home and tell their wives. Or maybe they'll call them on the way home so the gossip doesn't get cold. You're runnin' out of time." Lila left him sitting on the bar stool and picked up a coffeepot in each hand to refill cups as she made her way around the café.

"Sink or swim time," he muttered as he swallowed the last sip in his cup. Taking a long, deep breath, he crossed the wooden floor, his cowboy boots sounding like drumbeats. But the sound of them was nothing compared to the thump in his ears with every heartbeat. Without asking, he slid into the booth right beside Carlene. Hot sparks flashed through his whole body when their thighs touched and didn't disappear when she quickly scooted as far away as she could.

"Good mornin', ladies." He smiled brightly. "I see you like chocolate milk like your mama, Miz Tilly."

"And biscuits and gravy and waffles with peanut butter in all the little square holes," Tilly told him. "That's what we're havin' for breakfast this mornin'. What are you gettin', Mr. Jace?"

"I already ate but wanted to come over and talk to y'all. And you can call me plain old Jace, not Mr. Jace," he answered. "So you're in the second grade?"

"Third!" Tilly held up three fingers. "I'm almost nine."

"I see. Well, you sure are tall for your age," Jace said. "Before long you'll be taller than your mama."

"I was the tallest kid in my class in Florida," she said. "But I'd rather be short like Mama than stand out like an old wild sunflower in a bed full of pretty petunias."

"Who told you that you were an old sunflower?" Carlene asked.

"I heard one of the teachers at my school say that. I didn't tell you because..." Tilly concentrated on her waffles.

"Because your mama has a temper, right?" Jace asked.

"Yep, she does and sometimes"—she leaned forward a little—"I have one too. Mama says that it's good they don't show up on the same day."

"What else would you like to have like your mama?" Jace was amazed at how friendly the child was.

"Wellllll..." She drew out the word dramatically. "I'd like to have her straight blond hair, but she says that mine probably won't never change unless it gets gray when I'm old."

"Well, I think your red hair is beautiful and someday you'll love bein' tall," Jace said. "Where are you goin' this mornin', Carlene?"

"To Amarillo to buy groceries," she answered.

"And to take all them boxes to the animal shelter. We got all our stuff unpacked and we put Aunt Rosie's stuff in the empty boxes and my room has a pink bedspread and that's my favorite color," Tilly said. "Mama said that you went to school with her right here in Happy and that y'all went on dates. Do you have kids? I'm lookin' for some friends."

"I did go to school with your mama and..."

Carlene touched him on the knee. The heat from her fingertips burned through his jeans and he forgot what he was about to say.

"And?" Tilly asked.

It took a moment but then he remembered what she'd

asked. "And I don't have any children, but I'm sure that you'll make lots of friends tomorrow at school," Jace said quickly.

"How about you come by the house tonight and we'll catch up? Tilly and I will make some brownies. I remember that you really like them."

Carlene moved her hand but his leg still felt as if she'd branded him and he lost his train of thought again.

"Well?" she asked. "Do you have other plans?"

"No, ma'am. I'll be there. What time?"

A man should feel an instant, overwhelming rush of warmth when he looked at his child for the first time. When Rustin was born, Kasey said that tears had dripped from Adam's chin and that no one could drag him away from the nursery window. But Jace felt as if he were simply looking at his sister when she was a young girl.

"Say seven?" Carlene said.

"Seven what?" Jace asked, completely lost.

"O'clock this evening when you are coming to our house. Are you okay?" Carlene asked.

"I'm fine. Just woolgathering. Sounds good. I'll be there." He stood up and smiled down at Tilly. "You going to adopt a cat or puppy while you're at the shelter?"

Tilly's head bobbed up and down. "Mama said I could have a kitten if we ever got out of the apartment where we lived but I won't get it today. I have to think about it for a whole week and then I'll know what color cat I really want."

"Well, my sister has a new litter out in her barn. I'm sure she'd love for you to come out to the ranch and pick out one."

"Is there a black-and-white one? I kinda like that kind," Tilly asked.

"There might be. Want me to check it out for you?"

Tilly clapped her hands. "Yes. And if there's one with white feet, can you let me look at it?"

"I'll tell her not to give away any with white feet before you see it. See you this evening then, Carlene."

She gave a brief nod and then turned to stare out the window.

"And here's your breakfast." Lila stepped around him and set plates of food on the table. "Need anything else?"

"Hey, Jace." Paul winked. "I thought the disappearance of Henry Thomas was Happy's biggest secret. Guess I was wrong."

"Wouldn't know what you're talkin' about." Jace quickly escaped out to his car and looked at the two pictures of Tilly he'd managed to take—one through the window from a distance and one in the restaurant when he was fiddling around with his phone. They weren't very good, but he wanted Brody and the rest of his family to see her.

He stared at the pictures without blinking until his eyes were dry. Nothing. Nada. Not a single tear or a feeling of instant love for the child. Maybe he wasn't cut out to be a father. Maybe there was something genetically wrong with him.

He drove straight to the ranch house and found his mother in the kitchen, loading a box with some of her favorite pans. "You won't be using this big stock pot or this one that I like to make chicken and dumplin's in, so I'm takin' them to my new house."

Jace removed his coat and hung it on the back of a kitchen chair and tossed his black cowboy hat onto the other end of the table as he eased down into a chair. "Mama, come over here and sit with me a minute."

"I'm busy. Talk to me while I see if there's any more pans I want," she said.

"Mama, we need to talk." Jace's tone held an edge of desperation.

Valerie straightened up and pulled her phone from her hip pocket when it rang.

"Don't answer that, Mama. Let me talk to you first," Jace said.

Tall and slim built, Valerie could cut steel with her light gray eyes, and no one doubted that if she was angry, she would shoot first and ask questions later. Her hair had been as dark as her two sons' when she was young, but now it was sprinkled with silver and the crow's-feet around her eyes had deepened. Without a smile, she turned the phone off and laid it on the table.

She pulled out a chair and sat down. "Is your granny all right?"

"Granny Hope is fine."

"I can tell by your face this is bad news. Who's died?" Valerie asked.

"No one that I'm aware of." Folks said that a picture is worth a thousand words, so he slid his phone across the table with Tilly's picture right there.

Valerie held it up to see the picture better and frowned. "What does an old picture of Kasey have to do with the weird way you're acting this mornin'?"

"Look at her eyes."

"Why, that's not Kasey at all and this girl is too old to be Emma. Who is this child?"

"That would be Carlene's daughter, Tilly. She'll be nine next month."

Valerie studied it a few moments and slowly the confused expression on her face changed to disbelief. She dropped the phone as if it were a hot potato. "Holy mother of God."

"They had breakfast at the café this mornin' and you probably already have a dozen phone calls. I wanted to tell you first," Jace said.

"Did you know? For God's sake, tell me that you haven't kept this a secret for all these years and if you did that you did the right thing and have supported this child."

He shook his head. "No, ma'am, I did not know until I saw her yesterday. I've been trying to sort through my own feelings."

"What are you going to do?"

"Have no idea right now. Proceed with caution, I guess. Carlene thought she'd inherited Rosalie's house and they moved into it," Jace said. "I told her she could stay until the wrecking crew arrives. But I hope that she moves soon. Rosalie's house isn't fit for her to live in."

Valerie picked up his phone and stared, unblinking, at the picture. "I may not turn on my phone for a month. Not until this blows over. Does your grandmother know?"

"Yes, I do." Hope breezed into the house through the kitchen door. "I suppose that you're talkin' about Carlene's daughter, right? Gracie called me and that's why I'm here. What are we going to do about this, Jace? Everyone in town will know by sundown and we have to figure out how we as a family will handle this. It's not like Lila coming home. She didn't bring a child with her."

She removed the bright red scarf from around her neck, tossed it onto a chair along with her coat, and headed straight for the refrigerator. She pulled out a pitcher of sweet tea and carried it to the table with a couple of glasses.

"I'm going over to her place tonight to talk things over. Granny, I promise you I did not know about her being pregnant or..."

Hope hugged him and then sat down. "I know that. I trust you."

Valerie couldn't take her eyes off the picture. "It's uncanny how much she looks like Kasey and those eyes—oh my sweet Lord—those are yours for sure, Jace. How did this happen?"

"I expect it happened the same way all babies are made," Hope said bluntly, and rolled her eyes.

"What are we going to do about this child?" Valerie slid the phone over to Hope.

"Not 'this child.' That sounds like an orphan. She's your granddaughter and my great-granddaughter. She's family and Dawsons take care of their own. Holy smoke! She's the image of Kasey at that age," Hope said.

Valerie took the phone back and looked at the picture again. "Are you sure you didn't have any clue about this little girl? You and Rosalie were good friends. She went to visit her relatives once a year, so she had to know."

Hope threw up her hands. "Hey, she kept her secrets and I kept a few of my own. If you'll remember, none of us knew that she'd decided on not having a funeral or a memorial. Looks like she could have told us lots of things, don't it?"

"Lila and Carlene are planning a little get-together with a few friends on Sunday," Valerie said. "Tell me again that you didn't have any clue at all that Carlene was pregnant when she left town, Jace."

Jace toyed with his coffee mug, turning it around several times. "I had no idea and that's the truth. All I ever got from her was a postcard with no return address and she changed her phone number. When I asked Rosalie about it, she was all evasive."

"Rosalie told me once that she was going to college out

on the West Coast and living with her sister, who's in the military," Hope said.

Jace raked his hand across his square chin. "I didn't even know that much."

Valerie laid her hand on his arm. "We are all in shock but we'll get through it, and it's never too late to step up."

"And that means?"

"Well, it don't mean proposing to the girl," Hope answered. "But you should probably see a lawyer about child support and visitation if we all want to have a relationship with this child. And speaking of relationships..." Valerie handed the phone back to Jace and glared at her mother.

Hope pointed a finger right at Valerie. "Hey, it's not my doin' that Henry showed up at Christmas and decided to stick around at Nash and Kasey's a couple of weeks. He's loving getting to know those kids and Nash can use the help."

Jace could still see the shock on his grandmother's face when she opened the door and there was Henry Thomas. He and Hope had dated when they were teenagers and had lived on adjoining ranches. But he'd gone into the military and she'd married someone else. Then his father had gotten ill about the same time he'd retired, so Henry came home to help out. After both his parents died, he'd simply disappeared.

It had been the great mystery of Happy, Texas— something that folks still gossiped about—until a few weeks ago when he simply showed up again. Now he and Hope were...Jace frowned. Were they dating? Flirting? Whatever it was it sure put a new spring in his grandmother's step and he was happy for her.

"They say trouble comes in threes. I'm thinkin' it comes in fours," Valerie said.

"Four? Do you have a child we don't know about?" Jace asked.

"No, but sometimes raisin' a mother is as tough as a child. The way she and Henry are acting like a couple of teenagers, good Lord," Valerie sighed.

"Hey, now. I passed the legal age to be a consenting adult many years ago."

Valerie blushed. "Mama!"

"Well, I damn sure did, so don't lecture me. Besides, you should be careful—your turn could be next," Hope said.

"It's already my turn. I've got a granddaughter that I don't even know," Valerie said.

Hope snatched the phone from Jace's hand for another look. "No wonder Gracie called and said there was no doubt she was kin to us."

"There's certainly no reason to run a DNA test," Jace said. "And that child has no idea she's even kin to us. That's what Carlene and I will be talkin' about tonight."

* * *

Carlene and Tilly started at the bank in Happy that Tuesday morning. The teller behind the counter sent them to a small office down a short hallway to talk to someone who took care of new accounts.

A dark-haired lady with a wide smile and an expression that said she knew Carlene looked up from her desk. "Well, hello. I thought I might see you today."

"You did?" Carlene asked.

Who was this woman? Had she gone to school with Carlene or maybe spent a few Saturday nights out at the old barn with the group?

"Of course. You start teaching tomorrow morning so you

need to get your business taken care of today. To start with, you were on all of Rosalie's accounts. You will remember signing papers to that effect, right?"

"Yes." Carlene nodded.

The woman's voice sounded so familiar, but she couldn't place it.

"I got a friend named Natalie in Florida." Tilly pointed at the nameplate at the edge of the desk.

"Natalie!" Carlene said out loud. "You were a blonde in high school and you wore glasses." She glanced down at the nameplate right in front of her. "Natalie O'Dell. You aren't married?"

"Found out that blondes don't have more fun and I was married but that's been over for a couple of years now. Kind of had a thing for Jace that I couldn't get over but I can see why he couldn't be roped." Her eyes shifted toward Tilly for a second or two. "He's sure kept that secret well. Now what can we do for you today?"

"It's easy to keep a secret when no one knows about it. And I need to open a checking account," Carlene said quickly.

"Well, how about that? Bet that rocked his little boat." Natalie chuckled.

"Little bit. Did you ever move away from here?" Carlene tried to change the subject.

"Went to Tulia for a couple of years, but"—she shrugged—"my roots are here."

"Seems like Happy affects folks that way," Carlene said. "I'd like to know what's in all the accounts with my name on them."

Natalie hit a few keys, then rolled her chair back a couple of feet and retrieved a paper from the printer. "Here you go. That'll be her savings."

"Thanks." Carlene folded the paper and stuck it in her purse without even looking at the figures.

"Now on to the new checking account." Natalie turned her attention away from Carlene as she brought up another screen on her computer. "Do you think you'll like it here, Miss Tilly?"

"Well, I don't like the house so much, but Mama says we're goin' to find another one," Tilly answered honestly.

"What's wrong with the house?" Natalie asked.

"It smells funny and there's this dead tree in the corner and"—she lowered her voice—"I think I saw a mouse yesterday. But I didn't cuss—even though I wanted to— because that gets me into trouble."

Natalie giggled. "Outspoken just like another redhead I know real well."

"What other red-haired girl do I remind you of?" Tilly asked.

"A friend of mine. You'll probably meet her sometime before long." Natalie winked at Carlene. "Did you know that Kasey's livin' with Henry's nephew on Texas Star these days? Henry showed up at Christmas and is stayin' at the old place with them. I hear that it's only for another week or so but it's hard to believe he's back after all this time. Remember those stories the boys used to scare us with about him being killed in the barn and his ghost was still there? Scared me right out of..." She blushed and laughed. "Kids these days can't even go out there to party and have fun at the old barn anymore."

They finished their business and went outside to a beautiful sunny day. A brisk January wind blew out of the north. They passed a house on the west side of the street for sale and Carlene pointed at it. "What do you think? Buy a house or rent one?"

Tilly shrugged. "We never lived in a house till now. Just apartments in the same place as Aunt Bee. Can we get a swing set for the backyard?"

"Definitely." Carlene was glad that the comment Natalie had made about secrets had gone over the top of Tilly's head.

Tilly's eyes lit up. "And a trampoline?"

"No, ma'am. You know how I feel about those things."

"Well, shhh...crap!" Tilly muttered.

"Tilly Rose Varner!" Carlene scolded.

"I didn't cuss and Aunt Bee says that word all the time."

"That don't mean you can say it or any other bad word. Now let's talk about something else," Carlene said. "How about kittens?"

"Jace says he'll see about us gettin' one from his sister. Does she have kids? Will they be in school with me? You think I'll make friends with them?"

"Slow down. I hear that Kasey has three children. Two boys and a girl, but I would think they're all quite a bit younger than you are. However, you'll probably be seeing them in church and in other places, so maybe you'll be friends with them," Carlene answered.

How was Tilly going to feel about having cousins and all that family around her? It had always been just Carlene and her sister, Belinda, for the most part. Belinda's military posts changed every couple of years and she'd insisted that Carlene and Tilly move with her. Up until last summer, Carlene had had no trouble finding and keeping a teaching job wherever they went.

Tilly threw her hand over her forehead dramatically and said, "I bet them three kids will want all the kittens."

"We'll see." Carlene was just glad not to have to answer another question or make a promise. "Now off to buy food."

"And stuff to make brownies for Jace. Do you think he's pretty?"

Carlene laughed. "Do you?"

"I think he's sexy as…a word that Aunt Bee says but that I can't because you say it's a dirty word."

"Good grief. What do you know about sexy as…"

Tilly huffed and crossed her arms over her chest. "I'm almost nine and me and Natalie talk about sexy guys all the time."

"Like who?"

"Blake Shelton and Josh Turner and Dustin Bennett," she said.

"Who's Dustin Bennett?" Carlene frowned and fought the urge to flip off a man who cut in front of her and grabbed a prime parking space at Walmart.

"He's Natalie's new crush. He's in the fourth grade and he's got blue eyes and blond hair and he chases her at recess. He's real sexy," Tilly said wistfully.

"So Natalie is into the older guys, is she?"

"Yep, and they tried to fix me up with his friend Billy Smith, but it didn't work," Tilly said seriously. "I'm not ready to date just one boy."

"My God! You are eight, not eighteen," Carlene sputtered.

"Almost nine." Tilly shot a look her way as a reminder. "Besides, Billy Smith is a sissy. I could beat him up with one hand tied behind my back. I'm way taller than he is and he wears his jeans way down on his butt so folks can see his underwear. I can say *butt*, can't I?"

"Yes, but *fanny* sounds better." Carlene drove around the lot twice before she landed a decent parking spot.

Tilly rolled her eyes toward the ceiling. "Girls have fannies. Boys have butts."

Carlene undid her seat belt. "Is that so?"

"Yes, Mama, you got to keep up. Girls are pretty. Boys are sexy."

"But you said Jace was pretty," Carlene argued.

Tilly drew her eyebrows down. "That's not the right word. Sexy is what Aunt Bee would say, but his eyelashes are so long that I guess that's why I said pretty." Her expression changed to a cute smile. "When can I have makeup?"

"When you are twenty-one and only then if I think you are ready," Carlene answered.

"Mama!" Tilly groaned as she crawled out of the vehicle and tucked her hand into her mother's.

*   *   *

As soon as they got home and had the groceries unloaded, Tilly went right to her room to call Natalie. Carlene caught bits and pieces of the conversation as she told her all about Happy and the cowboy who went to school with her mama. And that the bank lady liked him but that Jace had a secret and Tilly was going to find out what it was.

"They don't miss a thing," Carlene muttered as she slid a pan of brownies into the oven and got her briefcase ready for the next day.

Every nerve ending in her body was on high alert and yet when she heard the crunch of tires on the gravel driveway at five minutes to seven, it was strangely calming. Jace had arrived. Now it was just a matter of convincing him to give her a few days to let Tilly settle into school before she told her. His hand was raised to knock when she swung open the door.

"Come in, Jace. Can I get you something to drink? Water, sweet tea, beer, a shot of whiskey?"

"Nothing, thank you," he said.

"Well, I'm having a shot." She went to the cabinet and

brought down a bottle, poured a double shot, and dropped a cube of ice into it from the refrigerator. "Take off your coat and hat and have a seat."

"Where's Tilly?" he asked.

"She's watching a movie in her room. I thought we'd talk before I call her out to have brownies with us."

"So?" Jace removed his coat and hat and sat down in the recliner across the room from the sofa.

Afraid to sit beside me, is he?

"I want to buy a place. I have a small savings that I can put with what you gave Aunt Rosalie for this property and I don't want to move twice. So tell me about any houses for sale right here in Happy."

He took a long breath. "There are a couple of nice places up for sale, but you know very well that I'm not here to talk about land or houses."

"I know you deserve an answer, and the only one I have to give you is that I didn't want to ruin your life. Or mine. We were eighteen—way too young to be making any kind of lifetime decisions. You would have hated being tied down to changing diapers when all your friends were having fun at college." Her voice was high and squeaky in her own ears.

"I would have done the right thing no matter what," Jace said coolly.

"Yes, but would you have been happy?" she asked.

He raked his fingers through his hair and his foot started to tap. "I had the right to know and to at least help with child support even if you didn't want to marry me."

She eyed him carefully. "You aren't sure how you feel about all this, are you?"

"Truthfully, no. But you've dropped this on me out of the clear blue. I feel like I'm trying to walk on water in cement boots, but, Carlene, we might have made it through the tough times just fine."

"Of course you would have, but I would have always felt like I ruined your life and you would have thought you'd been roped into a marriage that you weren't ready for. A marriage that *I* wasn't ready for. I already had to take care of a baby. I couldn't imagine trying to get used to a husband too," she argued as she sat down on the end of the sofa.

He stared at her for a full minute before he went on. "Maybe you are right, but we'll never know now, will we?"

She folded her arms over her chest. "Hey, I only found out the day before we left town. Daddy's new post came through a month earlier than we expected, so it was a rush move and I was still in shock. And it seemed like the thing to do at the time."

"Imagine how I feel after all these years," he said.

"So what kind of problem is this going to make for you?"

"Everyone in town knew the minute they saw her, Carlene. My whole family wants to see her, and I want her to know that I'm not a deadbeat dad who skipped out on you." He sighed. "I'm more than willing to pay child support, even back support. But truthfully, I've got to catch my breath here and figure things out."

"And Tilly has to get used to a brand-new school. Give us this week to get used to that, and I promise I'll tell her over the weekend. We can all sit down and talk about it together after I tell her," Carlene said.

She wiggled around so the spring pushing its way up through the cushion would stop poking her on the left cheek of her fanny.

Girls have fannies. Boys have butts. Tilly's words came back to her.

Jace was sitting on his butt, so she couldn't see it but she knew it still looked amazing. When his eyes caught hers, she quickly blinked and dropped her gaze to his mouth.

Dammit! Just looking at his lips made her want to kiss him and she should focus on the serious conversation they were having.

"Fair enough. Will y'all come to supper tomorrow evening so we can meet her?"

"That's way too soon for something that big. Let us all get used to the idea for a few days. How about waiting until Sunday? Lila is planning a little memorial for Aunt Rosalie. Just a few of her favorite songs at church that morning and then Sunday dinner at the ranch. That will be a good time," Carlene said.

"You always were as stubborn as a ..." He hesitated.

"As a Dawson?" she finished for him, and scooted over to the middle of the sofa to get away from the spring that was poking her on the fanny.

"I was going to say as a rebellious teenager."

"That's not as bad as a Dawson. You set your mind and your heels and God couldn't change it," she snapped.

She met his eyes.

Not a wise thing.

She quickly shifted her gaze and focused on his broad chest. His blue shirt stretched out over hard muscles that had known a lot of work in the fields, not in a gym or a health club.

"I know about the memorial. Granny is real happy about it."

She couldn't keep staring at his chest forever. Her eyes went to his big oval belt buckle with the Prairie Rose brand engraved on it. Heat started at her neck and traveled around to her cheeks as she thought about how many times she'd undone his belt. He said something but it was a buzz in her ears.

"So?" he asked.

"So what?" she asked, completely oblivious to whatever he'd asked before.

"Can I drop by and see her before Sunday?"

"Fine," she said.

"Fair enough. Now about those brownies?"

"We should talk about rent," she said as she got up and headed toward the kitchen.

"Make me a plate of brownies or cookies and deliver them every Sunday and that should cover it."

"Sounds like a deal to me. For every Sunday that I live here, I will bring brownies to church on Sunday for you," she said.

Jace held out a hand. "Shake on it?"

She braced herself for the vibes and wasn't a bit disappointed when the simple touch of her hand in his created sparks. She pulled her hand free and fought the urge to take a step forward, put her arms around his neck, roll up on her toes, and kiss him.

Footsteps in the hallway brought her back to reality with a jerk. Tilly came in wearing a big smile and carrying her stuffed gator in her arms. "What were y'all shakin' hands for?"

"A rent agreement until we can find a place," Jace said quickly.

Tilly followed her mother to the cabinet. "I'll pour the milk, Mama, while you put the brownies on the table. You like a little kick in yours, Jace?"

He followed behind them and frowned. "What?"

Carlene giggled. "Her aunt Belinda takes a little kick of Irish whiskey in her coffee."

"And we take a little kick of chocolate in our milk," Tilly explained. "Do you have a dog? I see you with a dog and not cats."

"Yes, I do have a dog but I like cats and, yes, I do want chocolate milk," Jace answered.

"What kind? Can I see it? Does it bite?"

"My dog is a flop-eared, redbone hound and his name is Red and you can see him anytime your mama wants to bring you to my ranch, and Red doesn't bite pretty little girls." Jace turned on the charm.

"When can we go, Mama? I want to see Red. Did you name him after that Blake Shelton song about a dog?"

"Yes, I did. So you like country music, do you?" Jace asked. "We going to sit at the table or take this to the living room?"

"At the table," Tilly said. "That's where the brownies are, and Mama put a pretty cloth on it and even lit a candle, so we'll have our party in here. Is this a date?" She picked up the chocolate syrup. "One squirt or two?"

"I think I'd like three," he said.

"That's the way I like it too," Tilly said.

"Must be—"

Carlene shot him a look.

He coughed into his hand and started again. "Must be the right way to drink chocolate milk."

"Are we sitting at the table or taking this to the living room?"

"At the table," Tilly said. "That's where the brownies are and Mama put a pretty cloth on it and even lit a candle so we'll have our party in here. Is this a date?"

"Depends." Jace pulled out a chair for her.

"On what?"

"Whether I like the brownies," he teased as he seated Carlene next.

"Are you bat-crap crazy? Who doesn't like brownies?"

"Tilly!" Carlene scolded.

"Well, I didn't say the other word." Tilly's eyes twinkled. "And only someone who was that crazy wouldn't like my mama's brownies. They're the best in the whole world."

Jace finally sat down across from Carlene. "Been a long time since I had them. She might have lost her touch."

"Boys!" Tilly rolled her eyes. "Why did God even make them?"

"To drive little girls bat-crap crazy." Jace chuckled.

"Well, it worked." Tilly took a brownie and pushed the platter toward him. "She puts caramel and nuts in them but that's only part of her secret."

"What's the rest?" Jace whispered.

"She lets me kiss the spoon before she stirs them up."

Jace winked at Tilly. "This is even better than I remembered. Must be her new secret that makes them so good."

"Do you like any other country singers besides Blake?" Tilly asked.

"Yes, I do." Jace bit into the brownie and something stirred in his heart.

"I like country music too," Tilly told him. "Blake is my favorite. I listen to him all the time, don't I, Mama?"

Carlene picked up a brownie. "She also likes the old artists like George Jones and—"

"George Strait," Tilly butted in. "I decided I want a black-and-white cat and it's supposed to have at least two white feet."

Jace took a couple gulps of the chocolate milk. "And you changed the subject. I remember when your mama did that."

"Did what?" Tilly asked.

"Changed the subject in the middle of the conversation," Jace answered. "I'll check on those kittens." Oh, yes, there was a definite flutter in his heart. She was funny and smart and so danged cute that it would be easy for her to wrap him tightly around her little finger.

"Good." She licked a brownie crumb from her fingertip. "You got my mama's phone number? I'd give you mine, but Mama says I'm not old enough for my own phone. I have to wait until I'm thirteen and I can't wear makeup until I'm twenty-one."

"You've got a smart mama," Jace said.

Tilly wiggled in her seat and then jumped up. "It might not be proper and all since we're all on a date, but I got to go to the bathroom." She pushed back her chair and was barely a blur as she left the kitchen.

"Kids!" Carlene giggled.

"And I want a black-and-white cat. Remember that, Jace!" Tilly yelled from the bathroom. "Huh-oh!"

Carlene didn't like the sound of that and was on her way across the room with Jace right behind her when Tilly called out again. "Water is runnin' out over the top of the potty and gettin' all over the floor."

"Can't say it hasn't been an interesting first date." Jace grabbed the plunger. "And this just proves my point about this house."

"Don't gloat." Carlene slapped his arm. "Now I know why Aunt Rosalie keeps the mop in the bathroom. And this is absolutely not a date."

"But I really do like those brownies." Jace winked at her and then went to work on the toilet until it flushed twice without a problem.

"Man, this has been a fun night. Can we do it again?" Tilly said from the doorway.

"Sure we can," Jace answered. "But I should be going now. Tomorrow is your first day of school here in Happy and it's probably getting close to your bedtime." He picked up his coat and hat and opened the door.

"Hey, Jace, thank you," Carlene said.

"Want me to come over when you..."

She shook her head. "Let me do it my way."

Chapter Four

The fifth-grade students were at their desks, feet on the floor and quiet for Carlene's first day, which was a miracle after a long holiday. They all stared at her as if trying to figure out if she was going to be one of those tough teachers or if she'd let them get away with murder. That first day was the most important one of the whole year to set the tone.

"Good morning. I'm Miss Varner and I'm very glad to be your new teacher. I know this is quite a transition for all of you. Losing a teacher in the middle of the year isn't easy and I'm sure you all loved Mrs. Anderson. She taught school here for many years and even though I didn't have the privilege of being in elementary school here, I do know her. I'll need your help to get to know everyone and if we work together it won't be any time at all until we have things running as well as they did for you and Mrs. Anderson," she said.

A hand went up near the back of the classroom.

"Yes." She checked the chart. "Melissa, what's your question?"

"Is Mrs. Anderson ever coming back?"

"I don't think so."

Another hand.

She ran her finger down the chart. "Yes, Thomas."

"We'll see her in church on Sundays, so that's okay, Melissa."

"Thank you for that, Thomas. Now let's get out our history books," Carlene said.

"You goin' to be as mean as Mrs. Anderson?" asked a kid from the back of the room without raising his hand.

"Ten times worse," Carlene said. "Any more questions before we get to work?"

A couple of kids shook their heads. Most of them got busy getting out their books. *One smarty pants taken care of,* Carlene thought as she started telling the children about the American Revolution. The morning went by fast and at noon she walked her children up the hall toward the cafeteria. She was near the door when she caught sight of Tilly heading outside with a little dark-haired girl. They were both talking at the same time, gesturing like crazy. Tilly looked across the room, pointed at Carlene, and waved. She looked happy, and Carlene breathed a long sigh of relief.

She turned back to her own students just in time to see one of her boys put his hands on the back of the girl in front of him and give her a shove. Like a row of dominoes, the little girl fell forward into the boy in front of her, who hit the scrawny kid in front of him, and they all wound up on the floor. The little girl was the first one up with her hands knotted in fists and then suddenly the boy who'd been in front of her was on his feet in a boxing stance. Carlene took a step forward and got between them and gave them her meanest teacher glare.

"What exactly happened here?" she asked.

The blond-haired boy she'd fallen into said, "She pushed me, Miz Varner."

"Did not. Andy Bob shoved me and that made me fall into Slade," the dark-haired girl declared. "They're both mean boys."

"Gloria ain't supposed to be in our grade. She's a fourth grader," Andy Bob argued.

Carlene turned to face Andy Bob. "Young man, I will not abide bullying. I don't care if Gloria is supposed to be in first grade or eighth grade. This is where she is and you'll respect her. Do you understand me?"

Andy Bob tucked his chin to his chest. "Yes, ma'am."

She turned her gaze to Slade. "How about you? Were you going to really hit a girl?"

"No, ma'am."

"What about you, Gloria?"

"I would've decked him if he'd hit me first. Andy Bob and Slade have been mean to me all year."

"Did you tell Mrs. Anderson?" Carlene asked.

Gloria shook her head. "I'm not a rat, and besides Slade is a teacher's pet. She wouldn't believe me."

"Am not!" he said.

"Enough," Carlene said. "I will not put up with bullies or fighting in my class. Not in class, in the cafeteria, or on the playground. If it happens, there will be severe— and I do mean really hard—punishment, so think twice before you're mean to another student. Now, let's go have our lunch. We've wasted five minutes of noon recess with this, but if it happens one more time, you'll all be writing essays in the classroom during playtime for a solid week."

Carlene carried her food tray to a table close to where Andy Bob and Slade were sitting so she could keep an eye on them. She'd taken the first bite of some pretty good meat loaf when another teacher sat down across the table from her.

"You handled that situation well. Andy Bob and Slade are cousins and they aren't bad kids unless they're in the same class all day. It's like they feed off each other's ability to get into trouble. If they're apart most of the day, it's not so tough but you've got them both."

"Guess I've got my work cut out for me. I'm Carlene Varner."

"I'm Regina Watson and I teach fourth grade. I had Gloria for about three weeks last year. She'd been home-schooled before that and probably should've been bumped up to sixth grade, but her parents were worried about her being with kids who were so much older. She's brilliant and that... well, you know," Regina said.

"Thanks for the background. It helps to know these things," Carlene said.

"If you need anything, my classroom is just down the hall from yours," Regina said. "I understand that you lived here when you were a teenager."

"Yes, ma'am. Graduated from here but we moved that summer."

"Married?" Regina asked.

"No, ma'am." Carlene had the distinct feeling that Regina was fishing. Talk travels fast in small towns. "Are you married?"

"Not yet but maybe by summer." She leaned over and lowered her voice. "I heard you and Jace Dawson were an item back in the day. Did you take this job so that—"

"No," Carlene butted in before she could finish.

"Miss Watson?" A little girl tapped Regina on the shoulder. "I don't feel so good. Will you call my mama?"

"See you later," Regina told Carlene. "Duty calls."

"Leave your tray. I'll take care of it for you," Carlene offered.

"Thanks." Regina tucked the little girl's hand in hers and hurried across the floor.

*   *   *

The wind whipped dead leaves against his legs as Jace held on to his hat and hurried across the yard to the house at the Texas Star Ranch, where his sister, Kasey, lived with Nash Lamont. She threw open the door before he made it across the porch. "Good mornin'. Think this little breeze will blow up a storm?"

He hurried inside and didn't stop until he made it to the kitchen. "That's a full-fledged norther out there, not a little breeze."

"Coffee is made. Help yourself and tell me about Carlene and your daughter. Folks say she looks like me and Emma." Kasey followed along behind him.

He hung his coat and hat on the back of a kitchen chair and poured two mugs of coffee. Then he pulled out his phone, found the picture, and handed it to Kasey.

She carried it to the table and slid into a chair. "My God, Jace. There's not a single doubt. Mama said that she could be my twin, but this is uncanny. What are you going to do?"

Jace paced the floor. "Everyone keeps asking me that question, and I don't have a clue how to answer other than try to do the right thing. I'm still in shock, sis. Carlene says that she'll tell her this weekend, and she's a real cute little kid. But the weird thing is that I..." He stopped and took a sip of coffee.

Kasey continued to stare at the picture. "All this turmoil has little to do with the child. It's got more to do with Carlene, right?"

Jace stopped and looked over her shoulder at the picture. "I can't get a handle on how I feel about her, and now there's a child she didn't tell me about. I like Tilly. She's a cute kid, but..." He paused again.

Kasey slapped his arm. "Wake up! You were barely eighteen and so was she. Marriage when y'all were that young would have probably been a disaster."

He rubbed his biceps and sat down across the table from her. "You're mean."

"Had to be. I had two older brothers."

"She's had nine years to tell me. I'm sure that Rosalie kept her informed."

Kasey handed him back the phone. "I'd bet Rosalie didn't tell her jack crap about you."

Her phone rang and she held up a finger as she answered it. "Okay, I'll bring it to the office. Thanks for calling."

"What?" Jace asked when she'd set the phone aside.

She headed toward the stairs. "Rustin forgot his homework. I need to take it to the school."

"I'll do it," Jace said. "That way you won't have to take the kids out in this miserable cold. Isn't Nash off to Amarillo to get sheep feed? Henry went with him this morning."

"Thank you, Nash," Kasey answered. "And, yes, he is, along with visiting the therapist. He's hoping that she says he only needs to come back every three months after this one. Things are going really well for us, Jace, and we're so happy."

"Still thinking about a spring wedding?"

"Plannin' it for the end of March. Nothing big—maybe a

small family affair at the church and then a reception in the fellowship hall. Nash still isn't really comfortable with big crowds."

"I hear that Henry is staying until the first of the week."

"Middle, actually. He's got flight reservations for a week from today. We're going to bring him with us to the little memorial on Sunday," Kasey said. "I'll run upstairs and get Rustin's papers. I appreciate you doing this for me and if you see Carlene, tell her that she's welcome here anytime."

He shrugged. "No problem at all. I'm on my way to Amarillo for a roll of barbed wire anyway."

"Maybe you'll see your daughter. One of these days that daddy feeling will kick in. It might be slow in coming and it might happen in an instant. Nash says that it was instant with Silas but that it took a little longer with Rustin and Emma. Your daughter—that sounds strange in my ears," Kasey said, and then yelled toward the dining room. "Emma, stop bossing Silas."

"Where are they?" Jace asked.

"I built them a tent with a sheet over the table. She wants to play Barbies and he wants to build a tractor out of Lego blocks."

Jace chuckled. "And you could hear Emma?"

"Like I said—the instinct might be lyin' dormant, but it will kick in and then you'll have kid superpowers too," Kasey said.

"Right now I'm just trying to wrap my mind around that word *daughter*."

"And the feelings that Carlene has stirred up, right?"

"Something like that." He sighed.

When Kasey returned with the pages of homework, he already had his coat and hat on and was waiting at the bottom of the stairs.

"You never did say why you stopped by this morning." She handed the papers to him. "Did you need something?"

"I wanted to show you the pictures of Tilly and ask if there's any kittens out in the barn big enough to give away."

"Old white mama cat has a litter of four out there ready to find a home. Why?"

"Tilly wants a cat and Carlene says that she can have one. Thought maybe I'd see if there was a black-and-white one in the litter."

"She's welcome to however many she wants," Kasey said.

"Thanks, sis. See you later and I hope you are right about that instinct stuff. Right now all I feel is turmoil." He gripped the two sheets of homework in one hand and held his hat on with the other as he jogged toward his truck.

Jace hadn't been inside the Happy Elementary School in years but like riding a bull or a saddle bronc, it all came back, bringing memories of several years of his life, both good and bad, as he went toward the principal's office. He dropped off the papers in the principal's office and had made it halfway across the playground without even a glimpse of Tilly when someone called his name. He turned around and saw Tilly and a little dark-haired girl that he recognized as the daughter of a hired hand at Prairie Rose running toward him. He let go of his hat to wave and it went tumbling across the dirt.

Tilly grabbed it as it rolled past her.

"Well, hello, Maribel and Tilly." He smiled.

"You already know Tilly?" Maribel asked.

"Yes, I do. How are you pretty ladies today?" Jace asked.

"Maribel is my new friend." Tilly handed him the hat. "Better get you a stockin' hat. It'll stay on your head."

"And me and Tilly are goin' to be best friends." Maribel beamed. "We're goin' out on the playground now and we're goin' to hide from the boys who chased us at the mornin' recess. Don't tell 'em where we are, okay?"

Jace made the sign of the cross on his chest. "I promise I won't."

Giggling and holding hands, they ran toward the swings. He hadn't taken two steps when another voice called his name. Thinking that he was only imagining that Carlene was close by, he turned slowly. Wearing a cute little skirt that skimmed her knees and a bright red coat with the collar turned up, she wasted no time covering the distance between them. She didn't stop until she was only inches from him, the sparks flying around like fireworks on the Fourth of July.

"Are you stalking me and Tilly?"

"Hell no! I came to bring Rustin's homework. But a heads-up, I've told my whole family about her, and she's made friends with a little girl whose father works on Prairie Rose. Please tell me that you haven't changed your mind about Sunday."

"I said I would be there and I will. It is for Aunt Rosalie, after all."

With her so close that he could get a whiff of her perfume with every breath, it was all he could do to resist drawing her into his arms and nuzzling his nose into her neck right there on the school yard. He blinked half a dozen times to recall whatever they'd been talking about. Oh, yeah! It was about her and Tilly coming to the ranch on Sunday.

"Okay, then. How's your first day of school goin'?" he asked, reluctant to walk away from her.

"Already had to break up a fight, so I've shown them I'm mean. Mrs. Anderson ran a tight ship, so that helps."

"She was my fifth-grade teacher. I could have told you that she was old school. Feet in front of you, sit tall, don't talk unless you raise your hand and never pass notes."

"And I bet you obeyed every one of those rules, right?" Carlene drew her coat tighter around her body and buttoned it.

"We won't talk about that. But if I remember right, you didn't have a halo and wings back when you lived here," he teased.

"Well, hello, Jace." Regina was suddenly between them. "Hope I'm not interrupting, but Carlene and I have playground duty until the bell rings." She looked from one to the other. "So sorry. I see that you were having a private conversation."

"Carlene and I go way back to our days at good old Happy High School." Jace smiled. "I should be going. Good day, ladies." He tipped his hat and caught one more sight of Tilly on the swing set as he was leaving. Her ponytail was sticking straight out, and from the look on her face, she and Maribel were having a contest to see who could make the swings go the highest. He wanted to go over there and push her, but that wouldn't be a good idea, so he watched her from his truck until the bell rang. If Carlene wanted to call that stalking, then so be it.

*　　　*　　　*

"Women should carry around hot flash pills for when they cross paths with the likes of that cowboy," Regina sighed as she and Carlene made their way to the edge of the playground to keep an eye on the kids.

"I'm surprised he's not married," Carlene said.

"Every woman in the panhandle has been after him and Brody for years. Lila came back to Happy and boom." Regina clapped her hands. "Brody is off the market, but we still have hope for Jace. What was he like in high school?"

"Sexy as hell," Carlene said honestly just as the bell rang and kids started inside in a rush. "And thank goodness for the bell," she muttered as she found her way through the maze of students to her room. She slumped in her chair, crossed her arms, and laid her head down on her desk. In five minutes a bunch of energetic students would burst inside the room, so she had to get control of the butterflies in her stomach.

It was time to get down to business, which meant she had to get the vision of Jace out of her head and think about math. But no kids rushed in, all excited from running and playing, hanging their coats on the long rack of hooks. She checked her schedule; physical education after lunch three days a week, music on the other two days.

She inhaled deeply and let it out slowly. "Thank you, sweet Lord. I need a thirty-minute break to get myself together," she whispered. "I was crazy to move here, but it seemed like Fate was pushing me. And now I'm talkin' to myself. What am I going to do?"

You are going to accept what you can't change. You knew what would happen when you took this job. Aunt Rosalie was giving advice again.

Carlene couldn't change the fact that she had to move out of the house. She couldn't change the fact that Tilly belonged to Jace. But she had a few weeks before she had to move and a few days before she had to tell Tilly about Jace. She raised her head. The plan was to get through the next three days, and then sometime Saturday she'd tell Tilly about Jace. Once she had a plan written in stone, she could face anything. She'd proved that in the past when she decided to bow out of Jace's life.

The afternoon went faster than the morning and when the final bell rang, Carlene's smile was genuine and not pasted on. Like always, Tilly came straight to her room, talking nonstop about her day just like she used to do in Florida.

"I'm glad we moved so you don't have to be a substitute anymore and can have your own room. Did you see I got a new friend, Maribel, and she's got cats at her house and her daddy works for Jace, that cowboy that came to our house and guess what, he was here at the school today and can we have spaghetti for supper?" She finally stopped to take in a lungful of air. "Maribel says that Jace is real nice and the ranch where her daddy works is real big and she gets to go four-wheel ridin' out there on it sometimes with her daddy. And can I go with her if I be real careful and guess what else?"

"Slow down." Carlene laughed. "I'm so glad you made a new friend, but we've got the rest of the afternoon and evening for you to tell me all this."

"Spaghetti?"

"Of course, and ice cream with caramel on top to celebrate us both getting through our first day at the new school." Carlene packed her well-worn shoulder bag with papers to grade that evening. "Ready?"

"Mama, I like that Jace cowboy. Why don't you ask him out on a date?"

Carlene had to think fast and even then she stuttered. "Girls wait for guys to ask them out."

"Why?" Tilly went out ahead of Carlene and waited for her mother to turn out the lights and lock the door.

"Because that's the way it's done."

"Not on television. The girls ask the boys out all the time," Tilly argued. "When I get big enough to go on dates, I'm going to ask the boys."

"Why?" Carlene asked.

"Because I want to. And, Mama, when I find a boy to fall in love with, he's going to be a cowboy like Jace. Why don't you call him and ask him to eat spaghetti with us."

"I will not, Tilly Rose Varner," Carlene gasped. "And please tell me that you didn't do that, either."

"Nope." Tilly crawled into the van and fastened her seat belt. "But I wanted to."

Jace Dawson wouldn't like being called pretty. She smiled.

Chapter Five

Tilly ran across the living room floor like a wild Texas tornado, slung open the door, and said, "Come in, Jace. Did you see if there was kittens in your barn?"

"There were a couple over at my sister's ranch," he answered.

Tilly hugged herself. "Did she say I could have one?"

"Carlene? Can Tilly have a kitten?"

"We could sure use a cat. Tilly says she saw a mouse the other day." Carlene shivered at the thought.

"You okay?" Jace asked with real concern on his face.

"I hate spiders, and Mama hates mice," Tilly explained.

"Well, then, it's a good thing I found a little black-and-white kitten for you."

Tilly shrieked with excitement. "That's just what I wanted!"

Jace smiled. "I seem to remember you mentioning it. Shall I bring her in or hold on to her until you get moved into your new place?" He looked at Carlene, eyebrow raised.

"If it will take care of mice, I've got no objection to having her right now. Bring her on inside." Carlene's heart settled to a steady beat as she made her way to the living room.

Carlene hadn't rolled into Happy expecting any kind of reunion with him. She'd thought that he was probably married and had a child or two and hoped that when he did find out about Tilly, it didn't cause a problem in his relationship. But she was sure enough wrong on every single scenario that had played through her mind.

Tilly danced around on one foot. "Do kittens chase off spiders too?"

"They might. I'll go out to my truck and get her. I'm sure she's gonna be real happy to meet you, Tilly."

Tilly did a couple of spins and squealed so loud that if there had been a mouse in the house, it wouldn't have quit running until it hit the New Mexico state line. When she settled down, she wrapped her arms around Carlene and hugged her tightly. "Thank you, Mama. This is the best day of my life," Tilly declared.

Jace brought in a box with a few holes poked in the sides. He set it on the floor and Tilly sucked in so much air that Carlene thought she might explode. Then she let it out in a long whoosh.

"This is better than Christmas," she said as she looked inside. "Oh, Mama, I love her already."

"You'll have to take her to the vet in a few months if you don't want two or three litters a year," he said.

"Thank you, Jace," Carlene said. "I'm sure she'll be babied until she thinks she's human instead of feline."

Jace dropped to his knees beside the box. "What are you going to name her?"

"What's her mama's name?" she asked.

"White Mama Cat is all I've ever heard her called. She's pure white and lives in my sister's barn."

"What's their daddy's name?"

"Don't have any idea who their daddy is," Jace answered honestly.

Tilly picked her up and held her close to her chest. "That's great! She's just like me. I don't know who my daddy is either. Mama says it don't matter because she can be my mama and daddy both. I guess that's what White Mama Cat told these babies. Well, come on, sweet darlin', you don't need a daddy in this house because my mama can be both to us."

Carlene didn't know whether to giggle or weep, so she just blushed and kept her eyes downcast. No way did she want to see what Jace was thinking. He'd never been able to hide his emotions and one look would tell her exactly how that last statement had affected him.

"Thank you, Jace. I'm going to take her to my room now. Mama, can I call Natalie and tell her? She's going to be so jealous that I got a baby kitten and she can't have any because her daddy is allergic. See there, baby girl, if we had a daddy, he might be allergic and you'd have to live in an old ratty barn," she crooned on the way down the hall.

Jace rolled up on his feet and sank down on the end of the sofa without an invitation. "I guess I just got told off right well."

"Might as well take off your coat. Want a cup of coffee or a beer or something?"

"I might take that shot of whiskey you offered last time I was here," he said.

"Ouch!" She jumped up.

"What?"

"This sofa is one thing I'm definitely not going to miss when I move into my new house. Its springs keep pokin' me. Two shots of whiskey coming right up."

"Didn't she ever ask about a dad?" he whispered.

She poured the last of the Jack Daniel's into two shot glasses. "Not until she was in first grade and there was a father-daughter dance at the school for Valentine's Day. Do they…"

"Yep, they still have the Happy Elementary School father and daughter dance at Valentine's. You think she'll ask me to go with her?"

"One step at a time." She set the whiskey on the coffee table and went back for two bottles of water. "How would you feel about it if she did ask you? How do you even feel about having a daughter, Jace? Are you all warm and oozy or kind of trying to figure things out?"

"I'd go if she asked me and yes, I'm trying to figure things out, Carlene."

When she returned and handed him the whiskey, he touched his glass to hers in a toast. "Here's to the future."

They downed the whiskey at the same time and she'd bent to reach for the water when a mouse darted across the coffee table, brushing against her hand in the journey from one end to the other. It bounded off the edge like it had a tiny parachute on its back, scampered across her bare foot, and did a couple of circles around the Christmas tree until it got its bearing and dashed off toward the kitchen.

Carlene tried to walk on air, but she had no wings. She jumped up on the coffee table and all four legs went out from under it. She was falling forward, hoping she didn't break a bone, when suddenly strong arms were around her, and her feet were dangling several inches off the floor.

All those old feelings she thought she'd buried swirled to the surface. Jace's eyelashes fluttered down to rest on his cheeks and her tongue darted out to moisten her lips. The kiss started out soft and tender, barely grazing her mouth; then it deepened into more, sending waves of desire through her body. Then just as quickly as it started, it was over and he set her on the floor.

"I told you this place wasn't fit to live in," he said.

"So I'll buy some mousetraps," she snapped. Why were they talking about traps when she wanted to kiss him again and see if the second one would buckle her knees as much as the first?

He took a step back. "Sorry about that. I got caught up in the moment."

"Don't apologize. Consider it payment for saving me from a bad fall."

"Well, darlin', you can fall into my arms any time you want to," Jace said with a wicked grin as he picked up all the pieces to the table and carried them toward the door. "One less thing you'll have to deal with when you move."

"Too bad I didn't destroy the sofa too," she muttered, still breathless and scanning every inch of the floor to be sure that wicked critter hadn't come back.

"What is going on? I was talkin' to Natalie and tellin' her about my cat and it sounded like an explosion in here." Tilly touched her on the arm.

Carlene's soul slowly settled back into her body as she gave the room another quick glance. "A mouse ran over my foot."

"Must've been a huge one to tear down the coffee table," Tilly said.

"I jumped on it," Carlene said.

"She tried to walk on air." Jace chuckled as he brought in

the litter pan filled with all the things her kitten would need. "It didn't work too well."

"If it'd been a spider, I'd be standin' on the back of the sofa." Tilly giggled and then turned serious.

Jace laughed out loud. "Let me know when and if you want me to help with anything. I've got some other errands to run so I'll be going." Jace picked up his coat. "Thanks for the drink. Seems like it tasted better out at Henry's old barn, don't it?"

"Everything tastes better when it's forbidden," she said.

"Ain't that the truth." Jace leveled her a look with his stunning gray eyes that made her weak in the knees. "Mind if I come around and see the kitten every now and then?" Jace released Carlene from his gaze and turned to Tilly.

"Anytime." Tilly waved back at him, then sniffed the air. "I smell..."

"Whiskey. Jace and I had a shot. You want a glass of chocolate milk and some leftover brownies for a bedtime snack?"

"When I get big, I'm going to drink whiskey. I like the way it smells," Tilly said. "But since I'm just a little kid, I'll have milk and brownies for now."

Carlene rolled her eyes toward the ceiling. When Tilly was born, Carlene didn't think she needed a father for her baby. After all, she'd grown up just fine without one. Oh, there'd been a father in the house all right, but she'd always felt like she was nothing but a disappointment to him. And that had been multiplied by a thousand when he found out she was pregnant. Her sister, Belinda, who was ten years older than Carlene, had stepped up and taken her in when their father declared that she was an embarrassment to him, her mother, and their careers.

But maybe Fate drove her back to Happy so that she

could have some help with the teenage years. With Varner and Dawson blood in her veins, Tilly was bound to be one determined, make-her-own-rules girl.

*   *   *

"Thank goodness for mice." Jace couldn't wipe the smile off his face as he drove toward town. But the humor was soon overshadowed by the big picture looming in the background. Tilly seemed to like him and she loved the kitten, but what would she think of him as a father? And had Carlene felt the same electricity that he did when they shared that amazing kiss?

Wake up and quit thinkin' life would have been a fairy tale if you two had gotten married.

"And where does that leave me today, right now?" he asked himself as he parked his truck in front of the sprawling ranch house on Prairie Rose Ranch.

A few weeks ago he thought he'd have loved having the big house all to himself. He'd been looking forward to his mother finally retiring and moving into the small two-bedroom house that she'd had built toward the back of the ranch. For the first time in his life, he'd be truly on his own.

But a couple days after she'd gone, the place felt too quiet, too empty. Jace had already started spending time at Hope Springs with Brody and Lila or over at Texas Star with Kasey's family.

Finally, with a sigh, he got out of the truck, braced himself against the ever-blowing wind, and hurried inside. An enormous living room that had entertained hundreds, maybe thousands of people in the past fifty years opened off the foyer. A stone fireplace covered one end with oak bookcases on either side. A buttery-soft leather sofa that did not have springs poking up through the bottom beckoned to him and he plopped down into the corner. Propping his feet on the coffee table and leaning his head back, he let the past half hour play over and over through his mind, from the expres-sions on Carlene's and Tilly's faces to that scorching hot kiss. He'd kissed lots of women in the past ten years but not a single one of them had affected him like Carlene did.

He didn't realize that he'd gotten to his feet and was pacing until Brody pushed into the foyer and called out, "Anybody home? Jace, you here?"

"In the living room," he raised his voice to say.

"Why are you sitting in the dark?" Brody flipped the light switch.

"Didn't realize I was," he answered.

"Kascy said you took a kitten to Carlene's. When is this coming out into the open so we can meet your daughter? Whole family is eager to see more than pictures on your phone. Mama even went to the school yesterday on a trumped up school board excuse, but she didn't see Tilly." Brody pushed through two swinging doors into the kitchen and returned with two longneck bottles of beer. "You look miserable. What happened?"

Jace took a bottle from Brody's hand and tipped it up for several long gulps before he sank back onto the sofa again. "I would have married her, Brody. I would have done the right thing and *not* just because she was pregnant."

"I know that. And the whole family knows it too. We've been over this before, so what's the real problem?"

"I'm so damned angry at her," Jace admitted. "It broke my heart when she moved away at the end of the summer. Then a week later she changed her phone number and I couldn't even get in touch with her."

Brody sat down on a recliner and popped the footrest up.

"That's probably about the time she found out she was pregnant and made up her mind for a clean break."

"I kissed her tonight," Jace blurted out.

"Did she slap you?" Brody asked.

"No, it was like this..." He went on to tell about the mouse and breaking down the old coffee table.

Brody chuckled through the story. "And where was Tilly in all this noise?"

"In her room talking on the phone with her friend in Florida. The legs just popped off the table and it went down with a thud; then Carlene was in my arms. Tilly came out after the kiss ended."

"How'd it affect you?" Brody asked.

"How'd that first kiss with Lila last summer affect you?" Jace shot back.

"If it's anything like that one was," Brody groaned, "you are in big trouble."

"Yep." Jace nodded.

*   *   *

Carlene didn't need a coffee table. It was just another piece of furniture to bump her knees on and have to dust. Besides, all vertical surfaces attracted junk like flies on honey. So why did it upset her so much to have broken it?

"It's not the table," she sniffled. "I'm supposed to be strong and fearless, and Jace saw me vulnerable and terrified."

Tilly bounced into the room after her bath, stopped so fast that her damp feet screeched against the hard wood floor, and pointed at the television. "Kill it, Mama. Hurry!"

Adrenaline rushed through Carlene's veins and she expected to see a mouse when she made herself look that way.

But it was a huge daddy longlegs inching its way to the floor. Poor Tilly was glued to the floor and shaking so badly that her finger trembled.

Like mice, the only good spider was a dead one, so Carlene quickly grabbed a paper towel and killed the wicked critter, carried it to the trash can in the kitchen, and tossed it inside. When she returned, Tilly was still standing in the same place, but she was calmly checking out the whole room for another terrifying varmint.

"I want another house tomorrow," Tilly said bluntly.

Carlene hugged her daughter and kissed her on the forehead. "We'll move, no doubt about that, but it will take me a while to find a place and get things arranged. Until then, if you'll let your kitten take care of the mice, then I'll do away with any spiders. Your aunt Belinda says that they're both more scared of us than we are of them and I bet they didn't know we were moving in here. Now that they do, they'll keep away from this place until we move out."

"If you hadn't already broke down the coffee table, I would have. That thing was as big as a bear." Tilly shivered again.

"Have you named your kitten yet?" Carlene asked to get Tilly's mind away from the spider. "Did Natalie have any good ideas?"

Tilly shook her head. "Next time I see Jace, I'm goin' to ask him what kind of names he likes for cats."

"What makes you think we'll see Jace again?" Carlene asked.

Tilly shrugged and pointed. "Look. She's comin' out here to play."

Carlene's phone rang, taking her attention away from the cute little kitten with her nose to the ground as if she were hunting. She fished the phone from her pocket as Tilly went to follow behind her new pet as she made her way to the Christmas tree and clawed at the trunk.

"Hello?" she said on the fifth ring.

"Hey, sis, how did the first two days of school go?" Belinda asked. "Did you run into you-know-who? Is he married?"

Carlene filled her in on the house news, her job, and then told her about the arguments she'd had with Jace but she didn't tell her about that kiss. "And then there was the mouse and the spider."

"Oh. My. Goodness. Both in one evening." Belinda laughed. "You broke the coffee table and what did Tilly do? Sprout wings and fly to the top of the fridge?"

"No, but she would have probably liked to," Carlene laughed.

"I'm glad you aren't staying in that place forever," Belinda said. "Use the money Aunt Rosalie left you and put a down payment on something decent. Why don't you just stay in a motel until you can find something else?"

"I'll look at a couple places over the weekend, I promise. There's two really nice little brick houses for sale not far from the school."

"Good. So Jace isn't married? Think he might still be carrying a torch for you?" Belinda said.

"I need to talk to Aunt Bee," Tilly said. "She might have good kitten names."

"Give her the phone," Belinda laughed. "And remember what Aunt Rosalie always said about things passing."

"This, too, shall pass," Carlene sighed. "But the distance between the beginning and the passing takes forever."

"Yes, it does. I read a sign last week that said, 'This, too, shall pass. It might pass like a kidney stone but it will pass.'" Belinda giggled.

Carlene laughed with her and was suddenly nostalgic about all the evenings they'd spent together and the way Belinda could bring her out of the doldrums. "Amen to that. More like a birthin' than a kidney stone. Sometimes the passing is difficult and painful."

"And when it's all over, the pain is forgotten. Now, let me talk to my niece and then I'll tell you all about this guy I met at work," Belinda said.

"You? A guy? Hold the presses!"

"Oh, hush or I won't tell you anything."

Tilly was sitting on the floor with her kitten in her lap when Carlene handed the phone to her. She started off telling her aunt Bee every single detail about her week.

"Bedtime," Carlene said.

"Love you, Aunt Bee. Oh, I forgot. The potty ran over too and there was water everywhere. Here's Mama."

"Good Lord! You've got to get out of there." Belinda's voice went all high and shrill.

"It's not the end of the world. Just a little...rustic. We're fine for now," Carlene said. "I'll find a new place soon, I promise. Now tell me about this guy."

She put the phone on speaker when it was time to tuck Tilly into bed. The tone of Belinda's voice when she told Tilly good night made Carlene go all misty eyed. She hadn't thought about how much Belinda would miss them.

Belinda had been the one who had been there through the whole pregnancy, who'd walked the floor with a crying baby until they'd figured out she was lactose intolerant and got her formula straightened out, and who'd read Tilly bedtime stories when Carlene had to grade papers in the evenings. Belinda was the one who'd insisted every time she moved that they do the same and who'd even helped her locate teaching jobs. No wonder her sister hadn't had time for a relationship for almost a decade—she'd been too busy helping take care of Tilly.

A fresh wave of guilt washed over Carlene. Tears streamed down her face. She'd been too busy to realize how much she would miss her sister until that moment. Talking to her was great but popping into her apartment right across the landing for a glass of tea or a bottle of beer—well, that wasn't going to happen. Not with Belinda at her new job in Hampton, Virginia, and Carlene in the Texas panhandle.

Things had happened so quickly. First Belinda came home with the news that she had been transferred from Eglin Air Force Base to one in Virginia and then Aunt Rosalie told Carlene about the job in Happy and it had kind of fallen into Carlene's lap. After that, there'd been a flurry of packing and cleaning the apartments where they lived and then Aunt Rosalie died.

She picked up the phone and hit the speed dial for her sister.

"Is everything all right?" Belinda asked.

"It's fine. I just wanted to say that I'm so, so sorry," Carlene sobbed.

"Because your daughter is asleep or because you are not over that cowboy?" Belinda yawned loudly.

"No, because I stole all those years of your life." Carlene hiccupped. "We should've moved out on our own so much sooner."

"Oh, hush! You're emotional because you finally have the time to miss me. I went through that three days ago and almost got on a plane to Texas. We're grown women. We made decisions and I'm not sorry for the one I made. Having Tilly and you in my life has been amazing. I wouldn't redo a single minute of it. Now paddle that guilt boat to shore and set fire to it," Belinda said.

Carlene managed a weak giggle at the visual. "I'm still sorry. If we hadn't been there, you would have found a wonderful guy years ago and had four kids by now."

"Honey, I'm amazing aunt material, but there's no mother instinct in me. It's debatable if I'll ever even be wife material. Now go to sleep and don't wake me up again, not even if a mouse is sitting on your pillow. Good night."

Belinda was bluntly honest and truthful, so Carlene didn't harbor any idea that she might be smoothing things over to make her feel better. No, sir, Belinda spoke her mind and liked being in control. That's why she had advanced so far in her military career.

She crawled into bed and shut her eyes. Every word that she and Jace had exchanged that evening flashed through her mind, like instant replays, some hanging around in slow motion while others sped through in fast forward. His eyes, looking all dreamy after that kiss, his strong arms breaking the fall, and most of all the way his lips felt on hers—she raised a hand to touch her mouth, surprised that it wasn't scalding hot.

"I really thought I'd moved on, but I guess I was just standing still and waiting," she said.

Chapter Six

Tilly hit Carlene's room on Friday afternoon in a dead run and had to grab the teacher's desk to stop herself. "Mama, Mama, guess what? There's a bronc bustin' tonight at the rodeo grounds and Maribel is goin' with her daddy. Can we go, too, Mama? Please, please, please!"

Carlene laid a finger over Tilly's mouth. "Calm down and take a breath. I thought you wanted to get rid of that tree tonight."

"I'll help do it tomorrow, I promise." Tilly made the sign of the cross over her heart. "Please, Mama."

"I reckon it won't hurt for the tree to stand there one more night but first thing in the mornin', it has to go. It's shedding worse and worse every day."

"Then we can go?" Tilly's eyes sparkled.

"Yes, we can go," Carlene agreed.

Tilly did a couple of fast spins and hugged Carlene. "Thanks, Mama! This is goin' to be awesome!"

Carlene remembered lots of rodeo events during the three years that she'd lived in Happy. Both Dawson brothers had ridden bulls at the first one she'd attended. That might have been the night she actually fell in love with Jace, even though it was a year before he actually asked her out on a date. Would Brody and Jace be riding tonight?

Before she could leave the school, Carlene stuffed all the papers she'd grade over the weekend into her bag, made sure that the desks were lined up and that everything in the room was in shape for Monday morning. While she worked, Tilly talked about all the kids in her class who wore cowboy boots to school.

"I got to call Aunt Bee before we leave for the bronc bustin' and tell her that I want to change my birthday present. I need cowboy boots for my birthday." Tilly rattled on and on as they crossed the playground.

"Hey." Regina was putting things into her pickup truck, parked right beside Carlene's minivan. "I've been trying to get away all afternoon to tell you about the event at the rodeo grounds tonight."

"Thanks. It's all Tilly's been talkin' about since the last bell rang. We might see you there?"

"Oh, yeah. Save you a seat?" Regina asked.

"I thought you were stalking Jace Dawson," Carlene teased.

"Nah, my feller, Randy Dickson, will be riding. He's not a pro by any means but he's all cowboy. If I get there first, I'll save room. Since it's a fund-raiser for that little boy in Tulia with cancer and the first event in several months, the stands will be packed."

"I'll look for you then," Carlene said, wishing Regina would have mentioned if Jace would be riding that night.

"I like her," Tilly said as soon as they were inside the van. "She'll be my teacher next year, right?"

"Most likely." Carlene was happy that Tilly had made the transition from one school and set of friends to another so easily. But then kids were resilient that way—much, much more than adults. Hopefully she'd accept the news of her father just as well.

When they reached the house, Tilly skipped across the yard and up onto the porch. She was so excited that she didn't even see two daddy longlegs beside the door.

Carlene checked the mailbox and removed a couple of utility bills still in Rosalie's name, of course, and a seed catalog. She stomped her foot. "I can't even go to the cemetery and put flowers on a grave. You could have lived with me and Tilly. We would have taken care of you. But whether you like it or not, we are having a memorial."

One foot was on the bottom porch step when her phone rang. She pulled her coat tighter around her body and sat down. "Hello, Mama. How are things in Alabama?"

"Your dad is being transferred to California. We leave next week. Love to come through Texas but they're going to fly us out and put us in temporary housing until our car and things arrive."

"Do you ever get tired of moving?" Carlene laid the mail to the side.

"I'm not your aunt Rosalie, Carlene. I wasn't made to stay in one place. That's why your father and I are such good companions," she answered. "I'll text you the address as soon as I know it."

"How's Dad doing with Aunt Rosalie's death? That's the last of that generation."

"You know your dad. He's not the sentimental type. I

barely knew her but then she was his grandfather's sister and wasn't actually related to me."

Carlene frowned. "Well, I am and I'm feeling guilty because we didn't come around more often."

"She came to see you and Belinda every year, so you did see her." Her mother paused and then changed the subject. "What's goin' on there?"

"Tilly has met and likes Jace," she answered.

Deborah's long sigh came through the phone. "That could be a good thing. At least he's not married."

"How did you know that?"

"I have my ways."

"Aunt Rosalie?"

"No!" Deborah almost snorted. "That old lady never did like me."

"Why didn't you tell me?" Carlene huffed.

"Well, you made it pretty clear you wanted a clean break, now, didn't you? Seems like your words were that you didn't want to ever hear his name."

"And that's when Daddy told me that I was going to live with Belinda." A cold north wind whipped Carlene's hair around her face and threatened to blow the mail off the porch. She stood up and quickly went inside the house.

"You caused it, Carlene. If you'd have had the good sense to use birth control—or not fool around in the first place!—you wouldn't have gotten pregnant."

"No use scolding me now." Carlene sighed. "I need to fix Tilly an after-school snack. Don't forget to text me your address."

"Will do," Deborah said, and hung up.

"No good-bye. No 'I love you.' And that's why I'm determined to be a good mother no matter what the sacrifice.

I don't intend for Tilly to ever feel unloved. And it's also why—"

"Who are you talkin' to, Mama?" Tilly bounced down the hall with her kitten wrapped in one of her doll's blankets.

"Your grandmother."

"Did you tell her about my kitten?"

"I thought you'd want to do that the next time she calls. Shall we have cookies and milk?" Carlene asked.

"I want a double kick in mine today." Tilly laid the kitten on the sofa but she quickly climbed down and scampered back to her room.

"You sure you want to go to this thing tonight? Would you rather go up to Amarillo, eat at Dairy Queen, and go to the movies? We've had a big week, what with moving in here and you getting all settled in school. It could just be an evening of me and you."

And I can tell you all about Jace and the Dawsons and try to explain why I kept it a secret.

Tilly got the milk and chocolate syrup out of the refrigerator. "Nope. I want to sit with Maribel and watch the horses. I've named my kitten. Want me to tell you?"

Carlene took a long, deep breath and let it out slowly. "Of course I do."

"Her name is Jasmine," Tilly said. "I wish you would have named me Merida instead of Matilda and then we could both be Disney princesses." She took her milk to the kitchen table and sat down. "Can I call Aunt Bee and tell her that I picked out a name after we finish our snack?"

"You'll always be my princess, no matter what your name is," Carlene said. "And you can call your aunt Bee while I take a bath. Now let's talk about what we're going to do this weekend, other than get that tree out of our house."

*   *   *

As she and Tilly walked across their lawn out to the dirt road toward the rodeo grounds, Carlene tried to keep the butterflies at bay. It was impossible not to let all Tilly's infectious excitement affect her. But most of the jitters was from knowing that Jace and the whole Dawson clan would be at the event since the Prairie Rose Ranch was the sponsor. By the time they reached the gate, her hands were shaking so badly that she dropped her wallet.

"I wondered if you might be here tonight." Paul McKay picked it up and handed it to her and lowered his voice to a whisper. "You do know the entire Dawson clan is sitting in the stands already?"

"Thanks." Carlene's hands continued to shake as she took the wallet from him.

"There's Maribel, Mama." Tilly tugged on her hand. "Over there on the bottom seat with a bunch of kids. Can I go sit with them, please, please, please? I won't go anywhere else less I come and tell you, I promise."

Carlene spotted an empty space two rows up from where the children had gathered. She could keep an eye on Tilly and still watch the bronc riding from that point. "Okay, but remember your promise. You have to stay right there," Carlene said.

"Maribel told me we get to yell for the ones we like. Kind of like Aunt Bee when the Dallas Cowboys are playin'."

Along with Maribel, several other little girls ran to greet Tilly and surround her as they all went back to their place on the bottom row.

Sitting down on the old wooden seats not far up from where Tilly was, she scanned the stands for Jace and his family. It wasn't hard to spot Kasey with that curly red hair so very like Tilly's. Evidently the tall, dark guy beside her was Nash Lamont, Henry Thomas's great-nephew. Paul's wife, Gracie, was holding a little blond-haired boy in her lap and an older child was seated on the other side of Nash. God could have been a lot nicer and given her a blond-haired child with brown or even blue eyes instead of a red-haired one with Jace's unusual gray eyes. But like Belinda often said, "Man plans and God giggles."

She recognized the gray-haired man sitting right behind Hope as Henry. She hadn't known him so well in Happy. He'd disappeared not long after she'd moved there but they'd rekindled their friendship in Florida when he recognized her and immediately knew that Tilly was a Dawson. He drove his ice cream truck right past her apartment a couple times a week. She and Tilly both got so excited when they heard the music playing. He'd always reminded her of Avery Markham, a character in the last season of *Justified*. What was his name? She touched her lips with her finger and tried to remember. It was someone Aunt Rosalie liked.

"Sam Elliott," she blurted out when it came to mind.

"I love his voice." Regina climbed up the bleachers and handed her a Coke. "Here. I saw you come in while I was in line for food and thought you might want something to drink."

"Thanks so much," Carlene said.

"So how do you think they're gonna take it?" Regina asked, nodding toward the Dawson family.

"Oh, I think they already know. I'm more worried about how Tilly is going to take the news," Carlene shared.

"The way all the Dawsons are staring right at her, you might want to tell her tonight," Regina said.

"Hello, ladies," Jace drawled as he took the bleacher steps two at a time.

Carlene looked up and felt herself sinking into his eyes—a dangerous place to dive into right there in public with his whole family not fifty feet away. She shifted her gaze to his long legs and thighs that filled out those tight-fitting jeans so well. She'd always been a sucker for a cowboy but it had gotten worse when she passed the city limits sign of Happy, Texas, last week.

Before she could recover enough to say a word, Jace was sitting beside her. "I see that Tilly has made a lot of friends. Glad to see her and both of you here tonight." He leaned around Carlene to ask Regina, "Is Randy ridin'?"

"Number six on the docket. How about you?"

"First one." He nudged Carlene with his shoulder. "You goin' to yell for me?"

"Sounds like you've got your own cheering squad down there with the kids. Is Brody riding?" Carlene was amazed that her voice was anywhere near calm. His cheek had brushed against her breast when he leaned back, and even through her jacket, it shot tingles down her spine.

"No, he's in the press box doing the announcing for us," Jace answered.

The weather satellite circling the earth probably picked up a big red spot of heat right where Carlene was sitting when his knee touched hers. Electricity sizzled all around her and the vibes made her feel like a minor earthquake had hit.

"Cold wind pickin' up." Regina shivered against the north wind that was creating miniature dust tornadoes out there in the arena.

"I found two more houses for you to consider buying," Jace said.

"I'm not looking for a place. Randy and I just moved in together," Regina said.

"I was talking to Carlene, but congratulations. You and Randy make a good couple," Jace said.

"Carlene, when you get ready to move, call me and I'll be glad to help," Regina said. "I was surprised to hear that you even moved into Rosalie's old house since the rodeo folks are tearin' it down soon."

"Hey, Jace!!" Maribel screamed so loud that every eye in the stands turned toward them. "Me and Tilly are down here and we're gonna holler for you."

He gave them a thumbs-up and turned to face Carlene. "Kind of nice to have a cheerin' squad of my own. I gotta go get ready. See you ladies later."

Carlene watched him swagger down the bleachers, jump the fence, and do a mock argument with the clowns on his way across the arena.

"He was flirtin' with you," Regina whispered.

"No, he wasn't. He's just eager for me to tell Tilly and get it over with. I'm not sure he even knows how he feels about all this," Carlene said.

"Honey, I'm a pro at the flirting game, so don't argue with me." Regina nudged her on the shoulder. "And about houses. Randy and I looked at one out at the edge of town going toward Tulia. It's a two bedroom but it's only got a couple of acres with it and we needed at least forty. Right on the highway and there's a For Rent sign hangin' on the barbed wire fence."

"Thanks, I'll take a look at it this weekend." Carlene smiled.

A booming voice from the press box filled the arena. "Evenin', folks. We're glad y'all came out tonight for the fund-raiser. Want to thank Donnie Turner for bringing his livestock up to this event and not charging us. And to our ladies from the rodeo association for taking care of the concession tonight. Now, is everyone ready for some fun?"

Whoops, hollers, and whistles answered him.

"Okay, then, in a few minutes my brother, Jace Dawson, will start off the bronc riding tonight. We've got a good lineup of cowboys for the evening, but before Jace comes out of the chute tryin' to hang on to that bareback bronc for a full eight seconds, let's hear it for our clowns."

A clown rode a stick horse out of a chute and put on quite a show before he fell off to the side and the other three clowns rescued him. Everyone's attention was on the spectacle in the arena. But Carlene's eyes were on Jace as he crawled down off the side of the chute onto the bronc's back. In a few seconds he'd come out of there in a blur with that horse's hind legs pointed toward the moon and its nose practically in the dirt as it tried to throw him off its back. She'd seen it all before and what had been exciting when they were in high school was far scarier than a mouse that evening. What if Jace was killed and she had to tell Tilly that she'd never know her father?

Want to go back and undo the decision to move to Happy? Rosalie's voice was in her head again.

No. But I do wish I'd told Tilly earlier about her father and that I'd really moved on like I thought I had.

"Listen to those kids. I believe they're louder than the whole Dawson clan." Regina broke into Carlene's thoughts. "Jace had better stay on that bronc's back the full time or they'll be so disappointed."

"And now coming out of chute number one is Jace Dawson riding Blaze of Glory. There goes his hat, folks. Will he make it the whole eight seconds?"

Carlene couldn't breathe or blink. With one hand tightly

under the rope and the other toward the sky, Jace was tossed back and forth like a rag doll as the horse's back bowed up in the middle one second and the next his hind legs tried to kick the stars.

You could have told her even if you didn't want him to know, Aunt Rosalie scolded.

She let out eight seconds' worth of pent-up air when the horn sounded that the ride was complete. The whole stretch of Dawson family, including Henry, was on their feet, clapping, stomping, and whistling. Then Tilly and Maribel led a chant over everyone else as they screamed, "Jace Dawson! Jace Dawson!" The pickup men rode out and helped him get free of the horse and immediately the second stall opened with another rider trying to beat the clock.

"Did you miss this when you moved away?" Regina asked. "Oh, look! Jace jumped the fence and is sitting with the kids. Isn't that sweet? All the children will go home tonight with stars in their little eyes."

Carlene wasn't even aware that she was standing but suddenly she was light-headed, so she sat down with a thud. From what she could see from her position, Tilly's eyes really were twinkling as she shook her head and said something that put a huge smile on Jace's face.

*   *   *

"We hollered for you," Maribel said.

"I heard you." Jace sat down between Maribel and Tilly. "That's what kept me on that buckin' bronc's back until they blew the horn."

"Someday I'm going to ride broncs," Maribel said.

"What about you, Tilly? You want to learn to ride?"

She shook her head. "Nope. I want to be a clown. That

looks like more fun. I like to make people laugh, and Mama can make me a clown outfit. Can you teach me how to be one of them?"

"Sometimes I'm the rodeo clown, so I expect I could give you some pointers if your mama don't mind," Jace answered.

The horn blasted loudly and Brody announced: "Fell a little short there, cowboy, but White Demon is a tough bronc. Let's give him a big hand while our next rider gets set. Only ten more rides and...gate is open and look at that cowboy ride, folks. Now that's worth comin' out tonight right there."

Kasey stopped in front of Jace. "Hey, you got your own fan club?"

"Yep, he does," Maribel said. "Me and Tilly is the bosses of it. The boys all got to do what we say or we won't let them be bronc busters when they grow up."

"You can't stop me from ridin', and you ain't the boss of our club. We done already had it made up before you girls got to the arena tonight," said a little freckle-faced boy.

"We'll make our own club, then," Maribel told him.

Tilly studied Kasey seriously. "Who are you? Have we met before?"

"I'm Jace's sister, and I don't believe we've ever met," Kasey said. "Who are you?"

"I'm sorry," Jace said. "Tilly Rose Varner, this is my sister Kasey, and, Kasey, this is Tilly. Her mama is the new teacher at the school."

"Well"—Kasey stuck out a hand—"I'm pleased to meet you."

Tilly shook with her. "You got the same color hair as me. Mama says that it's like oak leaves in the fall."

"That's what my mama used to say too." Kasey smiled. "Well, I'm going down to the concession stand. My kids are yellin' for candy bars."

Tilly's eyes lit up. "Mama told me that you have kids. Can I meet them sometime?"

"I've got three and they'd love to meet you. Their names are Rustin, Emma, and Silas."

Tilly clapped her hands. "Are you Jace's sister that gave me the kitten? I named her Jasmine. Maybe your kids could come see her sometime."

"Emma would like it that you named her after a princess," Kasey said. "Got to be going. Nice to meet you, Tilly Rose Varner. Nice name. I like it."

Tilly stood up on the seat and cupped her hand over Kasey's ear. "It's really Matilda Rose but I don't like Matilda too much. Mama said it was for her aunt, Matilda Rosalie Varner. Don't tell nobody, okay?"

"It's our secret," Kasey whispered.

Jace overheard the secret and smiled.

Maribel leaned around Jace's back and whispered, "What did you tell her, Tilly?"

"A secret because our hair is the same color," Tilly answered. "I'll tell you someday, but you have to tell me one when I do, so be thinkin' up a good one."

Jace glanced over his shoulder toward Carlene. He'd much rather be up there with her, snuggled up close with his arm around her, so close that he could catch a whiff of the same perfume she'd worn in high school, maybe even bury his face in her hair and kiss her on the neck.

"What are you lookin' at my mama for? Did she say I have to go sit with her now?" Tilly asked, bringing his head out of the clouds and back to the arena.

"No, I was just seeing if she was still in the same spot. I

think I'll go talk to her and see if she'll let you be a rodeo clown." Jace stood up.

"Look, it's my daddy's turn," Maribel shouted, and moved in closer to Tilly. "Scream as loud as you can, so he'll stay on till the horn blows."

Just like that, Jace was forgotten and a new hero had taken his place. Jimmy Vasquez was a fine rider. There probably wasn't a horse in the competition that night that could throw him in eight seconds, but Jace hated to give up the spotlight with his daughter.

"What just happened?" Carlene asked when he sat down beside her.

The chemistry between them jacked his pulse up even more than when he lay back on Blaze of Glory and got that rush of adrenaline when the gate opened. "Well, I managed to hang on eight seconds."

"I'm going to the concession stand to get Randy a beer. He's manning the gates now that his ride is over." Regina winked at Carlene as she left.

"Thanks for keepin' me company," Carlene said.

Jace nudged her shoulder. "I was real glad that I didn't bite the dirt since I had such a good little cheering squad. Did you know Tilly wants to be a rodeo clown?"

"I was afraid she'd want to try her hand at ridin' broncs after tonight. Other than being afraid of spiders, she's fearless."

"Does that mean you'll let me spend some time with her and show her how to be a rodeo clown?" he asked.

"Let's take this one step at a time. I'll tell her before Sunday and see how she takes the news. She's pretty headstrong," Carlene said.

"Kasey's hair and your temper? I wouldn't expect anything else. Will you call me after you tell her?"

"Yes, I will," Carlene promised.

"Thank you. I should be getting on down to the arena. I've promised that I'll help load the horses and do cleanup in the stands before I go home tonight," he said.

"You doin' cleanup? I'd rather watch that than see you ride."

"Oh, so you'd rather watch me bending over so you can see my butt? I got to admit, I'd rather watch you doing the same than watch you ride a bronc," he teased.

"Don't put words into my mouth," she said.

"Don't put visions in my head." He laid a hand on her shoulder.

Yep, there were the sparks again, proving once again that time and space had not erased that chemistry they had years before.

*　　　*　　　*

Nothing escaped Hope's eyes that night. Not the expression on Jaçe's face when he sat down beside Carlene the first time, or the way he interacted with the children or when he found an excuse of some kind to talk to her a second time.

Hope turned around and looked up at Henry. He'd been a handsome young man but he was a distinguished-looking older guy with his thick gray hair and that mustache. "If she doesn't get on the ball and tell that child what everyone in town knows, I'm going to do it myself."

"She's only been here a week. Give her a few more days." Henry's deep voice was the same as when they were teenagers, back when she'd been in love with him. But he'd gone to the military, angry at her because she wouldn't go with him. And she'd married the foreman of Hope Springs the next year. She'd loved her husband and they'd had good years together but she'd never been in love with him like she had been with Henry. Now Henry was back on the ranch next door, staying with Kasey and Nash, and those old feelings had sprung up again.

"What was she whispering to you, Kasey?" Hope turned to the other side.

"I'm sworn to secrecy, but it has to do with her name. Tilly is a nickname."

"For Matilda? That was Rosalie's first name and she hated it," Hope said.

"Something like that. You have to promise me you'll let Carlene take care of this news in her own way," Kasey said.

"Oh, okay," Hope agreed.

"Are the kids driving you crazy, Henry?" Kasey asked.

"Not at all. I haven't been to a rodeo in years and it's fun to see it through their eyes. So much more exciting than if I was here alone," he answered Kasey, but his eyes were on Hope, not the next rider out of the chute.

"Are you missin' Florida, yet?" Hope turned around again and looked up at him.

"Come on up here beside me. Us old folks don't hear as well as we used to, especially in all this noise," he said.

She didn't hesitate and in a few seconds she was shoulder to shoulder with him and suddenly felt like she was a young woman again. When Henry Thomas walked back into her life on Christmas Day, she'd felt like she was sixteen. He'd been her first love but now they were past seventy and their moment had passed years ago.

"Did I tell you that I knew about Jace's daughter for a couple of years?"

"You already knew? How?" She gave him her full attention.

"They lived not far from me in Florida," he answered.

"I knew who that little girl belonged to the first time I saw her."

"Henry!" a shrill voice squealed, and suddenly Tilly was right in front of them. "Where's your ice cream truck? How did you get here?"

"It's still in Florida and I'm visiting here. That red-haired lady that you met is going to be my niece when she marries my nephew. Do you have a hug for me?"

She slung herself into his arms and Hope felt a pang of jealousy. It was her great-granddaughter, for goodness' sake, and she wanted to hug her too.

"I'd like you to meet my friend, Hope Dalley," Henry said.

"Hello, Miz Hope. Are you kin to Jace? He gave me a kitten and I named her Jasmine and is there a lot of Dawsons in this town?" She stopped for air.

"Jace is my grandson and I like baby kittens and yes, there are a lot of Dawsons in this place," Hope answered.

"My mama is right up there." Tilly pointed.

Henry turned around and waved at Carlene. She waved back and again a little streak of jealousy struck Hope because Carlene had been able to spend time with him when she couldn't. When they both turned around, Tilly had already gone back to talk to Maribel.

"I wanted to hug her too," she said.

"All in due time. She's going to love you," Henry said.

Chapter Seven

Tilly tucked her hand into Carlene's on the way home from the rodeo grounds that night. The temperature had dropped and dark clouds shifted back and forth over the moon, so maybe the weatherman was right about a cold front blowing through.

"Did you know Henry is right here in Happy? I wish he woulda brought his ice cream truck with him, Mama. And there's a bunch of Dawsons in Happy and guess what, Henry has a friend named Hope. He never told us that." Tilly talked nonstop, barely giving Carlene time to answer one question before another popped into her head and out her mouth.

"I did know that he is here." Carlene caught a faint whiff of smoke.

"And you didn't tell me?" Tilly scolded.

A few more steps and the wind blew more smoke in her face. "I was plannin' on it but we've had so much happening this week."

Tilly's nose curled as she raised her chin and sniffed the air. "I hate the smell of cigarette smoke."

"Me too, baby girl." Carlene gently squeezed her hand.

They cleared the parking lot and Carlene could see a cloud of gray spiraling upward toward the dark clouds and dread washed over her. She lengthened her stride and Tilly had to do double time to keep up.

"Mama, why are you walking so fast? Is something wrong?"

"I hope not."

They were both jogging when they reached the edge of the yard. Smoke was billowing from the roof and bright yellow blazes were eating up the living room drapes.

"Jasmine is in there!" Tilly screamed, and took off for the front door in a dead run. "I've got to get her out."

Carlene's knees buckled and she wanted to drop to the ground and weep. But Tilly was about to rush into a burning living room, so she ran after her. "No, Tilly, don't open that door!" she yelled as she ran through a gray fog.

"I got to save Jasmine," Tilly coughed and yelled at the same time.

"I'll do it. Here, take my phone and go stand in the road. Call 911." Carlene threw up her arm and tucked her nose into it. "Promise me you will stay in the road. I'll get Jasmine."

Tilly took the phone and ran back toward the road. Carlene could hear her talking, but she couldn't see a thing. The back door was locked, but she saw the mop hanging on a hook and quickly grabbed it. Using the handle, she broke the window, slipped her hand inside, and twisted the doorknob. She tucked her nose into the collar of her coat and took a deep breath. The Christmas tree was a bonfire and the intense heat was almost more than she could stand, but she ran past it toward Tilly's bedroom, hoping the kitten was in there.

She was halfway down the hallway when she heard a pitiful meow to her right and a crash at the same time. She rushed into the small bathroom and found Jasmine behind the toilet. She grabbed her, tucked her into her coat, and ran for the back door. The fire and smoke were now billowing out the front window. Blazing and throwing heat, it had managed to make its way to the kitchen curtains above the sink. Her lungs ached and the kitten was squirming up next to her chest. Tears flowed down her cheeks, attempting to wash away the sting of the smoke, but all she could think about was getting that kitten out to Tilly.

She was bailing off the porch when two strong arms scooped her up. Even in his yellow turnout gear, she knew it was Jace holding her because there was that instant tingle on the back of her neck. When did he begin to work with the volunteer fire department and how did he get there so fast? Even in the chaos, she was so glad he was there.

"My God, Carlene!" he yelled as he ran around the side of the house toward the yard. "Why did you go in there?"

Her ears were ringing and she was having trouble catching her breath but she managed to cough and say, "Kitten. Is Tilly all right?"

"She's fine," Jace answered as he handed her over to an EMT, who immediately snapped an oxygen mask over her nose and stripped off her coat. She held on to Jasmine, and panic filled her breast as Jace disappeared into the grayness again.

"Mama! Mama!" Tilly's voice rushed to her on the north wind that was now blowing the smoke away from the road. "Mama! I got to see my mama. Let me go."

"Tilly, I'm fine," she yelled as loud as she could in between coughing fits.

Then suddenly the EMT was throwing a blanket around

her shoulders to stop the shivering. Strange that she could be that cold with all the heat from the fire. Her eyes fluttered and everything started to spin, getting faster and faster. A buzzing in her ears went from sounding like a bumblebee to a high-pitched screech.

"Mama, where are you?" Tilly's voice jerked her back.

"Right here." She focused on a little figure running right toward her with a taller one behind her.

"Mama!" Tilly crawled up in her lap and sobbed. "I was afraid you was dead."

"I'm fine." Carlene's voice was raspy and she could only get out a few words at a time, so she held up the cat.

"Jasmine! You saved her, Mama, but what's that thing on your nose? Are you going to have to keep it forever? Where are we going to stay tonight, Mama?" Tilly cuddled the cat in her arms and snuggled down even tighter against her mother.

She opened her mouth to answer and still yet another coughing fit stopped her. Before she could get control, Lila was at her side with a hand on her shoulder and one on Tilly's. "It's an oxygen mask so your mama can get her breath. She'll only need it for a little while. She breathed in a lot of smoke and her lungs need the oxygen. Have you got a place to stay tonight, Carlene?"

Jace answered before Carlene could say a word. "The fire is out, and she and Tilly can stay at the ranch with me tonight."

Carlene removed the mask. "I can get a motel room."

"Nonsense." Valerie and Kasey joined the rest of the family, surrounding the ambulance. "There's lots of room at the ranch house. You can stay there."

Carlene opened her mouth to argue but then clamped it shut when Henry caught her eye and mouthed, *"Do it."*

"Thank you." She took a deep breath. "We can find a house tomorrow."

"That won't catch on fire?" Tilly's tone was filled with fear.

Jace removed his headgear and his gloves before he reached out and touched Tilly's cheek. "We'll make sure your new house is safe before you move into it. I promise I'll check it all out myself."

Brody appeared out of nowhere, ashes in his hair and smudges on his face. "Is everyone okay? Does Carlene need to go to the hospital and get checked?"

"No," she said emphatically. No way was she leaving Tilly after a trauma like that.

"I want you to have oxygen for a while longer but I don't think you need to go to the hospital. You are a lucky lady. The bottom of your coat was singed pretty good," the EMT said.

Tears welled up in her eyes but this time they were emotional. Tilly could have easily been an orphan if that coat had caught on fire.

She's got a father. Aunt Rosalie's voice was so real in her head that she looked out over the top of the mask to see if she was there. *But she needs her mother.*

"Let me put Tilly in the van with Kasey's kids," Lila whispered. "She needs to get out of this smoke or she'll need a mask too."

"Thank you so much for everything. For showing up." Carlene covered her mouth when she coughed again. "For offering to let us stay at your house."

"That's what friends and family are for." Lila took Tilly's free hand in hers. "Hey, sweetie, let's go put Jasmine in the van with Kasey's kids. She's had enough smoke for one night."

"Mama?" Tilly looked up at her.

"Is it all right if I take them on to the ranch?" Kasey asked.

"My stuffed animals?" Tilly groaned.

Carlene was trying to wrap her mind around someone taking Tilly away from her when another fireman walked up behind Jace.

"Mama, I want to go away from this place," Tilly whispered.

"Yes, and thank you, Kasey," Carlene said.

"We'll take good care of her and bring her to Prairie Rose as soon as you get there." Kasey held out her hand toward Tilly.

Tilly kissed her mother on the cheek and hopped down off her lap. "Here's your phone, Mama. Call me soon as you get there."

"I will and you did good tonight, baby girl."

"So did you, Mama. Jasmine is alive. You are a hero."

Carlene caught Jace's eye as he stood next to her with all the Dawsons and firemen behind him. "I think these firemen are the heroes," she said to Tilly, but hoped that he understood how much gratitude she had for him for carrying her away from that burning house. When Tilly and Kasey were out of sight, she shifted her gaze from Jace to the new fireman and asked, "Is it over?"

"It's out but still smoldering. The bedroom doors were closed and the fire didn't get back that far but I'd guess there's smoke damage on whatever is in there. Looks like it started in an electrical outlet and spread to that old tree, then burned through the ceiling into the attic. Those old clothes stored up there fueled it," he answered.

"Attic?" Carlene's voice was little more than a squeak.

"Yes, ma'am. Rosalie had stored boxes and boxes full of

stuff up there. We'll keep a watch on things tonight in case it sparks up again," he said.

"Can we go inside and take out her things?" Lila asked.

He rubbed his chin and shook his head. "I can't let you in the front part of the house. Too much debris still fallin' out of the attic."

"I'll knock out the bedroom window and make a hole big enough for us to get through," Jace offered. "One hour, Randy, is all we'll need. We'll work fast and be out of here in no time."

"If there's a leak in any of those old gas lines, well, you know what could happen with nothin' more than a spark, so work fast."

"Couldn't we just get some of her things?" Lila begged.

"Only if one of us goes in with you and you hurry," Randy said. "I'm not supposed to let anyone go inside after a fire like this."

"We'll be quick, and I'll help them," Jace promised.

Carlene's breath came in short bursts. What-ifs flooded her mind—what if the fire had started at night while they were sleeping? What if there was a tiny leak in the ancient gas lines? What if she lost her precious daughter because of her stubbornness about living in the house when Jace told her it wasn't safe?

Carlene wasn't sure when Hope and Henry left but suddenly they were back with a whole box of trash bags and Valerie had taken charge, giving orders to everyone about how to take one bag, go inside, fill it, and then get out as fast as possible.

Carlene looked up to keep the tears at bay. Stars twinkled around the moon as if everything was right on earth. Her world had just fallen apart—again—and all she'd wanted was to give Tilly the security of putting down roots in a small town.

"You stay right here, Carlene. By the time Jody says you can go home, we'll have everything out of the bedrooms." Lila gave her another pat on the shoulder.

"I need to help." She reached for the mask.

Jace's big hand covered hers. "Not now. Let them take care of it." Despite the emotional upheaval inside her whole being, his touch made her feel safe and secure.

"Jace?" Her eyes met his.

He kept her hand in his and held it on his thigh. "It's going to be okay."

"Thank you," she whispered.

*   *   *

Jace drove home that evening with a truckload of black bags. He parked in the backyard, crossed his arms over the steering wheel, and laid his head on them. He'd really thought he'd lost both Carlene and Tilly when the call came in to the volunteer fire department. He'd been the first one out of the truck and ordered a rookie to stay with Tilly when he heard that Carlene had gone into the burning house for a kitten. When he ran around the house, the only thing on his mind was saving her. He'd just gone through the back door when he'd heard a crash and realized that she'd fallen..

His chest had been so tight that he could hardly breathe and sweat poured off him under the suit. Then there she was, covered in ashes with a little black-faced kitten poking its head out from the top of her coat.

"I could have lost them," he muttered. His hands trembled and tears left streaks down his dirty face. "I want to be a father and I want to be with Carlene but I'll have to go at it easy so I don't scare her away again."

He heard a truck pull up beside his but didn't raise his head until the passenger door opened and his mother crawled in beside him. "Everyone else is right behind me. Nash is going to help you unload while Brody gets all the equipment taken back to the firehouse."

"Why did you tell them they could stay with me on the ranch, Mama?"

"Because it was the right thing to do. For God's sake, Jace, what happened all those years ago is in the past and done with. Y'all can at least be friends for Tilly. It's not like she's goin' to live here forever and get in the way of your life. You can ask Tommy Wilson about that house he's remodeling to rent. It's out of town but the commute to school wouldn't be more than five minutes."

"She was going to tell Tilly about me this weekend. I imagine that's all shot to hell since the child has been through enough this past week," Jace said.

She scooted over in the seat far enough to put a hand on each side of his face. "This could be a blessing, son. It will give you a chance to get to know Tilly on a daily basis and better yet a chance for her to get to know you and us. Everything happens for a reason."

He held her hands for a moment and then let go. "Thank you, Mama. I was so afraid that they'd be hurt."

"I know, son, but they're fine. Now, it looks like Nash and Kasey are here," Valerie said as she crawled out of the truck.

Jace made it to the minivan's sliding door as it was opening. Tilly had a death grip on Jasmine and looked up at him with more than a little fear in her eyes.

"I need help."

He grabbed the kitten by the scruff of the neck and it went limp. "Where's Carlene?"

"Right here," she said as she got out of a truck that Lila was driving. "Tilly, are you okay?"

"Yes, Mama." Tilly ran over to Carlene and wrapped her arms around her mother's waist. "Did you get enough of that stuff in your nose?"

"I did but we both need a shower to get the smoke off us." She hugged Tilly and kissed the top of her head and then her forehead.

Brody and Nash each grabbed an armload of bags from the back of the truck and carried them to the back porch, then returned for the rest of them. Jace was suddenly more exhausted than he'd ever been after a fire before. His limbs felt like they weighed a ton. Cowboys didn't let folks see them cry but he was having trouble keeping the tears at bay.

"You and Carlene and Tilly get on inside and get cleaned up," Valerie said. "I'll start some laundry and then we'll have a drink. I think we all need it."

"Thanks, guys," Jace said when everything was unloaded.

"No problem. I seem to remember that you took care of my sheep when I had that bout of amnesia, so consider it payback." Nash smiled. "Speaking from experience here, Jace, sometimes it's darkest right before dawn."

Jace nodded. "Ain't that the gospel truth?"

*   *   *

Kasey hugged Tilly and then Carlene and whispered, "If you need anything at all, call me. I'll be here in five minutes."

Lila gave them both a hug and said, "Granny Hope is on her way over. She wants to help, so let her. And I'll check on you tomorrow but if you need to talk tonight or wake up with nightmares, call me."

"Thank you again, both of you, all of you." Carlene

didn't care who saw the tears running down her face and dropping on her smoke-stained shirt.

One by one the vehicles left and she and Tilly were left standing in the yard with Jace. With the way he affected her just by being close, she didn't need to live in the same house with him, no matter how big it was, but it was only for a couple of days. Kasey had said something about a rental property not far from town and she could check on that tomorrow.

When she walked through the back door at the ranch, she sure enough hoped that things looked better at dawn the next day because right then she wanted to curl up in a ball under a blanket with Tilly in her arms. The screened-in back porch at Prairie Rose was filled with black bags full of everything from their clothing, to Tilly's book collection, to stuffed animals. When she passed by them, she had to keep her eyes straight ahead or she would have broken down again and Tilly needed her strength to get through still yet another new place.

She stubbed her toe on a bag right by the door but Jace quickly wrapped his arms around her waist to keep her from falling.

With a gasp she tore herself from his arms. "Tilly's bear. I have to find it, Jace."

"Okay, then we'll drag this one in first. I see a stuffed animal paw sticking out the top." He slid it in the back door.

Carlene dropped to her knees with Tilly right beside her. They dragged out half a dozen items before Tilly brought out a pink bear and hugged it tightly to her chest. "That was scary, Mama."

Carlene drew Tilly into her lap and rocked her and the bear as Jace stood by and wished that he could offer his daughter that kind of comfort.

"Jasmine?" Tilly craned her neck to look up at Jace.

"She's fine. See?" He sat down on the floor beside them and put the kitten in her arms. "Do you think maybe we should put her in the pantry while we are going in and out? That way she won't run out the door and get lost."

"Yes, please." Tilly handed her back to Jace. "This is Rella." She held up her bear. "She smells bad right now but she'll be better when she's all cleaned up."

Jace shook the bear's paw. "I'm glad to meet you, Rella. I hope you like it here on the ranch."

Tilly put her ear to the bear's mouth. "She says to tell you thank you for saving her."

"She's very welcome." Jace rose to his feet with Jasmine in his arms. "I'll be right back."

Valerie pushed her way into the kitchen. "I made sure that Kasey's old room and the one right across the hall are ready for guests. Now, which bagful goes in the washer first?"

"Rella needs washing." Tilly handed the bear to her.

"Then we'll do a load of stuffies and then go on to cloth-ing. I laid out some things on your bed, Carlene. And there's a variety of soaps and shampoos in the upstairs bathroom. Help yourself and holler if y'all need anything else," Valerie said. "And, Tilly, Miss Rella will be clean and ready for bed in an hour."

Tilly sniffed the air. "I like this place better already. It doesn't smell like old ladies and mice."

"Good." Valerie smiled. "Jace, show them their rooms."

"Can I check on Jasmine one time?" Tilly asked.

"Sure you can." Jace held out his hand to help her up. "I'll take you to her."

Valerie shoved as many stuffed animals into the washer as it would hold and started it to running; then she sat down on the floor beside Carlene. "You'll have to decide when to tell Tilly about all of us, but I can't wait to get to know her better. I just want you to know that and to know that if you'd told us, things might have been different. Now I suggest that you go on upstairs with them. A hot shower will do you and Tilly both good."

"Thank you one more time." Carlene rolled up on her toes and headed into the kitchen. Memories rushed across the room to meet her. Over there by the sink was where she and Jace had been making out when Valerie almost caught them. Carlene had gotten her shirt buttoned but she had to hold her bra behind her back until Valerie left the room. And she'd done lots of homework sitting at the kitchen table with Jace on the other side. Yes, she'd had her feet in his lap but they'd managed to get the work done.

"You done good, Jace," Tilly said as she came out of the pantry. "Mama, Jasmine is asleep. Jace gave her a pillow and a blanket."

"That's great," Carlene said.

"She's happy," Tilly sighed. "Jace, can we really see all of this house? It's a whole bunch bigger than the one we were livin' in but if we need to, me and Mama can share a room. Hey, where's your dog? You said you got a hound dog named Red. Where is he?"

"Whoa, girl!" At least Carlene knew her daughter felt safe if she was already making plans and asking about the dog. "Take a breath."

"Red is out in the barn where he has a nice soft dog bed to sleep in," Jace answered. "You'll probably see him tomorrow. And we have plenty of bedrooms, so you don't have to share."

"Wow! Is this a hotel?" Tilly let go of his hand and crossed the room to her mother.

"No, just a big house that needs a little girl and a kitten in it," Jace answered. "If you ladies will follow me, I'll show you the way."

Carlene didn't need to be shown. She'd been in every room of the house at one time or another and could remember more than she wanted to about each one, but this wasn't the time to admit that in front of Tilly.

Tilly's eyes took in everything as they passed through a kitchen as big as their Florida apartment had been and then the huge dining room. "You sure this ain't a hotel?"

"Positive," he chuckled. "Hotels don't let cats in the kitchen."

"You're funny, Jace," Tilly giggled. "This looks like that fancy café where we went with Aunt Bee. Are we really goin' to stay here?"

"For a couple of days." Carlene remembered her first impression of the place. Jace had brought her home for Sunday dinner after church one day. She'd lived in big houses provided through her father's job but nothing ever had the warmth or the feeling of either Aunt Rosalie's small place or the big house on Prairie Rose.

"And through this archway is the living room. I'll leave a lamp on tonight in case y'all get hungry and want to find your way to the kitchen," Jace said.

Tilly's eyes darted around the big room with two separate seating arrangements—one facing the fireplace and the other the television. Finally, she looked up at Jace and asked, "Are you rich or something? Does *dynasty* mean 'rich'?"

"Dynasty?" he asked.

"Mama said you have a dynasty."

"Oh, she did, did she?" Jace grinned.

"Yep, and she said it was Piddly Rose Ranch."

"Prairie Rose," Carlene muttered as a blush turned her cheeks crimson red.

"That's it," Tilly said.

"I'm not rich, but I do own a really big ranch." Jace stopped at the foot of the stairs and motioned for them to go up before him.

When they reached the hallway, he opened the first door he came to. "This one is yours, Tilly. It was Kasey's room when we were all growing up."

Tilly grabbed Carlene's hand and squeezed. "I really like it but where's Mama goin' to be?"

"Right across the hallway," Carlene answered.

"It's a princess room, Mama. Just like the one in the book," Tilly whispered. "Can I let Maribel see it, Jace?"

"Anytime, darlin'," he said.

Carlene gave him a dirty look and he threw up a hand. "Just an endearment."

"Where's a deer?" Tilly asked.

"Not a deer, an endearment. It's a nice word," Carlene explained. "Let's go run you a bath so I can tuck you into this princess bed."

"Will Rella be dried by then?" Tilly ran a finger down the canopy bed with a pretty pink bedspread.

"If she's not, I'll bring her up here and tuck her in with you when she is," Carlene answered.

"Rella?" Jace whispered close enough to Carlene's ear that she caught a mixture of smoke with just a touch of beer. It was downright heady and she didn't need that on top of everything else that night, so she took a step back.

"Cinderella. That's her bear's name," she answered.

"I see." Jace crossed the hall and opened up her new room. "This okay?"

"Fine." Carlene glanced inside to see a queen-sized

poster bed, a recliner by the window, and a dresser with a double mirror. This was the very room where she and Jace had gotten dressed after taking a bath together. Thank goodness Valerie and Hope hadn't come home early that day.

"It's got its own bathroom and a walk-in closet. Mama kept it for the top buyers at the fall cattle sale. You should be comfortable here and you and Tilly can spread out your stuff in the bathroom. I use the one at the end of the hall. I remember some good times in this room and in that bathtub," he whispered for her ears only.

"We were two crazy kids," Carlene said.

"Oh. My. Goodness!" Tilly brushed past them and into the bathroom. "Look at the size of this tub, Mama. It's like a swimmin' pool."

"Standard-sized Jacuzzi," Jace said. "Y'all make yourselves at home. I'm going to grab a quick shower to get the smoke off me. There's cookies and milk if Tilly wants a night snack. And the bar is open if you want something stronger. I know I sure do." He glanced toward Carlene. "Treat this place as if it were your home and if you can't find something, just holler at me."

*　　　*　　　*

As soon as Jace finished his shower, he went straight to his room. Tilly's giggles drifted across the hallway and then there were low tones of a conversation between her and her mother. He vowed right then that he'd always be there for her and Tilly, and he'd do his damnedest to keep them safe.

His phone pinged and he picked it up to find a one-word message from Brody: *Talk?*

He hit the right number to call him back and Brody

answered on the first ring. "How are you doin' with all this? We would have been happy to have Carlene and Tilly here at Hope Springs, but Valerie had already given Lila the word before we even got there that she was going to stay with you, so we didn't interfere."

"Nobody interferes with Mama when she sets her head, but she has no idea that there's still chemistry between us. She wants us to be friends for my daughter's sake." His voice cracked. Just saying those two words, *my daughter*, out loud, made it more real.

"You okay, brother?"

Jace shook his head. "No, I'm not. I'm trying to be strong for their sakes, but dammit, Brody. I thought they were dead and then when Tilly was standing in the middle of the road all alone, crying...and Carlene was in that blazing house. I realized how much they both meant to me. Thank God the fire truck was at the rodeo grounds or it could have been worse."

"Well, I'm here if you need me. Lord only knows how often you listened to me whine about Lila when she came back to town," Brody said.

"I'm not whinin'. I'm just tryin' to..."

"I know, Jace, I know. Remember what a basket case I was when Lila went back to Florida and I thought I'd lost her?" Brody said. "Call or come on over anytime you need anything."

"Thanks." Jace ended the call and paced across the floor to stare out the window at the big black clouds gathering in the distance, covering the moon and stars as they pushed their way toward Happy, bringing, if the weatherman was right, two inches of snow, sleet, or ice to their area.

Through the wall, he could hear Tilly talking to her bear or maybe it was to her kitten, and then everything was quiet.

It was after midnight when he jerked on a T-shirt, slipped on a pair of pajama pants, and went downstairs. A good belt of Tennessee whiskey always helped him get to sleep.

He'd poured up a double shot and was humming "Tennessee Whiskey" as he carried it into the dark living room and sat down on the sofa facing the television. He sang along with the lyrics in his head that said she was as smooth as Tennessee whiskey, as sweet as strawberry wine, and as warm as a glass of brandy.

"Who are you singin' to?" Carlene asked from the sofa across the room.

Jace jumped. "Guess you couldn't sleep either, huh? Well, it's been a helluva week. And as for the song, it was about this girl I used to know a long time ago," he answered honestly. "We danced to this song once up in the hayloft."

"Oh, really," Carlene said.

"Oh, yeah," he said. "She moved here from California her sophomore year of high school and we teased her about her accent."

"I'm sure y'all's accents sounded strange in her ears if she was from the West Coast."

"Maybe. She'd only been out there a couple of years, so some words sounded like she'd lived in Mississippi and then she'd come off with some kind of hippie lingo," Jace chuckled.

"What happened to that girl?" Carlene asked.

"She moved away. She had an old aunt here in Happy and I tried to get her to give me the girl's phone number but she told me off right quick," Jace said.

"Maybe the girl and the aunt both had their reasons." Carlene's voice got closer with each word until she was standing in front of Jace. "Maybe she didn't want to ruin someone's life."

"Could be, but I sure did miss her. I guess that time probably changed both of us, though."

"Oh, it definitely did, I'm sure. And machines that could take you or that girl back in time haven't been invented except in science-fiction books."

"What are you drinkin'?" he asked. "I'll get you a refill if you'll sit with me a while?"

"Strawberry wine," she answered. "But no refills for me tonight. I've got a lot of work to do tomorrow and I should get up early."

"I've still got some left in my glass. Sit with me, Carlene."

She sank down on the other end of the sofa. Three feet separated them, but it might as well have been six miles, which was probably a good thing that evening. Crazy thing was that when he talked to her, it felt right and yet there was that niggling feeling in his heart that wasn't so sure he was ready for any of what had been thrown in his lap.

Jace let a sip of the warm whiskey burn away the smoke smell that still lingered in his mouth and nose. "You think things happen for a reason?"

"I hope so because if tonight doesn't have a reason behind it, then it would be doubly sad." She drank the rest of her wine.

He sat down beside her, close enough that sparks danced between them. He'd always been comfortable with her while they'd been dating and never ran out of things to talk about, but suddenly he was at a loss for words. Not wanting her to leave, he grasped at straws and finally said, "Granny says that you knew Henry in Florida. Did you know that he and Granny had a thing between them when they were young?"

"I saw the way they looked at each other at the rodeo

grounds. I wouldn't be surprised if whatever they had flared up again. How do you feel about that?"

"I thought my grandpa walked on water. I still miss him, but if Granny and Henry can rekindle something they had, I can only wish them the best. Not many people get a second chance."

Carlene stood up at the same time the moon peeked out from behind the dark clouds. Her slim body in a nightshirt that stopped at midcalf was silhouetted in the little bit of light that filtered in through the window. Her hair was pinned up with strands poking out every which way, making a halo around her head.

"Angel," he whispered, and covered it with a cough.

"What was that?"

"Just remembering that song again," he said quickly.

Carlene turned to walk away but then spun around. "That girl you mentioned was only doing what she thought was best for everyone."

"I wonder what she'd think now," he said.

"She might have changed her mind, but like I said one of those time machines hasn't been invented."

"If they do make one, you let me know. I'll buy the sucker and I'll drag that girl into it with me. We'll go back a few years and see where a different path might have led us."

"I'll call you if I hear they are up for sale." She disappeared into the darkness.

"I'd sell the whole ranch for one of those machines," he muttered as he went back to the buffet to pour another shot.

Chapter Eight

Carlene had slept poorly, waking every two hours and padding across the hall to check on Tilly. Nightmares had plagued her when she did sleep—basically the same one that involved losing Tilly to a forest fire when she ran into the blazing woods to find a kitten or a baby bunny or one time it was a stupid turtle. She'd awake in a cold sweat, sometimes with tears streaming down her cheeks. Then toward dawn she had a dream where she didn't tell Tilly about Jace and she died in the house fire. Tilly was devastated and she had to live with Jace without even knowing him.

When morning finally came, she was eager to get out of bed. She opened the curtains and stared out the window for a long time at a few snowflakes drifting down from gray skies. She'd wanted to give Tilly roots and doing so meant that she had to face this thing about her own father. It didn't take a therapist to know that she had issues with her own upbringing, with the emptiness that she'd always felt and the longing to have a father who loved her and supported her. She didn't ever want Tilly to feel like she had when she was growing up. And if telling her that Jace was her father would make her roots grow deeper, then Carlene was ready to do so—today.

Making the decision didn't mean that it would be easy. Just thinking about it twisted Carlene's stomach into knots. Finding out that she was pregnant and making the decision to raise her baby on her own was the toughest decision that Carlene had ever faced—until that morning.

"Just get it over with and be done with it. That's what Aunt Rosalie would say." She heard music and noises coming from the kitchen but none of that mattered. This was Tilly's first snow and she had to wake her so she didn't miss it. Texas weather was as unpredictable as a pregnant woman, so the sun could be shining in twenty minutes.

"Mama!" Tilly met her in the hall. "Come and see. It's snowing."

Tugging on her hand, Tilly led her into her bedroom and to the window. "Look, Mama. Do you think we can build a snowman? I can't wait to tell Natalie and Aunt Bee about my princess bedroom and the snow."

"Let's go outside and get a picture we can send them." Carlene went back to the bedroom for her phone with Tilly right behind her.

The snow had gotten a lot more serious when they reached the front porch and it had gotten colder through the night. The thin nightshirt that Carlene wore didn't do much in the way of protection, but she didn't plan on being out in the yard more than a couple of minutes. Giggling at Tilly's antics, she took several snapshots and then a thirty-second video to send to Belinda.

Suddenly a big red raw-boned hound dog bounded

from around the side of the house and put his paws on Tilly's shoulders. With one big slurp, he licked her face from chin to forehead; then all four feet were on the ground and he chased the snowflakes with her, carrying on like a puppy.

"Time to come in now or you're going to turn into a popsicle," Carlene yelled.

"Just one more on my tongue, Mama?" Tilly begged.

"One more and then we've got to get inside. When there's enough on the ground, we'll come back out and play. Then we'll have our clothes washed and we won't be out here in our nightgowns." Carlene leaned against the porch post even though it was icy cold to brace her hand. Belinda would love the second short video of Tilly wearing white in falling snow and all those red curls bouncing. On her phone screen, it looked pretty enough to be an advertisement.

"Time's up," Carlene called out.

"Okay, but we can come back later, right?"

"Right," Carlene said.

"Lovely." Hope startled her when she slung open the door to let them both inside the house. "Didn't mean to scare you, child. I came through the back door with a pan of cinnamon rolls for you girls' breakfast. And Valerie took a load of clothes home last night when she left. They're in the basket right there." She pointed to the stairs. "She tried to get something that you could wear today."

"Thank you. Seems like I keep saying that and it's not enough," Carlene said.

"It's plenty. Us country folks help out in times like this and besides we're..." Hope stopped and smiled at Tilly. "Looks like Red likes you."

"I sure like him. He's a fun dog but right now, I'm hungry. You said cinnamon rolls? Where's Henry? Did he come over here with you?" She rattled on as she headed for the kitchen with Carlene and Hope right behind her.

"Henry is over at Kasey's, I'm sure. And, yes, there are cinnamon rolls in the kitchen. I hope they're still warm. I'm sure glad you and your mama and your kitten weren't hurt."

Tilly wrapped her arms around Hope. "Me, too, but I'm not sorry the house got on fire. It had mice and spiders and I wanted to move."

Hope giggled. "Well, that's honest enough. Carlene, I didn't have anything to do today so I thought I'd help you with the rest of the laundry. I hope I'm not intruding. I've got another load of toys in the washer now. I don't know what you put in the dryer and what you hang up, so I waited until you could tell me how and what to do with the rest of your things."

"Thank you and you aren't intruding at all." Maybe God had sent Hope so that Carlene didn't have to tell Tilly that day.

"Thank you again," Carlene said.

"My pleasure." Hope smiled again. "Let's eat and then we'll get to work."

"Yes! But first I've got to check on— There she is!" Jasmine was sitting on the sofa washing her paws. Tilly ran over to her and kissed her on the nose. "How'd you get out of the pantry?"

"Jace let her out this morning when he left to do chores. When I talked to him, he said to be very careful not to let her out when I came in," Hope answered.

Carlene's phone rang and she smiled as she answered it. "Hello, Maribel. I bet you want to talk to Tilly, right?"

"Yes, ma'am. Is she all right? Did her kitten get hurt? My daddy says that you had to move to the ranch. Can I come and see Tilly?"

"Here, darlin', I'll let you talk to her." Carlene handed the phone off to Tilly.

Tilly carried it halfway up the stairs before she sat down. "Hi, Maribel. The Christmas tree was on fire when we got home."

"Five minutes and then you better come to breakfast or it will be cold," Carlene raised her voice to say.

"Okay, Mama," Tilly said.

A familiar flutter in her stomach told Carlene that Jace was in the house before she went from the foyer into the kitchen. He looked up from the stove and their eyes met for a brief second before he turned his charm toward his grandmother.

"Now, this is a treat to come in from feedin' chores and find your special cinnamon rolls, Granny. Go on and have a seat, Carlene. I'll bring one to the table for you. Coffee or milk?"

"Coffee," she answered, and tugged at the bottom of the nightshirt Valerie had left on the bed. No makeup, hair a fright because she hadn't even taken time to brush out the tangles.

Hope poured three cups of coffee and carried them to the table one at a time. "Tilly has Kasey's sass as well as her red hair?"

"She was a strong little girl last night." Jace set a plate in front of Carlene with two huge cinnamon rolls on it and went back to get his breakfast. "I see you still take your coffee black."

Carlene picked up the fork. Would it be totally against etiquette to comb her hair with it? "Yes, I do like it without additives. Aunt Rosalie said that anything other than black and strong was just murdered water."

"I remember her sayin' that. I got to admit that I'm

glad Lila has put together a little memorial tomorrow after church. But I have to tell you, it's gotten bigger than we planned, so it's going to be in the fellowship hall. So many people want to remember her," Hope said.

Carlene swallowed and took a sip of her coffee. "These are amazing, Hope, and I'm grateful for a memorial wherever it's held. It's still hard to believe that she's gone. We talked every week."

Jace's fork stopped midway from plate to his mouth. "You did?"

"Yes, we did. Sometimes she'd tell me some little something about Happy, like when there was a death or a marriage but not much. Mostly we talked about Tilly and my job and she'd tell me stories about when she was young. She really liked to talk about the old days," Carlene answered.

"I can understand that. Henry and I spend hours every night playing the 'remember when' game," Hope said.

Jace looked across the table. "Think we'll ever do that, Carlene?"

"What?" She blushed. Holy smoke! Hope was right there at the head of the table. They sure didn't need to be talking about the past in front of her.

"We could remember all those nights when the whole bunch of us kids gathered up at Henry's barn or down at the school playground." Jace's eyes held her captive for several moments before he looked down at his coffee.

Carlene shrugged. "That's the past and the future is more important. I've got to find a place to live," she said. "Thought maybe tomorrow after church Tilly and I might drive all over town and see what's for sale or for rent."

"You don't have to be in a hurry. What you and Jace had when you were kids is over and done with. Mistakes were made back then and we can't undo the past but we can move on to the future. You share a daughter and you can always be friends for her sake," Hope said in a low voice. "Stay here as long as you like. Let Tilly get to know the ranch and all of us."

"I made a phone call this morning," Jace said. "Tommy Wilson and his family have built a new house, and he's re-modeling his old one to rent out. It's not anything special. Two-bedroom frame house with one bathroom, but it's well built."

"Can I see it today?" Her spirits rose and excitement filled her whole body.

"No, but maybe in a week. He says it's not ready to show just yet and he's not planning to rent it until mid-February but if you want it, he won't put it on the market," Jace said.

That burst her bubble. "That's almost six weeks."

"Like I said, stay here until then." Hope smiled. "I know that place. It sits out on an acre or two of land and it's a nice little house. It would sure be worth waitin' for."

"Maybe something will come up sooner," Jace said quickly. "I get most of the news at the café or at the rodeo meetings, but you're really welcome to stay here until it does. And, Carlene, you don't have to tell Tilly about me until this kind of settles down about the fire."

"She's going to be a handful when I do, so you better get ready for it," Carlene sighed.

"Got a temper, does she?" Hope asked.

"Somewhat like a Texas wildfire and about as hot," Carlene answered.

"My mama was like that. She was as sweet as honey but when she was riled up, it was not a pretty sight," Hope said.

Tilly marched to the kitchen with her arms crossed over her chest. "There's another fire comin'? Where is it?"

Carlene looked up from her food. "No, we were talking about anger. So is Maribel coming over today?"

Tilly popped her hands on her hips. Other than her eyes shifting from her mother to Jace about three times, she might have been one of those statues of little girls that folks put in their flower beds.

"Well?" she asked through clenched teeth.

"Well, what?" Carlene shot right back at her.

"Are you my daddy, Jace?"

Chapter Nine

Time stood still and a heavy silence filled the room. Scenarios of how this would go down had played through Carlene's mind the past week but not a one of them was close to being right.

"If I am, how do you feel about that?" Jace asked.

"I don't like it," Tilly said with a sharp edge to her voice.

"You soften up that tone, Matilda Rose," Carlene said.

"Tell me outright, is Jace my daddy?"

"Yes, he is," Carlene said. "We were very young when I got pregnant and I never even told him, so don't be mad at him."

Tilly sighed dramatically. "Why'd we even come here? I don't want a daddy! We're doin' just fine the way we are, Mama, with you bein' a mama and a daddy both."

"I thought we were friends," Jace said.

"A real friend would've told me the truth instead of tryin' to act all nice." She spun around and stormed up the stairs.

Carlene pushed back her chair.

Jace followed her lead.

"Give it a minute," Hope said quickly. "Let her cool down before you both race up there and muddy the waters even more. This reminds me of when Valerie was about eleven years old and I was sure dreading having the sex talk with her. One day her father came into our bedroom and asked me if I had any idea what our child was reading. I told him that it was a well-known children's author, not knowing that that particular writer also wrote books with some pretty explicit sex scenes in it. I checked out what she was reading and figured that I could take it one of two ways. I could either be angry that she was reading something like that or relieved that she already knew and I didn't have to have that dreaded talk with her."

"And that pertains to this how?" Jace asked.

"Again, it's two ways. The story about Valerie has kept you from rushing up there and now Carlene doesn't have to worry about telling her anymore," Hope answered. "I expect you'd both better go now."

*   *   *

"How do you want to handle this?" Jace asked as he followed her up the steps.

"I have no idea."

"You had to have known when you moved here that she and I both would find out," Jace said when they reached the top.

"Yes, I did and figured it was time for both, but I sure didn't expect it to go down this way."

Neither did Jace. He'd had all kinds of visions about his first daddy moment with Tilly and not a one of them involved this scenario. He'd even dreamed about her the night before, dancing together at the father-daughter Valentine's Day affair. Didn't look like that was going to happen. Maybe this was an omen that he wasn't cut out to be a daddy after all.

There's a difference between a father and a daddy. His dad's voice in his head stopped him in his tracks at the top of the stairs. *Which are you going to be when you grow up?*

He remembered having that conversation when he came home fussing about Carlene's father never being around for any school functions.

Carlene rapped on Tilly's door. "All right if we come in and talk?"

"Nothing to talk about," Tilly said.

Carlene slung the door open. "I'm coming inside. And Jace is coming with me."

With his dad's words still in his head, he followed Carlene into the bedroom. Tilly was sitting in the middle of her bed with her pink bear hugged up to her chest.

Carlene sat down on the bed and wrapped Tilly and her bear up in her arms. "I should have told you sooner."

"Does this mean you and Jace are going to get married? Maribel said that her mama told her daddy you should have married him a long time ago."

Jace braced a shoulder against the doorjamb. "Tilly, I don't expect you to think of me as a..." He paused. It was time to make a decision. Did he want to be a father or a daddy? He inhaled deeply and said, "...as a daddy right now so maybe we could start off by being friends. I promise to tell you the truth from now on. It doesn't mean that your mama and I are going to get married. I found a house for you to move into, but it won't be ready for a few weeks. I was hoping that you and your mama would stay here until then so you don't have to move twice. Jasmine likes it here and I like having someone in this big old place to keep me company."

"And if we find something sooner, we will move out," Carlene said.

Tilly cut her eyes around at him. "Just friends?"

"I could teach you about bein' a rodeo clown and you could learn a little bit of ranchin' with me. And Red already likes you. And you could even get to know your great-grandma, Hope, a little better and your grandmother, Valerie. They'd both like that," Jace said.

"So many people. What if they don't like me?" she whispered.

Her anguish broke his heart. "I like you, so I'm bettin' they will too. And I'm sure they're also wonderin' if you're goin' to like them," Jace answered.

"You promise you won't boss me around?" Tilly crawled off the bed. "You can't tell me what to do. That's my mama's job."

He stuck out his hand. "Deal."

Tilly shook with him. "You did bring me Jasmine and I would like to be a rodeo clown."

Her tiny hand in his created a stirring in his heart that told him that he definitely wanted to be a daddy. He glanced up at Carlene and decided in that moment that he wanted to take a step even further. He wanted them to be a family.

"I'm bringing Tilly some cinnamon rolls and chocolate milk up the stairs," Hope yelled out.

"I can stay as long as we need to, Mama. Me and Jace can learn to be friends and I can get to know these other people. But I don't want a daddy, okay? He'll just be plain old Jace."

Tilly might have been talking to her mother, but her eyes

never left Jace's face. They pierced through his tough muscles right into his heart and dared him to disagree. He'd had his share of schoolyard fights as well as barroom arguments but that morning he simply nodded when he was confronted by an eight-year-old girl with steel in her gaze.

"And here it is." Hope brought in a wooden tray laden with breakfast. "Reckon we could have us a visit while you eat, Miz Tilly?"

"I'm really hungry, but I don't drink coffee."

"That's for me." Hope smiled.

"I believe you two didn't get your food finished." Hope set the tray down on the bed, took the pink bear from Tilly, and set it beside her, then slid the tray over her lap.

"I only get breakfast in bed when I'm sick," Tilly said.

"Today is a special day," Hope told her.

"I'll see you downstairs in a bit, young lady," Carlene told her. "You can play princess until you finish breakfast, but then we've got to get to work."

Tilly flashed a smile. "Then I will eat real slow."

As they closed the door behind them, Jace held out a hand and Carlene put hers in it. He liked the way her small hand fit in his but more than that he really, really needed the support, even if only for a few minutes.

"Don't let go."

"Why?" she asked.

"You're a strong woman, Carlene, but that about brought me to my knees. I need you right now even if it's only your hand in mine," he answered.

When they reached the bottom of the stairs, she whipped around, let go of his hand, and wrapped her arms around his neck. "I've worried about this day for years, and now that it's out in the open…"

He drew her close to his body. They needed each other

in that moment more than ever before at any time. "I know exactly what you're talking about," he whispered.

"You really don't mind that we're going to be here for longer than the weekend?"

"Not one bit. I was telling Tilly the truth when I said I needed the company." He massaged the tense muscles in her back. "This is a busy season on the ranch and you'll be at work every day. We'll probably only see each other in passing."

"You're right about that," she said with a nod.

One day at a time, Jace thought.

*   *   *

Hope sat down on the edge of the bed while Tilly dug into the breakfast with the gusto of a starving puppy. Watching her was like seeing Kasey at that age except for the gray eyes that in no way went with that deep red hair. It made for a striking look and Jace would have his hands full when the boys started coming around.

"So what do you want to be when you grow up?" Hope asked.

"A soldier like my aunt Bee," she answered quickly. "I like her uniform but maybe I could be a rodeo clown too. And I want to live where I can have animals so that Jasmine will have a place, too. What did you want to be when you was a little girl?"

"Well, when I was your age, I thought maybe I'd be a nurse but then I figured out that I didn't like needles, so I changed my mind and decided I'd marry a prince and go live in a castle in a faraway land." Hope hadn't thought of those things in years but then no one had ever asked her that question. She'd been groomed from the time she was born to run Hope Springs Ranch and there was no question about what she'd really be when she grew up.

Tilly giggled. "And he'd come and take you away on a white horse and you'd live happily ever after like in *Cinderella*."

Hope laughed with her. "My prince doesn't have a white horse but I understand that he's got an ice cream truck that is white with red writing on the side. Want to see it?"

"You have a real prince? One who's going to take you off to happily-ever-after?" Tilly's gray eyes popped wide open.

"I do." Hope pulled out her phone and flipped through several pictures. "And here he is in his ice cream truck."

Tilly giggled even harder. "That's not a prince. That's Henry. Me and Mama used to get ice cream from him when he went past our apartment in Laguna Beach. I like the Creamsicles and Mama always gets the kind with vanilla in the middle and chocolate on the outside."

"He told me that you did. Someday I'd like to go see the beach."

"You'd love it." She lowered her voice. "Don't tell Mama, but I sure do miss it. But I think it's funny that you call Henry a prince."

"He's a prince to me, Tilly. You see, a person can be many things to different people. Like your mama is your aunt Bee's sister and your grandma's daughter."

"And my mama," Tilly said.

"And Jace can be your mama's friend but he's also my grandson and Kasey's brother," Hope said.

"I said he could be my friend, too, but I don't want him for a daddy," Tilly told her.

"You got a problem with him bein' your mama's friend too?" Hope asked cautiously.

Tilly shook her head. "I told Mama to ask him out on a date but she said that girls didn't do that. I'm going to when I get old like Mama. What if a boy I like is too scared to ask me out? Then I guess I'll have to just ask him, right? They do it on television."

When Hope could speak, she said, "So you don't mind your mama dating Jace?"

"No, ma'am. She needs a friend to go places with since Aunt Bee didn't move here with us. And," Tilly said, "if she goes out with Jace, then I might get to go over to Maribel's for a sleepover, right?"

A wide smile spread across Hope's face. "Or maybe you and I could invite Maribel to come to my house for a sleepover and we'd have a night of movies and maybe make some cookies?"

Tilly clapped her hands. "That would be wonderful. You could be the fairy godmother and we'd be princesses."

"And if Henry drops by for a visit?" Hope asked.

"Tell him to bring ice cream," Tilly teased. "And we'll let him be the fairy godmother's Prince Charmin'."

Hope picked up the tray and stood up. "Sounds like a good plan to me. I suppose we should get down to the laundry room and help your mama get all your things washed so they don't smell like smoke when you put them in your dresser drawers and closet, right?"

"I really like this room and this house, Miz...What do I call you?" Tilly bailed off the bed.

"The grandchildren and the great-grands call me Granny," Hope said.

"Am I a great-grand?" Tilly asked.

"That's right."

"And I look like your mama. She's my..." Tilly frowned.

"Great-great-grandmother."

"Wow, that's a lot of greats. So you are Granny and my grandmother is Nanny. What is Valerie?"

"She'd be Grandma."

Hope started toward the door, expecting Tilly to be right behind her, but when she turned, she saw the little girl making her bed. "Rella, that's my bear, doesn't like to spend the whole day in a messy room. Mama told me that when I was just a little girl, so we fix the bed for her and keep things nice and neat."

"It sounds like your mama is pretty smart," Hope said as she and Tilly left the bedroom together.

"Yep, she is. I hope that the dryer is done. Rella gets lonely without her buddies."

"You met Emma and Silas and Rustin last night. Did you know that Emma gets lonely because all she's got is boys in her family? Think you can be her friend?"

"I never had a cousin. That's what she is, isn't it?"

"That's right."

"I guess I got room for another friend, but Maribel and Natalie are my best friends." Tilly stopped at the kitchen door and stared at her mother and Jace sitting at the kitchen table together.

"You okay?" Carlene asked.

"Yep, did you know that Henry isn't just the ice cream man? He's Granny's"—her brow wrinkled as she tried to figure out the relationship and then she blurted out—"boyfriend. Yep, that's what he is."

"Oh, really?" Jace asked.

"Yes, really, and I'll have no sass out of you this mornin', Jace Dawson," Hope declared.

"Henry's ice cream truck came by our house in Florida. Usually on Friday afternoon about four o'clock. We kind of recognized each other years ago," Carlene explained to Jace.

"Small world." Jace went back to his breakfast.

"Yes, it is," Hope said. "And that's the dryer buzzer. How about me and you take the toys up to your room and put them away."

"Okay, Granny." Tilly shrugged toward her mother. "She said that she is Granny and Valerie is Grandma. And Emma is my cousin."

"Oooookaaaaaay," Carlene drew out the word into a half dozen syllables.

Tilly sucked in a lungful of air and went on. "Cinderella is waiting for her friends. And she says that she likes it here. She didn't like Aunt Rosie's house too much. She was afraid a mouse would get on the bed and pee on her."

"Matilda Rose Varner," Carlene scolded.

"Well, she was," Tilly said.

"I'm glad that you and your bear both like it here," Jace said. "And you can stay as long as you want to."

"Thank you, Jace, but I reckon me and you will be friends or we won't by the time we move out. Will my birthday be here while we are still in this house, Mama?"

"Probably not," Carlene answered.

"Wherever we are living, can we have a party?"

"You bet we can." Jace agreed.

Hope's phone rang as she went to the laundry room to empty the dryer. She leaned her back against the dryer and smiled when Henry's picture popped up. "Why didn't you tell me before last night about Carlene and Tilly?"

"We made a deal the first time that I saw that little girl. She didn't tell Rosalie anything about me, and I wouldn't call you and tell her that I knew that daughter of hers is a Dawson. Guess both our secrets are out now," he chuckled.

"Yes, they are and thank God." Hope told him what had

happened that morning, including the pictures she'd send him later of Tilly catching snowflakes on her tongue.

"I'm glad that it's snowing while I'm here. I missed that in Florida. Not getting out in the miserable stuff to feed and break the ice on the cows' water, but the peace when all the earth is white and clean," he said. "So how's Jace and Carlene?"

"I'm surprised you didn't ask about Tilly."

"She's a firecracker. She'll find her way through the turmoil, but Jace and Carlene...they're trying to work out the wrinkles of the past just like we are and I know that's not so easy," he said.

"Granny, if your prince takes you away on a white horse, will he be my grandpa?" Tilly asked loudly.

"Like I said, a firecracker," Henry laughed.

"I'd say she's more like a bottle rocket," Hope answered, glad that Henry couldn't see the fiery red dots on her cheeks.

"See you tomorrow at the memorial," Henry said. "Have a wonderful day getting to know Miss Tilly Rose."

"I'm looking forward to both," Hope said.

Chapter Ten

Carlene chose a black dress that morning for Aunt Rosalie's memorial service at the church. She decided on a simple gold necklace and she pulled her blond hair back in a bun.

Tilly wanted to wear her Christmas dress, a blue and black plaid with a bodice of black velvet and Carlene didn't argue with her. They arrived at the church with Jace early enough to get a seat in the second pew. Tilly sat between them, but that didn't stop Carlene's heart from kicking in a little extra thump every time she glanced at him dressed in jeans, a white shirt and tie, and a Western-cut black corduroy jacket.

The preacher took the podium at exactly eleven o'clock. "Good mornin'. It's good to see a crowd on this snowy day, but I know Miss Rosalie Varner had many friends. It was her wish that there would be no funeral. I'm not brave enough or stupid enough to go against her wishes."

A few folks laughed, including Carlene and Jace.

"With that in mind, what we are having today is a little celebration of life. No reading of the day of her birth..." He paused for a moment. "Mainly because I'm not that stupid either. So we're going to sing a couple of her favorite songs and then we're going to let whoever wants to come forward do so to tell us what Miss Rosalie meant to them."

They sang "Precious Memories" and "When We All Get to Heaven." And then the preacher opened the service to anyone who wanted to step up and talk for a few minutes.

Hope was the first one on her feet and she took a moment to look out over the congregation before she started. "Rosalie Varner was the most aggravating woman I ever knew and one of the most generous. She was my mother's best friend and they organized lots of church socials and funeral dinners. She loved our little town and she's probably throwing a fit in heaven right now because we're doing this. Well, Rosalie, this is for us. I'm going to miss you and for the first time in my life, I get to tell you to sit down and hush."

Henry passed her as she went to sit down. Carlene noticed that for a brief second he locked little fingers with her. He adjusted the microphone. "When my mother was ailing and couldn't get to church, Rosalie would come to the house every Sunday afternoon. She'd bring a plate of oatmeal cookies or a blackberry cobbler, which were my mother's favorite desserts, and she'd sit with her for at least an hour and tell her everything the preacher said, what songs they'd sung that morning and who was at church. I appreciated that and I'll never forget her for it."

Carlene stood and made her way to the podium. "I loved my aunt Rosalie. She gave me the desire for roots and the love for this town. I hope that part of her will live on in me. Although her boots are way too big for me to fill, I'll do my best. Thank you all for being her family when we weren't here. Oh, and she made the best snickerdoodles in the whole world."

One by one, the folks came forward until the hour was nearly up and then the preacher took his place again. "Thank you all and, Carlene, Hope, and all Rosalie's close friends, I hope this has brought you a little bit of closure. Now we'll close with another hymn. If you'll all stand, we'll sing 'Just Over in the Gloryland' and then we'll go straight to the fellowship hall for a potluck dinner."

When they first walked inside, Tilly hung back but Jace held out his hand. "I'll be right here with you and your mama. And Maribel is right over there."

She put her hand in his and smiled up at him. "Do they all know that you are my . . . you know?"

"They do and it's okay," Jace said. "You ready or do you need a little more time? We can all three go back into the church and wait until you are comfortable."

"Tilly!" Maribel yelled, and waved. "Come on over here with us. We're all going to sit together."

It was the same group of little girls and boys she'd sat with at the rodeo. She let go of Jace's hand and looked up at her mother. "Will you be okay if I go with them?"

"I think so," Carlene said.

"Here." She picked up Jace's hand and put her mother's in it. "It'll help."

"It helps me for sure." Jace smiled.

Maribel crossed the floor and together they went to the other side of the room to the group of kids.

Carlene tried to pull her hand free but he held on to it.

"I need the support whether you do or not. This is a big day for me, Carlene. My first public appearance as a daddy," he said.

She craned her neck upward until she was sinking into his gorgeous eyes. He wasn't joking. He was truly nervous. She hadn't thought about someone as tough as a Dawson ever being insecure in any role, but Jace was. She squeezed his hand and took the first step toward the tables of food where the people were lining up.

* * *

Carlene took a few extra minutes after the church potluck and drove down south of town to take a peek at the house Regina had told her about. She almost missed the faded sign on the fence and had to brake hard to make the turn into the lane leading to a small frame house. From the outside it didn't look a bit better than Aunt Rosalie's place and she'd have a really big yard to be kept mowed. But she held out hope until she and Tilly got out of the vehicle and a skunk ran out from under the front porch with three babies behind it.

Tilly grabbed her nose. "They're cute, but this place stinks and look at all them spiders on the front door." She got back into the van and slammed the door.

There was no use in even looking at the place now. Tilly would never set foot inside the house. Carlene got into the driver's seat and really looked at the house. "Too much yard and I'm not sure we'd like living with skunks under the house."

Tilly exhaled with a dramatic whoosh. "Thank you, Mama. I'd have nightmares in that place."

She turned the van around and drove back to Hope Springs and parked beside Jace's truck.

"Thank goodness for rain boots," Carlene muttered as she stomped snow from her rubber boots at the door of the ranch house on Hope Springs. She'd forgotten about snow and cold weather and she missed Florida where anything white was warm sand, not freezing-cold snow finding its way down her back and freezing her cheeks. A shiver chased down her spine as she knocked on the door.

Tilly bent over and brushed the snow from her feet. "I need some cowboy boots. All of Kasey's kids have them. I saw them when everyone was huggin' us after our dinner at the church. I was the only one there in fancy shoes."

Valerie threw open the door and stood to one side. "Come right in. You can put your boots over there on the rug with everyone else's. I hear the kids are building a snowman this afternoon."

"Rubber boots beside all them cowboy boots," Tilly grumbled.

Valerie said. "So you want boots, do you? I hear your birthday is sometime in February, so maybe you could ask for them then."

Tilly slipped her hand into Carlene's like she always did when she was nervous. "Yes, I do and I told Aunt Bee. My birthday is February the twenty-fourth."

Jace stepped out of the living room. "Hey, I thought I heard your voices out here. Emma's been askin' where you were and when you'd get here. She's in the living room with a whole suitcase full of dolls."

"Will you come with me, Mama?" Tilly asked.

"Sure she will," Valerie said. "It's been a long time since she's been here, but it hasn't changed much."

"Thanks, Valerie," Carlene said. Ten years hadn't changed the house at Hope Springs any more than it had the one at Prairie Rose. There were just as many memories lurking around in the shadows at the sprawling house on Hope Springs. But there were more down at the actual springs where she and Jace had gone skinny-dipping more than once.

"So, how did the night go after y'all went up to bed? She didn't mention anything about it all day when I was in your presence," Jace whispered when Tilly let go of Carlene's hand and started toward Emma.

Emma squealed and hugged Tilly. "Play Barbies with me."

Tilly sat down where Emma had opened up a whole case full of dolls and clothing.

"I asked her about it at bedtime and she said she didn't want to talk about it," Carlene said. "I'm going to wait until she comes to me. Lord knows she's been through enough for one week."

"So have you," he said softly.

"Hey, Carlene, you got moved in over at Prairie Rose all right?" Brody called out from the sofa.

"Just about. What's goin' on with Aunt Rosalie's place now?" she asked.

"We've gotten all the utilities turned off and with that hole in the wall and this bad weather, I don't imagine there's much left worth saving. If there's anything in there you want to salvage, you might want to do it this week."

"I'll go take a look." She looked up into Jace's face. "If she misses me, tell her I'm in the kitchen."

"I will," he drawled.

Two words only but the electricity between them was so hot that it made her wish for one of those cardboard church fans. She stepped to the left to go around him and he did the same thing. She went to the other side and so did he.

"Shall we dance?" He drew her into his arms for a two-step and even provided the music by singing Blake Shelton's "Every Time I Hear That Song." He moved her across the living room and into the kitchen without missing a beat or a dance step.

"Do you realize that the guys are watching you and, sweet Lord, look at your sister's face," she whispered.

"Thanks for the dance, ma'am." He bent low and kissed the palm of her hand.

"Well, now, what's that all about?" Lila asked.

"I was trying to get around him and..." Carlene shrugged.

"Okay, okay. We'll discuss you and Jace another time. We're dyin' to know what Tilly said after I left," Hope said.

"She didn't want to talk about it, not all day or last night or this morning," Carlene said. "I'm sorry to spring all this on the family. We'll find a place as soon as possible. I intend to make a home here, but I want all of you to know that it's your choice whether you want to get involved with Tilly and that there's no hard feelings if you want to step away from it."

There.

She'd said her piece and now the ball was in their court.

Kasey threw an arm around Carlene's shoulders. "Me and my family sure want her in our lives. She's all Emma talks about. It's good to have another granddaughter in the family. And, Carlene, we want you in our lives, too, not just Tilly."

"And that goes for the rest of us," Hope said.

"Thank you," Carlene said. "But..."

"There are no buts in good relationships," Valerie said. "Now, Lila, Kasey, and Carlene, y'all start carrying bowls to the table."

"I figured they'd be furious," Carlene whispered to Lila as they took food from the kitchen to the dining room.

"When you guys were eighteen they probably would have been. But you're welcome." Lila smiled and gave her a wink.

"Welcome for what?"

Kasey leaned over and said, "Lila and I already paved the path for you, darlin'. We've done the heavy liftin'. Now you and Jace have a clear path if you want to take it."

Carlene patted them both on their shoulders. "Thank you, but what's in the past stays there. It'll be nice if Jace and I can be friends for Tilly's sake but I don't expect any more than that."

Who are you kiddin'?

*   *   *

Since he was a kid, Jace had loved the snow. His granny had passed down a rule to his mama that said that a kid could go out and play as long as they wanted but when they came in the house, they had to stay. There would be no running in and out to get warm and then going back out in the cold.

So after lunch while he was helping the two younger ones get bundled up in their coats, he wasn't surprised to hear those same words from Kasey and then for Carlene to echo them concerning Tilly. It didn't even shock him too much when Valerie pointed her finger and said the same thing to him.

"And Brody and Nash?" he asked.

"If they get sick, I don't have to listen to them whinin'. That's Lila's and Kasey's job. But it's still my job to help take care of you, so I get to boss you until you fix that little issue," Valerie said.

"Then I guess you'll be bossin' me for a long time," Jace teased, but he searched the room for Carlene until she was in his sight and hoped that he would be proven wrong.

"Karma can and will kick you in the butt," Brody said as he picked up Emma and carried her outside. Nash scooped up Silas. "Don't look at me. Kasey gave me my snow orders already."

"You aren't comin' out with us?" Tilly asked her mother as she zipped up her coat.

"No, I'm going to be in the house taking pictures through the window to send to Nanny and Aunt Bee." Carlene pulled out her phone. "First picture is of you and the kids, okay? Can you gather them up on the porch before you go out in the snow? And then I want one with all the guys and you kids."

"Thank you," Jace mouthed as he got into his place behind Tilly for the picture.

The excitement reminded him of the days when dozens of his Dawson cousins would come from all over Texas to Prairie Rose for Easter. They'd have a huge egg hunt in the pasture behind the house, and Valerie's rule for that was that any cowboy older than twelve had to help hide the eggs. The kids would line up across the fence line and wait for Valerie to drop a bandana and then they'd rush out in a dead run, most of the time leaving eggs behind them in their wake.

It might be a long time before Tilly called him Daddy, if she ever did, but today at least he got to help her build her very first snowman. And that was every bit as exciting as the egg hunts when he was a kid.

"Look, Tilly, it's almost over my snow boots," Emma said when Brody set her down.

"So how are we going to do this?" Jace asked.

"I vote that you and Tilly make the bottom since she's the oldest and it has to be the biggest," Nash said. "Silas and I will make the head and Brody and Rustin can make the middle section."

"I'm with Tilly," Emma said.

"Of course she is. Girl cousins have to work together," Jace agreed.

"I'm putting the arms and other stuff here on the porch," Hope called out.

"Thanks, Granny." Jace waved.

"Okay, ladies, let's get to work. We've got the biggest job there is." Jace patted snow into a round shape in his big hands and set it on the ground. "Now it's time to roll it into something big."

"Like this, Uncle Jace?" Emma pushed it across the yard a few feet.

"Just like that. When you get to the pecan tree, let Tilly turn it around and bring it back this way."

Emma struggled the last two feet but she made the distance and then handed the job off to Tilly. "Hard work. I'm goin' to make a snow angel while you get it all bigger."

"Flip it over so that it stays round," Jace said.

"What do we do when it's too big to turn over?" Tilly started to roll it toward the house.

"That's what I'm for." Jace followed behind her.

"What's a snow angel?" Tilly whispered.

"Turn around and look at Emma," he said.

"Oh!" Her eyes widened. "Can I make one of those so Mama can send a picture to Aunt Bee?"

"Sure you can. I'll roll this for a bit while you go make one right beside Emma's. That way there's a little one and a big one."

When he reached the porch, he turned it around and hiked a hip onto the porch. Not minding the cold that shot through his jeans, he watched the two girls as they made perfect snow angels. Their giggles were like the sweet sound of wind chimes as they echoed out over the ranch.

If he'd married Carlene back out of high school, they

could easily have four kids by now. *But would you be the same person you are today? At that age you weren't ready to start a family.*

"I am now," he muttered under his breath.

"What was that?" Brody asked as he and Rustin pushed their snowball toward him. "You'd better be doin' your job or our big old middle won't have a bottom to sit on."

"I was just mumblin'," Jace said. "And don't you worry about this part of the snowman. All I got to do is get it to size and place it in the middle of the yard. You have to set your part up on it."

"Which you and Nash will help me with, I'm sure." Brody flashed a grin as he and Rustin headed off in a different direction, leaving clear paths zigzagged out across the yard. "And aren't we glad that this held off until after the bronc ridin'?"

"Amen, brother." Jace suddenly had two little girls beside him ready to finish making their part of the snowman.

Months went by in Happy, Texas, with nothing but routine ranch work. Plow, plant, work cattle, make hay, fix machinery, rebuild fences. And then boom! Just like that, all kinds of fireworks could begin.

It was hard to believe that only a little more than a week ago Carlene had come back to town—even more difficult to think that the fire had happened only night before last. He was replaying every scene with Carlene as he rolled the big snowball across the yard. He didn't even realize how close he was to Tilly until she yelled at him.

"Don't mess up our angels," she scolded. "We want Mama to take pictures of them. This is so much fun. I built a little snowman at the beach with sand one time but this is the real thing. Will we get more snow?"

"Never know in January or February but by March it's

usually gettin' pretty warm," Jace said. "Aren't you girls about to freeze?"

"Yep, but I'm not going inside until we get him all finished," Tilly declared.

"Hey." Jace waved at the window where Kasey and Carlene were both taking pictures. "Kasey, bring one of Granny's old coats. Tilly's isn't keepin' her warm."

Kasey brought out a coat, handed it to Jace and said, "Roll up the sleeves and just put it on over what she's already wearing."

"Gotcha." Jace agreed.

"Better?" he asked when he'd put it on Tilly and buttoned up the front.

"I'm fat as the snowman now," she giggled.

"Not quite, and that poor old feller won't ever have pretty red hair," Jace told her.

"Like me." Emma said seriously.

"Like both you girls," Jace said.

"We've got our part as big as I figure we can lift him without gettin' out the tractor," Brody said.

"One more roll and we'll be ready for you," Jace called out from across the yard.

"We got the head all done, right, Silas?" Nash asked the toddler.

"Yep, Nashie and me all done." Silas said seriously.

Jace groaned when they lifted the midsection. "We should've gotten the tractor."

"I can help." Rustin joined the three guys and slipped his hands under a section.

"Me too." Silas put his little hands on the big round ball.

"Me too," Tilly declared as she joined in the effort with Emma right beside her.

"Okay, kids, one two three," Jace said as the middle came

up from the ground and set down perfectly on the bottom. "Couldn't have done it without y'all helping."

"Me head now." Silas danced around excitedly.

"Okay, you reckon you could help me with that?" Nash picked up the smallest perfectly round ball in one hand and Silas in the other. "Now, when I put it up there, you get it set just right, okay?"

"Tay," Silas answered.

*   *   *

Hope slipped away to her old bedroom, the one she'd shared with her husband, Wes, for more than forty years. It was still like she'd left it last spring when she moved into the ranch foreman's small house and let the grandchildren have the big house. Memories, good and bad, flashed through her mind as she sat down in the wooden rocking chair beside the window to watch the kids all play in the snow.

"I don't regret a single night that I had in this room," she said. "We had a good life, Wes."

Someone knocked on the door and she called out, "Come on in."

The door swung open and Henry filled the space. "I don't reckon I'd better. It wouldn't look too good. I was just wonderin' if maybe you'd like to put on a coat and go for a walk in the snow with me. We wouldn't be gone long."

"Nonsense. Leave the door open and come on in here. There's two chairs and a lovely view of the children out the window."

"Are you sure?" he asked.

"We are past seventy, Henry. I don't give a rat's ass what people think." She smiled and pointed to the other rocking chair.

He sat down and crossed one long leg over the other. "Do you ever wonder about our lives as teenagers if we'd had cell phones and could text each other?"

"I find myself just wishing I'd had your phone number the past decade," she said.

"Hey, I've been wonderin'. Did you set that Christmas tree on fire? Seems like it all was too much for fate. You knew that Rosalie's old house was a nightmare. You figured that Valerie would want to see her granddaughter so badly that she'd offer Carlene a place to live. So?" Henry drawled.

"I did not," Hope giggled. "But if I'd thought about it, I might have."

Henry chuckled. "Did you save most of Carlene's things?"

"All of it, including the kitten that Jace took over there," Hope said. "I'm going to send you some pictures and videos this afternoon. The kids are having such a wonderful time out there in the snow."

"If we were out there, we could make snow angels. I remember when we did that as kids."

"We were younger then. At our age, it would take a forklift to get us up out of the snow," she said.

"Speak for yourself, woman. I still run a mile on the beach every morning," he said. "And I know that you're still able to operate the ranch equipment and probably sit a horse real well too."

"Sold off the horses years ago. Nowadays we get around faster on four-wheelers. If you'll come back in the spring, we'll get a couple out and go for a ride," she said.

"Maybe we'll have a picnic at Hope Springs." He wiggled his eyebrows.

"Or in the loft of your old barn."

"We can't be at the barn anymore. Nash and Kasey might

catch us and then I'd have to make an honest woman out of you."

"Henry Thomas, you are flirting!"

"I just might be, but now I'm going to get out of here and at least sit on the porch a little bit. I might not see snow like this again for a long time," he said.

"Enjoy it," she said, and kept rocking.

She glanced over at a photograph of Valerie and Wes and went back to the window, where she could see Kasey's kids looking at Nash the same way. Tilly was having a wonderful time. Right now she only saw Jace as a friend, but give it a few weeks and all that could change.

Lila, Carlene, and Kasey were all outside now, taking pictures as the snowman got his final touches. Sticks for arms, buttons for his nose and mouth, and a carrot for a nose. The scarf, hat, and red-handled shovel made for pretty photos but Hope's favorite was still Tilly spinning around out there in the snow on Saturday morning, catching flakes on her tongue.

Her eyes went back to the collection of pictures that she'd left on the dresser. One of her and Wes on their twenty-fifth anniversary in a pretty gold frame.

"No, that one is in a silver frame. I took it with me when I moved. That is our thirtieth." She rose to her feet, picked it up, and the number 30 was on top of the cake in the midst of a pretty floral arrangement. For the first time she noticed Henry standing in a group of people over to the left and his expression said he'd rather be anywhere but at that reception.

"But his mother wanted to be there and he had to bring her," Hope whispered.

Until that moment, she'd never realized how painful it must've been for Henry to live next door for all those years.

When she did think about him, she'd figured that she'd broken his heart and he'd found lots of other women to take her place even if he didn't ever marry.

Now you have a second chance. Don't waste it.

*   *   *

"Granny, where are you?" Lila yelled down the hall.

"In my old bedroom," Hope hollered.

Lila and Carlene both poked their heads in the door.

"We're fixin' to make snow ice cream and we need you to come tell us your secret recipe," Lila said.

"Tilly has never had it but I remember yours being so good when I was dating Jace." Carlene recognized that expression on Hope's face. It didn't matter if a woman was eighteen or eighty—there was a look in her eyes when she was troubled about a man.

"I'll be glad to stir up a bowl for y'all. Tell Jace to bring in a big pan full of clean snow." Hope rose to her feet and looped her arm through Carlene's.

"Are you okay?" Carlene asked.

"I'm fine, honey. Just revisiting old memories."

"Old memories are good, but making new ones is even better," Lila said. "And I'm speaking from experience. We can hang on to the old but we can make new ones that are just as precious. I read a quote that said something about when opportunity knocks, invite it in and feed it chocolate cake because it's easier to deal with it right then than it is to chase after it when it's a mile down the road."

"That's pretty wise for a young kid." Hope squeezed her arm gently.

"Granny, I'm thirty. That's well past the young kid stage," Lila laughed.

"To me, that's still a baby."

"Hey, Granny!" Tilly yelled as she rushed into the house with the rest of the kids. "Look at our snowman. Isn't it gorgeous? And he's so big! Me and Emma and Jace made the biggest part."

Hope squeezed Carlene's arm. "Here's to letting go of the past and to all the new beginnings in the future."

"Amen," Carlene whispered.

Chapter Eleven

Usually Carlene dropped her shoulder bag on the sofa in the living room when she went into the house but for some reason, she'd taken it to the bedroom the day that Aunt Rosalie's house caught on fire. When she opened it that Sunday evening, she got a strong whiff of smoke as she strung the contents out on the dining room table. It was later than she liked to get started on getting all the papers graded, but Tilly had wanted to talk about every single detail of the whole day and it had taken a while for her to wind down. Now she was reading in her bedroom and Carlene was staring off into space rather than getting busy with spelling tests and history quizzes.

Jace slid a cup of hot tea over her shoulder and set it down between two stacks of paper. "Need some help?"

"Got any motivation hiding in your hip pocket?" She picked up the tea and warmed her hands with the mug. "Getting started is the hard part. After the first ten minutes, it usually goes pretty fast."

He took a step to the side and massaged her shoulders. "Who would have thought we'd be where we are today? You a teacher and me runnin' the ranch? We had different ideas that last summer we were together."

"You were going off to the big city, maybe Houston or Austin for an office job after college." She moved her hair to one side so he'd have better access. "I think you missed your calling. You should have been a masseur."

He expertly rubbed a knot from the base of her neck and then bent forward and kissed the soft part, sending ripples of warmth through her whole body. "And you were going to be a scientist and work for NASA if I remember right."

"So why aren't you a CEO of some firm?" she asked.

"I figured out real quick that I didn't like being inside when we did some job observations. And you?"

"Teaching lets me be out of school when Tilly is so I can spend more time with her."

"Unlike your parents?" He used his thumbs to work a knot out of her shoulder.

"Exactly. I'm surprised that you remember that."

"I remember everything about you." He moved to the other side of the table and pulled out a chair. As he eased down into it, his long legs brushed against hers and she whipped them off to one side.

"I didn't really have a father who was around much, so I figured Tilly didn't need one." A lump formed in her throat. A vision of her father's face when she told him she was pregnant passed through her mind. It was more than indifference or even disappointment; it was pure disgust. She'd braced herself that day and didn't shed a single tear, not even when she was sent to live with her sister in California. But after the fire, the memorial, and all that had happened, her emotions were running high and she couldn't shake that image of her father's face. All the strength she'd had that day when her mother put her on the plane for California and the determination that had held her together disappeared. She laid her head on the table and sobbed uncontrollably.

He reached across the table and laid his hands on hers. "I'm here for both of you, Carlene. I promise I'll be a daddy and not a father."

She raised her head. Uncontrollable tears still rolled down her cheeks like a small rushing river. "You can make that kind of promise?"

"I can, Carlene." His eyes were floating in tears. "Leaving Tilly in the road and expecting to find you dead in that house showed me exactly what you two mean to me."

"I believe you," she said.

*   *   *

Jace took a quick shower and slipped on a terry robe before he hurried across the hall to his bedroom. Throwing himself back on the bed, he stared at the shadows on the ceiling. Ever changing as clouds chased across the moon, they seemed to echo his mood that evening and his feelings. Nothing was steady and everything was unsettled.

He flipped on a lamp to chase away the shadows and picked up a book he'd been reading from the nightstand. It couldn't keep his attention, so he laid it aside and put earbuds in to listen to music. That always made him sleepy and he had hundreds of songs on the player. Randy Travis's deep voice singing "Diggin' Up Bones," which said that he was resurrecting memories of a love that had died.

"Dammit!" He turned off the music.

Dressing in a pair of flannel pajama bottoms and a white

tank, he marched down to the dining room. She glanced up from the last stack of papers on the table and smiled.

"Okay, let's do this and get it done," he said.

"What?"

"Tilly was so happy today at Hope Springs and I want her to always be that way."

Carlene finished the last paper and put it in her bag, zipped it shut, and stood up. "And that has to do with what?"

Jace crossed his arms over his chest. "She told me that you looked at that old place south of town and that it's just not fit for you to live in. I don't want you to even look at other houses. I want you to live right here."

"Tell you what I'll do. I'll take a look at that one for sale that's close to the school but if it's a no-go, we'll stay here until your friend's place is ready. How's that for a compromise?"

"If it's the best I can get, I'll take it, but I'm really ready..."

She marched around the table and poked him in the chest. "I appreciate that you are willing and ready to be a father—"

"Daddy!" He covered her finger with his whole hand. "You had a father. I had a daddy and that's what I'm going to be and I don't want Tilly living six miles from the ranch."

"We're both too emotional tonight to make a decision like this. Let's compromise. I won't look for another place for a week and see how she adjusts."

"Fair enough." He gazed into her eyes.

The tip of her tongue darted out and moistened her lips. He brushed a strand of hair back from her face and lowered his lips to hers. Her arms went up around his neck, sending sparks dancing around them like they were standing under a shower of Fourth of July sparklers.

He slipped an arm under her knees and another across her back, scooped her up, and carried her to the sofa, where he sank down in the cushions with her in his lap. The kisses deepened and his heart pounded in unison with hers, doing double time as he slipped his hand under her shirt and deftly unfastened her bra. Massaging her bare back sent him into instant arousal but he wanted to take this slow.

His hands skimmed her ribs, but his lips didn't leave hers. She moaned slightly at his touch. Then her fingertips tangled themselves in his dark hair and the other hand found its way up under his shirt to twirl his chest hair. He stood up to take her to his bedroom and she wrapped her legs around his waist. They were near the bottom step when Tilly yelled from the top of the staircase.

"Mama, there's a spider on the ceiling in my room. Come kill it."

Jace set Carlene down and took the steps two at a time. "Where is it? I'll take care of it for you."

*   *   *

"Damn spider." Carlene held on to the newel post and panted for a couple of minutes before she put a foot on the first step.

"Mama," Tilly singsonged from the hall. "It was big and black and hairy, and I want to sleep in your bed tonight."

"I'm on my way. Is it dead?" she called out.

"Jace took care of it." Tilly met her halfway down and grabbed her hand. "He says that it's the first one he's seen in this house in years, so I bet it caught a ride with us from that old place. But I can't sleep in my room tonight."

"I looked under the bed and in every corner and there's no spiders anywhere," Jace said from the top of the stairs.

"I still better sleep with my mama tonight," Tilly said.

"Want me to get your bear?" Jace asked.

"No, I can get it. I'll get her and get out real quick. Rella don't know you, so she might be afraid if you grab her." Tilly let go of Carlene's hand and made her way into the room on her tiptoes.

"Sorry," Carlene said softly.

"Not as much as I am," he whispered, and brushed a quick kiss across her lips.

"Who's mad?" Tilly brought her pink bear and a stuffed gator. "Rella might get lonesome, so Gator needs to sleep with us too."

"And the kitten?" Jace asked.

"Spiders don't scare them and she's asleep on her pillow. I don't want to wake her up." Tilly yawned.

"Well, then good night, ladies."

"Night." Tilly took her animals into the bedroom and then called out, "Thank you, Jace."

"You are welcome," he said, and then lowered his voice to a whisper just for Carlene's ears. "And don't tell me about colicky babies. An eight-year-old can put a kink in a night just as well."

She laid a hand on his arm, took a step forward so that her mouth was right against his ear. "Just think how many sleepless nights she'll cause as a teenager if she's anything at all like we were."

"Holy crap!" he mumbled.

A smile covered her face. "Welcome to fatherhood."

He was still standing in the middle of the hallway with a stunned expression when she gently closed her bedroom door.

"Mama, do we have hurricanes in Texas?" Tilly was busy getting Rella and Gator situated on her side of the bed.

"No, we do not." Carlene put emphasis on the last word. There was no way she was going to tell her daughter about tornadoes at that hour of the night. She ran the big bathtub full of water and sank down into it. She might have turned on the jets but they made so much noise that she couldn't hear Tilly; besides, Carlene needed quietness to surround her so she could think.

She'd been in love with Jace in high school—that much she was sure of and had a daughter to prove it. But what was tonight? Her brow furrowed into dozens of wrinkles as she analyzed her feelings and what the consequences could have been if she'd gone to bed with him.

Carlene flipped the lever to drain the tub and stepped out. Wrapping a towel around her body, she checked her reflection in the mirror. "What do you think, Miss Varner? Do we settle for friends with benefits? Do we even want more than that?"

Her reflection didn't offer a bit of help, so she turned away from it, got into her pajamas, and went to bed. She kissed Tilly on the forehead and shut her eyes but sleep was a long time coming that night. Her hormones and desires were still on high alert, needing fulfillment like they'd never needed since Jace Dawson had been in her life. She'd had a total of three dates since Tilly had been born, and in every instance she'd been bored out of her mind and couldn't wait to get home. But not with Jace... a few kisses and touches and she couldn't control herself.

The next morning, Jace had breakfast ready when she made it to the kitchen. "Good mornin'. How'd you sleep last night?"

"Not so well," she answered honestly. "How about you?"

"Horrible. What are we doing, Carlene?" he asked.

"Taking it a day at a time, I suppose, since that's all we can do."

"We proved that the chemistry is still there between us." He moved across the floor and drew her to his chest.

"Good mornin'. Do I smell bacon?" Tilly rubbed sleep from her eyes. Rella was tucked under her arm. "Gator was still sleepy, so I covered him up and didn't wake him."

Jace took a quick two steps back. "Yes, ma'am, you do smell bacon and I'm making omelets to go with it." He smiled. "What do you take on yours?"

"Cheese, tomatoes, and mushrooms." Tilly hugged Carlene and then sat down in a chair. "Can I have a glass of milk?"

"Want a little kick in it?" Jace's eyes glittered.

"Double shot. It's Monday." Tilly folded her arms on the table and laid her head on them. "Jace, why don't you homeschool me? I could sleep until noon every day."

"A rancher is up with the chickens and goes to bed after the cows," Jace said. "If you stay home every day, you'll have to be up and ready to work at dawn and not stop until dark."

"Well, then I'll just go on to school with Mama," she sighed.

"Might be the best idea." Jace gave Carlene a sly wink.

"Oh!" Tilly's head popped up. "I didn't call Aunt Bee and tell her about Jace stayin' on the horse until the horn sounded or about the house burnin' or nothin'. I need to do that on the way to school."

"I called her Saturday morning and caught her up on everything," Carlene said. "Right now you need to eat and get ready to go. We've got less than an hour."

*　　*　　*

The sun was out and the warmth was putting a dent in the snow, but the roads were still slick, so it took Carlene five extra minutes to get to school. The yard duty teacher told them that all the kids were staying in the cafeteria until the first bell rang, so Tilly headed off in that direction.

It seemed like ten years ago instead of only two days since Carlene walked out of her classroom on Friday. Half expecting to see a big change of some kind, Carlene held her breath as she unlocked her door and flipped on the lights. But there it was, just as she'd left it, and that brought a measure of comfort. She needed for one facet of her life to be solid. She removed her coat and hung it on the back of her chair and was unloading her bag when her cell phone rang. It was on the fifth ring when she found it at the bottom of her big purse and answered it without even looking at the caller ID because she recognized Belinda's ring tone.

"Hello," she said.

"Hey, did you find a house over the weekend?" Belinda asked.

Her sister wasn't going to like what she had to say, so Carlene sighed and then talked fast, telling her everything, from the way Jace held her hand at the memorial, to the promise and the breakfast he'd made, and to their visit to the skunk house.

"I'm glad that Tilly is taking it in stride, but she's a tough kid and I'd expect that from her. I'm not happy about you living in that house. You need to get past your infatuation with Jace Dawson." Belinda had her no-nonsense voice out that morning. "But none of it surprises me, except that Tilly didn't make you sign her over to me when she found out about Jace."

"Fat chance. Go have your own babies," Carlene said.

"I'm lookin' forty right in the eye and I never did want kids, but I'd sure take Tilly if you'll let me adopt her. Then you and the hot cowboy can romp around in the hay all you want. But you might want to learn a lesson and use double protection," Belinda teased.

"Keep dreamin'," Carlene said. "Now tell me about this guy you're dating."

"Nothing to tell. He's military, of course, and he's damn fine-lookin' and real good in bed. That's about it. Oh, and he does like Jack Daniel's better than Jim Beam, so that's a plus."

"Well, that's a definite plus but if he drinks light beer, throw him to the curb." Carlene told her about Tilly asking Jace if he needed a little kick for his glass of milk.

"Ah, proof positive that she could easily be mine," Belinda said. "Got to go for now. I'll talk to you and Tilly later and then I'll tell you just exactly what she thinks of having a daddy. And, Carlene, be careful. Not only with protection but also with your heart. Bye now."

The phone went dark before Carlene could even tell her good-bye. What she hadn't told her sister played back through her head—the way Jace's hands felt on her bare skin, the dreamy look in his eyes right before their lips touched, the chemistry between them that separated them from the rest of the world for a little while that evening.

"The past is gone. I burned that bridge," she whispered.

But the future lies ahead of you and that bridge is real sturdy. The voice in her head definitely belonged to Aunt Rosalie.

Chapter Twelve

A thunderstorm howled outside as Jace finished a long, hot shower and slipped into a pair of pajama pants and a T-shirt. He was on his way downstairs when he heard Tilly wailing. Not crying, but a pitiful sound as if she'd lost her best friend. He took the steps two at a time and hurried into the kitchen, where she was on the floor, hanging on to Carlene's knees and sobbing uncontrollably.

He dropped down next to her and wrapped her up in his arms. "What's happened? Are you hurt?"

"Jas...mine," she howled.

"What about Jasmine? Is she hurt?" Carlene asked.

Jace's eyes went to Carlene with silent questions.

She shrugged. "She rushed in from the utility room like this. I don't know."

"I just wanted to see if the snow was mel...ting...," she said between sobs. "So I looked out the back door."

"What about Jasmine, sweetheart?"

"She ... ran ... outside."

Jace jumped to his feet and ran to the back door, where he crammed his bare feet into a pair of work boots and grabbed the first coat he could put his hands on. "I'll find her, Tilly."

A hard north wind slammed the rain against his face and lightning split the sky in long jagged pieces, followed by low-rolling thunder—but none of that mattered. His daughter was upset and he had to fix it.

Continually wiping water out of his eyes and pushing back his dripping wet hair, he checked under the bushes around the house first but came up empty-handed. Surely that kitten wouldn't have gone any farther than the yard with all the noise. He was on his way to broaden his search to the truck and van parked out in the yard when he heard a meow off to his right. A long lightning streak gave enough light to show Jasmine huddled against the gatepost.

"Kitty, kitty," he called softly.

Heading that way slowly so he didn't spook her, he took a step at a time and talked to her in a soft voice that he hoped was soothing in the downpour. He reached the gate and bent to pick her up, still sweet-talking her. But a flash of lightning, followed immediately by a clap of thunder that could be heard all the way to the Gulf of Mexico, startled him so badly that he covered his head with his hands. When he looked down, the kitten was nothing more than a black-and-white streak headed out across the pasture toward the barn.

He put one hand on the fence post and jumped the fence in one easy motion, then headed off the way he saw the kitten go. Another streak of lightning gave him a glimpse of Jasmine making a beeline to the barn. Trouble was, that was where Red would be curled up in a stall on his dog bed. Not that he'd hurt a kitten, but she'd be terrified of a big red dog if he came toward her and could possibly run outside. Then he'd never find her and Tilly's heart would be broken.

Jace took another running step and his foot sank into a puddle of water and snow mixture that overflowed over the top of his boot. "Damn, that's cold," he muttered as he kept going.

Just before he got to the barn, he saw Jasmine dart inside. In spite of the shivers from the cold water sloshing in his boot, he doubled his pace and hurried inside the barn, where he shut the door firmly. Now she was trapped and he'd be able to find her.

Red came out of his stall, wagging his tail and wanting Jace to pet him. Completely winded and shaking from the cold, Jace sat down on a bale of hay and scratched Red's ears.

"Did you see a little black-and-white kitten that looks like a half-drowned rat?" he asked.

Red yipped and laid his head in Jace's lap, but when he figured out how wet it was, he quickly backed up several feet.

"I don't blame you a bit, but it's time to start the search. You might as well go on back to bed because seeing you will scare her." He stood up and pulled the coat around his chest and the front overlapped by three inches. That's when he realized he'd grabbed his dad's coat. It was hanging on the rack the day his dad was killed in a tractor accident and no one could bring themselves to move it.

"I'd appreciate any help you could give me, Dad. It'll take some doing for me to ever fill this coat, but I'm willing to try," he said.

That's when he heard the mewling somewhere behind him. Red's ears perked up and he went into hunting mode, his nose to the barn floor. He chased a mouse out of a corner, then turned and headed toward the tack room with Jace right behind him. He entered the room and stopped immediately, going into a point toward the worktable.

One more tiny little mewling sound took Jace right to the kitten. She was cowering under the table. Dripping wet, big eyed, she came right to him when he called her that time. He picked her up and dried her off as best he could with a paper towel before he tucked her inside the coat, next to his chest.

"Thanks, Red. You done good, old boy. You can go back to bed now," he said, and then looked up toward the ceiling. "And thanks, Dad."

The rain was still coming down in sheets, but the thunder had rolled off toward the northeast. He cracked the barn door with one hand and held on to the place where Jasmine was cuddled up next to him with the other one.

Afraid that if he went too fast he'd spook the kitten, he took off for the house in a fast walk. Halfway there, he stepped in the same puddle with the other foot and now both boots were sloshy with cold water, but he didn't let it slow him down. He could see Tilly's face in the kitchen window and he had to get Jasmine to her.

He was to the gate when lightning lit up the sky and a mesquite tree crackled somewhere not far behind him. Immediately a loud burst of thunder followed it and Jasmine clawed her way from his chest, up across his neck, and climbed down his back like he was an oak tree. Then she darted under the fence and took off for the porch, made a left-hand turn, and scaled the hedge. He found her sitting in the middle of the snow-covered leaves, hissing at him and baring her little claws. He reached through the dormant limbs to snatch her up by the back of the neck. She went limp and he eased her out to keep from scratching her.

Tilly slung open the door when he took the first step onto the porch. With her arms out and tearstains on her cheeks, she smiled up at him. And despite the cold outside, despite his slushy boots—that smile warmed him to the center of his heart.

"Oh, Jace, you saved her! You are a hero." Tilly hugged him tightly.

He put Jasmine in her arms. "She's pretty wet."

"Come here, baby girl. You must never do that again. You scared me so bad." She grabbed a towel from the laundry basket, wrapped the kitten in it, and crooned sweet words to her the whole way to the living room.

He hung his dad's coat back on the hook and turned to find Carlene behind him. Her eyes were soft and she had a small smile on her face. "That was a good thing you did."

"Well, I wasn't gonna leave a kitten in the cold. Besides, I couldn't bear seein' Tilly cry like that."

"Well, cowboy, you'd better get out of those wet clothes and into the shower and get warmed up. I'll clean up this mess. The things we do for our child."

He dripped water all the way up the stairs to the bathroom. The warm water felt like prickles on his chilled skin at first but after a few minutes, it started to heat up his body and he stopped shaking like a leaf in a windstorm. So now Tilly was our child—not Carlene's daughter or his but theirs together. Seeing Tilly's smile and hearing Carlene say those two words was worth the whole cat-rescue mission.

When he made it back down the stairs, this time in a gray sweat suit, Carlene met him halfway across the floor and handed him a glass with a double shot of Jack Daniel's in it.

"You need to warm up your insides, too, after a chill like that," she said. "And thank you one more time."

"It was worth it. Our child"—he liked the sound of that—"is happy now."

"Yes, she is," Carlene said.

They'd barely made it to the sofa when a loud rap on the door was followed by Hope's voice out in the foyer. "Y'all at home?"

"In the livin' room. Come on in," Jace yelled.

The sound of two people stomping snow from their boots on the rug inside the door filtered to the living room. Then there was a low rumble of whispers before they actually appeared in the doorway.

"Hello, Henry and Granny. What are you doing out in a storm like this?" he asked.

"Can I get you something to drink?" Carlene asked.

"I'd like a shot of Wild Turkey and I bet Henry would like a beer," Hope answered for both of them.

"You know me too well." Henry's old eyes glowed when they looked at her.

"I'll get those for you. Y'all have a seat." Carlene rose from the sofa. "You want another one, Jace?"

"Yes, please."

He sank down into a recliner, expecting Henry to sit on the other one, but he and Hope both chose the sofa. There was two feet of space between them, but Jace could almost see the sparks when they looked at each other. He'd known that Hope and Henry had an infatuation when they were younger and he'd said he was all right with it but there was still a little jealousy that sparked when he thought of his grandpa.

Tilly came into the room from the kitchen holding Jasmine in one of her doll's blankets. "Hello, Henry. Hi, Granny. Jace, you are a hero. She's going to live."

"What happened?" Hope asked.

"She ran outside in the rain." Tilly went on to tell the whole story, making it far more dramatic than it was. "I thought she'd drown for sure, but Jace saved her."

Henry's eyes glittered, but he didn't laugh at Tilly. "It must have been terrifying."

"It was," Tilly said with a sigh. "I watched out the window and I thought Jace would never come home with her. She's so little and it was a big storm. But she says she's learned her lesson and she'll stay in the house from now on."

"Well, I hope she doesn't forget," Henry said.

Carlene returned, carrying a tray with a glass, a bottle of Wild Turkey, and a tray of cookies. She set it on the coffee table and took a seat on the recliner beside Jace.

Hope poured a little more than a double shot into the glass and took a sip. "We'd like to have a family dinner Wednesday night to celebrate Henry's last evening with us."

"Sounds like fun. If it's all right with Carlene, can we host it here at Prairie Rose? We haven't had a family dinner here since Mama moved to her new place."

"Well, I was going to ask Brody and Lila, but if you'd like to do it here, Valerie and I'll do the cookin' since you'll be in school all day, Carlene." Hope took another sip of her whiskey.

"Whatever y'all want is fine with me. I'm sure Tilly will love having her cousins here to play."

"Mama, may I have a glass of milk, please? With a kick? And a small saucer without a kick for Jasmine. She's havin' trouble gettin' over this," Tilly said.

"Of course, sweetheart," Carlene answered.

"Kick?" Hope whispered to Jace.

"Chocolate," he said out the side of his mouth.

Carlene went back to the kitchen and Tilly plopped down

on the arm of the chair her mother had vacated. "You never told me that you knew Granny and Jace when we were in Florida, Henry."

"I knew your granny when she was your age. We were friends."

"I have a new friend. Her name is Maribel," Tilly said. "Oh, I should call her and tell her all about how Jace saved Jasmine."

Henry nodded slowly and seriously. "It's a good thing to have friends in times of need."

Carlene returned with a tray bearing a glass of chocolate milk.

"Can I take it upstairs, Mama, and use your phone to call Maribel?"

"If you are very careful and don't spill it but Jasmine has to drink her milk in the utility room. I put a full saucer out there for her," Carlene said.

"But, Mama, she's still upset from bein' out in the rain," Tilly declared.

"That saucer of milk stays in the utility room, young lady," Carlene told her.

Tilly took the chocolate milk and picked up her mother's phone from the end table. "Yes, ma'am."

Henry waited until she was out of the room to chuckle. "You two have got your work cut out for you."

"Don't I know it." Carlene took another gulp of beer.

"And I'm learnin' it real fast," Jace agreed.

Chapter Thirteen

On Tuesday morning, Tilly was fidgety on the way to school. She sighed and turned the radio station five times before Carlene pulled the van into her space in the school parking lot.

"Mama, can we talk?" she said as Carlene reached to open the door.

"We've got five minutes," Carlene said.

"If you was to marry Jace...well, I liked it bein' just me and you," she stammered. "But if you was to fall in love with him, would that mean you wouldn't love me as much?"

"Do you love Jasmine?" Carlene asked.

Tilly frowned. "Of course I do."

"Do you love Aunt Bee?"

"Why are you askin' me that?"

"Does that make you love me any less?"

"Of course not," she blurted out.

"I love you more every single day of your life, Matilda

Rose Varner. It's impossible that I could ever not love you as much as I do right now or more, but don't worry about me getting married anytime soon."

"Not even to Jace?"

"Not even to Jace."

"Okay, Mama. That makes me feel better, but if you change your mind about Jace and you'll still love me, I might be all right with it." Tilly grabbed her backpack. "There's Maribel. I've *got* to get me some cowboy boots."

"Wow! Just wow," Carlene gasped.

*   *   *

From the time Tilly and Carlene got home from school on Wednesday, Tilly couldn't wait for her cousins to arrive for their family dinner. She ran back and forth from the kitchen where Valerie and Hope were cooking to the living room window to see if the kids were out there yet.

"Anything I can do to help?" Carlene asked.

"Set the table, please," Valerie said. "Just the napkin and cutlery. We're doing buffet style, so they'll get their plates and drinks right here on the kitchen table."

"Yes, ma'am."

Jace entered the room and her pulse raced. She moved to the next place setting and he went right along with her.

"I like this scene. Us having dinner at our house," he said.

"Tilly and I are looking at one on Sunday. That little yellow brick not far from the school. It's for sale and the price is good," she said bluntly.

"You said you'd stay until—" he started.

"I said I'd stay if this one wasn't right. I need to look at it," she answered before he could finish the sentence.

"Can I go with you?"

"No, it needs to just be the two of us," she whispered.

"I hope you hate it."

Kasey, Nash, and the kids came in through the kitchen. Emma barely stopped long enough to hug her uncle Jace and then her red braids flew out behind her as she ran to find Tilly.

"Whoa! Take off your coat," Kasey yelled.

"I got it," Lila said. "Need help with the other two?"

"Nash has got them corralled," Kasey said. "They've all been pretty excited about tonight."

"Where's Henry?" Hope asked.

"He's bringing over the work truck. Said he might want to go for a drive after dinner," Kasey said.

Hope raised her voice above the children's giggles. "Hey, Carlene, when I came by on Sunday, I lost an earring. I think it's probably up in Tilly's bedroom. Think you could help me search for it?"

"It should be right around the bed if it's up there," Carlene said as they started that way. "Was it expensive?"

"A half-carat diamond stud," Hope answered.

"Oh my!" Carlene gasped.

They were halfway up the steps when Hope whispered, "Don't panic. I didn't lose my earring. I just said that so I could get you alone. We need to talk."

That was scarier than the thought of a half-carat diamond sunk down in the plush carpet. "About?" Carlene asked.

"Wait until we get to the bedroom and shut the door," she said. "It's personal."

Carlene's mind spun around so fast that she couldn't latch on to a single thought. When they reached Tilly's room and shut the door, Hope sat down on the edge of the bed and sighed. Carlene shoved a stuffed Olaf from *Frozen* off onto the floor and sank down in a ladder-back chair.

"Is this about Tilly? I'm not going to ask Jace for support. I've raised her on my own for..."

Hope shook her head. "There's no doubt about that, child. This is about me, not you, and certainly not my great-granddaughter."

"Are you sick?" Carlene's heart took a tumble. Jace would be devastated if Hope was terminally ill.

"I hope not!" Hope giggled. "Okay, the only way I know how to do this is to spit it out. I'm worried about all this change in my life and in yours. I loved my husband, but I'm not sure I was in love with him, and now I could have a shot at a second chance with the man I was in love with and you're in the same boat and I thought maybe we could talk."

"You've always been a strong woman, Miz Hope. I can't imagine you not taking the bull by the horns and spitting in his eye."

"Thank you, but I don't feel so strong right now."

"You've got what Aunt Rosalie called the what-ifs. What if the family is against your decision to be more than friends with Henry? What if you are tarnishing the beautiful marriage you had with Wes if you got involved with Henry?"

Hope patted her hand. "You are a wise kid. Have you been plagued with these what-ifs too?"

"More than you'll ever know."

"You are young." Hope left her hand on Carlene's. "I'm past seventy. Maybe I've wrung all the good out of my life that is possible and Henry and I should just be friends." She looked down at her body. "Gravity has taken over every bit of this thing. What used to be tight now sags. I don't want him to see me like this. In his memory I've still got perky boobs and a smooth butt."

"And in yours, he's still got a broad chest with black hair on it and no wrinkles in his face, right?" Carlene said.

"What if I've forgotten how to..." She hesitated and looked up at the ceiling.

"I reckon it's like riding a bicycle."

"Never did learn to ride one. Had horses in my youth that I could ride and then we traded them in for a four-wheeler."

Carlene scooted over closer to Hope. She draped an arm around her shoulders and said, "I have stretch marks and I'm scared to death of letting Jace see me. And I'm afraid that this is just a passing fancy that will end in hard feelings between us. Tilly doesn't need that." She took a deep breath. "Jace was my first love and..." She paused.

"And since then?" Hope asked.

Carlene shook her head. "Then there was a baby. No man wants to date a woman with wet spots on her shirt from leaky breasts."

"And after she was weaned?"

Carlene inhaled deeply and let it out very slowly. "It was too complicated. I went out with a few guys but why start something with no future? I'd made up my mind to keep my baby and bein' both mother and father takes a lot of time and energy. It doesn't leave much time for flings or even relationships. And thinkin' of her with a stepfather didn't sit too well with me."

Hope nodded along with every sentence. "I'm wondering how a stepfather will sit with Valerie. I'm probably too old to even entertain such things."

"Age doesn't have much to do with it." Carlene hugged her. "I know that Jace has had other women, and..." Another long pause. "There is chemistry but now I'd always wonder if he wanted a relationship with me so he could have Tilly. It's very complicated."

"You kids use that word a lot but I guess in this situation

it's justified. Thanks for the visit, Carlene." She pulled a diamond earring from her pocket and dropped it on the floor.

"Would you look at that? We found it." Carlene smiled.

"Sometimes all a diamond has to do is sparkle a little bit for us to find it."

*   *   *

When Hope called on Tilly to say grace, the child bowed her head and said, "Father, bless this food and all the folks who put it on this table. Thank you for Jace because he saved Jasmine. And thank you for giving me and Mama this nice place to stay and for givin' me some new cousins and aunts and uncles and grandmas. Please tell Mama not to make me eat brussels sprouts even though we have company. In Jesus's name, amen."

"Jasmine?" Lila whispered for Jace's ears only. "Is that the cat?"

"Yes." He whispered.

"Jace saved her from drowning and that makes him a hero. I thought she'd die and go to heaven for sure," Tilly piped up from across the table.

"I got a daddy in heaven," Emma said seriously.

"I'd like to know what's wrong with brussels sprouts?" Henry changed the subject. "I was thinkin' about maybe making an ice cream flavor like that."

"Yuk!!" Emma and Rustin said at the same time.

"Go ahead and make that for the old people, but I'm always goin' to buy Creamsicles," Tilly said. "You goin' to buy a nasty old green popsicle, Jace?"

"No, thank you. I'd rather have an ice cream sandwich," he answered.

"Mama likes those too," Tilly said. "Did y'all have an ice cream truck in Happy when you was kids?"

"No, but we did have an old hand-crank ice cream maker that we still get out on the Fourth of July," Jace answered.

That brought back a memory of a bunch of kids who borrowed the ice cream freezer to take to Henry's old barn the spring before Jace and Carlene graduated. They made frozen daiquiris in it and every kid there was more than a little drunk when they went home.

"Daiquiris?" Carlene leaned over and whispered.

"Back of my truck afterward," he said softly.

She blushed and he thought it was adorable.

The evening went by fast, according to Tilly. But to Jace's way of thinking, the hands on the clock above the mantel had gotten stuck. He loved his family, but he liked spending his evenings with Carlene and Tilly much better.

Tilly covered a yawn with the back of one hand and waved good-bye to her little cousins as they pulled away from the driveway. "Mama, I'm tired. I'm going to get my bath and read a book to Rella and Olaf. I like my cousins but I miss bein' the only child when we have family around."

"You'll get used to it," Jace said. "Maybe I could read a story to you and Rella and Olaf and tuck you in tonight."

"You can read me a story, but Mama has to tuck me in," Tilly said.

"Fair enough. You just call me when you get finished with your bath and I'll come right on up," Jace said.

She turned around halfway up the stairs. "If there's any more spiders in my room, will you kill them for me?"

"Of course I will. I'm the biggest meanest toughest spider killer in the whole state of Texas," he said.

She went on up the stairs and he turned to find Carlene leaning on the doorjamb with a big smile on her face.

"What?" he asked.

"You're doin' good on the friendship thing," she answered.

The sparkle in his eyes lit up the whole room. "She's a good kid. You've done an amazing job, Carlene."

"It's been tough staying on the parent side of the line and not stepping over onto the friendship side. But the way I figure it is that she'll have lots of friends in her lifetime. Some will be there forever. Some will be gone tomorrow. But parenting goes beyond that."

Jace sat down on the third step and stretched out his long legs. "I'm all right to be her friend for now but I'm finding that I do want to step over the line into parenting someday."

Carlene sat on the second step but her legs didn't reach as far as his did. "Just don't rush it. Anything worth havin' is worth waiting for."

*   *   *

Carlene didn't know if she was giving advice to herself or to Jace. Miz Matilda Rose was independent—of that, Carlene had no doubt because she'd raised her to be that way. She had no idea whether Tilly would accept Jace as a father, but she did know her daughter wouldn't be pushed into anything.

"I guess Granny and Henry are proof of that waiting thing," Jace said. "Did she really lose an earring?"

"Why else would we be in Tilly's room searching for it?"

"Because she wanted to talk to you about all this." He waved a hand to take in the whole universe.

"Tilly's room is like Las Vegas."

"What's said there stays there, right?" he asked.

"You got it," Carlene said. "What did you and Henry talk about at the barn when you went out there after dinner?"

"What's said in the barn stays in the barn." One of those impish grins covered his face that reminded her of Tilly. Their daughter might look like her aunt Kasey, but she sure had her daddy's mannerisms as well as his height and his eyes.

Our daughter, Aunt Rosalie's voice in her head said with a giggle. *You always told me that you weren't sharin' or tellin'. And here you are after only a week doin' both.*

You didn't leave me much choice when you sold the house and left that damned Christmas tree to dry up in the corner, Carlene argued.

"Who are you fightin' with?" Jace asked.

"I didn't say a word," she protested.

He nudged her on the shoulder. "Not out loud. Was it Granny?"

She pushed back. "I'm fine with Hope. I'm fine with Valerie and Kasey and Lila."

"Then who?"

"Aunt Rosalie," she said honestly. "Sometimes I get so mad at her for dying and yet still poppin' into my head with her sass."

"What happened when you told your dad about the baby? Did she draw him closer to you and did y'all finally have a decent relationship?"

"Far from it. He was disgusted with me and they shipped me off to live with Belinda. I went to college and she helped me with the baby," Carlene said.

"I'm so sorry, darlin'."

She shrugged. "Like I told you before, I was the accident. They only wanted one child and Belinda was the glory girl. I had a nanny for the first several years of my life and then Daddy was sent to Amarillo for three years. Mama decided that we'd live in Happy because Aunt Rosalie could help keep an eye on me. I was too old for a nanny and too young to be left on my own when they had business trips and job stuff to do, but you probably remember me whining about all this when we were dating."

"How is he with Tilly now?" Jace twirled a strand of her hair around his finger.

"He didn't speak to me for six months. When Tilly was born, though, he did come to the hospital, and he told me that he would pay for my education if I stayed in college."

"That was a start, right?"

"No." Carlene shook her head. "I told him that I'd take out loans, get scholarships and grants or whatever it took but I'd made my bed and I'd lie in it and I didn't need his help. I paid off my student loans last May. Daddy has come around somewhat. He likes Tilly in small doses and tolerates me. But Belinda has been my rock for the past ten years."

"I would have married you," Jace said.

"I have no doubt about either one, but pregnancy won't hold a marriage together. I wasn't ready, and besides, I'd have always wondered if that's the only reason you married me and you could have come to resent me and Tilly."

"Hey, Jace, me and Gator and Rella are ready for you to read to us," Tilly yelled.

"Duty calls." He brushed back Carlene's hair and kissed that soft spot right under her ear. "And, darlin', we won't ever know now what might have happened if we'd married young, but one thing I do know, I'd be tuckin' her in tonight as well as reading a story to her."

Carlene stayed on the step but she could hear his deep voice reading the first chapter of *Harry Potter* to her. She wondered why Tilly had chosen that book—she'd heard it read more than once.

Her phone pinged and she found a text from Belinda: *Call me.*

She quickly hit the speed dial and her sister picked up on the first ring. "How did the dinner go?"

"Went fine. It's kind of scary how well these people are accepting me," Carlene answered.

"They have to take the cow if they want the calf," Belinda laughed. "Dad and Mom are settled into their new place and have invited us to come out and spend spring break with them."

"Shall I pack my evening dresses?" Carlene's laughter had a bitter edge.

"We could take Tilly to Disneyland and do some fun things," Belinda said.

"Or I could stay here and go to Kasey and Nash's wedding. I wouldn't be surprised if they invite Tilly to do something, like maybe sit at the guest table."

"Be careful. You've had enough heartaches," Belinda told her. "I hear a voice in the background. Where are you?"

"Right now I'm sitting on the stairs and Jace is in Tilly's room reading *Harry Potter* to her. I'll go up and tuck her in for the night after he finishes the chapter," Carlene said. "Did Daddy ever read to you?"

"Of course he did, when he was home. If not, then my nanny read to me," Belinda answered. "I read to you, remember?"

"I do." Carlene answered. "And I loved it, but then you joined the service when I was only eight."

"You could read by then, so it wasn't a big deal," Belinda said. "Did Aunt Rosalie read to you?"

"Lord, no!" Carlene giggled. "She did make cookies and shovel out advice in bulk. I ate the cookies and ignored the advice, as you well know."

"Then pull up your big girl panties and thank God that life taught you how to stand on your own two feet and not depend on anyone to take care of you," Belinda scolded.

"You took care of me." Carlene shut her eyes and visualized her tall, dark-haired sister who looked like their father.

"No, honey, I simply gave you a place to live until you could get your own apartment. You weren't always wise in your choices but you were damn sure big enough to accept the consequences. Enough of this heavy conversation. How are you and Tilly settling into ranch life?"

"No problems. You should come visit us. We're looking at a house to buy next Sunday and there's one for rent coming up the middle of next month, so ranch life might not last long."

"I just might do that before I'm shipped off to Germany. Want to go with me? I bet you could get a teaching job on the base."

"Oh no," Carlene gasped. "When?"

"Mid-April. I could find a place for you by the time you finish up the school year there. Think about it. Good night."

"You can't throw that on the table and then hang up," Carlene snapped.

"Yes, I can and I will," Belinda said, and the phone went dark.

"Mama, it's your turn," Tilly called out.

She put the phone in her pocket, tucked her feelings away inside her heart, and went to tuck the covers up around Tilly's chin.

Chapter Fourteen

Hope dropped Henry at the airport, then cried all the way back to Happy, where she went to the cemetery instead of the ranch. Wes's tombstone was a huge chunk of gray granite with his name engraved on one side and hers on the other.

She sat down in front of it on the icy-cold ground and traced her name with a forefinger. Sighing when she reached the last letter, she reached up to her neck and touched the little gold locket. One decision made when she wasn't even old enough to order a shot of whiskey had determined her whole life. She couldn't leave her family or the ranch. Henry wouldn't stay and fight their opinion of him. She'd made the decision to stay and he'd gone. Then when he came back more than twenty years later to take care of his mother, they just steered clear of each other as much as possible.

"I loved you, Wes. You were an amazing husband and

father." She laid a palm on his name. "This happiness I feel now shouldn't have so much guilt attached to it."

The crunch of tires on frozen ground took her attention away from the tombstone. A shiny white Caddy stopped not five feet from her and a woman with dyed black hair, high-heeled shoes, and a fancy little business suit gracefully got out of the driver's seat. She carried a huge armload of red roses and a confused expression covered her thin face.

"Hello," she said with a flat accent as she laid the flowers at the base. "Were you a friend of Wes's?"

"Yes, I was," Hope answered honestly. "Evidently you were too."

"I was his fiancée. He left East Texas to take a job as a foreman here, and I was supposed to join him," she said. "I come here once a year to put flowers on his grave."

Hope got to her feet. "Why didn't you join him?"

"It's a long story," she said. "And you are a complete stranger to me."

"I've got time." Hope sat on the tombstone, her legs covering up her name. She patted the other side. "Might as well sit a spell and sometimes a stranger is a good person to talk to because they won't judge you."

The woman sat down on Wes's side of the tombstone. "I loved him from the time I was thirteen and he loved me. He had the opportunity for two jobs that year. One only thirty miles from where we grew up in the northeast corner of Texas. The other one was here and he made the choice to come here because it was a bigger ranch."

"And you found someone else?" Hope asked.

"No, he did. He said that he'd always love me but..."

Hope's chin quivered. "But his future was here in Happy, right? He could make more, be more, and have a better place in life?"

"Something like that," she said. "My heart was broken. I made a career for myself and married three times. No children, didn't want any if I couldn't have them with him, but he and his wife had a daughter. I couldn't seem to find happiness until I retired and then I got in touch with him. We met in Amarillo for dinner and it was like we'd never been apart. That was fifteen years ago today, January twelfth. He's been dead thirteen years this summer."

Hope was speechless.

"It feels odd tellin' this to a stranger. How did you know him?" the lady asked.

"We were both in the ranchin' business," she whispered.

The woman stood up. "I used to hate the woman who had more money than I did, who could give him a better life, but I don't anymore. She got to live with him and have his child but I kept a huge chunk of his heart. We had two and a half good years together before he died."

"You mean . . ." Hope left the sentence dangling.

"He always felt guilty for cheatin' on her. I never had a day's worth of guilt, though. She got the best of him but I got the last of him. Well, thanks for listenin'. It's a long trip here from where I live now but it's good for me to remember him this way. Will you be tellin' his wife what I said?" She asked.

Hope shook her head. "Wes was my very good friend and I'd never tarnish his reputation with his family."

She circled around the end of the Caddy, got inside, and rolled down the window. "I don't ask for forgiveness because I knew exactly what I was doing and I'd do it again but I'm glad we met today, Hope."

"How did you know?" Hope asked.

"I was at his funeral," the woman answered, and drove away.

Hope sat down in front of the tombstone again, this time with a thud. She picked up the flowers and flung them with a good strong right arm. They hit a tall stone a few yards away and red rose petals floated down like bloody snowflakes.

"Why, Wes?" She slapped the tombstone.

Have you really got the right to get mad? Did you give him your whole heart? All those years when Henry lived across the fence, you often wondered what it would have been like if you'd gone with him. You made that decision before Wes started courting you. Up until then he was just flirting. She didn't recognize the voice in her head speaking the truth but it didn't stop the tears.

She got into her truck and drove out of the cemetery with the radio blaring out "Linda on My Mind," by Conway Twitty. She drove east toward the ranch but instead of turning down the lane, she kept going until she was down at the bottom of the Palo Duro Canyon. She pulled onto a side road and stopped the engine. How many times had Wes lay beside her with another woman on his mind like Conway sang about in the song?

Her phone pinged and she dug it out of her purse.

There was a short text: *Being with you is like heaven.*

Then there was a link to an old Conway Twitty song, "I May Never Get to Heaven."

She listened to it six times before she laid the phone to the side. "So we both had our secrets, didn't we, Wes? I'll keep yours and not share them with anyone but I'm not going to feel guilty about Henry. Not ever again."

*   *   *

Carlene brought two hyper little girls home with her that Friday afternoon. They barely stopped in the foyer long enough to hang up their coats before they chased up the stairs to Tilly's room. In ten minutes they were back down in the kitchen for cookies and milk, to pet the cat, and then off they went back upstairs again.

Someone rapped on the back door and Hope poked her head inside. "Anybody home?"

"Me and two little wild girls. Enter at your own risk," Carlene answered. "Want a glass of sweet tea?"

"I'd rather have something stronger. How about we break out the Pappy Van Winkle and have a double shot?" Hope tossed her jacket onto a kitchen chair and headed straight for the buffet in the dining room.

"I reckon it's five o'clock somewhere," Carlene laughed.

"I don't give a damn if it's barely breaking dawn. I need a drink." Hope poured two healthy double shots and handed one to Carlene. "I'm fixin' to give you some advice and you can take it or leave it. Pappy is too expensive to throw back like cheap whiskey, so let's take this to the living room."

"Yes, ma'am." Carlene carried her glass with her as she followed Hope. "What's happening? Did you and Henry break up?"

"Nope, but he's invited me to Florida and I don't know what to do about that. I thought it would be easier once he was on the plane and gone, but it's not. I miss him already and he's not even home yet." Hope sipped the bourbon.

Carlene kicked off her shoes, pulled her feet up on the sofa, and let a small sip of the bourbon lay on her tongue a moment before she swallowed. "Lord have mercy! This is some fine stuff."

"It damn sure better be at more than five hundred dollars a bottle but we're facin' life today." Hope sat down and touched her glass to Carlene's.

"What happened?"

"I got my eyes opened wide today. I'm not going into the details and I deserve exactly what happened. Matter of fact, I set the whole thing in motion." She touched the gold necklace around her neck like she did pretty regularly. "So I can't blame anyone but myself but I'm burying the past and I want you to do the same."

Carlene took another sip of the bourbon. "Okay, I guess. Are you all right?"

Hope shook her head. "No, I'm not all right but I will be. Conway Twitty is one of my favorite artists and he sings a song called 'A Bridge That Just Won't Burn.' Call it up on your phone and let's listen to it."

Carlene set her drink on the massive coffee table and quickly found the song, turned up the volume on her phone, and set it between them on the sofa. "Does this have some meaning for you today?"

"Both of us. You and I are both standing on bridges that won't burn. Jace never completely got over you and Henry for sure didn't get over me. We need to realize that, especially you, Carlene, because you've got a lot of years in front of you. Most of mine are behind me but by damn I will never waste another one," Hope said.

"But did we get over them?" Carlene asked as she listened to the lyrics.

"No, we did not," Hope said emphatically. "If you'd gotten over him, you'd have managed to get yourself into a relationship. If I'd gotten over Henry, I would have taken a couple of widowers up on dinner offers. We have to bury the past, darlin', and open the door to the future. We tried, but the damn bridges just won't burn, just like the song says. So we're goin' to grab this bull called Future and we're goin' to hang on for the full eight seconds."

"Yes, ma'am." Carlene nodded. "You sure you don't want to tell me what got you so worked up today?"

"It wouldn't matter or change a thing if I did tell you. Just take my advice and give Jace a chance. He's happy when he's with you. It won't be easy, but it's doable and I'm here if you need me." She finished off the bourbon and set the empty glass on the table. "Now I'm off to start the first day of the rest of my life. It might last two years or ten or if I'm really lucky, me and Henry will live to be in our nineties and we'll have twenty, but by damn they will be wonderful years."

"I bet they will. And, Hope."

Hope shook her head. "That's Granny to you, child."

"Okay, then, Granny." Carlene smiled. "Thank you."

"Thank you." Hope bent to hug her. "For listening to me without demanding more than I could give."

Carlene wasn't sure what set Hope off that day or what had set off the cussin' factor—she'd never heard Hope Dalley say *damn* that many times in one conversation. But she appreciated being made to feel like a friend and part of the family.

As Hope left by the back door, Jace came inside. She shook her finger at him and said, "You leave that Pappy alone. That was for us girls because we needed to get things settled."

"What'd I do?" he asked as he sank down into a recliner. "And what in the world were you two talkin' about that made her get out the Pappy?"

"Tell the truth, I'm not real sure, but I believe it had something to do with a bridge that won't burn." She hit the button on her phone to replay the old Conway song. "We listened to this while we drank a double shot of the best bourbon I've ever had."

Jace got up and crossed the room and sat down so close

to her that sparks lit up the room. He draped an arm around her and tipped up her chin with his fist. The first kiss was kind of sweet but it didn't take long for them to heat up to the boiling point.

"What's that all about?" she panted when they heard the girls running down the stairs.

He slid to the other end of the sofa. "If I can't have a shot, then at least I can taste it on your lips. I got to admit that's a better way to drink it anyway. And, honey, I expect she's thinkin' about Henry but I can understand that song very well. I tried to burn the bridge between me and you in my time, but just like he says, the one with you in the middle ain't the burnin' kind."

"Maybe you just haven't had the right kind of kindlin'," she teased.

"I found her." Tilly's voice floated down the stairs. "We'll take her back to my room and you can hold her."

"They must've been chasin' the cat," he said as he touched the phone and the song played again. "May I have this dance?"

She let him pull her up and put her arms around his neck. He pulled her close and let his hands rest on the small of her back as they did a slow two-step to the music. "The song says that he threw away the pictures but I didn't, Carlene. I kept them right along with the last note you sent me."

"Mama, when's the pizza going to be ready?" Tilly yelled from the top of the stairs.

"One hour," she raised her voice to say.

"Good. We've got time to play Barbies. Do I hear Blake?"

"No. We're listenin' to Conway," Jace hollered, and then lowered his voice. "Speaking of that." He two-stepped over to the coffee table and without letting go of Carlene, he leaned over and hit a few icons and "I May Never Get to

Heaven" started. He swayed with her to the slow music and whispered the words in her ear as Conway sang them.

His warm breath sent shivers from her scalp to her toes. When the song ended, he kissed the palm of her hands one at a time, slowly. "I did come mighty close to heaven and I was too young to even know it."

With the warmth of the expensive bourbon heating up her insides along with those hot kisses and the heat from being so close to his body for two songs, she felt like she was floating as he led her back to the sofa. He picked up her phone once more and then laced his fingers in hers, holding her hand across the middle cushion on the sofa.

"That is what I was listenin' to when I was out plowin' today," he said. Randy Travis began to sing "Spirit of a Boy, Wisdom of a Man." Tears welled up in the back of Carlene's eyes, but she wouldn't let them fall.

"We live with the decisions that we make in our life like he says. I'm not sure if I would have had the wisdom of a man. Maybe you were right about me just having the spirit of a boy in those days, Carlene. I like to think I would have but who knows. What I do know is that I can't undo or redo that part but I can tell you that I'd give up the spirit to have the wisdom. Give me a chance."

"You want a chance. I want time," she said.

"Fair enough," he said. "Reckon Granny would miss it if we had a shot of Pappy?"

"I'm not brave enough to take a chance. Maybe we ought to just have a shot of Jack Daniel's," she said. "The Pappy is for really special times, remember?"

"I kinda thought this was very special," he said. "I'm beginning to figure out what's important in life, so that means it's an amazing day, right?"

"Not even that sexy smile will work on me. I'm not gettin' in trouble with Granny and I wouldn't be surprised if she marked that bottle with a scratch," she said.

"So you think my smile is sexy?" It grew even bigger across his face. "That's as good as a shot of Pappy any day of the week, even Sunday."

"It sounds like a herd of elephants coming down those stairs but I know it's two little girls." She stepped away from him.

"How about we save that Jack Daniel's until they're in bed?"

"Deal." She smiled back at him.

Chapter Fifteen

The sun might be shining brightly or gray clouds could hang low in the sky, but there was always wind in the panhandle of Texas in January. That Sunday morning, a gentle breeze barely ruffled Carlene's hair as she went from the porch to her van.

"Today is a good day." Tilly fastened her seat belt. "We get to buy a house. I get to go to Maribel's after that and then when I get home, Jace said he'd take me out for a ride on a four-wheeler. Do you think he'll let me drive it?"

"Number one," Carlene said as she backed the van out and headed to church. "We are looking at a house, not buying it. Number two, you can't drive a four-wheeler today."

"Well, maybe it's not a good day after all," Tilly pouted.

"You do get to go to Maribel's. One out of three isn't so bad that it will ruin your complete day," Carlene told her.

"If I wear my bicycle helmet, can I drive it?"

"What does it mean when I say no?"

Tilly sighed. "It means no. And I don't suppose we're going to buy the house?"

"That has a better chance than you driving the four-wheeler," Carlene answered. "Are you ready to move?"

Tilly shrugged. "I love it on the ranch, but if we're goin' to leave…"

"Got mixed feelin's about it, right?" Carlene made a left turn out onto the road from the lane. "One part wants to live there forever and the other part doesn't want to say goodbye to the ranch and Jace so you might as well get it over with if you have to move again. Am I getting close to what you feel?"

Tilly's head bobbed. "I like it when it's just me and you, like it always has been. Livin' on the ranch is fun but it's like a vacation. And I really do like Jace as a friend, Mama. But he can be our friend no matter where we live, right?"

Carlene snagged a parking spot not far from the front door of the church. "And when the vacation is over, it's time to go to our real home. And yes, Jace can be our friend no matter where we move."

"Why didn't Jace come with us this mornin'?"

"He had to leave early so he could teach Sunday school today. The guy who usually takes care of the teenage class has the flu, so Jace is standing in for him today."

"Is he comin' to lunch with us?" Tilly asked.

"Not today. It's just me and you, kid." Carlene lowered her voice to a growl like a character from a cartoon.

Tilly giggled. "I like that, Mama. Just me and you."

Because the church was packed that morning and they'd arrived at the last minute, Carlene and Tilly had to sit in the back pew beside some folks she didn't know. They sang a congregational hymn and then the preacher took the podium.

"Good mornin'. It's good to see all the seats full this mornin'. To start off, let's all recite the Lord's Prayer because that's what's been on my mind this week."

Everyone bowed their heads. Tilly didn't stumble over a single sentence but at the end she muttered, "And please make my mama change her mind about me driving a four-wheeler."

The preacher cleared his throat and went on. "Some of us think we've got to have a new car every year or a big fancy house to live in or maybe enough money to keep us until the end of our days, but what Jesus prayed for was simply that he'd be given his daily bread. Not enough to last a week or a month but just for today..."

Carlene's mind wandered to buying a house, which was far more than bread for just today. It was putting all her money—and possibly borrowing more—into it. She wanted something that Tilly would call the home place when she was older. A place where she'd have memories in every corner, a house that would call her soul back to it so that she could revisit all the good times.

With all the moving that Carlene's family had done, she'd never had that and it was the one thing missing in her life. She caught sight of Jace sitting about three pews up from her. Just looking at the back of his head created a soft flutter in her stomach. Prairie Rose had been and was his home place and she'd always envied him that.

Carlene visualized Tilly leaving the house with a boy for her first junior high Christmas dance. That segued into her prom dress hanging on the back of her bedroom door for a month before the actual night that she'd wear it. Then there would be college friends who came home with her for the weekend and a wedding dress in the far distant future.

And if she gets pregnant right out of high school or

before—the voice in her head was definitely Aunt Rosalie's—*that might blow all those plans to the devil.*

Carlene glanced over at Tilly and a vision of Jace with a loaded double-barrel shotgun in his hands popped into her head. And right along with it was Belinda's warning when Carlene told her that she'd taken the job in Happy.

"You can't unring a bell when the whole state heard it. You better be sure you're ready for the consequences when you make that decision," Belinda had warned.

If she stayed in Happy, then Tilly would have her home place and she'd have the prom dress and the small town atmosphere. But the price would mean that she'd have to share it all with Jace because he was her father. However, if she took Belinda up on that offer to go to Germany, Tilly would never have roots but Carlene wouldn't have to share very much of her daughter's life with Jace.

She opened her hands, palms up, and stared at them. In the right one was roots; in the left was "just you and me." The decision didn't have to be made that minute or even that day or that week but until it was, Carlene would have no peace. She slowly closed her left hand. The roots would be worth it all.

"And now I'm going to ask Fred if he will deliver the benediction," the preacher said, and Carlene bowed her head.

Since she and Tilly were on the back row, they were the first ones out that morning. They shook the preacher's hand and were driving toward the café before anyone else.

"I didn't even get to see Maribel," Tilly whined. "I know she was there because she told me that she would be and why are you in such a hurry?"

"We have one hour until we go see the house. If we don't get to the café pretty fast, we'll have to wait for a table and might not even have time to eat. You want food or to talk to your little friend that you'll see at two o'clock anyway?"

Tilly placed a hand over her stomach. "It's growlin'. The muffins we had for breakfast are all gone and it wants a hamburger and maybe a piece of chocolate cake."

"Don't know if Molly made cake today. You might have to be satisfied with a piece of pie." Carlene whipped into a parking lot where half a dozen other vehicles were already parked. "The other church must've let out a few minutes early."

"Why do we go to the one that we do?" Tilly asked.

"Because that's where Aunt Rosalie went and where I did when I lived here in Happy," Carlene answered. "I see a whole string of cars and trucks on the way. We'd better get a move on it."

Tilly grabbed her mother's hand when they were out of the minivan and Carlene was glad that she was wearing flat shoes because she was practically jogging when they reached the café. Carlene went straight for the bar, where she and Tilly claimed two stools.

"I like sittin' here but there's a booth," Tilly said.

"And four people can sit there," Carlene said.

"What can I get you?" Daisy asked. There was no doubt that Daisy was Lila's mother but she wasn't nearly as tall as her daughter.

"Two burger baskets. Mustard, no onions, and fries. Root beer for both of us," Carlene answered.

"Easy enough." Daisy yelled the order through a small serving window. "Figured y'all would be eating at Hope Springs today with the family."

"We're going to buy a house," Tilly said. "And then I'm goin' to Maribel's."

"Well, now, that sounds like an exciting day for sure." Daisy smiled. "Which house are you lookin' to buy?"

"The little brick one about a block from the school. Price seems reasonable and it's close to work," Carlene answered.

"You look close at that place," Daisy whispered. "Last bunch that lived there were renting it and they were not gentle with it."

"Thank you."

"Hey, Jace." Daisy waved toward the door. "Booths are taken but we've got a couple of bar stools left."

He chose the one on the other side of Tilly. "Just a burger basket with mustard and no onions and onion rings. Sweet tea, please, Daisy. I've got a rodeo meeting at one so I'm pushed for time."

"No onions but onion rings?" Tilly frowned.

"I don't like raw onions, but cooked ones are pretty good. So I hear you are ridin' four-wheelers today?"

Tilly rolled her eyes at Carlene. "Ridin', but not drivin'."

"One more of those little insolent looks and you'll be cleanin' your room instead of ridin'," Carlene told her.

"And you're going to look at a house?" Jace changed the subject.

"Yep," Tilly answered.

"Think you might like moving again, Tilly?" Jace asked, but his eyes were on Carlene.

"You'll still be my friend even when we move. Mama said so," Tilly said.

"Well, thank you," Jace said. "You'll be my friend, too, no matter where you live."

"Natalie is my friend and I moved from Florida so maybe," Tilly said, as if trying to convince herself.

"Order up!" Molly called from the kitchen, and three red plastic baskets appeared on the shelf.

Daisy set them on the counter along with a bottle of ketchup. She quickly filled three glasses with their drinks and then picked up another plate from the shelf and carried it to the far end of the café.

"What's goin' on with the rodeo?" Carlene asked between bites.

"We were discussing the demolition of Rosalie's place. If there's anything you want, you might want to get it soon."

Carlene couldn't think of a single thing she wanted except maybe the sugar bowl with the yellow flowers on the side that had always sat in the middle of the kitchen table. She and Jace had sat at that table for after-school snacks, and the last time he was in the house, he'd had brownies and milk with her and Tilly. The sugar bowl would always remind her of the happiness they'd shared, both past and present.

"After I take Tilly out to Maribel's house, I'll go by there," she said. "Anything that you want, Tilly?"

"Nope. You want something, Jace?" she asked.

"Not from there." His sexy eyes met Carlene's over the top of Tilly's head and the look he gave her spoke more than the three words from his mouth.

*   *   *

The Realtor, Joan Richmond, turned out to be a tall brunette who wore jeans and cowboy boots. She met them outside the house, handing Carlene her card with one hand and extending the other one to shake. "This is a sweet little property but it does need a little cosmetic face-lift. The lady who lived here died and her daughter tried using it for rental property for six months but she figured out how much of a hassle that can be, so she put it on the market about a year ago. Things don't move very fast here in Happy."

She unlocked the door to the house and a blast of stale air hit them in the face. "With some paint and new carpet, it could be a nice little home for two people."

The walls and ceilings had been white at one time but

they were nicotine stained now and the brown carpet would definitely have to go. "Yes, the last renter was a smoker and in full disclosure, it was a known drug house. But like I said, the price is low and it can be made into a lovely home with only a little money and a lot of elbow grease."

Tilly barely glanced at the room that would be hers. "I don't like this house. It's ugly and it smells awful. Don't make me move here, Mama."

"Well, now, darlin', your mama can fix the smell and it would be very pretty with some flowers out front and a cute little picket fence around it." The Realtor smiled.

Carlene mentally tallied up the cost of the remodeling along with putting up that cute little fence and quickly decided that this was not the place for Tilly to put down her roots. "Thank you so much for driving up from Tulia to let us look around but this won't do. If you get anything else in this price range but in better shape, call me."

"I happen to know that the owner would be willing to take less than the asking price," Joan whispered. "I'm not supposed to tell you that because it cuts down on my commission but I'd really like to move this property."

"No, thanks," Carlene said. "But again I appreciate you taking time on your Sunday afternoon to show it to us. Let's get you over to Maribel's, Tilly."

"If you change your mind"—Joan sighed—"you've got my card."

Carlene tapped the hip of her denim skirt. "Right here in my pocket."

Ten minutes later she was a mile north of Happy at a small house not far off the highway. Maribel hopped off the porch steps and waved, and was crossing the yard before Carlene even came to a full stop. Tilly had unhooked the seat belt, grabbed her tote bag with her jeans and sweatshirt inside, and jumped out of the van the moment the back door slid open.

Maribel's mother, Gloria, rounded the end of the house and yelled, "Come on inside. I've got a pot of coffee on."

Carlene rolled down the window. "I should be going. I'm supposed to stop at Aunt Rosalie's house this afternoon."

Taller than Carlene by several inches, dark haired and long legged, Gloria soon covered the distance between house and vehicle. "Next time then or anytime you want to stop by. All Maribel has talked about is how much fun she had at the ranch with Tilly."

"That's all I've heard too. And the invitation goes both ways, Gloria. You and Maribel are both welcome at the ranch anytime."

"I'll drive her home about five."

"I'll have the coffee ready." Carlene smiled.

"Maybe next time but thank you. I'll have to get right back to get supper done in time for evening church." Gloria waved over her shoulder.

Carlene drove back into town, made the turn down Main Street, and went out to the dirt road beside the rodeo grounds. There were half-dozen trucks parked near the gate, not far from the concession stand where the guys must've been having their meeting. Whether Jace was riding that weekend or not, Tilly would want to go to the event, so Carlene mentally planned the week to include Saturday at the rodeo grounds. That would mean looking at another house that someone at school had mentioned might be available to rent soon.

Aunt Rosalie's house looked downright pitiful, like a little old lady who'd gotten lost. Carlene sat in the van for a long time, letting the memories and things that Aunt Rosalie had told her come back to mind.

"She did things her way right up to the end and even past her life. I'm going to be just like her when I'm old."

She reached behind her seat and picked up an empty tote bag and then opened the door. The smell of smoke filled her nose as she walked up onto the porch. It had been more than a week and they'd had a big snow since the night it burned, but evidently charred wood that was already a hundred years old held the scent for a long time. She walked inside.

The ugly sofa had been soaked and now had mildew growing on the cushions.

Surprisingly enough the cabinets in the kitchen weren't so badly damaged even though everything in them was covered with soot. She found the sugar bowl still in the middle of the table. Then she remembered that there were two albums of family pictures in the hall closet. There was the stench of old house mixed with smoke on them but she could take the pictures out and put them into new albums.

She shoved them down into the bag and smiled at the memory of Aunt Rosalie telling her about each picture and showing her that their names were written on the back. She'd started toward the outside when she heard a vehicle coming to a stop. Her hands were black, so she looked around for a paper towel but there was nothing to be had.

"Thought I might find you here," Hope said at the doorway. "I keep baby wipes in the truck for the great-grandkids. Come on out here and we'll get you cleaned up in no time."

"You're a lifesaver." Carlene put her keepsakes in the van on her way to Hope's truck.

"I wanted to talk to you about that conversation we had yesterday. I was angry and very upset and I shouldn't have burdened you with it." Hope yanked half a dozen wet towels from a round container and wiped Carlene's hands like she would a child.

"So are you and Henry still renewing that old friendship?" Carlene asked.

"Several times a day either by phone or by text. I love this new technology. I'm seriously thinking of going down there for a few days just to see how things are away from this area, but it won't be for revenge."

"Revenge? What happened?"

"I shouldn't have let that word slip out. Forget it. Hit the delete button." She waved her hand in the hair. "I want to go see Henry in his new world. Right now I'm not sure either of us can leave the place that we've built, so we might always have a long-distance relationship." Hope pulled down the tailgate, hopped up onto it, and patted the spot beside her. "It's not a bad day. Sit with an old woman and let her pretend she's as young as you are and we're friends."

"You will never be old, Hope Dalley, and we are friends." Carlene bounced up beside her. "Aunt Rosalie was one of my best friends and she was old enough to be your mama, so age has nothing to do with friendship."

A smile deepened the wrinkles in Hope's face. "You flatter me but I love it."

They sat there for a full three minutes, swinging their feet like little girls. "We need ice cream cones or lollipops," Carlene said.

"Red suckers. Those round ones that last a whole day. Cherry flavored." Hope said.

"I'll have them on hand for next time. So you and Henry?"

"Will forget about sagging skin and wrinkles."

Carlene giggled. "No rose petals on the bed or candles and wine chillin' in a crystal bucket?"

"More like a Viagra on the nightstand and two cold beers in the refrigerator," Hope laughed.

Carlene blushed. "Miz Hope!"

"Hey, I'm not stupid, girlfriend. I know all about those little blue pills." She lowered her voice and an impish grin covered her face. "At our age, at least I don't have to worry about protection."

Carlene clapped a hand over each ear. "I can't hear this. You've always been right next to the angels in my eyes."

"Me, an angel? Not this girl. How about you?"

"Don't think so and my daddy will be glad to introduce you to his older daughter. She's the one that got the wings and halo. The younger one is more than a little bit of a disappointment."

"He'll wake up one of these days, darlin'." Hope slung an arm around her shoulders. "Valerie and I were pretty stiff-necked this time last year but we've loosened up a lot, so don't give up hope on your dad. We both threw us a fit when Lila came back to town and then when Kasey moved in with Nash we pitched a bigger one."

"I heard about that," Carlene said.

"I imagine you did. We would have interfered with both of them but we would have been wrong and we'd have destroyed lives if we had. So we're holding back with you and Jace. Besides, you're kind of holding an ace in this card game. Valerie is in love with Tilly."

"I want..." Carlene took a deep breath and then went on. "I want Jace and Tilly to have a good relationship. I should have told him about her before now. And I want her to be a part of the family, to have roots here in Happy."

"But if there's ever going to be anything between you and Jace, you want it to be for you, not just because of Tilly, right?"

Carlene swallowed hard. "And I'll never know, will I?"

"Follow your heart. That's the advice I'm giving both of us." Hope eased down off the tailgate and held out a hand to help Carlene. "The heart don't know how to lie and it's painfully honest."

Carlene took her hand and landed on both feet. "I'll try, Granny."

"Trying is all any of us can do. I'll see you at the bull ridin' on Friday night. Bring a quilt. The weatherman says it'll be cold but we can bundle up and please sit with the family."

"Thank you. I will." Carlene hugged her and got into her own vehicle.

She checked the clock on the dashboard when she parked in front of the ranch house—two forty-five. That meant she had a little over two hours before Gloria brought Tilly home, plenty of time to get caught up on all her papers and be ready for Monday morning at the school.

After both of the places she'd been in, walking into the ranch house was pure heaven. No stained, smelly carpet. No smoke lingering in the air. She caught a faint whiff of Jace's shaving lotion and followed it up to the second floor, where she found him standing in the doorway to his bedroom.

"Did you buy the house?"

She shook her head. "Tilly hated it and anything that needs that much work on the surface is bound to have problems underneath what is visible."

"Well, that makes my day brighter. Go by Rosalie's?" he asked.

"Got a few things. I'm good with them burnin' it or tearin' it down."

A grin turned the corners of his mouth up. "Want a beer to celebrate?"

"Celebrate what?"

"That we have a couple of hours all to ourselves."

Chapter Sixteen

Yes," she said.

"To what?"

"A beer." A grin covered her face.

He laced his fingers in hers and together they went to the living room, where he pulled her down on the sofa onto his lap. He pushed her long hair back and trailed soft kisses from her neck to her lips. When he deepened the kiss, she decided that he'd been right about the fancy whiskey. Getting the taste of beer from his kisses was downright exhilarating.

"Still want that beer?" he asked.

"I had it like you had the whiskey yesterday," she answered. "Kind of reminds me of those first kisses we had out in Henry's old barn."

He ran a rough palm down her cheek and kissed her on the tip of her nose. "I wonder how many notches there'd be on the ladder up to the loft if everyone carved out a little nick to celebrate their first kiss."

"I wonder if the first nick would belong to Granny Hope and Henry?"

"Or maybe it would be for Henry's daddy and Granny's mama. And it could go way back from there because my ancestors settled right here and Henry's were right next door."

Carlene cupped his face in her hands. In the past ten years, his dark beard had gotten heavier. He'd shaved for church this morning but was already a little scruff. He took her hands in his and looked deeply into her eyes. "I've got something to say and it's not easy."

"I guess you'd best spit it out, then." She held his gaze.

"After you left, I tried to get Mama and Brody both to let me stay home and not go to college. Brody didn't get to go what with Grandpa and Dad dying the same summer and I felt guilty about leaving him with so much to do. But they convinced me and..." He paused. "I was angry that you'd gone and you didn't even keep in touch."

"And there were a lot of college girls, right?"

He almost blushed. "I kept my grades up and I didn't do the fraternity thing but I partied on weekends."

"Bet it wasn't out in a barn with the music on a pickup turned up loud enough that it scared the buzzards off their roosts." Her mouth turned up in half a smile.

"No, it was with a fake ID in bars and when I graduated and came back to Happy, there were other women too. But..." Another hesitation.

"I didn't expect you to be celibate, Jace."

"I just want you to know that I had the test run last week and it came back that I'm okay," he said.

"Test?" She frowned.

"HIV and all STDs." He spit it out in a hurry and then blushed.

She moved from his lap to the other end of the sofa. "I never thought of that."

"I thought it best to come clean before we…"

"So you think we are going to?" she asked.

"If and when the time is right. But I wanted to be honest with you, Carlene. What about you?"

"I don't need to take a test," she said.

"I see." He stood up, left the room, and returned with two icy cold bottles of beer. He offered her one and then downed a fourth of the other one before coming up for air. "Are you going to look at any more houses?"

"Why did you change the subject?" She sipped at the beer. It tasted better on his lips than right out of the bottle.

"Because you moved away from me."

"I needed to think for a few minutes. I can't do that when I can feel your breath on my skin," she told him. "Yes, I will look at the other house, but if it's anything like the one Tilly and I looked at today, then I won't be interested in that one either."

He sat down and she stood up.

What comes natural—that's what Hope had said.

Don't analyze anything to death or worry it into the dirt—that's what Aunt Rosalie told her when she found out that Tilly was a Dawson. Just make up your mind and don't look back.

She set the bottle on the coffee table and settled back onto his lap. "The reason I don't need to take one of those tests is because I haven't been with anyone other than you."

"My God, Carlene, that's ten years," he said.

She shrugged. "Morning sickness. Colic. Diapers. A few dates that ended at the door with good night kisses but that's all I've got for my ten years."

"Are you serious? You are so beautiful I'm surprised that

guys weren't lined up at your door and Tilly would simply be the icing on the cake. To have you and an amazing daughter both would be like gettin' a slice of heaven."

"You see things different because you are her father." Carlene cuddled against him with her head on his chest.

"No, I'm her daddy, and those other men are all idiots." He paused. "But that's okay."

"Oh?" She leaned back so she could see his eyes. "Why's that?"

"They didn't see the diamond but I do, which makes me the luckiest cowboy of all," he whispered as his lips found hers in a scorching hot kiss that left them both breathless.

She grabbed the top snap on his shirt and gave a tug and every one of them popped open. Running her fingers through the soft, dark hair on his chest, she leaned forward and captured his lips again. His hands trembled as they inched under her sweater. Carlene shut her eyes and sent up a silent prayer that no one interrupted them because she was so ready for this.

No candles. No champagne. No rose petals strewn over the bed. Just a good wide sofa with a throw over the back if they got chilled. It was perfect.

He slipped the bright blue sweater up over her head and gasped at the sight of the blue lacy bra. "It's too pretty to take off, but I want to feel all of your skin against mine."

She whipped the straps down and tossed it toward a recliner. Then she pulled his shirt down over his shoulders and laid her bare breasts against his chest as she wrapped her arms around his neck. "Skin on skin, like this?"

He stood up with her, keeping her close, and unfastened the zipper and button on her denim skirt. She did the same thing with his belt and jeans and then somehow without stopping the kisses, they were totally naked.

"More like this." He hugged her so tightly that she could feel every tense muscle in his body. "I missed you so much, Carlene. Don't ever leave again."

"I don't intend to," she said.

He picked her up in his arms and carried her up the stairs to his bedroom, where he kicked the door shut with his bare foot and gently laid her on the king-sized bed. "That sofa is too narrow."

She giggled. "This is almost as big as the hayloft where we were the last time."

"I remember waking up at dawn and you were wearing my shirt. It came to your knees and you had straw in your hair. The picture has been burned into my mind for ten years, at times when it shouldn't have been." He lay down beside her.

She flipped over to stretch out on top of him. "I remember that morning. I looked over my shoulder and you were raised up on an elbow staring at me. I felt strange, as if something had ended."

"And now." He captured her face with his hands. "Today is a new beginning." After a long, lingering kiss, he rolled her to the side. "Be still, darlin'. I want to touch your body and..."

"Stretch marks and all? It's changed since our graduation night."

He kissed each of the faded marks and then trailed more kisses from there to her lips. "They're battle scars."

"Ten pounds and six ounces of battle and a C-section after ten hours of labor," she said.

"I'm so sorry I wasn't there," he said. "But I'm here now, Carlene, and..."

Words stopped as she pulled him on top of her body and guided him to her.

Afterward, she couldn't form a single thought other than being thankful that he was holding her. All the bones in her body had turned to jelly. Somewhere beyond that bedroom was a world with problems and decisions to be made but at that moment it had ceased to even exist. She wanted to stay here forever and never open that door to let in the outside world, or to leave the one that she and Jace had created.

His hand found hers and closed around it but he didn't say anything. She snuggled even closer to his side and pulled the down comforter up from the side to wrap them into a fluffy, white cocoon. Then she laid her head on his chest so she could hear his racing heart and fell asleep.

She awoke with a start to something moving fast and then she recognized the sound of a vehicle outside. Jace had jerked on a pair of jeans and a shirt and was running out of the room. She sat up, yawned, and pulled the comforter up under her arms and then realized where she was and what the noise outside meant. She jumped off the bed so fast that she got a head rush and raced to her bedroom, where she quickly found a pair of pajama pants and a shirt in a drawer and put them on. She was halfway down the stairs when she met Jace coming back up, his hands full of the clothing they'd left in the living room.

"Your shirt is on backward and wrong side out," he said.

She righted things the rest of the way down the stairs and hurried into the living room just before the front door burst open.

"Mama, I'm home!" Tilly called.

"In here," Carlene responded as she crossed over into the foyer. She waved at Gloria from the door and mouthed a thank-you.

Gloria's hand stuck out the window and then they were gone.

Tilly frowned. "Why are you wearin' that?"

"You woke me from a nap. I got comfortable and went to sleep. So, did you have a good time?" Carlene asked.

Tilly put her hand in Carlene's and led her to the sofa. "You didn't use a coaster and these bottles have sweated, Mama."

"Must've fallen asleep before I finished mine."

"Did Jace fall asleep too? There's two," Tilly said.

"No, I just didn't finish mine," Jace said from the doorway. "Got called away and just now gettin' back to it. Probably gone stale by now. Did you have a good nap, Carlene?"

"Best in a very long time."

Jace picked up the beer and carried it to the kitchen. He returned in a few minutes with a wad of paper towels and wiped up the condensation that had settled on the table. "There, not even a ring."

"Did Mama tell you that we don't like the house?" Tilly fell back on the sofa and stared at the ceiling. "I bet Jasmine would hate it too. It smelled like nasty old cigarette smoke."

Jace sat down in the recliner and popped the footrest out. "Yep, she did. What did you not like about it other than the smoke?"

"The carpet was even worse than Aunt Rosalie's and the cabinet doors under the sink wouldn't shut and there was a cracked window in the bathroom," she answered. "And it didn't feel right, so I'm glad we're not buyin' it."

"Well, I sure wouldn't want you to live in something like that." He picked up the remote, surfed through a dozen channels, and settled on a bull-riding event.

"Maribel says that her daddy is ridin' in one of them." Tilly pointed in that direction as she got to her feet and removed her coat and hat. "You goin' to ride?"

"You think I should?" Jace asked.

Her eyes twinkled. "Yep and I can be a clown, right?"

"Not this week, princess." He smiled. "You've got to get trained and that will take at least six months. You've got to learn how to dodge in and out away from the bulls and broncs so they don't stomp you and leave scars on your pretty face."

"Well, rats! Mama, can I use your phone to call Natalie and Aunt Bee? I want to tell them about the four-wheelers. I want one of my own for my birthday."

"That's a bigger present than a pair of boots." Carlene handed her the phone from the coffee table where she'd laid it earlier that afternoon.

"And I want a clown outfit too. I need it for my lessons." She skipped out of the room and was already talking to Natalie when she started up the stairs.

"Whew!" Jace wiped the back of his hand across his forehead. "I didn't mean to fall asleep, darlin'. I couldn't find your bra when I was gathering up your things. They're hiding in the liquor cabinet when you want to sneak them back upstairs."

She peeked over the back of the sofa and there was a blue lacy bra peeking out from underneath. For the second time in half an hour, she got a head rush when she hopped up too fast and rounded the end of the sofa. She jerked it out and pulled off her shirt, put the bra on quicker than the speed of light, and sat back down.

"I had to rush to even be decent," she explained. "Thank goodness most everything slipped under the sofa instead of lying right out in plain sight."

"No complaints here, darlin'. I get to see part of you all naked again." Jace teased.

"Where are we, Jace?" She turned toward him.

"In the living room and we just escaped a near-death experience," he joked.

"You know what I mean." She narrowed her big brown eyes at him.

"Where do you want us to be, Carlene?"

She shrugged. "I don't know."

"Well, when you figure that out, you let me know and I'll join you," he answered.

*　　　*　　　*

"Anybody home?" Valerie's voice carried from the kitchen.

"In here, Mama," Jace yelled back at her, but didn't move off the recliner.

"I'm on my way to the church but wanted to run by for a few minutes and talk to you. I'm glad you are both here. Where's my granddaughter?" Valerie set a plate of cookies that smelled of cinnamon on the coffee table.

Carlene picked up one and groaned. "Snickerdoodles are my favorite and these are still warm."

"Right out of the oven. I'd say that they're Jace's favorites, but he'll devour anything sweet." Valerie pulled a wooden rocker up to where she was sitting between them.

"Amen to that." Jace winked at Carlene.

Valerie brushed imaginary dust from her black dress slacks. "I don't need an immediate answer to what I'm about to propose. I just want you to think about it. I heard that you didn't like that house, Carlene."

"News travels fast." She finished the cookie and reached for another one.

"Well, I didn't want to interfere until you made up your mind."

"Just spit it out, Mama," Jace demanded.

"I want to offer Carlene five acres anywhere on this ranch to build a house on. That way Tilly will grow up right here on her ranch close to you. You and Carlene can go on about your lives and when you each marry other people, it won't uproot Tilly."

Marry someone else? Was Valerie crazy? And Tilly having a stepmother? God Almighty! That was enough to start Carlene to packing for a move to Germany for sure.

"That's very generous of you, Valerie, but I'd have to think long and hard about that before..."

Valerie nodded. "It would help Tilly put down roots to be near her family, and you..."

"I won't say no right now, but I'm not sure it's a good idea." She'd already committed to a lot and this would be a giant step. She glanced over at Jace to see how he was taking this idea, to find an expression on his face that looked like he'd been sucker punched. His jaw worked like he was chewing gum but his lips were clamped shut.

"Fair enough, but the offer is good anytime you want to take me up on it," Valerie said.

*   *   *

Jace's hands knotted into fists and his stomach twisted up into a pretzel at even the mere thought of Carlene dating, kissing, or going to bed with another man. He glanced over her way and saw that her cheeks were dotted with high color. In that moment, he realized just how far he'd come in his thinking and his desires the past week.

Valerie stood and shook the legs of her pants down over her boots. "Did you know that your grandmother is planning to go to Florida for a week?"

Jace didn't want to talk about his grandmother. He

wanted his mother to leave so he and Carlene could discuss this idea that Valerie had thrown out. He damn sure didn't want to think of Tilly having a stepfather, or…His brain almost exploded at the thought of Carlene having more children with another man.

"Are you serious? She hasn't left the state in my lifetime."

"And she's never flown, but I guess that's on her brand-new bucket list," Valerie said.

A heavy silence filled the room when she'd left. Jace finally reached for the last cookie on the plate, broke it in half, and handed the bigger piece to Carlene. "Well, no one can ever look back in the history books and say that this day was boring."

"I'm not going to build a house on this ranch. It would be too awkward if…"

"I could not bear to be that close if you married someone else," he admitted honestly.

"That's what I mean by awkward," she said. "But I appreciate your mother's offer, and I know she's only got Tilly's best interest at heart. I'm going to get a glass of tea. You want anything?"

"Yes, please. Tea is fine," he said. "Did you know this thing about Granny going to Florida?"

"She mentioned it. So she's really not left Texas in fifty years?" Carlene stopped midway across the floor.

"If Happy didn't take up portions of two counties, I'd probably be safe in saying that she hadn't left the county but I can assure you that she hasn't been out of the panhandle."

"Wow! That is some serious roots." Carlene kept walking. "I may grow up and be just like her."

"I hope so," Jace muttered under his breath. He wanted her to have roots so deep that she'd never leave him again.

With her head down and her bottom lip pushed out in a pout, Tilly arrived in the room a couple of seconds before Carlene returned with two tall glasses of tea. Tilly threw herself on the sofa, put the back of her hand over her forehead, and groaned.

"Are you sick?" Jace asked.

"No, she's sulking," Carlene said. "Aunt Bee said you couldn't have a four-wheeler because they are dangerous and if you begged she'd take back the cowboy boots and get you a tarantula in an aquarium, right?"

"Grown-ups are so mean." Tilly turned her head to the side and refused to look at either Jace or Carlene. "How'd you know what she said? Have you been talkin' to her?"

"I didn't tell her a thing about a four-wheeler." Carlene handed off a glass to Jace and crossed her heart with a finger. "But she's a smart lady because she knows I would have taken it back to the store if she'd had one delivered here."

"Then I want my ears and belly button pierced." Tilly sat up and tilted her head defiantly. "And I want little diamond drops for my ears and one of those three diamond dangly things for my belly button. And maybe a tattoo of angel wings on my ankle."

"No!" Jace said.

"Hey, you don't get to boss me." Tilly's voice carried an icy edge with it.

"Then I'll say not only no, but also hell no!" Carlene said bluntly. "And you'd best drop that attitude."

"How old do I have to be to get piercings and tats?" she asked.

"Forty." Jace answered quickly.

"When you are out of college, have a job that pays three times what mine does as a teacher, and you are sober when you go into the tattoo parlor," Carlene said.

"If I promise not to get those things, can I have a four-wheeler for my birthday?" Tilly asked. "Please, ma'am and"—she turned toward Jace—"please, sir."

"If you promise not to get them, I might not give you a tarantula in an aquarium. I might just get you a plain old black fuzzy spider in a big pretty bowl," Carlene said.

"You win!" Tilly sighed. "I'm going to go call Natalie now."

"Well played." Jace smiled.

Carlene touched her glass to his. "Thanks for the help. Forty, huh?"

"I thought forty would be a good age to let her start dating and the way I figure it, if she was old enough to date, then she could make up her own mind about tattoos and pierced ears. But I got to admit when she looked at me with those big old beggin' pretty eyes, I was ready to ask her what color four-wheeler she wanted."

"You done good, as Aunt Rosalie used to say," Carlene said.

Chapter Seventeen

That Friday night, Carlene followed the aroma of grilled onions and nachos to the concession stand at the rodeo grounds, but before she got in line, Tilly tugged on her hand.

"I gotta go to the bathroom, Mama. And it can't wait."

Carlene stepped away from the crowd and tried to keep up with Tilly. There wasn't a line in the ladies' room, so Tilly darted into one stall and Carlene took another one. Tilly finished first and was washing her hands when Maribel and Gloria arrived. Gloria pulled a paper towel out of the dispenser, got it wet, and was cleaning nacho cheese off Maribel's face and shirt when Carlene made her way to the second wall-hung sink.

"This child is every bit as messy as I am," Gloria fussed.

"Tilly, ask your mama if you can go with us," Maribel whispered.

"They're sittin' with me, Carlene," Gloria said over the noise of two running faucets. "And I don't mind a bit if Tilly joins us."

"Okay, I'll be with the Dawsons." Carlene rinsed her hands, reached for a paper towel, and remembered that she'd left her purse on the hook in the stall. When she reached for it, it fell to the floor and everything spilled out around the toilet. She whispered a couple of cuss words and bent to retrieve everything.

"We're right in front of you, so that works well," Gloria raised her voice to say.

"Thank you!" Carlene hollered back.

She'd just gotten her purse put to rights when she heard her name as a couple more women dashed into the ladies' room. She slid the lock home on the door, put the lid down on the potty, and sat down. Peeking out the crack between the door and the hinges, she watched them as they leaned over the sinks toward the mirrors. One was touching up her lipstick, the other fluffing out her black hair.

"Do you think she'll take Jace off the market?" Black Hair asked.

"I don't think so. That was just a teenage fling." Bright Red Lipstick used a tissue from her purse to blot her lips.

"She's livin' out there on the ranch," Black Hair said.

"That's Hope's doin'. She and Carlene's aunt Rosalie were thick as thieves, so she probably feels like she should offer. Poor old lady don't know that Carlene is going to fleece them good. I bet if Jace did marry her, she'd divorce him in a year and demand half of Prairie Rose."

"Or maybe she'll just get pregnant again and he'll marry her this time around," Black Hair giggled.

Carlene put her head between her knees. It was their comment about her getting pregnant again that caused the world to spin around like a Class 4 tornado had taken up residence right there in the stall. She hadn't even thought of birth control on Sunday. It was too late to run up to

Amarillo for a morning-after pill and way too early for a pregnancy test.

Finally, she was able to stand up and make it to the vanity, where she washed her hands and counted the days. She'd always been on-the-dot regular, so she only had three days to wait until she knew for sure.

"To take a chance like that once can be blamed on being a crazy teenager," she whispered to her reflection in the mirror. "But I'm a grown woman and this is inexcusable." She looked up toward the ceiling. "Lord, if you've got any magic powers, please use them and I promise to be more careful from now on."

From now on? Aunt Rosalie's voice yelled so loudly in her head that she turned quickly to see if someone had entered the bathroom without her knowing it.

She picked up her purse and shook her head as she left the restroom and made her way to join Lila at the concession stand.

"We saved a spot for you," Lila said. "Jace is the fifth rider tonight."

"Brody announcing?" Carlene asked.

Lila flashed a brilliant smile. "Yes, I almost had a heart attack the last time I saw him ride." She stepped up to the window and rattled off half a dozen items.

The prickly feeling on the back of Carlene's neck announced Jace's presence even before she looked over her shoulder to find him right behind her. "Tilly said I might find you here. I need a beer."

"Still doin' your ritual before every ride?" Carlene asked.

"Oh, yeah," Jace answered. "Two sips of beer, flex my hand six times before I grab the rope, and look up at the moon."

"I'd forgotten the moon," Carlene said, "but I remembered the other two."

"And if it works and I stay on eight seconds, then I get the rest of the beer. If not, then I have to pour it out and I sure hate to waste good beer."

"But sometimes it's worth it, right?" she teased.

"Oh, yeah." One eyelid slid shut in a sexy wink.

"About Sunday. We need to talk," she said.

"Anytime." He cocked his head to one side.

"What can I get you, Carlene?" Regina asked from inside the concession stand.

"A nacho supreme with peppers, two beers, two Snickers, and a hot chocolate with a lid on it, please."

"Two beers? Who are you sittin' with tonight?" Jace frowned.

"Nachos for me. Candy and chocolate for Tilly. One beer for me. One for you," she said.

"Well, thank you. It ain't often a pretty lady buys me a beer."

Regina handed him a cold can and he tipped his hat at both the ladies. "This will be my lucky night for sure."

"Does that mean you are gettin' lucky with him?" Regina asked out the side of her mouth when she slid the order onto the window ledge.

Carlene felt the blush before it ever hit her cheeks.

"No need to answer that. Your bright red cheeks are tattlin' on your thoughts," Regina giggled.

"It's this cold wind and my fair complexion," Carlene argued. There would be no more getting lucky with him until one of them had protection. She remembered the machine in the ladies' room and the blush deepened.

"I'll see you at school tomorrow and believe me, I will know by the expression on your face." Regina shook a finger at her.

"I never was a good poker player." Carlene paid for her items and headed for the stands.

*   *   *

Jace took two sips of beer, flexed his hand six times, and glanced up in the stands. He could hear his brother's voice announcing that he was the next rider, and Tilly was jumping up and down, leading all the kids around her in the chant of his name. Carlene was sitting with his family, her eyes on the chute gate. He gave the men the sign, and suddenly the gate was open. The bull's hind legs pointed at the sky and that's when he remembered that he'd forgotten to look up at the moon.

It was too late now, so he hung on and did the best he could, but four seconds into the ride, the bull slung him off the side. He couldn't free his hand from the rope and the bull kept whipping him around like a rag doll. He felt the impact of tons of mean animal when a hoof came down on his cowboy boot and again when the side of a horn slapped him across the cheek. Then he was free from the rope and the bull snagged a horn under the back of his vest and flipped him ass over cowboy hat out into the arena. Dust and dirt flew every which way when he landed flat on his back, knocking the wind out of him.

His last thought as he tried to force air into his lungs was that he should've looked at the moon. And then everything went black.

His first thought when he opened his eyes to the bright lights above the arena was that Tilly was going to be disappointed. He inhaled deeply and groaned.

"Don't think anything is broken, but we need to take him in for stitches on that cheekbone and a couple of X-rays."

Whoever was speaking sounded like they were talking up from the bottom of a barrel of water. "He's going to be one sore cowboy for a couple of weeks."

Then he heard a voice screamin'. "Turn me loose. That's my daddy and he's hurt and I need to talk to him and you better let me go or I'll kick you in the shins again."

Jace heard Tilly's voice and forced himself to sit up so that she'd know he was okay. It hurt like hell and two clowns helped him to his feet. If his ankle was only badly bruised, he damn sure never wanted to have a broken one. And that was minor compared to his ribs and cheekbone. And where in the hell was his hat?

The crowd was on their feet, screaming and chanting his name. He wiped the blood from his cheek and scanned the stands for Tilly but couldn't find her. Had he imagined her hollering?

Then suddenly she was beside him, her arm around his waist. "Lean on me. Me and Mama will take care of you."

"Little girl, you can't possibly go in the ambulance with him," the paramedic said.

"I'm goin' and there's nothin' you can do about it," Tilly told him.

"She's my daughter," Jace said, pride in his voice even though he could hardly stand all the pain in his body. "I wouldn't cross her if I was you."

The ambulance was waiting at the end of the arena, which wasn't far, but he was more than ready to sit down—until he saw Carlene's ashen face and stiffened his spine. "I'm fine, darlin'. Just a little dustup."

"We're takin' him for stitches and X-rays," the paramedic said.

"We'll meet you at the hospital," Carlene said. "Come on, Tilly. We'll follow them and get there at the same time."

Tilly shook her head. "I'm ridin' with him. He needs me to hold his hand."

"Please," Jace said. "I really do need her."

"I'll be right there to keep her in the waiting room," Carlene said.

Tilly stepped up on the running board and sat down on the narrow bench. "You do what you got to do."

"Yes, ma'am." The paramedic frowned.

Jace stretched out on the gurney and someone closed the doors. It was only a fifteen-minute trip from Happy to Tulia and they made it in ten minutes. Tilly held his hand the whole way.

They wheeled him into the emergency room and right on back to a room and Tilly still did not let go of his hand. When the nurse told her that she should go sit in the waiting room, she shot her a dirty look and said, "My aunt Kasey and aunt Lila are takin' care of my mama. I'm takin' care of my daddy, and I'm not leavin'."

"I'm going to be fine, sweetheart," Jace told Tilly. "I've fallen off bulls before and got hurt a lot more than this time."

"Promise?" Her chin quivered. "Pinky swear?"

He stuck up a hand and she locked her pinky finger with his.

"Okay, I believe you because when you promise, you do what you say."

The doctor peeked around the curtain. "Hear the bull got the best of you, Jace?"

"Yep, Doc."

"And he's a lucky bull," Tilly said.

"How's that, young lady?" The doctor set about cleaning the cut on Jace's cheek.

"He's still alive. I wish I could've shot the sorry sucker," Tilly said.

"This Kasey's daughter?" the doctor asked.

"No, she belongs to me." Jace smiled and then grimaced.

"Well, she's sure got Kasey's spunk. What's your name, child?"

"I'm Matilda Rose. What's your name?"

"Doctor Jim is what all these Dawson kids call me. I reckon you can too."

"Pleased to meet you. Can you fix my daddy?" she asked softly.

"Looks like we can use some glue and strips this time rather than stitches," Doctor Jim said. "Our EMT didn't think the ribs or ankle was broken, but I'll feel better if we take X-rays. Should have you ready to go in a couple of hours. And, Matilda Rose, you cannot go to radiology with him."

She glared at the doctor.

He didn't blink.

She crossed her arms over her chest. "I'll wait right here, then."

"Deal," the doctor said. "And if you'd like, we can even let your mama or Jace's mama wait with you."

"I'd like Granny Hope better," Tilly said. "Mama don't do too good when there's blood on someone that she likes a lot."

"You think..." Every word made Jace's ribs and face hurt worse. "That she..." He managed to fill his lungs. "Likes me a lot?"

"You better check him for one of them cussion things, Doctor Jim. He's talkin' crazy."

"Oh, yeah? What makes you think that?"

"If a kid like me knows that my mama likes him, then he ought to know too," she said.

"You are right." Doctor Jim smiled. "I'll check him real good."

The doctor motioned toward the nurse. "Let's get some strips on that cut to hold it together and then we'll get him down to X-ray," the doctor said as he deftly cleaned the cut on his cheek and applied several strips. "I'll be back as soon as we know something. I expect he'll need some crutches for a few days and lots of ice packs."

"T-bone or sirloin?" Jace asked, glad that Doc Jim was able to take care of the gash on his face without shots. He'd always been the biggest baby of the three Dawson kids when it came to anything to do with needles.

"Frozen peas work even better and you don't waste a good steak." The doctor pulled back the curtain to leave. "Evenin', Hope. Is the whole family in the waiting room?"

"All but Brody and we've got him on speed dial," she answered. "What's the verdict?"

"Got the face fixed. Don't think there will be much of a scar. He'll have a big bruise and one black eye for sure, maybe two. He's about to leave for X-rays and then I'll know more but I'm thinkin' nothing is broken. Think you can keep him off bulls and broncs now?"

"I'll do that, Doctor Jim," Tilly declared. "Granny, you can sit here with me."

As they were rolling him out of the room, Jace looked back at Tilly. She held Hope's hand and waved at him with the other one.

"She called me Daddy." He whispered even if it did hurt like hell.

*   *   *

Lila, Kasey, Nash, three kids, and Valerie surrounded Carlene in the emergency room waiting area but she felt like she was in a vacuum and all the oxygen was slowly evaporating. She paced the floor from one end to the other and back again, wondering if she should demand the right to push through those doors so she could be with her daughter.

"He'll be fine," Valerie said, but her tone said that she didn't know if she was trying to convince Carlene or herself. "This is crazy. He's taken a fall dozens of times and never gotten hurt beyond a bruise or two. Brody was a different story. He's had a broken arm and a cracked collarbone."

"Just hope that he doesn't have a concussion and think y'all are married," Nash teased.

He didn't look at the moon. He forgot the last thing in his good luck ritual. Carlene wanted to hit something. The vending machine would do just fine. She started toward it and stopped. That would just break her hand and she'd have a lot of explaining to do.

Emma's little chin quivered. "Is my uncle Jace goin' to die?"

"No, baby." Valerie picked her up and hugged her tightly. "Doctor Jim is going to fix him right up and we'll probably take him home tonight, but he won't be doin' much ridin' for a while."

"I'll ride for him," Emma declared.

"Not until you are a lot older," Kasey told her.

"Screw it," Carlene muttered as she headed toward the admitting desk.

Before she reached it, Hope pushed through the doors with Tilly right beside her. "He's back from X-ray and nothing is broken or cracked, but he's goin' to be really bruised up and sore."

"And he's really mad because they had to cut his boot off." Tilly went straight to her mother and wrapped her arms around her waist. "But I told him that I'd give him my birthday boots."

Hope dabbed at her eyes. "Sweet kid y'all got there, Carlene."

"I'll text Brody," Lila said.

"I'll call Jimmy—that's Maribel's daddy, Carlene—and tell him he's in charge of the ranch for the weekend," Valerie said.

"And you'll let us know if you need anything at all, Carlene?" Kasey began to gather up her kids.

"I'll be over first thing in the morning to help Jimmy," Nash said.

"And I'll be there to do whatever needs done," Hope said. Family.

Supporting one another was what it was all about and what she'd wanted for Tilly when she moved to Happy, but seeing it all come together put tears in Carlene's eyes. Her insides were still all aquiver at the thought of losing Jace and she could hardly sit still. Knowing that he was all right didn't calm it instantly.

"Thank you," she whispered.

The doors opened again and a nurse brought Jace out in a wheelchair. He caught Carlene's eye and said, "We got a family reunion goin' on out here? Where's the fried chicken?"

"We'll get it on the way home," Tilly told him. "You want chicken strips or chicken on the bone?"

"I'd rather have your mama's fried chicken and it can wait until dinner tomorrow but I would like a double-meat cheeseburger and some fries," Jace answered. "But since they've cut one of my boots all to pieces, we'll have to use the drive-through window."

"I suppose we can manage that." Carlene wanted to rush to his side, push that tall dark-haired nurse to the side, and smother Jace with kisses. She wanted to tell him that she'd been scared out of her mind when he didn't get up and then again when she saw blood on his face and all over his shirt. But she couldn't, not with his whole family surrounding him.

"If whoever is takin' him home will bring their vehicle to the doors, I'll roll him out to it," the nurse said. "Who do I give all these instructions to?"

"I'll take them." Carlene reached out. "And I'll be driving him home."

"Okay, then, he's to stay off the foot and ice it for the next four days. Ice packs should stay on it twenty minutes at a time several times a day," she said. "Doctor Jim says to call for an appointment if you have any trouble."

"Thank you," Carlene said. "We'll be sure he follows the directions."

Hope draped an arm around Carlene's shoulder and whispered, "If you need me, I'll postpone my trip to Florida. But right now you go on and get your van and I'll wait right here with Tilly."

Carlene had managed to put on a cool, calm, and collected front in the waiting room. But that all ended the second she slammed the door and reached for her seat belt. What if he'd been killed and she was pregnant again? What if she'd never gotten to say she still loved him and probably always would? Just thinking about him lying in a casket sent tears rolling down her cheeks.

"Get a hold of yourself." She slapped the steering wheel. "You're no good to anyone acting like a big baby."

She took a deep breath, dried her eyes, and started the engine. She drove up to the doors and the nurse got Jace settled into the passenger seat while Tilly strapped herself into the backseat. The nurse slid a pair of crutches into the minivan, laid the paperwork in Jace's lap, and slammed the door.

"What a night," Jace said when they were under way. "I was serious about the cheeseburger, though. I'm starving."

"Me too," Tilly said.

"You really scared me," Carlene said.

"I forgot to look at the moon and about the time I realized it, I remembered you saying that we needed to talk and I lost all concentration. What do we need to talk about?"

"Later," she said.

"BC?" he asked.

"Something like that," she answered.

"What's BC?" Tilly asked from the backseat.

"Bull crap," Jace answered quickly.

"So can I spell bad words, like SOB?"

"No, you can't," Carlene answered.

"Grown-ups don't play fair." Tilly put the buds to her MP3 player in her ears and looked out the side window.

"She called me daddy more than once," Jace whispered.

"I think everyone in the stands heard her the first time." Carlene pulled into the drive-through at Sonic and rolled down the window. "So a double cheeseburger basket?"

He nodded. "And a chocolate milkshake."

Tilly pulled out one earbud. "I want the chicken strip meal deal and a strawberry shake."

Carlene made the order, including only a milkshake for herself. There was no way she'd be able to swallow food or keep it down. She got like that after every single big incident. She managed to keep up a rock-solid front but when it was over, she felt as if her whole insides were shaking for hours.

"Not hungry?" Jace asked.

"Still a little bit jittery," she answered honestly.

"I'm okay," he whispered.

"I know that now, but when you didn't get up and then

I saw the blood…" She took a deep breath. "That was the second longest drive of my life and it was only fifteen miles." She reached for her purse, but he quickly pulled a credit card from his shirt pocket and handed it to her.

"Got a little blood on it but I don't reckon that will show up when you scan it."

She nudged him with her shoulder. "Don't tease, Jace. You could have been killed."

He laid a hand on her knee. "But I wasn't. If I'd looked at the moon, I woulda been fine. I'll never make that mistake again. Don't worry, darlin'. I'm fine."

"This time," she muttered.

"Want me to stop ridin'?" he asked.

"Even if I did, I wouldn't ask you to quit something that you like to do," she answered.

"Ask me how much I like it tomorrow when every joint in my body aches. Right now my ribs are tellin' me that they did not appreciate bein' abused. And we won't talk about my poor hand that got hung up in that rope or my ankle or the scar that is liable to ruin my looks forever."

"Humph," she snorted. "As if one little scratch could have that kind of power."

"So you think I'm good-lookin'?" He raised an eyebrow.

"Does it matter what I think?"

"Honey, you'll never know how much it matters. And here's our food."

"Did I hear food?" Tilly said from the backseat.

Removing the paper from his burger, Jace asked, "What was the longest ride that you ever had? You said that was the second longest and it's only fifteen miles."

"From here to Georgia ten years ago," she answered.

*   *   *

With the help of the crutches, Jace made it inside the house, but maneuvering the porch steps was not an easy task. He'd just gotten that pair of boots broken in well and every step reminded him that when his ankle healed, he'd have absolutely no use for one boot.

"Might as well have thrown away my money," he grumbled.

"You still carryin' on about the boots, aren't you? You still got one. Look at it like this. If you keep ridin', it could come in handy later on down the line. Or maybe you ought to learn to ride in your bare feet." Carlene unlocked the door and held it open for him.

"Sassy piece of baggage, aren't you?" He grimaced when he accidentally set the foot down.

"Always have been and don't intend to change now," she told him. "I'll get you some pajama pants from your room and you can use the downstairs bathroom for showers over the weekend."

"I can go up the stairs to my bedroom," he declared. He wasn't an invalid and those steps couldn't be a bit worse than what he'd already been through that night.

"Are you crazy?" Tilly popped her hands on her hips and did a head wiggle. "If you fall backwards, you could kill yourself. Climbing those steps with crutches is BC."

"BC?" Jace caught Carlene's gaze over the top of Tilly's head.

"Bull crap and don't fuss, Mama, it is," she said.

"Okay, then, Miz Prissy Butt, what do you think I should do?"

"Sleep in the recliner. It'll keep your foot propped up and we can put pillows around you. We had to do that when Aunt Bee sprained her ankle when she was doin' obstacle courses," Tilly answered. "And I'm not a prissy butt. I'm going up to get a shower and go to bed now. Mama, can I have the phone to call Aunt Bee? I told her I'd call her after the bull ridin'."

Carlene handed over the phone and Tilly raced up the stairs.

"Man, she uses big words," Jace said as he made his way slowly to the recliner.

"She's spent her whole life with adults," Carlene said. "I'll get your loungin' pants and then help you get into them."

Jace wiggled both eyebrows at her. "But first you have to get me out of these clothes and help me take a shower. Or maybe we'll just both get naked and shower together."

"I don't think so, cowboy. I can help you get undressed but you can manage the shower all by yourself. Remember this next time you try to stay on a bull's back for eight seconds. I'm going to get a couple of ice packs ready for you."

"Hey!" He started for the bathroom. "I hung on for a lot longer than that. I just wasn't on his back the whole time. I'll be waiting for you. If you change your mind, just come on in wearin' a smile and a robe."

"You got a condom?" she asked.

His gray eyes widened. "What did you say?"

"You heard me."

"Got a whole box yesterday." He lowered his voice. "They're in my nightstand. Bring as many as you think we'll need. I'm so sorry about Sunday. I shouldn't have..."

"Get well and then we'll talk about whether they'll go out of date before they get used." She bounced up the steps, blond ponytail flipping to one side and then the other.

Yep, that was his Carlene, the girl he'd fallen in love with all those years ago and had never gotten out of his mind or his heart.

Chapter Eighteen

Jace felt fine on Saturday morning—until he moved or inhaled deeply to get a whiff of bacon and coffee that floated in from the kitchen. He popped the recliner footrest down and picked up his crutches. It was exactly two miles across the floor and foyer to the bathroom, or so it seemed that morning with every bone in his body whining at every step. Even the leg that hadn't been hurt ached, and all the hangovers he'd ever had couldn't compare to the pounding in his head.

He felt better after he'd brushed his teeth, but he was totally exhausted when he made it back to his recliner. His blanket had been folded and stacked with the pillows in the corner of the room. A mug full of coffee and two white pills waited for him on a side table. He swallowed them with a sip of coffee and propped his crutches on the back of the sofa before he eased down on the recliner with a groan.

Carlene brought in a tray of food and he groaned louder.

"I can't chew. Brushing my teeth was a chore with this cut on my cheek."

"I imagine standing on one leg to do anything in the bathroom wasn't easy, but you've got to have food with those pain pills. I figured you'd have trouble eating for a couple of days, so you've got a glass of chocolate instant breakfast and a bowl of oatmeal with brown sugar and maple syrup this morning." She set the tray over his lap and tucked a big white napkin into the neck of his muscle shirt.

"I'm reduced to wearing a bib," he fussed.

"It's either that or raising your arms up to get the shirt off when you get something on it. Your choice, cowboy," she said.

"Thank you for breakfast and for sleeping on the sofa last night. You didn't have to do that," he said.

"And what would have happened if you'd fallen and really broken a bone or two? I'll be on that sofa until you can make it up the stairs to your bedroom." She pointed at her folded bedding at the end. "And I imagine Tilly will be on that one." She pointed the other direction where the child was still sleeping. "It's only for a few days and until then these are very comfortable."

He tasted the oatmeal. "This isn't instant."

"Tilly gags on the instant kind so I quit making it years ago." Her voice dropped to a whisper. "We should talk about the real BC stuff while she's asleep."

"I apologize again. I just assumed you were on the pill and I shouldn't have," he said between bites.

"And I was too taken up in the moment to think about that," she said. "So you don't get to carry the whole burden. We'll know in another day or two for sure but I think that"—she lowered her voice even more—"ovulation was over by then."

"If you are, we can do it right this time and get married." Hope fluttered in his belly that she would be so that she would marry him.

"No, I will not marry you, Jace."

"But...," he started to argue.

"That's not an excuse for marriage and neither is a daughter that you didn't know you had."

"We are a great team. We can be great partners and we're Tilly's parents," he said.

"There's more to it than that, Jace, and you know it."

"Well, we're damn good at sex." He chuckled.

She swatted him on the arm. "There is no excuse for marriage and there's only one reason," she told him.

"And that is?"

"You figure it out and we'll have another discussion later. I see a little girl starting to wiggle over there."

"Before she opens her eyes, a kiss would go a long way in healing this poor old broken-down cowboy," he teased.

Carlene propped her hands on the arms of the chair, leaned over the breakfast tray, and gave him a quick peck on the cheek that didn't have strips on it. Before she could straighten up, he cupped the back of her head with one hand and tipped her chin up with the other one. Then his lips closed on hers in a searing-hot kiss that burned out any thoughts of pain.

"See, I'm better already. I'll be ready to do chores by tomorrow mornin' if you'll repeat that process about once an hour."

Sparks were still floating around the room when she took a couple of steps back.

"You can't tell me that you don't feel the electricity every time we're close to each other," he said.

"Honey, there was never a doubt that we had chemistry or that it will ever disappear. But we have to ask ourselves if it's a lasting thing or a flash in the pan. We've both proven that we can live without each other."

"But were we happy doing it?" he asked.

"We survived," she answered. "Or at least I did."

"Survival and happiness are two very different things, darlin'," he said.

"Do I smell bacon, Mama?" Tilly sat up and yawned.

"Yep, you do, and oatmeal just the way you like it." Carlene moved across the room and started folding the bedding that Tilly had used. "Food is all on the stove. Juice is in the fridge. I'll be there in a minute."

Tilly rubbed the sleep from her eyes with her knuckles and stared at Jace. "Are you okay? I mean really, really okay? You didn't try to go up the stairs, did you?"

"It'd take more than that sorry old cranky bull to kill me. I'm tough and I listened to you and slept in the chair. It wasn't so bad," Jace told her. "Did you sleep well?"

"Yep." She jumped off the sofa and quickly helped Carlene get the rest of the bedding folded. "What are we doin' today?"

"What would you be doin' if you were still in Florida?" Jace asked.

"This is Saturday, so me and Mama would do our chores, then go to the beach," she said wistfully. "I miss the beach, Mama."

"We'll go back someday for a vacation. Maybe we'll meet Aunt Bee there for a week this summer," Carlene said.

"And Jace can go with us and maybe we'll find a big shell and we can have a picnic and..."

His heart fell when she didn't call him Daddy, but he pasted on a smile when she invited him to go to the beach with them. "That sounds like fun, but what about crutches in the sand?"

"You'll be well by then and ridin' bulls and broncs but

if this happens again, you can't never ride no more, so you better be careful," Tilly said seriously.

"Yes, ma'am." He winked at Carlene.

*   *   *

It was going to be a long, long day for Hope. She'd gotten up an hour earlier than usual and made two batches of banana nut muffins before the sun even came up. She'd take two dozen to Kasey and a dozen to Lila and the last twelve over to Prairie Rose. She'd start with telling Carlene her plans. Once she said them out loud, then she'd have the courage to tell the rest of the family.

She was so glad to see the kitchen lights showing through the window when she parked in the backyard that she almost forgot to pick up the muffins when she got out of her truck. Tilly was sitting at the table when she breezed into the house and set the basket on the table.

"Banana," Tilly squealed. "My favorite. Can I have one now?"

"Sure. Where's your mama?"

"In the living room with Jace. They were talkin' grown-up stuff when I woke up, Granny, but I pretended to still be asleep so I could listen. Mama said she wouldn't marry him and something about him bein' my daddy wasn't a good enough excuse," she said.

"Oh, really." Hope pulled out a chair and sat down.

"They thought I was still asleep. I used to keep my eyes shut when Mama and Aunt Bee had coffee on Saturday mornings so I could listen to big people talk," Tilly whispered.

"Hey, when did you get here?" Carlene carried a tray to the cabinet, refilled a coffee cup, and eyed the muffins. "Are those banana nut?"

"Yep, and they're still warm," Tilly said.

Carlene put four on the tray, along with two cups of coffee. "Well, thank you, Granny. They look scrumptious. Want me to add a third mug?"

"No, I'm good, but I'll join y'all so I can see how Jace is doing," she said.

"Hey, Granny, thanks for the muffins," Jace said when Hope walked into the living room.

"How'd you know?"

"I could smell them across the room. What are you doin' up and around this early?"

"After last night when you just laid there on the ground and I was afraid that you'd never get up, I've changed my outlook a little," she said. "I'm leaving for Florida tomorrow after church. I'm stayin' a week at least, maybe longer. I'm not putting off anything ever again. I'm past seventy and I'm livin' on borrowed time as it is."

"Good for you," Carlene said. "I'll miss you but go and have a wonderful time. I'm plannin' on celebratin' your hundredth birthday with you, so don't give me that crap about borrowed time."

"Well said, Carlene, but, Granny, are you sure about this? You've never flown, much less alone, and a whole week away from Hope Springs and Happy?" Jace asked.

"I'm ready for a new adventure. It might be a little scary, but Henry is waiting on the other end, so the end justifies the means," Hope answered.

"Who's takin' you to the airport?" Carlene asked.

"I am. I'm capable of driving in Amarillo and I can ask questions if I'm lost and besides I have a cell phone."

Tilly stepped inside the room. "Can I go with you, Granny? I've flown lots of times and I can show you how it's done."

"You've got school, young lady," Carlene said.

Tilly crossed her arms and huffed. "Rats! I miss the beach and gettin' an ice cream from Henry."

"I'll bring you a shell or two. I've never seen the beach. You want to go with me over to your aunt Kasey's and aunt Lila's to deliver muffins? You could tell me all about it."

"Give me five minutes to get dressed." She was gone in a flash.

"I should've asked you first, Carlene," Hope said quickly.

"No problem." Carlene grabbed the last muffin from the tray. "This one's mine. I didn't bring all of them in here for you, Jace Dawson."

*　　*　　*

Carlene watched out the kitchen window as Hope drove away with Tilly. It wasn't easy sharing her but if she wanted her daughter to grow long, sturdy roots, it was necessary. She heard the sound of crutches on the wood floor. Still, she stared out the window, trying to figure out how to even begin to talk to him and how to make him understand. It wasn't until the hair on her neck began to prickle that she looked up into his eyes.

"Would you really not marry me?" he asked.

"I really would not," she answered.

"What if after six months we were so in love that we wanted to spend the rest of our lives together?"

"I might consider it." She moistened her lips with the tip of her tongue.

"What if after three months?" He lowered his voice to a sexy whisper.

"The answer would be no."

"Why?" His thick, dark lashes fluttered shut to rest on his cheekbones.

"Because—" She got one word out and then his lips were

on hers. A sweet kiss with no tongue but so passionate that if he'd asked her to marry him right then with the wedding held in the kitchen, she would have said yes.

His lips left hers and he carefully took a backward step and stared wistfully out the window. "I hate being cooped up."

She wiggled around him, dropped a tea bag into a cup of water, and put it in the microwave. "Then do something to pass the time. Read a book. Watch a movie. Want me to get out the Legos so you can build a tractor?"

"We could open up that box up there in my nightstand," he teased.

"Yeah, right. Look at you, Jace Dawson."

"I can dream." He headed for the living room, then stopped and looked over his shoulder. "When I'm well?"

"We'll break out the Pappy for a shot to celebrate when you are well." She brushed past him and flopped down on the sofa. She hadn't made plans for that day but she had entertained notions of going to Amarillo to do some shopping for a dress for Tilly that would serve for both an Easter dress and the Valentine's dance.

The sofa was at least six feet long, but he eased down so close to her that their sides were pressed close together. The crackle of the electricity between them sounded loudly in her ears. When he traced the outline of her lips, her heart threw in a couple of extra beats.

"You drive me crazy, Carlene," he whispered.

"I thought I was over you." She tangled her fingers in his dark hair and brought his lips to hers.

"So did I, but it looks like we were both wrong." He draped an arm around her shoulders when the kiss ended. "Please give us a chance."

"Hey, how's the invalid?" Brody yelled from the front door.

She moved to the recliner. "We can talk later."

Chapter Nineteen

Carlene was in the kitchen getting the last of the dishes from lunch loaded into the dishwasher when a rap on the back door was followed by Valerie popping her head inside. "Have you eaten? There's leftover pot roast on the stove," she said.

"I stopped at the café. Jace in the living room? How's he doing?"

"Go see for yourself." Carlene said and hit the button to start the dishwasher. She could only imagine how Valerie must feel. Had it been Carlene's son out there in that arena with blood on his face and unable to sit up, she would have probably fainted.

Carlene followed her into the living room, where Valerie kicked off her shoes and slumped down in a rocking chair with a long sigh. "How about some hot chocolate or coffee?"

"I'd love a cup of chocolate. Thanks," Valerie said. "Okay, son, give it to me straight. How are you?"

"I'm not ready to get back on a bull this week but maybe by the next event, I will be," he joked. "Seriously, Mama, I hurt but I'll heal."

Carlene made three cups of hot chocolate and carried them to the living room on a tray. "Tilly's napping but she'll be up in a little while."

"Mama's worried about Granny," Jace said. "I told her that she'll be fine." Jace took the cup of chocolate from Carlene and winked. "She's got a phone and Henry will be there to pick her up."

The brush of his hand against hers and the wink sent delicious little tingles through her body. Carlene quickly picked up the second cup and handed it to Valerie. "Granny is like a little girl on her first trip to Disneyland."

"I'm learning what they mean by the sandwich generation." Valerie blew on the chocolate and took a sip. "Very good. Nice and rich. I hate that instant stuff. It's barely more than chocolate-flavored water. How'd you get it ready so quick?"

"I make a slow cooker full about once a week, pour it into an empty milk jug, and then all we have to do is heat it in the microwave," Carlene answered.

"Sandwich generation?" Jace asked.

"I'm in the middle of my own kids plus grandkids on one side and then have a mother who's acting like a teenager on the other side," she explained. "What if she decides to move down there?"

"Not Granny. She's too rooted in ranchin' to leave it behind," Jace chuckled.

"And he's too rooted in the beach and sand to leave there," Valerie said. "So where does that leave them?" She took another sip of the chocolate. "I'll tell you exactly. Miserable because they want to be together."

Carlene poured chocolate for herself. "They'll figure it out. We can't do it for them. Maybe they'll split the time and live in Florida part of each month and here the other part."

Jace poured half coffee and half chocolate. "Granny's worked hard her whole life, Mama. We can't begrudge her a few adventures. You should be thinkin' of going on a few yourself."

"You sayin' I'm old?" Valerie frowned.

"I'm sayin' that you have worked hard your whole life just like Granny and it would be good for you to have some fun," Jace said. "How long has it been since you were outside the state of Texas?"

Valerie's dark brows drew down even farther. "Probably when we all drove to Las Vegas during Brody's senior year. That next summer we lost my daddy and yours as well, so we all had to buckle down and run two huge ranches."

"Why don't you and your Sunday school class plan a cruise?" Carlene asked. "You could fly down to Houston or Fort Lauderdale..."

"No, thank you. If I went on a cruise, it wouldn't be with that bunch of women." Valerie finally smiled. "They'd have me ridin' to hell on a rusty poker if I had a drink. I'd rather go by myself on one of those fifties things where they have shows all week with music from that era. I hear they even have Elvis impersonators."

"Aha!" Jace pointed. "You have been thinkin' about it."

"Thinkin' and doin' are two different things," Valerie said quickly.

"Just like dreamin' and doin'," Carlene said. "But that does sound like fun. Belinda and I looked at that cruise once because Tilly loves oldies. If they had a country music cruise with some of the stars on it, she'd go with you for sure."

Valerie finished her chocolate and stood up. "Did you decide if you'd like to build something here on the ranch or are you still set on living in town?"

Carlene shook her head. "Haven't had time to think about it but I don't know that it would work too well." The idea of Tilly ever dealing with a stepmother still fired up Carlene's anger.

"Keep thinkin'." Valerie set her cup on the tray. "I'm going home and wait for Mama to call me when she gets to Dallas. I swear raisin' parents is a helluva lot tougher than raisin' kids. With kids you've got some control. Parents are a whole different matter."

"Hey, where are all y'all?" Brody stuck his head around the door frame. "Lila and Kasey are going to Amarillo to Walmart and want to know if you'd like to go with them, Carlene."

"If you're goin', can I have Tilly for a few hours? I'll wait until she wakes up." Valerie's dark eyes lit up. "We can play games or watch kid movies. I've got dozens of them at my house, so she can choose."

Tilly yawned as she entered the living room with her kitten in her arms. "Do you got the one about Dory?"

"Yes, I do," Valerie said. "It's one of my favorites."

"Please, Mama," Tilly begged. "Grandma needs me."

"I could do some grocery shopping and we do need a few things from Walmart. Are you sure, Valerie?" Carlene asked.

"I'll stay with old hop-along here," Brody said. "We can find a good bull ridin' on television and maybe he can get some pointers on how to stay on the critter."

"Hey, now!" Jace protested.

"Why don't you run upstairs and get some pajamas and that teddy bear you like, Miz Tilly?" Valerie looked across the room at Tilly. "We'll get all comfortable and throw some popcorn in the microwave. And don't rush to get home, Carlene. I'll love havin' the company. She'll keep me from worryin' about Mama until she's safe on the ground in Florida."

"Mama, can I?" Tilly asked.

"I bet Rella would love to spend some time with Grandma." Carlene smiled. "Go on and get your stuff all ready."

"I'll just be a minute, Grandma. Rella will be so happy that she can go. Gator can keep Jasmine company while we're gone." The last words were said when she was half-way up the stairs.

"Tilly sure reminds me of Kasey at that age. She had more energy than both of us boys put together," Brody said.

"She's got a never-ending supply. Sometimes I wish I could borrow some of it." Carlene sighed. "Thanks, Valerie."

"I'll just step out here in the foyer and call Lila if you want to go, Carlene," Brody said.

"I'd love to," she said.

"And I'll go up and help Tilly," Valerie said with a better attitude than the one she'd brought in earlier.

"And I can think of lots of ways we could spend the afternoon if you weren't going shopping," Jace whispered when Carlene reached for his cup.

"Down, cowboy!" She pointed at him.

"Any way you want it, darlin'," he said.

She was blushing scarlet when she passed Brody on her way up to change clothes.

*   *   *

If Jace had to be laid up in a recliner again for a whole afternoon, he would have rather been stuck in the house with Carlene than his older brother, but he couldn't begrudge her some time away from the ranch. Lord only knew how much he'd love to go somewhere that afternoon.

Brody picked up the remote and found a station that was doing a rerun of a bull riding in Central Texas and the two of them were laid back watching it as all the ladies left the ranch. As soon as they'd cleared the driveway, Brody turned off the television.

"Grab them crutches and let's break out of this joint. There's a bull up on the other side of Claude that I want to go look at." He picked up a pillow and headed to the kitchen and came back with two ice packs.

"I've got a cooler already in the backseat to keep the second one cold."

"God bless you, brother." Jace grinned.

"I'd be crazy if I had to sit in the house two whole days. Besides, I really want your opinion on this bull. He's young, but he's got a lot of potential and the price is really good because Danny Richmond's widow is downsizing." Brody led them back through the kitchen where he and Jace grabbed old work coats from a couple of hooks by the back door and put them on. "You in the market for any heifers about to drop calves for Prairie Rose? Danny's stock is some of the best in the area."

"I figured his widow would keep things going forever," Jace said.

"She ain't Granny." Brody opened the pickup door for Jace and tossed his crutches in the back. "Now put your foot on this pillow and slap an ice pack on it; then when Carlene gets home you can truthfully say that you remembered to ice it twice while she was gone."

"And I'll tell her that the new cows arriving tomorrow just dropped down from the sky." Jace chuckled. "I'll tell her the truth."

"Must be gettin' serious if you're doin' that." Brody fastened his seat belt and started the engine. "So talk, little brother. Tell me how things are really goin'."

Jace slowly shook his head. How could he tell Brody how he felt when he couldn't put it into words himself?

"I don't know exactly, but I don't want them to leave the ranch," he started. "I'm trying to remember that saying about giving someone wings and letting them fly and if they come back it shows that they love you. I don't want to give her wings. I don't want her to fly away with my daughter. I want them to have roots so deep here in Happy that going to Amarillo is a big deal."

"Sounds like you're ready to be a husband as well as a father," Brody said.

"That feelin' started the morning after they moved in. Since the accident on Friday night, it's gone to a new level. It's goin' to kill me to see Carlene move Tilly away from the ranch. I get up in the mornin' thinkin' about them and count the hours until they come home in the afternoons."

"Sounds like you've come a long way from the last time we talked," Brody said.

"Miles and miles," Jace said. "And I have no idea how to make Carlene understand that my feelings aren't the same as when we were a couple of crazy kids, that they've gone a lot further than that."

"I found my way through the maze and I've got faith that you will too. I've got a confession. Lila and I are so jealous of you having Tilly and Kasey's family that we're not putting off a baby of our own. We threw away the birth control pills last night."

"Whoa! That's great news." Jace raised his hand for a high-five.

Brody slapped hands with him. "Please don't tell anyone. I'm past thirty and even if it happens quickly, I'll be past fifty when the first one is through college, and Lila wants a big family."

"Me, too, but"—Jace paused, took a deep breath, groaned with the pain it caused, and then went on—"only with Carlene."

"Love always is," Brody said. "Heard someone say on television a while back that life only moves one way and you have to go with it. So get that ankle well so that you get your walkin' boots back on. Life and love both are goin' to leave you in the dust if you don't get with it."

Jace pushed the button on the stereo and the country station Brody listened to the most was playing "Livin' on Love" by Alan Jackson.

Brody kept time by tapping his thumbs on the steering wheel. "Ever wonder what would have happened if Granny had married Henry instead of Grandpa? If he'd been Mama's daddy instead of Grandpa, we might have all been military brats instead of ranchers."

"Ever wonder where you'd be if you'd married someone else and then Lila came home? You still had deep feelin's for her for sure and that couldn't be changed, but what would have happened if you'd been married and had a child or two? You'd have never, ever left them because you're not made that way," Jace said. "Listen to us, rambling on about all these what-ifs like a couple of old ladies."

Brody laughed as he turned off the highway onto a county road. "Good thing that we're nearly to the ranch where we can talk bulls and lean on rail fences like men, ain't it?"

"You got it." Jace removed the ice pack and tossed the pillow into the backseat.

Delores Richmond removed her work gloves as she came out of the barn when Brody parked beside the corral filled with four bulls.

"Hey, Brody, I've been watchin' for y'all."

"Hello, Delores. I hate to see you sell out. Y'all have been a big help to all the cattle ranchers in this area," Brody said.

"Besides, you make the best apple pies at any ranchin' party." Jace got the crutches in position when he slid out of the passenger's seat.

"Well, Jace Dawson, what happened to you?" Delores asked.

"Had a misunderstanding with a bull last night."

"Looks like he won," Delores laughed.

"Nope, I did." Jace argued but he had a wide smile.

"You boys come on out here to the corral. Bulls that I'm interested in sellin' are right there and we'll go take a look at the heifers after that," she said.

Tall and lanky, she wore a dusty work coat, scuffed boots, and a cowboy hat. Strands of brown hair had slipped away from a ponytail hanging down her back. She moved in long strides toward the fence and pointed out the bulls by name. "I thought when Danny died that I'd keep the place, but my neighbor has made one of those deals I can't turn down."

"You gonna stay in the area?" Brody asked.

"I'll be movin' out to Virginia where our kids live now. How is Hope?"

"Right now she should be in the air. She's flyin' to Florida for a week's vacation on the beach," Brody answered.

"Good for her. She should be spendin' some time doin'

fun things. I intend to do something other than look at the south end of a northbound bull for the rest of my lifetime."

Jace chuckled. "You got some fine-lookin' stock here. It'd bring a high price at your fall sale. Only time I was up here was about twelve years ago and I came with Grandpa to your sale. I remember eatin' some real good barbecue."

She shook her head at Jace's crutches. "I was so glad when Danny got too old to ride bulls and broncs. Scared the bejesus out of me every time he got on one. You married?" she asked as they made their way back to the trucks after they'd seen all the stock.

"No, ma'am."

"Well, take some advice from an old woman. Don't get married before you get your fill of excitement. A good woman won't ask you to give it up, but every ride will age her ten years. You boys talk it over and let me know in the next couple of days if you're interested in buying."

"Yes, ma'am." Jace got into the truck again.

He weighed the pros and cons of that conversation as he and Brody talked about the two bulls and buying all the heifers. They finally decided that it was too good of a deal to pass up and that they'd buy two bulls and all the heifers and split them between the two ranches. Brody called Delores before they'd gone a mile back toward home and made her an offer. She took it and the deal was done.

Delores's words were still haunting Jace on the ride home, along with all the other advice he'd been weighing.

Life only goes in one direction.

Be willing to give up bulls and broncs.

The first he could believe 100 percent. The second was going to require a little more thought.

Chapter Twenty

Henry met Hope halfway across the baggage area of the airport. She walked right into his open arms and wrapped her arms around his neck.

"I missed you so much." He cupped her cheeks in his big hands and brushed a sweet kiss across her lips.

"Me too," she whispered.

He brought her fingertips to his lips and kissed each knuckle. "Those are the best two words I believe I've ever heard."

"You haven't lost a bit of your charm." Hope smiled.

"Only with you, darlin'." He kept her hand in his until they'd retrieved her two suitcases. "I had to park quite a ways, so you can enjoy the warm sunshine right over there on that bench while I go get the car."

Bright sunshine warmed her face as she watched the people leaving the terminal. Young folks with their arms around each other, maybe returning from a honeymoon.

Parents corralling young children, who were so glad to be free from the confinements of the airplane. Older folks waiting for taxis, probably glad to be coming back home after visiting their children and grandchildren. There was life in every stage around her and she hadn't felt so alive in years.

She thought of Lila and Brody, who'd only been married a couple of months. Of Nash and Kasey, who were starting off their relationship with three children underfoot and doing a fine job of it. Then there was Carlene and Jace, who were meant to be together and would be if they could get past their own trust issues.

A lady with slightly blue-tinted hair sat down beside her. "You comin' or goin'?"

"Just got here. Waitin' for my ride," Hope said.

"Me too. My great-grandson is coming to get me. He's getting married this weekend. Ever been to Florida before?"

Hope shook her head "No, ma'am. And this was my first time to fly too."

"I hear some Southern accent. Where are you from?"

"Texas," Hope answered.

"Two of my children live in Abilene, so I have to go there at least once a year."

"Where do you live?" Hope asked.

"Upstate Pennsylvania. Up in the mountains. Is that good-looking man getting out of the truck your ride?" She pointed to Henry.

"Yes, ma'am." Hope smiled.

"Well, you kids have a good time," the lady said.

"Kids?" Hope laughed.

"Honey, I'm ninety-six years old. I bet neither of you are a day over seventy. In my eyes that makes you a kid," she said.

"You enjoy the wedding." Hope headed toward the door that Henry held open for her.

It was all relative. In her Texas world, Hope was the oldest relative, but today she was a kid and it felt good to be one again. When she started feeling old, she fully well intended to remember that comment from the sweet little lady.

"How far is it from here to home?" she asked.

Henry flashed a smile. "I like that you called it home. It's about an hour. I've got some steaks marinating for supper. We'll eat on the deck where we can catch the evening breeze off the ocean. Maybe if you're not too tired, we'll even walk down to the beach and you can get some sand between your toes."

"You live right on the beach?" she asked.

"It's a small house, but there's a lovely beach right off the deck. You can go barefoot all week if you want."

"It's still colder 'n a mother-in-law's kiss in Texas, so I'm lookin' forward to warm days and seeing the ocean for the first time," she said.

"It's the Gulf, darlin', not the ocean," he told her.

"Is the water salty?"

He nodded.

"Then it's the ocean to me. But what appeals to me more than the ocean is just bein' with you, Henry. I don't care what we do as long as I can spend the time right beside you."

He wiggled his eyebrows. "Right beside me. I thought I'd take the fold-out sofa and give you my bedroom."

She laid a hand on his thigh. "Darlin', you will not be sleepin' on the sofa and neither will I."

"I'd love to wake up with you beside me every morning, Hope," he said softly.

*   *   *

Carlene had just checked out at Walmart and she was sitting on the bench in the foyer. A lady came out of the store with a cart piled so high that she could hardly see over it. When she saw Carlene looking her way, she smiled and said, "Moving into a new house. It's amazing what all I didn't have."

"I'll be doing the same thing in three weeks," Carlene said.

"Good luck. It's a big job." The lady disappeared out the automatic doors.

Three weeks—in that short amount of time Carlene and Tilly would leave the ranch. Thinking about leaving Jace behind, even when she'd only be across town, made her misty eyed, but before a tear could streak down her cheek, her phone rang.

"Mama, Grandma wants to buy me a new dress for the father-daughter dance for Valentine's Day. She says that we can go shoppin' for it on Tuesday night. She's goin' to pick me up at school and she says you can come, too, if you want."

Carlene shut her eyes tightly. It was happening—and sharing her daughter wasn't easy but every decision came with consequences.

"Are you there, Mama?" Tilly asked.

"Yes, I'm here and I think it's a lovely idea. You and Grandma can spend the whole evening together and I trust her to help you pick out just the right dress. But tell me, who are you going to ask to go with you to the dance?"

Tilly sighed. "Is it goin' to hurt your feelin's if I don't ask you this time, Mama? Maribel told me about it last week and I've been hopin' that it wouldn't make you sad if I asked

Jace. Maribel is takin' her daddy and do you think it's all right if I ask him?"

"Of course. That doesn't make me sad or hurt my feelin's. Are you havin' fun with Grandma?"

"I love Granny Hope but I really, really love Grandma the most. Don't tell Granny Hope, though. She might cry."

"Cross my heart." Carlene smiled. "It's our secret and I'm glad you're having a good time."

"Bye, Mama. We're goin' to watch Dory."

"Bye, love you to the moon and back," Carlene said.

"Bushels and pecks and a kiss on the cheek," Tilly giggled.

Carlene sighed heavily as she hung up and Kasey plopped down beside her.

"Was that Tilly?" Kasey asked.

With another sigh, Carlene said, "I wanted roots for her, but it's hard lettin' go. It's just been me and her and my sister for so long."

"I understand," Kasey said. "I liked when my first husband was in the army and we could be away from so much family. Adam and I had each other—and the kids when they came along—and we were forging ahead with our own lives."

"Why'd you come back here, then?" Carlene asked.

"Well, after Adam died, Granny turned the ranch over to Jace and Brody last spring and my lease was up on the house I was living in. My brothers needed me to help get them through the transition and I needed to move on and away from all those memories. Then last fall everything started to snowball. Brody got married and Mama decided to let Jace have Prairie Rose and Nash moved in next door."

"Does it feel right?" Carlene asked.

Kasey nodded very slowly. "Finally, lookin' back, it all

came together perfectly. So what about you and Jace? Mama says that she offered to give you a parcel of land to build a house on so Tilly could grow up on the ranch."

"It would be too awkward. Jace and I..."

"What if he got married?" Lila joined them, catching the last of the conversation. "I'm sure that Carlene is thinking of that scenario. There she'd be on the land with the new wife and Tilly would be running back and forth between her house and the ranch house. Lord, it could turn into a nightmare. Can't you just picture Carlene running by to see if Tilly was there and catching Jace and his new bride in bed?"

Carlene felt the blush starting at her neck but there wasn't a damn thing she could do about it. The picture Lila had painted was burned into her brain like it had been branded there. And the new wife was tall, had gorgeous dark hair and big blue eyes, and she shot pure evil at Tilly every time she looked at her.

"Okay, ladies," Carlene said. "Let's go get something fattening like one of those oversized muffins at the coffee shop and a cappuccino with so many calories that it makes the bathroom scales moan."

"And get that picture of Jace's new wife out of your head, right?" Kasey said. "Hey, don't look at me like that. Those spots of red on your cheeks are not from too much makeup and believe me, if Lila had just said all that about Nash, I'd be thinkin' up ways to get away with homicide."

Lila leaned over the cart and whispered, "If you ever want some help gettin' rid of a body, me and Kasey will be there with three sharpened shovels before you can hang up the phone."

"Just call and say the word," Kasey giggled.

Carlene stood up and started pushing her cart toward the door. "You two are hilarious, but I got to admit it's good to know you've got my back. It's good to have family close by. Other than those years here with Aunt Rosalie, I never had that. I was always jealous of Jace when we were dating because of that very thing." She lowered her voice to an evil whisper. "Though, Kasey, you'd be killin' your own brother's wife."

"Sometimes blood isn't thicker than water," Lila threw over her shoulder as they pushed their carts out to Kasey's vehicle.

A quarter moon hung proudly in the midst of millions of twinkling stars that evening when Kasey parked in front of the ranch house. She didn't waste any time getting out of the minivan and grabbing up an armload of bags to help Carlene get her things into the house.

"Thanks so much for the day," Carlene said as they both entered the house.

Kasey went straight to the kitchen and set the bags on the table. "It was like a breath of fresh air to get out with you and Lila. We've got to do this more often."

"Mama, Mama." Tilly ran into the room. "Hi, Aunt Kasey."

"Hi, kiddo." Kasey gave her a hug. "Did you have a good time at Grandma's today?"

"Yes! And, Mama, Grandma wants to know if I can spend the night. I packed a bag and got it all ready in case you said yes and—"

"And I promise to get her to school on time. I'm picking up Rustin in the morning for Kasey too. We've had such a good time that neither of us want it to end," Valerie said as she made her way into the kitchen.

"I'll remember to brush my teeth and Grandma is going to braid my hair tomorrow. She knows how because Aunt Kasey has hair like mine and she used to fix it in French braids. Please, Mama." Tilly hugged Carlene tightly.

"I can attest to the fact that she does beautiful braids on curly hair," Kasey said. "When Emma starts school, she's going to come to my house every morning just to help with her hair."

"Oh, I am?" Valerie raised a dark eyebrow.

"I'll ask nicely later. Bye, y'all." She waved on her way out.

"Mama?" Tilly asked.

"Yes, of course you can go spend the night with your grandma. Call me when you are tucked into bed so I can tell you good night," Carlene said.

"I'll see to it and thank you, Carlene." Valerie smiled and then lowered her voice. "That kid has stolen my heart."

"I'm sure the feelin' is mutual." This meant that she and Jace would be alone in the house.

They were on their way out when Valerie turned back around. "Jace is upstairs in his own room. He said he was feelin' better and he wasn't spending another night in that chair. His daddy was like that, too, impossible to keep down."

"Has he had supper?" The idea of having the whole night with Jace created excitement all though her.

"Didn't ask. Figured if he could get up the steps, he could get down them to fix himself something. He's a big boy. Don't worry about him." Valerie waved over her shoulder.

Carlene put away the perishables and loaded all the toiletries into one of the empty bags. Then she grumbled all the way up to the second floor. Some men were so damned stubborn that they couldn't listen to orders. The doctor said for him to be careful for at least four days. His door was wide open so she waltzed right in without even knocking.

She folded her arms over her chest and tried to shoot her meanest look across he room but Lord have mercy, he was downright sexy. Wearing a white undershirt that stretched out over all those ripped stomach muscles and a pair of Texas Longhorn flannel pajama pants, he looked like the poster cowboy for some kind of whiskey commercial.

She was quick to note that his king-sized bed took up a big portion of the room. A recliner was situated on the far side between the bed and a window that overlooked the front yard. A wall-mounted television hung above a tall chest of drawers that had a few pictures of his family arranged neatly on it. Nothing spectacular about the room except the faint scent of Stetson—and a little whiff of that always took her thoughts back in time to the bed of his truck or that old barn over on the Texas Star.

"Did you have a good time with the girls?" he asked.

"Clearly I can't even leave you alone for a couple of hours without you getting into trouble," she huffed.

"I'm tired of the chair. Come here, darlin', and stretch out beside me." He patted the spot beside him on the big bed. "Besides, I'm almost well."

She crossed the floor and sat down on the edge of the bed. "Almost only counts in horseshoes and hand grenades."

"You got a hand grenade in your bra?" he teased.

"You never know what I might have hidden away just for stubborn cowboys who won't listen to doctor's orders," she answered.

"Lie down here beside me and let me hold you," he said.

She glanced at his ribs and shook her head.

"This is my good side. It's the other one that's bruised and it's a lot better."

She absolutely should not get into bed with him. That was just asking for trouble. But no matter how much her mind argued, her heart won out. She kicked off her shoes and cuddled against him. "You'll be honest and tell me if it hurts, right?"

"This will heal me quicker than anything," he whispered as he buried his face in her thick blond hair.

Lying there in the crook of his arm with her head on his chest brought back memories of the last night they had together in the old hayloft. She'd bit back the tears and kissed him good-bye after midnight. She'd known that she was pregnant and the timing couldn't have been better with her father's transfer to Georgia. She'd never thought she'd see the town again, much less spend time in Jace's arms.

Now, hot desire felt like whiskey in her veins.

He moved his head away from her hair but then toyed with a strand of it. "It's so silky. Did you girls get into trouble today?"

"What's said on a shopping trip stays on a shopping trip. It's another Las Vegas thing. Did you get into trouble today? Other than coming upstairs when you weren't supposed to?"

"I guess I'd better fess up to all my sins today," he said.

"Please tell me that you did not get on a bull," she gasped.

"I did not get on a bull, but I will as soon as I'm able. We've got a feisty one over on Hope Springs that I might try out before I go for a rodeo-trained one again. You know what they say about gettin' back on a horse soon as it bucks you off."

"Maybe the fact that the bull got the best of you is reason enough not to get back on it," she said.

"All you have to do is ask me not to, darlin'," he said.

She rose up on one elbow and kissed him on the tip of his nose. "And when you are fifty, you'd resent me for it. If you didn't rope a bull and ride him while I was gone, then what do you have to fess up about?"

He traced the contours of her face with a forefinger, and just that light touch sent goose bumps down her arms. He could recite the phone book in that slow, Texas drawl and she'd start taking off her clothes if she didn't get control. She moistened her lips as his dark lashes lowered, and then his lips were on hers. She felt a flash of heat as the tender kisses sent hot sparks all around the room.

"I don't want to hurt your cheek," she murmured, forcing herself to pull away.

"This is healing it," he said.

She checked his expression and sure enough there was a grimace. "Healing, my fanny. You're in pain."

"Worth every second of it. Sleep with me tonight, Carlene."

"You can't...we can't," she stammered.

"I want to feel you in my arms and I want to wake up tomorrow with you beside me. Who knows when we'll have a night to ourselves again?" He ran his palm down the length of her arm and even though her sweater kept his touch from her bare skin, there was still the same feeling as if she'd been strip-stark naked.

"Please?" he asked. "We can watch a movie together or just lie here and talk about the future."

"Not the past?" she asked.

"That's done and gone but the future is a bright new day." He smiled. "But I do have some mighty fine memories of the past."

"And the present?" she asked.

"Want to hear my confession?"

She wasn't sure that she did and yet curiosity got in the way. After all, what could be a bigger thing than him not obeying one blessed thing the doctor said?

"Today Brody and I went up by Claude and bought

cattle. They'll be arriving tomorrow. But I took a pillow and ice and did what the doctor told me about keeping my foot elevated and iced."

"Jace Dawson!" She sat up in bed and moved away from him. "You're worse than a kid. I can't leave you alone for five minutes."

"Which means you better sleep with me tonight or else I might get in my truck and go up to Amarillo to the Rusty Spur after you start snoring." His eyes twinkled.

"I do not snore," she protested.

"Rephrasing that. You purr in your sleep."

She slid off the bed. "I'm going to take a shower and wash my hair."

"And then you'll come back to bed with me?"

"We'll see."

His eyebrows drew down into a single line. "That's what you'd tell Tilly."

"When you act like a child, you get treated like a child."

He chuckled and picked up the remote. "If I fall asleep before you get back, wake me up for a good night kiss."

Carlene didn't even look over her shoulder but went straight to her room and fell backward on the bed. She could not spend the night with him. She wouldn't sleep a wink and she had school the next day. Her phone rang and she had to find it in the bottom of her purse. The Pistol Annies' "Hush, Hush" was the tone that played when Belinda called, so she didn't even look at the caller ID.

"Hello, sister," Carlene said.

"Do you have a purse full of condoms?" Belinda asked.

"My God...what...why...," Carlene stammered.

"I just talked to Tilly. She called me on Valerie's phone and told me that she was spending the night. That means you and that sexy hunk of cowboy are alone in that house and I'm just reminding you that—"

"Hush," Carlene butted in. "He's hurt and couldn't..."

"Whoa!"

Carlene could visualize Belinda throwing up a palm.

"Do you really think that he couldn't figure out a way? If so, then you aren't ready to live on your own after all. You'd better let me find you a job in Germany and grow up some more."

Carlene shook her head. "I'm not leaving Happy."

"Then there's nothing left for me to do but have a box of condoms sitting on your porch on the first day of every month. What size do I send?" Belinda asked.

The blush came close to igniting the chenille bedspread. "Good God!"

"Oh, I've got the site right here and they have extra large. That sound about right?"

"Sweet Jesus!" The red cheeks were burning over into Carlene's eyeballs and frying them right out of her head.

"Honey, prayer does not keep you from getting pregnant. I'll just order the one-size-fits-all and hope for the best. Hey, here's some that glow in the dark."

"I'm not going to have sex with him tonight," Carlene declared.

"Good! That eases my mind but I'm ordering two boxes and overnighting them. They'll be on the porch when you get home tomorrow night," Belinda said.

"Don't you dare! What if Tilly finds them?" Carlene told her.

"Okay, okay. Promise me you'll be careful and I'll hang up so you can at least kiss him good night," Belinda giggled.

"We haven't talked about your new feller. What size does he need?" Carlene turned the joke around.

"Oh, honey, they don't even make them big enough, so I'm on the pill." Belinda's laughter echoed loud enough that Jace could probably hear it in his room.

"Hush!" There was that hot feeling in her cheeks again.

"You already said that once. Don't repeat yourself. Good night, sis."

"Night." Carlene laid her phone on the nightstand and headed toward the bathroom.

A few minutes later, with a towel around her hair and another one around her body, she stood in front of the dresser with a drawer pulled out. What should she wear to bed if she did decide to cross the hall and crawl into bed with him? She picked up the red silk, spaghetti-strapped slip of a gown that Belinda had given her for Christmas.

"No, that's just askin' for trouble." She laid it back down.

Finally she chose a pair of faded pajama pants with Rudolph the Red-Nosed Reindeer on them and a T-shirt that hung almost to her knees. She checked herself in the mirror. Not one sexy thing about her that night and if she was lying beside him at least she'd know if he crawled out of bed and tried to get down the stairs alone.

With the towel still around her hair, she padded barefoot across the hall to his room. He was watching reruns of *Justified* on television but his eyes left the television and were glued to her when she crawled into the bed with him. The dreamy look on his face said that her sister could be right—he might figure out a way to have sex even if he did have to endure the pain.

She sat cross-legged in the middle of the bed and towel dried her hair, then fished a comb from a pocket and started getting the tangles from her long, blond hair. In seconds he was behind her and had taken the comb from her hands.

"Let me, darlin'," he drawled.

She had no idea that hair could be sensitive but each time he gently worked a tangle out, a little burst of fire, ice, and desire mixed together and shot through her body. She bit back a groan, but it didn't escape him.

"Feels good, does it?" he whispered in her ear.

The warmth of his breath was the last straw. Forget the tangles and the fact that he was hurt. She could damn sure do the work, and she'd never get to sleep with the ache in her insides. She turned around and threw a leg over each of his until she was sitting in his lap. That hardness pressing against her belly told her that he was more than ready.

He tossed the comb on the floor and his lips found hers in a kiss so passionate that it jacked up the ache in her insides another notch or two. She ran her hands up under his shirt and splayed them out over his hard chest.

"You're so beautiful," he breathed as he removed her shirt between kisses. "I want to hold your naked body next to mine."

"Honey, I want more than that," she said. "Where are those condoms?"

"In the nightstand," he answered huskily.

She rolled off the bed, shucked out of the rest of her clothing, and smiled when she noticed the size on the box. Ripping open the package, she turned to help him take off his pajamas to find him naked. He reached out and she put it in his hands. He rolled it on and braced his back on the headboard.

"Now where were we?" he asked.

"Right here." She flipped a leg over his lap again and guided him into her.

"Oh, God!" he muttered.

She smiled. "Prayer won't help you now, darlin'. You belong to me."

His hands cupped her butt to steady her movements. "I'm not sure that I've ever belonged to anyone else."

When he groaned, she slowed down the rhythm. "Am I hurting you?"

"Hell no!" His voice was raspy.

With one swift roll, he was on top of her. The headboard sounded like a bass drum on the wall. Nothing mattered but this moment.

Then everything exploded and he rolled to the side, panting as badly as she was, his head on the pillow, his fingers lacing with hers to close up the distance between them.

"I'm almost healed," he said between breaths.

"Almost?" She got out one word.

"Second dose should do it."

"Why mess with perfection?"

"You will sleep with me, naked so I can feel your warm body next to mine, right?" He inched over close enough that he could kiss that soft spot right under her ear.

Shivers raced all the way to her toes.

"Feels good?" he asked.

She whipped around and met his eyes. "You know it does. Let's take a shower together and then come back here and feel good all night."

"We've already had showers," he said.

"And I can't go to school tomorrow smelling like sex," she declared. "Believe me, the teachers I work with…"

"I understand." He reached for his crutches. "Besides, we've never had a shower together."

"We've skinny-dipped together in the springs," she said.

"Want to go down there and do it again instead of a shower?"

Her arms went around her body as she slid off the bed. Just thinking about getting into the springs' icy-cold water was enough to put chill bumps on every inch of her body. "No thank you!"

"We'll save that for summer, then," he said.

Summer. He was thinking that they might still be together by then?

Carlene's pulse raced just thinking about a future with Jace as she led the way to the bathroom. She'd never thought that such a thing could even be remotely possible. *What will be, will be and what won't be just might be anyway.* Aunt Rosie's saying came back again to her mind.

Chapter Twenty-One

On Monday as she was leaving school, Carlene got a text message from Hope with only one word: *Amazing.*

She quickly wrote back: *As in?*

The answer was: *Everything. There?*

She hit the tiny keys as she walked to the van: *Same.*

Tilly skipped along beside her. Although the wind was chilly, the sun was shining and a few little white snow flowers were peeking up from the cold ground, a harbinger of spring and the end of winter. Maybe what she and Jace had experienced the past few days was like those tiny blossoms, showing her that better things were ahead if she could put her trust in him.

"Mama, I like it here." Tilly slipped her hand into Carlene's. "I'm glad we moved and I'm real glad that we got to go live at the ranch and that I got a Grandma Valerie and cousins and..." She stopped to suck in a double lungful of air.

"Do I hear a *but* in all those *ands*?" Carlene knew her daughter and something was on her mind.

"But I'm afraid to ask Jace to go to the daughter-daddy dance. He's been real nice and we're friends like I said we might be, but, Mama, he might not want to be a daddy and he might say no and that would be awful." Tilly sighed.

"You never know what he might answer if you don't ask the question." Carlene unlocked the van door remotely.

"That's what Grandma said. I talked to her and to Aunt Bee about it, but I'm still scared. Will you go with me to ask Jace?" Tilly's voice sounded desperate.

"Of course I will. You just tell me when," she said as they both got into the van.

"I was thinking at supper tonight and oh, dang it, I forgot. Grandma wants me to go shopping with her right after supper to get some things for the church for the dance." Carlene checked the rearview mirror before she backed out. "Do you have homework?"

"No, ma'am. Not a bit," Tilly answered.

"Then you can go with your grandma." Carlene headed toward the ranch.

"Yay!" She pumped her fist in the air. "You won't be lonely, will you? I been leavin' you a lot lately and I went last night to buy a dress. Oh no! Was it bad luck to buy the dress before I even asked him? Is that crazy, Mama? I see now why you say that boys ought to ask girls. This is tough. And one other thing, Mama. Are we really goin' to move into another house? I'm not sure I want to move again. I like it on the ranch."

"We are going to look at another one pretty soon now. One that we can rent, not buy, so it won't be a permanent thing."

"Good." Tilly's sigh was definitely one of relief.

"Will you miss me if I go with Grandma?" she asked again.

Carlene pretended to pout. "I'll probably cry the whole time you are gone."

Tilly inhaled deeply, raised her shoulders almost to her ears, and then let it all out in a whoosh. "I guess I'd better stay home, then."

Giggling, Carlene looked into the rearview mirror. "I was teasing. I wanted you to have family and get to know them. I'm just fine, darlin'. I want you to go. I was only teasing."

"For real? I could make you a cup of tea or some milk with a little kick in it before I go," Tilly said.

"You know, a glass of your special milk sure might be good. Thank you," Carlene said as she turned into the lane toward the house.

"We take care of each other," Tilly said seriously.

Red bounded off the porch and wiggled from nose to tail when Tilly got out of the van. She dropped to her knees and giggles filled the air when he licked her across the nose. Carlene leaned on the fender and drank in the sight. This was exactly what she wanted for her daughter instead of living in an apartment in a different town every two years.

From the prickly feeling on her neck and a faint whiff of Stetson cologne, she knew that Jace wasn't far behind her. When he parted her hair and kissed her neck, every sane thought in her head disappeared.

"I missed you today," he said.

"Jace!" Tilly squealed. "You don't have your crutches."

"Retired them, princess," he said.

"Princess?" She stood up and twirled a couple of times. "You think I'm a princess?"

"I've been leanin' that way ever since you moved into

the ranch house with me, but then you modeled that pretty dress you and your grandma bought last night and it erased all doubt. All you need is a tiara and folks will be bowing at your feet and kissing your ring," he said.

Another giggle and a cute little curtsy said that she liked what he said. "Well, now that you said that, will you go to the daddy-daughter dance with me?"

Carlene took a step to the side so she could see Jace, but he was a blur. He picked Tilly up and swung her around in circles until they were both dizzy. "Oh, my darlin' princess, I would be so honored to escort you to the dance. Do you think you should have roses or orchids in your corsage?"

Carlene's heart nearly burst with happiness to see her daughter's face. And Jace looked like someone had just handed him the keys to paradise. This was truly what she wanted when she moved to Happy and she felt so blessed in that moment.

"What's an orchid?" Tilly plopped down on the cold ground. "I'm dizzy like when I stay on the merry-go-round too long."

Red sprawled out on the ground beside her and laid his big head in her lap.

"It's a beautiful purple flower," Carlene answered.

"I want pink roses and, Mama, can I have a tiara for my hair?"

"Yes, you can." Jace answered before Carlene could utter a word. "It can be my present to you for letting me take you to the dance."

"For real?" Tilly's eyes popped open wide. "Mama?"

"I guess a princess does need a tiara but it can't be a really big one. You need to save that one for something special," Carlene agreed.

"But, Mama, this is a special day. But I don't want a big

one, just a little one with sparkly diamonds," she said. "Can I go call Aunt Bee and tell her that Jace said yes? I thought it would be harder to ask him but it just popped right out of my mouth. You need to try it, Mama. You don't have to wait for him to ask you if that's what you're waitin' on."

She danced off to the house with Red trailing along at her side. He flopped down on the porch and she slammed the screen door behind her. Jace picked up Carlene and twirled her around like he'd done Tilly.

"Jace, you are going to hurt yourself," she scolded, but she loved every minute of being in his arms.

"I can't even begin to tell you how happy this makes me, darlin'. When she tried on that pretty dress last night, I thought my heart might jump right out of my chest. She's so beautiful and, oh, Carlene, I get to be her daddy," he said breathlessly.

"Please tell me this isn't just a spur-of-the-moment thing and you really do want to be her daddy," Carlene whispered.

"It's a forever thing," he answered as he brushed a soft kiss across her lips. "And are you going to let her get ahead of you in this dating game? When are you goin' to ask me out?"

"What makes you think I want to go out with you?" She teared up but quickly wiped the one that escaped away with her hand. A forever thing—that carried a lot of weight and even though she'd turned the corner when he got hurt and she was terrified that she'd lose him, was she ready for a forever thing?

Yes, I am, she thought as she hung on to him in her dizzy state.

"Hey, now." He draped an arm around her shoulders. "I'm not bein' romantic here, darlin'. I need a little help getting into the house. This foot is killin' me, but I was determined to wear my boots today. Now it's swollen up and I'm goin' to have to ask for help to get my boot off."

"Why would I want to go out with a limpin' old cowboy who can't even stay on a bull's back eight seconds?" She paced her steps so he wouldn't have to go too fast. "You shouldn't have picked her up or me either and carried on like you weren't hurt."

"Didn't think," he groaned.

"You've probably set yourself back a week," she scolded.

"And it was worth every minute. I'll be ready for our date on Friday night, though, I promise," he said as he limped up the stairs and into the house.

"I didn't ask you for a date."

"Well, we're goin' on one. I've asked Mama to keep Tilly. She's goin' to invite Maribel and take the girls to get their toenails done." He made his way to the recliner and stuck up a boot. "Please."

Carlene straddled his leg, cupped the boot heel in one hand, and got a firm grip on the toe with the other. It wasn't her first rodeo when it came to taking off Jace's boots but no matter how hard she battled, the damn boot would not budge.

"You didn't ask me if she could do all that and I'm her mother." She gave it another tug but it was firmly stuck. "One more try and then I'm getting the scissors. Why didn't you just wear sneakers?" She got a firm grip and he put his other foot on her butt. When she pulled, he pushed and both Carlene and the boot went flying across the room.

The boot landed about a few inches from where Jasmine had been stalking one of her toys. She jumped three feet straight up and a black-and-white flash of fur turned around midair and headed toward the kitchen, wadding a throw rug up in a ball as she tried to get traction.

Carlene wound up on the sofa, muttering swear words

under her breath that would blister the paint off the wall. She came up shaking her finger at Jace. "Next time I'm cutting it off, I swear. So you better think twice before putting them on again while that ankle is still healing."

"How am I going to two-step with you on Friday night if I can't wear boots?" he asked.

"I guess you aren't. Not unless you want to wait until the next Friday night." She righted herself and crossed one leg over the other. "By then you might be able to wear boots."

"It's a date, then. We'll just go to dinner and maybe to the canyon to look at the stars this Friday. We used to spend some quality time parked in the canyon, remember?"

"I'm changing the subject," she said as heat traveled from her neck to settle in her cheeks. "We're havin' chili for supper. You want it as a chili pie, on top of a plate of nachos, or with crackers or corn bread?"

"A bowlful with corn bread and a plate of nachos on the side and a cold beer. I smelled it cooking when I got home a while ago and my stomach has been whining," he told her. "Thanks for getting the boot off, darlin'."

"Like I said, scissors next time."

*　　　*　　　*

Jace was restless after Valerie and Tilly left. Not even reruns of bull riding entertained him and with ice packs on his swollen foot, he couldn't very well pace the floor. There were things that needed to be said and he'd never been too good with serious words. He could tease or flirt any hour of any day, but to really expose his deep-down feelings wasn't easy—not when he'd grown up in a world where men were tough, both inside and out.

He was still deep in thought when Carlene came to get the ice pack and put it back in the freezer until right before bedtime when she'd make him be still for another twenty minutes.

"Let's go for a drive. I'll even sit in the passenger's seat and let you have the wheel if you'll get me out of this house," he said.

"Where do you want to go?" she asked.

"Down in the canyon," he told her. "To our old parking spot so we can talk."

"About?"

"Us." He popped the recliner's footrest down and got to his feet. "See, most of the swelling has gone down and I promise I'll wear shoes tomorrow instead of boots."

"I'm not pregnant," she said bluntly. "So we don't really have to talk."

Jace tried to ignore the twinge of disappointment in his belly. "Well, I still have some things to say and I'd really like to go for a drive."

"Even though it's chilly, the stars are out. Do we need to take a blanket or . . . " She let the sentence hang.

"Our quilt is in the toolbox." He limped toward the coat rack and helped her get into hers before putting his on.

"And how many other women have you taken to our spot and told them how special they were since that quilt was made by your great-grandmother?" she asked on the way outside.

"Honey, that's our quilt. No other woman has ever touched it or been to our spot, either. Those are sacred things and I don't share them." He settled into the passenger side and tossed the keys over onto the driver's seat.

"For real?" She started the engine and drove down the lane.

"Absolutely." He turned on the radio to the old classic country music station. "This okay?"

"Tilly and I love the old artists." She kept time with her thumbs on the steering wheel as George Jones sang "A Picture of Me Without You."

"That song pretty much says it all," Jace whispered.

"Yep, it does, but—"

He laid two fingers over her lips. "No buts. Let's just listen to the songs and let the words sink in until we get to our spot."

"Are you breakin' up with me before we even go on our first real date?" she asked.

"We've been on dozens and dozens of dates. We even attended two proms together," he said.

"But that was ten years ago. We haven't been on a date this time around," she argued.

"Then the answer is no, ma'am, I am not breaking up with you. I'm lookin' forward to an evening of two-steppin' with you in a real bar instead of in a barn or out in a pasture," he said.

"Hey, now! I love that barn and all the fun we had out in the pasture. Nothing in a bar could be a bit sexier than dancin' under the stars to 'Good Directions.'"

He turned off the radio and started hummin' the song. "I bet you did think that this was where rednecks came from when you landed here from the big California city."

"Kind of." She agreed. "But Lila and all y'all took me right in and pretty soon I was wearin' cutoff jean shorts and cowboy boots with everyone else."

"And lookin' downright cute in them." He reached across the console and laid a hand on her shoulder. "You still got a pair that you could wear for me this summer?"

"Got the shorts but not the boots."

"Honey, that can be fixed real easy."

"As if." She pointed toward the radio. "I remember this song. It's Sara Evans and we danced to it at the springs right after we went skinny-dippin' the week after graduation. We were naked and it was a hot night," she said.

"The lyrics talk about loving the way you wore those worn-out jeans and how the skies were blue and would never turn into rain. Who would have thought they could be so wrong?"

"Rain nothing," she said as the road started down a steep incline into the canyon. "I believe what I faced was a full-fledged storm."

"Me, too, when I figured out that you were gone and I'd never see you again." He laid his head back and shut his eyes. Even after the song ended, it played through his head a couple more times before he opened his eyes and started to recognize familiar landmarks. The tall formation rose up like an enormous chimney; its rusty red color visible in the moonlight was the first thing he noticed. Then they passed the sign telling them they'd passed over a fork of the Red River but there was no water, just a dusty river bottom that might have a trickle when the spring rains came around.

"Any of this bring back memories?" he asked.

"Every single bit. We climbed to the top of that chimney thing one night and made out under the stars," she said as she made a sharp right and brought the truck to a stop in front of a locked gate.

"You remembered," he said.

She killed the engine and turned around in the seat. "You said you wanted to go to our spot, so here we are."

"No, let's get the quilt out and crawl into the bed of the truck like we used to," he said.

"It's your party." She opened the door.

By the time he got around the truck, she'd already pulled the tailgate down and was opening the toolbox. She brought out the familiar old quilt and pulled it up over her body as she braced her back against the cab. The moonlight lit up her blond hair and half her face, leaving the rest in shadows. He'd dreamed of her just like that way too many times to ever count on his fingers and toes.

Wrapping an arm around her shoulders, he pulled her close enough that their bodies were plastered together and he used the quilt to form a cocoon just big enough for two people.

"So when are we going to have this big talk?" she asked.

"I'm not good at this, so bear with me," he said. "I knew I'd be sad when you moved away, but I wasn't prepared for the emptiness or the pain. You'd become such a part of my life that I felt like half my heart was gone. I figured I'd get over it at college but I didn't. I learned to live with it and thought maybe love wasn't meant for me. I'd be the uncle who spoiled Kasey's kids and then when Lila came home and Brody...well, you know that story. Anyway, I thought I'd just add their kids to my list of nieces and nephews to love." He stopped and buried his face into her hair, inhaling deeply. It smelled like coconut and something slightly vanilla just like he remembered from all those years ago.

"And how about now that you have a daughter? How has that changed your outlook?" she asked.

"I'm gettin' to that," he said. "I was nervous about you coming back to Happy. I didn't know if you were married and I couldn't imagine living in a town this small and maybe having to see you with another man in church."

"I couldn't believe that you weren't married. I guess it's a good thing you didn't fall off that bull before now or one of the women in the panhandle would have lassoed you for sure," she teased.

"What's falling got to do with anything?" he asked.

"With your bum ankle, you couldn't run away as fast. They'd catch you for sure." She nudged him gently on the shoulder.

"I don't think so." He tucked her hand into his. "In order to give my heart to another woman, you would have to have given it back to me first."

"Is that why you brought me out here? To ask for your heart?"

He brought her hand to his lips and kissed the knuckles. "No, darlin', it's to try to make you understand that I've fallen in love with Tilly. I want her to have my name. I want to go to the courthouse and make her a Dawson like she should've been all along."

She started to say something, but he shook his head. "Let me finish. I adore our child. I can't imagine loving a little kid more than I've learned to love her. It wasn't an instant thing, either. I didn't look at her in Rosalie's house and have sudden fatherly instincts rush over me. It was shock and anger all mixed together. But the shock and the anger went away and something else started. All I can do is explain it like this. She giggled and a little seed was planted in my soul. It's been growing really fast and now it's tall as corn on the Fourth of July in these parts."

Everything stood still at night in the canyon but some where off in the distance a coyote howled and another one answered him in the opposite direction. Other than that, it was so quiet that collecting his thoughts for the hardest part of what he had to say came fairly easy. After all, he was talking to Carlene, the woman who really knew him better than anybody in the world.

"Is that all?" she asked.

"No, it's not. That was the easy part. Carlene, if you didn't have Tilly, I'd still want a relationship with you. She's just the icing on the pretty cupcake. I know you think that if we'd married young it would have been a mistake and if we married now it would only be because I feel guilty because of her but that's not true. I loved you then even though I was too young to really know what love was. I loved you when I thought you were gone forever and that love only brought me misery and left me with good memories. And I still love you now that you are back in my life. I'm not askin' you to say it back to me but I want you to know how I feel and to give our relationship a chance."

"Who told you that you weren't good with words?" She shifted her position until she was sitting in his lap. "Whoever it was is crazy."

He dropped her hand and looked deeply into her dark brown eyes. "Then you'll give us a chance?"

"Yes, Jace Dawson, I will," she whispered as their lips met in a kiss that lit up the sky far more than all the sparkling stars in the universe.

Chapter Twenty-Two

January 24. Carlene didn't need to mark it on her calendar because it was branded right into her brain. She might remember it in future days even more than any other day in the year because it was the night Jace said that he loved her, just the way she was, and always would. Sitting in the canyon wrapped up in an old quilt with frayed edges wasn't what some love stories would consider romantic. But his words and the emotion in his voice when he'd said them were more important than wine, roses, and a fancy place.

But...there always seemed to be a few *buts* in life. Number one *but*: She still needed her own space and time to build this new relationship. Number two *but*: Even though he'd only asked her to give them a chance, if he had asked her to dash off to the courthouse to apply for a marriage license, she would have said no. And last but not least, number three *but*: She wanted him to be sure about giving up his favorite-uncle role and make time to really contemplate being a full-time daddy.

Now it was two days later and Carlene still hadn't sorted out all the *buts* plaguing her. Tilly was at her grandmother's house for the night and most likely half the day on Saturday. Carlene had dressed in six different outfits for her date with Jace and found something wrong with every one of them. Even though she'd spent most of the night on Wednesday and Thursday in his bed, barely making it to her own room before Tilly awoke, she was as nervous as a hooker in a church revival.

He was ready because she'd heard him going from his room downstairs. From the sound, he wasn't wearing boots and he was still limping. She checked the clock and sank down to the floor in front of the closet doors. Why was this so difficult? He'd seen her in ratty pajamas. He'd seen her naked. He'd seen her in church clothes and what she wore to school, so why was tonight such an issue?

"Because it's a date," she mumbled as she dressed in the very first outfit she'd tried on—skinny jeans, knee boots with a three-inch heel, a bright blue sweater, and a clunky gold necklace with multicolored stones. She checked her reflection in the mirror. Her makeup was perfect and the curls in her hair hadn't fallen out, so she took a long breath as she shut the door behind her.

When she was halfway down the stairs, he stepped into sight. His jeans were creased and stacked up on his boots perfectly. The black pearl-snap shirt hugged his body as if it had been tailor made just for him.

When her feet hit the bottom step, he drew her into his arms and held her tightly.

"You are simply stunning tonight, darlin'," he said.

"And you are simply sexy," she whispered. "But cowboy boots?"

"These are a size too big. They belonged to my dad and it was a joke that neither Brody nor I could ever fill his boots," he said.

"Guess all it takes is a sprained ankle," she said.

"Yep." He reached for her coat and helped her into it. "I'm thinkin' about a steak house in Amarillo and then we could go see that new Western movie that's just come out."

"I'm thinkin' about a good rib eye and then comin' back home to make our own Western movie." She smiled up at him.

"You got a video camera?" he teased.

"No, but I can prop up my phone and take videos with it..."

"You're killing me, woman," he groaned.

There's something to be said about riding half an hour with someone you are so comfortable with that you don't need to fill the airspace with words. That's what Belinda said once upon a time about one of her boyfriends and Carlene could say a hearty amen to the quote that evening.

When they reached the restaurant, she waited for Jace to open the door for her. He'd called ahead for reservations, so the waitress led them straight to a little table for two in a back corner. A jar candle lit up the table but the lights in the rest of the place were dim.

"Oh, Jace, this is so romantic," she said.

He removed her coat and handed it along with his to the waitress. "We'll have two sweet teas and an appetizer tray with fried pickles and pepper poppers to start with."

"Be right back with those." She disappeared into the shadows.

He pulled out a chair for Carlene and kissed her softly on the forehead when she was seated. "I never thought this night would be possible. Thank you for giving it to me, Carlene."

"You are so welcome, but, darlin', I'm sharing it with you, not giving it to you," she said.

"And that is the beauty of our relationship, isn't it?" He reached across the table and took both her hands in his. "I love this place where we are right now, Carlene."

"Me too."

The waitress returned with their drinks. "Would y'all like a sample of our famous red wine?"

"No, but we might like a glass of white wine with our dessert," Carlene answered.

"Appetizers are almost ready and our wine list is at the back of the menus," she said.

"I guess that's my cue to look at something other than your beautiful face," Jace told her.

Carlene blushed—again. "You are a hopeless romantic."

"Only with you."

"Bull!" She almost snorted sweet tea.

"It's the truth. I can sweet-talk or flirt with any woman, but it's only serious with you and then I'm about half tongue-tied for fear it'll come out corny. You deserve so much more than this old rugged cowboy," he said. "But there's the waitress bringing our appetizers and we'd better make a decision about our order."

She scanned the menu and quickly made up her mind to have the smoked prime rib and wondered why she couldn't figure out life as quickly as she could dinner.

*   *   *

After spending the night in bed with Jace, she didn't think he was tongue-tied at all and not a single word had come out corny. The next morning she slipped back into her room before Tilly awoke. If it hadn't been so early she would have called Hope because she wanted to talk to another woman—one who would understand what she was going through. Belinda would tell her things were moving too fast. Lila and Kasey would gather her into the family with open arms. As she dressed she was mentally planning to slip away for a little while that evening and have a long visit with Hope.

She thought about it all day and was still trying to analyze the whole thing as she and Tilly headed home that evening after school. "I'm so confused," she whispered.

"About what, Mama? We turn left on the highway and then left again to get to the ranch. Are you okay?" Tilly stopped her chattering about school and leaned forward as far as the seat belt would allow so she could look at her mother.

"I'm fine, darlin'," Carlene answered. "Did I tell you that Aunt Belinda is going to Germany? I was surprised since she only moved a couple of months ago from Florida, but this is a big promotion and she's real excited about it."

Tilly threw the back of her hand across her forehead. "This is terrible. Can we go visit her sometime? Can she come see us? Will she stay there forever?"

Carlene chuckled. "And she said that she could find me a job if we wanted to move."

Tilly stared out the window until Carlene parked the car in front of the house. Red bounded off the porch and Jasmine was sitting in the living room window staring out across the yard.

"If Aunt Bee can come see us or we can go see her, I

don't want to move there, Mama." Tilly didn't seem to be in a hurry to jump out of the minivan and greet Red or dash into the house to play with Jasmine.

"Of course she can, and I bet we can save up the money to go see her maybe at Christmas," Carlene answered.

"I want to be here on the ranch for Christmas, Mama, but maybe we could go this summer or she could come by on her way to Germany."

"I thought we were looking for a house," Carlene said.

"We are." Tilly pushed the button to open the door. "But that doesn't mean we can't be at the ranch for Christmas day. But I don't want to leave Happy, not ever. I want to be like Aunt Rosie and live to be a hundred and die right here."

"She wasn't a hundred," Carlene said.

"She sure looked like it." Tilly hopped out of the vehicle, wrapped her arms around Red, and kissed him on the nose. "If they let dogs go to school, I'd take you with me. I bet you get lonesome here without me."

*   *   *

Jace had made it a point the last week to work a little break into his day by showing up at the house within minutes of when Carlene and Tilly got home from school. But that Monday afternoon as he was driving toward the house in the old work truck, his phone rang.

"I thought we had the fence bull tight, but I'm beginning to think that's just a figment of our imaginations when it comes to Sundance," Brody said. "He's broke through it and is knee deep in a mud lolly."

"I'll be there in ten minutes."

Red and Tilly were making their way toward the house and Carlene was getting out of the minivan when he reached the yard. He braked and told her where he was going and that he'd see her later at supper time. The expression on her face said that she was troubled about something. He didn't have time to stop and talk, but he sure hoped it had to do with school and nothing was going on that would slam a bulldozer into their new relationship.

Brody was a muddy mess when he reached the place where an old farm pond had almost dried up. He had a rope around Sundance's neck but the rangy old bull wasn't moving an inch.

"You going to have to ride him out of there like you did when he wouldn't get out of the springs last year?" Jace asked as he got out of the truck.

"This is worse," Brody said. "It's not that he's too stubborn this time, but he's actually stuck and can't move. Tie the rope around the trailer hitch and let's try to pull him out."

The bull threw back his head and bellowed as if he were agreeing with Brody. Jace took the rope from his brother's hand and whipped the end around the hitch. He got inside and very slowly pulled ahead until he felt the line get taut. He rolled down the window and yelled, "Ready?"

"No more than five miles an hour. I don't want to break one of his legs. Devil that he is, he's our best breeding bull," Brody hollered back.

Jace clutched and let it out easy as he barely pressed the gas pedal. Sundance protested, but then there was a loud sucking noise as he left the mud and found solid ground. Jace kept his eyes on the rearview mirror until the bull was completely away from the mud before he braked and turned off the engine. When he reached the back of the truck, Sundance had his old head hung over the tailgate as if looking for food.

"You sorry rascal. You don't get treats after a stunt like that." Brody was covered in mud from his thighs down. "I pushed on him until my eyes crossed and he thinks he deserves food. He may get to spend a week in a barn stall with nothing but bare rations." He lowered the tailgate and sat down to catch his breath.

Jace got out of the truck and leaned on the back fender. "Y'all make quite a pair. I'm surprised that either of you came out of this one without a broken leg. We could have sold him for dog food, but you wouldn't be worth much."

"Hey, don't you tease me about that. You're still limpin' around like an old man. I'm just glad you can drive and helped us out." Brody removed his gloves, jerked a red bandana from his hip pocket, and wiped his face. "That stuff is cold as ice."

"We'd better get him on back to the barn," Jace said. "He'll need to be hosed off and kept inside for at least a day unless you want to get out the hair dryer like we did when we took our calves to the show barn."

"He's not gettin' that kind of treatment but I will use warm water so he doesn't come down with pneumonia. What makes him bust out of a perfectly good pen and go straight for water?"

Jace chuckled. "His mama didn't potty train him right."

"I'm not in the mood for jokes," Brody declared as he scooted back into the truck bed. "You goin' to stick around and help me get him cleaned up or is your woman waiting on you?"

"My woman?" Jace frowned.

"You know exactly what I'm talkin' about. You've been moon-eyed for weeks and even more so these past few days. So is she buyin' a house or stayin' on at Prairie Rose?"

"We'll talk about this when we get Sundance to the barn.

He's shivering. Thank goodness this isn't breeding season." Jace hurried around the truck and hopped into the driver's seat again. Leaving the window down so he could hear Brody if he needed to and keeping an eye in the rearview to make sure Sundance hadn't stopped, he thought long and hard about his brother's questions.

Just the idea of that big house without Carlene and Tilly in it put a lump in his throat. Dawson men did not show emotion and they damn sure did not cry, so he swallowed several times.

Sundance didn't even balk at having to go into the barn but hung his head and followed Brody inside like a little puppy. He went straight for the middle of the barn where the faucets and the drain were located and stopped.

"So what are you going to do about Carlene?" Brody pushed.

Jace sighed. "I don't want them to leave, but I guess it's like her tellin' me that she can't ask me to stay off bulls and broncs," he said as he stretched out the hose and adjusted the water temperature to lukewarm. "If I do give up riding just for her, then will I resent her later in life? If I ask her to stay and she does it in the heat of the moment and then resents me for it later, how will that affect us as a family?"

"So you've wrapped your mind around you all being a family?" Brody took the hose from him and started washing Sundance.

"I didn't realize I had until this minute." Jace pulled on a pair of heavy rubber gloves and went to work rubbing the mud from Sundance's thick black coat.

"There comes a time, maybe not today or tomorrow, but soon when you're going to have to have a serious talk with her," Brody said. "At least she's here in Happy. I had to fly all the way to Florida to have that talk with Lila."

"I had a talk with her last Wednesday night and I told her exactly how I felt." He moved to the bull's back legs.

"Are you afraid to lose her or afraid that you'll regret giving up your bachelorhood?" Brody finished rinsing Sundance and led him back to a stall, where the bull went straight for the feed box.

"Maybe a little of both," Jace said.

"Well, you got some thinkin' to do, so give me a ride up to the house so I can get out of these clothes and take a shower." Brody headed out of the barn toward the truck. "But don't hesitate too long or you might lose her. Believe me, I've been down that road, and it's the emptiest feeling in the whole world."

*   *   *

Carlene had put a roast in the slow cooker that morning before she left for school. She whipped up a little quick instant peach cobbler that only took half an hour to bake and made mashed potatoes, glazed carrots, and buttered green beans. She was setting the table when Hope breezed into the house through the back door.

"I've waited all day for you to get home."

Hope beamed with happiness.

"Can I set an extra place for you? Jace said he'd be here in about twenty minutes and there's plenty." Carlene stopped long enough to hug Hope.

"No, darlin'. I'm going to the café with Valerie. She'll pick me up here in fifteen minutes, so we have to talk fast. What's going on with you and Jace? You are radiant," Hope said, and then lowered her voice. "Are you pregnant?"

"No, ma'am! But we've been on a real date and"— Carlene dropped her voice to barely a whisper—"we are sharing a bed even though I have to be careful that Tilly doesn't find out. But let's talk about you."

"I love Florida and I'm in love with Henry. We've decided that we'll give it a few months of him coming here for a week in one month and me going there for a week the next one."

"What about the family? What will they think of you going away to visit him?"

"What can they say? Kasey is living with Nash and you're living with Jace, so they'd better not give me any sass," Hope said. "Marriage is just a piece of paper to satisfy the law but real marriage is a commitment in the heart. I've made that commitment. And I don't know where we'll live, but we'll figure it out along the way. Right now I'm content to be happy."

"Oh, Granny, I'll miss you so much," Carlene said wistfully.

"Hey, we've got phones and text and FaceTime. And you can visit me and I'll be home a few days every other month. I couldn't stay away from y'all forever and Henry will come with me, so we'll never have to fly alone again after these next few months," Hope said.

"Sounds like you've put a lot of thought into this," Carlene said.

"I have but I'm going to ask you to keep it a secret. The rest of the family needs to be broken in easy to the idea and we thought a few visits between now and July would do that job real good," she said.

"So tell me how you liked the beach." Carlene finished setting the table for three.

"There are no words. It's the most peaceful place I've ever been. I cried when I had to leave it yesterday and I missed it five minutes after I was in the air. I can't wait to get back to it—and Henry. But it's his turn to fly here in February. He's coming for Valentine's Day and then he'll be here in the middle of March for the wedding."

"That makes him coming here two months in a row," Carlene said.

"Yep, it does, so I'm flying back with him right after Kasey and Nash's wedding and staying for two weeks." Hope picked up a spoon and tasted the cobbler. "Very good."

"Thank you. It's just a thrown-together dessert." Carlene checked the time and then filled three glasses with ice.

"There's Valerie," Hope said when a horn sounded loud and clear. "I guess she and Tilly have really struck up a good friendship. I'm so glad. She needs that right now with all these changes. Secret?"

"My lips are sealed but, Granny, I'm so happy for you that I could dance a jig on Main Street."

"And I'm every bit that happy for you, darlin' girl." Hope opened the door and Jace came inside as she was leaving. She stopped long enough to hug him and then hurried on out to Valerie's truck.

"Still limpin'. Think it'll ever be good enough for you to ride another bull?" Tilly appeared in the kitchen.

"Sure, my foot will heal enough to ride bulls," Jace answered. "But the real question is whether I'll want to." He shot a look over the top of Tilly's head, catching Carlene's eye and speaking to her without saying a word. "Supper sure smells good. I'll get washed up and tell you all about Sundance while we eat."

Carlene wanted to hug herself, to dance a jig right there in the kitchen, or to join Jace in the bathroom and kiss him until they were both panting. That he would give up riding for her was a big, big step.

*   *   *

"Who's Sundance?" Tilly stopped folding napkins.

"He's a bull and he really does like water." Jace disappeared and came back a few minutes later wearing a clean T-shirt and with clean hands and face. Dinner was on the table and Carlene was pouring three glasses of sweet tea.

"So, hurry up and bless this food so that you can tell me about Sundance. I like that name. If I ever get another cat, I might name him that." Tilly pulled out her chair and sat down.

Jace said a quick grace and then entertained them with the stories of all the times that Sundance had gotten out of the fence. "Once he wandered back to the springs. That waterfall beside where we buried Anna, and we couldn't talk him out of the water. We pulled on the rope and finally Brody got angry and hopped on his back. He went to buckin' and carryin' on like a rodeo bull. Then a few weeks later Lila did the same thing and he didn't even flinch, just followed her out of the water like he was mesmerized by her."

"Us girls got a way with animals," Tilly said. "That's why I've changed my mind about bein' a rodeo clown. I'm goin' to college and I'm goin' to be a veteran so I can take care of the cows on Prairie Rose."

"You mean a veterinarian," Carlene said.

"That's it. Aunt Bee is a veteran."

"So you want to be a rancher?" Jace asked.

"Yes, I do, only I want to be a smart one that can take care of her own herd of cattle. I'm thinkin' about askin' for my first calf for Christmas. I reckon I can have a herd by the time I get through high school," she answered.

"Smart girl." Jace's smile lit up the room.

And here's the perfect opportunity, handed to you on a

silver platter. You should jump on it, the voice in his head said loudly.

"You have to be very smart, and it takes a long time to be a veterinarian," Carlene said.

"But you could learn a lot just by living here on the ranch. I could teach you like my grandpa and my daddy taught me about cattle, so you'd be ahead when you did get into vet school." Jace talked to Tilly but his eyes were on Carlene.

"I don't think building a house on the ranch is a good idea," she said softly.

"Me neither," Jace said. "Why should you build a house when you're already comfortable here?"

"What are you saying?" Carlene asked.

"Yes!" Tilly squealed. "I didn't want to move again. I want to live here forever with Jace and Red and Jasmine and learn how to do all this ranchin' stuff. Can I go with you next time that Sundance gets in the water? I bet I could ride him right out of it just like Aunt Lila did."

"One vote is in." Jace continued to stare into Carlene's eyes. "I'm asking you to stay here in this house and not move out."

"And?"

"I will give you time. Today that's what I'm asking. You know how I feel. I told you earlier, but I don't want you to feel pressured to rush into anything."

She inhaled deeply and let it out in a whoosh. "And you? Will you feel pressured and regret asking this?"

"Are you talkin' big people? I can't understand a word of what you are sayin'," Tilly fussed at them.

"Yes, we are," Carlene answered.

He leaned forward and took her hand in his. "I'm ready for this, Carlene. I think I've been ready for this day my whole life but we both had to go through the obstacle course to get here."

"And where do we go now that we've made it over the hurdles?"

"I'll leave that in your hands. You tell me when you are ready for the next step and we'll take it together."

Tears formed behind those big, beautiful brown eyes and he had to blink several times to keep from crying with her.

He brought her hand to his lips. "If you want to say no, then I'll understand."

"I want to say yes, not no," she whispered.

"But?" he asked.

"A wise woman told me once that there are no buts in a good relationship," she said.

Jace pushed his chair back and pulled her to a standing position. He wrapped his arms around her and hugged her closely. Then he felt a tap on his shoulder and looked down to see Tilly with her arms wide open.

"Does this mean we might be a real family someday?" she asked.

"Yes, it does." Jace picked her up and included her in the hug.

Chapter Twenty-Three

Two weeks later

He's not going to stand me up, is he?" Tilly touched the tiny tiara set in a bed of curls on top of her head. "Why didn't he come home for supper? We have to be there in half an hour and he's not even dressed. Mama, I told Maribel and all my friends that he was bringin' me to the dance and I was having a real corsage."

"Do you trust him?" Carlene asked.

"Of course I do. He said we'd be a family someday, but I wish someday was already here because then he wouldn't forget my special night. Do I really look all right, Mama?"

"You just keep smiling and you're absolutely beautiful," Carlene said. "I've got a special present for you from Aunt Bee." She brought out a lovely white faux fur cape with a hood and satin ribbons to tie at her throat.

Tilly squealed when Carlene draped it around her shoulders. "Take a picture so I can send it to Aunt Bee." She struck a pose and Carlene snapped a photograph with her phone.

Before Tilly could even look at the outcome on her mother's phone, someone knocked on the door and she frowned. "Nobody ever knocks. Who is it, Mama?"

"I have no idea. Why don't you open the door and find out? It might be for you instead of me."

"Aunt Bee?"

"Got to open the door to see," Carlene said.

Tilly threw it open and Jace stepped inside. He wore a Western-cut suit with a tie and his boots were shined so well that Carlene could see the reflection of Tilly's little pink leather shoes in them.

Jace held out a corsage box. "I'm all thumbs when it comes to things like that so I'd appreciate some help."

"You came. You didn't forget," Tilly sighed.

"Of course I didn't forget. I even shined up my truck so it would be nice enough for a princess to ride in. Reckon we could get a picture together before we leave. Your grandma and the whole family want to see you tonight, but I told them this was our date and they'd have to just be happy with pictures," he said.

Carlene put the corsage on Tilly's wrist while Jace got down on one knee and patted it for Tilly to sit on. She took her time arranging her cape and crossing her legs at the ankles before she nodded at Carlene to snap the pictures.

"Y'all better go on so you aren't late," she said. "Have a great evening."

"Of course we'll have a good night," Tilly said. "My daddy and I are going to dance every single dance. I'm the happiest girl in the whole town tonight, Mama."

"I'll have her home by ten," Jace said hoarsely.

"Nine forty-five." Carlene tried to play the concerned parent, but she couldn't keep the smile off her face.

Jace hugged her and whispered, "She called me daddy for the first time since the rodeo event."

"That's what I've been waiting on. I'm ready now for that next step in this relationship business, but we can talk about it when y'all get home."

He kissed her on the forehead. "This is definitely a Pappy Van Winkle night. Are you going to say yes?"

"To the whiskey, yes."

"To the question we both know I've been itchin' to ask?"

"Ask and see. Right now you've got a daddy-daughter dance to go to."

His lips found hers in a kiss so filled with love that it brought tears to her eyes.

Chapter Twenty-Four

Tilly chatted the whole way to the school cafeteria but her entire demeanor changed when she got out of the truck. She hung back, bit her lip, and frowned. Country music floated out every time the doors opened and little girls were practically dragging their fathers across the parking lot.

"I'm scared. I can't dance," she blurted out.

He tucked her small hand into his. "It's easy. You put your feet on mine and learn the steps that way."

"Really?" A tiny smile tickled the corners of her mouth.

"Yep. But haven't you been to these with your mama?"

"Dancin' with Mama is different than dancin' with a daddy," she whispered.

He opened the door for her and her grip tightened on his hand. "You know something?" he whispered. "This is my first daughter-daddy dance and I know you've been to one or two with your mama. So will you show me what to do?"

"I guess we'll just have to help each other." She marched

through the door but didn't let go of his hand. "Let's get some cookies and punch first and then we'll dance. Too bad they don't have milk. I could use something with a little kick to it."

"Me too," Jace said, but he sure wasn't thinking about chocolate milk.

Folding chairs were lined up around the wall but few of them were occupied. Little girls were either dancing with their dads out in the middle of the floor or they were gathered in groups whispering and giggling. The fathers who weren't dancing were hanging around the refreshment tables, most likely talking about cows, hay, and calving season.

The DJ for the evening put on a slow song and Jace tossed his empty cup and napkin in the trash can. He held out his hand toward his daughter and smiled. "May I have this dance, Miz Tilly?"

Her smile lit up the whole room as she let him lead her out onto the dance floor. He put his hands on her shoulders and she slipped hers around his waist. "Now what?" she asked.

"Now you just take two steps back and one to the side, then two steps forward," he whispered. "Keep time with the music."

"This is easy," she said after a few seconds. "And it's fun. When there's a fast song, can you teach me how to do that too?"

"You bet I can." His heart doubled in size.

*   *   *

Seconds took hours; minutes took days that evening as Carlene busied herself with school papers. She finally took a long bath and read a few chapters of a romance book. Still, it seemed like they'd been gone a week when she finally heard the sound of the truck pulling up in front of the house. Then all quiet ended.

"Guess what, Mama? Daddy and I danced fast dances and slow dances and we had cookies and punch and then we danced some more and my daddy was the best one there tonight." Tilly bounced around like a windup toy. "It was epic, Mama. It really was."

"Epic?" Jace helped Tilly remove her jacket and then hung his beside hers.

"That's the new *awesome* or *fabulous*," Carlene informed him.

"Then it was the most epic evening ever." He slid down on the sofa beside Carlene.

"I'm going to go change out of my pretty dress and call Aunt Bee. Is that okay, Mama? And then I'll come back down and have a glass of milk with a kick in it. Next year at the dance I want you to be one of the mamas who helps serve the 'freshments and you need to make a big punch bowl of chocolate milk, okay?"

"Sounds like a great idea to me." Carlene smiled.

"Talk?" Jace asked after Tilly raced up the steps.

"Yes," she said.

"Okay, I can't bear the thought of you leaving. I can't even imagine living in this house without you. I love you so much, Carlene," he said.

"Yes," she said again.

He cocked his head to one side.

"Yes." Her eyes danced with happiness.

"You're tellin' me that you won't move out and that you love me too?"

"Yes." She cupped his cheeks in her hands.

He leaned forward and kissed her with so much passion and love that it sent tingles all the way to her toes.

"Aunt Bee ain't home." Tilly stopped at the doorway and stared at both of them. "You kissed my mama, Daddy."

"I did because she just said that she'd live here and not move away. How are you with that idea?" Jace asked.

"Does that mean that we're a family?" Tilly asked.

"What do you think of that idea?" Carlene asked her.

She bounded across the floor and landed in their laps. "I love it. Do I get to be a real Dawson?"

"If you want to be." Jace wrapped his arms around both of them in a three-way hug.

"I do, Mama. I really do want to be a Dawson."

"Then I guess that's decided too," she said.

"And the other question?" Jace asked.

"You have to ask?" Carlene said.

Leaving them both sitting on the sofa, he dropped down on one knee and took Carlene's hand in his. "I don't have a ring tonight, but we can pick one out tomorrow. I love you, Carlene. I loved you when we were kids and I still do. Will you marry me?"

"Yes," she said.

He leaned in and brushed a sweet kiss across her lips that held the promise of a better one later that evening. Keeping Tilly's hand in his other one, he shifted his gaze to her. "Tilly, I didn't even know about you until a few weeks ago but I love having you for a daughter and I especially like it when you call me daddy, so will you let me marry your mama and will you be my daughter?"

"Do I get a ring too?"

"No, that honor is saved for the boy who comes along

who will treat you right, respect you, and who can get past my judgment."

"Yes," she said without hesitation.

"I am the luckiest cowboy in the whole state of Texas." He gathered them together for another hug.

Epilogue

One year later

There wasn't a cloud in the sky when Hope and Henry stepped out of the airport in Amarillo that February afternoon. While he went for their rental car, Hope sat on the bench out front with their luggage at her feet.

Flashes of the past year crossed her mind as she waited alone, the brisk north wind chilling her face and hands. She'd thought she'd have a heart attack when Henry first showed up at the ranch—mercy, could that have been fourteen months ago? It seemed like it was only yesterday. After a summer and fall of courting and flying back and forth so they could spend time together, she and Henry had gobirthtten married at the courthouse with only the family surrounding them the day before Thanksgiving. That was three months ago and the honeymoon hadn't ended. And if she had anything to do with it, it never would.

She closed her eyes and thought about their Florida house located right on the beach. She could feel the warm sand on her bare feet, smell the warm winter rains, and almost hear the sound of the ocean. She was so deep in thought that she didn't even hear the car come to a stop beside the curb. She blinked and there was Henry getting out, with a big smile on his face.

"Hey, sweetheart, you ready to go surprise this family you brought me into?" Henry opened the door for her.

"Darlin', I believe that it's the other way around. Nash is your nephew, so you brought me into your family," she teased as she stood and kissed him on the cheek.

"We'll call it a joint venture." He drew her close and tipped her chin up.

"We're in public, Henry," she whispered.

"I don't give a damn. I'm in love with you." And then he kissed her right there in front of the terminal.

When it ended, her heart was thumping. "Think we'll have time to go by the house before the party?"

"I don't reckon we will but we'll make up for it afterward."

*　　　*　　　*

Nash jerked off his dirty work clothes, took a quick shower, and hurriedly dressed for the party. Then he rushed to help Kasey, who was struggling with Silas that afternoon. He was having a difficult time getting through the terrible twos. Hopefully when he had his birthday in May and moved on to the three-year-old stage, it would be better.

"Daddy, you better get on in there. You're the only one

that can do anything with him." Four-year-old Emma sighed from the top step of the staircase. "Silas is a brat. You better help."

"On my way." Nash blew her a kiss.

She caught it and stuffed it inside the pocket of her cute little skirt.

When Nash made it to the boy's bedroom door, Silas was squirming against Kasey, who was trying to put on his boots.

"Daddy." Silas held up his arms.

Nash held him close and whispered, "There's going to be cake and cookies and ice cream and maybe even pony rides at the party. Why don't you want to go?"

"Need boots," he said simply.

"I've got your boots right here." Kasey held them up.

"Need workin' boots."

"Why?" Nash asked. "I'm wearin' my good boots."

Silas leaned back far enough he could look down. "Ohhh...kay. Need good boots."

Nash set him on the edge of the bed and Kasey handed Nash the boots. He slipped them on Silas's feet and put him on the floor. "You ready for cake?"

"All ready now!" His smile lit up the whole room.

"Looks just like Adam," Nash said.

"Maybe so," Kasey told him, "but he's definitely your child."

Nash pulled her close to him and laid his hand on her pregnant belly. "I can't believe we're getting two for one on the first try."

"Can you imagine two boys in the terrible twos?" she said.

"I'm here and we'll get through every phase together." He bent and kissed her belly. "I never thought I'd ever be this happy, Kasey."

"Me neither. God sure blessed me when he put you into my life."

Nash rose to his full height. "Not as much as he did me."

Kasey took his hand. "It's party time."

"Are we still talkin' about a birthday party?" He wiggled his dark eyebrows.

"For now, but one never knows about later," she whispered seductively into his ear.

*   *   *

Brody hurried back to the house from a rodeo meeting, getting there just as Lila was dressing the baby, Daisy Hope, in a pink dress. He leaned against the nursery door for a second, taking in the scene. His emotions were overwhelming to the point that they almost brought him to his knees. He'd thought that he could never be happier than he was the day that Lila said she'd marry him, but that was barely the tip of the iceberg.

She looked up and smiled and he crossed the room in a couple of long strides, slipped his arms around her waist, and kissed her on the neck. "The princess is almost as beautiful as the queen of my heart. Let me help."

"All that's left is putting her socks and shoes on." Lila whipped around, moistened her lips, and rolled up on her toes for a long, steamy kiss. "And the princess outshines the queen. She can wrap a tough old cowboy right around her little finger."

He chuckled. "Yes, she can and there no words to tell you what you and this baby mean to me, darlin'." He started a string of steamy kisses that went from her neck, across her cheek, and ended at her lips.

Breathless, she took a step back. "We have to stop now or we'll never get to the party."

His blue eyes glimmered. "We might have a party of our own, but you're right. This is Miz Daisy's first party and it's liable to cause her to be a rebellious teenager if we don't get her there on time."

"Oh, honey!" Lila handed him the pink satin shoes, both of which fit in her palm. "There's nothing we can do or not do that will prevent that from happening. Look at who her mama and daddy are. There's not a snowball's chance in hell of her being anything but rebellious."

"I have a set of rules that we will follow. Number one is that she can date when she's sixteen, but I'll be sitting in the front seat with her until she's thirty." He kissed each tiny toe before he put her shoes on. His voice rose several octaves when he talked to her. "You got your mama's pretty dark hair and her nose and her pretty lips. Yes, you do, darlin' daughter."

Lila laid a hand on his shoulder. "But she got your gorgeous Dawson blue eyes."

"I had to give you something, didn't I, princess?" Brody crooned in a high-pitched baby-talk voice. "Now she's all ready, Mama. I've got her baby seat in the chariot and her adoring family is waiting to see her."

"Is the red carpet rolled out?" Lila teased.

"Always and forever, wherever we go—for you and her both," Brody answered.

*   *   *

Jace draped an arm around Tilly's shoulders as they watched out the window for the first guests to arrive for her tenth birthday party. Her red hair was braided and her gray eyes, so much like his own, glittered in anticipation of the family all gathering for her special day.

"A watched window never produces people." Carlene came up beside him and he drew her close with his other arm.

"Yes, it does. There's the first ones." Tilly took off in a run toward the door to greet them.

Jace took that opportunity to spin Carlene around to face him. "I love you to Pluto and back, Mrs. Dawson."

"Pluto?" She only got out one word before his lips were on hers in a searing kiss.

"Yes, darlin', Pluto. That's a lot farther out there than the plain old moon."

"Aunt Bee!" Tilly's squeals filled the house.

"Oh. My. Goodness!" Carlene whispered. "Did you know?"

"Can't lie to you. And believe me it's been hard for me to keep the secret." He turned her around to face the door and held to her waist in case she fainted. "And there's more."

"I hear there's a birthday going on here," Belinda said. "And look who I brought with me." She pushed her mother and father into the living room ahead of her.

"Jace?" Carlene muttered.

"Surprise." He leaned over and kissed her on the cheek. "For you and our daughter both."

"Come in, come in. I'm so glad you could…"

"We are on our way to Florida for a meeting," her father said. "We had an extra day."

"I can't believe how much Tilly has grown in only a year," her mother said.

"Look, Mama!" Tilly pointed to the window. "It's Granny and Henry! Ooooh, this is going to be the best birthday party ever."

Jace bent forward, kissed Carlene on the cheek, and

whispered, "You go get your folks something to drink and I'll play host for a little while as the people arrive. I'm as excited as Tilly that Granny and Henry came home for the party."

*   *   *

"Thank you," Carlene said softly. "For everything."

Another quick kiss on the ear and he stepped back.

"I'm so glad to see all of you." Tears welled up in Carlene's eyes as she hugged each of them. "I feel like it's my birthday instead of Tilly's. Can I get you something to drink?"

"I'd take a beer," her father said.

"And I'd love some good old Southern sweet tea." Her mother smiled.

"Coke." Belinda nodded.

"With a little kick?" Tilly winked at Belinda as she ran to the door to open it for Hope and Henry.

"Only way to drink it." Belinda grabbed another quick hug as Tilly passed her.

Carlene led the way to the kitchen and then to the dining room, still feeling like if she pinched herself, she'd wake up and find the whole past year had been nothing but a beautiful dream.

Tilly danced out of the living room, grabbed her aunt Bee by one hand and her grandmother by the other, and dragged them away to meet her cousins when Nash and Kasey and Brody and Lila all arrived at the same time.

"Well?" Her father tipped up his beer.

"Well, what?" she asked.

But before he could say another word, Tilly returned and took his big hand in hers. "Come on, Grandpa. You got to see baby Daisy. She's just the cutest thing ever. I want a sister so bad. I'd be happy with a brother but boys are such a pain in the ass. I mean butt."

Carlene's father chuckled and let Tilly lead him into the living room.

Valerie was the last one to the party and brought the cake. She set it on the dining room table with the punch bowl and all the fancy crystal. "Everything looks beautiful, Carlene. Presents first and then party?"

"I think so," Carlene said. "And thank you for everything."

"Hey, that little girl couldn't have stolen my heart more if I'd gotten her at birth than she has now. So shall we give them thirty minutes to visit and then announce that it's time to open the gifts?" Jace asked.

"Sounds like a plan to me." Carlene looped her arm through Valerie's. "My folks and my sister are here."

"And so are we," Hope said from the doorway.

"Mama!" Valerie drew Carlene to Hope and they had a three-way hug. "What a wonderful surprise. Tilly will remember this day forever."

The next half hour went by fast and then Tilly was the center of the party as she opened one present after another, including a new pair of boots from Hope and Henry to replace the ones she'd outgrown.

After the first one, Carlene nudged Jace on the shoulder. "Darlin', we don't need twenty pictures of her with each present."

"There can never be too many of her," he said, and snapped another one.

"Give me your phone." Carlene reached out a hand. "My battery is almost gone, and I want to take some with you and her together when she opens your special one."

He handed it off to her and crossed over to sit beside Tilly on the sofa. He picked up a small box wrapped in red and tied with a pretty silver bow. "And this one is from me."

She tore into the paper and flipped open a pink velvet box to reveal a necklace with a heart-shaped pendant hanging from it engraved with *Daddy's Girl*. She gasped, jumped up to show everyone, and then barreled into him, knocking him sideways as she kissed him all over his face.

"I love it, Daddy. I'm going to wear it every day and never take it off," she said. "Will you put it on me right now?"

Carlene shot at least a dozen pictures of that event before she switched it over to video mode and said over the noise. "Hey, you've got one more present. It's from me and your daddy both."

Tilly picked up the last one, a tiny box all wrapped in the same pretty paper. Valerie touched her on the shoulder. "Let me take a picture of the three of you for this one."

"Oh, no, I want to capture both of their faces, but thanks," Carlene told her.

Tilly ripped off the paper and opened the box to find a key and a tiny baby ring. "What's this go to, Mama? And this little gold ring is way too little for me. Does the key open a jewelry box to hold my new necklace and does this little ring go on a bracelet?"

"That's the key to your brand-new four-wheeler. It's waiting for you in the backyard," Jace answered. "If you're going to be a rancher and help me bring in cattle for working this spring, you need your own ride."

She was speechless and then she jumped up and did a stomp dance right there in the living room. "I'm going to be the best rancher in Happy, Texas. I'm going to grow up and be just like my grandma and my granny. This is the best day of my whole life. I'm so glad that we moved here!"

Valerie frowned. "Did the jewelry shop give you the wrong ring?"

"Think about it, Tilly," Carlene said. "What have you been asking for ever since Daisy was born? I thought maybe you'd like to give that to your baby brother or sister sometime at the end of October."

"Oh! Oh! Oh!" Tilly raced across the floor but Jace beat her to Carlene. Bless Valerie's heart; she grabbed her phone in time to film the whole scene.

"I only found out this morning for sure and I wanted to surprise you," she said as Jace held her tightly and Tilly kept kissing her face.

"I'm truly the luckiest cowboy of all," Jace said.

While everyone had birthday cake and the kids all had milk with a little kick in it, Carlene escaped to the kitchen. She was making another pitcher of chocolate milk when her father joined her and Jace slipped up beside her.

"Well?" her father said again.

"Well, what?" Carlene asked.

"Well, I'm proud of you. Just wanted to tell you that. Got another beer for this old man who is going to retire after this duty station?"

Jace gently squeezed her hand.

Carlene smiled and said, "Y'all could consider retiring here in Happy. We'd love to have you and Mother."

Yes, it made her feel good that he finally said those words, but somehow it dimmed in the light of all the happiness she'd found on the ranch the past year and now a new baby coming would be like icing on the cake.

"It's something to think about," he said as he took the beer from her hands.

He took a drink and went back to join the party, and she looked up into Jace's stunning gray eyes. He cupped her face in his rough hands and kissed her with so much passion that it made her knees weak.

"Thank you for giving me such a wonderful life." He laid a palm on her belly. "I love you so much."

"Rightbackatcha, darlin'. You'd better love me a whole lot because enduring those terrible twos like Silas is in right now will be a test of our marriage for sure." She laid her hand over his.

He grazed her lips with a soft kiss. "Together, we can conquer the world, darlin'."

Get an early look at the first book in the Longhorn Canyon series featuring more sexy, rugged cowboys!

Cowboy Bold

Coming in Spring 2018

Come on in," a man with a deep drawl yelled when Retta knocked on the door of the bunkhouse with a carved wooden sign above the door that said BOYS.

Feeling like she was entering forbidden territory, she eased open the door and peeked inside. A man was sitting on the sofa staring at a laptop on the coffee table in front of him. Without looking up, he raised his hand and motioned to her.

She quickly crossed the room. "I'm Retta Palmer. I'm a few minutes early."

He stood up, towering above her five feet eight inches. Her eyes went from his broad chest to the clearest blue eyes she'd ever seen. Dammit! She'd always been a sucker for blue eyes.

He stuck out his hand. "Cade Maguire. Please, have a seat."

"Thank you." There was a slight flutter in her chest when he took her hand and gave it a firm shake. His smile was genuine but there was sadness in those striking blue eyes.

He'd told her his name on the phone when she called for an interview. With a voice like Sam Elliott, she'd expected him to be a much older man, maybe one with a gray mustache. She'd figured that he'd be a cowboy—after all, he owned a ranch. But in her wildest dreams, she never thought Cade would be close to her age and have the most mesmerizing crystal-clear blue eyes.

He led the way from the middle of the floor to a small seating area. His wide back and biceps half the size of her waist stretched the knit of his blue shirt. Her gaze drifted down the taper toward his waist and on farther to his butt that filled out those tight-fitting jeans really well.

God almighty, but he was a fine specimen. However,

Retta had vowed to never get involved with a cowboy, a rancher, or a farmer of any kind—even if this one did make her pulse race. He turned around and motioned toward a comfortable chair on the other side coffee table in front of the sofa.

She sat down and crossed one leg over the other. She shouldn't have worn jeans and boots. That would give him the idea that she was a cowgirl, which she was not, but all of her business clothes were at least two sizes too big these days, leaving her with jeans, boots, and a few plaid shirts.

"The weatherman is calling for high nineties," he said.

"That's summer in Texas." She smiled. Always made a little small talk to put the person being interviewed at ease before the real questions started. She'd used that tactic before so she wasn't surprised.

"So you drove down from Oklahoma today?"

"Yes, sir, Mr. Maguire."

"Cade," he chuckled. "No one even calls my father that."

"Then Cade it is." She smiled.

"Okay, Retta, I'll tell you what the job entails and ask a few questions and then answer what questions you might have." He eased down onto the sofa.

He glanced at the laptop. "You've got a degree in business and worked for an oil company until three years ago and then there's nothing listed."

"Where Corn Don't Grow" played through her mind. That had been the very song that had spoken to her when she was growing up on a small ranch in Oklahoma. Every day she thought if she could just move to a place where corn didn't grow, she'd never look back with a single regret.

"My father took sick, so I went home to help out." This wasn't her first rodeo at being interviewed or being the one asking the questions either.

Don't talk too much. Answer his questions completely and honestly but don't give away your whole life story. He's only interested in the job he's hiring you for, not anything personal. That's the motivational speech she gave when the company sent her out to talk to college graduates looking for jobs in the oil industry.

"Did he recover?" Cade asked.

"No, he lost the battle with cancer three months ago."

Again, his eyes locked with hers and there was that flutter again. "I'm so sorry for your loss."

"Thank you. It took a while for me to get things settled. Everything is sold and finished now." She focused on his forehead.

"And why do you want this job?" he asked.

"I've got experience in these kinds of surroundings. I know a bull from a steer and I can saddle up and ride a horse even though I prefer a four-wheeler. I've worked with several leadership groups in my previous jobs and I can teach kids teamwork. And the job ends July Fourth, which is a perfect time because I have an interview with an oil company on July fifth."

"You've worked with adults. Ever had a bit of experience with kids? These are ten- to twelve-year-old girls from the inner city who are tough as nails. What makes you think you can control them?" He kept his eyes on the computer.

"I was a Sunday school teacher to girls who were eight to twelve years old in the church where my dad went. I helped with the Bible school programs all three summers while I was there. I've served as counselor, supervisor, and sponsor for two trips to summer church camp and twice I took my girls to southeastern Oklahoma for short missionary trips," she answered.

"So what did you do on those trips?" He looked up and

their eyes caught in the middle of the distance separating them.

"First one, we painted an elderly couple's house for them. Second time, we worked on a small farm, picking vegetables and fruit and selling it in a roadside fruit stand for them. It taught my girls to work and to help others," she answered, amazed that her voice sounded completely normal with those blue eyes boring into hers.

"You had a small farm when your father passed away. Why didn't you stay there?" He blinked and looked down at the computer.

She uncrossed her legs and leaned forward slightly. "I left that lifestyle right out of high school because I didn't like it. Only went back because I'm an only child and my father needed me. Now I'll be moving back to the place where I belong."

"Fair enough. There will be four little girls, ages ten and eleven this year, living here in the bunkhouse." He hesitated.

She waited for the question a full thirty seconds before she leaned back in the rocker and smiled. "Which means there will be lots of giggling and whining and I can expect it to lean more toward whining. I have cousins that age and once upon a time I was a little girl so I know what I'm signing up for, Mr. Maguire. Any more questions?"

"No, but I will be honest. I ran the references you listed," he said. "And your previous employers said that you'd be excellent in this position."

"So am I hired?" She shot another smile his way but avoided his eyes. If she got the job, she had to remember to look at the cleft in his chin, or his ears, or even his mouth but to never fall into those cool blue eyes again—no, not his mouth, never the lips because that brought on thoughts of kissing.

"I'll show you the girls' bunkhouse and if you are still interested we'll talk salary." He stood to his feet, crossed the floor in a few long, swaggering strides, and held the door open for her. "It's only a few yards from here, so we'll walk."

"I saw it as I drove down here from the ranch house. Stopped to ask exactly where to go and a sweet lady named Ruby told me." She passed him close enough to get a whiff of the remnants of his shaving lotion. Without thinking, she drew a long breath and let it out slowly. Yep, the scent was Diesel Fuel for Life, a masculine cologne that did wicked things to her hormones.

"You okay?" he asked.

"Fine. Ranch. Farm. It all smells like dirt and hard work," she answered.

"Wonderful, ain't it?" He shortened his step to keep up with her but it still only took two minutes to go from one building to the next.

He opened the door and stepped to the side to let her enter first.

She scanned the large room. No television but there was a bookcase full of age-appropriate books.

"I see the question in your eyes. They can get video games and television at home. As you can see, this is the living room and the little kitchen will be for you and the girls to prepare snacks. You will need to make a list for my cook each day to keep whatever they like or want. If you take the job, you can have today to unpack your things and tomorrow one of us—our foreman, Levi; my brother, Justin; or I—will get you familiar with the layout of the Longhorn."

"Longhorn Canyon Ranch. I can understand the Longhorn but I don't see a canyon anywhere."

His chuckle was as deep as his voice. "My great-grandparents built this place from scratch and we've always had Longhorn cattle on it. My great-grandmother lived on the edge of Canyon Creek, so they combined the two when they needed a brand. I'm a die-hard Texas Longhorn fan, so I love the ranch's name."

"I won't hold that against you," she said seriously.

"OU?" He almost groaned.

"Boomer Sooner!" she answered with a smile. "And this year we'll whip your butts."

"Want to make a bet on it?"

"I'll be long gone by the second week in October but if I was here, I'd gladly take your money away from you," she said.

"Hey, now!" He opened the doors into four small bedrooms, each with a twin bed, a desk, and a dresser with a mirror above it and a tiny closet. "Each girl has her own room. All exactly alike so no one is special."

"Did you go to UT at Austin?" she asked as she followed him to the fifth door.

"Played for them. Helped bring home the Gold Hat in '09."

"And helped them give it back to Oklahoma in '10," she said.

"You know your football," he said. "Why would you live in Texas if you are an OU fan?"

"I like Dallas," she said. "But I'm as die-hard Sooners as you are Longhorn."

"I doubt it," he chuckled. "But let me show you your quarters now."

She expected him to show her a bedroom like the other four but she was wrong—again. A queen-sized bed took up a very small portion of the big room. Nightstands on either side, a big ten-drawer dresser, a walk-in closet, and a private bathroom with an oversized tub.

"Wow!" she whispered.

"This is the original bunkhouse. When it was built, the foreman at that time was about six and a half feet tall. He asked for a tub big enough for him to soak away the aches of the day. When we threw up walls and made this into a retreat type of bunkhouse, we left the tub. The boys' place doesn't have a tub, but it does have two shower stalls. It was built when the ranch outgrew this little one."

If he'd shown her the tub first, she could have already been unloaded and ready to go to work. After having nothing but a shower stall for four years, she could already envision bubbles and bath salts and reading a thick book.

"If you are interested in the job." He quoted a salary that was twice as much as she expected. "In addition to that, you get room and board, which includes three meals in the big house and two snacks a day right along with the kids."

"I'll take it." Had she really said that out loud? She'd meant to say that she'd think about it until tomorrow. The money was excellent. Benefits fabulous. But she should ask how closely she'd be working with the cowboys. Did she turn the children over to them each day or was she expected to go on every adventure with them? What was her job description past listening to four little girls whine and giggle?

"Great!" he said. "Can you start work today? I'd like for you to get to know the lay of the ranch and be familiar with everything before the kids arrive day after tomorrow. They always get here on June first and leave the morning of July fifth."

It was too late to back out now. "I can do that."

"Contract is on the computer. I'll make a couple of adjustments and if you've seen enough, we'll both get it signed. If you've seen enough, we'll go back down to the boys' place and get it signed."

Until her signature was on the paper, she could still back out. That's what she kept telling herself from one building to the next. But her father had taught her that a Palmer's word was worth more than any legal document and she'd said she would take the job. Once inside, he went straight to the computer, hit a few keys, and then whipped the screen around to her. She read through the one-page contract. Payment upon completion of the program and would be forfeited if she left before the last day. Any accidents happening during the program would be covered by the ranch insurance. Pretty basic stuff really. She hit the SIGN HERE key and it was done.

"That does it. I'll print out a copy for you and bring it with me when I come and get you for supper this evening. Right now I'll help you get unloaded."

"Thank you." She wondered why she'd done the first impulsive thing in her life that day and on a ranch of all places.

*   *   *

With a name like Retta, which had to be short for Loretta, Cade had looked at the only résumé left on the computer and wished he was doing any job other than that one. But then a cowgirl walked in and he'd felt a stirring in his heart that he hadn't felt in a long time.

She pointed. "That's my truck and my stuff."

Her truck had probably been bright red at one time but it definitely showed signs that it had been left out in the weather instead of in a garage. She must've caught his expression because she turned around with a frown on her face.

"What?"

He shrugged. "Since you don't like ranchin', I figured you'd be driving some kind of low-slung sports car."

"My cute little yellow Camaro went the same way as the farm—to pay off all the medical bills, but I'm debt free and this old girl has a lot of miles left in her."

He threw up his palms defensively. "Hey, I like trucks. I drive one and if you'll look up toward the house, you'll see three parked out front."

"Saw them when I drove in. Nice trucks." She deftly unfastened a tie-down and pulled two suitcases from the bed of the truck.

"This is all?" Cade was amazed at only one more suitcase and three boxes.

"Like I said, the medical bills are paid. Thanks for the help."

"No problem." He hoisted two boxes onto his shoulders.

She went ahead of him, set the suitcases on the porch, and held the door for him. "Just put them in my room and I'll take care of getting the rest of it."

"I'm a big boy but my mama would tack my hide to the smokehouse door if I let a lady carry stuff. I'm already in hot water with her if she finds out that you opened the door for me."

"Does she live on the ranch too?"

"No, ma'am. She and Dad moved out around Sweetwater three years ago but they come home for Christmas and the whole family always meets in Dallas for the Texas–Oklahoma game every year." He set the boxes in the corner of the living area.

"I've missed the last three games. Watched them on

television but it wasn't the same. Oklahoma can whip Texas's butt this year to celebrate me being right there in the stands again." She wheeled the suitcases into the bedroom.

"In your dreams," he chuckled as he started back out for the last boxes.

"Hey, now, this is serious business," she called after him.

"Don't I know it and I'll be on the winning side," he yelled.

"And that, Mr. Maguire, is in your dreams," she hollered.

Holy hell! Was he flirting? And with a woman he'd met only a half hour before? That was entirely too bold, even for Cade Maguire, who always took the bull by the horns and spit in his eye.

Another bantering remark came to his mind but he clamped his mouth shut. He set the last two boxes inside the door and said, "We have supper at six o'clock. I'll be here about five-thirty to take you up to the house."

"I can see the house and find my way. You don't need to do that," she said.

He picked up a dark brown cowboy hat, settled it on his head, and tipped his hat toward her. "Then I'll see you there between five-thirty and six. The boys and I like a good cold beer before supper but we can make you a drink if you want something different."

"I'll be there on time," she said.

With his long strides, it only took a few minutes to go from the girls' bunkhouse to the big house located about a hundred yards away. He circled around and went in through the back door, kicked off his good boots, and shoved his feet down into a pair of scuffed-up work boots and then headed to the refrigerator for a quart jar of sweet tea to take to the field for Justin.

"Did you like her better than the rest of them?" Ruby was taking a blackberry cobbler from the stove when he made it to the kitchen.

"I did," Cade answered. "And she'll be joining us for supper tonight."

Ruby would never make a good poker player because whatever she thought was right there on her face as surely as if it were on a flashing billboard. "Not that I'm one to meddle but..." She rolled her brown eyes.

Ruby had been the cook at the ranch since before Cade and Justin were born and even though she was well past sixty, she swore they'd take her out of the kitchen feetfirst. Her husband, Willy, retired two years ago but Ruby said there was no way she was staying home with him twenty-four/seven.

"But what?" Cade asked.

"She stopped by here to be sure where it was she was supposed to be interviewed. She's real pretty and them brown eyes would remind you of Julie," Ruby said.

"Not so much. Julie's were darker brown and had little yellow flecks in them and that part of my life is over." He didn't want to go there because it was the one time in his life that his confidence had been shaken to the core.

"Okay, then, I'll set another plate for supper. I hope she likes pot roast." Ruby shoved a forefinger up close to his nose even though she had to stand on her tiptoes to do it. "Sayin' it's over and believin' it's over and actin' like it's over are all different things."

He grabbed her finger and twirled her around in a swing dance movement. "That was two years ago, Ruby, and it won't happen again. Don't worry about me."

"You rascal, you've messed up my hair." She patted at her short blond hair with an inch of gray roots showing.

"You still got spring in your step. You should go with me and the boys out dancing some Saturday night," he said.

"Did that woman's brown eyes make you crazy? I'm too old for shenanigans like that. Lord have mercy! I'll be seventy in the fall."

"Don't you lie to me, Miz Ruby. You're not a day over fifty." He gave her a quick hug and headed out the back door.

"You are full of horse crap but it's good to see you with a smile on your face for a change. Don't forget your tea," she yelled.

He came back, picked it up, and blew her a kiss on his way out. A vision of the last time he saw Julie came back to him. It was the night before their wedding the next day and he blew her a kiss when he walked off her porch at ten minutes to midnight.

With the shake of his head, he tried to erase the memory and got into the old work truck that didn't look a bit better than Retta's. He set the tea on the floor in front of the passenger seat and shifted into low gear. Then another picture flashed through his mind of Julie holding a jar just like that for him as they drove out to the old hunter's cabin at the back side of the ranch for a picnic.

He turned on the radio to take his mind somewhere else but that didn't help when "Deju Vu" started playing. Like Lauren Duski sang about, there were weeks when he didn't even think of Julie—and then it would all come back in a flash, especially when he saw a woman with beautiful brown eyes like Retta's.

He parked the truck and picked up the quart of tea. A trail of dust floated out behind the green tractor coming toward him. The smell of freshly plowed dirt and hot sun rays beating down from a cloudless sky—this was living worth giving up everything for.

The tractor came to a stop a few feet in front of the truck and Justin hopped out of it. "I hope that tea is for me. I'm spittin' dust. Did the new woman get hired?"

"Yes, it is. I figured you'd be needin' something to drink. And yes, I hired the new woman. She's a city girl but she was wearing boots and jeans. Lived on a ranch until lately. Her daddy died and she's eager to get back to the big city life. I brought you a jar of tea." Cade held out the jar.

Justin took it from him. "Thanks." He removed the lid and took a long drink. "You can have the tractor. My butt was beginning to feel like it was grown to the seat. I'm going to go help Levi fix fence the rest of the day so I can stand up."

"I'll gladly plow a field or even string barbed wire, I'm so happy to have those interviews done. You want to show Retta around the ranch tomorrow?" Cade removed his hat and used it for a fan.

"Nope. I'm going to the store with Skip to get supplies for the boys. And Levi is getting a marshmallow roast ready out in the corral for their first night here. I can't wait to see Benjy. How about you?"

"It's kind of bittersweet. Love to see that kid and yet this is his last year," Cade answered.

"Okay, then, I'll take the truck out to the far pasture where Levi is stringing fence. You can drive the tractor back to the barn when you finish plowing this pasture." Justin handed him half a jar of tea. "You might need this. See you at home in a couple of hours."

"Ruby made pot roast. Don't be late." He waved as Justin drove away. Then he got into the tractor cab and fired up the engine. There were a few things on his schedule that he couldn't move around, so Retta would simply have to go with him.

He'd barely gotten the tractor turned around when his blue tick hound ran up beside him and barked loudly several times. He braked and slung open the door and Beau scrambled up across him and took his place in the passenger's seat.

"Needin' a little air-conditioning, are you? Let me tell you about this woman who's goin' to be with us on the ranch for the next five weeks. I think you'll like her, Beau, old buddy." He reached across and scratched the dog's ears with his free hand. "But don't get too attached. She's a city gal and she won't be stayin' with us."

About the Author

Carolyn Brown is a *New York Times* and *USA Today* best-selling romance author and RITA Finalist who has sold more than 3 million books. She presently writes both women's fiction and cowboy romance. She has also written historical single title, historical series, contemporary single title, and contemporary series. She lives in southern Oklahoma with her husband, a former English teacher, who is not allowed to read her books until they are published. They have three children and enough grandchildren to keep them young. For a complete listing of her books (series in order) check out her website at CarolynBrownBooks.com.

Hometown Cowboy

Sara Richardson

Prologue

Funny how you can remember every detail about the most significant day of your life. Not the best day of your life necessarily, but the day that shaped you, the day that you were forced to find your strength.

Lance Cortez wandered to the bay window in his living room and stared out at the land that had been in his family since the Spaniards had crossed the mountains into Colorado and founded the town of Topaz Falls.

From his house situated on the valley floor, it seemed he could see every acre, from the razor-edges of Topaz Mountain to the pointed tips of the evergreens that studded the steep slopes. Even in the dimness of that eerie space preceding the dawn, he could make out the stables up the hill, the bullpens across from the pasture, and the house farther on down the hill where his father still lived. The house where he'd grown up. It was a ranch style, built from the logs of those trees on the mountain. Anchored by a wraparound porch.

Sixteen years ago, before dawn, he'd stood on that porch right there and watched his mother walk out of his life. He didn't know what had woken him that day. Maybe the sound of the dog barking or the door creaking. But when he'd stumbled down the hallway, he'd caught her dragging her suitcase across that old porch.

"Where are you going?" he'd asked, not liking the weakness that had started to spread over his body like a dark shadow. Something in him already knew. She'd been distant for months, there but not.

· His mother had paused on the sidewalk at the bottom of those porch steps, but she hadn't looked at him. "I have to go away for a while," she'd said. "I can't do this anymore."

He'd wanted to ask why, but couldn't. He couldn't open his mouth, couldn't unfist his hands. She was leaving them. And he wondered if it had anything to do with the underage drinking ticket he'd gotten two days before. At fourteen, he knew he was a holy terror.

Or maybe it was the fact that his father was away so much, traveling to the rodeos, giving all of his time to a sport his mother hated.

"I'm sorry, Lance," his mother had said. There were no tears in her eyes, but her voice caught. "I'm so sorry."

That word gathered up the sadness that had weighted his bones and spun it into a whorl of anger. If she was sorry then why was she going?

"I hope you'll understand someday."

He didn't. Sixteen years later, he had yet to understand how a mother could walk out on her husband and three boys who needed her. He'd been fourteen. He could take care of himself. But what about Lucas? At ten, he'd only just started the sixth grade. And Levi. Hell, he was still wetting the bed at seven.

Without another word, she'd walked away and hauled her suitcase into the old pickup. Energy had burned through him, tempting him to run down those steps and somehow force her to stay. He couldn't, though. He knew it. He saw it in her eyes.

She'd already left them behind.

The engine had started and the tires ground against gravel. Lance had watched until the darkness swallowed the taillights and she was gone.

When he'd stepped back into the house, he was a different kid. Refusing to shed even one tear, he'd made himself a cup of coffee and omelets for his brothers. When his father came back that afternoon, he'd told him she was gone.

They'd never said another word about it.

In the months and years that followed, he'd tried to make up for her abandonment. He'd quit being such a delinquent. Watched over his brothers when their father was out searching for something to remedy his own pain. Became a bull-riding champion in his own right. But he couldn't undo the damage she'd left in her wake. It took seven years after she left for things to fall apart.

He wished he would've been watching Levi that night he'd set the fire. Wished he'd been able to stop it before it killed the livestock. Wished he could've stopped it before it ruined them all. Lucas had wanted to take the blame, to protect their younger brother just like he always did, and Lance let him. They'd made a plan. Kept quiet about it. He'd been so sure Lucas would get off easy.

But he'd been wrong. Even though his brother had been

only seventeen, they'd charged him as an adult and sent him to prison.

Nothing had ever been the same after that. Levi threw himself into bull riding and hadn't been home in years. After Lucas got out of prison, he refused to come home. He'd gone on to work for a stock contractor down south and hadn't been home since.

All because of one day. One rejection. One person who was supposed to care for them turning her back instead.

Funny how you remember the details of days like that. The words, the sounds, the feelings that'd turned your body cold. Funny how you spend every day for the rest of your life trying to forget them.

Turning his back on the view of that porch, Lance headed for the kitchen.

It was time to put the coffee on.

Chapter One

Sorry, sir." Jessa Mae Love threw out her arms to block the heavyset man who tried to sit on the stool next to her. "This seat is taken."

He eyed her, the coarseness of his five o'clock shadow giving his face a particularly menacing quality. Still, she held her ground.

"You been sittin' there by yourself for an hour, lady," he pointed out, scratching at his beer belly. "And this is the best spot to watch the game."

"It's true. I have been sitting here for a while." She smiled politely and shimmied her shoulders straighter, lest he think she was intimidated by his bulk. "But my *boyfriend* is meeting me. We have an important date tonight and I know he'll be here any minute." She checked the screen of her cell phone again, the glowing numbers blaring an insult in her face. Seven o'clock. *Seven o'clock?*

Cam was never late. He'd been planning this date for

more than a week. Since she was coming straight from the animal rescue shelter she owned, they'd agreed to meet at the Tumble Inn Bar for a drink before he took her to the new Italian restaurant on Main Street. "He'll be here," she said to the man. "Cam is *very* reliable."

"Whatever," the man grumbled, hunching himself on a stool three down from her.

Signaling to the bartender, she ordered another glass of pinot. "And why don't you go ahead and bring a Bud Light for my boyfriend?" she asked with a squeak of insecurity. But that was silly because Cam would be there. He'd show up and give her a kiss and apologize for being so late because... his car broke down. Or maybe his mother called and he couldn't get off the phone with her.

"He won't let me down," she muttered to cool the heat that rose to her face. He would *never* stand her up in this crowded bar—in front of the whole town.

Everyone considered the Tumble Inn the classiest watering hole in Topaz Falls, Colorado. And that was simply because you weren't allowed to throw peanut shells on the floor. It was nice enough—an old brick auto shop garage that had been converted years ago. They'd restored the original garage doors and in the summer, they opened them to the patio, which was strung with colorful hanging globe lights. Gil Wilson, the owner, had kept up with the times, bringing in modern furniture and decor. He also offered the best happy hour in town, which would explain why it was so crowded on a Wednesday night.

She stole a quick glance over her shoulder. Were people starting to stare?

Plastering on a smile, she called Cam. *Again.*

His voice mail picked up. *Again.*

"Hey, it's me." She lowered her voice. "I'm kind of worried. Maybe I got the time wrong? Did we say we'd meet at six? Or seven? I guess it doesn't matter. I'm here at the bar. Waiting for you..." A deafening silence echoed back in her ear. "Okay. Well I'm sure you're on your way. I'll see you soon."

She set down the phone and took a long sip of wine. Everything was fine. It was true she hadn't had very good luck with men, but Cam was different.

She drummed her fingers against the bar to keep her hand from trembling. Over the past ten years, she'd been *almost* engaged approximately three times. Approximately, because she wasn't all that sure that a twist tie from the high school cafeteria counted as a betrothal, although her seventeen-year-old heart had thought it to be wildly romantic at the time. Little did she know, one year later, her high school sweetheart—the one who'd gotten down on one knee in the middle of the cafeteria to recite one of Shakespeare's sonnets in front of nearly the whole school (did she mention he was in the drama club?)—would go off to college and meet the Phi Beta Kappa sisters who'd splurged on breast implants instead of fashionable new glasses like Jessa's. Breast implants seemed to get you more bang for your buck in college. Who knew?

She pushed her glasses up on her nose and snuck a glance at the big man who'd tried to steal Cam's seat earlier.

"Still no boyfriend, huh?" he asked as though he suspected she'd made up the whole thing.

"He's on his way." Her voice climbed the ladder of desperation. "He'll be here soon."

"Sure he will." The man went back to nursing his beer and tilted his head to see some football game on the television screen across the room.

She was about to flip him off when an incoming text chimed on her phone. From Cam! "It's him," she called, holding up the phone to prove she wasn't delusional.

"Lucky guy," Big Man muttered, rolling his eyes.

"You got that right." She focused on the screen to read the text.

Jessa, I left this morning to move back to Denver.

Wait. *What?* The words blurred. A typo. It must be a typo. Damn that autocorrect.

"What's the word?" Big Man asked. "He comin' or can I take that seat?"

"Um. Uh..." Fear wedged itself into her throat as she scrolled through the rest of the words.

I didn't see a future for me there. In Topaz Falls or with you. Sorry. I know this would've been better in person, but I couldn't do it. You're too nice. I know you'll find the right person. It's just not me.

Yours,

Cam

"Yours? *Yours?*" Ha. That was laughable. Cam had never been hers. Just like the others. Hadn't mattered how *nice* she'd been. She'd been jilted. *Again.* This time by her animal rescue's largest donor. And, yes, the man she'd been sleeping with...because he'd seemed like a good idea at the time. Women had slim pickings around Topaz Falls, population 2,345.

"Is he coming or not?" Big Man asked, still eyeing the empty stool.

"No. He's not coming." A laugh bubbled out, bordering on hysteria. "He broke up with me! By text!"

A hush came over the bar, but who cared? Let them all stare. Poor Jessa. Dumped again.

"It's not like he's a prize," she said, turning to address them all. "He's a technology consultant, for God's sake. Not Chris Hemsworth." Not that she knew what being a technology consultant meant. But it'd sounded good when she'd met him after she found his stray puggle wandering downtown six months ago. Peabody had pranced right up to her on the street and peed on her leg, the little shit. Now, Jessa was a dog person—an *animal* person—but that puggle had it out for her from day one.

When Cam had come in to retrieve his little beast from the shelter, stars had circled in her eyes. He was the first attractive man she'd seen since all those bull riders had passed through town three months ago. So unfair for those smokin' hot cowboys to gather in town and get the women all revved up only to leave them the next day.

In all honesty, Cam was no cowboy. Though his slight bulk suggested he spent a good portion of every day sitting in front of a computer screen, his soft brown eyes had a kind shimmer that instantly drew you in. He'd been good to her— taking her out to fancy restaurants and buying her flowers just because. Also, because she'd saved his beloved varmint from the potential fate of being mauled by a mountain lion, he'd made monthly donations to the shelter, which had kept them going.

Now he was gone.

"I can't believe this. How could he break up with me?"

Everyone around her had gone back to their own conversations, either unwilling to answer or pretending they didn't hear. So she turned to Big Man. "I guess you're happy about this, huh? Now the seat's all yours."

He didn't even look at her. "Nope. I'm good right where I am, thanks."

Oh, sure. After all that, now he didn't want to sit by her? "Fine. That's fine. It's all fine." Raising the glass to her lips, she drained the rest of her wine in one gulp.

"You know what?" she asked Big Man, not caring one iota that he seemed hell-bent on ignoring her. "I'm done." This had to stop. The falling in love thing. It always started innocently enough. A man would ask her out and they'd go on a few dates. She'd swear that this time she wouldn't get too attached too soon, but before she knew it, she was looking up wedding venues and bridal gowns and honeymoon destinations online. She couldn't help it. Her heart had always been a sucker for romance. Her father had said it was her best quality—that she could love someone so quickly, that she could give her heart to others so easily. He got it because he was the same way. Her mother, of course, labeled it her worst quality. *You're simply in love with the idea of being in love*, her wise mother would say. And it was true. Was that so *wrong*?

"Hey, Jessa."

The gruffness of the quiet voice, aged by years of good cigars, snapped up her head. She turned.

Luis Cortez stood behind her, hunched in his bowlegged stance. Clad in worn jeans and sporting his pro rodeo belt buckle, he looked like he'd just stepped off the set of an old western, face tanned and leathery, white hair tufted after a long ride on his trusty steed.

"Hi there, Luis," she mumbled, trying to hold her head high. Luis was her lone volunteer at the shelter, and he just might be the only one in town who loved animals as much as she did. He'd also been her dad's best friend and since she'd come back to town last year to settle her father's estate, she'd spent a lot of time with the man.

Maybe that was part of her problem with finding the love of her life. She spent most of her free time with a sixty-seven-year-old man...

"You all right?" Luis asked, gimping to the stool next to her. Seeing as how he was a retired bull-riding legend, it was a wonder he could walk at all.

"Uh." That was a complicated question. "Yes." She cleared the tremble out of her voice. "I'm fine. Great." She would be, anyway. As soon as the sting wore off.

"Thought you and Cam had a date tonight." Luis shifted with a wince, as though his arthritis was flaring again. "Where is he anyway? I was hopin' I could talk him into puttin' in his donation early this month. We gotta replace half the roof before the snow comes."

Cam. That name was her newest curse word. *Cam him! Cam it!* Feeling the burn of humiliation pulse across her cheeks, she turned on her phone and pushed it over to him so he could read the text. "Cam broke up with me." Luis had obviously missed the little announcement she'd made earlier.

He held up the phone and squinted, mouthing the words as he read. The older man looked as outraged as she was, bless him. "Man wasn't good enough for you, anyways, Jess. He's a damn fool."

"I have a knack for picking the fools." Just ask her mother. Every time she went through one of these breakups, Carla Roth, DO, would remind her of how bad the odds were for finding true love. Her mother had never married her father. She didn't believe in monogamy. *One person out of six billion?* she'd ask. *That is highly unlikely, Jessa.*

It might be unlikely, but the odds weren't enough to kill the dream. Not for her. Neither was the lack of any significant relationship in her mother's life. Jessa had grown up being shuffled back and forth—summers and Christmas in Topaz Falls with her father and the rest of the year with her college professor mother who didn't believe in love, secretly watching old romantic classics and movies like *Sleepless in Seattle* and *You've Got Mail* with wistful tears stinging in her eyes.

"Don't worry, Jess," Luis said in his kind way. "You'll find someone."

Big Man snorted.

Before she could backhand him, Luis gave her shoulder a pat. "My boys ain't married yet," he reminded her, as if she would *ever* be able to forget the Cortez brothers. Every woman's fantasy.

Lance, the oldest, had followed in his father's footsteps, though rumor had it this would be his last season on the circuit. He trained nonstop and had little time for anything else in his life, considering he left the ranch only about once a month. The thought of him married almost made her laugh. Over the years, he'd built quite the reputation with women, though she had no personal experience. Even with her father being one of his father's best friends, Lance had said maybe five words to her in all the years she'd known him. He seemed to prefer a woman who'd let him off the hook easily, and God knew there were plenty of them following those cowboys around.

Then there was Levi. Oh, hallelujah, Levi. One of God's greatest gifts to women. She'd had a fling with him the summer of their sophomore year, but after that he'd left home to train with some big-shot rodeo mentor and rarely came home.

There was a third Cortez brother, but Luis didn't talk

about him. Lucas, the middle child, had been sent to prison for arson when he was seventeen.

"Sure wish I'd see more of Levi," Luis said wistfully. "He ain't been home in a long time."

Her eyebrows lifted with interest. "So, um..." She pretended to examine a broken nail to prove she didn't care too much. "How is Levi, anyway?"

"That boy needs to get his head out of his ass. He's reckless. He's gonna get himself killed out there."

Jessa doubted that. Levi Cortez was making a name for himself in the rodeo world.

"Lance, now, he's the only one of my boys who's got his head on straight," Luis went on. "He always was a smart kid."

From what she'd seen, the oldest Cortez brother had never been a kid, but she didn't say so. After their mom ditched the family, Lance took over a more parental role. Not that she had any right to analyze him. "He's handsome, too," she offered, because every time she did happen to run into him, his luscious eyes had completely tied up her tongue. Yes, indeedy, Lance happened to be a looker. Though it was in a much different way than his cocky brother. "He looks the most like you," she said with a wink.

Luis's lips puckered in that crotchety, don't-want-to-smile-but-can't-help-it grin she loved to see. Her dad used to have one like that, too.

"Anyway...," the man said, obviously trying to change the subject. "What're we gonna do with Cam gone? I assume he didn't leave any money behind for the shelter."

"Not that I know of." Apparently, he hadn't left anything. Not even the toothbrush she'd kept at his house, Cam it.

"You got any other donors yet?"

"Not yet." She'd been so preoccupied with the most recent love—infatuation—of her life that she hadn't exactly made time to go trolling for other interested parties. Her dad had a big heart, but he'd always hated to ask for money, so when she'd come to take over, the list of benefactors had been...well...nonexistent. In one year, she'd already used most of what little money he'd left her to purchase supplies and complete the critical repairs. She could live off her savings for a couple more months, and at least keep up with the payroll, but after that things didn't look too promising. She'd probably have to lay off her night shift guy.

With Cam's generosity, she hadn't been too worried. Until now, of course.

"Don't you worry, Jess. Somethin'll work out." Luis's confidence almost made her believe it. "You're doin' okay. You know that? Buzz would be proud."

She smiled a little. Yes, her father definitely would've been proud to see his old place cleaned up. When she'd finished veterinary school and started on her MBA, he'd been so excited. He'd owned the rescue for thirty years but had never taken one business class. Which meant the place never made any money. He'd barely had enough to live on.

She had planned to change all of that. They'd planned it together. While she worked her way through business school, they'd talked on the phone twice a week, discussing how they could expand the place. Then, a month before she finished school, her father had a heart attack. He'd been out on a hike with Luis. Maybe that was why the man felt the need to take care of her, check in on her, help her fix things up around the house.

Familiar tears burned. She'd never blame Luis, though. That was exactly the way her dad would've chosen to go. Out on the side of a mountain, doing something he loved.

"We'll find a way, Jess." Pure determination turned the man's face statuelike, making him look as pensive as his eldest son. "All we need is some inspiration." Which he always insisted you couldn't find while stuck indoors. "I'm headin' up the mountain tomorrow. You wanna come?"

She brushed a grateful pat across the man's gnarled hand. "I can't, Luis. Thank you."

As much as she'd like to spend the day on the mountain, drowning her sorrows about Cam and the rescue's current financial situation in the fresh mountain air, she had things to do. This breakup had to be the dawn of a new era for her. She was tired of being passed over like yesterday's pastries. To hell with relationships. With romance. She didn't have time for it anyway. She had walls to paint and supplies to purchase and animals to rescue. Which meant she also had generous donors to find.

She shot a quick glance down at her attire. Might be a good idea to invest in herself first. Typically, she used her Visa only for emergencies, but this could be considered disaster prevention, right? She needed a new wardrobe. Something more professional. How could she schmooze potential stakeholders looking like she'd just come from a half-price sale at the New Life Secondhand Store?

"You sure you don't want to come?" Luis prompted.

"I'd love to but I have to go shopping." Right after their book club meeting, she'd enlist her friends to help her reinvent herself so she could reinvent her nonprofit.

By the time she was done, the Helping Paws Animal Rescue and Shelter would be everything her father dreamed it would be.

It would keep the memory of his love alive.

Chapter Two

Easy, now, Wild Willy." Raising his hands in stick-'em-up surrender, Lance eased closer to the barn stall, where his favorite training bull was backed against the wall, snorting and pawing at the ground like he was seeing red. *Fuck.* Sweat soaked the bull's brown coat and for some reason those horns looked even more lethal in the dim light.

On a normal day, he didn't enjoy standing eye-to-eye with one of his bovine athletes—especially before he'd finished his coffee—but this mean bastard had given him no choice.

Just as the coffeepot had started to hiss, Tucker, the stable manager and training wrangler, had come barreling into Lance's kitchen hollerin' about how Wild Willy had gone ape shit in the field. Seemed his favorite cow was flirting with another bull. In the process of proving his manhood by charging Ball Buster, Wild Willy had stepped in a hole and come out of the debacle with a limp. Which meant Lance had the pleasure of assessing the injury to see if they had to call out the vet.

"All over a woman," he muttered. Last he'd checked, he was a bull rider, but some days he felt more like he was stuck on an episode of *The Bachelor*.

"Trust me, fella," he said, easing closer to Wild Willy, who'd calmed some and was now chawing on a bundle of hay. "She's not worth it." Relationships in general weren't worth it. "You're better off alone." Why put in all of that effort when almost every relationship ended with two people walking in opposite directions? Or two cows, in this case. "All right, Wild Willy. Let's get a look at that hind leg." Keeping a safe distance on the outside of the pen, he tested the bull with a sweep of his hand down its flank, which only riled it up again. The dumbass jolted away, slamming its rear end into the wall.

Shiiiiit. Whipping a bandanna out of his back pocket, Lance mopped sweat from his forehead. "You're not gonna make this easy on me, are you?" he asked, backing off to give Wild Willy some space.

The bull tossed its head and snorted a confirmation.

"Don't forget who feeds you. I *own* you." And he needed this big guy right now. Only a few weeks until World Finals, and he had a hell of a lot of work to do to get ready. This season had pretty much sucked. Only one title and a whole lot of back talkin' from fans about how he should've retired two years ago.

"Well, maybe I'm not ready to retire," he said to the bull. Hell, he was only thirty. He could still go out on top. Even with his joints creaking the way they did. He'd ignored pain before, especially when he had somethin' to prove. This wouldn't be the first time.

But it might be the last.

No. Couldn't think about that. Couldn't think about how everything he'd worked for his whole life would likely end after this competition. What would he have after it was over?

Instead of dwelling on that fun question, he faced the bull. He'd rather face a lethal bull than uncertainty any day. "Steady now." He ripped the bull's halter off a nearby nail in the wall. "Don't make me get the tranquilizer—"

"Lance?" A woman's voice echoed from outside the stall. Not just any woman, Naomi Sullivan, the ranch's bookkeeper and all around caretaker of the whole lot of them. "Are you in there?" she called again. And she didn't sound calm.

Raising a finger to Wild Willy's snout, Lance tried to match the crazy in the bull's eyes. "This is not over." He tossed down the halter and stepped outside into the early morning sunlight. The sky was still pink. It cast a bluish haze over the hand-hewn log buildings that made up the Cortez Family Ranch. Smoke still puttered out of the main house's chimney from the fire he'd started in the woodstove last night. That's how early it was. Too damn early for another crisis, but from the looks of Naomi's bedraggled reddish hair and wide green eyes, something had her panties all bunched up.

Naomi had been a family friend forever. The sister they'd never had. So he could tell when she was stressed. And now would be one of those times. "What's up?" he asked, thinking of nothing but the steaming hot coffee waiting in his kitchen.

"Sorry to bother you." She was heaving like she'd run all the way up the hill from her house. She lived with them on the ranch. After her husband had taken off and left her with a baby girl ten years ago, Lance had offered her a job and invited her to move into the guesthouse on the property. Not that she was a charity case. She was damn good with numbers. Always had been. However, she did tend to run high in the drama department.

He gave her a smile to simmer her down. "You're not bothering me. Everything all right?"

She looked around as though torn. "I'm worried about your dad. I haven't seen him since yesterday." In addition to doing the books for the ranch, she kept an eye on his father, which had become a heroic task as of late. As if she hadn't already proven herself a saint, the woman had offered to cook and clean for Luis. She was the one who made sure he took his blood pressure meds.

"He said he was going for a hike and wouldn't need dinner," Naomi went on. "But when I brought over his breakfast this morning, he wasn't around."

Of course he wasn't. Because lately his dear old dad had taken to wandering off without bothering to tell anyone where he was going. If he wasn't volunteering at that animal shelter in town, he was somewhere out on the mountain, head in the clouds as he relived better days.

Naomi wrung her hands in front of her small waist. "I noticed his backpack was gone. Along with his sleeping bag." She reached into her pocket and held up a prescription bottle. "But he left his medication behind."

Which meant a thousand things could've happened to him out there. He could've gotten disoriented. Could've passed out. Could've lost his balance and fallen off a cliff. He was sixty-seven years old, for shit's sake. A fact Lance had to keep reminding him of over and over. He didn't belong out on that mountain alone.

"I'm worried about him." Naomi was on the verge of tears now, and if there was one thing he hated more than having to act like his father's babysitter, it was a woman crying. "Should we call out search and rescue?"

Hell no. He didn't say it, but he wasn't about to call out search and rescue. They'd called those guys six times in the past year, all because Luis Cortez had taken to wandering off alone somewhere on the three thousand acres they owned. God only knew how much of the taxpayers' money they'd already wasted. Not to mention he didn't want to put any lives at risk for a man who was probably just out for an extended stroll.

Lance laid a hand on Naomi's shoulder and steered her back toward her house. Looked like his training would have to wait. Again. "I'm sure Dad's fine. Probably just wanted a night under the stars." That's what he usually said when Lance dragged him back home from one of his impromptu camping trips. A new layer of sweat burned his forehead. If the man kept wandering away he swore he would implant a GPS chip into his father's arm so he could start tracking the old coot.

"What if he's hurt?" Naomi asked, grabbing his arm like she needed support. "Oh God, Lance. I should've checked on him last night. After everything he's done for me, I hate to think of him out there alone."

"Hey." He stopped and turned her to face him. She seemed to worry about everything. Everyone. And he knew the weight of that burden. She didn't need it. She had a daughter to raise. Much as she mothered him, he took it upon himself to protect her, to make sure she didn't have to worry.

"He's *fine*. Don't forget, he does this all the time." His father was worse than an untrained Labrador the way he got distracted and roamed away. "I don't want you to worry, got that? I'll take care of it." The same way he always did.

"How do you even know where to look?"

"I don't. But Jessa might." She spent more time with Luis than pretty much anyone. If it was any other woman, he'd worry she was on a gold-digging expedition, but Jessa didn't exactly scream temptress.

Naomi's face brightened. "Great idea. Jessa will know how to find him."

"Sure she will." He prodded her up the porch steps. "Now you go on in and take care of Gracie. Tell her we can do a riding lesson this afternoon, if she's up for it." Naomi's ten-year-old was currently the only female he chose to spend time with and that was just fine with him.

Naomi shook her head with a wide smile. "*If* she wants to? Are you kidding? You should hear her bragging to all of her friends about how she has the most handsome riding instructor in the whole wide world. She actually told them all you look like Ryder from *Tangled*. You should've heard the squealing." She trotted up the steps to her modest guesthouse and turned back to him with a smirk on her face. "Me? I'd take Gerard Butler. No offense."

"None taken." They'd determined long ago that they'd be a bad fit. Course, he'd be a bad fit with pretty much anyone.

"See you later." Naomi waved him off. "Tell Jessa I said hey. And be nice to her, Lance. I saw her at book club..."

He happened to know that book club was a fancy way of saying wine and chocolate club, but whatever.

"She got dumped again."

Shiiiiit. Wasn't this his lucky day? "As long as she's not crying," he muttered, heading down the road. Boots pounding the packed dirt, he passed the main house, passed that steaming hot cup of coffee waiting in his kitchen, and kept right on movin' until he'd reached his truck, cursing the whole way.

* * *

This couldn't be right. Jessa turned to get a profile view of her body. *Hello!* When she saw that the label on the bra said Bold Lift, she'd had no idea what it meant. In a matter of two minutes, she'd somehow gained at least two cup sizes. She gawked at herself in the mirror. *Wow.* Those babies were really out there. When she looked down at her toes, her chin practically hit her cleavage. Not to mention the straps were already digging into her skin. Why did satin and lace feel so itchy compared to cotton?

Turning her back on the spectacle in the mirror, she gazed longingly at an old cotton bra hanging on the knob of her closet door. But no. *No.* It was time for her to kick it up a notch. She had a lot to offer and she was about to show it to the world.

When she'd called her mother last night to inform her that she'd lost her main donor (carefully omitting the fact that he'd also happened to be her boyfriend), the woman had gotten right down to business. "You'll only appear as professional as you feel," she'd said. Then she'd advised her on how to build a wardrobe that would help her "dress for success."

Jessa had written everything down.

Expensive undergarments. Check! Even though the bra squeezed her tighter than a corset, she'd wear it. Along with the new thong she'd bought to match. Because smart, stylish women apparently wore uncomfortable undergarments.

Carefully avoiding a glance at the backside of her body, she backed out of her bedroom and into the small bathroom. When it came to how she looked in a thong, she subscribed to the ignorance-is-bliss mentality.

After doing her makeup the way she'd learned on Pinterest last night, she dashed to the closet to select one of the new outfits she'd bought. Today was a big day. She'd set up meetings at the local real estate office, the bank, and the town chamber to see about developing some partnerships with businesses in town. Not that any of them had seemed particularly excited to talk to her, but she'd change their minds. Which meant she had to look her best.

To her credit, her mom had never nagged her about the way she dressed, though it was obvious that style had never been important to Jessa. It'd never mattered what she wore, seeing as how she spent her time with animals. She'd been bled on, vomited on, pooped on, peed on…so she'd never actually had a reason to wear nice clothes. Most of her life, scrubs, yoga pants, and T-shirts had suited her just fine.

But Dr. Carla Roth was refined, elegant, brilliant, and incredibly sophisticated. Even as a professor, her mother wore beautiful silk blouses and wrap dresses with heels. At a cocktail party, the woman glittered like royalty. She'd won three of the university's largest grants by simply charming old men at various university functions.

Unlike Jessa, her mother had never had her heart broken. Not once. And that was exactly the kind of woman Jessa needed to become.

Her book club friends—Naomi Sullivan, Cassidy Greer, and Darla Michelson—had been all too eager to help her craft a new look.

The whole group had led her down Main Street, parading

through the clothing boutiques, arms full of adventurous new garments for her to try on.

But now, hanging in her closet, the skirts and brightly colored tunics didn't appeal to her the way they had last night when everyone was oohhhing and aahing at her in the dressing rooms.

She snatched a flowery blouse off a hanger. What did that go with again? Was it the blue skirt? The red capri pants that her friends swore made her look exactly like Katharine Hepburn? All the new colors and patterns in her closet started to blur together in a whorl of confusion. *Whoa.* This could take a while. She needed coffee. Stat.

Leaving the clothes behind, she dashed through the living room to the kitchen and scooped heaping tablespoons of coffee into the French press. The familiar scent of her morning routine soothed the mounting tension from her hands. She could do this. She could match a shirt and shorts, for the love of God. It wasn't rocket science. She had an MBA, Cam it!

After filling the kettle, she set it on the stove and cranked the burner. It was the flowery shirt that went with the capris, right?

Shit. She had no idea. It was time to call for backup. Snatching her cell phone off the counter, she summoned her mother.

"Hello?" Her mother sounded a bit out of breath, which meant Jessa had probably interrupted her morning yoga practice.

"Hi, Mom," she said, glancing down at her body. Come to think of it, she might benefit from a morning yoga practice, too. The only morning practice she embraced regularly involved pastries.

"Jessa?" her mother wheezed. "Is everything all right, honey?"

"Everything's good!" she said, trying to sound chipper. "I bought all those clothes you told me to get."

"That's wonderful! I'm so happy for you." Her mother sounded more relieved than happy. "You're *finally* investing in yourself. It's going to make such a difference. You won't believe what new clothes can do for your self-confidence."

"Yeah. Um. It's pretty exciting." But it'd be even better if she could actually *dress* herself in the new clothes. "So listen. I have some important meetings today and I'm not sure what top to wear with my red capri pants."

"Hmmm..." Her mother mused as though this decision ranked right up there with purchasing a house. "Were you able to find a white asymmetric blouse?"

"Uh—" What was an asymmetric blouse again?

A knock sounded. At the front door. Yes, that would be the door, which was neatly centered between the two large bay windows a mere twenty feet from where she stood. In the kitchen. Wearing only a bra and thong.

Okay. She edged her back against the refrigerator. Sheer curtains had seemed like a good idea when she'd picked them out last year, but she was starting to regret that decision. Clearly, she hadn't thought through the implications of what would happen when she wanted to make herself a cup of coffee dressed only in a thong and Bold Lift bra.

"Jessa?" her mother said loudly. "Did I lose you?"

"No. I'm still here," she whispered.

Another round of hearty pounding pried a squeal from her lips. What the hell was happening? Who'd knock on her door before seven? Was her house on fire or something?

"Honey? Is everything all right?" her mother asked.

"Yes," she hissed. "But I'll have to call you back." Before her mother could answer, she clicked off her phone and set it down. Holding her breath, she stood perfectly still and quiet—minus the loud drumbeat of her heart.

The knocking didn't stop.

"Hello?" A man's deep rumbling voice sent her heart off to the races again. There was something vaguely familiar about it...

"It's Lance Cortez. I need to talk to you."

Lance! Oh. Holy. No. This was *not* happening. She gazed longingly at the other side of the living room to the safe darkness of the tiny hallway that led to her bedroom. There was no way she'd get through there without him seeing *some*thing. Like her ass, maybe. Cam it!

Get the front door with the windows, the ignorant Home Depot salesman had advised. *It'll let in the most light.* Yes, and now it would also give Lance a clear view of a very full moon.

She flattened her body against the cabinets, craning her neck, and sure enough, he stood right there on her front porch, now peering through that lovely window on the door.

Oh, God. Her lungs heaved so hard it felt like the Bold Lift Bra was about to bust at the seams. *Calm down*, she instructed herself. *He'll go away.* He had to go away.

"Jessa! I know you're in there. Your car's here," he called again, rapping the door with that big manly fist of his. "I need to talk to you. It's an emergency."

Tell me about it! Maybe she could call 9-1-1 and have him escorted off her porch...

Footsteps thudded on the front porch, moving closer.

Sweet lord! Lance Cortez was peeking through the bay window!

"Hang on a sec!" she yelled, then hit the deck, pressing her body against the wood floor. Lifting her head, she assessed the distance to the hallway. It might as well have been twenty miles.

Okay. Think. What would Naomi do? That was an easy one. She never would've gotten herself into this situation in the first place because Naomi had the ability to get dressed without the assistance of coffee.

"Jessa, I really need a word," Lance called again.

"Be there in a minute!" Despite the fact that she was basically naked, sweat itched on her back. Her room. She had to get to her room. And there was only one way. She'd have to army crawl. As long as she stayed on this side of the couch, Lance probably wouldn't be able to see her from the window. It was risky, but what other option did she have? He obviously wasn't going away.

Here goes. Trying to remain one with the floor, she squirmed forward, shimmying past the bookshelf. *Squirm, pull, squirm, pull.* She edged against the couch, bare skin grazing the cold wood planks.

Yes. Yes! It was working. Almost halfway now...

A scratch stung her hip as something sharp caught the delicate strap of her thong.

Uh oh. Contorting her body, she tried to get a better look. A loose staple from the re-upholstery job she'd done on the couch had hooked her adorable brand-new panties. *Cam it!* She should've known a staple gun wasn't enough to hold a couch cover together. *Thanks a lot, Pinterest.*

"Jessa!" More pounding.

"Hold on! Give me a minute!" she called, trying to wring the panic from her tone. What the hell was his problem, anyway? Couldn't he take a hint? She pushed onto her side to free herself from the staple, but her legs smacked into the end table. The whole thing toppled over with a deafening crash. *Ow! Shit!* She rolled over, gripping the backs of her calves. At the same time, the thong stretched, ripped, and snapped, falling to the floor underneath her.

"Jessa?" Lance yelled through the door. "What was that?" The doorknob clanged like he was trying to get in. "Is everything okay?"

Hot tears filled her eyes. "Fine!" Minus the throbbing in her legs and the fact that she'd just shredded a fifty-dollar thong.

"Are you sure?" he persisted, the sonofabitch. "That sounded bad. Is the key still out here?"

The key? Oh, dear God, the key! Her dad had always left a house key underneath the flowerpot...

A new wave of terror surged, blinding her with white-hot fear.

The sound of metal clanged in the lock.

"No!" She squealed, scrambling to hide herself behind a small square throw pillow from the couch. "Please! Don't come—"

The door sprang open.

Right as Lance stepped around the couch, she shifted the pillow to cover her lower hemisphere.

"What're you—?" He halted like he'd been shot, his gaze bouncing from her eyes to her bra and then, sure enough, down to the pillow.

"Turn around! Cover your eyes," she wailed. For the love of God! Humiliation curdled into anger. "Why'd you have to come in? Who just barges into someone's house, huh?" Why couldn't he have waited on the porch like she'd asked?

"Uh..." He seemed to be frozen in place. "Sorry. I heard the crash. Thought you were hurt..."

Was he gawking? His lips had parted with surprise. And then there were his eyes. Wide and unblinking. Men didn't usually look at her like that...

"What the hell happened?" he asked, finally finding the decency to turn around and stare out the bay window.

Securing the pillow against her lower abdomen with one hand, she covered her Boldly Lifted chest with her arm in case he decided to peek again. "I had a bit of an accident." She should make something up. Something really exciting. Something like she and a mystery man were playing this kinky game...

"Are you hurt?" Lance asked, his head swiveling toward her again.

She kept herself covered. Oh, yes. She was hurt. On more than one level. "I'm fine," she choked out. "Can you get my robe? It's hanging up in the bathroom at the end of the hall."

"Right. Your robe." He sort of side-shuffled his way down the hall and back, before tossing the robe at her without turning around.

Clutching her salvation, she scurried up to a standing position, the backs of her calves still aching, and wrapped the fabric around her, tying the belt securely at her waist.

Lance peeked over his shoulder as if to check on her, then turned all the way around.

She wasn't sure if she was out of breath due to the terrible thong ordeal or to the fact that the elusive Lance Cortez looked so different up close. She's seen him around town since she'd been back, but she'd never *looked* at him that closely. He'd never looked at her the way he was now, either.

Eyes open slightly wider than a normal person's, lips parted like he couldn't remember what it was he'd wanted to say.

Yes, well, neither could she. Not with the sight of his dark hair, which curled slightly at the edges. It was mussed like he'd been nervously running his hand through it all morning. And those eyes. An arctic blue-gray. Cutting. He wore a dark red flannel shirt with the sleeves pushed up over his bulky forearms. His jeans were faded and worn like he worked hard, which she'd heard he did.

"So..." His voice had this deep soothing reverberation that made her want to curl up against him. "Did you fall or something?"

Or something. "I was in the kitchen making coffee," she informed him, trying to smooth her hair into soft waves like it had been before she'd gone to battle with the couch. "Wasn't expecting anyone to show up at my door..." Especially the enigma that was Lance Cortez. "So I panicked and was trying to get back to my room without giving you a show." Which was clearly too much to ask from the universe.

"Oh." His gaze seemed to fixate on the leopard-print thong that lay a mere two feet from his boots.

As swiftly as possible, she swiped it off the floor and shoved it into the pocket of her robe. "Um. Did you need something, Lance?" Because her humiliation meter was about tapped out for the day and it wasn't even seven o'clock.

"Right. Yes." That intense gaze pierced her eyes. "Dad spent the night out on the mountain and I need you to tell me how to find him."

The news shocked her into stillness. "He spent the night out there?" Luis hadn't said a word about camping when she'd talked to him Wednesday night. Though he did camp occasionally, he usually told her his plans.

"I'm sure he's fine," he went on. "His sleeping bag is gone, which means he planned on being out all night. But he didn't bring his meds."

Though she tried not to panic, her mind hopped on a runaway train car of worst-case scenarios. So many things could've happened to him...he could've taken a fall. He could've gotten turned around. He could've had a heart attack like her father...

Lance's weight shifted. He cleared his throat. "So, have you seen him?"

"Not since Wednesday." It was hard to swallow past the emerging rock formation in her throat. Because Luis had asked her to go up the mountain with him. And she'd said no.

"Are you okay?"

"I'm..." What if something had happened to him and he was all alone because she didn't go with him?

A shrill whistle sliced into her thoughts.

Lance looked around. "You got water on the stove?"

Blinking fast enough to sop up threatening tears, she nodded quickly. "I was making coffee..."

"Coffee sounds great," Lance said. And if that wasn't shocking enough, he sat himself down on her couch.

Heat blanketed her, making the robe feel like a fur coat. He wanted to sit and have coffee with her? While she wore her robe? "But...um...maybe...well...okay..." The words stumbled over one another, mimicking the erratic beat of her heart. *No. Don't you dare*, she told that stubborn thing.

No matter how beautiful Lance Cortez was, she was done with romance.

Chapter Three

He'd only stayed for the coffee, so he'd best stop looking at Jessa like she was on the menu.

Lance did his best to reel in his tongue and crank his jaw closed. But... *damn.*

It had to be the thong. And the bra. And the robe. Who knew Jessa Mae Love owned sexy lingerie? Not him. It would've been better if he'd known, if he'd been prepared to see her like that—all half naked and done up like a no-strings-attached fantasy. Her legs were much longer than he'd ever realized. Long, tanned, and defined. Lethal combination. Must be all of that hiking she did.

Though he knew better, his gaze followed her to the kitchen. Yes, Jessa had spent every summer in Topaz Falls for as long as he could remember. He'd known of her, even a little bit about her, considering their fathers were more like brothers than friends. He'd seen her around the ranch, but he'd never looked at her too closely. How could he have ever missed that bust, which he'd gotten a nice view of before he remembered his manners and turned away. He may not get out much, but he was still a man. And he had perfect eyesight. He noticed things like that. Somehow on Jessa, he'd missed it until the moment he'd seen her lying on the floor. All of a sudden, there they were, two perfect breasts staring him in the face, and he was awake on a whole new level. Even without coffee.

The unrecognizable woman in front of him—could he even call her Jessa anymore?—worked quickly in the kitchen, clutching the top of the robe like she wanted to bolt it together. He almost wished she could.

After she'd removed the screaming teakettle from the stove and poured water into a French press, she sort of scuttled past him. "I should go change," she said in a huskily sexy voice that didn't seem to fit her. Or at least it hadn't. Before the lingerie...

"I'll throw on some clothes," she went on, nervously shifting her eyes. "Then we can talk about Luis."

Yes. Clothes. That would be best. Because if she put on more clothes, maybe he could focus on something besides these details he'd never noticed about her. Like the soft way her blondish hair cascaded past her shoulders. Or the way her earnest, unsure, brown-eyed gaze had stirred something inside him. Instead of answering her, he simply averted his eyes and nodded, giving her permission to go, giving himself space to get his shit together. Because he'd just spent a good five minutes checking out Jessa Mae Love. Town animal activist. Best friend to his sixty-seven-year-old father. Which was weird.

God, this was so weird...

"Um. Be right back." Her skin blotched bright pink before

she whirled and scampered down the hall, that short robe riding up enough to make his eyes pop open wider so he could get a better look before he checked himself again. Jessa Mae Love. He tried to picture her the way he'd always seen her—wearing tan hiking pants, a T-shirt, hair pulled back tightly into a ponytail, and those eyes obscured by thick-rimmed glasses. But the image kept morphing back into sexy robe babe. No way would he get her out of his head now.

He pushed off the couch and did a lap around her living room to get the blood flowing somewhere besides his crotch.

Trying to distract himself from the action happening in her bedroom down the hall, he looked around. The house was the typical 1940s bungalow. Jessa's father, Buzz, had lived there for more than thirty years. A few years ago, his father had dragged Lance to a poker game here. Back then, dark wood paneling covered the walls. A hazy smell of cigar smoke contaminated the furniture. It'd been the typical elderly bachelor pad—everything old, moldy, and most likely purchased from garage sales. But Jessa had really lightened things up.

She'd painted the wood paneling bright white and knocked down the wall that used to separate the kitchen from the small living room. There were pops of orange and turquoise in pillows and curtains. Instead of trinkets, a wall of white bookshelves was filled with academic-looking hardbacks. He paused in front of the white sofa and studied the picture that hung on the wall behind it. Jessa and Buzz standing on Topaz Mountain. He leaned in closer. She had on the typical Jessa uniform—pants and a loose-fitting T-shirt—but on closer inspection, it did appear that the woman had always been more well-endowed than he'd given her credit for...

"Sorry that took so long."

He spun, knocking his knee on the edge of an old trunk that acted as a coffee table, and held back the wince.

"I'll get the coffee. Should be done now," she murmured, nervously fisting her delicate hands.

"Sounds good." His head *was* pounding for a hit of caffeine, but the rest of his body pounded for different reasons. Apparently, Jessa had suddenly decided to start wearing shorts. Short shorts and a faded V-neck T-shirt that pointed his gaze to the very spot he'd been trying to avoid.

"Have a seat." She gestured to the couch and sashayed across the room and into the small kitchen.

For the second time that morning, he had to remind himself to close his mouth. He sank to the couch, glancing at the picture book on her coffee table instead of her ass. Which was shaped and firm, he couldn't help but notice. And if he sat here much longer, he might be tempted to do more than notice, which meant he should fast track this little meeting.

With that in mind, he shifted forward, widened his stance, and rested his elbows on his knees. "So, got any idea where my dad might be?"

"I'm not *exactly* sure," Jessa answered, working quickly to fill two mugs in the kitchen. "But if I had to guess, I'd say he's somewhere up near the north ridge."

"And the north ridge is...?" His face heated. Yes, he owned the land, but he never had time to get out and explore it. Not the way Jessa and his father did.

"It's about eight miles up the mountain." Carrying two steaming mugs, Jessa walked—no *swayed* those curvy hips—back across the living room and handed one to him. She sat on the very edge of a leather chair opposite the couch. "I saw him Wednesday," she said, her brown eyes reddening. "He asked me if I wanted to go up with him. And I said no." The last word teetered on the edge of a whimper.

Oh, shit. Don't do it. Don't cry. "He'll be fine," he said before a tear could fall.

Jessa bit into her lower lip. Something he might like to try sometime...

"I thought he'd ask Tucker to go with him since I couldn't. No one should be out there alone. Ever." A tear did slip out then, and he shocked himself by reaching over to cover her hand with his. Not because he wanted to touch her. Hell no. That had nothing to do with this. Her dad had passed away last year and it obviously still got to her, that's all. He could imagine how that would feel. Didn't know what he'd do if he lost his own father. "Dad's out there all the time," he reminded her. "He likes to be alone. And it's not your responsibility to babysit him." That burden rested solely on his shoulders. And with his training schedule, he hadn't done much of a good job of it lately.

Jessa stared at his hand covering hers like she didn't quite know what to make of it. Yeah, neither did he. So he withdrew it, lifted the coffee mug to his lips, and took a good long sip. Heaven. It was liquid heaven. Bitter but creamy. Exactly the way he made it for himself. The realization shook him up again. He set down the mug before he spilled it. "You put a tablespoon of cream in it." Real cream. None of that fake flavored shit.

Jessa startled, her eyes worried. "You don't like it?"

"No. I mean...yes." He paused to unscramble his thoughts. "That's exactly how I make it." But she hadn't asked him if he wanted cream.

A soft smile plumped her lips and made them look as delicious as the coffee. "That's how Luis drinks it every day at the shelter. I figured maybe that was how you liked it, too."

"Good guess." He sipped again, hoping the caffeine would clarify his thoughts, because they kept wandering and now was not the time to get distracted by a woman. He had to find his dad so he could get back to the ranch and take care of Wild Willy. Otherwise he wouldn't be able to resume his training and then he'd be five hundred miles up shit creek.

"So he didn't tell you where he planned to camp?" Jessa asked, crossing those long legs. Her voice had a formal ring to it, like she was about as uncomfortable with the current situation as he was.

He focused on his coffee. "No. But he does this all the time." Definitely more than Jessa knew about.

"He can't sit still," she said through a fond smile. "He hates to be confined."

"Yeah, well, if he doesn't start sitting still more often, I'll *have* to confine him." He couldn't watch the man 24/7. Not with Worlds coming up.

Not that he needed to have that discussion with Jessa. He'd already said too much.

Lance finished off his coffee and plunked the mug onto the trunk. "So can you tell me how to get up there? To the north ridge?"

"There's really no easy way." She stood and collected their mugs, rushing them to the kitchen. "You'll have to take the ATV up most of the way," she called as she rinsed them in the sink. "Until the talus field. Then you go on foot about another mile or so until you see the outcropping."

The what huh?

She traipsed back to her chair and sat. "Then you run

into the boulder field." Her eyes glittered with excitement. "That's where it gets fun."

"Sounds simple." Yeah, about as simple as getting his body to behave when he took his gaze to the point of her V-neck shirt. Holy hell. This was gonna take him all day.

"It's actually pretty complicated. I'll have to come with you," she murmured, the rounded apples of her cheeks flushing with an intensity he'd never seen on her face. Of course, he'd never really looked before.

"You want to come?" His mouth went dry. He'd have to spend the whole day trying not to notice how sexy she suddenly was?

"I *have* to come. There's no way you'll find him on your own."

Damn it all. She was right.

* * *

Jessa did her darnedest to stuff down the worry that threatened to make her seem overdramatic. Lance was so calm about the whole thing. So sure his father would be fine. Luis went out on the mountain all the time. Sometimes alone. He knew the terrain. Knew every survival skill he'd ever need...

She gazed out at the peaks from Naomi's front porch, where she and her friend had gathered to wait for Lance to bring down the ATV. The mountains looked beautiful, powdered with snow at the very tops, the late fall sun casting a spotlight on every chiseled detail. *He'll be fine*, she told herself again, trying to mentally separate today from the trauma of last year. And yet her stomach refused to settle.

In an attempt to distract herself, she filled Naomi in on her eventful morning.

"Let me get this straight." Her friend's luminous green eyes doubled in size. "Lance came *in*to your house. Sat on your couch. And had coffee with you?" she repeated for what had to be the fifth time.

Jessa's skin warmed as though the high-altitude sun was beating down right on her face, but nope, they were nice and shaded. It was simply a hearty Lance Cortez–induced blush. Not even the brisk mountain breeze could douse it, though goose bumps prickled her legs. God, she shouldn't be wearing shorts on a search-and-rescue operation. But they'd left her house in such a hurry she hadn't even had time to change into more appropriate attire.

A few feet away, Naomi's sweet daughter, Gracie, sang to herself on the porch swing.

Jessa leaned in close so the girl wouldn't hear. "*Yes*. He came into my house. And I was naked," she moaned, reliving that humiliating moment when Lance had stepped around the couch and the bottom fell out of his jaw.

Naomi's eyes narrowed in a way that quirked her lips. "Better naked than wearing your old hiking pants," she offered.

"Thanks." She'd hoped a quick chat with her friend would bolster her confidence, seeing as how she had to spend an entire day with Lance and somehow not succumb to her typical awkward ways, but so far the woman wasn't helping. "This isn't funny! You should've seen the way he looked at me." At first he'd looked shocked, then it seemed more like lust, but then, as he'd finished his coffee, his expression had looked almost disgusted. "I don't think he likes me very much."

"Lance doesn't like anyone," Naomi reminded her. "But that's why this is so perfect."

"I'm not following." This didn't sound perfect to her. She had to spend a whole day with someone who didn't like people. And he was so beautiful to look at. Which meant she was guaranteed to make a fool out of herself again.

"He's tough to read," Naomi admitted. "But it's the perfect opportunity for you to try out your new look. See if you can win him over. It'll be great practice for finding donors for the shelter."

Now it was her turn to laugh. "Win him over? Lance Cortez?" That was like a duck trying to win over a lion. "Do you know me at all? I have no clue how to charm a man."

"Well you coulda fooled me," her friend said, looking her up and down. "Seriously. You look hot. The contacts, the makeup, the hair…" She reached over and fluffed the soft waves Jessa had blown dry earlier. "You've always been beautiful, and now everyone's going to know it."

Jessa smoothed her hair nervously. "I'm not sure it'll make much of a difference."

"Trust me," Naomi insisted. "It *will* make a difference. You look great," she emphasized. "Pretty soon you'll have donors lined up down the block."

"If you say so." But after Lance came over, she canceled all of her meetings. Donors weren't her biggest concern today. Not right now. She squeezed her friend's hands, feeling her own tremble. "Do you really think Luis is okay out there?" she asked, almost breathless. Memories of getting the phone call that her father had collapsed out on the mountain bore down on her.

"I was worried, too, honey," Naomi said, not letting go of her hands. "But Lance is right. His dad is a true mountain man. He's not lost. He's not missing. He just needs to be more responsible and remember to bring along his medication next time."

"Right." She nodded as though the words had alleviated her fears.

"You and Lance will find him," Naomi went on, turning back to the driveway.

Somewhere in the distance, an engine sounded. Nerves gripped Jessa's stomach. She hoped so. She hoped they'd find Luis right away. She also hoped she could spend the day with Lance and somehow resist that dark, hot cowboy thing he had going on...

But when he came speeding around the corner on the ATV, dirt flying from the wheels, that hard body tensed and strong, her heart floated away from her again.

He skidded to a stop in front of the green lawn and pulled off his helmet.

"Uncle Lance!" Gracie squealed, launching herself off the porch and into his arms just as he stood.

Laughing, he swung her around, and that smile on Lance's face—the unguarded expression of happiness—bolted Jessa's feet right to the wooden planks beneath her. Then and there her heart dissolved into warm mush and something inside her sang. She knew she could never see him the same way again.

Lance glanced over at her, some of that messy dark hair spilling over his forehead, and their eyes locked. The singing turned into a warm hum. It was like that scene in *West Side Story*, when Tony and Maria first see each other across the dance floor. Everything else blurs into a meaningless background and it's just the two of them, staring longingly into each other's eyes. Well, she was longing. It was hard to tell what he thought.

Lance was the first to blink. "Hey, Jessa," he said casually, like the universe hadn't just exploded into a million glittering diamonds that made everything sparkle. Was she imagining it or did his voice gentle the syllables of her name?

"Hi." Jessa nearly sighed.

"All right, buckaroo." Lance set a still-giggling Gracie gently on the ground. "I've got to go. But we'll get to that riding lesson later."

The girl's eyes were sparkling the same way Jessa imagined hers still were. "Promise?" Gracie asked, hands clasped underneath her chin, the little charmer.

"Pinkie swear." He held up his little finger to finalize the deal and Jessa could've sworn her ovaries ached.

Naomi pushed her from behind, and it was a good thing because otherwise she might've stood in that spot all day long staring at Lance.

"So you two have a good time," her friend said, giving her another good nudge in his direction. "Let me know as soon as you find Luis. Tell him I'll have his lunch waiting."

"Will do." Lance looked at her. "Ready?"

No. She was clearly not ready, seeing as how she could feel her heart starting to wander away from her again. Somehow, with one look, Lance had obliterated her ambition to put romance on the backburner.

Oh God. If that had happened with one look, how would she spend the whole day with him? She shot a desperate look at Naomi, but her friend only nudged her toward the steps, her whole face beaming a calculated smile.

As if she knew Jessa was already in over her head.

Chapter Four

White-hot rays of sun cut across his vision and blinded Lance the second he turned back to the ATV. It was a damn good thing the sun blinded him, too, because *something* had to direct his attention away from Jessa so he'd quit noticing how the brightness lit her long, sleek hair. And how her hips swayed in that womanly way. Not to mention how her tanned legs tensed with her steps, shaped and strong but delicate, too.

Damn those shorts. Who the hell wore shorts on a rescue operation, anyway?

Someone with sexy legs, jackass. Not like it was a crime. The woman was allowed to wear whatever she wanted. He never used to care what she wore before. Until sexy robe babe, that is. He kept his head down and navigated the path across Naomi's lawn. *Man.* His father owed him for this mess. If the man would've stayed put, he never would've had to call on Jessa. Never would've noticed her sex appeal. *This is Jessa Mae*, he reminded himself for the hundredth time.

Blinking against the morning sun, he casually sauntered to the driveway. Jessa had already made it to the ATV, booking it down the walkway as if she could feel the snort of a pissed-off bull on her tail. Seemed she wasn't thrilled about spending the day with him, either. When she'd seen him swinging Gracie around, the woman's face had been stony and expressionless. She'd stared at him for a full minute at first, and her eyes had avoided him ever since. Kind of the way he attempted to carefully avoid looking at her. But that was about to get a lot harder because dear old Dad had taken the other ATV out for his little escape, which meant there was only one left. For him and Jessa. To ride together...

Without glancing back at him, she plunked one of the helmets onto her head and tugged the chinstrap into place. Then she swung a leg over the machine and took the handlebars in her hands, staring straight ahead.

"What are you doing?" Lance asked quickening his pace.

Jessa cranked on the handle, starting the thing up. "I'm driving," she yelled over the engine noise.

He skidded to a stop. "*You're* driving?" He hadn't counted on... spooning her from behind.

"You don't know where to go," she yelled again, handing over his helmet like she wanted to get this over with. "I bet I know exactly where he went."

He reached over her and shut off the engine. "You can tell me where to go. *I* should drive."

Jessa didn't budge, but she threw up the face shield on her helmet. "I've been up there a lot more than you have. *I* know the terrain."

"And *I* can handle the ATV," he said, before he thought

better of it. Not that he wanted to insult her, but she was pretty petite to maneuver a machine like this. Especially with the weight of two riders.

Fire filled her narrowed eyes. "I'm driving," she said, turning the key to start the engine back up. "So you can either get on the back or I'll go by myself."

"Fine," he ground out, pulling the helmet down so she wouldn't see the scowl that tightened his face.

Careful not to touch her, he eased his leg over the seat and slid on, bracing his hands against his thighs, unsure where else to put them.

Jessa glanced over her shoulder. "You need to hold on," she advised him, flicking the helmet's shield up so he could gaze into her exotic brown eyes. They flashed with determination but wouldn't quite meet his.

"I am holding on." To himself. That was much safer. He didn't want to feel her soft skin beneath his fingertips. Didn't want to feel anything for her at all.

With a slight shrug, Jessa flicked down the helmet's face shield and turned back to the handlebars.

He clamped his legs tight and secured his feet on the ATV's sturdy base. That'd be enough to hold him in place. How fast could Jessa possibly drive any—

The engine squealed then clinked, there was the grind of metal gears, and they shot off like a missile on target.

"Shit!" His arms flew up and before the momentum threw him right off the back, he wrapped them around her waist, pulling his chest against her back to steady himself.

Her shoulders tensed against him, but she kept her head straight, focused on driving, and it was a damn good thing because they must've been going twenty miles per hour straight up the side of the mountain. "You always drive like this?" he growled over the wind. He'd have to think twice about letting her and his father go up the mountain together again.

"I just want to get there," she yelled back, turning enough that he could see the worry tensing her jaw.

Right. She'd lost her father only a year ago. On the same mountain they were currently blitzing up. And he couldn't imagine that...losing his dad. He'd already lost Lucas, then Levi. One by one the people he'd cared about had walked out of his life. If he lost his dad, he'd lose everyone who mattered. Everyone he had left. Friends weren't the same. Parents anchored you to your heritage, reminded you who you were when it got hard to remember. Far as he knew, Jessa didn't see her mom much. She'd been close with her dad. An ache snuck into his chest as he peered at her profile. Beneath her helmet, her face had hardened into a mask of desperation.

He didn't like seeing her that way. Worried. A little scared. It did something to him, made sympathy prickle through him, which made his arms soften around her...more like he was holding her instead of holding on for dear life. "Hey." He leaned in close so he wouldn't have to shout so loud. "He's all right." This was Luis Cortez they were talking about. The man who'd wrestled a mountain lion off one of his horses, according to local legends. "He's probably gonna be all pissed off that we came up here after him." In fact, he knew his dad would be pissed.

The ATV slowed, then stuttered to a stop, reducing the engine noise to a low hum. Jessa glanced back at him. "Do you really think so?" she asked in a small wobbling tone. Even with the face shield in place he could see the paleness that had taken over her complexion.

"Yeah." He flicked up his face shield, then went for hers so their eyes could lock. So he could reach through her fears. "And I'll tell you one thing," he said with a smirk. "I'm riding down the mountain with *him*."

A shadow of a smile flickered across her lips. "You don't like my driving." The revelation seemed to amuse her. "That's surprising considering you ride maniacal bulls for a living."

"That's a hell of a lot safer than sitting behind you on this thing." He meant that in more ways than one. Because the sun haloed her in a mystifying glow and for the first time ever he realized she wasn't only pretty. Jessa was stunning—beautiful and real and deep.

"Hey," she scolded, her eyes narrowing. "I'm being safe. I'd never endanger—"

"I'm teasing you," he interrupted before she got her leopard-print thong all bunched. "Trying to lighten things up."

"Oh." She looked down.

"I'm not worried about him, Jessa," he said more softly. "Really. The only reason I rushed over to your place was because he doesn't have his blood pressure medication." He grinned at her. "That and I've gotta get back to my training. The sooner we find him the sooner I can get back on my bull."

"Right. Thanks, Lance." Jessa's eyes shied away from his, unsure and guarded and humble. She cleared her throat and lowered the shield to cover up her delicate face, which definitely wasn't pale anymore. Color had shaded her cheeks with the same heat he felt flickering somewhere deep.

Her scent reached him, floating into the cloud of exhaust that had started to dissipate. Some type of vanilla, but light and subtle. It'd been a while since he'd inhaled a woman's scent and a sigh expanded through him, ending in a sharp pain that descended behind his ribs. He'd lusted after plenty of women. The buckle bunnies who'd followed him around the circuit in the early days, who'd always made good on their promise of offering him a fun, uncomplicated night. That had been a different kind of ache, though. It'd never traveled any farther north than his brass belt buckle.

"Ready then?" she murmured, the words muffled. Scooting herself into position, she clamped her hands onto the handlebars again, then cranked the engine.

"Ready." Heart pulsing in small bursts of a long-forgotten desire, Lance threaded his arms around her waist again, letting her back rest against his chest, this time with no hesitation.

* * *

Heaven help her, Jessa had to start focusing on something besides the way Lance's hardened muscled chest shielded her back. The way his sinewed arms guarded her in a strong embrace. *Something else … something else …*

The cool, crisp air. The rays of sun poking through white puffy clouds overhead. Pine trees, tall and gangly. *Shit!* She dodged one that seemed to jump out of nowhere, jerking the handlebars in a way that brought Lance even closer.

"We almost there?" he asked through her helmet. And yes, she'd be the first to admit that the last twenty minutes of her driving hadn't been the best in her life. But he was the one to blame for that. Being all sweet to her. Draping his body all over hers from behind. That had made it a bit hard to concentrate on not hitting broad tree trunks or massive boulders. "Getting close," she yelled so he wouldn't hear the tremble in her voice.

She'd sworn off men, damn it. Sworn off love. All well and good in her head, but God, she wished she could cut out her heart and leave it behind. Already it had ballooned in her chest, rising higher, soaring with the same sappy emotions that had gotten her into so much trouble in the past. And who was she kidding? Lance. Lance Cortez! Bull-riding god who'd been known to shack up with the groupies who made it their life's mission to sleep with a bull rider. Or all of the bull riders. She swore those women kept a checklist in their back pockets.

That thought was all it took to deflate her heart. It couldn't take more disappointment. More pain. Lance Cortez had a certain reputation. Rumor had it that he'd never spent a full night with a woman. He'd slept with plenty of them, but he never stayed in their bed until morning. Remembering that made it easier to focus. They were out here to find Luis. That was all.

Standing up a bit, she peered over the next small rise. This was one of the trickier spots. She slowed the ATV, easing it up the side of a steep incline so Lance wouldn't be thrust into her again. They were getting close to the boulder field, the place she and Luis always parked when they hiked together.

Easing herself forward, she made a futile attempt to put space between her back and Lance's chest, leaning over the handlebars as she navigated the rocky slope. Just as they crested the rise, a smear of blue caught her eye. Luis's ATV. She plowed straight for it, then cranked the brake, skidding to stop right next to it. Hands shaky and tingling, she ripped off her helmet and let it fall to the ground. "He's not here." She glanced around. They were high enough that the trees had thinned; only an occasional gnarled pine tree twisted from the snow and wind during the harsh winters. But there was no sign of Luis. No backpack. No evidence of a camp.

"He must've gone off on foot," Lance said from behind her.

An ominous feeling swept over her, thinning her breath. She stared at the boulder field, the scattered granite that stretched all the way to the mountain's pointed summit. "I thought we'd find him here." She'd been so sure. They'd gone off on foot many times, but always in different directions. And there weren't many places to camp past this point. The terrain got rocky, steeper. Less than a mile up from this place was the spot where her own father had collapsed. Where his heart had given out. Panic fluttered her nerves.

"He couldn't have gone very far," Lance said, coming up beside her, seeming to assess the land. "Looks pretty unforgiving." For the first time gravity weighted his tone.

"It is," she whispered. She and Luis had hiked around here. Once, she'd even gotten him to take her to the spot where her father had died. Tears bit at the rims of her eyes.

From here, it took about another twenty minutes to hike up to the place Luis had taken her father that day. Was that where'd he'd gone? Did he visit the place often? Was it still as hard for him as it was for her? Before she could stop them, the tears spilled over in warm streaks, sadness flowing out of her once again.

"Hey." Lance rested a hand on her shoulder. "You okay?"

"Yes." But the tears kept streaming out and she was powerless to stop them. "Sorry," she muttered, annoyed with herself. She hadn't counted on this being so hard. "I'm worried." And God, she missed her father. Missed being someone's little girl.

Taking her shoulders in those large manly hands, Lance helped her climb off the ATV and turned her to face him, crouching so their eyes were level. "Dad's fine. Trust me. I know."

"How?" she whimpered.

He shrugged, shook his head a little. "This'll sound crazy, but he and I have this connection. If something was wrong, I'd know. I'd feel it."

The words almost prompted a sob. Why hadn't she known? The day her father had died, she'd gone about her life, seeing her furry patients, meeting her roommate for a drink during happy hour. That's where she'd been when she'd gotten the call. She should've felt something...should've felt the loss even before she knew. He was her father.

She gazed at the boulder field, everything blurred and gray despite the bright sunshine, and once again she wondered if he'd suffered. If he'd been in pain. If he'd been scared. Luis hadn't told her much, couldn't seem to talk about it. But he'd said her father had gone ahead and was already on the ground by the time he got there.

"Don't cry, Jessa." Lance held her face in his hands and swiped away the tears with his thumbs. "Like I said, he's okay. I know it. We'll find him."

She nodded, attempting to sniffle back a year of sadness. "I believe you." And yet she couldn't get a grip, not up here so close to her dad's final moments. "It's just...my father." She swallowed so hard her throat ached. "Sometimes it's hard to be up here." God those tears burned her eyes. "I wish I would've been with him. I wish I could've been holding his hand when he...:" She couldn't bring herself to say it. It was so horrible. So, so horrible to think of him out here in pain and terrified as the world dimmed and life faded from his body. Instinctively, her hand reached up to finger the necklace he'd given her. It had been his last gift. A rose gold heart with a small diamond embedded inside.

"It's real pretty," Lance said, looking down at the charm. "He give it to you?"

She nodded, tensing her throat so her voice wouldn't wobble. "I miss him. I should've been around more."

She half expected Lance to lecture her on living in the past, on not letting the regrets take over, like so many other people had done. Instead, he pulled her against him, wrapping her up in the comfort and peace of a long, sturdy hug. And despite the potential dangers, she let her head rest against him. She breathed in the calming scent of leather and coffee.

"I wish I knew what those minutes were like." The minutes before he closed his eyes and gave in. Maybe that would bring her peace. Maybe it would give her the permission to let her regrets go.

Lance moved back slightly and took her chin in his hand. She felt the roughness of his skin, the calluses, the coarseness of scabs from healing scrapes. Gently, he tilted her head up until she was staring straight at the sky. So blue, the color itself seemed alive, bottomless in its perfection. Fluffy clouds billowed and moved and floated, a fluid dance. And the sun, so bright and clear it seemed to make everything sparkle.

"That's what he would've been looking at," he murmured, the deep vibration of his voice close to her temple. "The sky, the mountains."

Jessa let her eyes soak it all in until she felt so full with

the beauty and wonder of the world, she had to close them.
"It's beautiful." Didn't matter how many times she saw it.
This view, these mountains, that endless royal sky always
struck her. And her dad had loved it, too. He would've
wanted this to be the last thing he ever saw.

"It's peaceful up here," Lance said, looking up, too.
"Maybe a little what Heaven's like."

The words held a gift, a surprise ray of hope that pene-
trated her doubts. "You believe in Heaven?"

Those lips quirked in a small smile, and even though he
was so dark, with that mussed hair and tanned sun-drenched
skin, his eyes were lit with energy. "I like to believe there's
something more."

More. The word spread over her like a healing salve, al-
leviating the lingering throb from the wounds of loss. All
these years, she'd been wrong about Lance. She'd thought
him to be closed off and grouchy, a man of few words who
got annoyed easily, but now she realized she'd misjudged
him. He might not do small talk, but a seven-word sentence
from Lance meant more than paragraphs from most people.

Her eyes opened and color flooded in. The first thing she
saw were his lips, right there, inches from hers. The tendons that threaded her joints together loosened and sparks
crackled in her heart. She inhaled his musky scent, let her
gaze rest in his. Such beautiful clear eyes. Deep and wise.
And yes, she seemed to be moving in closer now but she
couldn't fight that pull, couldn't stop the hard cry of need
and desire that pushed her into him. Her palms came to rest
on his chest as her lips grazed his. But that one light touch
wasn't enough. Wasn't nearly enough...so she went for it—
a full-on kiss, lips fused to his, sighing, searching...

Except his chest tensed and he seemed to step back. An

icy realization splashed her face, dousing the passion that had ignited. Lance didn't want to be kissing her. He'd offered her a kind word because she was upset. That was all.

That was all.

Throat thick and pulsing, she slowly eased back, the warmth that had bathed her lips turning cold.

Lance stood stock-still, his own lips parted, arms out as though he'd lost his balance, chest suspended like he wasn't sure if he should breathe in or out.

"Oh my God." Invisible flames of humiliation licked at her cheeks. "I'm so sorry." She'd freaking kissed him! Less than a day after swearing off men, she'd let that swirl of emotion and desire and hope sweep her up into its kingdom of seduction. Her skin tingled. The sunlight seemed too bright. "I didn't mean to...I shouldn't have..." *Kissed* him. On the lips. Like they'd been transported into some sappy chick flick. They were supposed to be searching for Luis! Holy baldheaded cats, what the hell was the matter with her? She couldn't even go one day without swooning. She needed help. Romantics Anonymous. *Hello, my name is Jessa and I'm addicted to love...*

Might as well face it.

Lance simply stood there, saying nothing, an unreadable expression frozen on his face.

Not surprising. He was clearly in a state of shock. Or disbelief? Repulsion? It was impossible to tell. That fight or flight survival instinct kicked her hard under the ribs. "We should find your dad," she said quickly, turning so he wouldn't see the fierce blush that had brought her about two inches from passing out. "Let's go this way."

With desperation in her steps, she tromped toward the boulder field before she could screw up anything else.

Chapter Five

Two seconds ago, he could've sworn Jessa's lips were pressed to his, warm and wet and the slightest bit naughty. If it hadn't been for the smear of some honey-flavored lip gloss on his bottom lip, he would've thought he'd imagined the whole thing because she was gone. As in out of sight. And he was still standing in the same position he'd assumed when she knocked his world off its axis and kissed him.

Shit. He'd screwed that up. Royally. Who could blame him, though? He'd never expected *Jessa* to press herself against him and kiss him. Never expected the rush it brought in him, either. She'd caught him off guard, knocked him off balance. And yes, he could see how stiffening and stepping back may have sent her a certain message, but it was a reflex. Either regain balance or land on his ass. His body had reacted and made the choice for him.

He squinted in the direction that Jessa had stormed off.

The boulder field was sloped and she'd already disappeared on the other side of the rise. "Jessa!" he yelled, not exactly sure how to find her. But he had to. Had to find her, somehow undo the awkwardness he must've made her feel. And they still had to find his dad, too. So he stepped off the way she'd gone, trying to follow her path. He skirted around a hunk of granite as tall as him. Went over a smaller boulder, then hoisted himself up and gazed around. *There.* She was weaving her way through the rocks about thirty yards up.

"Hey!" he called again. "Wait up." He climbed down, trying to formulate an explanation in his head. Except he didn't have one. Usually when women started crying in front of him, his forehead would crank itself tight and he'd slowly back away, scanning for a fast escape. But he kind of hadn't minded comforting Jessa. He certainly hadn't minded the feel of her soft breasts against his chest and her silky lips locked on his...

In fact, he didn't mind this whole excursion as much as he'd thought he would.

Though Jessa slowed her pace, she didn't stop to wait for him. Her chin had lifted with determination, her eyes focused ahead and her arms swooshing at her sides.

The sight drew out a smile. Sure, he felt bad that she seemed embarrassed, but God she was captivating with that fortitude. Continuing on like the whole thing hadn't bothered her at all. He'd met women before who would've whined about his reaction, who would've gone for the guilt trip. Not Jessa. She'd simply hauled off and left him standing there like she didn't need him anyway.

By the time he'd closed in on her, he was out of breath. "Are you okay?" He tried to hide the wheeze in his lungs through a hearty throat clearing.

"Spectacular," she muttered, stomping on.

His hand snagged her shoulder and forced her to stop. "Come on. It's not a big deal." At least it shouldn't have been. Hell, he'd been kissed by his fair share of women. A couple had even caught him off guard before. None had rendered him unable to walk, however. Or to think straight. His eyes searched hers.

They were dark, but the sunlight made the flecks of bronze in them glisten. There was a force in her gaze. She didn't shy away or narrow her eyes angrily at him. She simply stared back, open and unfazed.

"I was surprised," he admitted, leaving out the whole truth. Surprised and thrown off balance by his body's fast response to her. "And I—"

"Can we forget it?" she interrupted. "Please? I'm just emotional. Maybe even a little hormonal this week. You know how it goes."

"Uh." No. He didn't. He *really* didn't.

"And let's face it," she went on. "You're PDF, so it's not my fault, exactly."

"PDF?" he repeated. He sucked at acronyms. Had to use Google to decode most of Levi's Facebook posts. He'd never been good with words. *PDF...PDF...* "Poor dumb fool?"

Those glistening baby browns rolled. "Pretty. Damn. Fine. Don't you get out?"

"Not as much as you would think," he admitted. Lately he hadn't gotten out at all. He was supposed to be training his ass off.

"So you can see how something like that would've happened," she said, lifting her chin again. "The emotions. The whole smoldering cowboy thing you've got going on. But I'd really appreciate it if we could forget it. Like, completely erase it from our memories. Because, Lance, I've sworn off men. Romance. All of it, really. Gotta shift my focus, you know? Don't need it messing up my life anymore. So please. This never happened."

He'd never enjoyed a woman babbling. Ever. Until today. "Okay. I guess. But—"

"Nope. See, 'but' is a segue back into the same topic we just agreed to forget. As in never mention it; never even *remember* it. We entered into a verbal agreement, which can be legally binding in the state of Colorado," she finished, looking quite proud of herself.

"Can it now?" He didn't even try to hide his amusement. He'd known Jessa for years. Or at least he'd known about her. To him, she'd always been Buzz Love's daughter, the gangly girl with the glasses. He thought her to be nice though somewhat shy, maybe even awkward. But they'd never had a real conversation before this morning. She was actually fun to talk to.

"Yes," she uttered with a definitive nod. "As a matter of fact it can."

"What if I said go ahead and sue me?" He pressed his gaze into hers again. "Because I'm not sure I'll be able to forget. I didn't *mind* you kissing me."

She laughed. "Right. You didn't mind." The words mocked him. "Your shoulders felt like concrete. And the way you stepped back...I actually thought you were gonna bolt." But she waved a hand through the air as if it didn't matter. "Listen, I get it. You're Lance Cortez. Sort of famous. Rugged. Hot. I'm just Jessa. Normal girl who smells like animals half the time."

Not right now she didn't. Right now she smelled like the vanilla beans Naomi sometimes set around his father's kitchen. And what was wrong with normal? Kind of refreshing to have a woman say things like they were instead of what she thought he wanted to hear for once.

"Besides all of that, I've sworn off kissing." She turned away and started to hike again, giving him no choice but to follow.

"That seems a little extreme." He kept his eyes focused on the ground so he wouldn't trip over a rock and look like a dumb ass. "Isn't there something else you could swear off? Sugar? Chocolate? Alcohol? Seems to me kissing is one of those things that's actually good for you." Especially when it led to sex. Weren't there a bunch of health benefits associated with sex? Sure seemed like it. Not that kissing Jessa would lead to sex. Because how weird would that be? Having sex with this woman who hung out with his father? Who wanted marriage and kids and the whole bit so badly she'd been engaged multiple times? His body didn't seem to think it would be weird, though. The quick flash of a conjured image was enough to activate the launch sequence. Steam seemed to radiate off his face and cloud the brisk mountain air.

"Actually, I happen to think alcohol and chocolate are much healthier than kissing. At least in my experience," Jessa insisted, scrambling to climb over a tall boulder that blocked their path. She moved effortlessly. Her feet and hands knew exactly where to go. While she finessed it, he awkwardly scaled the thing with sheer strength.

When they'd gotten past the obstacle he slipped in front of her. Wouldn't be as easy for her to get around *him*.

"So that's it then," he challenged.

"That's it." Her gaze didn't waver and he didn't doubt that she meant it.

"Oh, wait. Actually, one more thing. I'd really appreciate it if you didn't say anything to anyone else. The girls would *kill* me if they knew I'd already slipped up and—"

A shrill whistle cut her off. For a second he thought he'd imagined it, but then it rang out again.

"Luis," she whispered, gripping Lance's coat. "That's your dad."

* * *

"How do you know it's him?" Lance jogged alongside her, seeming to be hardly out of breath while she hiccupped and gagged on the thin mountain air.

"He told me if I ever needed help out here, I should whistle exactly like that," she sputtered, clutching at the pains needling her chest. And then Luis had said he'd find her. He'd told her if he ever heard that whistle, he'd rescue her. A second wind lifted her head and churned her legs faster. "We have to find him." Her eyes drank in the endless blue-gray peaks spread all around them. He could be anywhere. Who knew where that whistle had echoed from...

The shrill sound pierced the air again. They were getting closer. Jessa skidded down a steep section of loose talus, losing her balance and flailing to catch herself.

Lance held on to her arm. "Take it easy. Don't need to do two rescues."

She ignored him, ripping out of his grip. "He's in trouble," she wheezed, her heartbeat throbbing in her temples. Luis was in trouble and he was alone.

Another whistle veered her to the left. She slowed to pick her way down a boulder-strewn slope. So close. It sounded so close...

"There!" Lance darted in front of her and pointed toward a huge rounded boulder.

She strained to see.

Luis stood near it, still and alert.

"Are you okay?" blared from her mouth with surprising force, given how she could hardly breathe.

The man spun and relief whooshed in, filling her lungs, calming that surge of adrenaline. He looked like the same Luis, nothing broken, nothing bleeding. His white hair was bedraggled, but other than that, he seemed fine.

Lance made it to his father before her. "What the hell, Dad?" Now he did seem to run out of breath. And he looked pale, too. Rattled. Like maybe he'd been as worried as her on their little sprint down here.

Jessa doubled over to catch her breath.

"What's the problem, son?" the man asked, clearly clueless as to how worried they'd been.

"What's the *problem*?" Lance's tone inched toward a yell.

"We thought something terrible happened to you," Jessa broke in, before Lance could jump all over him. "You were gone all night. And no one knew where you went." She wasn't yelling, but a bit of a whimper snuck through. If anything had happened to him—

"Course I was gone all night," he said, as ornery and gruff as ever. "I have every right to go out and camp on my land whenever the hell I want."

Jessa cut a glance at Lance. His face had gone red. Molten.

"The hell you do," he ground out. "It's not safe for you to come out here alone."

Now that she agreed with. What if her father had been out here alone when he'd had the heart attack? They never would've known what had happened to him. They may have never found his body. She pressed the back of her hand against her lips before a sob snuck out.

Luis seemed to assess her with those watery gray eyes. "I didn't mean to worry anyone," he said more gently. "I'm fine. Everything's fine."

"Then why were you whistling?" she whispered, still battling how the memories of her dad and her relief at seeing Luis swirled her in a fog of emotion.

"Can't find the damn ATV," Luis said, gazing around. "Woke up at sunrise and been lookin' for it ever since. Left it parked right here. I know I did. Someone must've taken it."

"No," Lance snapped, his body rigid. "Actually you didn't leave it right here."

The worry that had just started to dissipate clouded Jessa's heart again. "You parked it where we always park," she said, studying him, searching his eyes for a sign that he remembered. "Over on the east side of the mountain."

Luis simply blinked at her. He looked...confused. Disoriented. And she'd never seen him that way out here. He always knew where things were, which direction was which, how to get from one point to another. On all of their hikes, he'd been the one to lead her.

"This *is* the east side," he insisted, with a stubborn lift to his stubbled jaw. "I ought to know. This is my land."

She glanced at Lance, but he simply shrugged it off. His head tilted to the right. "Topaz Mountain is right there, which means that way is east. You must've gotten turned around." Whirling, he pointed toward the ridge. "The ATVs are this way. Let's go."

Luis stepped off, too, hiking up the backpack that held all of his gear and passing his son as though he had something to prove. Jessa followed behind, watching him, and something was definitely off. His feet seemed to be stumbling more than usual. Was his balance unsteady?

When Luis had gotten far enough ahead of them that he couldn't hear, she jogged to Lance. "Something's not right," she said.

"Tell me about it." He shook his head. "He can never admit when he's wrong about anything."

She tugged on his arm until he stopped and faced her. "That's not what I mean."

"So what do you mean?" he asked, inching into her space. He was so broad she couldn't see around him. His thick callused hands came to rest on his hips.

Her heart fluttered like a caged butterfly searching for a way out. "I just... I've never seen him get turned around out here."

Once again, Lance's shoulders lifted in that laid-back-cowboy shrug. "It could happen to anyone. Especially if he didn't sleep all that great. He's probably tired."

No. It'd happened to her multiple times but it didn't happen to Luis. She glanced at the older man, still stalking toward the east side of the mountain in a huff. "What if something's wrong? Health-wise or something?"

Sympathy softened Lance's eyes. "It's not like what happened to your dad. Nothing's wrong. I see the man every day. Trust me. He's healthy as a horse."

A sigh sank in her chest. Maybe Lance saw only what he wanted to see. "What if we hadn't come looking for him? How long would it have taken him to find his way?" Or would he have wandered off and gotten lost? If he couldn't even find the ATV, what else would he forget?

"He would've found his way eventually," Lance insisted, as though he was unwilling to consider the alternative.

Well, it was easy to see where he'd gotten his stubbornness. Jessa raised her head and stared him down. "I don't think he should go out alone anymore."

"I couldn't agree more," he said, checking behind his shoulder as though he wanted to make sure his father was out of earshot. "Which is why I'd like you to stay with him for a while."

Her mouth fell open. "Excuse me?" She must not have heard him right.

"I can't babysit him every second. Not for the next few weeks. I'm training for Worlds."

Right. The biggest competition on the bull-riding stage. A laugh tumbled out. "So you want *me* to babysit him." Did he even realize how ridiculous that sounded?

Lance took a step closer, and it wasn't fair how those large silvery eyes of his could look so pleading. "He already spends most of his free time at your rescue thing anyway."

Rescue thing? Heat swathed her forehead. "I'm pretty sure you meant to say my father's animal rescue organization, which happens to be his legacy." *You hot jackass.*

"Right." His lips twitched as though he was trying to hold back a smile. "That's what I meant. You already spend a lot of time with him. We can tell him your house is being fumigated or something and you can move in with him for a few weeks. The upper story of his house is furnished and everything."

"Oh, well in that case." She let the sarcasm in her tone speak for her. "Are you crazy? The man is sixty-seven years old. He's not going to let me babysit him." If he realized what was really going on, Luis would have a conniption.

"He likes you," Lance countered, his eyes melting into some kind of irresistible plea. The same one she often saw on wounded animals. Good God. Sometimes life just wasn't fair.

"In fact, I think he might like you better than he likes me," he said, going for the kill shot with a delicious little smirk. "I can't keep my eye on him when I'm out training. And I don't trust him to be alone. Can't have him wandering off anymore."

Under the power of his gaze, her will had started to cave, but she shook her head, desperately holding on to the shard of pride she had left. "No. I'm sorry. I *do* have a life, you know. I can't drop everything and babysit your—"

"I'll give you half of my winnings," he interrupted.

Jessa staggered back a step. This was absurd. "I won't take your money."

"Fine, then. I'll donate it to your shelter. Half of everything I win at Worlds."

Half of everything? She didn't know much about bull riding, but she knew those purses were worth a lot of money. "That's . . . wow . . . a chunk of change . . ."

He stepped in closer, lowered his head to hers. "I'm gonna win this year. I just need the time to train."

Determination had steeled his face, his voice, and she didn't doubt he'd win. He'd won a World title before, though it had been years back. But he was the real thing—the rider who persevered through every injury, through every disappointment. And given how disappointing she'd heard the past year had been for him in the arena, he'd do whatever it took to get one more title. "I don't want to take your winnings." But she kind of did, too. Not for herself, but for the shelter. That'd give her plenty to make the repairs and improvements they needed, to buy supplies and upgrade their facility until she could establish a good donor base.

"I'm not doing it for the money," Lance uttered, his voice full of conviction.

No. It clearly went much deeper for him. She could read it in his eyes. He had something to prove to the world. She'd seen the articles in the town newspaper. She'd heard what everyone was saying. While Luis had somehow managed to continue competing as a living legend until the age of thirty-eight, they thought Lance had lost his spark. Some people in town said he should've quit a long time ago. How would that feel? To always be stuck in the shadow of your great father? To have the world thinking you're done before you're ready to be?

"Please, Jessa," he said laying a hand on her forearm and effectively wiping out her last scrap of dignified resolve. "I need your help." Judging from the twitch in his jaw, those might've been the most difficult words he'd ever managed to say.

Yeah, who was she kidding? She couldn't say no to the man. Couldn't turn down a large donation to the shelter.

"Fine. I'll do it," she said, starting to walk past him.

On one condition, she should have added. That he'd steer clear of her so she wouldn't lose her heart again.

Chapter Six

Topaz Falls didn't exactly offer much in the way of nightlife. Not that Jessa had ever minded. Since she'd moved here full time last year, her idea of nightlife had been snuggling up with whatever animals she was caring for at the time and enjoying a rom com movie marathon from the comfort of her couch. But one Friday evening last winter, as she was getting settled in for one of her favorites, she realized she was out of chocolate truffles and she simply couldn't watch the fabulous *Chocolat* without any chocolate. So she'd thrown on a hat and a coat and braved a blizzard to walk eight blocks to The Chocolate Therapist, the town's only confectionery and wine bar.

Normally the town was dead at nine o'clock on a snowy Friday night in December, and sure enough The Chocolate Therapist had been closed. Her heart had sunk until she'd noticed a light on somewhere near the back of the store. In a move of desperation, she'd knocked on the door.

The owner, Darla Michelson, had answered. She had one of those friendly inviting faces, with dancing blue eyes and smile lines instead of crow's-feet, all framed by an unruly but adorable nest of curly black hair with hip red streaks. In a halo of light, Darla had hurried to unlock the door and when Jessa explained the situation, the woman had invited her in and had not only filled up a takeout box with the creamiest, loveliest truffles she'd ever seen, Darla also invited her to stay for the book club meeting she was hosting in the back room.

She might not have if she hadn't been freezing, if her pinky toes hadn't been numb. The prospect of staying somewhere warm and cheerful, with that rich chocolate scent billowing all around her, far outweighed the cold, lonely walk home. Darla had taken her coat and poured her a glass of mulled wine that tasted like Heaven. Then she'd taken her into a small back room, which happened to be set up like the coziest living room Jessa had ever seen. There were an overstuffed couch and two lopsided recliners clustered around an antique coffee table. Happy pink and green pillows freshened up the worn sofa while polka-dotted lampshades brightened the whole space.

Cassidy Greer, who was a local EMT, and Naomi had popped off the couch enthusiastically to greet her. They were so warm and friendly, bright rays of sunshine in the winter of her lingering grief. That night, for the first time since her father had passed away, the feeling of loneliness that had shrouded Jessa fell away and the first signs of spring started to bud in her heart.

After that, every week, she headed to The Chocolate Therapist, and it really had become her healing. The chocolate and wine, yes of course, but even more so these women who'd become like her sisters. Maybe it was their shared grief. Darla had lost her husband to cancer two years before, which made her a young widow at thirty-four. Sweet young Cassidy had lost her brother Cash in a bull-riding accident five years previously. And Naomi had been left behind by a husband who wanted nothing to do with her or their amazing daughter. That first night, they'd bonded. Pain has a funny way of bringing people together, and they'd spent the whole night sharing their life stories over countless mugs of mulled wine and God only knew how many boxes of truffles. They were all so different—on the book side of things Darla preferred straight-up smut, Naomi was addicted to self-help books, Cassidy read only suspense and thrillers, and Jessa, of course, was all about sweet character-driven romance novels that told idyllic stories with happy endings. Their vast differences didn't matter, though. They hardly ever discussed the books they were reading, anyway. Every discussion somehow diverged into talking about life, their problems, and the joys or hurts or triumphs they were facing.

Jessa had never had a group of friends like that before, with whom she could say anything she wanted without guarding herself or considering how silly or ignorant or pathetic she might sound. With them she could just be.

So when Darla called an extra meeting, Jessa had hurried right over, expecting to discuss their latest selection. But instead of their normal discussion, it had started to feel like an interrogation. Like always, they were gathered around the coffee table. Red sangria had replaced the mulled wine once the snow had started to melt. Tonight, Darla had made the most addictive chocolate-covered strawberries—white, dark, and cinnamon flavored. Everything had been going wonderfully, until Jessa mentioned Lance's proposition. That's when the gasps and questions had started.

"Lance asked you to move in with him?" Naomi demanded, dabbing a smear of chocolate from the corner of her lips.

"Isn't that a little fast?" Darla chimed in, leaning over to refill her sangria for the fourth time in an hour. Owning a wine bar means you build up quite the tolerance.

"Yeah, you've been on only one date," Cassidy added. Though she had the most somber blue eyes Jessa had ever seen, Cassidy's grin revealed her dimples. She was the quietest in the group, but also could win the award for the wittiest. Not to mention the most reliable. She covered weekends at the shelter so Jessa could have some time off.

They were teasing, she knew that, but she wished she could fan the blush away from her face. The truth was, she knew it was a bad idea, moving to the ranch, babysitting Lance's father for the next couple of weeks. Especially with the way Lance affected her. She'd kissed the man after being in his presence for all of an hour. Not that she could let these women ever find out. She'd never hear the end of it. They were already teasing her enough. And that had to stop before she crumbled and told them everything.

Trying to maintain an air of indifference, she leaned back into the couch cushion as if their chatter didn't faze her. "First of all, he didn't ask me to move in with *him*," she said for at least the fifth time. "He asked me to move in with his *father*."

"That's not weird or anything," Cassidy quipped, sharing a look with Darla.

Jessa gave the women a look of her own. "Second, we have *not* been on any dates. This is strictly a business ar-

rangement." And she intended to keep it that way. All she'd
have to do is recall the repulsed stiffening of his upper body
when she'd gone to kiss him. That should make it easier.

"He's already seen you naked," Naomi pointed out before
popping another strawberry into her mouth.

"Bet he wouldn't mind seeing that again," Cassidy teased.
"Like tonight. In his bedroom."

Jessa squirmed. Could not let herself go there. Lance was
off-limits. So was romance. And sex. Definitely sex because,
in her opinion, those two things went together.

She picked up her glass and took a sip to cool herself
down. When was the last time she'd broken out in a sweat
simply sitting still?

"I've always wondered how Lance would be in bed,"
Darla said, licking the chocolate covering off a strawberry.
She tended to wonder that about everyone. Did a lot of ex-
perimenting, too, though she claimed she'd never fall in love
again. "I bet he's rowdy." She bit into the strawberry with a
gleam in her eyes.

"That's something I hope I never have to hear about,"
Naomi answered sternly. Though she was close to Lance,
Naomi had been Lucas Cortez's high school sweetheart until
he'd gone and gotten himself sent off to prison for arson. She
still talked about him sometimes, though. Seemed to wonder
what could've been, like everyone does once in a while. Or
more than once in a while if you were Jessa. Which is exactly
why she'd sworn off men for now. "You can tease me all you
want, but nothing is going to happen between Lance and me."
He'd made it perfectly clear. "He promised to donate money to
the rescue. That's the only reason I agreed." That and Lance's
ridiculously convincing wounded puppy eyes.

"Maybe he wanted you around more," Naomi suggested.

Jessa only laughed.

"I'm serious," her friend insisted. "I never dreamed he'd ask someone to move to the ranch. He usually avoids people at all costs." She tilted her head and studied Jessa in a way that made her want to hide. Naomi had one of those intense gazes that made you wonder if she could read your mind. "But he obviously doesn't mind having you around. Which is a little suspicious. He could've asked *me* to keep a better eye on Luis. I already live there."

"You've got enough to do," Jessa shot back, refusing to let hope root itself in her heart. "He knows Luis and I are friends. That's all it is." He knew the man wouldn't put up a fight if Jessa moved in. Luis would do anything for her and his son knew it. "Couldn't be better timing, actually," she said in her best businesslike tone. "Because I'm not interested anyway." Or at least she shouldn't be. Therefore, she'd simply avoid Lance, keep an eye on Luis, and start making plans to upgrade the shelter. That would keep her busy, and before she knew it, the time would be up.

"If your face gets this red when you're not interested, I'd hate to see what happens when you *are* interested," Darla said sweetly.

"It's warm in here," she lied. Actually, there was a wonderful cool breeze floating through the open window.

"I have a feeling it's about to get hotter," Naomi said, elbowing Darla. The three of them laughed in that happy tipsy way.

Jessa fought off another blush with a sip of sangria. She held an ice cube in her mouth and simply rolled her eyes at them, denying that thoughts of Lance generated any heat within her. Which only made her skin burn hotter.

She had only one more night to fix that problem.

* * *

His father had gotten older, no doubt about that. Lance
eyed him from across the kitchen table. Wisdom pooled
in the grayness of the man's eyes, but they sagged, too.
Jagged lines that had started as crow's-feet at the corners
now fissured down into his cheeks, which were wrinkled and
spotted with age. Most times he didn't look at his father's
face for too long, but now he forced his gaze to be still, to
note the details, the changes.

If it were up to him, he'd still see Luis Cortez the same
way he had when he was a boy. He used to stand on the
corral fence whooping while his dad rode, his spirit and
strength a force Lance had dreamed of one day harnessing
himself. Didn't matter how many times he was thrown, his
father always got up, shook off the dust, and shoved his
foot right back in that stirrup. Nothing could break the man,
nothing inside the corral and nothing outside the corral, either. Even after his mother had left and Lance had worried it
might break them both, Luis had simply soldiered on. But no
one was indestructible. Not even the toughest cowboy. Life
wears on you, little by little, not shattering you all at once,
but chipping away from the inside where the damage isn't
always visible. Lance had lived enough to know that.

"What're you still doin' here?" Luis asked, scraping the
last of the eggs and crumbled bits of bacon off his plate and
shoveling them into his mouth. "I thought you'd be training
on Ball Buster this mornin'."

"I'm waiting until Jessa gets here." And trying to figure
out how time had gone so fast, how his father had gone from
an unbreakable wrangler to an old man who lost ATVs. He
shook the thought away. It was age, that's all. Old people

forgot stuff. It was bound to happen to Luis sometime. Lance reached for the coffeepot and poured himself a refill. "You're okay if she stays here for a while?" he asked, cupping his hands around the mug. The robust scent sparked the memory of drinking coffee with Jessa yesterday, which conjured up the images of her lying almost naked on the floor again.

"Why's Jessa coming?" his father asked from behind a blank stare.

Worry dulled his body's sudden arousal. "We talked about this last night." Maybe the man's hearing was going out...

"Right," Luis said gruffly, eyes cast down at the table as though he was trying to remember.

"Her place is being fumigated," Lance reminded him. "She's got an insect problem."

Luis grunted his disapproval. "She shouldn't have to pay for something like that. What's she got? I could take care of it for free."

A grin broke through Lance's concern. His dad might be aging, but he'd never quit striving to be the hero. Age couldn't take away something like that. "She wanted to leave it to the professionals this time," he said before Luis could ask more questions. "So can she stay here or not?"

"Course she can. Got that whole upstairs that don't get used anyway."

"Great. She should be here by eight." At least he hoped she'd be there. She'd sure left in a hurry after they'd gotten Luis back down the mountain. He'd hoped they'd have time to go over the plan, but next thing he knew, Jessa was gone.

"Well, I'd best get moving." His father stood and carted his dishes to the sink. "I was gonna head up for a hike before I mend the corral fences later on."

Shit. Lance had meant to have a little talk with him about the whole hiking alone thing last night, but hadn't gotten around to it. Okay. He'd completely avoided it. But it looked as though it might be time to force the issue. He stood, too. "I don't think it's a good idea for you to go up the mountain on your own anymore."

Right on cue, his father's shoulders straightened. "Pardon?"

"You forgot where you parked the ATV," Lance said, trying to be careful.

"I didn't forget," Luis shot back. "I was this close to finding it." He held an inch of space between his thumb and pointer finger. "Another ten minutes and I would've been on my way down. You didn't need to come find me."

Of course not. Luis Cortez didn't need anything from anyone. Lance tried to quiet the fight rising in his father's eyes. "All I'm saying is, I'd like you to take somebody with you. What if something *did* happen? I don't want you out there alone."

"Nothin's gonna happen," his father insisted. "I don't need a babysitter out in my own backyard." He went to walk away but Lance stepped in front of him.

"I'll get you a satellite phone then." With a GPS tracker. That way he'd always be able to find him.

"I'm not bringing a phone into the wilderness. I go to get away from that shit."

"Come on, Dad. I'm just—"

A knock sounded at the front door.

"Good morning," Jessa called through the screen.

Sighing out the disgruntled annoyance, Lance gave his father a look before winding through the living room, then down the hallway to the front door.

Jessa stood on the other side. She was dressed differently—more like the old Jessa, in a faded yellow T-shirt and long hiking shorts. Her feathery blond hair had been loosely pulled back and that easy smile was intact. Lance had an urge to hug her. Somehow the sight of her made his body lighter. She was so…easygoing. And that was a rarity in his life at the moment.

"Hey." He stepped out onto the porch and closed the door so his father wouldn't hear anything.

"Everything all set?" she whispered. Her hand curled over the handle of a small wheeled suitcase.

"Yeah. I told Dad your place has an infestation. He's fine with you staying a few weeks." As long as he never found out the real reason…

"Great." She went to pick up her suitcase, but Lance reached out and snatched the handle before she could grasp it. It was light, as unburdened as she seemed to be. "One other thing you should know. I was trying to talk to him about not going up the mountain alone anymore," he half-whispered.

Jessa laughed and somehow the heartiness of it tempted him to join her.

"Bet that went over well," she said.

"Yeah. Not so much." But just being near her for two minutes had purged the tension from his head. "I told him I'd get him a satellite phone, but he wasn't interested."

"I'll work on it," she promised.

He set down the suitcase. "Thank you."

"I can't make any promises. He might not listen to me, either."

"No." He stepped closer. "Thank you for being here. For doing this."

"Oh." She stumbled back a step as if she'd been caught off guard. "Sure. It's nothing."

That was the biggest understatement he'd ever heard. "Actually, it's a lot. And I really appreciate it." She had no guarantees going into this. She didn't know if he'd win, if she'd get anything out of it. Somehow that made it more generous. "There's no way I could handle all of this on my own with the finals coming up," he admitted. Hell, he'd have to put in twice the training hours as those twenty-something guys he was going up against or he'd be humiliated on the biggest stage in bull riding. And there it was...his greatest fear worming its way to the surface of his life. That he really was washed up and too old like everyone said.

"I'm happy to help," Jessa said, smiling again but still keeping her distance. "I love your dad."

She might love his father, but after the awkward exchange yesterday, she didn't seem to want to be anywhere near *him*. Unfortunately for her, Lance wasn't in a real big hurry to get inside.

"Besides that," she went on, "you promised me enough money to make a difference at the shelter. And I happen to think you'll win."

"Really?" She'd be about the only one in the world.

"Sure." She seemed to look him over, size him up. "You've got more experience than those young guys, which means you probably have more composure. You know what to expect. And it looks to me like you're still in pretty good shape." Her eyes shied away from his. "So yes. I think you'll win this year."

The words left his tongue fumbling for something to say. It's a gift when someone believes in you at a time no one else does. When you've lost some of the belief in yourself. Before he could say anything, the front door opened.

"Jessa." Luis already had on his hiking backpack, the stubborn bastard.

"Morning, Luis," she greeted warmly as she leaned in to hug him.

His dad's face seemed to soften whenever Jessa was around, as if she were the daughter he'd never had. "I was headed up the mountain," Luis said, nowhere near as ornery as he'd been with Lance.

Her eyes lit with genuine excitement. "I'd love to come with you. Maybe we should bring the fishing poles."

"Good idea," Luis agreed, already clomping down the porch steps. "Lance can get your things to your room."

"Oh, perfect. Thank you." She winked at Lance and it said so much, that they were co-conspirators, allies, and maybe even friends.

Clutching her light, carefree suitcase in his hand, he turned and watched the two of them hike up the driveway.

Jessa had come for his father, to watch over him, to take care of him. So why did he want her to be here for him, too?

Chapter Seven

So far so good. Jessa tossed another fence post into the ATV's trailer and clapped her gloves together. Clouds of dust puffed into the air, disappearing against the sky's blue radiance. So far she'd managed to avoid Lance all morning. The hike with Luis had eaten up a good three hours, and it had been nothing short of spectacular—the sky clear and blue, just the right breeze sighing through the pine trees. Luis had been in top form, his pace quick and his footsteps sure. Without even a slight hesitation, he'd led her right to the pond nestled into the swell of land at tree line, and between the two of them they'd caught five rainbow trout. Hers had been the largest, she'd pointed out. Luis had simply smiled in his long-suffering way.

Her concerns about being in such close quarters with Lance had started to dissipate with the morning's chill. This wouldn't be so hard. Luis liked to keep busy and the two of them would spend a good portion of time at the shelter during the week. That would leave little time for running into Lance. This morning when she saw him on that porch, a whole flock of butterflies had migrated into her chest, nesting all around her heart and humming with that tantalizing purr. That's why she couldn't allow herself to be close to him. Not alone, anyway. She didn't trust herself one iota. Something else took over when Lance gazed at her. Some*one* else. Her inner slut.

"You got all those posts loaded up already?" Luis careened around the corner hauling a sledgehammer over his shoulder, and for the life of her she couldn't figure out what she'd been so worried about. Apparently the whole getting lost in the mountains thing was an isolated incident because today, Luis looked strong and determined and completely capable. There was nothing feeble about him.

Jessa glanced into the shed where she'd been searching for the fence posts he'd asked for. "I think that's all of them." When Luis said he had to mend some fences on the property, she'd jumped at the chance to help him, just in case he had any more balance issues. But he seemed fine. Plus, it had given her an excuse to hide in the shed and stay busy so she wouldn't risk a Lance sighting.

"All right, let's head on up to the corral then." Luis slid onto the ATV, but Jessa froze next to it.

The butterflies still hibernating in her chest stirred. "The corral?" As in the place where Lance would be training?

"Yeah. Got a bunch of fences all but fallin' down up there." Luis cranked the handlebar and the ATV roared to life. "Gotta get 'em fixed up 'fore one of the horses gets out," he shouted above the noise.

He released the brake and nodded her over. Jessa moved slowly toward the ATV, like her shoes were made of lead.

She'd promised to help Luis with the fences, so she couldn't back out now. Hopefully Lance would be so busy he wouldn't even notice her.

She climbed onto the ATV and buckled her arms around Luis's waist.

Instead of peeling out and tearing up the driveway like he so often did, Luis eased the ATV along. He peered back at her. "Is there somethin' goin' on I don't know about?"

Her shoulders locked. Had he figured out this whole thing was a sham? "What do you mean?" she managed to reply without an echo of fear. Lance would kill her if Luis found out what they were doing.

The ATV stopped. Luis turned his upper body, those wise eyes studying her. "I mean you and my boy seem to have gotten close," he said behind a hint of a smile. "I was surprised when he asked if you could stay with me."

She gulped back a relieved breath. "We're just friends. He's trying to help me out."

The man gave her a nod, then turned around and they puttered along again. "I wouldn't be put out. If it was more than that."

She forced a laugh but it felt like the beef jerky they'd snacked on earlier had gotten stuck in her throat. There *shouldn't* be anything more. He'd backed away when she kissed him, and given the man's reputation, anything more would only lead to heartbreak for her. "Nope. Nothing more." The bat-shit crazy butterflies in her chest called her bluff.

Thankfully, Luis let it go. She'd never been a good liar and had never been good at hiding her emotions, either. They always made their way to her face, out there for the world to see. Which was why she couldn't face Luis. As soon as he parked the ATV, just down the hill from the corral, she slid off and started to unload the fence posts, working with a repetitive precision. She would not look at the corral. She would pretend it wasn't there. She would—

"Come on, Uncle Lance! Hold on!"

Jessa's head snapped up and her eyes honed in on the very scene she'd been trying to avoid. Oh, hell-to-the-no. Across the corral, Gracie stood on the second fence rail, teetering precariously on her sparkly pink cowgirl boots while she gripped the top rail with her hands. Naomi stood next to her, body set as though ready to catch her daughter. Tucker, the Cortez's stable manager, stood next to Naomi, eyes glued to a stopwatch.

Before she could stop herself, Jessa darted her gaze to the right and yes, ladies and gentlemen, there was Lance Cortez in all of his bull-riding glory. Chap-clad legs cinched down over the steer's wide girth, back arched, free arm whipping over his head in a graceful rhythm. Sweat drenched his blue T-shirt, making it cling to every chiseled muscle, and that black cowboy hat on his head made him look downright dangerous.

The maniacal bull snorted and jackknifed his body, but Lance held on, those powerful arms fully engaged, and God they had to be as big around as the fence posts she was loading. Then there were his hands. There was something so seductive about large, rugged hands skilled in the art of holding on. She'd like to bet they were skilled in other arts, too.

A slow heated breath eased out as she thought about all of the places those hands could hold her body.

Lance continued the dance—that's how he made it look, graceful and choreographed—riding that steer like he owned it. In complete control.

Wooooowwww. She couldn't move. Couldn't take her eyes off him.

His body was actually built for this, muscle stacked on muscle, tendons as thick as ropes. The more the bull bucked, the more Lance seemed to come alive.

Awe surged through her, nearly buckling her knees, turning her arms weak.

The fence post dropped from her hands and slammed onto her toes. Pain shredded through her feet.

"Ow!" she screamed as she fell to her knees to push the thing off.

The post rolled down to the ATV.

"Oh no!" she heard Gracie screech. "Hold on, Uncle Lance!"

Jessa looked up. Lance had turned his head in her direction, which threw off his form. The beast below him bucked and kicked its legs in the air.

Jessa scrambled to her knees.

Lance was trying to recover, hands both grasping, but his body was being tossed violently. With a final snorting fury, the bull threw his head back, a horn connecting with Lance, then leaped and sent him flying toward the fence.

"Oh God!" Jessa shot to her feet and hobble-ran the perimeter. It was horrible seeing him sprawled there. He could be dead!

Tucker was already out in the corral, luring the bull away from Lance. Somehow Jessa managed to squeeze herself between the fence posts and sprint to him, but her foot caught a rock. Momentum pitched her forward and launched her right on top of Lance.

His wide eyes stared into hers. They were open. And he was breathing.

"Are you okay?" she choked out. The lingering pain in her toes throbbed with the fast pulse of her heart.

"Of course I'm okay," he said with an amused smile. "That's not the first time I've been tossed, Jessa."

His eyes were so pretty. Grayish blue with heavy thick lashes.

"Are *you* okay?" he asked, lifting his head.

Oh. Right. She was still lying on him. "I'm fine," she said quickly, rolling off to the side, then standing before he could get a glimpse of the humiliation that radiated across her face.

Lance stood, too. His shirt was torn and blood stained the right side beneath his chest plate.

"You're bleeding." She reached out to touch the wound, but he stepped back quickly.

"It's fine. Ball Buster caught me with his horn. Again, not the first time."

So back off, his movements seemed to scream. The same humiliation that heated her face traveled down her throat. She glanced around. Naomi and Gracie were staring. Luis was on the other side of the fence watching the whole spectacle. Tucker had corralled the bull and was now gazing at her and Lance, too. The same question seemed to have stumped all of them: Why had she panicked and run to him when no one else watching—even the ten-year-old—seemed the least bit concerned?

Why indeed.

"I'm sorry," she half-whispered. "I mean, I thought you were hurt..."

"I'm fine," he said again, this time with a gruff undertone. "It's part of the job. I'm used to it."

"Right. Good. I'm glad you're fine," she muttered, turning to slink away. "I should get back to the fence, then."

Truth was, she never should've left the damn fence. Never should've glanced at him. Never should've agreed to this in the first place. Her toes scuffed the dirt as she walked away from him. From everyone.

"That was a good one, Uncle Lance," she heard Gracie prattle behind her. "And it was so funny when Jessa fell right on top of you!"

Yeah. Funny. Jessa kept walking. Fast. Head down, arms pumping at her sides, propelling her away from the girl's giggles.

She knew Naomi was behind her, and it didn't matter how fast she walked, somehow her friend matched her stride.

"So wow, you're really not interested in him, huh?" the woman teased.

Jessa stopped. Luis had started digging out a fence post nearby and he didn't need to hear this. "Why would I be interested in him? Every time I get near him his body goes rigid like he's terrified I'll actually touch him. Like he might get cooties if he lets himself get too close." She *shouldn't* be interested. He'd sent plenty of vibes to ward her off. Instead she seemed to want him more. Go figure.

"Come on." Naomi swatted at her. "It's no big deal. I bet no one else could tell. They don't know you like I do." She elbowed her as though trying to make her smile. "They probably just think you're a drama queen."

"Only when Lance is around." She peeked over her shoulder. Tucker was playing chase with Gracie and Lance had disappeared. "I shouldn't be doing this. Staying here."

"Lance would be lucky to have you." Naomi hooked her arm through Jessa's and started towing her toward Luis. "In fact, you're too good for him. The man hasn't had a real relationship with anyone. Ever. And you want it all. Dating. Romance. Marriage. He's completely ignorant. Trust me."

"I know." She sighed. "So what should I do?"

Her friend pulled her in for a half hug. "Stay and help Luis," she whispered. "And see Lance for who he really is. Not for who you want him to become."

* * *

Son of a— That hurt like hell. Lance gritted his teeth and pressed a bandage into the gaping wound Ball Buster had slashed across his ribs. Somehow the bull had managed to get under his chest plate and give him a nasty cut. Not to mention that weight of a serious bruise crushing the air from his lungs.

He latched the first aid kit and hung it back on the nail behind the stable door. When he'd heard Jessa cry out in pain, he'd turned, which gave Ball Buster the perfect opportunity to kick, toss his head back, and catch Lance with his horn. Damn it, he should've stayed focused. Should've tuned out everything else. Usually he could. Except when Jessa was around, evidently.

"You okay?" Tucker stuck his head into the stables. "Didn't realize you took off."

"I'm good." He braced his shoulders so his voice wouldn't wheeze. His whole chest ached like a mother, but no one else needed to know that. He couldn't slow down on his training. Couldn't lose a day. His longest time all morning had been six seconds and that wasn't gonna cut it for Worlds.

"That last one was only four," Tucker informed him. "Not your fault. You got distracted." The man raised his brows and looked him over. "Not like you to get distracted out there."

"Yeah, well, I'm not used to hearing women scream," he grumbled.

"That's surprising, given your revolving bedroom door," Tucker said through a hearty laugh.

Lance shook his head. He'd set himself up for that one. Wasn't worth reminding Tucker that he'd grown up since his early days on the circuit. "I'm not used to hearing *Jessa* scream." That was the plain truth of it. It'd scared him, the pain in her voice. Pulled him right out of the zone.

His friend stepped into the shadows, a funny grin on his face. "I like Jessa. She's good people."

"Yeah." Clumsy, but a good person. She'd pretty much be a saint in his book if she could stick it out with his father for the next couple of weeks.

"So..." Tucker leaned against the wall. "Somethin' goin' on between you two?"

"No." Lance dodged past him and headed out the door and into the sunlight. "Nothing's going on." At least nothing he needed to discuss with Tucker. "She's doing me a favor. Staying with Dad so I can train and not worry about him." Tucker would never give up his secret.

"That all she's doin'?" Tucker called from behind him.

Lance stopped. "Yes." He turned. "Why?"

His friend smirked. "She sure seemed worried about you."

"She's probably not used to seeing stuff like that." Most people were shocked the first time they saw a rider get thrown. Usually it looked worse than it was. Not today, but usually. Thankfully she'd walked away before she could see how much pain he was in. Knowing Jessa, she'd force him to go to the hospital to have his ribs looked at. And he sure as hell couldn't fit that into his schedule today.

"Maybe I'll ask her out," his friend said, poking him in the ribs.

Pain splintered through his bones. *Motherfucker.* Lance sucked in a breath and held it until the stabbing sensation subsided.

"You wouldn't mind, would ya?"

He didn't know if his blood ran hot because of the pain he was in or because of the smug look on his friend's face. He shouldn't mind. Tucker wasn't a bad guy. He was funny, as loyal as they came. The man would do anything for anyone who needed help. But he couldn't stomach the thought of his hands on Jessa. "She's taking a break from dating," Lance informed him. "Said she's sworn off the whole thing so she can focus on the shelter."

"Don't seem right. A woman as good-looking as Jessa not dating anyone."

"Yeah, well, what're you gonna do?" He was fine with it. Her not dating anyone. Didn't bother him none. The thought of her dating someone else? Now that was a different story. One he didn't care to analyze. He straightened his shoulders, battling a wince. "Make sure Ball Buster is ready. I'm going again."

"You sure?" Tucker stared at him like he'd lost it. "Maybe you ought to call it a day. That was a nasty fall. You're movin' kinda slow."

"I'm going again," he repeated. And this time, it didn't matter who screamed. He would hold on for eight seconds.

Chapter Eight

Jessa stood at the kitchen window halfheartedly scrubbing dinner dishes in the sink while she watched the sun slide behind Topaz Mountain. She'd lived in the mountains for almost a year, but the sunsets still stunned her. Darkness had started to spread down the mountain, inviting the sky to come alive with surreal bursts of orange and pink.

She sighed, arms and back weighted with a day of work.

"You don't gotta do the dishes." Luis lumbered over to her. "You're the guest. I can handle it." He eased the lasagna pan off the counter.

"Don't be silly." She turned to smile at him. "I actually like doing the dishes." Strange. At home, she let them pile up in the sink until she *had* to do them. But here, after sharing dinner with someone, it made her happy to stand at the sink, the feel of her hands drenched in the warm, sudsy water. It was nice, not being alone for a meal. It felt more purposeful, somehow.

"Fine, then. But I'm on dish duty tomorrow." Luis set the pan back on the counter. His hands trembled like they had all throughout dinner. Small little tremors she'd pretended not to notice, even when he'd dropped his fork, when he'd knocked over his glass.

Damn arthritis, he'd said, but she'd never noticed tremors before. Stiffness, sure. But not the shaking. She'd casually asked him what his doctor thought about the arthritis, if he was taking anything for it, but he'd quickly changed the subject.

Without turning her head, she stole a quick look at him over her shoulder. While they were eating the lasagna Naomi had brought over, Jessa had noticed the signs of fatigue tugging at his eyes. They'd had polite conversation, but he hadn't said much. The spark he'd had while hiking and working on the fences earlier seemed to have dimmed.

She turned her attention back to the window, to the sunset. "You can go to bed if you want." It was almost seven and they'd had a full day. Back when her father was alive and she'd visit, he'd always fall asleep in his chair after dinner. Until she woke him and sent him off to bed. "I can finish up here."

"You sure you don't mind?" Luis shocked her by saying. She'd expected an argument. "After all that work, I'm done in for the day." Weariness softened his typical gruff tenor.

Jessa shook the water off her hands and turned. "I'm sure. I'll finish up in the kitchen, have a cup of tea, and probably head to bed myself." Well, maybe not bed, but a little book therapy. After the whole debacle with Lance, she'd downloaded a new book on her Kindle. *You Don't Need Him: How to Make Yourself Believe It*. It had gotten three and a half stars...

"All right, then. See you in the morning." Luis plodded out of the kitchen and disappeared down the hallway.

Jessa did her best to sigh out the concern that knotted her stomach. Luis had every right to be tired. He was almost seventy, after all. The man had earned the right to go to bed before eight o'clock at night. She snatched another plate off the pile, plunging it deep into the sink and scouring until the last bits of tomato sauce had been cleaned off.

Outside, the shadows had deepened. Instead of brilliant colors, the sky had muted into a rose-tinted softness, the mountains forming a jagged, dark silhouette. Inhaling the crisp, wood-scented air through the open window, she finished up the last of the dishes and swiped a towel from the stove to start drying.

A click sounded at the back door, interrupting her soft humming. Lance walked into the kitchen, still dusty from his day out in the corral, although it appeared he'd changed into a clean T-shirt.

"Hey." She tried to say it casually, but the quick ascent of her heart made her voice effervescent.

"Hey." He looked around the empty room. "Where's Dad?"

"He seemed tired," she said, focusing hard on drying the dish in her hands so she could avoid the insta-blush that plagued her when she looked directly into his eyes. "Are you hungry? I can reheat some of Naomi's lasagna…"

"Nah. I'm fine, thanks." He walked over and leaned against the counter next to her. "How'd today go?"

His nearness sent her heart spiraling. Damn infatuation. "Things were good," she murmured. "Great actually." Minus the memorable scene of her tackling that man right there. But it was best to make this conversation strictly business.

"We were out on the mountain for a good three hours and there were no problems at all," she reported.

"Good. That's great." Lance stuffed his hands into his pockets and simply stood there gazing at her.

Which made her work extra hard on drying those plates. When she'd finished and stashed them in the cupboard, Lance still stood there. She couldn't take the silence anymore. "So I'm sorry about the whole falling on you thing," she babbled. "I didn't mean to, it just looked like you were hurt—maybe even dead—and I kind of panicked, which I now realize was ridiculous, but at the time I didn't think it through..." *Stop talking. Please stop talking.* But her mouth rarely obeyed her brain. "I didn't *mean* to land on you. I tripped," she said, as though he'd demanded an explanation. "There was a rock and I didn't see it and—"

"It's fine," Lance said through the beginning of a smile. "It didn't bother me."

Mmm-hmmm. Right. She turned to him, not caring that her face was on fire. "The thing is... it kind of seemed like it *did* bother you. Like you got all rigid and glared at me. So I wanted you to know, I didn't mean to make a scene." Though it seemed to be one of her specialties in life.

"You're right." He wore a full-on smile now, the one that quirked his lips and tugged at the corners of his eyes. "I did get all rigid and glare at you."

Well, at least he admitted it. "Don't worry. It won't happen again." Because she would keep her distance. No more humiliating herself in front of Lance. Tomorrow was a new day.

Lance said nothing, but his eyes stayed with hers as he started to roll the edge of his T-shirt, up over the button fly of his jeans, up over a carved, tanned six-pack...

Heat sparked in her chest. She shouldn't be looking. Shouldn't be *ogling*. What was he doing? This was highly unfair...

Finally, he rolled the shirt up his chest...

"Holy mother of God." She gawked at the blood-soaked bandage and the purple and blue splotches that mottled his skin.

"That's why I was so rigid," he said, rolling the shirt back down. "And that's why I glared. It hurt."

Air hissed out of her mouth. "Lance. Geez." How in the world was the man even standing? Breathing?

"It's not as bad as it looks. I've had worse."

Worse? Her ribs ached just thinking about it. She shook her head and tossed the towel aside. "Why do you do that to yourself?" She couldn't imagine it. Couldn't imagine subjecting herself to pain like that day in and day out.

"Why do you rescue wounded and lost animals?" he asked her pointedly.

"Because I love it." She did, but that wasn't the whole reason, and it seemed Lance knew that, because he waited for her to expand.

"And...?" he prompted when she didn't speak.

Damn, he was more perceptive than she'd given him credit for. "Aaannd," she sassed. "Because it's something I can do to carry on my father's legacy." It gave her a connection to him, a way to honor him.

"We have a lot in common," he said as though resting his case.

Maybe so. But dwelling on the things they had in common would not help her put out the flames of infatuation. "You need to redo that bandage," she said, changing the subject. "Did you even clean the wound?"

"No," he admitted, standing straighter. "I was training all afternoon."

Now it was her turn to glare at him. "*Training?* Your ribs might be broken. And not to mention, that cut should probably be stitched. It's definitely going to scar."

"It's not a big deal," he insisted stubbornly.

Not a big deal. Ha! He might be perceptive but he was not as smart as she'd thought. "Have you ever heard of infection? You would not believe the infections I've treated. Wounds fester, Lance. They get full of bacteria and then they get worse and worse until—"

"Fine," he interrupted before she could offer him the gory details. "I'll wash it out."

"Wash it out." She shook her head, already heading for the first aid kit she'd seen in the bathroom earlier. "We can't just wash it out. We're using the strong stuff." She marched back into the kitchen and laid out the kit, seeing what she had to work with.

"Take off your shirt," she ordered.

"Gladly." That naughty smile of his flashed, but she shamed him with a look. This was not a joke. She's seen animals go septic as the result of an infected wound.

He peeled off the shirt gingerly, as if every movement caused him pain, and she forced herself not to examine the muscles, the hard flesh. She had to go into full doctor mode.

Leaning in, she carefully removed the bandage and examined the wound. It had started on one side as a puncture wound, then tore across his flesh with jagged margins. "This is going to hurt," she informed him.

He squeezed his eyes shut. "It already does."

Jessa glanced around. He wouldn't make it through this without something…

There. On top of the fridge sat a small collection of Jack Daniel's bottles. She hurried over and reached for one, then unscrewed the cap. "Here." She held it out to Lance.

He accepted with a grin. "You trying to get me drunk?"

"Yes," she confirmed, digging through drawers until she found a clean rag. "Trust me. You're going to want to be good and drunk for this." Especially if one of his ribs happened to be cracked underneath that gash. The thought brought on a shiver. How had he trained all afternoon with an injury like this?

"All right, then. Bottoms up." Lance raised the bottle to his lips and took a hearty gulp.

Jessa ran the washrag underneath scalding hot water and squirted on some of the antibacterial soap. "Take another shot," she said, inspecting the wound again. A bandage wasn't gonna cut it. They needed something to hold the edges together.

Lance obeyed, albeit wincing. He set down the bottle and swiped his arm across his mouth. "God, that stuff is awful."

The words surprised her. "You don't drink?"

"Sure, a beer once in a while. When I'm not training. But I've never liked the hard stuff."

"Well, you'll like it now. Trust me." She nodded toward the bottle.

Making a disgusted face, Lance downed another shot. "Gah." He pushed it far away. "That's enough. I'll be fine."

"Suit yourself." Jessa approached him with the cloth. "I'll start by cleaning the edges of the wound. We have to clear away the dried blood so we can flush it out." It was best to start prepping him now. This would be the easy part.

Lance straightened his upper body, tensing those carved muscles. "Right. Okay. Go for it."

Doctor mode, she reminded herself, deliberately overlooking the way his upper body flexed. It was just flesh and muscle. *Lots* of muscle...

Ahem. She steadied her hands and carefully pressed the cloth against his skin, lightly running it along the cut's borders.

His chest expanded with a breath, and he let it out slowly.

"Am I hurting you?" she asked, already knowing the answer.

"No worse than I've been hurting," he answered with gritted teeth.

She pulled back a little. "I'm trying to be careful." But that would be difficult as soon as she got into the wound. Hence the use of whiskey. "I have to flush it out a bit." She hurried to the sink and filled a glass with hot water. "This'll sting," she warned. Holding a towel beneath the cut, she poured water over the damaged flesh.

Sure enough, Lance flinched, but she kept her hand and the towel strong against his lower chest.

When the cup had emptied, she blotted the wound with the towel. "You really should have this stitched up," she said again.

"I'm not going to the hospital." His voice had gotten a bit lazy. It appeared the whiskey had done its job.

"Well, I can try to pull it all together with butterfly strips." She riffled through the first aid kit until she found the antibacterial ointment, gauze, and tape.

With the cleaning part over, Lance seemed to relax. "So why did you think I was glaring at *you* earlier?" he asked, searching out her eyes.

Shrugging, she carefully swabbed the ointment thoroughly over the wound. "I guess I thought you were annoyed."

His shoulders flinched, but he seemed focused on her instead of the pain. "Why?"

"Because I made a scene." With a towel, she carefully cleaned off the excess ointment, then cut the gauze. "Because I was worried about you." Using some butterfly strips, she secured the bandage and pulled the edges of his skin together.

"Why would I mind if you were worried about me?" he asked, gazing down at her, his eyes soft and open.

"I don't know." She gently pressed her fingers against the wound, making sure the dressing would hold. "You seemed put off. Just like you were when I accidentally kissed you."

Lance's breathing had gone shallow, but he didn't wince. "I already told you. I didn't mind the kiss. You're the one who said you shouldn't be kissing anyone."

"I shouldn't," she insisted defiantly, peeling the paper off a large bandage, and thanking God she had something to focus on besides his eyes. She plastered the sticky waterproof covering over the dressing and stepped back to admire her work. Yes, her work. Not his pecs...

"Then why did you kiss me?" Lance asked. His voice had deepened, no longer flippant and teasing, but somewhat solemn.

He asked as though he really wanted to know.

Because I couldn't stop myself. Because he'd been so kind and careful and comforting to her that morning. Because his lips were warm and somehow soft, even though the rest of him was so rugged. She cleared her throat. "I already told you. I was extra emotional that day."

His eyes narrowed. "You sure that's all it was?"

"Of course," she lied, straight to his face, locking her jaw for good measure.

"That's a shame. Because I happen to think you're PDF, too." There was a light in his eyes—a heat that made them downright dangerous.

She looked away. "That's the whiskey talking, cowboy," she said through a forced laugh.

His huge hand reached up and cupped her cheek, steering her gaze back to his. "No. It's not."

Air lodged in her lungs, giving her chest that wonderful, tight sensation, like any moment it would burst open and the flood of desire would carry her away.

No. No more getting carried away.

"It's not the whiskey," he murmured, his face lowering to hers. "You're stunning. And funny. And good."

See him as he is… Naomi's words echoed back to her. She did. She saw everything in his eyes. They were so close. So clear. Holding her gaze with a shameless tenderness.

"Kiss me again, Jessa," he tempted. "And I'll prove how much I don't mind."

This time she did laugh. She couldn't hold it back. Pressure had built inside of her, and it had to come out somehow. "You're not attracted to me." Lance Cortez didn't *want* her…

He took her hand and pressed her palm to the crotch of his jeans.

Beneath her fingers a hard bulge made her gasp. *Wow.* Okay, so that was quite impressive…

"That's how much I want you," he uttered. "I haven't kissed you. Haven't even touched you. I'm hard just looking at you. Just being near you." He let go of her hand.

She quickly pulled it to her side. She was not supposed to be doing this. Not now. And yet she couldn't run away. Couldn't even move. Lance still had his shirt off. Oh, why did he have to have his shirt off? He had a body made for touching. So tight and hard, sturdy and strong.

He watched her, saying nothing. Doing nothing. Just watching her.

Naomi had a point. He wasn't marriage material. But should that matter? It wasn't like she was ready to get married tomorrow or anything.

And Lance was still standing there. Shirtless. Watching her with those sexy heavy-lidded eyes.

This was her problem. She overanalyzed things. Thought too much. Tried to plan. A very good-looking man was standing right in front of her. Muscles gleaming in the soft light. Wanting her so badly his groin had to be aching. Asking her to kiss him.

Screw it. No more planning. She might have sworn off relationships, but technically she hadn't sworn off kissing. A surge of adrenaline empowered her. "You're sure?" she asked, desire flooding her throat. Her feet shuffled closer to him, until she stood against his solid body. "You want me to kiss you? Because your life might never be the same after this."

"That's quite the promise." His gaze lowered to her lips.

Jessa swallowed hard. Had she ever kissed a man? Well, besides that awkward moment with Lance on the mountain. She'd never instigated it. Men usually kissed her. Should she just go for it and press her lips into his? Maul him? Ease into it?

"You sure know how to build anticipation," Lance teased.

Her face flamed. "Sorry. I'm…I guess I've never been the one to start it…" And awkward Jessa was back.

"I can start it," he offered. "If it makes you feel better."

"Um, yes please."

His smile grew and his gaze captured hers. They were magnetic, those eyes. The power of his gaze held her still, everything except for her shoulders, which rose and fell with expectant breaths. Nerves seemed to flow through her blood and lodge in her chest, filling it until it pulled tight at the seams again.

Taking his sweet time, Lance slid his fingers underneath her chin and drew her face to his, eyes watching hers—no, conquering hers—overriding the subtle knowledge that this was not the best idea she'd ever had.

"I thought you weren't supposed to be doing this," he murmured, his lips nearly fused to hers.

Talk about building anticipation. That deep, rich coffee scent. The way the stubble on his face grazed her skin. Jessa's head got light. "I talked myself into it," she whispered, bracing her hand securely against the countertop next to him so she didn't collapse.

"I'm glad." His fingers stroked the skin at her jaw as his lips lowered over hers.

Her eyes fell shut and blocked out everything except for the feel of his mouth, the curve of it, the wet warmth, the way his lips melted into hers. They were firm, but tender, too, so skilled and wonderful it broke open her chest.

Heat flowed in until she was dizzy with it, drowning in it, but just as she lost the power to stand on her own, Lance's hands moved to her hips and hitched her closer to his body. She let herself lean into him, sliding her hands up his ripped chest, lightly sweeping her fingers over the bandage. God, he was perfection.

His lips moved to her ear, while his fingers carefully brushed her hair out of the way. "I think you're right," he breathed. "My life might never be the same." His tongue traced the ridge of her ear while his heavy breaths grazed her neck and made her legs falter.

He must've felt her wobble, because he wrapped his arms around her and crushed her body against his. "Damn, Jessa..." He kissed his way down her neck. "You smell good."

"Vanilla sugar shower gel," she gasped, letting her head tilt to the side.

"Mmmm. I like it." He slid his tongue back up her neck and his lips found hers again. This time he kissed her harder, like he wanted more.

Yes. More. There could be so much more...

Lance shifted, guiding her until her back was against the refrigerator. Things were falling, magnets and papers, but none of that mattered because Lance was pressed against her, his tongue stroking hers, his hips grinding against her body. The feel of him hard and desperate against her sent her heart spiraling. A frantic moan escaped, and Lance smiled against her lips. She let her head fall back so she could draw in a breath, but she hit the refrigerator.

A loud crash froze her. Lance pulled away. Those bottles of Jack Daniel's that had been on top of the fridge now lay next to their feet.

"At least they didn't break." Lance started to laugh but she pressed her hand against his mouth. "It's not funny! What if your dad—"

"What in God's name is that racket?" came from down the hall.

"Oh no," she hissed. "Oh God..."

Lance still had a big silly grin on his face. "It's nothing, Dad," he called, but the man came charging around the corner anyway.

Jessa pushed back and pretended to inspect the bandage. "Well, there we go. Everything looks good." She glanced up and forced a smile, but she'd like to bet he could see the vein in her forehead pulsing. "Hey, Luis. Sorry about the noise. I was bandaging Lance up and we accidentally knocked over the bottles." Her bright red face had to be a dead giveaway that the whole sentence was a lie. Not to mention her dilated eyes.

"Uh. Thanks, Jessa," Lance said, reaching past her for his shirt.

"No problem," she intoned, as if answering a complete stranger. "Next time, don't wait so long to get it cleaned up."

A spark smiled in his eyes. "I definitely won't."

Whew. She fought the compulsion to fan her face with a towel.

"Guess I should get going then." Lance clapped his dad's shoulder on his way out the door. "Night, Pops."

Luis didn't respond. He simply watched his son leave, then he turned to Jessa. "So nothing's going on between you two."

She invoked her laser focus to put away the first aid supplies. "Uh-huh. Nope. Nothing."

"From what I could tell that was a whole lot of nothing," Luis muttered as he plodded back down the hall.

That was one way to put it. A whole lot of nothing.

Chapter Nine

The world came back into focus slowly, the way it did when he woke from a dead sleep. Cold air blasted his face. The door slammed shut behind him. Lance stuttered to a stop on the front porch. He should go back in there. Shouldn't end the night with Jessa like that. Should he? Hell. He didn't know. It was still hard to think, but it had nothing to do with the shots of whiskey he'd downed.

He faced the door. What had just happened in there? He'd never planned on kissing her. He'd only wanted to check in, make sure his dad hadn't given her a hard time today. But then she'd ordered his shirt off. And the way she got so close, her delicate fingers pressing against his skin. It should've hurt like hell while she worked on him, but instead it only charged him up, making his body ache with the need for more until it was all he could think about.

She'd taken her time cleaning the cut, applying the bandages so carefully. She'd taken care of him. No one had ever taken care of him...

On the other side of the door, lights glowed. Which meant she hadn't gone to bed yet. Knowing his father, he'd gone back to bed right away. Probably pretended he didn't suspect anything, just like he always had when Lance was growing up. If he pretended he didn't see, they didn't have to talk about it. For once, he was glad Luis didn't like to meddle.

He took a step toward the door, the porch's bright light casting his shadow across the wooden planks.

The ache for a woman's soft touch gripped him. He could still feel her body under his hands, petite but toned. Could still feel her lips burning against his. But he really shouldn't go back in there, because this time he might not be able to stop himself, no matter who walked into the room.

A dog's low bark drifted somewhere behind him. He didn't even have to turn around to figure out who it belonged to. Bogart, Naomi's German shepherd, came trotting regally up the porch steps. Which meant Naomi wouldn't be far behind. He should've anticipated that, seeing as how her house was right across the driveway. She'd probably been spying.

"Well, well, well." Naomi walked into view beneath the porch light, staring up at him like a pissed-off librarian, mouth in a thin line, arms crossed in a stance of unyielding disappointment.

Yeah, there was no way out of this. Lance sauntered down the steps to meet her.

"What're you doing here?" she asked before he could say hello.

He reached down to pat Bogart's perked ears. "Came by to check in with Jessa." The wind picked up, carrying the strong pine scent. He should've been cold without his coat on, but the fire Jessa had lit inside him was still going strong.

"Mmm-hmm. Mmmm-hmmm," Naomi mocked. "You came to check in." Her narrowed eyes invited him to a silent interrogation, which he avoided by glancing down at the dog.

He sucked at lying. "Hey there, Bogart. Out for your nightly stroll?"

"Don't try to change the subject." Naomi's growl was almost as low as the dog's. "Seriously. Your hair is sticking up like someone just ran her fingers through it. What happened in there?"

Actually, he still wasn't exactly sure, but Naomi wouldn't let him off that easy. He leaned a shoulder against the front porch column. "I really did come to check in."

She raised her brows, admonishing him to continue.

"But then she saw the damage Ball Buster inflicted earlier, so she wanted to fix me up." He lifted his shirt to show her the bandage.

The woman rolled her eyes with a hearty shake of her head. "Fix you up?" she snorted. "So let me guess. You took your shirt off to show her the goods and she threw herself at you."

"It was definitely my fault," he admitted. Things had started out innocently enough. She'd seemed genuinely horrified when she saw the wound. Then he had to go and dare her to kiss him again. He shook his head. "She didn't throw herself at me." He'd gone after her. He didn't know what it was about Jessa, but he seemed to lose what little self-control he had when she was around.

"Damn it, Lance." Naomi took a shot at his shoulder.

At least she didn't nail him in the ribs. He backed away before she got any ideas. "We just kissed." Even as the words tumbled out, the argument fell apart. It'd turned into more than a kiss in about two seconds. Two more minutes and he would've had her clothes off. He would've been buried so deep inside her he might never have found his way out.

"Jessa doesn't know how to just kiss," Naomi informed him, one hand placed on her hip in a sassy way that reminded him of Gracie.

He might be losing his touch, too. Used to be a kiss was simply a necessary stepping stone to get a woman where he wanted her, but he couldn't get Jessa out of his head. Hell, he could go for another round of kissing right now. Maybe at his place, so his father wouldn't interrupt this time...

"Oh no you don't." Naomi shook a finger in his face. "You and Jessa is not happening. So stop thinking about it."

He shoved away her finger. "How do you know what I'm thinking?"

"Oh please. Your eyes are all glazed over and you're practically drooling." Her glare could've incinerated him. "Don't do this to her, Lance. She's not like those women who follow you around everywhere."

Actually, that had stopped a long time ago. "They're not there to see me. Not anymore." There were younger guys. Guys who were happy to take them home for a night.

Naomi glared up at him, jutting out her right hip slightly, a signal that she was about to change her approach. "Do you want to get married? Have kids? Has that changed for you?"

"No." Didn't have to think about the answer. He'd never wanted that. Any idealistic views he'd had about love had been obliterated the day his mother looked him in the face, then turned her back on him. He didn't intend to build a life with someone only to watch it fall apart the way it had for his father. The way it had for their family.

"Jessa does," Naomi said. "She wants all of that. A commitment. A family. A man to spend the rest of her life with. She believes in that. We might not, but she does."

"I know." People talked about how many times she'd been engaged. He doubted she'd ever gone on "just a date." She seemed to want something that'd last a lifetime. Everyone in town knew Jessa had that dreamy-eyed view of love. Sometimes he envied that. It wasn't like her parents had some fairy-tale romance, but she still held on to the hope it could happen. What would that be like? He had no clue what it felt like to believe in something.

Naomi stepped closer. She was short, but she sure could look intimidating when she wanted to. "She's been jerked around enough. I can't be responsible for it happening again."

"You? Why would you be responsible?"

"I'm the one who helped her change her look so she could start winning over donors for the shelter. And I told her to use you as a guinea pig. I told her to try to win you over."

That was worth a laugh. "You told her to use me?" Not that he minded...

But Naomi wasn't seeing any humor in the situation. "Come on, Lance." She sighed. "You never even noticed her until she started to dress sexier. Until she wore her contacts. Put on makeup."

Maybe not, but he hadn't had a reason to notice Jessa, either. He didn't exactly get out much. Besides, it wasn't the makeup. He couldn't give a damn about the makeup. That's not what tempted him to kiss her tonight. That's not what drove him to keep kissing her until his mind and body were lost in fantasyland. "She wasn't wearing makeup tonight. And why would you tell her to change her look?" Why did women do that to each other?

"She *wanted* to," Naomi shot back. "And I never thought you'd take advantage of it. I never thought she'd fall for *you*, of all people."

Fall for him. He thought about the way she'd touched him. The way she'd smiled up at him. It all seemed genuine, but…"Maybe she's not falling for me. Maybe it's all part of your little plan."

"No." Naomi's head shook the possibility away. "When she ran over to you today…I knew. She cares about you. And you can't take advantage of that. It's not right."

He blew out a breath. Wow, women sure knew how to use guilt to trip people up. "I didn't mean to take advantage of her." He hadn't meant for anything to happen between them. Maybe if he hadn't seen her naked…

"You and Jessa want two different things. She has a big heart, Lance. And I don't want her to get hurt again." That was the final blow. It didn't matter how much he wanted to kiss her again. Didn't matter how much she turned him on.

"I don't want her to get hurt, either." She deserved to find what she wanted. He couldn't stand in the way of that. "I'll talk to her. Tomorrow. I'll get things straightened out."

But first he had to straighten himself out.

* * *

Morning looked different after sharing a hot kiss with Lance Cortez. Jessa opened her eyes. After last night, everything was different. Sunlight flooded the room, streaming lazily in through the large picture window that framed Topaz Mountain. The cliffs appeared to be so close it seemed she could reach out and brush her fingers along their rugged peaks. She stretched out in the creaky bed and let the rays of light warm her face. She'd never dreamed she'd be so comfortable staying in Luis's house. The room was so simple—a brass queen bed, an old scratched antique dresser, and a wooden rocking chair in the corner. There were no frills, no pops of color, but somehow the simplicity of it put her at ease. You didn't need much when you had that view staring you in the face first thing every morning.

She closed her eyes, letting herself fall back through the hours to last night. A deep vibrato still fluttered her heart. Had Lance really kissed her? Had he really said he wanted her? The images were so soft and hazy, overcast by a thick cloud of desire.

And yet the memories sizzled through her, an assurance that it was real. It had all happened. The kiss, his strong hands on her body, his tongue against her skin. Her body woke with a start, feeling the sensations again.

Noise sounded from downstairs—the creaking of the kitchen's wood floors, running water. Luis must be up.

A shot of embarrassment jolted her out of bed. She rarely slept past seven and it was almost eight. Quickly, she shed her flannel pajamas and pulled on yoga pants and a long-sleeved T-shirt. Stopping in the bathroom, she smoothed her hair and pulled it back into a ponytail. Her eyes looked tired, but happy, too, as though she was still luxuriating in the exhilarating pleasure of being touched and held.

She'd *never* been touched and held exactly the way Lance had done it.

A bounce snuck into her step as she made her way down the narrow wooden staircase. She found Luis in the kitchen.

"Good morning." She greeted the older man with a happy wave. She couldn't help it. Everything felt lighter. It was so freeing not worrying about things with Lance. Not devising a strategy for how to avoid him or overanalyze what last night meant. It had felt so natural and easy. They'd had fun. He'd been good to her. And that was all that mattered. Instead of lying awake agonizing over what might come from it all, she'd slept deeply and restfully. Such a contrast to pretty much every other man she'd ever kissed.

"Morning." Luis nodded with a small smile. He had to have known there was more going on than they cared to admit last night, but she knew him well enough to know he'd never bring it up. He was a *live and let live* type of person.

Jessa sashayed past him and filled a glass of water. She liked to down eight ounces first thing every morning. "Can I make breakfast?" she asked, after she'd finished the glass. Nothing said Sunday morning like her father's sweet potato and egg hash.

"Nah, you don't have to cook for me, Jessa." Luis slipped on a heavy flannel coat. "Besides, Sundays we all go up to Lance's place for breakfast. Me and Naomi and Gracie."

"Oh." Her heart thumped a bit harder. One kiss and she'd been conditioned. She heard the man's name and instantly her lady parts warmed right up.

"Better get your coat," Luis added. "Cold out this morning. The dew's as thick as icing out there."

"Um." She sneaked a quick glance at herself in the microwave's spotted glass. So yeah. She definitely wasn't looking her best. She hadn't showered, hadn't even officially gotten dressed.

She reached up and patted the straggler hairs into place. "You know, I can stay here. I'm sure he doesn't need one more person to feed."

"Unless I miss my guess, he'll want you there." Luis looked her over, those kind eyes crinkled and wise.

And...omniscient. That was the word. Though they were watered down with age, Luis's eyes were so focused and intent they seemed to see everything. "He'll be glad to see you. Trust me. I know my son."

Would he? The thought baited a smile. Would he be as happy to see her as she would be to see him? Already her heart was twirling like she had when her mother would dress her in a frilly skirt.

"Let's get a move on. Luis waved her over to the front door. "We don't want the grub to get cold."

Her hesitation melted away. Luis knew his son. And things didn't have to be awkward. They'd kissed, that's all. Okay, made out. But only for about three minutes. He'd probably made out with a lot of women for much longer than that.

She pulled her coat off the rack and slipped it on, then bent to jam her feet into her shoes. "Should we bring anything?" She'd seen some fruit lying around. She could cut it up and make a salad...

"Nah. Lance cooks for everyone on Sundays." He held open the door for her. "Not sure where he learned. I never could do much in the kitchen."

She paused on her way out to the porch, nerves boiling with the anticipation of seeing him. "You're sure he won't mind if I come?"

Luis looked at her, his face serious and sincere. "You're practically part of the family. I always promised your dad we'd watch out for you if anything ever happened to him. He'd want you to be part of our family."

Unexpected tears pricked at her eyes. Luis had said things like that before, but she'd never felt it hit so close to her heart. In a way, she did feel like she fit. She'd agreed to stay only to do Lance a favor, but truthfully she loved it at the ranch—the surrounding peaks, the old creaking floors, the acres of open space surrounding them. The people. "Thank you." She squeezed his shoulder and followed him down the steps to the driveway.

It *was* chilly, but beautiful, too. The early morning sunlight gleamed so bright it almost hurt to look. Thick morning dew made the ground sparkle. They crunched over the dirt in a sort of awed silence, taking in the pure air, the warm sun, the shimmering blue sky. The closer they got to Lance's house, the more her insides warmed, the more her heart beat with eagerness. Even though she couldn't wait to see him again, it wasn't because she wanted something out of him. For once in her life, she had no expectations. She simply wanted to be around him. To know him better. To see him smile like he had last night.

The thought made her smile as she followed Luis up the porch steps.

She'd heard Lance had built his own house a few years ago, and it was gorgeous, all log and stone. A wraparound porch wound around the entire thing, making it cozy and welcoming. She passed a wicker swing, which looked like the perfect spot to sit out with a glass of wine on a cool autumn night...

"Here we go." Luis opened the front door, not bothering to knock.

The inside of Lance's house was as impressive as the outside. Jessa crept across the slate-tiled entryway, trying to take in everything at once. The comforting smell of black coffee, the warm tones on the walls, the framed scenes she recognized from around the ranch. The main floor was a completely open concept, a living room with leather furniture clustered near a large stone fireplace on one wall. Beyond that, the space opened into the masculine gourmet kitchen with dark wood cabinets and grayish concrete countertops.

A large dining table sat in front of a beautiful bay window, and it was already laden with dishes and food—some sort of decadent-looking coffee cake, a pan of eggs, a plate of crisp bacon.

God, it smelled heavenly.

A set of French doors near the kitchen busted open. Gracie came skipping through, followed by Naomi and Lance.

Oh, Lance. A faint humming purred inside her. If it was possible he looked even better than he had last night. Fitted faded Levi's and an unbuttoned flannel with a tattered henley underneath.

Heat flashed the way it had when he'd first pressed his lips into hers.

"We saw some deers!" Gracie cried, skipping over. "A mama and two little ones."

"Wow." Jessa knelt down to her level and folded her into a hug. "I'd love to see them," she said, as though she didn't see deer walking down the street every day in Topaz Falls.

Naomi ruffled her daughter's red curls. "You could've seen them if this little princess hadn't scared them away."

"I was trying to be quiet but they were so cute." Gracie grinned up at her, those jewel-like eyes shining. "One of the babies got this close!" She held her hands about six inches apart while her mother laughed.

Jessa laughed, too. The little girl had some mad skills in the art of exaggeration.

As soon as the laughter faded, an awkward silence settled. Awkward because Lance still stood by the doors, his arms crossed, staring at her.

"Come on, sweet girl," Naomi said, steering her daughter away. "Let's get those grubby hands washed up before breakfast."

As she passed, Naomi gave Jessa a small smile. A tad sympathetic?

Unease spread through her, taming the elation she'd felt since she'd woken up. Why was Naomi looking at her as if she felt sorry for her?

"Grub ready yet?" Luis asked his son, heading for the table without waiting for an answer. "I'm starvin'."

"Uh. Yeah." Lance seemed to shake himself out of whatever held him in a trance. "Just about. You can have a seat if you want."

Luis didn't have to be told twice. He crossed to the far end of the room and sat himself at the head of the dining table.

Lance approached Jessa, but he didn't look at her. Not really. His eyes shifted. "You came." The words weren't happy. They weren't even welcoming. And for someone who'd been so adamant about kissing her last night, he sure was keeping a chilly distance intact.

"Um, yeah." She tried to make eye contact with him, but he looked away. "Luis insisted. I hope that's okay."

"Sure." He seemed to shrug it off like he didn't care either way before he left her standing there and went to the coffeepot in the kitchen.

Gracie skipped back into the great room. "Papa!" Since Naomi's parents had moved to Florida a few years ago, Luis was the closest thing Gracie had to a local grandpa.

He rose from his chair and lifted her into the air while she squealed. Then he set her down in the chair next to his, and their heads bent together as she chattered about the deer.

Jessa watched Lance move stonily in the kitchen, her feet rooted to the floor. Suddenly she felt like she shouldn't be there. Like she didn't belong after all.

Naomi came to stand by her. A little too close. "So how was your night?" she whispered.

"Oh. Fine. Good." She squirmed out of her coat and walked over to hang it on the rack near the front door so they were out of earshot.

"Anything unusual happen?" Naomi asked too innocently. She obviously knew something had happened, and why should that surprise her? The woman lived right across the driveway from Luis.

"How did you know?" Jessa sighed.

"I saw Lance leaving." Naomi glanced toward the other side of the room, where everyone was still otherwise occupied.

"It was nothing," she insisted feebly. Obviously. Lance was completely ignoring her.

"Nothing? Really? Because your face is beet red."

"It's warm in here." She tugged her shirt out a few times to let in some air.

Her friend yanked on her elbow and pulled her closer to the front door. "Have you changed your mind? About banning relationships from your life for a while?"

"No." But she had to admit she could. She could change her mind pretty easily with the right motivation. "We kissed. It's not like I'm hearing wedding bells or anything."

"Good." Naomi let her go. "Because we've already talked about this. He's not commitment material."

"Maybe that's because he hasn't met the right woman." She was just thinking out loud here, but that would make sense. Lance didn't have much time to date. The women she'd heard he'd been with weren't exactly commitment material, either. Besides... "I'm not in a hurry for anything to happen. I liked kissing him." She wouldn't even try to deny it. "But I don't need some big commitment right now anyway."

Naomi rolled her eyes. "Sure, you say that now. But what about in a month when you're more invested? What happens then?"

For once, she didn't know. And she didn't have to. "I'll work that out then."

"And get hurt again," her friend said gently. "Trust me. Lance has baggage. You don't want to be the one to have to deal with his mommy issues. That's exactly why I—"

"Hey, Jessa."

Her head snapped so fast she felt a pull in her neck. Lance was looking at her now. He was even talking to her.

"Can you help me get the drinks ready?" he asked, still hanging out by the coffeepot.

Naomi rolled her eyes, but Jessa simply bumped past her. "Sure. I'd be happy to."

Chapter Ten

Jessa drifted to the other side of the counter and glanced at him as though waiting for instructions. Which was good. Distance would be key for this conversation. When he'd walked in and seen her standing there it hit like a shock-wave. He noticed her lips first. The lips that were so smooth and giving against his last night. Then her eyes. Friendly and open, smiling in a way that made him want to smile, too. She had on yoga pants that showcased her tight ass. The tight ass his hands had held just last night. It pretty much looked like she'd rolled right out of bed and come on over. Seeing her disheveled in that sexy carefree way made his brain give out and the little speech he'd rehearsed last night faded into the desire to touch her again.

But he couldn't. So she'd stay over there and he'd stay over here and then maybe he could remember what it was he was supposed to say to her. He checked on the others, who were seated at the table, already piling food onto their plates while Gracie informed them of every fact she knew about deer.

"Sooo . . . should I pour coffee for everyone?" Jessa asked, stepping into his line of vision.

Their eyes connected and he forced himself not to look away again. "In a second." He shuffled a few steps closer. "Actually, we need to talk first."

Something changed on her face. Her smile fell away, and the bright, wide eyes that kept demanding his attention narrowed. "Okay. So talk." She folded her arms and leaned against the counter, glaring as though she already knew what he was going to say.

Damn it. How had he planned to start this again? "Well . . ." He cleared his throat. The noise level over at the table rose as Gracie giggled about something his dad had said. Jessa didn't seem to notice. Her glare was relentless.

He blew out a breath. If anyone wondered why he didn't do relationships, this would be a good example. He sucked at having honest, hard conversations. Since there was no easy way to put it, he'd best just get it out there. "I shouldn't have kissed you," he said, quietly enough that the others wouldn't hear.

Jessa's unreadable expression didn't change but her jaw twitched. "And why is that?"

Why was that again? Staring at her made it hard to remember. He glanced down at his plain, uncomplicated boots. "I'm pretty sure we want different things."

When silence thrummed into his ears, he looked up at her.

Her facial expression hadn't budged an inch. "What is it you want, Lance?" The words came out solid and hard. She didn't seem to care much if anyone else heard.

He shoved his hands into his pockets so he wouldn't flip

off Naomi from across the room. What the hell did she know? Talking had been a bad idea. "I want simplicity."

Jessa shocked him with a smirk. Where had all this attitude and sass come from? He'd always heard she was a softie. He must've heard wrong.

"And what is it you think I want?" Her tone came within an inch of mocking him.

"Uh." Was this a trap? He'd learned early in his dating career never to answer a question that could have potentially catastrophic consequences. Truth was, he didn't know what she wanted. Not exactly. He knew what Naomi thought Jessa wanted. But Jessa was waiting.

He blew out the frustration in a hefty sigh. "Look. This isn't about you. I don't do relationships. I'm not interested in that." Life was so much easier without those ties. "I shouldn't have taken those shots last night." Not that he could blame his body's reaction to her on the whiskey. "You're great, but—"

"Did I do something that led you to believe I wanted a relationship with you?" she interrupted in that same bold, *screw you* tone.

"No." *Wow.* This was the last time he'd follow Naomi's advice on anything. Talk about a crash and burn. "But Naomi seemed to think—"

"Did it ever occur to you that maybe *I* wanted a fling?" Jessa marched closer. "That maybe I'm sick of relationships and just want to have fun with no strings attached for once in my life?"

"No." Somehow he managed to get the word out even with his jaw hanging open. That had definitely never occurred to him.

"Would it be so hard to believe that I'm not out searching

for a husband?" she demanded, hands positioned on the rounded curve of her sexy hips.

"Well..." What could he say to that without risking her foot in his balls? She'd built quite the reputation for herself. Wasn't his fault word got around. "Isn't that what you want?"

She laughed. The woman laughed at him. "*You* kissed *me*." Her pointer finger slashed the air between them. "*You* said you were attracted to *me*."

"I am." Damn was he attracted to her. Her shoulders were straight and tight, her perky breasts begging for some attention. And her face had flushed with the same passion he'd seen last night.

"Then what the hell is your problem, Lance, huh?" she demanded.

When she put it that way... he glanced over at the table again.

Gracie and his father were still chatting while they ate, but Naomi was glaring at him. *Oh, right.* That kicked his memory into gear. He was supposed to be putting boundaries between them to save Jessa some heartache. "I don't want you to get hurt." He felt like he was reading a damn script. What he really wanted to tell her was that he'd never been more turned on than he was right now and would she like a tour of his bedroom?

"Maybe I'm the one who'll hurt you." Her head tilted in a flippant gesture. "Did you ever think about that?"

"Noooo," he admitted. But he could be down with some pain...

"Screw you, Lance. I don't need your pity *or* your protection." She marched over to him, and he felt his heart lift at the prospect of her body being against his again.

"You know what I *do* want?" she asked, her voice lowered into an alluring growl.

He could only shake his head. Shock and intrigue surged through him in a way he'd never felt.

"I want some fucking coffee." She bumped past him to the coffeepot. Without a glance back, she filled herself a mug and sashayed over to the table, leaving him staring after her, his body as primed and ready as it'd been last night.

* * *

She was so done. And not just with breakfast, either. Jessa blotted her mouth with a napkin and tossed it onto her empty plate. Lance might be a complete jerk-wad, but he knew how to make breakfast. Normally, she would be a polite guest and offer to help clean up the dishes, but she had to get out of there. Now.

All through breakfast she'd felt Lance's eyes searching her out. But she had studiously avoided him, gushing over Gracie instead. Thank God there was an adorable ten-year-old at the table to distract everyone from the fat-ass purple polka-dotted elephant in the room. Because Naomi had obviously discussed last night's kiss with Lance in great detail, and Luis might be nearing seventy, but he wasn't blind. He had to have witnessed something of what had transpired between her and Lance in the kitchen—an encounter that still had her knees quaking, by the way.

So during the meal the adults in the room had hardly looked at one another, instead enthusiastically indulging Gracie's spirited ideas about how adding pigs to the ranch could be super fun. Because look how much Wilbur livened things up in *Charlotte's Web*. Gracie was always on a mission to bring more animals into the fold. She was a girl after her own heart.

A lull in the conversation presented Jessa with the opportunity she'd been waiting for for at least a half hour. "Well, this has been great," she said, her gaze skimming right over all of them. "But I should check in at the shelter. Make sure Cassidy's holding up okay." It wasn't like Cassidy couldn't handle it, but Jessa couldn't handle *this*. The poor brokenhearted Jessa routine. When she'd realized what Lance was trying to get at in the kitchen, something inside of her had erupted. She was *not* emotionally fragile. And she sure as hell didn't need a man—even Lance Cortez—to be her key to a happy life.

She was done being poor nice Jessa.

The eruption had left behind a force that built inside her, fortifying her. With this newfound courage, she popped right out of her chair. "Thanks for a lovely breakfast," she said to no one in particular. But she did beam a real smile at Gracie. "See you soon, sweet girl."

The girl blew her a kiss, which Jessa returned before she spun and made a break for the door.

"Wait." A chair scraped the plank floors and before she could get too far, Lance slipped in front of her. She forced herself to stare back at him, working her mouth into a line of indifference. "Yes?"

"Don't you need help at the shelter today?" he asked, widening his eyes and glancing in his father's direction.

Right. She was supposed to be on babysitting duty. After everything that had transpired between them, that's what it came down to. That's why she was here. Lance hadn't forgotten and she shouldn't, either. Irritation simmered, but she didn't want to take it out on Luis. It wasn't his fault his son was clueless.

"Actually I could really use some help." Blocking out Lance, she turned to his father. "Do you have time to come today? I might have to do inventory on supplies."

The older man's mustache twitched. "Sure," he said. If he was trying to hide his amusement, he was doing a terrible job. "Gets me outta doin' the dishes." He planted a kiss on the top of Gracie's head and dragged himself out of the chair.

"Great. Thanks." With a prim smile, she sidestepped Lance and led a hearty charge out the front door to the tune of the "Hallelujah" chorus playing in her head. Not surprisingly, Lance didn't try to stop her.

Outside, the day had brightened and the scents of fall permeated the air—dried grass, crisp leaves. Not that she enjoyed it. Her volcanic heart still fumed. As far as she could remember, she hadn't said anything pathetic to Lance. Sure, she'd tried to kiss him, and yes, she'd admired him, but she wasn't Scarlett freaking O'Hara. She hadn't been *pining* after him. She hadn't begged him to kiss her. And maybe she would enjoy a fling. She didn't know for sure, but it was possible. Now she'd never know, since Lance had gone and made it a huge deal.

We want different things. God. How did he know anything about what she wanted? Her feet pounded the dirt harder. He didn't. Mostly because he hadn't bothered to ask her.

Luis tromped along by her side. "You want to talk about it?" he asked in his pleasant way.

"Not especially." There was nothing to talk about. Nothing to think about, except the work she had to do today. Swearing off men had been the right decision all along, but then Lance had come along and screwed it up by kissing her, before doing a complete one-eighty and telling her he wasn't looking for a commitment.

And people thought *she* had issues.

After running into Luis's house to change into some jeans and her *Stay Calm and Help Animals* T-shirt, she led Luis to her truck, which was parked off to the side of his garage. Driving away from the ranch felt freeing. She flicked on the radio and let the country music coax out the tension.

Luis stared ahead, his fingers drumming on his knees to the beat. "Lance took it the hardest when his mom left," he said, his jaw tight. "I never knew what to do. How to talk to him about it. We just tried to survive."

The words caught her off guard. Even though they'd spent a lot of time together, Luis had never mentioned his ex-wife before. She turned down the radio. "Sometimes that's all you can do," she said, her shoulders softening.

"Point is, he didn't learn anything good about relationships. Not from me," the man went on, though he didn't look at her. Luis didn't have to expand. She'd heard the rumors about him after his wife left. He'd had affairs with married women, taking full advantage of his status as a renowned bull rider. For a while, he'd been quite the Casanova. But she didn't hold that against him. She knew how it felt to have a broken heart, to search for something that would soothe away the loneliness, even if it was only temporary.

Luis stared blankly out the windshield. "It's one of the things I regret the most."

Letting silence settle, Jessa turned onto Main Street. The sidewalks were full of people strolling, pausing to window shop at the eclectic mix of boutiques and shops. It was a beautiful day, bright and vivid, yet she couldn't help but feel that a cloud hung over them. Sure, Lance hadn't had it easy after his mom left, but a lot of people hadn't. And Luis had already paid a steep price for his actions. He'd lost a son. After Lucas was sent to prison, the man had cleaned up his act. From what she'd heard, he stayed home with Lance and Levi more, tried to fix things with his boys. People *could* change. But they had to want it.

Stopping at the lone traffic light, she waved at Mrs. Eckles, who owned the bakery across the street. "I didn't exactly learn about healthy relationships from my parents, either," she reminded Luis. But that didn't have to stop her from having a healthy relationship with someone else. "And you know what, Luis? Lance's issues aren't your fault." He had a choice. He could decide what he wanted for his life. It seemed he already had, so there was no point in dwelling on the situation. "Anyway, we don't have to talk about Lance. Like I've said before, there's nothing to talk about." They had a business arrangement and things had gotten too personal. She wouldn't make that mistake again.

On the south end of Main Street, she veered to the right and pulled up in front of the shelter. The building itself wasn't attractive. Before her father had bought it, it had been an old diner, a plain square brick building with a shingled roof. Some people around town called it an eyesore, but it served its purpose. Before Buzz had passed, she'd planned to give it a facelift in hopes that would help donations. Things hadn't exactly worked out that way. Her dad had left behind a couple of debts and after she'd paid them off, she needed what remained to keep things running month-to-month, to pay Cassidy and Xavier, her night shift guy, so she didn't have to be there 24/7.

She parked in the space next to Cassidy's SUV and cut

the engine. It looked like the sign above the door had lost another bolt. It was tilted like it was about to fall to the ground.

Luis noticed her looking at it.

"That's nothin'. I'll get on a ladder and get it all fixed up," he said, unbuckling his seat belt.

She climbed out of the truck, hauling along her bag of paperwork she had to finish up. "Thanks, Luis." Seriously. What would she do without him? Lance might be paying her to stay with the man, but she should be doing it for free, given how much he did to help her out.

"You deserve to be on the payroll," she told him, leading the way inside. The bell chimed a cheerful welcome.

"Nah. I don't need the money," he insisted.

And it was obvious she *did* need some money. Jessa looked around the reception area at the front of the building. Buzz had unearthed the two oak desks from a trash heap in the rubble of a dilapidated building. Sturdy as a rock, he'd claimed, even though they both leaned slightly to the left. And those desks weren't the only monstrosities in the room. The stained gray carpet was pulling up around the edges. It had been snagged from the array of paws that had walked or pranced or scampered or cowered on its surface. Two overstuffed chairs he'd found at a garage sale provided the only seating in the room.

She sighed deeply. It wasn't the neatest place, but it was hard to keep things neat when you had a revolving door of animals coming in and out.

"Hey there." Cassidy walked out from the back room, where they kept the animal pens and supplies.

"Hi," Jessa said brightly, doing her best to cover up her earlier irritation. "How're things going?"

"Good..." Her friend drew out the word as though she

was confused. That would be because technically Jessa wasn't supposed to come in on Sundays. Her friends were always on her about being a workaholic and making sure she took at least one day off during the week. So much so that Cassidy had volunteered to hang out on weekends for a very reasonable wage.

Before Cass could ask her why she'd come in, she got right down to business. "So how's the pig?" The day before Cam had broken up with her, someone had called to report a potbellied pig that was seen wandering around the park. Jessa had found the sweet thing down by the river, and she didn't look healthy. Too thin and very lethargic. She'd brought her in and posted signs around town, but so far no one had claimed her. Which meant she'd likely been abandoned by someone passing through town.

"The poor baby won't eat," Cass said. "I tried everything you recommended, but she just kind of nibbles, then goes back to sleep."

"I figured that might be the case." Which gave her the perfect excuse to come in on a Sunday. She'd already started the pig on antibiotics but might have to up the dosage. "That's why I thought I'd better stop and check in. I'll go take a look." She slipped past the desk and hurried to the back room. Though she'd given the pig the largest crate they had, it had curled up in the farthest corner, snout burrowed into the soft blanket Jessa had used to make a bed. When she unlatched the crate, the pig's head lifted, but it didn't move.

"Come here, sweetie." Carefully, Jessa lifted her out and held her the same way she'd hold a baby. Based on the pig's small size, she'd guess her to be less than a year old. "Why would anyone ever leave you behind?" she cooed, petting her soft head. "You're so pretty, yes you are." Downright irresistible, if you asked her, with that shiny pink snout and those black-and-white spots. "Such a pretty piggy."

"Think she's gonna make it?" Luis asked from behind her.

"She might have a touch of pneumonia, but we'll take care of her." Jessa scratched the pig's ears and it lifted its snout into the air. "You like that, don't you," she murmured.

The pig gave the cutest little grunt, proving that a little love can help perk up anyone.

"Would you mind if I brought her home?" Jessa turned to Luis. I'd like to keep a closer eye on her."

"Fine by me." Having brought up three boys, Luis seemed to be fazed by nothing. He'd told her plenty of tales of Lance and his brothers bringing home snakes and mice and spiders.

"Not sure Lance'll like the idea, though. He's always sayin' animals belong outside."

She couldn't fight a wicked grin. Even better.

"Got a name for her?" the man asked, scratching under the pig's chin.

Jessa held her up and carefully looked her over. "Ilsa," she said, satisfied. "Because she's fancy." And because she loved *Casablanca*.

Luis grunted out a laugh. "Never met a pig named Ilsa."

"You named her?" Cass asked, walking through the door. "Uh-oh. In my experience naming an animal means it'll be part of your family forever."

"I'd be fine with that." Jessa couldn't take in every animal that came through the shelter's doors, but Ilsa was obviously special.

"So you could've called to check on the pig, you know," her friend said as though she was hurt. "I could've handled it until tomorrow."

Guilt turned Jessa's stomach. "Oh, I know. Of course you could." That wasn't it at all! "It's just…" She paused. There was no way she'd get out of this without telling her the whole story, which she couldn't do in front of Lance's father. She turned to him. "Luis, do you mind getting started on inventory in the storage room?"

"No problem," he said, tipping his cowboy hat in Cassidy's direction as he slipped by.

Once he was gone, Cassidy plopped down at the desk with the aged computer, then rolled another office chair close and pointed at it. "Spill it. What are you doing here? You're supposed to be enjoying a day off."

Jessa sat and settled Ilsa on her lap. She *would've* been enjoying a day off if things hadn't gotten so awkward back at the ranch. In a hushed tone, she shared the whole story in what had to be record time.

Cassidy's eyes grew wider and wider. "Wow. So what're you going to do? You going to stay there?"

"I feel like I have to." She'd made a deal with Lance. Besides, she needed the money. And now she wouldn't feel bad at all taking a cut. She didn't want to give him the satisfaction of bowing out because things had gotten a little uncomfortable.

"I can't believe you kissed Lance Cortez," Cassidy blurted. Her eyes bulged and she covered her mouth. "Sorry. But that's crazy. Was it good?"

"No." *Yes it was*. Her heart sighed. *Sooooo good*.

"I can tell when you're lying, you know."

Jessa simply petted Ilsa's coarse hair and planted a kiss on the pig's head. "I wonder why someone didn't want her," she said, trying to get Cassidy to focus on something besides Lance.

Luis came back, lugging along her father's old metal tool-box. "We're almost out of dog bones," he informed her. "But from what I can tell, everything else looks fine."

Of course it was fine, because she'd done the inventory three days ago. Jessa fanned her face. "Okay," she sang. "Thanks, Luis. I'll add dog bones to the list."

He secured the toolbox under one arm and hooked the other around the ladder they kept behind the counter. "I'm gonna head out and get that sign fixed."

After he'd moseyed through the door, Cassidy looked at Jessa with shiny eyes, a grin brimming. But before the woman could ask more questions, she glanced at the call log on the desk. "Has anything else come in today?"

Cassie snorted. "No. But Hank Green called. Twice in the past half hour, even though I told him you're not in today. I offered to help him out, but it's not me he wants." She wiggled her eyebrows.

Damn it. Not exactly the kind of call she'd hoped for. Give her a fawn tangled in a fence any day over Hank Green. The retired grocery store manager had had a thing for her ever since she'd worked there the summer she'd turned eighteen. He made passes at her every time he saw her.

She sighed. "What's the problem?"

"His cat is stuck in a tree. Again." Cassidy laughed. "He probably *put* him up there so he could call you."

"Oy." Hank did have some delusions about the two of them driving off into the sunset together. Despite the fact that he was a good forty years older than her and she'd tried to tell him repeatedly he wasn't her type.

Cassidy patted her hand sympathetically. "I told him he'd have to check in with you Monday if he wanted to talk with you."

Except that would mean she had nothing to do here today. No reason to keep Luis here, which meant they would have to go back to the ranch. And she dreaded that even more than she dreaded Hank's awkward passes. "Actually, I think I'll go over there." She rose from the chair and started to collect everything she'd need for Ilsa—the crate, the antibiotics, a special bottle so she could help her put on some weight. She could easily drop the pig off at the ranch before heading over to Hank's place.

When she turned around, Cass was gaping at her. "That'll only encourage him, you know."

"The poor cat. It's not his fault his owner is nuts." She crossed to the other desk and pulled out her medical kit from the drawer, just in case Butch the wonder cat was injured during the rescue.

"I'm sure he'll get him down if you don't come," Cassidy muttered.

"I wish I had your faith." But Hank could be quite persistent. She'd been witness to that. "Anyway, this is exactly what I need today. A distraction." A reason to avoid the ranch. Okay, a reason to avoid *Lance*. "I'll bring Luis with me."

"Oh, that'll help." Her friend rolled her eyes. Hank had always had it out for the Cortez boys—called them hoodlums and troublemakers—and now the rivalry between Hank Green and Luis Cortez was legendary. "You might want to bring some rope in case there's a brawl and you have to hogtie the two of them."

"Everything'll be fine," she insisted. Even if it wasn't, it would be a hell of a lot easier than facing Lance again today.

Chapter Eleven

Though she couldn't say much for the man himself, Jessa had always loved Hank Green's house. Located only a few blocks off Main Street, it had that old, small-town curb appeal, with rounded Victorian bay windows and pointed eaves. Pale bricks set off the blue shutters and an intricate white front porch wrapped the length of the house in a charming elegance.

"Hank Green needs your help about as much as Lance needs mine," Luis mumbled as she pulled up to the curb.

"I feel bad for him," Jessa said through a sigh. "He's lonely." So he called her over to help with his animals occasionally. What was the harm in that? Though he was in his late sixties, the man had never been married, never had any family, so she could understand why he'd want some company. "Besides," she continued, withdrawing the keys and unclipping her seat belt, "I can't ignore an animal in distress." The poor cat was probably terrified.

"You sure do have a big heart, Jessa." Luis pulled himself out of her truck, and did she imagine it or was he wincing more than normal?

Before she could make a full assessment, Hank waved from the front porch.

"Jessa. Thank God you're here," he called, teetering down the steps while he clutched the rail. The rim of white hair on his head had been neatly trimmed, and the bald spot on top shone in the sun. "Butch is terrified up there. I can hear him meowing."

Luis snorted and Jessa shoved a gentle elbow into his ribs. "Be nice," she whispered. "At least you have Lance and Naomi and Gracie around."

A small smile fumbled on his lips. "And you," he said. Which made *her* smile. Though she missed her father with heart-aching sorrow, having Luis sure helped.

Hank lumbered down the walkway toward them.

Ah, geez. He'd put on his dress slacks, with a sweater vest and bow tie. If only she could convince him dressing up for her wasn't worth the effort.

"What're you doing here, Cortez?" he asked, as though perturbed that he had some competition.

"Luis is helping at the shelter today," Jessa answered for him. The less these two gentlemen talked, the better off everyone would be. Way back in a previous life, Hank had accused Levi, the youngest Cortez, of shoplifting from his store. Levi, of course, always claimed innocence, and when Luis went down there to straighten things out, it had ended in a brawl that had the town sheriff locking up both men overnight.

Hank still eyed Luis warily. "I've told you, Jessa. *I* can help you at the shelter." He shifted his body as if to block out

Luis and focus solely on her. "I have nothing but time on my hands, and as you know, I *am* an animal lover."

"Lover," Luis scoffed under his breath. Jessa did have to admit that Hank somehow made that word sound rather dirty.

Instead of indulging Hank's offer with an acknowledgment, she brushed past him and continued up the walkway toward the house. "So where is poor Butch?" she asked.

"He's out back. About halfway up that blue spruce." Hank hustled to her side, leaving Luis to walk behind them. "I don't even know how he got out..."

Once again, Luis snorted.

Jessa shot him a look over her shoulder. Hopefully it said, *Let's not make this more painful that it has to be.* Though she had a hard time choking back a laugh. "How high up?" she asked in a businesslike tone. If she could keep them on track, this wouldn't have to take long and she wouldn't risk the two of them getting into another brawl.

"Oh, I don't know..." The man led the way around the side of the house on an intricate stone path that weaved through his prize-winning rose garden. "Maybe twenty feet up."

"Twenty feet?" Was the man trying to kill her? "You could've called the fire department," she reminded him. That was the sort of thing the small-town Topaz Falls Fire and Rescue was famous for. Rescuing kitties, helping little old ladies cross the street, putting out one hell of a scorching calendar every year...

"I did call." Hank escorted her past the large white gazebo in the backyard. It was gorgeous. Flawless and lavish, adorned with hanging baskets of every kind of flower. God, maybe she should just give in and marry the man. He had the best yard in all of Topaz Falls.

"The fire department refused to come."

Yeah, and she was Dolly Parton. The thought brought on a serious cringe. Hank probably *wished* she were Dolly Parton...

This time Luis coughed behind her, but at least he was keeping his mouth shut. She gave him a surreptitious grin before glancing up into the blue spruce that towered over a white picket fence on the back perimeter of the property.

At least twenty feet above the ground, the cat crouched on a wide pluming branch, its face obscured by the pine needles.

Oh, wow. Yeah. That cat was stuck. "Have you tried calling to him? Luring him down with treats?" she asked, shading her eyes from the overpowering sun.

"Of course," Hank assured her emphatically. "I've tried *everything*. I'm so distressed by the whole thing. Butch hates heights."

Again, Jessa called his bluff. Butch did, indeed, look terrified. But there was no way he'd climbed up there by himself. Cassidy was right. Hank had probably hauled over the ladder and stowed the cat up there as a ploy to get her to come over.

"Maybe he'll come down when he sees your beautiful face," Hank murmured, leaning too close for comfort. The smell of Pepto-Bismol wafted around her, stealing the sweet scent of roses from the air.

With a quick sidestep she escaped the assault, drawing closer to Luis.

"The thing is, I can't keep climbing up your tree to get your cat down, Hank." This was the fifth time in less than two months. But this was also the highest she'd ever found Butch.

"I understand," he said through a martyred sigh. "Don't worry. I won't ask for your help anymore."

"There really is a God," Luis muttered, though not nearly soft enough.

Hank whirled. "What the hell does that mean, Cortez? Do you have a problem with me?"

"I think it was you who had a problem with me," Luis shot back.

Jessa stepped between them. "Luis, can you please go get Hank's ladder out of the garage?" she asked in her sweetest-daughter-in-the-world voice. Her father had never been able to resist it, and it appeared Luis couldn't either. He turned away, mumbling some very colorful names for Hank, and hoofed it to the path around the side of the house.

Whew. Crisis averted. Lance would kill her if he knew she'd let his father get into it with Hank Green.

Lance. Right on cue, her stomach dropped and her heart twirled and the warmth of the sun seemed to slip inside her skin.

"So what's the plan?" Hank's low and gritty tone snuffed out the sudden fire burning hot and low in her belly. Well, there it was. Her remedy for shamelessly swooning over Lance. She didn't have to worry about that when Hank was nearby. "Um." She pushed her bangs off her forehead and gazed up again.

Butch was still perched in place, frozen into a fluffy cat statue. She moved closer to the tree. "Here kitty. Come on, Butch, baby. Come down now."

The cat crouched lower and mewed. There was no way in hell he was coming down on his own. Which meant she would have to go up and get him. "We need the ladder." Luis must've found it by now, but he was probably taking his time so he could cool off.

Hank slipped in front of her, gazing down on her with an affectionate look that deepened the creases in the corners of his beady gray eyes. "Jessa...while we wait, I want to thank you. For coming. You're always there for me when I need something."

"Technically I'm always there for Butch—"

Hank didn't seem to hear. "I hope you'll let me take you out to dinner this time. Only to thank you, of course," he said quickly. "Someplace nice. Maybe the Broker?"

"The Broker?" She almost laughed. "But that's in Denver."

"Exactly. We could make it a weekend trip..." Mr. Green rubbed his hand on her shoulder.

She swatted at it like she would a pestering fly. "I'm sorry. That's not going to happen. *Ever*." And the touching her shoulder thing...that had to stop, too.

"*Ever*?" he repeated, as though mortally wounded.

A sigh lodged in her throat. The poor man. He wasn't so bad. Hell, at least he had good taste. And at least he didn't look at her like she was some pathetic groupie. "I'm not in a good place for anything like that right now," she said gently.

His lips pursed while his head bobbed in a brave nod. "I understand. I can wait."

Never. She'd told him never. Ain't no way he could wait that long...

"Mew." The cat's soft call commanded her attention. Jessa stood on her tiptoes and tried to see through the pine needles.

"Mew." Butch inched forward on the branch as though ready to jump down to the next one.

"That's it!" Jessa scrambled up the first couple of

branches until she was about five feet off the ground. "Come on, Butchie. Come here." She pulled herself up higher. Somewhere beneath her something cracked.

"Here. I'll give you a boost," Hank offered, raising his hands and cupping them against her ass.

"No thanks," she squawked, darting up to the next branch. The tree was thick and sturdy, shaking only slightly while she climbed higher. After pulling herself up a few more branches, she had to stop. The branches were getting thinner and there was no way they'd support her weight. Butch had climbed down a ways, but he was still a few feet above her. "Here, kitty," she crooned softly. "Come on, now. I'm right here. Jump down and I'll catch you."

The cat crept closer to the edge of the branch, head low, wide, terrified eyes focused on Jessa.

"Okay. It's okay." Hooking one arm around the trunk, she shimmied up one more branch and reached until her fingertips tingled. "There." She grabbed the skin at the back of Butch's neck. The cat hissed and squirmed but she secured him against her chest, gasping and sweating. Carefully, she picked her way back down the tree and dropped to the ground. Heaving from the effort, she handed Butch over to Hank. "Don't let the cat get out again. I can't keep doing this."

The man's chin tipped up defiantly. "If you'd agree to dinner, I wouldn't *have* to keep calling."

Shaking her head, she turned away from him and started toward the path. What could be taking Luis so long?

"Maybe you'd rather have breakfast?" Hank persisted, coming alongside of her.

Wordlessly, she shook her head.

"Coffee?" he tried.

She stopped walking and faced him. "Sorry. It's not going

to work out." This time she patted his shoulder in an effort to ease the dejected look he gave her. "What about Helen Garcia?" she asked. Helen had been the librarian since the turn of the century. "She's so smart. And ... organized." That was about where the list of her attributes stopped.

"Jessa, I know there's a slight age difference, but—"

"Slight?" she interrupted.

"I think you're the loveliest woman in the world," he finished a little desperately.

Okay, so sweet and subtle was not going to work with Hank. She had to give it to him straight. She started walking along the path so she wouldn't have to look into his eyes. "I appreciate that. Really. But it's not going to happen. I don't look at you like that, and—" When they came around the corner of the house she stopped cold.

The ladder lay in the center of the yard, crushing Hank's perfect green grass.

"My grass," he gasped, stalking toward the ladder.

Worry filled her stomach like a cold hard stone. "Where's Luis?" she choked out. The ladder looked like it had been dropped, but he wasn't there.

"I don't know, but this'll ruin my grass." Hank struggled to drag the ladder to the driveway while she scanned the empty street.

Luis wasn't there. He was gone.

Somehow, Jessa faltered to the garage, her eyes searching. It was empty. "Where could he be?" she blurted, frantically looking around.

"Knowing Cortez, he's in the house going through my things," Hank replied tightly. He marched to the garage door and threw it open. "That family is all the same. Thieves, the lot of them."

She reprimanded him with a glare. "None of them are thieves," she said sternly. "But maybe he went in for a drink. Or maybe he had to use the bathroom." Of course that was it. He had to be in the house. Jessa gulped a breath to steady her heart. He hadn't disappeared, for God's sake. She followed Hank inside, inhaling the musty scent of an old closed-in house, searching room by room, not really seeing anything but somehow finding her way. He wasn't in the kitchen or the living room or the dining room or the main floor bathroom. She bolted up the rickety staircase. "Luis?" she screeched, throwing open the upstairs bedroom doors. The house sat in a heavy silence. She broke it again with another shout, half stumbling back down the steps.

Hank met her by the front door. "He's probably gone into town for pie and coffee," he said, his nose scrunched with distaste. "You can't count on the Cortez family for anything except trouble."

"No," Jessa wheezed. Not Luis. He wouldn't leave her when she needed his help. He wouldn't have left the ladder lying in the middle of the front yard. "Oh God." Sidestepping Hank, she broke through the front door and sprinted down the driveway to the sidewalk. Trying to breathe, she looked up and down the deserted street. "Luis?" she yelled.

Nothing. No response. Hands shaking, she dug her keys out of her pocket and flew to her truck.

"Sorry, Hank!" she yelled, fumbling to unlock the doors. "Please call me right away if Luis comes back!" Before he could respond, she thrust herself into the driver's seat and gunned the engine until the truck shot away from the curb.

Chapter Twelve

One more fall like that and he'd be seein' stars. Lance hoisted himself off the ground. Not gonna lie, it was getting harder to get up. That was the third time in an hour Ball Buster had thrown him. Good thing Tucker was a regular master at corralling the mean son of a bitch so he hadn't trampled him.

Shit. He hunched, trying to even out his breathing, which was a hell of a lot harder than it sounded with the laceration and bone bruise sending flames up his rib cage.

"Hey, you okay, man?" Tucker jogged over to where Lance limped near the fence. "You're lookin' tense out there."

Tense. That was one way to put it. "I'm fine," he lied, guarding his right side. Damn bone bruise. Sure wasn't making his training any easier. Every time that pain zinged through him, he also thought back to when Jessa had touched him there. When she'd run her hands over his skin, her fingers light and gentle. That only led to another problem that pretty much made it impossible for him to ride in comfort.

"Maybe you ought to call it a day," Tucker suggested, handing him his water bottle.

Lance removed his hat and took a good long swig. He couldn't call it a day. Not until he'd gotten the better of Ball Buster. There was no way he'd be able to compete at Worlds if he couldn't even stay on that damn bull for more than three fucking seconds.

He shoved the water bottle back into Tucker's hands. "Here. I'm going again. Let's get him ready."

The man shook his head like he wasn't sure if he should pity Lance or argue. But he knew the sport. He knew what it took.

Lance climbed the fence and jumped down on the other side. He removed his gloves to check the tape on his hands. It was already frayed and torn. He'd have to rewrap—

"Lance!"

Naomi raced around the edge of the corral.

Damn. She had that look of drama about her.

"I just got a call from Ginny Eckles," she yelled as he walked to meet her. "It's your dad. She found him in front of the bakery, and something's wrong."

The pain in his ribs intensified with the hitch in his breathing. "What do you mean something's wrong?"

Naomi was wheezing like she'd sprinted all the way from her house. "She said she tried asking him some questions but he wouldn't answer. He wasn't acting like himself."

Oh for chrisssake. "Where the hell is Jessa?" he demanded, as if Naomi were her keeper.

"I don't know," she shot back with just as much attitude.

"I asked Mrs. Eckles if he was alone and she said he was. She said Luis didn't seem to remember where he was supposed to be."

"Of course he remembers," Lance grumbled, already unbuckling his chaps. His dad wouldn't forget where he was supposed to be. He was probably just being ornery. Which Jessa could've prevented had she kept an eye on him like she was supposed to.

Naomi stooped to help him get the chaps off. Always the mother. "She thinks someone should pick him up. I'd go but I have to pick up Gracie at a friend's house on the other side of town in five minutes."

"I'll get him," Lance said, kicking off the leather gear. "Tucker, go ahead and get Ball Buster settled in the stables," he called to his friend. Looked like he was done training for the day after all.

The man tipped his hat and approached the bull while Lance followed Naomi down to the driveway.

"I tried to call Jessa's cell a few times, but she didn't answer," Naomi informed him, almost like she didn't want to get her friend in trouble.

His face steamed. "Don't worry about it." Not like he could blame all of this on Jessa. Knowing his father, he'd probably lost her on purpose.

"Maybe she's really upset," Naomi said. "About your talk this morning."

"She didn't seem upset." The memory of her coy smile tugged at his gut. She seemed fine. Confident. Strong. Like a woman who could hold her own. "You're wrong about her, you know," he told Naomi. "She's stronger than you give her credit for." Strong and sexy. Enticing with that body of hers. Not that he wanted to get slapped...

"Don't you get any ideas," Naomi warned. "I don't know who that woman at breakfast was, but it wasn't Jessa. It was an act. And I don't blame her. You practically humiliated her."

"On your advice," he reminded her.

They parted ways, but before Naomi climbed into her car, she shot him a glare. "You just keep your distance. Take my word for it." Before he could answer that he was done taking her word for anything, she disappeared into her car and peeled out.

Shaking his head, Lance climbed into his truck and drove down to the highway. As far as he could tell, Jessa was a big girl and could take care of herself. He might not go out of his way to pursue her, but if something clicked between them one night, he'd let it happen. Not that he'd be dreaming about that moment. Not dreaming...fantasizing. About those slender fingers grazing his skin again, about the sexy dip in the curve of her upper lip. About the delicate weight of her body against his, all soft curves and creamy flesh...

Shit, he just about missed his turn. He jerked the wheel in a quick left and slowed as he cruised down the strip. Sure enough, a small crowd had gathered in front of Butter Buns Bakery. He slowed and pulled over to parallel park at the curb. This didn't look good.

The people who'd gathered around Luis parted as Lance jogged down the sidewalk.

"Get the hell away from me," his dad was shouting at Mrs. Eckles.

"Whoa." Lance rushed to his father's side. "Dad. What's wrong?"

"He's very agitated," Mrs. Eckles prattled in her know-it-all way. She shook her head, the bifocals strung around her neck clanking. "All I did was ask if he needed something.

He looked so confused. And when I told him I was going to call over to your place, you should've seen him. Cursing and screaming like a lunatic."

"She was badgering me," Luis put in, glaring at Mrs. Eckles like he wanted to pop her in the face.

Damn, this went way beyond ornery. "I'm sorry about this, Mrs. Eckles," Lance said, delivering the words with a polite smile. But chaos raged underneath it. What the hell was his father's problem? Making a scene like this in the middle of town? "I'll get him home." He clamped a hand onto Luis's shoulder and dragged him away before the woman decided to press charges.

His father jerked out of his grip. "I don't need you coming to pick me up. Acting like I'm the one who's crazy."

Lance growled out a sigh. Is that what happened when people got older? They stopped caring what everyone thought and did whatever they wanted? "Where's Jessa, Dad?" he asked, trying to control the venom in his tone.

"How the hell should I know?" his father shot back.

That forced him to a stop. "Because you left the house with her. To go help at the clinic."

A look of understanding dawned in his dad's blank eyes.

Tremors took over Lance's stomach. "Don't you remember?"

"Of course I remember," his father snapped. "I wanted to go for a walk, that's all. I got thirsty and I wanted to go for a walk."

Lance studied him. The man's hands were trembling. Sweat glistened on his forehead. "Are you feeling okay?" he asked.

"I'm fine," his father said, a little softer. "Just so thirsty."

Relief swept through him. He'd probably gotten dehydrated. At some point, he'd have to talk to Jessa about making sure Luis drank plenty of water. "All right, old man," he said lightly, steering his father toward the truck. "I think I've got an extra water bottle in the tr—"

"Luis!"

Lance spun. Jessa sprinted toward them, her arms flailing, long hair sailing behind her.

"Where have you been?" she rasped, pressing one hand against her heaving chest.

Damn...the way she filled out a shirt...

"I went for a walk," Luis muttered, refusing to look at Jessa.

"A walk?" she choked out. "A *walk*?" If it was possible, her face got redder. "How could you do that, Luis? Huh? How could you just walk away without telling me where you were going?"

A couple passing by on the street paused to stare at Jessa.

Yeah, she was a little fired up. "Dad needs some water. He's thirsty." Lance slipped an arm around her waist and tried coaxing her to the truck so they could move this discussion somewhere more private.

"I have the right to go for a walk if I want to," his father insisted.

Jessa halted and squirmed out of Lance's grip. "I asked you to get the ladder out of Hank Green's garage. And you never came back." She turned to Lance, her eyes wild with indignation. "And then I found the ladder lying in the middle of the front yard and Luis had simply disappeared."

What was he supposed to say? He couldn't make excuses for his father's behavior.

"I was thirsty," Luis said again. "I wanted something to drink."

"Then you should've told me that," Jessa whispered, as though she was still having a hard time breathing. "I could've gotten you a drink, Luis." She swayed a little, as if the stress of losing his father had gone to her head. Once again, Lance secured an arm around her, trying not to notice how good she smelled.

This time, she allowed him to lead her to the truck. Luis got into the passenger's seat and Lance handed him a water bottle from a cooler in the back.

Jessa had leaned against the bed of the truck, staring off into space as though trying to collect her wits.

"He didn't mean to scare you," Lance said, coming up beside her and nudging her shoulder with his. "He's always had a mind of his own. But he doesn't do stuff like that on purpose."

"He never does stuff like that to me, Lance," she said quietly. Her face turned to his, and for the first time he noticed the red rims around her eyes. She'd been crying. Some protective instinct ballooned inside him and he wanted to wipe away her tears and make sure she never had another reason to cry.

Yes, Jessa was strong. She had a lot of sass. But she was also compassionate and seemed to feel everything so deeply. Maybe he appreciated that about her even more than he appreciated her sexy legs.

"I'll talk to him. Make sure he doesn't do it again," Lance promised, and God help him, he couldn't keep his hands off her. He trailed his fingers at the base of her jaw, sweeping back the strands of hair that had escaped her ponytail.

"I think..." Her gaze strayed from his. "I think something's wrong."

"What do you mean?"

"With your father. I think something's wrong with him."

"He got thirsty and he's used to doing what he wants when he wants." That was it. The older he got, the more stubborn he got.

"Lance..." Jessa took his hand in hers and it felt so out of place but so right, her soft smooth skin covering his rough callused knuckles. "I think you need to take him to the doctor. To have him checked out."

"What?" He pulled his hands to his sides.

Jessa peered up at him, her face steeled as it had been earlier that morning when they'd had their little chat in the kitchen. "He's had short-term memory loss twice now..."

"That's not memory loss." His hands twitched and he pulled them into fists. Clearly, the man was fine. "He got turned around in the mountains. And today he just wanted a damn drink of water."

"So he left a ladder in the middle of Hank Green's yard and walked ten blocks to Main Street for a drink?" she challenged. "Why didn't he go into the house to get a drink?"

"He hates that man." Everyone knew that. Jessa knew that. Why had she even taken him there? That was probably what started this whole debacle. "He'd never set foot in Hank Green's house willingly."

Jessa stepped up to him. "I think he got disoriented. I think he didn't remember where he was or what he was supposed to be doing." Anger flashed in her eyes. "He wouldn't walk away like that when I asked him to do something. He's never done that."

Lance threw up his hands. What did she want from him? "Cut the man some slack," he said, dismissing her concerns. "He's almost seventy. He probably shouldn't be carrying ladders around anyway."

Jessa glared at him for a silent minute. Then she strode close and got in his face. "I know you don't want to hear this. But something's wrong with him."

She was right about one thing. He didn't want to hear an uneducated diagnosis. "He was at the doctor three months ago and he's healthy as a horse." Those were the doc's exact words. Trying to appease her, he laid his hand on her shoulder. "Now I'm gonna take him home. Let him rest. I'll see you later." He turned and headed for the truck before she could argue.

Chapter Thirteen

There was a reason Darla had named her establishment the Chocolate Therapist. She firmly believed that every problem could be solved with the right wine and chocolate pairing. And in Jessa's experience, she was almost always right.

In need of some serious therapy after that little exchange with Lance, Jessa marched herself down four and a half blocks and charged through the familiar stained-glass door.

A few patrons sat around the tall pub tables, leaf-peeping tourists from the looks of their designer clothing. All of them had flights of wine and an assortment of truffles to match.

Somehow just inhaling that rich, cocoa scent made Jessa feel better already.

Darla was stationed behind the counter, walking a young couple through the menu, so Jessa slunk to the far corner stool at the main bar and plopped herself down, replaying that conversation with Lance again.

He probably shouldn't be carrying ladders around anyway.

As if Luis disappearing was her fault. Her shoulders sank lower. She only wanted to help the man, and yet Lance had completely dismissed her like her opinion didn't matter at all. It wasn't just the situation with the ladder. She'd noticed the tremors, things she'd originally written off as his arthritis acting up, but now she wasn't so sure.

"Wow, who pissed in your coffee today?" Darla appeared before her with a tray of truffles and a flight of reds.

Her angel of mercy.

The woman set the trays on the counter beside Jessa and pulled over a stool. "Looked like you could use something strong, so I brought all darks and a bittersweet."

"Perfect," Jessa, said before popping one of the cocoa-dusted confections into her mouth. Then she sipped on the first glass. Closing her eyes to hold on to the taste, she swallowed. "Better already," she said with a sigh.

"You want to talk about it?" her friend asked in a tone that wouldn't take no for an answer. Who was Jessa kidding? Her face was an open comedic tragedy. She'd never been one to hide her emotions.

"This arrangement is more complicated than I thought it would be," she admitted, going for another truffle. The chocolate melted in her mouth.

"What is? Staying at a ranch with a sexy *single* cowboy while you babysit his aging father?" Sarcasm dripped from her smile. "How could that possibly be complicated?"

Yeah, yeah, yeah. She'd set herself up for this. It had all seemed so simple. Until her body and heart betrayed her and attached themselves to a man who had zero ability to commit.

"All right. This looks bad. What happened?" Darla asked, leaning her chin into her fist as though she knew they'd be there awhile.

"You have customers to take care of." And she felt more like wallowing alone.

"Beth can take care of the customers and I can take care of you." Out of all of them, Darla happened to be the most motherly. Well...if your mother liked to make off-color jokes, flirt with much younger men, and only wear shirts that showed plenty of cleavage.

"Come on," Darla prompted. "You'll feel better if you talk about it."

Not likely. But she relayed the entire story anyway, popping the truffles into her mouth and washing them down with sips of the decadent wine between sentences.

Darla said nothing. She wore the same concentrated expression she did whenever she was testing out a new recipe.

"So that's it, I guess. I think something's wrong with Luis. Lance doesn't care what I think." That about summed it up. He didn't respect her enough to value her opinion.

"Am I missing something here?" Darla leaned in, her dark eyes wide and emphatic. "Isn't *he* the one who asked for your help? For you to stay with his father and keep an eye on him?"

"Yes." Exactly. He wanted her there, but he didn't want to hear what she thought.

"Here's what you're gonna do, honey," Darla said, waiting until Jessa looked her in the eyes. "You're gonna drive back to the ranch. March that cute little ass of yours right up to Lance's front door and ask him if he still wants your help with his father."

Jessa tried to take mental notes. That sounded easy.

"Then, when he says yes—because he *will* say yes—you're going to tell him he doesn't get to ignore you. Since you are doing him a favor, he will listen and consider what you say." A grin broke through her titanium expression. "Then you tell him he's not allowed to kiss you again unless he intends to fully finish the job."

Jessa rolled her eyes. "I'll take everything else and leave out that last part."

"Come on." Darla swatted at her. "What good is taking on a second job if you can't take advantage of some of the perks?" She nibbled on a truffle. "Trust me, honey. Lance Cortez's body is one hell of a perk."

That was one way to describe it…

"Besides, maybe if you two really got it on, all this tension would go away and you'd be able to move on."

Jessa choked on a sip of wine. "I don't think so." If she was going to stick it out at the ranch until Worlds, she couldn't make things more awkward than they already were.

"Here." Darla reached into the pocket of her apron and dug out some wrapped truffles. "Take these with you. A new blend. Pop one in your mouth before you talk to him." Her eyebrows arched. "Trust me."

Jessa held out her palm and carefully examined the dark mounds of goodness. "Isn't chocolate an aphrodisiac?" Because she didn't need any help in that area. Not with Lance.

Darla simply gave her an innocent smile before she stood and waltzed away.

* * *

All the way to Lance's house, Jessa practiced. She practiced saying exactly the words Darla had given her. She practiced in a bitchy voice, an apathetic voice, then decided that was too much and tried to add a note of sympathy. All in all, she must've said the words fifty times and yet as she climbed the stairs to his front porch, her mind blanked.

But there was no turning back now. Before she could overthink it, she knocked on the door. A sudden explosion of nerves blew inside her and she quickly unwrapped the truffle that had been melting in her pocket and popped it into her mouth. Some brand of heavenly merlot leaked through the chocolate, bringing a symphony of fruity notes. *Good, fun-loving lord*, enough of these chocolates and she'd never need sex again.

The door opened and Lance stepped out. He was dressed in a faded gray T-shirt and sinfully tight worn jeans. They should be illegal in all fifty states, those jeans.

Okay. So maybe never needing sex again was a bit strong...

"Hi," he said, straightening as though he was surprised to see her. "Everything okay?"

Right. That was her cue. Everything was *not* okay. But she couldn't seem to manage the words. "Um." She cleared her throat so she didn't sound like Lauren Bacall. "We need to talk." Because she had stuff to say. Lots of important stuff...

She tried to play back Darla's badass lecture in her mind, but a steady humming drowned it out.

"Okay..." Lance stepped aside and made room for her to walk past him. On the way, she caught that alluring scent that seemed to cling to him. Something woodsy and sexy. *Keep going*, she reminded her feet. She couldn't stand too close to him.

"Can I get you something to drink?" he asked politely,

leading her through his family room and into the kitchen, where they'd had their little exchange earlier. Just like that morning, she positioned herself far away, on the opposite side of the kitchen island.

"No." No drinks. She had to get this over with. She braced her hands against the countertop and looked at him directly before she lost the nerve. "You don't get to ignore me," she announced, and wow, Darla would have been so impressed. She sounded *pissed*.

Lance blinked at her.

Courage bloomed. "I mean, I'm only trying to help, and you acted like I'm causing some big problem for your father. Instead of listening to me, you load him up in the car and get out of there like my concerns don't matter. Do you have any idea how worried I was?" She started to pace. Once she got going, it was hard to stop. "I searched everywhere. I ran up and down the block looking in everyone's yard, going up to neighbors' doors and asking if they'd seen him. In case you haven't noticed, Lance," she said glaring at him again, "I care about Luis, too." A silent round of applause broke out in her head. She'd done it! Without letting him get a word in, even.

Lance's eyes were darker, narrow. She braced herself for a defensive tirade like he'd thrown at her earlier, but instead he sighed. "You're right." His hand raked though his hair. "I'm sorry."

"You know what, Lance," she said before she'd had time to process the words. *Hold on.* He hadn't argued with her. He'd…apologized? Just like that? "Huh?"

"You're right." The man's normally broad and powerful shoulders seemed to have bent under some unseen weight. "I shouldn't have brushed you off."

She should be gloating. That was exactly what she'd

wanted him to say. But the clear dejection that pulled at his mouth halted the victory party. "Okay, then. Thank you." The words sounded hollow and awkward. There was no script for this. Darla hadn't told her what to say if Lance started apologizing...

"I should've heard you out. I'm under a lot of pressure right now." His jaw tensed as he studied her, almost like he wanted to say something more, but decided against it.

"Because of Worlds?" she asked, trying to read what he wouldn't say.

Instead of answering, he walked to the table and picked up a magazine, then tossed it on the counter in front of her. "Because of this."

She grabbed the newest copy of *Rodeo World News* and her heart sank at the article's title: "Hometown Letdown."

Her eyes scanned the editorial—written by an anonymous source—which detailed Lance's fall from the highest acclaim in the rodeo world. It outlined his entire career—the early years of his success, the World title years ago. Then it detailed his fall from glory. The disappointing times, the disqualifications, the fact that he'd barely even qualified for Worlds this year. *He has proven that he's not his father, the great Luis Cortez, who at thirty was taking the top score in every competition...*

"They've decided I'm done. Useless. According to the fans, my career should've ended years ago," he said, eyes fixed on the article.

"Unbelievable." The words were cutting. Degrading for a man who'd won so many titles, who'd once been a hero. She read the last sentence: "Lance Cortez was once the greatest rider in the world. Now he's one of the greatest examples of what happens when you don't know when to quit."

A stab of pain lodged itself at the base of her throat. "This is crap," she said, tossing it back on the counter. Her hand shook with the absurdity of it. "Utter and complete crap. You've given your life to this sport." And when he was winning, everyone loved him. They couldn't say enough about him. Hell, there was a whole display about him at the public library...

"Maybe it's not." He raised his head and looked at her but didn't seem to see her. "Do you have any idea what it's like to read that? To hear the world saying you're done before you feel ready?" Those fierce bluish eyes steeled. He snatched the magazine and tossed it into the trash can. "Everything I've given my life to for the past fifteen years is over."

Jessa watched him pace the kitchen, words and anger and passion converging. There was no script for this. No plan for the sympathy that spilled out from inside her. "I can't imagine what that would be like," she said quietly, wishing she had more to offer him.

Lance stopped and turned to face her. "I don't know who I am outside of it. Outside of being my father's son. Outside of the arena. Outside of that world."

She got that. Sometimes when things changed so fast, when all of a sudden life looked different than it had the day before, you had to be reminded of who you were. That's what had happened when her father passed away. She was no longer a daughter and everything in her life was up for grabs.

She closed the distance between them with purposeful steps. "You're a good person, Lance. A good son. You've taken care of your dad. You've worked your ass off and you've accomplished more in fifteen years than most people do in a lifetime." The words were softer than she meant for them to be, more weighted with emotion than the conviction she wanted to offer him. "You can win." She'd seen him out there—that will, the sheer determination that drove him. "I know you can win." She wasn't sure exactly how, but her hand came to rest on his forearm, fingers lightly curled around his skin.

"Don't touch me." He staggered backward. "Not right now." There was a warning in his tone that matched the agony in his eyes.

Her hand froze where his arm had been. "Okay." She studied him, trying to understand what he wasn't saying, but his eyes wouldn't meet hers. What was he thinking? Had she made him angry again? "Did I say something wrong?" she asked quietly. She didn't know what to say, how to ease that tortured expression on his face.

Lance finally looked up, eyes smoldering with a passion she'd seen in him only out in the corral. "You tempt me to forget all of it," he uttered. "You make me think it doesn't matter."

Shock thundered through her. She braced a hand against the countertop and gaped at him. "Wh…what?"

"God, Jessa." He half-laughed while his head shook slowly back and forth. "You don't even know how beautiful you are, do you?"

The words were so unexpected she almost didn't believe them. Lance Cortez was calling her beautiful?

He stepped up to her, and he seemed to be moving so slowly. But maybe it was just the shock of what he was saying…

"When you're here I have a hard time focusing on my training…"

Her lungs locked in anticipation exactly the way they had last night when he'd covered her mouth with his. "D-do you...want me to leave?" she stuttered. She was pretty sure that wasn't what he meant, but sometimes it was best to be a hundred percent certain.

"No." His hands went to her cheeks, his callused fingers stroking them softly. "It wouldn't matter. I'd still see you." He leaned in closer, so that his lips were inches away. "I'd still feel you..."

"What happened to wanting different things?" she sputtered, her throat aching with the desire to lose herself in the feel of his lips over hers, his hands on her body.

"Right now, I only want you," he growled, his shoulders rising and falling with heavy breaths. His hands anchored her face while his lips came for hers—*claimed* hers—ravaging them in a frenzy of desperation and need.

Every fragment of self-protection she'd managed to piece together shattered in the sheer extravagance of his hot mouth, his tongue gliding over hers, his strong hands sliding down her neck, then caressing their way down her chest.

He groaned into her mouth as he brought his hands lower, running his fingers over her breasts.

Greed surged through her, heating the blood in her veins until even her legs tingled. Everything in her core tightened in a hard pull of sensuous tension. Right now, she only wanted him, too. *Needed* him to satisfy this overpowering hunger he'd provoked in her. Taking his bottom lip lightly between her teeth, she bit down and pushed him against the counter, somehow tugging his shirt up and over his head on the way. Stealing a second, she stopped to admire him, the hard muscle of his chest, the sinewed flesh stretched over his abs. His jeans sat low on his carved hips. The bandage she'd dressed him in last night was still intact, purple bruising visible around the edges. She touched it carefully.

"I don't need a nurse right now." His voice ground low in his throat. A sexy grin flashed before he came at her again, this time bypassing her lips and launching a thrilling assault on her neck. It was melting her, his lips, his tongue on her skin. He edged her back against the wall and captured her hands in his, raising them up until her arms were braced above her.

God, her body was so tight, so ready, she needed him to free her, but before she could beg, he pulled off her shirt in one smooth motion. Kissing her lips, then her cheeks, then her jaw, he worked his arms around her, pulling her in tighter and unhooking her bra with one hand. His other hand tore the flimsy satin away from her body but she couldn't see where it ended up because the magic of his mouth and hands teasing at her nipples blurred her vision. He buried his face in the valley of her, sighing, uttering helplessly desperate little noises.

Ragged breaths stole her thoughts. Her hands raked his thick, luxurious hair as he kissed and sucked and nibbled until she quaked with need. *Now.* She wanted him to fill her, to take her. Right. Now. Her hands clawed at his belt buckle until it somehow came unclasped and she could rip open the button fly of his jeans.

His forehead fell to her shoulder as she slid her hands down his hips, pushing down his boxers and jeans, and wrapped both hands around the hard length of him. She started moving her fingers, tightening the pressure, but he grabbed her wrists and brought them back above her head, pinning them against the wall and kissing his way to her ear. "You first."

She kept her hands raised over her head as he kissed her mouth deeply, his fingers undoing her jeans and pushing them down her hips.

His hands cupped her ass, then one of them slid down and hiked up her leg until her knee was at his waist. The other hand snaked around her body, slicing through the swollen flesh between her legs in one long stroke.

"No need for that," she murmured breathlessly. She was so hot, so primed, she only wanted him to break her apart. Now.

The grin flickered on his lips again. He finished removing his jeans, pulling out his wallet and riffling through until he found a condom. Impatiently, he ripped open the package and had that thing on before he'd made it over to where she stood.

Her heart beat against her ribs, pounding blood all through her.

Lance slipped his hands under her and hoisted her up, bracing her back against the wall as he drove into her in one long, hard thrust.

The heated grinding pried a moan from her lips. Her fingers dug into his shoulders as he slid out painstakingly slow, watching her eyes the whole way. By the time he thrust again she was panting, bearing her hips down to meet the rhythm he was using to tease her.

"God, Jessa." He grabbed a fistful of her hair, taking it roughly back from her face, and kissing her harder, deeper. The motion of his hips came faster, all power and strength, surging into her, lifting her higher, grazing the hot wetness. Her legs tightened around his waist, heightening the sensations, until it was all she felt…him. Everywhere. Inside of her and outside of her. With a tortured grunt he thrust again and this time she couldn't hold on. With a cry of exhilaration, she let go, abandoning herself to the release of blinding sensations, floating atop wave after wave of exquisite pleasure.

Lance brought one hand to her face and tipped up her head. A spark seemed to bind their eyes together. He pushed into her faster, harder, until a long groan punched out of his mouth and his body quaked.

Winded, but somehow still holding her up, his shoulders slumped against hers. A lazy grin took over his lips and she leaned her head down to kiss them again. They were so decadent, those lips of his...so wonderfully sensual and giving.

Lance set her feet on the floor and kissed her back, wrapping her in tighter, pulling her naked body snugly against his, and they seemed to fit so perfectly together.

"You're somethin', Jessa Mae," he said, his hungry gaze lowering down her body.

"I could say the same about you." Not once in her life had sex been so spontaneous, so instinctual and free-spirited. So close to the movie sex scenes that she'd always thought were contrived and unbelievable.

One time with Lance and she was a believer.

He took her hands in his, towing her closer. "So that was unexpect—"

The doorbell chimes cut him off.

Jessa snapped her head to stare at the front door on the other side of the great room. "Who's—"

"Uncle Laaa-aance!" The door muffled Gracie's singsongy voice.

"What is she doing here?" Jessa hissed, pushing away from him, breaking their bodies apart.

His eyes squeezed shut. "I'm supposed to give her a riding lesson."

"When?" Not to be dramatic or anything, but one minute ago the girl could've walked in on them having sex in his kitchen!

He glanced at the clock. "In two minutes."

"Holy shit. Good God, Lance." She scrambled around the floor, rummaging through the discarded clothing.

"I'll tell her to go away," he said, his mesmerized eyes locked on her body.

"You can't tell her to go away! Put these on." Jessa hurled his pants and boxers at him. Then his shirt. *Oops.* That was her shirt. *Aha!* His was pooled on the island. She ran over and snatched it, shaking it out so she could pull it over his head.

A knock sounded on the door. "Hello?" It was Naomi! The heavy wood started to creak open.

Jessa hit the floor next to Lance, scooting her knees into her chest and hiding herself behind the island.

He finished buckling his belt with amazing precision, given their current dilemma.

"There you are," she heard Naomi say from across the room, thank the lord.

There was a pause.

"Why didn't you answer the door?" her friend asked, a familiar skepticism creeping in.

Lance cleared his throat. "Um. Sorry. I was...on the phone."

Wow, he was good under pressure. He almost sounded bored. And then there was her...her pulse was racing so fast and hard, it felt like her heart could tear out of her rib cage at any second.

"Oh."

Jessa held her breath. Would Naomi get suspicious and

come over to the island? She edged her back against the cabinets.

"Why is Jessa's truck out there?" the woman asked.

Damn her!

"Dunno." Lance snuck a glance down at her, flashing that grin so fast she almost didn't see it, then he walked away. "Looks like someone's ready to ride, though," he said. And he must've twirled Gracie around because she giggled and squealed.

Slowly, Jessa let out the breath she'd been holding. Footsteps traipsed away from her until they grew faint.

"I wore my pink cowgirl hat," Gracie chirped as the front door opened.

When it closed, Jessa let herself collapse on the floor. Staring up at the ceiling, she tried to grasp what had happened. One minute she was reprimanding him and the next she was practically begging him to ravage her. And it might have been fast but...wow. For some reason that had made it even better. It had never happened that fast for her. Ever.

Trying to breathe like a normal human, she sat up and started dressing herself. She never did this...a quickie in the kitchen with a man she wasn't even *dating*. What the hell had come over her?

Shaking her head at herself, she shimmied on her jeans.

It had to be that damn chocolate.

Chapter Fourteen

Uncle Lance, why aren't you listening to me?" Gracie demanded, waving a hand in his face. Her glittery pink nails caught the sunlight and practically blinded him.

"Oh. Sorry, buckaroo." He shook himself conscious. Normally, he wasn't one to dwell on the past, but he couldn't seem to bring himself back into the present. Not after that mind-blowing rendezvous in his kitchen. It had been so good he might never get himself out of the past. And it wasn't like Gracie needed a ton of supervision. Not on Esmeralda. The mare had been his mother's horse way back when. She was as old as the sun and lumbered along steady and slow no matter what a person did with the reins.

"I asked if I'm holding on right," Gracie said, her bottom lip pouting slightly. She sat up taller on Esmeralda's back. "Because someday, when I'm a beauty queen, I'll need to know how to hold on the right way."

He grinned at her. "You're perfect. Just don't grow up and become a beauty queen too fast."

"Too late for that," Naomi mumbled beside him. "I swear...I don't know where she got her diva tendencies."

He swung his head to give her a proper look of disbelief. "Really?"

"What?" she demanded, just like her daughter.

He gave her a dose of raised eyebrows and braced himself for a fist in his biceps, but she only laughed. "So I like pink. And sparkles."

"And drama," he added, making a silly face so Gracie would laugh.

"Speaking of..." Naomi tugged him back a step while they watched Gracie make another leisurely round along the fence. "You do seem a little checked out. Who were you on the phone with when we came in?" Her expressive green eyes reflected the sunlight. She was already gloating.

Aw hell. He was busted. Naomi knew good and well he avoided the phone like he avoided her drama. "It was a wrong number," he said, heading for the safety of Gracie's presence.

"Where was she hiding?" Naomi asked, following him closely. "And what the hell was she doing in your house in the middle of the afternoon?"

He stopped and faced her. "If only that was your business."

"Oh, it's my business," she fired back. "Jessa is my friend. I thought we were in agreement on this." Her eyes narrowed as though she was calibrating her intuition.

Shit. That wasn't good for him.

"You slept with her didn't you?"

"Technically no." There was no sleeping involved. No lying down, even.

"Damn it, Lance," she said, smacking a hand against her thigh.

"We don't say 'damn it,' Mommy," Gracie called over. "That's a bad word."

Lance busted out laughing.

"You're right, peaches," Naomi muttered through clenched teeth. "What I meant to say is, 'How could you let this happen?'"

He shrugged, waiting until Gracie and Esmeralda had ambled to the other side of the corral. "It just happened. Okay?" He still wasn't sure how. When Jessa had said those things to him, told him she believed in him, something else took over. He couldn't stop himself. Couldn't hold back. Part of him had thought that once it happened, he'd get it out of his system and he'd be able to stop thinking about her. To see her without wanting her so badly it made him ache.

Man, had that backfired. That little tryst had only intensified the thoughts, the physical response to her. Next time it wouldn't be fast and frantic in the kitchen. He'd take his time with her.

"So what does this mean?" Naomi half-whispered. "Is Jessa okay?"

"She sure seemed okay." Way better than okay, actually, given her sexy cries there at the end...

"I mean are you guys together? In a relationship?"

"Not that I'm aware of." Though they hadn't really made time to discuss the details. "This morning, she said that wasn't what she wanted."

"Of course she said that, you idiot."

"We don't say, 'idiot,'" Gracie admonished. "Remember, Mommy? It's not nice to put people down."

Lance laughed again. He loved that girl.

"Right," Naomi said behind a plastic smile. "Thanks for the reminder."

Esmeralda hobbled away from them for another spin around the corral, and Lance took the opportunity to argue his case.

"Why does everything have to be defined right now?" Hell, he and Jessa hadn't even defined anything. He sure wasn't stupid enough to discuss the terms of their relationship with Naomi before he'd talked to Jessa about it. Relationship? Wow...had he ever used that word before? Maybe not, but he didn't exactly mind the sound of it as much as he once had.

"Well, I'm just wondering what you plan to do now," Naomi badgered in her little sister way. "Maybe it's time for you to deal with your commitment issues so you can actually have a healthy functioning relationship with someone."

If a man said that to him, he might haul off and throw a punch. "What the hell is that supposed to mean?"

"'Hell' is a bad word!" Gracie informed him from the other side of the corral.

"Right," he muttered, wondering what would happen if she wasn't around to keep them all in line. "I meant to say heck." He turned to Naomi. "What the *heck* does that mean?"

"You know what it means."

"I've never met anyone worth committing to," he said. That was all. Good women were hard to come by. She couldn't blame that on him.

"No," Naomi argued. "You've never let yourself *trust* anyone. Not since your mom left."

He opened his mouth to object, but she went on. "I know you better than almost anyone, Lance. You have serious trust issues."

Anger rose like a shield. "You're one to talk." She hadn't even dated anyone since Mark took off.

Instead of lashing back at him like he expected her to, Naomi laid a hand on his arm. "Exactly. Which means I can recognize it."

The admission disarmed him. What could he say to that? "Maybe it'll never be possible for me." Maybe his mother's abandonment had jacked him up so bad, he'd never have a relationship. Maybe he didn't even want to try.

"So what're you gonna do?" Naomi asked again.

"I don't know." It wasn't like he'd planned to have wild passionate sex with Jessa. He'd been in a rough place when she walked in. And right when he saw her everything seemed better. The opinion of the rest of the world hadn't mattered so much. She might be the only person in the world who believed he could compete at Worlds. Who believed he could win one more title.

"Oh my God," Naomi gasped. "Did we walk in on you two?"

"Not exactly." The memory of Jessa crouched behind the island next to him baited a smile. That could be their secret, though.

"Is she still at your house?" the woman blurted. "You have to go talk to her! You have to make sure she's all right!"

"She's all right." And yes, he'd talk to her. Later. He wasn't going to stress about it. Wasn't going to force things. And he sure as hell wasn't taking Naomi's advice again. "But after we're done here, I'm gonna call Tucker and have him bring out Wild Willy." The bull should be healed up by now and he needed to get serious.

Two minutes before Jessa had shown up on his doorstep,

he'd been this close to quitting. But she'd given him the determination to train and to fight and to keep going.

And now, he'd do whatever he had to do to get back in that arena for one more dance.

* * *

She should probably leave Lance's house, seeing as how *he'd* been gone for a half hour. Jessa had managed to retrieve her clothes—which by divine intervention had been strewn around the floor *behind* the kitchen island, saving them both from a potentially awkward conversation, had Gracie happened to have caught sight of a pair of women's underwear lying out in the open.

After she'd dressed, she'd teetered around the kitchen on her still wobbly legs doing the few dishes that sat in his sink and walking around the living room like it was a museum, noting the beautiful prints hanging on the walls and the detailed woodwork and the titles of the vast array of books he kept on the shelves.

You could tell a lot from a person's book collection and Lance's was extensive. He liked local history and cowboy legends. Political thrillers and classics like Dostoyevsky and Tolstoy. She wouldn't have pegged him for an intellectual, but then again, Lance was too layered to be pegged at all.

She knew she should leave, but she liked being there. She liked learning about him. She liked seeing how he organized his space and life. And yes, she liked *him*. Not just the sex, which had been…wow. But it went deeper than that. His tenderness. His loyalty. His sensitivity. He obviously didn't want people to see those things in him, but she did.

The more time she spent with Lance, the more he revealed his true heart to her—the one that had been wounded and left him wandering, much like her own. And the more she saw of his heart, the more she realized she could love this man. If she let herself. She could. That was a dangerous prospect. Because she already knew he didn't let himself love anyone.

So she had to leave. Walk out his door and not look over her shoulder. Accept the fact that things wouldn't be the same when they saw each other again. He'd be distant like he had been earlier. And she'd be unsure.

Steeling herself, she made her way across the sitting room and peeked out one of the front windows to make sure she wouldn't be caught. If she was honest, part of her hoped Lance would come back and find her there, that they could hold on to the connection that had rooted them together when he was looking into her eyes, holding her body, kissing her. It would be like a scene from a movie. She'd swing open his front door and he'd be standing there, just about to walk in because he'd realized he couldn't live without her. Then he'd kiss her and while he was kissing her, he'd sweep her into his arms and close the front door—locking it this time—and maybe he'd take her on the soft leather couch...

But Lance didn't come. No one was outside, and while disappointment weighted her chest, that was perfect because at least she wouldn't get caught sneaking out of his house. Quickly, she opened the door and slipped outside, eyeing the horizon for any glimpse of Naomi or Gracie. Once on the front porch, she ran, stumbling down the steps before racing to her truck. She climbed inside and sped down the road to Luis's house, taking an extra few seconds behind the wheel to collect herself so she didn't seem harried and panicked.

Carefully she straightened her hair, glancing in the

rearview mirror. God, she *looked* like she'd just had passionate sex. Her face was even still flushed.

Shaking her head at herself, she climbed out of the truck. Hopefully Luis wouldn't notice...

"Hey there." The man himself greeted her from the rocker on his porch as if he'd been sitting there waiting for her. He'd even brought out little Ilsa. The pig was curled up on his lap.

"Hi," she said brightly, going to sit by him. She loved his rocking chairs. He'd made them himself from the thick aspen branches he'd found on the property.

She settled in and stared out at the view. If Luis had noticed her sitting in the truck trying to primp herself back to normal he didn't let on. And he didn't ask why she'd just driven down from Lance's place.

He probably didn't have to.

"So how's our patient?" she asked, reaching over to ruffle Ilsa's ears.

"Seems fine." He handed over the pig and Jessa nuzzled her against her cheek. Ilsa still smelled like the scented shampoo she'd used when she'd bathed her.

The rocking chairs creaked for a few minutes before Luis turned to her. "Sorry I left Green's house like that," he said gruffly.

"No." She patted his hand. "It's okay. I probably overreacted." That morning already felt so long ago. So much had happened between then and now.

"Nah. It was a fool-headed thing to do," he mumbled as though angry at himself. "There's no excuse."

That was what bothered her. Luis never did fool-headed things. He'd always been careful and deliberate. Not rash. He thought things through.

She glanced at him, trying to interpret the disheartened expression on his face. A glimmer of intuition flared inside her and she drew in a breath of courage. "Are you sure you're okay, Luis?" Because he'd left the ladder in the middle of the yard. And even if he *had* been angry at Hank or even if he'd really been thirsty, he would've propped up the ladder near the house or left it in the garage...

"There's nothin' for you to worry about," he said, clearly not answering her question. He could've simply said no, but he hadn't.

Worry weaved itself into the threads of her fears. "If there was something, you could talk to me about it, you know." Though she hadn't meant for it to, emotion laced the words. "I could help you figure it out." She would do her best. In so many ways, this man was all she had left of her father. They'd shared years together. He'd known her dad even better than she had.

Luis rocked in his chair, his old hands gripping the armrests. "It's tough getting old," he finally said. "Feeling your body give out on you."

Give out on you how? she wanted to ask. What wasn't he telling her?

"Makes you think about all the things you'd do differently." He was gazing off to the mountains in the distance as though seeing a whole lifetime of regrets play before him.

The sad pull to his lips clawed at her heart. "What would you do differently?"

"Too many things to list," he said with a humorless laugh. Then he turned to her, those eyes watery and sure. "But you know what I regret the most?"

"No," she said, her eyes locked on his.

"I regret not making things right with Lucas." He looked

away from her again, but not before she saw tears brighten his eyes. "I was hard on him when they came for him after he set that fire. Said a lot of things I can't take back."

For the life of her, she could never imagine Luis saying a mean or hateful thing to anyone. But he'd likely been different back then.

"I'm sure he knew you were just angry," she offered. The fire had tarnished the Cortez family name. It divided the town, hurt Luis's own legacy...

"I told him I never wanted to see his face again." The old man's hands trembled and his grip on the armrests seemed to tighten. "But I didn't mean it. Didn't mean one word of it."

"Of course you didn't," she whispered, hidden tears thickening her throat. This poor man. Living with that grief all these years. "Have you ever tried to contact him?"

"I've kept up on him." His gaze lowered to the ground. "Through other people. He works for the McGowen Ranch down in Pueblo. Tried to send him a letter years back, but didn't ever get a response." Another garbled laugh sputtered out. "Can't say I blame him. He's built a good life for himself. Even after all he went through. No thanks to me."

"You're the one who gave him a foundation," she pointed out.

"But I should've been there for him," he said sternly. "I should've helped him through it."

"You did your best." In her estimation, every parent screwed up in some way or another. But Luis loved his boys. That was obvious. "I mean, look at Lance. And Levi. You have a great relationship with them."

"Not with Levi. He don't ever want to come home. Stays out on the circuit, away for his training." The man looked at her with that hollow gaze again. "Truth is, Jessa, my boys deserved better than me. All of 'em."

That wasn't the truth. Not at all, but she knew nothing she could say would take away his regrets. The only peace he'd find was through rebuilding what he'd lost with Lucas.

"I sure wish I knew 'em now." She barely heard the words above the rocking chair's creaking. "The way I know Lance."

"I'm sure they wish they knew you, too." God, she'd give anything to have her father. He wasn't perfect, but he was still her dad. Surely Lucas felt the same way. "I wish they knew you the way I know you. I wouldn't have survived this past year without you, Luis."

That earned a small smile. "I could say the same," he said, patting her hand. "Buzz would be proud of you."

"Thanks," she whispered. So much of who she was had come from her father. And that had to be true for Lucas and Levi, too. No matter what had happened in the past, Luis was still part of who they were. No one knew that better than her. Her dad's death had left a gaping hole in her life, but Lucas and Levi still had their father. And what if something was wrong with him? Then they might not have him much longer. She studied the tremors in Luis's hands. What would Lucas and Levi think of the symptoms Luis was obviously battling? Would they say it was nothing like Lance had?

Apprehension built inside her. They should at least know what was going on with their father. If Lance wouldn't tell them, someone else should.

She stood abruptly, cradling Ilsa against her chest. "I should go inside. I have some work to do." For starters, she had to contact the McGowen Ranch and talk Lucas into coming home.

Chapter Fifteen

Lance slung his dirty chaps over the stable's gate and brushed the dust off his jeans. He'd had a stellar training day, no doubt thanks to Jessa's pep talk and the extracurricular activities that had taken place in his kitchen. God, had it been almost a week ago? Ever since, he'd been out in the corral at the first light of dawn until well after sunset, occasionally breaking to eat or drink something. All in all, he'd managed to bring up his time consistently to eight seconds. His ribs and back might be aching now, but it was a good ache, familiar and dull. The kind of ache that told just how hard his muscles had been working.

Every day, Jessa's words had driven him. Along with thoughts of seeing her, being with her again. He fantasized about her all the time, but instead of distracting him, those thoughts now drove him. She drove him. But between his training and her and his dad's long hours at the shelter, he hadn't seen much of her. A wave here. A quick hello there.

It was not enough for him. Anticipation had built all week, and he couldn't hold it off anymore. Soon, he'd leave for Worlds. He couldn't miss out on spending some time with her before then.

So, desperate or not, he'd decided to show up at Luis's for dinner tonight. Then maybe the two of them could get out for a walk. Or a drink back at his place.

He hauled his gear onto the shelf and stepped out of the barn into the dusky evening. The sun was already sinking behind Topaz Mountain, giving the world that surreal pinkish glow. *Perfect mood lighting*, he thought as he trekked down the driveway to his dad's place. He really should stop at home and clean himself up, but if he did, he'd risk missing dinner. Besides, maybe after dinner, he could convince Jessa to soak in the hot tub with him. Just the two of them. Under the stars...

He almost broke into a jog as he veered to the left and over the small rise to Luis's house. Jessa's truck sat out front, but there was another truck, too. One he didn't recognize. Wouldn't be right of him to barge in on dinner if they had company, but he couldn't turn around, either. Not knowing Jessa was there. Not when the thought of seeing her made him ache like this.

So he hurried up the porch steps and pushed through the door without knocking. "Hello?" he called inside the entryway, where he stopped to stomp the dirt off his boots.

"Lance?" Jessa careened around the corner and hurried down the hallway.

"Hey." He let his eyes drink her in, the soft hair that framed her face, the smooth skin that had felt so soft against his lips. She wore tight tapered jeans and a long white shirt, casual, but seductive in his eyes. She could be wearing a snowsuit right now and she'd look seductive. God, he could come apart just looking at her.

But then he noticed the thing at her feet. He blinked. A small black-and-white pig. On a harness and leash? "Uh. What's that?"

Jessa looked down as though just remembering she was taking a pig for a walk. *In* the house. "Her name's Ilsa."

"*Ilsa?*" He laughed.

"Yeah," she shot back. "What's wrong with that?"

"Just seems like there's something more suitable. Like Ham Bone. Or Pork Chop. Or Bacon," he said, eyeing the critter like he was hungry.

"Don't even think about it." Jessa scooped the thing up into her arms. "I didn't know you were coming," she said, glancing nervously over her shoulder.

"I wanted to see you." More like *had* to see her. Had to touch her again. Had to kiss her. He closed the distance between them and skimmed his hand along her lower back, nudging her—and the pig—closer.

A pink glow lit up her face just like the sunset outside.

Voices drifted from the kitchen but he tuned them out. He didn't care who was in there. He needed a minute alone with Jessa. Now if he could just figure out how to ditch the pig...

"Lance..." Jessa's breathing had quickened, and her eyes seemed as hungry as he felt. But then she glanced back over her shoulder again. So distracted. He'd have to take care of that right now. First, he gently took the pig out of her hands. The thing squealed and squirmed as he set it on the floor, then it took off down the hall. Which was fine with him. They could discuss the pig later.

"I missed you," he said, sliding his hand up her back and pressing her against him, meeting her lips in the middle. The need for more of her swelled, threatening to rip him apart. He kissed her harder and her mouth opened to his, a small moan stirring the lust he felt into a fervor.

"Wait," Jessa gasped against his lips. She pushed back. "Just hold on. We have to talk."

Right. Talk. He suppressed the urge to take her hand and tow her back to him. They probably should discuss what happened between them. He still hadn't apologized for abandoning her in the kitchen. "Sorry I had to run out on you," he said. "I didn't want to. Believe me." If she needed proof, he'd be happy to offer it. All she had to do was feel him against her to know how much he wanted her.

"It's fine," she said brushing him off with another glance toward the kitchen.

Right. The company. The voices. They'd go. In a minute. But first he had more to say. He had to tell her what her words meant to him. How they'd given him a second wind. "I wanted to thank you for—"

"You don't have to thank me," she interrupted quickly. "But I think we should talk about—"

"We can talk about it later. Right now, there's something you need to know."

"Jessa!" The call came from the kitchen and knocked the air out of Lance. That voice. He hadn't noticed when it was subdued and murmuring, but now...

No. No way. That couldn't be Lucas.

But his brother appeared in the hallway. No longer a kid, instead a man with familiar blue-gray eyes. His hair was shorter and neater than he used to keep it, and he looked clean-cut for a rancher.

Shock bolted Lance's heart to his ribs. What the fuck was he doing here?

He said nothing as his brother walked toward them. It'd been so long since he'd seen him. Since they'd agreed it would be best if he cut ties and never came home…

"This is what I was trying to tell you," Jessa whispered. Or maybe she didn't whisper. Maybe Lance just couldn't hear past the blood pounding in his ears.

"Surprise," Lucas said with a healthy apprehension weighting his eyes. They'd agreed he wouldn't come back. It was best for Luis that way. Best for Levi. For the family.

The shock of seeing him started to thaw. "What're you doing here?" he asked, carefully controlling his tone. He didn't want to startle Jessa, but what the hell? No warning or anything. He'd just decided to show up after years of being away?

Lucas and Jessa shared a look. They *shared* a look. And suddenly, he had a bad feeling.

"I called him," Jessa said firmly. "And Levi. I asked them to come home."

He didn't look at her. Couldn't. His eyes were locked on Lucas. "You should've told me." He wasn't sure if he was saying it to his brother or to the woman he'd slept with.

Lucas stepped up to him. "I didn't have time. Jessa told me she's worried about Dad and I wanted to come as soon as possible."

His head turned slowly, like someone was cranking it click by click, until he was staring at Jessa's worried expression.

"Luis and I had a talk," she said, wringing her delicate hands. "And he said how much he missed Lucas and Levi. Given the incidents he's had lately, I thought it would be nice for them to come."

Nice. She'd thought it'd be nice. Well, she didn't know a damn thing about his family. About what they'd been through. Anger prickled his neck. What the hell had she been thinking? She should've talked to him first.

He faced his brother. "Can you give us a minute?"

Lucas slipped in front of Jessa. It'd been years, but obviously his brother could still recognize when he was pissed.

"Don't blame her. She's trying to help." Lucas seemed unfazed by all of it. But then he'd always been the mellow one. The one who didn't worry, who didn't carry the weight of the damn world on his shoulders. That's why they'd decided it should be him who went away. By the time he was fourteen, Levi had already gotten caught stealing twice. He'd thrown a rock through the ice cream shop's storefront and shattered the whole damn thing. He'd been so angry at Luis, who was always out with a different woman, and he'd taken it out on the town, targeting the places where the women worked.

That's why Levi had gone to the stables that night. He'd seen Luis messing around with the commissioner's wife. So he found some gasoline and a lighter. He hadn't meant to hurt anyone, he'd said later. He was just so angry.

Lance didn't have anger issues, but he was stressed all the time. So he drank. Had two underage tickets under his belt by then. But Lucas...he was too serious for stuff like that. Serious about school. Serious about following the rules. Serious about Naomi.

So they were sure he'd get a slap on the hand. Community service. Maybe house arrest. But they hadn't counted on the judge being the commissioner's golf buddy. It seemed he wanted to punish all of them. When Lance heard they were charging him as an adult he'd tried to beg the judge to reconsider. But the man had dismissed him like he was a stray dog, threatening to have him arrested if he came back.

"It was time for me to come home, anyway," Lucas said quietly, as though he'd resigned himself to whatever consequences this little reunion would bring. "Don't you think? Dad's getting older. I want to be around."

Maybe it *was* time. But he should've had a say in it. They should've discussed this, planned out how it would go. Jessa had taken that away from him. As if she had some right to play the healer for his family. His jaw pulled tight as he stared back at Lucas. "Give. Us. A. Minute."

His brother looked at Jessa.

"It's fine," she said, glaring back at Lance and crossing her arms in a fighter's stance. She wasn't afraid of him and it was a damn good thing because they were going to have a serious chat about her butting into his family's business.

Lucas anchored a hand on Jessa's shoulder and gave it a squeeze before walking away. Seeing him touch her like they had some kind of bond didn't do much to douse the anger.

As soon as his brother disappeared Lance faced her. "You had no right to do this."

"What do you mean I had no right?" she fired back. "This isn't about you, Lance. This is about your father."

Exactly. It was about his father and Luis already carried enough guilt. How'd she think he'd feel when he learned Levi had started that fire because he'd caught him in the stables with someone else's wife?

"Do you know what Luis told me?" Jessa asked.

It must've been a rhetorical question because she hardly paused.

"He told me that his biggest regret in life is not making things right with Lucas. Did you know that? Do you know how much it tears him apart?"

He almost laughed, it was so absurd. That was nothing compared to what he'd regret if he found out the truth. "You don't understand." The anger had drained away, but he tried to hold on to it. Anger was easier than the other emotions he was going to have to deal with now that the past stared him in the face. "You have no idea what you've done."

"What *I've* done?" she repeated, her face hardened with indignation. "What I've done is brought your brothers home. And you know what? When your father saw Lucas walk through that door, he was so overjoyed he cried. He *cried*."

That revelation freed the guilt. It flowed out, overpowering everything else. He'd done what he thought was best at the time. They all had. Hell, they were only kids. The day they'd hauled Lucas away, they'd all changed, each trying to atone for it in their own way. Luis stuck around the ranch more, cooked dinner, helped with homework, all the stuff he'd been too distracted to do before. And Lance and Levi trained, taking out the anguish in the arena as if that could bring back their brother.

But it was too late.

"Lance..." Jessa moved closer, studying him carefully. "Why are you so upset? Don't you want your brothers around? Tell me how this could possibly be a bad thing."

"I can't." They'd never told anyone. They'd tried to protect their father. But there'd be no way to keep the secret now. It would come out. Everything would come out.

"What's up, bro?" Levi bounded down the hall and captured him in a bear hug, lifting him off his feet. Typical. They'd always protected him from ever having to deal with reality. He was the party boy, the fun one. Which was ironic, considering he had more to lose right now than any of them.

"Let's head out to the old watering hole and celebrate the

fam getting back together." Levi slung an arm around him. "What do ya say? Drinks are on me."

Jessa still stared at Lance, her eyes focused and intent, demanding an explanation, but he turned away and clapped his long-lost brother on the back. "As long as you're buying, I'm in."

God knew, he could use a drink right now.

Chapter Sixteen

Well, this is awkward. Jessa sat in the back seat of Lance's extended cab, wedged between Levi and Lucas. No one had said a word since they'd gotten in the truck, the jovial tone of the reunion between Luis and his two sons deadened by the eldest son's stony-faced silence.

For the life of her, Jessa couldn't figure out what she'd done wrong. Lucas and Levi had obviously simply needed an invitation to come home. When she'd called them, both of them had been concerned about their father. Both had said how much they'd missed him. *And* Lance, for that matter. Levi had gotten away from Oklahoma as soon as he could and Lucas had picked him up at the airport in Denver. Now all three Cortez boys were together with their father and no one was saying a damn word.

She drummed her fingers on her thigh. She'd had a feeling Lance would be surprised to see his brothers, but this is not how she'd pictured things going. Lucky for them, she'd always been good at breaking the ice.

Scooting forward, she peered between the seats at Lance and Luis. "So how was your training today?" she asked politely.

"Fine," he muttered.

"Training?" Levi, who was sitting behind his oldest brother, ruffled Lance's hair. "Decided not to hang up the spurs yet, eh, old man?"

"Nope." Jessa watched Lance's grip tighten on the steering wheel.

"So, Lucas," she turned to him, hoping to steer the conversation away from Lance's retirement status, which had definitely been a sore subject lately. Having Levi poke fun at him would not end well. "How are things at the McGowen Ranch?" she asked, as if she had some sort of clue as to who the McGowens were and what they did on their ranch.

"Good," he answered dutifully, but he was eyeing Lance as though watching for an impending explosion.

Another silence fell like a heavy blanket, smothering her visions of a happy reunion for a father and his sons. Yes, okay, she was a bit idealistic, but she'd imagined chatter and laughter, not a wary distance. Even Levi, who was always the life of the party, seemed subdued, staring out the window like he wanted to avoid eye contact with everyone else.

Caving under the weight of their solemnity, she remained silent, pulled out her phone, and dashed off a text to Cassidy, Naomi, and Darla.

Meet me at the Tumble Inn ASAP. In case they didn't feel the urgency, she added a *911.* Those girls had known the Cortez family longer than she had, *better* than she did, considering Naomi had seriously dated Lucas before the fire. And Levi had been like a brother to Cassidy before her brother Cash had passed away. Maybe they could help her figure out what was going on, because she was not making progress.

Good thing the Tumble Inn was only an eight-minute drive from the ranch or she might have had to start singing to break up the silence. *No one* would want to hear that.

When they arrived at the bar Lance took his sweet time parking, she couldn't help but notice.

They all piled out of the truck like they were about to head into a funeral instead of the lone country western bar in town.

She hadn't been to the Tumble Inn since the whole Cam fiasco, and now she remembered why. A huge banner hung below the sign.

Two-step Night.

Fabulous. Since she was young, Jessa had absolutely no rhythm. Her mother had attempted to put her in ballet, but after she'd knocked into another girl and caused a domino effect of toppling ballerinas during her first recital, she'd walked away from dancing and never looked back. In college, she'd tried to take a ballroom dancing class and had somehow managed to break her partner's foot during the fox-trot, so nowadays she pretty much avoided any establishment that centered around dancing.

The Cortez brothers followed their father to the entrance, but she hung back.

"I let some friends know we were coming," she called. "I'll wait for them out here."

"Sounds good." Levi was the only one who acknowledged she'd said something. "Make sure you save me a dance when you get in there," he called, working his magic charm with a wink and dimpled grin.

The man had no idea what he was asking. "Sure, I'll do that," she lied. Once she got inside, she planned to order a nice, easygoing glass of chardonnay and park it at the bar for the evening. No breaking her friends' feet tonight.

The men disappeared into the bar right as Darla and Cassidy pulled up in Darla's BMW. Naomi was a few minutes behind, probably because she had to find a sitter.

They all congregated in the middle of the parking lot.

"You told us you'd never step foot in this place again," Darla accused. Though she'd had only a few minutes' warning, the woman had somehow managed to primp and change into a low-cut shirt that displayed her cleavage.

"I didn't exactly have a choice," Jessa said, gathering them in closer. "Lucas and Levi came home and—"

"What?" Naomi interrupted, suddenly appearing pale. "What do you mean Lucas came home?"

Jessa took in the shocked—no, make that horrified—look on her friend's face. Guilt churned her stomach. She should've warned them, but she'd gotten so caught up in the plans, not to mention a crazy week at the shelter. "I called them because of the issues Luis has been having," she half-whispered, watching the doors. "He told me he missed them, so I got in touch and asked them to come home."

"I'm shocked Levi actually listened to you." Cassidy's normally sweet tone had turned bitter.

Oh boy. She really should've thought all of this through. Darla was the only one who didn't seem disturbed by the Cortez family reunion.

The woman elbowed Jessa. "Way to go, girl. About time we got a few hot men back in this town."

Naomi whirled and made a move toward her car. "I'm not going in there."

"You have to!" Jessa caught her arm before she could escape. "It's been horrible since they got home. I thought I was helping but ever since Lance saw his brothers, they're hardly speaking to each other. I don't understand."

"They went through a lot," Naomi informed her, wrenching out of her grasp. "We all went through a lot when Lucas got sent away." Emotion trembled through the words.

But that was a long time ago. It wasn't too late to work things out, even for Naomi and Lucas. Once she got over the shock of it, surely she'd be glad he was back. "I need some support in there, girls." She had no idea what to do. How to make everything better. She needed backup.

"I'm in." Cassidy sighed. "As long as there are margaritas involved." She patted Naomi's arm sympathetically. "It's not like we'll have to talk to them. In an hour this place'll be packed."

"Yeah. We can hang out on the dance floor," Darla offered with a wicked gleam in her eyes. "Or on the mechanical bull."

"I'm not going near that thing." Jessa would leave bull riding to the professionals. "Besides, we'll be too busy to dance. We have to figure out how to get these guys talking so they can get past their issues for Luis's sake." All the man wanted was for his family to be together, and thanks to Lance's rude entrance, they couldn't even give him that.

Before anyone else tried to bail, she swung one arm around Cassidy and the other around Naomi.

"I don't know how I'll face Lucas," Naomi said through a steady exhale. "I mean, I haven't seen him since he was arrested..."

"Can't blame him for not coming back." Darla followed them across the parking lot. "The whole town wanted to hang him."

Maybe back then, but things were different now. Jessa held open the door for everyone. "I never knew him that well, but he seems like a great guy." He'd been so polite to her on the phone, kind even. A little soft-spoken. Thoughtful with words.

"He was always a great guy," Naomi said, pausing before the open door as though gathering courage. "That's why I never believed he'd set the fire."

"It was years ago." Cassidy took Naomi's arm and led her inside. "And things were bad before the fire. They all fell apart after their mom left."

Was that all it was? Were they all still dealing with the resentment of their abandonment? Jessa stepped in behind her friends and let her eyes adjust to the dim lighting. Most of the tables were empty, as it was still early for the party crowd. Thankfully, no one was out on the dance floor, though music played in the background.

The Cortez men had all claimed stools at the bar, sipping their beers while seeming to avoid eye contact.

"Look at them," Jessa grumbled. "After years apart, they have nothing to say to each other?"

"Sure they do," Darla said, sashaying her way to the bar. "Men just need a little help getting the conversation going, that's all."

Cassidy followed Darla, but Jessa had to practically push Naomi. When they finally made it to the bar, her friend slipped behind her as though searching for protection and stared at the floor.

"Well, well, well," Darla said, her voice shattering the

icy silence. "It sure is good to see you boys back in town." She pulled up a stool next to Levi and plopped down. "My friends and I would like a round of margaritas, Rico," she called to the bartender.

"You got it, *mi bombon*."

Ah yes. Every male in town thought of Darla as their chocolate sweetheart. She charmed them all, just like she was doing now, chatting easily with Levi and Lance about the ale they were drinking.

Not everyone was listening, though. Lucas had turned around and was staring steadily over Jessa's shoulder.

"Naomi?" He rose slowly and bypassed Jessa.

Offering Naomi courage with a smile, she stepped aside to retrieve her margarita from the bar and to give them a minute, but stayed close enough that she overheard the nerves in her friend's tone.

"Hi, Lucas," Naomi almost whimpered.

"Hi," he murmured with this sort of awed expression on his face. It was the sweetest thing Jessa had seen since Lance had told her she was beautiful. Since he'd looked at her the way Lucas was looking at Naomi now, like he wanted to take in all the details and remember them. Like he was powerless to look away.

That lost-in-the-moment look only proved that the Cortez men might be made of steel but underneath that, they had this raw passion that ran much deeper than their brooding stares. She should know. She'd felt that passion seep into her skin and set her whole body ablaze...

Levi appeared in front of her. "How about that dance?" he asked, holding out a hand like a true Southern gentleman.

"Oh. Um." Her cheeks pulsed. "Actually, no one's even out on the dance floor."

"So?" She remembered that grin from her high school summers. The grin no girl could deny...

Jessa glanced at Lance. He'd set down his beer and was watching her, his jaw set in a hard, angry line.

And wasn't that just typical? He seemed to be pissed off at her. Again. It'd become a pattern with him. One minute he was ravaging her up against a wall and the next he was glaring at her in a pout. Well, screw that. She faced his younger brother. "You know what? I'd love to dance with you." He was fun, after all. And wearing boots, which would hopefully protect his feet from any significant damage.

"You're not gonna regret this," he promised, leading her to the dance floor.

She laughed. "Let's hope *you* don't regret it." She probably should've had him sign a waiver or something.

"Not possible," he insisted, taking her hand in his and guiding her in front of him. He wrapped one arm around her waist and drew her close, but thankfully left a respectable distance intact.

The song was slow and twangy. Surprisingly, Levi made it very easy to follow his moves.

"You're a good dancer," she said, grinning up at him as he swayed her around the floor.

"I find that dancing only helps my chance at winning a woman's heart," he replied good-naturedly.

"I find that dancing only increases *my* potential for a lawsuit," she confided.

He laughed. "Not when you're dancing with the right person." In perfect rhythm with the music, he twirled her, then reeled her back in and dipped her low. With her head upside down, she caught a view of Lance, who still sat at the bar, but he'd turned around and made it no secret that he was watching her. The dangerous look on his face dried up her mouth.

Levi pulled her back up and resumed their graceful two-step.

Not even the look on Lance's face could deter her from finishing this dance. It actually gave her the perfect opportunity to figure out what was going on between the brothers. She smiled at Levi. "Things seem a little tense between you guys."

"Do they?" he asked, spinning her again.

"Yeah. Did you all have some big fight or something?" she asked innocently. They must've had some kind of falling out. If she could figure out what happened, maybe she could help them get past it.

His charming grin dimmed. "Let's just say some of us have moved on from the past and others are stuck in it."

"You mean—"

"Mind if I cut in?" Lance had left his post at the bar and somehow sneaked up behind her.

"Course not," Levi said, opening his arms to let her go. "She's all yours."

There was never a truer statement spoken in the English language. Seeing Lance, hearing him ask to dance with her, kindled that familiar music in her heart, and yes, right now she did belong to him.

He stepped against her, resting that large skilled hand on the very small of her back, pressing her close to him, not leaving any of the respectable space intact. His other hand swallowed hers, but instead of holding it loosely the way Levi had, Lance threaded his fingers through hers and fused their palms together.

The heat from his body seemed to flow into hers as he

moved against her, sparking her lower half until she wasn't sure she could keep her feet from stumbling.

The song was something sweet and light. Lance moved with the music effortlessly, not carefree and entertaining like Levi had been but deliberate and precise.

There were a few other couples on the floor, but now they seemed so far away under the power of Lance holding her.

"I can't stand seeing you dance with my brother," he said against her hair, as though he was too afraid to look into her eyes.

Jessa could hardly find her voice. "Your brother was the only one talking to me." Somehow the words managed to hold a good amount of attitude, which was impressive, seeing as how all she wanted to do was melt into him.

"I was surprised," he said, pulling back to look at her. His eyes were serious but they held glimmers of light. "Shocked. And I wasn't the only one." He turned to gaze across the room to the table where Lucas and Naomi sat.

"I didn't think about that," she murmured. "I was only thinking about your dad. About how much he seemed to regret what happened with Lucas. I wanted to help."

He smiled, and that smile had the power to change the world. Or at least her world.

"I know," he said, sliding his hand up her back, caressing in a way that made her want to arch into him. "And things'll be fine." He said it like he might be trying to convince himself.

"Why aren't things fine now?" she asked.

His hand slipped low to her waist again, guiding her as they swayed to the music. "It's complicated."

"Families usually are." Or at least, that's how she imagined a family would be. "But even with the complications,

I'd give anything to have a family." She'd always longed for that, a place where she fit. And he might not be willing to tell her any secrets, but she'd give up all of hers if it helped him smooth things over with his family.

Lance stopped moving and gazed down at her. "Don't you have your mom?"

"She's all I have." Not that she could complain, but… "I always wanted brothers and sisters." She used to beg her mother to have another baby. Or adopt.

He pulled her close again, and now his gaze strayed. "Yeah, well, having siblings isn't always easy. Trust me."

"I do trust you." But he didn't trust her. Lance was good at kissing her, touching her, and, let's face it, giving her more pleasure than she'd experienced with any man, ever. But when it came to trusting… that wasn't exactly his strength. "No matter what it is, you guys can work through—"

"Jessa?" Cassidy tapped her on the shoulder. "Can I have a word with you real quick?"

"Oh." She hesitated. They were finally getting some-where with a real conversation. "Right now?" she asked, hoping her friend would give her a minute.

"Yeah," Cassidy said apologetically. She leaned closer. "We have a situation."

The gravity in her tone forced Jessa to pry herself away from the luxurious warmth of Lance's body. "Be right back?"

He nodded and reluctantly let go of her hand.

Cassidy pulled her away, in the direction of the ladies' room.

She almost had to jog to keep up. "What's wrong?"

"Naomi. We need to get her out of here."

"Why—"

As they neared the ladies' room, the sound of sobbing echoed.

Jessa turned the jog into a sprint. "Good God, what happened?"

"Not exactly sure," Cassidy said as they pushed through the door.

Jessa ran to the open stall and found Naomi sitting on a vacant stool with her face buried in her hands. "I can't do this," she wailed. "I'm sorry. I wasn't prepared to see him."

Lucas. Jessa sank to her knees in front of her friend. "Oh, honey. I'm the one who's sorry. I should've told you he was coming." She knew how much Naomi still thought about him. She should've prepared her for this.

"I loved him so much," Naomi sniffled. "We never had any closure. And he's the same. Kind and thoughtful." She swiped at the tears on her face. "God, I could've married him. We would've been happy. Instead I made a mess of my life with Mark."

"You didn't make a mess of anything," Cassidy insisted, squeezing into the stall with them. "You have a beautiful daughter."

"Exactly," Jessa agreed, squeezing Naomi's hand. This had obviously been a bit too much for her. "Don't worry. We'll take you home. You don't have to stay."

They could stop by Darla's place and calm her down with some wine and chocolate. That always seemed to do the trick when one of them was upset about something.

"Okay," Naomi said, tearing off a piece of toilet paper to dry her eyes. "Just give me a minute to get myself together."

"Take your time, honey." Jessa sighed, her heart aching. Looked like a conversation with Lance would have to wait.

Chapter Seventeen

Lance moseyed over to where Lucas sat at a table. Last he saw, Naomi had been sitting with him, but she seemed to have disappeared. "Hey." He pulled out the chair across from his brother. He'd seen him only a few times since he'd left town. They'd met in Denver, just for a quick lunch or dinner if one of them was going through, but they'd always tried to avoid the subject they now had to discuss. And after they'd avoided it so long, he almost didn't know how to bring it up. "Where'd Naomi go?" he asked. Wouldn't hurt to keep avoiding it a little longer.

"Not sure." Lucas stared blankly at the full beer bottle that sat in front of him. "Didn't realize how much I'd missed her until I saw her."

"Yeah, I wondered about that." Couldn't have been easy for Naomi, either. Back in high school the two of them were pretty hot and heavy, and then one day Lucas was just gone. From all of their lives.

"She looks good," his brother said, taking a drink.

"You never ended up with anyone else." And Lucas could've found someone by now. He didn't seem to carry the baggage Lance did, even after prison. He wasn't bitter about any of it. Their mother leaving, the heavy-handed sentence he'd received...

"I've gone out with plenty of women," Lucas said, staring at his hands.

Guilt bore down on Lance once again. If they hadn't thought up that plan to protect Levi, he had no doubt Naomi and Lucas would be together right now.

"Wasn't in the cards," his brother said with a shrug.

"Because we wrote the cards." He'd never regretted it more than he did right now. When Lucas was gone, he didn't have to think about it, didn't have to face the consequences of covering for Levi. "I'm glad you're back." That surprised him. The shock had worn off and now, sitting across from him, he could see having Lucas around again. Once they waded through the shitstorm that would surely hit.

"Nice try." His brother took another sip.

"I wasn't expecting to see you. But Jessa's right. Maybe it's time." Maybe he wouldn't be able to move forward until he'd dealt with some things from his past. Something about dancing with Jessa, kissing Jessa, making love to Jessa, made him want to move forward.

"I'm not staying long."

That might be his fault. "You can stay. We'll figure out how to tell Dad everything. We'll fix it." Or at least they could try.

Lucas stared past him. "It's not worth going back. Not now."

One hour ago, Lance'd thought the same thing. But Jessa had changed his mind. "He should know the truth."

"And what would that mean for Levi?"

Lance glared over at their younger brother, who now had yet another woman out on the dance floor. What did that make? Four in the span of a half hour? Their little secret obviously didn't weigh on him. Likely because they'd always protected him. He'd never dealt with the consequences for anything.

"What would the truth mean for you?" Lance asked, looking at Lucas directly. It'd mean he'd be exonerated. At least in the eyes of the people who still despised him, who still held the fire against him. Hell, he'd noticed the whispering when people had started to trickle into the bar. The pointing. They'd all taken tables far away from Lucas—the hellion who'd burned down the stables and managed to kill the town's dreams of ever hosting another rodeo.

People in small towns like this held grudges. They wouldn't forget.

"We should keep things the way they are." Lucas had never been one to stir up trouble. "I'll stay for a while, spend some time with Dad, and lay low. Then I'll go back to work."

Except Lance couldn't get Jessa's words out of his head. She'd give anything to have a family—to have siblings—and his were right here, but he couldn't stay connected with them. "We have plenty of work around the ranch. Been leaning toward starting our own stock contracting operation." Once he retired, it would be a natural next step. "There'd be a place for you, too." Given that Lucas had gotten the McGowens' operation out of financial ruin and made it one of the most lucrative in the region, his brother could probably run things a hell of a lot better than he could.

Lucas smirked at him. "No one in this town wants me back. You know it as well as I do."

"That would change if everyone knew the truth."

"Then they'd go after Levi. That's why we protected him. And Dad." He leaned forward, his eyes never looking so much like their father's. "I knew what I was doing, Lance. And I'd do it again, too."

Of course he would. But if he had it to do over again, Lance wouldn't let him. He wouldn't let someone take the fall for something he didn't do. For something he never would've done. "I think we should tell Dad at least. Even if no one else ever knows."

"Not now. Not this trip." His brother looked over at their father, who was arguing with Gil about something. "Maybe I'll pop back in before winter for a few days." He shifted his gaze to Lance. "Jessa seems to think something's not right with him."

"He's fine." Lance brushed aside his concerns. "Just getting ornerier in his old age, that's all. He seemed happy to see you—"

"Look at you guys." Levi bounded over and grabbed a chair, turning it backward, then straddling it. "Why aren't you dancing? Plenty of women to go around."

"Not really in the mood to dance," Lance shot back. Unless it was with Jessa, but she'd been gone a while now.

"So…" Levi eyed him. "You and Jessa, huh? Should've picked up on that earlier. I wouldn't have asked her to dance if I'd known."

Nope. Not going there with Levi. He'd been gone all these years, had hardly called at all, and now he thought they could talk about Lance's personal life. They had a hell of a lot to work through before they got there. "There's nothing to know," he said with a look that would hopefully shut him down.

"Right," Levi mocked. "I saw how you were dancing with her. It was a lot different from the way I danced with her."

"Maybe you suck at dancing." He attempted to slip a warning into his tone.

"I definitely don't suck." Confidence had never been one of Levi's weaknesses.

"Are you two together?" he pressed.

"No." Technically they were not together. Not that they'd had any time to discuss their status...

"Do you want to be together?"

None of your damn business. But he went with the easier answer. "No."

"Sure seems like there's something there to me," Levi taunted. His brother had never known when to quit.

"We hooked up once. It was nothing." Classic code for *I'm not discussing this with you.* Especially when he hadn't even discussed it with her.

"So you wouldn't mind if I asked her out?" Levi clearly knew the answer to that question, judging from the smart-ass grin on his face. "'Cause she was into me once. We made out behind the barn the summer of our sophomore year, you know."

"Actually, Levi, it was behind your garage."

Shit. Lance checked over his shoulder and sure enough, Jessa stood behind them, no longer looking soft and sweet. Nice of Lucas to alert him to the fact that the woman they were talking about stood a mere four feet away. How long had she been there?

She stayed where she was, keeping her distance from the table. "I just came to tell you I have to go." The words sounded hollow. "See you later," she said to no one in particular, then spun and met Naomi, Cassidy, and Darla near the doors.

"You might want to follow her," Levi said, clapping Lance on the shoulder. "She seems pretty pissed."

Thanks to him. Instead of indulging his brother's arrogance, he leaned back into the chair. "She's fine." He hoped. Not much he could do about it after he'd told them he wasn't interested. He'd talk to her later. Right now ... "We have to figure out how we're gonna tell Dad the truth about the fire."

That got Levi's attention. His back went straight as a fence post. "What do you mean?" Yeah, now he wasn't playing the funny, spoiled-boy role. He looked worried.

"We're not telling anyone anything," Lucas said, as if that was the end of the discussion.

But it wasn't. Not if Lance had anything to say about it.

* * *

She really should've seen that coming.

Jessa tuned out her friends' chatter and sipped her wine, fighting to keep her expression neutral. Difficult, considering the humiliation still burned inside. Of course Lance wasn't interested in her. She'd known that in her head. To be fair, her judgment had been severely compromised by that heated passion they'd shared in the kitchen, but still. This was Lance Cortez. Self-professed commitment-a-phobe. So it was silly that a tiny seed of hope had embedded itself so deeply in the overly fertile lands of her heart. Silly and not a mistake she would make again. Lance seemed to excel in sending mixed signals, but she wasn't up for games anymore. And she would not wait around for a man to figure out what he wanted.

"How was it seeing Levi again?" Darla asked Cassidy. They'd all gotten settled back at the Chocolate Therapist, Naomi squished between Jessa and Cassidy on the comfy couch.

"He hardly said two words to me." Cassidy laughed. "I think he's afraid of me."

"He hasn't changed at all," Naomi chimed in. "He was always the party boy. Always the center of attention. Never wanted to deal with anything real."

Though Cassidy was a few years younger than them, Jessa had always wondered about her and Levi. At one time, he'd been so close to her family. "You two never dated?" she asked. Out of everyone here, she had the least background information, seeing as how she'd been around only in the summer.

"God, no." Cassidy's nose wrinkled with disgust. "I thought Levi was hot. Like every other girl in town. But Cash wouldn't let me near him. He was over at our place all the time. Especially after his mom took off. But after the accident..." The words trailed off.

"You want my opinion, I think he took Cash's death hard." Darla leaned over and topped off all of their glasses. "It seemed like he blamed himself."

Cassidy's expression darkened. "It wasn't his fault. It's the sport. It shouldn't even be legal." Since her brother had been killed during a competition, Cassidy despised bull riding, though on a normal night—a sober night—she rarely talked about it.

"You okay, Jessa?" Naomi asked her. "You're awfully quiet." Her sweet friend happened to be doing smashingly well after a potent elixir that consisted of prosecco and lavender liqueur.

"I'm great," she fibbed. She didn't need a chorus of *I told you so*'s ringing out all around her.

"Sure looked like you and Lance were having a *wonderful* time," Darla mentioned with a probing arch of her eyebrows.

"Yeah," Cassidy agreed. "Things were looking pretty hot between you two on the dance floor."

She evaded all of their curious stares with a long, savoring sip of wine.

"Of course they were hot," Naomi said with a giggle. "Once you have sex with someone, you tend to dance a little differently." Her eyes went wide and she slapped a hand across her mouth.

"Sex?" Darla repeated.

"Sex?" Cassidy echoed.

Well. Apparently it was harder to keep secrets at the Cortez Ranch than she'd thought. Calmly, Jessa set down her wineglass. "He told you?" she asked Naomi, wishing her voice didn't sound so strange. It was one thing for her to be humiliated in private, but now his rejection was about to go public.

"No." Rounding her eyes apologetically, Naomi rested a hand on her leg. "He didn't tell me. I figured it out and he didn't deny it."

That was *so* much better.

"Oh my God!" Darla wailed. "I can't believe you've been holding out on us!" She scooted to the edge of her seat as though the suspense was killing her. "When? Where? How?"

"How?" Jessa rolled her eyes. "*You* of all people know how it works, Darla."

Her friend laughed. "Truer words."

"But we *do* need details," Cassidy urged impatiently.

"Fine." They'd never let her get out of there until she spilled her guts. Might as well get it over with. "We were in his kitchen. *Talking*. And..." The images of him holding her body flashed. She couldn't stop them. They took her over...

"And?" Darla prompted.

Jessa sighed. "And it just happened. One minute we were talking. The next kissing. Then..." She let them fill in the blank.

"In the kitchen?" Darla mock-whined. "I love kitchen sex!"

"Pretty hot," Naomi agreed. "Not that I would remember. It's been years for me, ladies," she said a bit sloppily. "I mean *years*."

"Okay, honey. Maybe we should take a little break from this." Cassidy slipped Naomi's drink out of her hand and set it on the coffee table. "So are you two together, then?" she asked Jessa. "Because it sure looked like it."

"No." She steadied the tremble out of her voice. "We are *definitely* not together. He doesn't have feelings for me." She'd simply walked in on him at a vulnerable moment and they'd both let down their guards.

"How do you know he doesn't have feelings for you?" Naomi asked too loudly. "Because I've known him forever and I have to say...he looks different when he talks about you."

"No. Trust me." Jessa tried to laugh, but it felt more like a gag. "I overheard him tell his brothers he doesn't have feelings for me. So..."

"Are you serious?" Cassidy nearly spilled her drink.

"What an ass," Darla said, looking truly pissed on her behalf.

"I doubt he would tell his brothers if he *did* have feelings for you." Naomi reached for her glass again, her glare warning Jessa not to take it away. "It's not like they're close or anything. You saw how they were acting tonight."

"Maybe not, but we all know how Lance is." Hell, he'd told her himself how much he loathed the prospect of committed relationships. "You're the one who told me to avoid this in the first place." Then she'd thought maybe she really did simply want a one-night stand. Something easy, uncommitted. But that hadn't worked for her. Because now she knew what it could be like with Lance, how he could touch her and satisfy her and how his gaze could pierce her heart. She knew, but she couldn't have him. Lesson learned.

"Wow." Cassidy shook her head slowly back and forth. Being as busy as she was, working two jobs and going to nursing school, she didn't have a lot of her own drama. But she always confessed to loving other people's drama. "So now what're you going to do?"

"Nothing." Jessa shrugged, as though it would really be that easy to move on. "It's fine. It was fun and everything, but I'm not looking for someone like Lance, anyway." Besides, he'd gotten what he wanted. Now he'd probably leave her alone.

"Well you can't *stay* there," Darla scoffed. "For God's sake, here you are doing him a favor and he totally takes advantage of the situation."

"It's not his fault." She wasn't some naïve teenager. She'd wanted it. She'd wanted him. And the sad truth was, she still did. Even hearing those words play back in her head. That's why she had to leave the ranch. She couldn't see him every day. Not the way her soul seemed to crackle to life whenever he was near.

No. She had to walk away. Ever since she'd gone to stay

with Luis, she'd felt like she was part of a family, but it wasn't real. "You're right." She took in a breath of courage. "I need to move back home. Lucas and Levi can help out now, keep an eye on Luis."

"Exactly." Darla refilled her wineglass. "If Lance can't see what a treasure you are, he doesn't deserve you anyway. If you ask me, the best one out of that bunch is Lucas."

She had a point. While Lance seemed suspicious and closed off and Levi was capricious, Lucas was serious and quiet, but also tender, given what she'd seen when he'd been with Naomi earlier. "He really seems like a good man," she said to Naomi. "Maybe you two could reconnect..." Someone had to find a happy ending in this whole thing. And no one deserved it more than Naomi. Not after what she'd been through with her ex.

"No." Her expressive green eyes teared up again. "He's only here for a short time. Then he said he's headed back to the McGowens' place." She blotted her eyes with the sleeve of her shirt. "He seems happy. Like he's built a good life for himself down there."

A good life, but maybe not the best life. From the way he'd looked at Naomi, Jessa could swear he'd give up everything to be with her. "He wouldn't want to come back?" she asked. "Even to be with Luis?"

"He's convinced no one in town would want him back here." Naomi sighed. "Not after everything that happened."

"But that was years ago," Cassidy said. "Surely everyone's over it by now."

"Ha." Darla rolled her eyes. "Not around here. They wouldn't trust him. They'd be watching his every move. Sorry, honey. But I don't blame him for not wanting to come home."

"It's okay." Naomi finished off her drink. "It's not like we even know each other anymore."

"Except you still feel a connection to him." Jessa didn't usually resort to stating the obvious, but how could Naomi give up that easily?

A smile brought life to Naomi's eyes. "He was my first love. So I'll probably always feel connected to him."

"That's exactly why you should give it a chance," Jessa argued.

"You watch too many Hallmark movies," Darla said in her dry way.

"Maybe I do." But those stories kept her heart searching for something real and true. And not just for herself, either. "I think if you have a chance at finding true love, you should take it." No matter what. While the rest of them rolled their eyes and laughed in their *Oh, Jessa* way, she studied Naomi. She had no doubt the woman was scared. She'd been burned in the worst way possible, and now she didn't want to even consider the possibility that the man she loved might still be in love with her, too.

That was okay, though, because Jessa wasn't afraid. She had no problem launching her own secret investigation into the possibility. She had plenty of experience with these things. All she had to do was talk to Lucas.

While she might be surrounded by cynics, she still believed. No matter what happens in her own life, a true romantic never gives up on love.

Chapter Eighteen

Jessa zipped up her duffel and did a quick sweep around the room. She'd managed to shower, get dressed, and pack her things all within twenty minutes. The voices and breakfast noises from downstairs had lit quite the fire under her.

From the sound of things, all three brothers were downstairs with their father.

Levi had crashed in the other main floor bedroom of Luis's house and Lucas had stayed at Lance's place, she found out after she finally made it home around one o'clock in the morning.

Not home.

This was not her home. Luis was not her father. And Lance, while a good lover, was not boyfriend material. So, yes. It was time to go. She had to do this fast. Like ripping off a piece of medical tape that had gotten tangled in her hair while she was attempting to bandage a wounded squirrel with a major attitude problem. It'd happened to her only three times, but it hurt every time. She'd learned from experience, the faster you ripped, the faster you got through the pain.

Bravely, she stepped into her flip-flops before kneeling down to clip Ilsa into her harness. "Time to go home, lil' sweetie." She patted the pig's head affectionately. At least she wasn't going home alone. "We'll have so much fun. We can make popcorn and watch movies. You'll love it." Holding the leash in one hand, she hoisted her bag onto her shoulder. Eventually she'd have to come back for Ilsa's crate, but she wasn't about to ask for help loading her car.

Keeping her spine straight under the guise of confidence, she walked regally down the narrow staircase with her adorable little piggy and halted in the kitchen.

The men were all there together, and they were four peas in a pod. It wasn't their looks so much as their mannerisms, the way they ate, the way they sat hunched slightly, laid back and comfortable. She was glad to see they weren't silent strangers anymore, but talking easily about the ranch.

"I can help get things started," Lucas was saying. "At least from a distance. If you need me to consult on any purchases or—"

"Oh, hey, Jessa." Levi was the first one to notice her.

Lance straightened and turned around.

She looked through him. "So, the fumigator people let me know that my house is done." She gripped the suitcase strap tightly in a fist. "Which means Ilsa and I can move back home and you guys can have the place to yourselves again."

Lance's chin dipped forward slightly as he studied her from across the room. She didn't let her gaze settle in his.

"Thanks for letting me stay, Luis." She quickly led Ilsa over and planted a kiss on the man's cheek.

"Not a word about it." He reached up and pulled her into a half hug that dangerously weakened her resolve. "It's great having you here, Jessa," the man said, cutting a stern look at his firstborn. "Don't be a stranger, now."

"Why don't you stay for breakfast?" Lucas offered, rising to pull out another chair for her.

She swallowed hard. The threatening tears heated her throat. "Actually, I should get going so I can drop off my things at home before I head to the shelter." She turned before they could read any trace of sadness on her face. "But I'm sure I'll see everyone soon." Without a more formal goodbye, she stooped to pick up the pig and walked out, keeping her head low as she made her way down the porch steps. "Here we go." She opened the driver's-side door and settled a snorting, grunting Ilsa on the passenger seat. As she loaded her bag into the back, the screen door banged open behind her.

She didn't turn around. Didn't have to. She could feel Lance behind her, feel him looking at her. Unable to face him, she climbed into the truck next to Ilsa and slammed the door shut. But the damn window was open, and before she could peel out he leaned in to gaze at her with those perceptive silvery eyes. "I'm sorry," he said, slanting his head convincingly. "For what I said last night. I didn't mean...well...it wasn't what it sounded like."

Jessa kept her gaze centered on the windshield. She couldn't look at him or he'd see everything. "It's fine," she insisted, shoving the key into the ignition. "You don't owe me an apology." Technically, he didn't owe her anything. That one morning in the kitchen, she'd told him she wasn't interested in a relationship, either. She'd pretended to be just as detached as he could be.

"Come on, Jessa." His hand rested on her thigh and sent sparks shooting up her chest. "Levi was being an ass. Okay? I was just trying to shut him up."

"Sure. I get it." She moved her leg so his hand fell away, so he couldn't influence her with his touch. "The kitchen thing was..." Incredible. Impressive. Ravishingly hot. Not that she'd admit it right now. "...Fun. But you don't owe me anything. It just happened. Not like I'm expecting you to change your whole philosophy on relationships or anything." A humorless laugh slipped out. "I mean, I knew what I was signing up for. It was only a one-time thing and you—"

He pressed a finger against her lips to quiet her. "Let me take you out."

"What?"

"On a date." He paused as though the words had surprised him, too, but then he nodded. "Yeah. I want to take you on a date."

"A date?" she repeated through a laugh.

"Yes. Is that so hard to believe? Isn't that what people do when they like someone?"

"People, yes. But you?" As far as she knew, Lance had never *dated* a woman. He'd met women at bars. He'd met women out on the circuit. He'd for sure had women in his hotel rooms. But he didn't date.

"Why not me?" he demanded with that sexy half grin that had gotten her into so much trouble in his kitchen.

"Listen..." She raised a hand to stop him right there. "I know what you're trying to do here."

"Do you?"

"Yes."

He leaned in through the window, moving his face dangerously close to hers. "What am I trying to do, Jessa?"

Seduce her again. He was so damn good at it. Those eyes. They could practically undress her. "Um." She attempted to focus. "You're trying to make me feel better about things. Because let's be honest. I don't do one-night stands. Or one-afternoon stands. I've never done that. So maybe you feel bad and now you think you're obligated to take me on a date, but—"

This time he lowered his lips to hers.

A sharp breath sliced through her lungs, cutting them open. God, it was the best kind of pain...

He pulled back. "Or maybe I just want to take you on a date." His eyes held her in a daze. "Maybe I don't want you to go home. Because that means I won't see you every day. And maybe I *want* to see you. Maybe I was just trying to get my asshole brother off my back. And maybe I really do like you, Jessa. Did you ever think of that?"

One kiss and her lungs were nearly out of air. "That possibility hadn't occurred to me," she whispered, which brought back his grin.

"Please go on a date with me, Jessa. I'll beg if I have to. I'll get down on my knees right outside your truck."

He was teasing her again and damn it, she couldn't *not* smile at the man. "Um..."

He draped his arms over the open window and leaned close again. "Pretty please?" Tenderness crinkled the corners of his eyes. "You have to know I'd never tell Levi anything about how I really feel. We don't have that sort of relationship."

That was true. From what she'd seen, the eldest and youngest Cortez brothers had some competition between them.

"Let me take you out. I'll make it worth the trouble." The

promise in the words matched the one beaming suggestively in his eyes.

"Okay." She relented through a put-out sigh, hopefully covering the sudden rush that had her body humming. "Sure. Why not? I *guess* I'll go on a date with you."

His eyes brightened. "When?"

Yeah, like she had any ability to think through her schedule with her heart racing this way. Let's see...he was leaving on Friday for Vegas, so..."Thursday?" she tried.

His lips quirked with exaggerated disappointment. "That's a long time to wait."

Okay, so it didn't matter what she had going on. Based on her kitchen experience with the man, she'd cancel everything. "Wednesday?"

"Much better," he murmured, giving her lips a long, sexy glance. "I'll pick you up. Six o'clock." He glanced at Ilsa. "Leave Pork Chop at home and wear jeans."

Before she could ask him why, he walked back into the house.

* * *

He could get used to this. Having his brother home. Lance tossed his gloves onto the stable's shelf. He'd been out training this morning, and somehow with Lucas out there, things had gone smoother than they had in a long time. Not that Lance didn't appreciate Tucker, but Lucas had a way with animals. Somehow he'd calmed Wild Willy at the right moments and gotten his engine going when necessary. "Thanks for helping out today," he said, hanging the halter on a nail.

"You've still got it, you know." Lucas paced the length of the bull run, seeming to inspect it. "Same thing that made

Dad great." He ran his hand along the rotted fence railing. "Even with this shitty setup, you've got the perseverance. You can get the win this year."

"Hope so." Lance joined him near the fence, noticing for the first time how shitty it was. "Haven't had much time for keeping things up around here lately." That wasn't his thing. The equipment. The facilities. He wanted to ride. He wanted to raise bulls. "We're gonna need help getting our operation off the ground. Can't do it myself."

"I can make some notes while I'm here. Look around and give you suggestions." Lucas stuffed his hands into the pockets of his Wranglers and strode out of the stables and into the sunlight.

Lance followed. It was a hot day for the elevation. Had to be at least eighty. He slipped off his hat and swiped at the sweat that ran down his temples. "I'd sure appreciate it." He'd appreciate it even more if his brother would stay on at the ranch. He could use the expertise. But he knew when to push and now was not the time.

After latching the stable door, he followed his brother down to the driveway.

"Where's Levi anyway?" Lucas asked. "He could get his lazy ass out here and work on some of the fences for Dad."

"Think he finally went to bed." After Jessa had left the Tumble Inn last night, Lance hadn't seen much of a point in hanging out, so he'd brought Luis and Lucas home. Levi, of course, had wanted to stay. Hadn't come home until dawn, when they were getting breakfast on. Always the life of the party. Some things never changed. Lucas knew that as well as he did. When it came to the ranch, they wouldn't be able to count on Levi for much other than scoring them free booze.

"Things okay with Jessa?" Lucas asked as they neared Lance's place.

Other than the fact that he had no fucking clue what he was doing? "Think so. I'm taking her out on Wednesday." That was a real shocker, even to him. When he'd seen her loading up her bag in her truck, desperation had washed over him. He'd felt like he was losing her. Which was insane considering he'd never had her in the first place. At least not officially.

"You're taking her on a *date*?" his brother repeated with a low whistle. "Wow. So it's serious then."

The mocking tone hoisted Lance's defenses. "It's a date. Not a marriage proposal."

Lucas stopped walking and faced him. "Have you ever met a woman you *wanted* to take on a date?"

Sure. Of course he had. He scrolled through recent history. Okay. So it'd been a while. "Haven't had much time to date," he pointed out. He'd been too busy building a career.

"You don't have much time now," his brother countered. "But you're making time for this date."

Damn Lucas's insightful, philosophical nature. He never could be just another ordinary guy who stuck to safe topics like sports and rodeo gossip. He had a point, though. Lance had never bothered much with real dates. "Jessa's different." Than any other women he'd ever met. Or slept with. She didn't try too hard. Didn't fake it. She was genuine and empathetic. Honest. Real...Damn, he was whipped.

"Seems to me like she's worth a date," Lucas said, grinning as though he'd read all of Lance's thoughts. "Dad already loves her, you can tell that much. She's like the daughter he never had."

"She loves him, too." Took care of him exactly the way a daughter would...

"She worries about him," his brother said pointedly.

That knot of tension pulled in his neck. "And I keep telling her he's fine." If there was something to worry about, Luis would tell him.

Lucas rubbed at his forehead. Something he used to do when he was nervous.

"What?" Lance asked.

His brother gazed past him, out to the mountains. "He has tremors. I noticed during breakfast. His hands shake. Sometimes his head, too."

"He's gotten old." Not to be a dick, but his brother hadn't been around. He didn't know. "His arthritis flares up sometimes. That's all it is." He'd seen the tremors, too. Asked his dad about them, even. "He's almost seventy."

"You sure it's not more than that?"

Before he could answer, Naomi's car bounced up the driveway and parked in front of her house across the way.

The door opened and Gracie jumped out. "Uncle Lance! Uncle Lance!" She sprinted over and launched herself into his arms.

He swung her up into the air and twirled her around before setting her feet back on the ground. "Hey there, Gracie. Where've you been?"

"I was at my art class!" She held out a paper in her hands. "Look! I drew a picture of you riding Wild Willy."

Lance bent to study the paper, gawking at the fatheaded stick figure as though it were a work of art. "Wow." As he stood, he happened to catch a glimpse of Lucas.

His brother stared at Naomi as she walked toward them.

"Who are you?" Gracie asked, pointing a finger at Lucas.

Naomi approached looking downright spooked, so Lance answered for her. "This is my brother. Lucas."

The girl sized him up with a long glare, her lips puckered as though deep in thought. "So you're sort of like my uncle, too?"

That brought a smile to Lucas's face. He knelt in front of her. "Sure. I'd be happy to be your uncle." He stuck out his hand. "It's very nice to meet you, Gracie. Your mom is an old friend of mine."

The girl's eyes went wide. "Did you know my dad, too?"

"Oh no, honey. He didn't." Naomi lied. Mark had been Lucas's best friend in high school. Naomi's face flushed and Lance had never seen her look so flustered. "Why don't you go and get your backpack out of the car. Okay?" She sent the girl off with a light pat. "I'll be over in a minute and we can have a snack."

"Okay!" Gracie shot away from them, bounding over the ground like a happy golden retriever.

Naomi faced them, but she wouldn't look at either one of them. "Sorry about that. She's never met a stranger."

Lance stayed quiet. She definitely wasn't apologizing to him.

His brother stepped closer to her, still looking at her like she was some sort of goddess. Lance almost shook his head. And Lucas thought *he* was pathetic with Jessa.

"It's okay," Lucas said. "I'm glad I got to meet her. She's beautiful. She looks so much like you."

The compliment was met with a cold shoulder. Naomi turned. "I should get going. Gracie is always starving in the afternoon." She started to walk away, but Lance couldn't let her.

"Wait." He hooked a hand onto her shoulder and steered

her back to them. "I was thinking maybe you could sit down with Lucas and show him the books."

Her normally rosy face looked colorless. "Oh."

"He'll be consulting on our stock contracting operation," he went on before she could say no. "Might be good for him to get an idea of how our budget is allocated."

"Sure." It came out in a nervous whoosh of air. "Uh." She stared at the ground. "Yeah. Maybe this afternoon. Just...just stop by whenever." She turned and hurried away.

She hadn't even made it to her door when Lucas punched him in the arm. "Why the hell did you do that?"

Seemed Lucas didn't like people interfering in his love life, either. "It won't kill you two to spend a little time together."

Lucas glanced over at Naomi's house. "Spending time with me might kill *her*, from the looks of things."

Naomi had definitely been rattled. But not because she hated Lucas. "And why do you think that is?" Lance asked in the same mocking tone Lucas had used on him earlier.

"Same reason no one else wants me around here," his brother muttered. The moron.

Lucas turned and started for Lance's house.

Lance followed him up the porch steps. His brother had lost everything because of a decision they'd made when they were kids. He'd lived through the hell of prison time. Of being blackballed by his hometown. If anyone deserved something good, it was Lucas. "She might be worth coming back for."

His brother's back went stiff the way it used to before they'd start throwing punches. "I can't live here under a label. I'm not like you. I don't want to put myself out there for the judgment. Down at the McGowens' place, I have my freedom. I am who I am. Not the kid who screwed up." A small smile reminded Lance of Luis. "And I'm not one of the Cortez brothers. Not the son of Luis Cortez. No offense."

"None taken." Lance got that. Not wanting the labels. Hell, he'd been labeled his whole career. First as a superstar who was following in his great father's footsteps, now as a has-been.

It sounded good, having that freedom. Setting your own expectations instead of trying to live up to everyone else's. For years, the risk of failure had stalked him, driving him to become what the world needed him to be.

And now, it almost felt like it was too late to become anything else.

Chapter Nineteen

So...she was going on a date. Lance was taking her on a *date*. With Ilsa trailing behind her, Jessa pushed through the door of the shelter in a starry-eyed sort of wonder that made everything seem lovely and clean. She hardly noticed the dingy floors or the peeling drywall. The smell of dog food and animals.

She was going on a date!

"Wow, someone's chipper for a Monday morning." Xavier, her night shift guy, was hunched at the computer with his hand plastered to the mouse like he'd been in that exact position all night. Probably playing Dungeons & Dragons or something. Not that she cared. As long as someone was here to answer phones and take care of any animals that came in, he could do whatever he wanted.

Jessa floated over to the desk gracefully—probably looking like Grace Kelly in *High Society*. Well...minus the glamorous dresses, makeup, and heels. But those things weren't practical for taking care of animals and cleaning out kennels. Giving up the fantasy, she plopped down in the chair next to Xavier and pulled Ilsa into her lap. "Can I help it if it's a beautiful morning?" She swept an arm toward the streaked, grimy window. "I mean look at it. The sun is shining. The sky is so blue and perfect." That was how the world had looked ever since Lance had officially asked her out earlier this morning.

He eyed her travel mug suspiciously. "What'd you put in your coffee this morning?"

"Oh, Xavier." She sighed happily. "I don't need anything in my coffee. I'm just reveling in the beauty of the day." It wouldn't hurt him to get out and enjoy the sunshine. That long black hair of his made his skin look so pale...

"I'm headed out." He shut down the computer and shoved some books into his camo messenger bag. "No calls last night."

"Okay," she sang, scratching behind Ilsa's ears. "Enjoy the day! Maybe you should go for a hike or something. Get a little exercise."

He looked at her like she was suggesting he jump naked into a frigid mountain lake. "Why would *anyone* want to hike?" he asked in his bored monotone. "The only way I would ever hike is if the zombie apocalypse happened and I had to escape."

"That's a cheerful thought," she said, humming the sweet melody that seemed to radiate from her heart.

With a pronounced roll of the eyes, he grunted a wretched goodbye and trudged out the door, ducking his head as though anticipating the sunlight with horror.

Poor man. All he needed was a lovely goth-leaning Dungeons & Dragons princess to brighten up his world. Maybe she should start an online dating profile for him...

Instead, she logged on to the computer and checked her email, then updated the shelter's Facebook page with an adorable picture she'd snapped of Ilsa. Which gave her an idea...

Now that she'd left Luis's house, she couldn't possibly take Lance's money if he happened to win the competition. Even if she did, that wouldn't help her build a long-term donor base. It would only offer a quick, temporary fix, which was all her father could ever seem to find. *But...* if she could launch some type of brilliant social media campaign, maybe she could reach out to donors all over the country. She could have her old MBA study group help her out. Back in school, they'd worked on that kind of thing all the time together. Marketing had been her weakest area, but maybe the rest of the group would offer some pro bono work to beef up their own PR.

Her fingers tapped the keyboard excitedly as she typed out an email. Maybe they'd even know a developer who could build her an online donation page...

The door swung open, sending in a lovely autumn-scented breeze. Jessa pressed send and inhaled deeply, waving at Evie Starlington, who should have been a glamorous actress with that name, but she wasn't. She was a stained-glass artist. A recent transplant from Denver. Jessa had gone to her art show at Darla's place a couple of months ago and she'd hit it off with the woman right away. She was in her mid-sixties, but as hip as a teenager with her pink-streaked hair and bohemian clothing. Today, she wore a gauzy skirt and a peasant blouse with rainbow-colored tassels.

"Good morning," Jessa called, rising from the desk. She set Ilsa on the floor and the pig scurried quickly underneath the desk to hide. She was still working on socializing her.

"It is a good morning, isn't it?" Evie replied, snuggling a ball of fur tightly against her chest. "It got even better when I found this little charmer hanging out on my couch this morning." She held out a familiar cat. The very cat Jessa had rescued from a tree the other day.

"Oh, Butch." She took the cat out of the woman's hands.

"I have no idea how he got into my house," Evie said. "I did leave a window open last night…"

"Well, for being an inside cat, Butch here likes to go on adventures. Don't you, boy?" She held up the cat and he licked her nose as though he remembered her as his savior. "I know the owner. Hank Green. I can call him and have him pick him up." And in the process of returning the cat, shoot down every pass he made at her…

"If you wouldn't mind, that would be appreciated." The woman reached over to scratch behind the cat's ears. "Though I have to say, I did enjoy my short time with him. It was nice sharing coffee with someone. Even if it was someone else's cat."

A pang of sympathy dimmed her own happiness. Poor Evie. She seemed lonely. Her husband had passed away last year. That's why she'd moved away from Denver. She needed a new start, she'd said.

"Here." Jessa held out the cat. "Why don't you hold him while I call Hank?" And actually, the woman could stick around and meet him. He definitely wasn't Jessa's cup of tea, but he wasn't much older than Evie and they were both single.

While Evie sat in a chair gushing over Butch, Jessa hurried to the phone.

"Y-ello," Hank answered.

"Hey, it's Jessa. Butch is here at the shelter."

"What?" The word hurled through a dramatic gasp. "Why, I didn't even know he was gone!"

Uh-huh. Sure. He'd probably sent Butch out again and was getting ready to call her. Despite that, she smiled. Hank was lonely, too. And she knew how that felt. "Miss Starlington brought him in. Do you know her?"

"No. I can't say that I do."

"She's a wonderful woman. New to town." She battled the urge to start listing off all her best qualities. Shouldn't work too hard to sell her. "Somehow Butch managed to climb in her window."

Movement scratched on the other side of the line. "Well, thank her for bringing him in, will you?" he said dismissively. "I'll be right over. Then maybe we can grab a cup of coffee together..."

"Actually, you can thank Miss Starlington yourself," Jessa said before he could finish asking her out. "I'll ask her to stay until you get here."

"But—"

"See you soon!" With an extra flourish, she clicked the off button, then tossed the phone on her desk. "Hank will be over in a few minutes," she called to Evie. "Can I get you a cup of—?"

The door swung open again. *Wow*, busy morning. Jessa turned, expecting an animal situation, but instead Luis ambled in.

She popped up from her desk. "Hey, Luis. I wasn't expecting you today. Not with Lucas and Levi home."

His eyes didn't meet hers. In fact, his head stayed low enough that she could hardly get a look at his face. "I need to talk to you," he said quietly, too seriously.

The happiness that had been floating inside her all morning turned to stone. "Oh. Sure. Of course," she sputtered. She picked up Ilsa's leash and started walking toward the back room, but then noticed Evie watching them. She paused. "Have you met Evie?" she asked him. "She's new around here. An artist from Denver."

"Pleased to meet you," he said in his gentlemanly way. He crossed the room and held out his hand. The two of them shook.

Jessa tried to smile past the panic bells clanging in her heart. "Luis Cortez is..."

"I know who he is," Evie said with quite the blush. "I followed your career for a long time. It's so wonderful to meet you in person." The warm smile the woman offered him was rewarded with a humble grin.

"My career ended years ago," he said, his tone brushing away all of those famous belt buckles he'd earned.

"Maybe so, but you'll always be a legend," Evie said kindly, and suddenly Jessa regretted inviting Hank Green over.

Luis was still smiling when he shoved his hands into his pockets and strode toward the employee lounge.

Jessa followed, tugging Ilsa along behind. Whatever he wanted to say, he didn't want to wait. "Evie, Luis and I are going to have a chat in the back. Can you wait for Hank to come and pick up Butch?"

"Of course." She settled back into the chair. "I'm happy to."

They'd hardly cleared the door before Jessa turned to Luis. "Is everything okay?"

He faced her directly, steeling his hunched shoulders. "Truth is, something's not right. It hasn't been for months." His old hands folded in on themselves, fingers weaving together.

"Wh-what?" Her legs trembled, forcing her to sink to the beat-up leather couch. She swept Ilsa into her arms, holding her close for comfort. The pig nuzzled her snout into Jessa's neck.

Luis sat in the chair across from her, his expression resolute. "I get dizzy sometimes. Lose my balance. Other times I'm confused…"

The bottom dropped out of her lovely happy morning. "Oh, Luis…" *No. Please.* She couldn't do this. She couldn't face the thought of losing him, too.

He shifted, but his gaze still held hers like he was forcing himself not to look away. "When I dropped the ladder in Green's yard…I got disoriented. Couldn't remember what I was supposed to be doing. Don't even know how I ended up down on Main Street."

Don't cry. No crying. She touched a finger to the corner of each eye to catch the tears before they fell. "Have you been to the doctor?" she asked, holding her voice together with a thread of denial. Maybe he wasn't sick. Maybe he really had just been dehydrated that day…

"Yes," he said, abolishing her hope. "A couple times. The doc's done some tests. But he wants me to see a specialist in Denver. A neurologist. On Thursday."

A neurologist? This time there was no stopping the tears. They slipped down her cheeks one by one. She could be strong for him, but she couldn't promise not to show emotion. "Do you need me to come?" she half-whispered, trying to get a handle on her squeaky tone. "I can talk to Lance—"

"No." The firm denial cut her off. "I want you to come. No one else. I'm not telling Lance."

She shot to her feet, holding tightly to Ilsa, her pulse racing. "But Lance should know. He'd *want* to know."

"Not yet," Luis said stubbornly. "Not until I get a diagnosis. He's training. I can't distract him from what he needs to do."

"But..." She sank back to the couch, the gravity of what he was asking too much weight to bear. How could she not tell him? How could she go on a date with him and not tell him his father might be sick? "It's only a competition," she breathed. This was his father's life...

"It's more than that to him," Luis said sternly. "It's what he lives for. And I won't be the reason he fails."

Anger tore through the sadness. "That's ridiculous—"

"Please." The one word held enough sadness to smother her indignation. "I need to know you won't tell him. Not until I'm ready. I don't ask you for much. But I need this."

She pressed her hand against her mouth to hold in a sob and nodded. "Fine," she murmured when she could speak. "I won't tell him. But you'll have to. Eventually."

He nodded. "After the competition."

"And what about Lucas and Levi?" They'd only just reconnected with him...

"I'm not gonna saddle them with this now," he said, looking away from her as if he knew exactly what she thought about that plan.

Because she hated it. The thought of him going to a specialist—maybe hearing a grim diagnosis—without his boys there made her nauseated. "They're your family." She tried to say it gently, but conviction hurtled out.

Luis gave her a sad look as he reached across and patted her hand. "And I'll tell them when the time is right."

* * *

Lance fumbled with the buttons on his shirt. Been a damn long time since he'd worn a dress shirt. But he figured Jessa was worth the trouble, even if the collar did pinch at his neck. He tucked the shirt into his jeans and cinched his belt buckle. A fancy shirt was one thing, but he'd stick with jeans, thank you very much. Besides, what he had planned for their date tonight would require jeans. And with that thought...

He strode out into the living room. He never got nervous around women, but something in his gut churned. Which could mean only one thing. He had it bad.

"Whoa." Lucas stood in the kitchen helping himself to a beer. He whistled. "Someone must have big plans tonight."

Lance positioned himself on the other side of the counter, doing his best to appear casual. "How do you figure?"

His brother eyed him as though racking up a list of reasons. "For starters, you tucked your shirt in."

Lance looked down. *Yeah, okay.* That was a dead give-away. "So?" he challenged, just like he used to when they were kids. That usually ended in a scuffle around the floor until one of them had the other pinned. But tonight he didn't feel like messing up his hair.

"Where are you headed?" Lucas asked, the smirk on his face making him look thirteen again.

Lance evaded his brother's amused eyes. "Gonna pick up Jessa. Take her up to the lake." A romantic evening picnic. Not that he could take credit. He'd Googled romantic dates in the mountains...

"A picnic?" His brother's jaw hung open.

Yeah, it kind of shocked him, too. But what could he say? "I like her."

"So I see." Lucas took a swig of beer and set the bottle on

the counter. "I'm happy for you. She seems close to perfect for you." The smirk reappeared. "Nice. Kind. Compassionate. Someone to balance you out."

"What the hell is that supposed to—"

The door pounded open and Levi hustled in. "Got any beer around this place? Dad's out."

Probably because Levi had downed it all. Didn't take that kid long to put back a case of beer.

"Plenty in the fridge," Lucas said, moving out of the way so Levi could open it.

He snatched a lager and popped the top like he'd been waiting for a year.

"Ahh…" He swiped his arm across his mouth and looked at Lance as though noticing him for the first time. "Why the hell are you dressed like you're doing a photo shoot for *Rodeo News*?"

"He has a date," Lucas answered for him. "With Jessa."

Damn. If only he could sucker punch him like he used to.

"Knew it." Levi's palm smacked the countertop. "It was so obvious. You were all over her at the bar."

"Noticed you avoided Cassidy," Lance said. He still knew how to put Levi in his place when the situation demanded.

Sure enough, his brother's gaze dropped to the floor.

"Did you even say a word to her?" After being her brother's best friend and practically growing up as part of the family, a hello wouldn't have killed him.

"Cassidy hates me." He took a long pull on the beer and when he set it down the spark was gone from his eyes. "She hates everyone who has anything to do with riding."

Lance doubted that. Cassidy didn't hate Levi. His brother simply felt guilty for being there when Cash died. For not being able to prevent his accident, as if he were God or something.

"Come on, you two." Lucas shook his head at the two of them. "How about we stop trying to push one another's buttons and get along? I'm only gonna be here a few more days, then I gotta head back to the McGowens'."

"A few more days?" That was it? All these years Luis had been waiting for Lucas's return, and now he was staying only a few days.

"I've got stuff to take care of down there. They rely on me."

"I gotta head back to training soon, too," Levi said, finishing off his beer. "Not everyone qualifies for Worlds with just their name." He gave Lance a pointed look. "Some of us gotta work for it."

Lance's temper flared. He *had* worked for it. His whole life. He'd given everything to it. But Levi knew that. Once again, his younger brother was just trying to poke the dragon. Besides, they had other things to discuss. If they were both leaving soon, they didn't have much time. He glanced at the clock. He had to leave in ten minutes, but they had to do this now. He walked to the counter and pulled out a stool, sitting down across from his brothers. "Since you're both here, there's something I want to say." He didn't give them a chance to respond. "I think we should tell Dad. Everything."

Lucas braced his hands against the countertop. "We've been over this."

Maybe so, but their last go-round hadn't convinced him of anything. "I think he deserves to know the truth." If he stood in the man's shoes, he'd want to know.

"There's no point," Lucas growled, more riled up than he should've been. "Not right now. What's done is done. Let's leave it be."

He couldn't. Not anymore. Not for Lucas and not for Levi. Not for their father. "No one else has to know. But he should."

Levi looked back and forth between him and Lucas, his expression unreadable. "Lance is right," he finally said.

"What?" Come again? Had those three words really just come out of his younger brother's mouth?

"You're right," Levi said again, with more conviction this time. "He should know the truth."

Wow. Lance could only stand there blinking like a fool. He'd never thought Levi would be the one to agree on this. Maybe his brother *had* grown up some out there in Oklahoma...

"You don't know what the hell you're talking about," Lucas argued. "You don't want him to know the truth."

Their youngest brother slammed his beer onto the countertop so hard Lance couldn't believe the bottle didn't shatter.

"How do you think I felt knowing you were in prison because of something I did?" he demanded. "I ruined your life."

"We didn't exactly give you a choice," Lance reminded him. He'd never thought about what it had done to Levi. It'd never seemed to bother him. He'd obviously hidden it well.

"Exactly. You didn't give me a choice." His brother's eyes had darkened. "But I could've spoken up. I could've said something. If I had it to do over, I never would let you take the fall for me."

Lucas sighed as though he was more tired than angry. "You were a kid. Hell, we were all kids. We didn't know anything."

That was the truth. For the most part they'd been on their own to make life's big decisions. And there'd been plenty of times they'd screwed up. They could always right those wrongs, though. It wasn't too late. "We can make it right now."

Lucas studied Levi. "But you have your whole career ahead of you..."

"I don't need you to protect me anymore," their younger brother said with more conviction than Lance had thought he was capable of.

Lucas still looked as surprised as he felt. "No. I guess you don't."

Levi walked over and tossed his beer bottle into the recycling bin. "They couldn't prosecute me anyway. You've already served the sentence. So yeah, it might suck if everyone else found out. They might hate me. But I won't go to prison."

Lucas still looked undecided, but Lance wasn't. "We can tell him tomorrow. At dinner," he said. "But right now I have to run." Wouldn't do to be late for Jessa. She'd already forgiven him for being an ass once. Or twice. Didn't need to add poor punctuality to the list.

"Have fun," his brothers said in unison as he trotted out the door.

Didn't need to tell him twice. It'd been only a few days since he'd spent time with her, but it felt more like months.

Outside, the early evening sun backlit the mountains with a vibrant haze. He climbed into the truck, appreciating the view as he drove toward town. Normally, he didn't consider himself an optimistic sort of fella, but it seemed things were falling into place. His brothers were back home, which meant the family was back together. After all these years, they'd put the past to rest. Worlds were coming up fast, and he'd never felt more ready for a competition in his life.

And all of it was thanks to Jessa.

Chapter Twenty

It was becoming apparent that perhaps Darla hadn't been the best choice in reinforcements to call when Jessa had started to freak out about her date with Lance. The woman had come right over and talked her into wearing her brand-new flowy, low-cut sundress that clearly said, *Make love to me in a flower-dappled meadow.*

And yes, she had to admit, it was the perfect outfit for a first date with a man who'd already convinced her he was worth the effort. But there was a slight complication. She shouldn't go on a date with him. Not when she was leaving for Denver at six thirty in the morning with his father for a secret doctor's appointment. "He told me to wear jeans," she said, glancing at herself in the mirror.

Darla only laughed. "He doesn't want you to wear jeans. When he sees this dress, he'll forget all about jeans," she promised.

"I shouldn't go. I could tell him I have the chickenpox,"

Jessa squeaked, fisting her friend's shirt desperately in her hands. "Or measles. Or a bad case of the stomach flu..." A rising panic crowded into her chest, jamming up her throat. She glanced at the clock. Lance would be there in ten minutes!

"No." Darla plucked Jessa's hands from her clothing and backed away, straightening the wrinkles out of her shirt. "You are going on this date," she said sternly. "I mean, come on! Lance never asks anyone out." Her hands flew up. "Think of what this means. This is like a record. Maybe you'll end up in the Guinness World Records or something."

Jessa deflated to the couch, suddenly exhausted from the weight of carrying such a heavy secret. "I can't go. I can't." How could she look into that man's perceptive eyes and pretend everything was all right?

Darla plopped next to her. "You *have* to go," she argued. "You look gorgeous. And you don't want to discourage his interest in you, right?"

Jessa stared at her hands, trying to even out her breathing. "Well. No. I guess not." She liked Lance. Okay. She more than liked him. But that was the problem. She'd learned enough about him to realize that keeping any sort of secret about his father would be considered an unpardonable sin in his book.

"Come on." Darla gave her shoulders a quick massage, like a coach pumping up a boxer for a big match. "Just forget about everything else and have fun tonight. Let it all go."

"I want to." She wanted to waltz out that door with him and let him sweep her off her feet like they'd been caught up in one of those wonderful Humphrey Bogart movies. Not like it would be all that hard for him to sweep her off her feet. He'd already laid a serious claim on her heart. She wanted to hold his hand and kiss him and, well, depending on where things went, maybe more than kiss him. But. "I feel like I'm lying to him." In a moment of desperation on the phone, she'd given up Luis's secret to Darla. Not that she had to worry. The woman was a vault.

"Pshaw." Darla waved away her concerns. "You're not lying. You're withholding. Totally different," she said, as though she'd suddenly become a relationship expert. "You have to respect Luis's wishes on this, Jess. This is his decision. Not yours."

And that was the sad truth of it. "I know."

"Luis is right. This would completely throw Lance off right before the biggest competition of his life. Is that what you want?"

"No." He needed this win. He needed to go out on top. Surely he'd understand. She was just trying to do what was best for him.

"Now, I'm gonna take off before he gets here and sees me giving you a pep talk." Darla pushed off the couch and walked across the room to the dog bed Jessa had brought home for Ilsa. The pig squealed when she picked her up, but Darla carefully calmed her with a smooch on the head. She'd agreed to watch Ilsa tonight. Just in case things went late.

But Jessa couldn't let things go late. She couldn't sleep with Lance! Not when she was keeping something from him...

"Call me the second you get home," Darla said for the hundredth time. "Got it? I want details. I want to know *everything*."

She followed her friend to the door and opened it for her, then leaned down to kiss Ilsa's snout. "I'm not sure there'll be anything to tell." How could she say one word to him without everything coming out? Let alone kiss the man? It would feel so wrong...

"Oh, there'll be something to tell," Darla insisted on her way down the porch. "Trust me. That dress won't let you down." With a suggestive lift of her eyebrows, she traipsed down the porch, wiggling her fingers in a wave.

Jessa didn't wave back. Her arms felt too weak to move. She tapped the door closed with her toes and paced the living room. Usually the anticipation of seeing Lance brought on the butterflies, but now it had unleashed something far more intense. What if Lance could read the secret on her face? What if she accidentally mentioned something about their trip to Denver? What if—

The doorbell chimed.

Her head whipped around. Lance's sturdy build crowded the window.

"Okay," she breathed. "Okay." Too late to cancel. Too late to make up some sort of illness. Darla was right. She wasn't lying. After it all came out, she'd simply explain to Lance how important the secret had been to Luis. He would understand. He had to understand.

Slowly, she shuffled to the door, her insides quivering the whole way. She reached for the knob and suddenly the damn thing felt like it was solid steel. Somehow she managed to get the door open, even with her failing muscles. And that image of him standing there... that burned into her brain. He was dreamy... a rugged cowboy fantasy. Dark tight jeans. Black button-down shirt tucked in so as not to hide any of his goods. His hair had been somewhat tamed but not to the point of looking like he cared all that much, and God, that made him sexy.

"Hi, there," she said as casually as she could, considering the pulse in her throat.

"Hey." His gaze lazily trailed down her body and back up to her eyes, and the desire she saw there rendered her speechless.

"I know I told you to wear jeans, but that's one hell of a dress, Jessa Love," he uttered in a rather provocative, scraping tone that tempted her to do away with the dress altogether.

Instead of disrobing, she turned away to snatch her purse off the sofa table. And to talk her cheeks out of a blush. "Thanks," she muttered as soon as she could speak.

When she turned around, he stood closer, almost right against her, and even though he hadn't touched her yet, she felt him, inhaled that dangerous scent that made her think of the powerful trees lining the mountains outside.

"I thought we'd go for a picnic." His gaze lowered to her cleavage as though he wanted her to know how much he appreciated it. "That sound okay with you?"

A picnic. It sounded perfect. In the great outdoors, maybe she could think about something besides leading him right into her bedroom. Skip the small talk. Skip the food. Who needed a date when Lance was so good at seducing her? *Ahem.* Yes. A picnic would be much safer. "I love picnics," she told him, going to the closet to pick out a sweater. Delicate and white to match the dress.

"Can't say I've ever been on a picnic," he said, holding open the front door for her. "But I figure it'll be a nice evening up at the lake."

"Mmm-hmmm," she squeaked, hightailing it down the sidewalk to his old pickup. She'd already climbed in and gotten belted before he could open the door for her.

Lance hoisted himself into the driver's seat and started the engine. As he pulled away from the curb, he glanced over at her. "You okay?" he asked, more unsure than she'd ever seen him.

"Yes." A fake laugh tumbled out. "Of course I'm okay." Oh God. She might as well have said, *No, Lance. I'm not okay. I'm taking your father to Denver in the morning.* She was terrible at pretending.

Sure enough, he gave her a skeptical look.

"Um." She scraped at a piece of nail polish on the tip of her finger. *Think. Think, damn it.* Maybe sex would've been a better idea. Then she wouldn't actually have to talk to him. "It's just...it's been a stressful week."

His eyes watched the windshield now as he navigated the town streets. "Things at the shelter okay?"

"Yes." As far as she could tell. Though she'd been a bit distracted lately, courtesy of that man sitting right there. "Just a lot to do."

The truck lurched to a stop as he waited to turn onto the highway. "My offer's still good, you know." His hand swept down her arm and brought on a rush of longing. "Even though you're not staying with Dad anymore, I'll still donate half my winnings to the shelter."

Her shoulders went stiff. "You don't have to do that," she choked out. He shouldn't do that.

"I want to." He sped onto the highway, sneaking glances at her as they headed toward the ranch. "You've done a lot for us, Jessa. Bringing my brothers home...helping out Dad."

Her hands squeezed into fists. She was still trying to help out Luis. She had to remember that. "It's nothing," she insisted, staring out the passenger window, watching the familiar mountains roll by. They'd turned off the highway and onto the ranch's vast acreage and were heading up the same switchback road she and Luis took on the ATVs. The secret seemed to sear against her chest, but she battled back an urge to tell him. "So how are things going with your brothers?" she asked in an attempt to take the focus off her.

"Things are pretty good." He kind of laughed. "Surprisingly."

That drew her gaze to him. "Why is that surprising?"

"Let's just say there've always been some things between us." He focused on the road as though he wanted to evade her eyes. "But we're dealing with them. Finally. After all these years, I think we can be like a family again." There was a gravity in his voice, half hope, half fear. But when his face turned to her she saw only strength. "Thanks to you."

Guilt spilled through her again, forcing her to look away. "I can't take credit for that." After he found out about his father's situation, he likely wouldn't be singing her praises anymore.

Silence ensued as the truck crawled up the steep incline. When the road leveled out, he glanced over at her again. "I didn't think I'd be thankful for them coming back. But I am. And Dad is." His eyes locked on hers. "I haven't seen him this happy in a long time."

She felt the color drain from her face. His father was not a safe subject right now. Not at all. "How's training coming?" she rasped, hoping to divert the conversation away from Luis. She couldn't talk about him at all or she might burst into tears. She'd nearly driven herself crazy looking up his symptoms on the Internet, fearing everything from a brain tumor to dementia to Alzheimer's.

"I feel ready," Lance said, parking the truck near the short path that led down to the lake. "I don't think I've ever felt this ready for a competition."

"I'm glad." It was the most genuine thing she'd said since he rang her doorbell. She was glad for him. After the hell everyone was giving him, he deserved to win.

Which is why she wouldn't tell him. As soon as he came back from Worlds, he'd find out everything. Right now, she had to give him space to concentrate. Comforted by the thought, she climbed out of the truck, thankful for the fresh air, the expanse of space between them. Maybe out here in the openness things wouldn't feel as intimate. Maybe she could keep her distance.

While Lance unloaded a huge basket from the bed of his truck, she wandered to the path. Evening was just starting to settle, hushing the world, making everything glow. God, it was romantic. The lighting, the soft breeze, the faraway rush of a stream. The peace of it made reality seem a little farther away, like they really had entered some dream world where happiness could never come to a screeching halt with one diagnosis, with one little lie. Her body let go of some of the tension it had been carrying as she inhaled the scent of honeysuckle and pine. So lovely, these mountains. So far away from everything else.

"Hope you like cheese. And wine," Lance said, coming up behind her.

She turned, letting herself take him in, letting her eyes linger on his. "I like both." She smiled at him. And it felt real. Not forced. "That's quite the basket. I'm so impressed," she teased, eyeing the huge woven work of art he carried.

"Borrowed it from Naomi," he admitted with a grin. "I was just gonna pack it all in a good old saddle bag. But I figured we might not want hay in our food."

She laughed, and somehow it made a surge of tingling anticipation slip through her hesitations. Lance had gone to a lot of trouble planning this date. A picnic. Something intimate and sweet. He could've taken her to a restaurant, but instead he'd brought her out here. The effort he'd put in warmed her.

They walked in an easy silence down to the lake. She'd been there a couple of times, fishing with Luis, mostly, but she'd never seen it at dusk. When the trees opened into a clearing, she stopped suddenly. It almost looked fake. The glassy surface, smooth and turquoise, fed from the glacier nestled between two cliffs above. The setting sun streaked the sky with colors, reflecting off the water. "This is incredible," she breathed.

"Yeah. Sometimes I come up here at sunset. It's probably the most peaceful spot on the entire ranch." Lance led her down to the water, where a big flat rock sat mere feet away from the shoreline.

"This is where I usually sit." He lowered the basket to the ground and took out a red-and-white-checkered tablecloth, shaking it slightly before he spread it out.

"It's perfect." She sat, letting her legs stretch out in front of her, crossing them at the ankles as her skin soaked in the gentle evening sun.

Lance sat beside her, pulling things out of the basket, one by one. A plastic-wrapped plate of some yummy-looking cheeses, a container of grapes, a platter of what looked to be prosciutto and salami. Then, two wineglasses and a bottle of merlot. He uncorked the wine and poured a glass for each of them. Then he held his out to her, a sparkle of mystery in his eyes. "To great views," he said, eyeing her dress again, and this time she let herself blush.

"To great views," she repeated, clanking her glass against his.

He pulled out two plates and served her. It was all perfectly thought out. The saltiness of the cheese with the bitterness of the wine and the sweetness of the grapes. The two of them ate leisurely while the pink hues deepened in the sky.

Jessa set down her wineglass, still mesmerized by how the lake's surface mirrored the sky. "So what do you think about when you come up here?"

Lance gazed up at the peaks above them. "Life. Competitions. Sometimes my mom." That last sentence seemed garbled with an emotion she couldn't quite peg. Anger? Resentment? Sadness?

She munched on the amazing Brie he'd selected and sipped her wine. "Did you stay in touch with her? Ever hear from her?"

Instead of answering, he shook his head. Then he popped some grapes into his mouth, chewing thoughtfully before he swallowed. "For a while I thought she'd come back. That she'd realize her mistake and make things right."

By the sound of things, he'd given up on that dream a long time ago. But she'd never been one to lose hope easily. "Maybe she still will," Jessa said, her tone treading carefully.

"Nah. She would've already. If she wanted to." He set his plate on the ground next to the rock and hunched, resting his elbows on his knees. "I've looked for her more than once. Didn't find anything. She obviously doesn't want to be found."

The pain on his face ground itself into her heart. What would that be like? To have this important piece of your life missing? Did he feel incomplete because of it? "You boys deserved better," she said, covering his hand with hers. His was warm and rough. Battered by the constant tug-of-war with leather. She loved the feel of it. Of him. His hands were so distinct, the lines and ridges and scars…

Lance scooted closer to her. "You didn't have it so easy with your family, either, huh? Always going back and forth the way you did." His arm settled around her.

"No." She let herself lean into him. "That's true. But both of my parents were always there for me." They may not have been in love, but they both loved her. She'd never had to doubt that. "I consider myself very blessed to have had that."

Lance peered down at her, his eyes searching hers. "How do you do that?"

She turned to face him. "What?"

"See the best in every situation. In everyone?"

Maybe because she'd overdosed on romance her entire life and now she thought only in terms of happily-ever-afters? That didn't sound very intelligent. "I guess I like to focus on what I have instead of what I think I need. I only see the things I'm grateful for."

His face lowered to hers. "Want to know what I'm grateful for?" he murmured, nearly against her lips.

"What?" she breathed, her heart pounding its way out of her chest.

"That dress." The grin that accompanied the words was downright naughty. And close. *So* close.

She laughed as his lips nudged hers, and he laughed, too, but only for a second before he pulled her closer, teasing her with a scrap of his extravagant mouth against hers. The heat on their lips thawed the fears and the hesitations that had chilled her heart before. Because she loved kissing him. Loved how his firm lips moved against hers, slow and sensual. Savoring. She loved the feel of his hard chest under her palms, the way his hands held her, the way his stubble scraped her skin.

"You really know how to plan a date," she whispered against his neck.

Carefully he lowered her back to the rock, then hovered over her while he traced her collarbone with his finger. "It'll only get better," he promised,

"Can't wait," she whispered, bringing her lips to his again. Losing herself in the rhythm of his kiss and the peaceful breeze and the glowing sunset, she took Darla's advice.

She let the secret between them go.

Chapter Twenty-One

This evening wasn't supposed to be about sex, but God almighty was it hard to convince his body of that. Especially with Jessa underneath him, making those hot little noises while he kissed the soft warm flesh of her neck. He wanted sex. No. He should rephrase that. He wanted sex with Jessa again. Slow this time. Deliberate. So he could touch every inch of her skin. Taste it with his tongue. So he could revel in the sensation of burying himself inside her again, taking her to that place where her control shattered and she clung to him as she rode out the pleasure he gave her...

His hands fisted and he pulled back, eased himself onto his side next to her. He wanted her more than he'd ever wanted a woman, but he wanted more than her body. Tonight was not about sex. It was about taking her on a date. When he'd picked her up, she'd been distant, and who the hell could blame her? They'd already had a quickie in the kitchen but since then, they'd hardly talked. Had hardly spent any time alone, getting to know each other the way a woman like Jessa would want to. She might say she was fine with a fling, but he knew better. She'd never given herself away to just anyone. Hell, that's what made her special. He knew she wanted more. And she deserved it, too.

"Everything okay?" she asked quietly, touching her fingers to her lips. Even in the dusky light, he could see the rosiness of her cheeks, heated and alive, the same way his body felt.

He gazed down at her, playing with the strands of hair around her face, breathing in her sweet honey scent. "Everything's more than okay." Because he had her here, alone. Because right now in this moment, she belonged to him. He couldn't say what would happen tomorrow, where tonight would lead them, but right now he had everything he wanted. "Are *you* okay?"

She smiled up at the stars that were starting to prick the sky with their twinkling light. "Yes, Lance. I am definitely okay." Her gaze met his, and he had to hold his breath and count backward from ten so he wouldn't say screw getting to know her and maul her instead. He could do this. Talk to a woman he was interested in. Talk without expecting anything else. They had a lot of things to discuss. He knew a lot about her but he didn't know *her*.

She turned on her side, so that her perfect breasts pressed against his chest. Instead of caressing them the way he'd been fantasizing about, he rested his hand on her hip. "I figured we should talk some. Get to know each other."

Jessa busted out laughing.

"What?" he demanded, though her laughter lured out a grin. She had a great laugh. Happy and buoyant. A laugh that could make even the biggest miser smile. He needed more of that laugh in his life.

"Sorry," she managed to say through a lingering giggle. "I'm sorry." She made a face as though she was struggling to put on a more serious expression. "So what do you want to know about me? Favorite color? Favorite food?" Judging from the glimmer in her eyes she was teasing him.

And he liked it. "Bra size," he shot back, though he'd had enough experience to guess she was safely within the C category.

"Why don't you take a look?" she said, temptingly.

He could. He could take the thing off with his teeth right now. But he'd already decided. Next time he made love to Jessa, it wouldn't be on an uncomfortable rock in the great outdoors. It would be in his king-size bed, where they could spend the entire night exploring each other, where he could take his time figuring out how she liked it best. Where he could send her over the edge as many times as she'd let him and then they could fall asleep with their naked bodies tangled together.

He eased out a breath. "When's your birthday?" he asked, jaw tensed with restraint.

Jessa propped herself up on her elbow and gave him that soft smile that made him want to trace her lips with his tongue. "September. The sixteenth."

He nodded as though checking her answer off the list. He tried to think of another stupid question, something insignificant, but the truth was he didn't care what her favorite color was. He didn't care what she liked to eat. That would all be learned in time. What fascinated him most about Jessa was her heart. The woman had been hurt. Engaged a couple of times, rumor had it. She'd been cast aside. Abandoned just like him.

But she had this resilience he envied. Only one person had re-jected him in his whole life and yet in that one moment he'd shut himself off to the very connection he was starting to feel with Jessa. He'd ridden bulls, been bucked around, thrown. He'd broken too many bones to count. But this...this terrified him. The risk seemed so much greater than just his own life. Yet he didn't want to turn back. He didn't want to run scared this time. Jessa had managed to do what no other woman could all these years. She'd earned his trust.

He braved a look into her stunning eyes. "What do you want most in life?" he asked her, wondering if maybe he could offer it to her.

Her expression sobered. She rolled onto her back and stared up at the sky again.

Figuring it might make it easier for her to answer, he did the same.

Wind rustled the pine needles and made the water quietly lap at the shoreline. He said nothing, though Jessa's silence tempted him to let her off the hook.

Finally, she sighed, as though she'd resigned herself to honesty. "Love," she murmured as though somewhat ashamed. "That's what I want most in life. To love someone wholly and truly. And to have them love me back."

The words struck him with their simplicity. Wasn't that what most people wanted but were too afraid to admit? He leaned over, kissing her tenderly yet firmly. When he pulled back, his heart pounded. "I don't know how to do that," he admitted. To love someone. Even more than that, to let someone love *him*. "But maybe I can learn."

Jessa turned her body to his again, placing her palm at the curve of his jaw. "You're far better at it than you think you are," she whispered. "You love your father." Was it tears that made her eyes brighter? Or just the deepening darkness? He didn't know why that filled her with so much emotion, but he loved that in her. Loved how she let herself feel. He stroked her cheek, steering her lips back to his, and this time the kiss felt deeper, more meaningful. It was even harder to pull back, harder to keep his hands from wandering all of the places they wanted to go. Instead, he drew her into a tight embrace, trying to convince himself he was satisfied simply holding her. "Come with us. To Worlds." The words surprised him as much as they seemed to surprise Jessa. He hadn't planned on saying them, on inviting her. But he wanted her with him.

She pushed back and sat up. "What?"

"Come to Vegas." He sat up, too, gazing into her eyes to convince her. "We'll get you your own suite. Dad would love it."

Her head tilted to the side. "You want me to come along for your dad?"

"Yeah." He bit back a smile. She was much smarter than that, but she apparently wanted to make him say it. "And maybe I want you there for me, too." He wanted her light. Her laugh. Her smile. Her happiness. It wouldn't be easy for him to face his critics, the people who were hungrily awaiting his downfall. But something told him he could manage it better if she were with him.

Jessa's whole face lit. "Okay," she said slowly, as though it was sinking in. "Yes. I'd love to go with you."

"Okay," he repeated, already making the arrangements in his head. He'd have his agent set everything up, find her plane reservations, get her the best suite at the hotel. "You'll have a great time," he said, kissing her sweet lips again. "I promise."

She kissed him back, clinging to him, running her hands down his chest. Before they could travel any lower, he pulled back and cut off the kissing. "Right now, though, I should get you home," he growled, breaking apart their bodies before he wasn't able.

"You sure?" she whispered.

No. He was not at all sure. But the cold hardness of the rock was enough to remind him. "This isn't the most comfortable place to make out," he said.

"I noticed." She laughed. "And I really do need to get home," she agreed, scrambling off the rock and to her feet as though her balance had been compromised.

He could relate. He steadied her with a hand against her lower back. "We can go on a date in Vegas." He packed plenty of heat into the suggestive expression. "Then you can spend the night. If you want to."

The slightest hesitation flickered across her face but then she smiled. "Sure. It'll give us something to look forward to."

Hell yes, it would. He'd be counting down the minutes.

* * *

Doctor examination rooms were all the same. Bland white walls. Lights too bright. Inevitably one cheesy framed picture that someone had likely ordered as part of a special offer per dozen. From the chair where she sat next to Luis, Jessa studied the amateurish painting of an eagle perched on the sturdy branch of an evergreen tree. The creature's eyes glowered at her from all the way across the room. Not exactly the most comforting image while waiting to hear your fate.

A clock on the wall ticked off the seconds. Earlier, while she'd killed time in the waiting room, Luis had undergone some tests. Then the nurse had invited her into the exam room while they waited to hear from the doctor. And they'd been waiting ever since.

Luis sat tall and composed, much better off than she was, evidently. The anticipation of waiting for the doctor was slowly killing her. Her knee pumped with the frantic beat of her heart. What was taking so long? Had they found something terrible? Why hadn't the doctor come in yet? She watched the clock, tucking her hands under her thighs so she wouldn't fidget.

"You okay?" Luis asked, without turning his head to face her.

"No. I'm not." She couldn't lie. He'd see right through her, anyway. "This place is terrible. So depressing. I mean, would it hurt to put some color on the walls? And what's this?" she demanded, snatching a magazine off the small countertop next to them. "*Financial Times*? Are you kidding me? Who wants to sit in here and read boring old investment articles?" Indignation rolled off her face in waves, giving release to her misplaced anger. Sometimes anger was easier. Because truth be told, she was downright scared. The *what-if*s had been stirring a potion of fear that boiled in her stomach. She wanted to run from here. Far away. Before they found out the worst.

And God, she couldn't let herself think about last night. How perfect it had been. How truly wonderful Lance had treated her. Even while she'd withheld the knowledge that his father might be dying of some horrible disease...

"Everything will be all right, Jess," Luis said with a quiet confidence.

That only got her more riled up. "What if it's not?" Her throat was raw. How could she go through losing another father one year after her own had left her? Yes, that was selfish, but there it was. She loved Luis, and the thought of watching him suffer made her want to double over.

The old man patted her hand with warm affection. "I'm not worried, honey. Don't matter what the doc says. I've got everything I've ever wanted. My boys are all home. Together. Don't matter what's wrong with me." He spoke as though he knew something was wrong, as though he'd already accepted it.

So why couldn't she?

"Saw Lance's truck drive in awful late last night," Luis mentioned casually. "I reckon you two had a good time on your date?"

"A great time." The flashbacks of Lance touching her and kissing her with such tenderness filled her with warmth and longing. It was the best date she'd ever been on...

"You didn't tell him about the appointment?" his father asked carefully.

Her eyes fell shut. "No. I didn't."

"Sorry, Jess. I know that had to be real hard."

"It was." She tried not to glare at him. She loved the man, but she hated this. "I don't want to lie to him."

"I'll tell him when the time is right. I promise. As soon as—"

The door swung open, leaving the promise unfinished. Jessa snapped her spine to full attention as the neurologist— a short man with a neatly trimmed rim of graying hair— walked in.

"Sorry for the wait," he said briskly as he plunked himself on the rolling stool across from them. "I wanted to take a few extra minutes to go over your test results." He fumbled through a manila folder and Jessa glimpsed stacks of pictures. MRI scans, charts, diagrams. She turned to look at Luis, her mouth gaping. He must've been undergoing tests for months...

The doctor focused only on Luis, his expression a mask of polite detachment. "Based on all we've learned over the past months, and my conversations with your primary physician, I believe we have a diagnosis."

Jessa inhaled deeply, trying her hardest to be brave, trying to find strength for Luis. She snuck her hand over to his, holding on tightly, desperate to siphon some of his courage.

"I believe you're battling Parkinson's disease. And it would appear you've had it for some time," the doctor went on in a monotone.

"That's what Dr. Potter thought." Luis's voice didn't even waver. He wasn't surprised. He'd known for months. But Jessa was reeling. In anger, in sadness, in fear of how Lance would handle a blow like this...

"There's no way to know how quickly it will progress or exactly how the symptoms will manifest. Parkinson's is difficult to define. Each patient is different." The man handed Luis a large envelope. "Here are some resources. Potential treatments. Results from the latest trials. There are definitely methods we can try to slow down the progression. Medications, certain therapies."

"Is it fatal?" Jessa choked out, needing to know the prognosis.

"Not necessarily." For the first time since he'd come in, the doctor acknowledged her with direct eye contact. "But there are complications. It makes life significantly more challenging due to the mental and mobility implications."

"Okay," she whispered, nodding, trying to swallow past the emotion that snagged her throat. "Okay."

"I'd like to set up a meeting in two weeks. To give you time to digest this and read through the literature we've provided." The doctor stood, already on his way to the door. "Then we can formulate the treatment plan you feel is best for you and your situation."

He spoke like this was an everyday occurrence, like he hadn't just upturned Luis's world with one sentence. Fury climbed up to Jessa's face. She stood, too. "That's it? Shouldn't we start treatment now? Shouldn't we discuss all of the options now?" Her voice teetered on the brink of a breakdown, but seriously? They shouldn't waste any time!

The doctor looked at her patiently. "We find it's best in these situations to allow patients some time to process everything before we move forward with a treatment plan."

Her hands fisted tightly, the anger needing release. "But—"

"It's all right, Jess." Luis rested his hand on her shoulder to quiet her. "Thank you, Dr. Ellis." While Jessa wanted to wring the aloof doctor's neck, Luis reached out to shake the man's hand. "I'll see you in a couple weeks."

After the door closed, Jessa turned away from Luis so he wouldn't see her tears, but he wouldn't let her hide. The man took her arms in his hands, turning her to face him. "I'm not afraid. Not stupid enough to think it'll be easy, but I don't fear it, either." He offered her a comforting smile. "I have everything I've ever wanted," he said again. "My boys are home."

"So you'll tell Lance?" she asked, her voice watered down with tears.

"After the competition," he promised, pulling her into a reassuring hug. "After the competition, I'll tell them everything."

Chapter Twenty-Two

Hell yes. Lance swung himself up into the driver's seat of his pickup. He'd just finished kicking Wild Willy's ass. Clocked his best time yet. As in ever. Right after he'd hung it up for the day, he'd rushed through a quick shower and even slapped on some cologne. He may have told Jessa he'd take her out in Vegas, but he couldn't wait that long. Besides, they were supposed to leave tomorrow night for Worlds, and he wanted to bring her up to speed on the details. They'd already added her to the plane reservations and the suite had been booked. One of their suites wouldn't get much use, but it was best to keep up appearances.

Lance sped down the drive, kicking up a trail of dust behind his wheels. He could've called her first, but where was the fun in that? Since he'd dropped her off and kissed her on her doorstep last night, he'd been aching to see her, to feel that soft body of hers against his. It'd taken him ten minutes of sitting in his truck to actually pull away from her house.

He would've gone in, if she'd invited him, but she hadn't. After they shared a rather hot kiss that could've been considered a warm-up for other stuff, she'd said she had an early morning and should get inside. And he'd had to talk himself down the whole way home.

Figuring she'd still be at the shelter, he headed in that direction, tapping his hands to the rhythms playing on the country station. During his jaunt down Main Street, he waved to Kat Temple, the lone female deputy within a hundred-mile radius, and even at Hank Green, who was walking his cat on a leash. Because why the hell not?

Outside the shelter, he didn't see Jessa's car, but he parked anyway. He could wait until she got back if need be. Once he approached the windows, though, he saw that the lights were on, so he tried the door. It was open.

Cassidy sat at the front desk, working on the computer. She sat straighter as he came in.

"Hey," he said. "Didn't expect to see you here today." Far as he knew, she covered only on the weekends or when the boss was away. "Is Jessa around?"

"Oh." Her blue eyes grew round and her gaze wandered. "Um. No. Actually. She's not here." There was no evidence of her typical friendly smile. Why did she look so worried?

"What about my father?" he asked, his stomach coming unsettled. Something wasn't right. According to Levi, Jessa had picked up Luis early that morning. He'd told him they had a lot to do at the shelter today...

"Um. Your dad's not here, either."

"Where are they?"

"They're out," she said, staring hard at the computer screen. To avoid his probing gaze, if he wasn't mistaken.

"Out where?" He hadn't meant for it to sound so harsh, but this was starting to feel like a game.

"On a call."

"Oh." Why hadn't she said that in the first place? From the intensity of her worried expression, it had to be something bad. "Where are they? Maybe I can help out."

"I'm not sure," she mumbled, but Cassidy was a very bad liar. Her eyes shifted too much. And her voice carried the hoarseness of a bald-faced lie.

"What do you mean you're not sure?" He pinned her with his eyes, trying to read what she wouldn't tell him. "If she called you in to cover for her, she must've told you where she was going."

A sigh broke through her tight lips. "I think it's best if you talk to Jessa. Okay?" Without waiting for an answer, she went back to typing.

He reached over her and shut off the damn monitor. "What the hell is going on?" Something big, judging from the way she was putting him off. And he didn't like being the only one in the dark. "She wouldn't have called you in for an hour or two..." He knew that much. And Jessa rarely went out on calls outside the county limits.

"I'm not telling you anything," Cassidy said stubbornly. "It's not my place or my business. Understand?"

No. He didn't understand. Didn't understand how worry could boil up in his gut this way when he'd felt fine only five minutes ago. Was Jessa all right? Had something happened to her? "Is she with Dad?" He let his eyes beg. "Please. You at least have to tell me that." So he'd know whatever she was off dealing with she wasn't alone.

"Yes." Cassidy sighed. "She's with your father. He asked her to go to Denver with him today."

That stood him up straighter. "What?"

"That's all I'm gonna say." She walked to the door and held it open for him, gesturing for him to leave. "If you want to know more you'll have to talk to them. Okay? I'm guessing she'll have him home within the hour."

He lumbered out the door in a stunned fog. Last night, Jessa had said nothing about taking his father to Denver, but she must've been planning on it. Why would she keep something like that from him?

He wasn't sure he wanted to find out.

* * *

Jessa couldn't remember the last time she'd been silent for more than an hour. Even when she was home alone, she had a tendency to talk to herself. But most of the ride home from Denver, Luis had been quiet and introspective, as if processing what he'd learned. And she knew he had to process it alone. He wasn't like her. He didn't verbally analyze everything, so she'd let him be while she listened to the sad country songs playing on the radio.

Now that they'd almost made it back to the ranch, the urge to burst into tears intensified again. It wasn't like Luis would die in three months; she knew it could be worse. But she couldn't help wondering how long it would be before he'd have to give up the hikes he loved so much, the time wandering in the wilderness that seemed to keep him sane. *That* would slowly kill him.

"I sure appreciate you coming," he said, turning his head in her direction for the first time since they'd gotten in her truck.

"I'll do anything I can to help." She'd research until they

found the best doctors, the latest treatments. "As soon as we get home from the competition, we need to sit down with Lance and go over everything the doctor gave you." Then they could come up with a plan...

"We?" Luis asked, as though he hadn't heard right.

With all her apprehension, she'd forgotten to mention that she was tagging along to Vegas. "Lance asked me to come." Even with the sadness weighting her heart, she smiled. "I hope that's okay."

"It's more than okay," he said, smiling, too. "I couldn't be happier."

She knew he wasn't talking only about Vegas. As she veered onto the country road that led to the ranch, hope swelled inside her, seeming to stretch her ribs, to give her more room to breathe. They would get Luis through this. All of them. Together. "It won't be easy to keep it from him." Even for one more week.

"I know," he agreed. "But it's best."

She turned into Luis's driveway. "We might have to agree to disagree on—"

Her mouth froze open, the rest of the sentence disintegrating in an explosion of panic. Lance sat on Luis's front porch. As the truck rolled toward him, he looked up. Even though she couldn't see his face, she knew. He'd found out where they'd been.

"Oh God." She slowed and parked, but let the car idle. Her heart idled right along with it.

"You go on home, Jess," Luis murmured, unbuckling his seat belt. "I'll handle this."

It was tempting to take him up on that, to avoid the impending confrontation, but she couldn't. "No. I'll stay." How could she turn around and leave when Lance's expression had twisted with suspicion and anger? She had to make him understand. There'd be no way to protect him from the truth now.

Grasping at courage, she cut the engine and slowly withdrew the keys.

Luis got out first. While she struggled to find her balance, he approached the porch. "Hey, son. You've got some questions, I reckon."

Jessa hung back, bracing one hand against the truck's fender to steady herself.

Without looking in her direction, Lance walked down the steps to meet his father. "What were you doing in Denver, Dad?" he asked, and Jessa didn't recognize that voice. She'd never heard it before.

"That's my business," Luis said, not unkindly. "I'm allowed to have my own life. Don't have to answer to you."

Ignoring him, Lance turned to her. The indifference on his face sent a blow to her heart.

"Why did you go to Denver?" He repeated the question, but this time directed it at her.

Jessa eased in a steady breath, trading a look with Luis. She couldn't lie to Lance. Not right to his face. And he wasn't about to let this go. He knew something was wrong.

"I had an appointment," Luis told his son before she could speak. "And I asked Jessa to take me."

"What kind of appointment?" Lance asked impatiently.

Jessa crept closer to him. They had to tell the truth. Didn't Luis see that? The longer he stalled, the angrier Lance would be.

"I had to see a doctor. A specialist."

"A specialist." He seemed to carefully control his voice, but Jessa recognized the fury rising in his eyes, and she couldn't take it, couldn't force him to keep guessing.

"Luis saw a neurologist today," she blurted. "They diagnosed him with Parkinson's."

"What?" Lance staggered back a step, his eyes widening with a sudden wrenching pain. "Jesus, Dad." The words were breathless. "How could you keep that from me?" He shook his head as though he couldn't believe it, then set his sights on her. "And how the fuck could you pretend everything was fine? Last night. You knew. And you let me think everything was dandy." His hand raked through his hair as he paced away from them. "Jesus."

"Don't blame Jessa," Luis said, matching his son's furious tone. "It wasn't her fault. I told her to keep it quiet. I wasn't ready to tell you."

"You weren't *ready*?" Lance yelled. "Well, shit, Dad. By all means, take your time."

Jessa flinched.

"Easy, son," his father reprimanded. "Why don't we all go inside? We can tell you what the doc said. Get everything sorted out."

But Lance didn't seem to be in the place to sort anything out at the moment. He still paced in front of Jessa's truck, back and forth, staring at the ground.

She glanced at Luis. "Can you give us a minute?"

Luis hesitated, as though worried what Lance might do or say. But she could handle it. She could handle him. If they were alone, she could remind him of the connection they'd built. Just last night he'd said maybe he could learn to love, learn to let someone love him. He was still that man. He might be angry, but he was still the same Lance who'd taken her on a picnic in the mountains. "It'll be fine," she assured Luis, shooing him toward the front door. "We'll be in soon. Then we can all talk through this together."

The man nodded silently, but the look he gave his son sent a clear message. *Be careful.* Then he walked up the steps and disappeared into the house.

The hard slam of the screen door seemed to shake Lance out of his daze. He spun to face her, his face still flushed with anger, his eyes hard and distant. And who could blame him? She'd just unloaded this horrible news on him, without warning. He had to be in shock. Had to be reeling the same way she had in the doctor's office.

She approached him slowly. "I wanted to tell you," she said, reaching for his hand so she could thread their fingers together. "But I had to respect Luis's decision. He didn't want to distract you before Worlds. And it was his news to tell you. Not mine."

Lance yanked his arm away. "I didn't spend last night with him," he snapped. The ice in his tone sent her back a step. Her arms fell to her sides. She was losing him. Or…she'd already lost him. "I'm sorry. Maybe we should go inside—"

"We don't need you here for this discussion," he said, turning his back on her.

"Lance." She followed him up the steps. "Please. I was only doing what he asked me to do. I want to stay. I want to *help*." She touched his arm, tried to bring him back to her. "We can get him through this. The doctor said there are treatment options. Things that will slow the progression."

Shrugging away from her touch, he assessed her from behind a curtain of apathy. "Go home, Jessa. You're not a part of this family."

The words drove into her, sharp and cutting. And he knew. He knew exactly what kind of damage he'd just inflicted. Because she'd told him. What she wanted most in the world, what mattered to her more than anything in life. Loving and being loved. Those family connections she'd longed for to anchor her but had never managed to build.

Tears stung, but she would not give him the satisfaction of seeing them fall. "You're right. I'm not part of this family." Instead of shying away like he obviously wanted her to, she marched right to him, piercing his eyes with hers. "But I could've been." Her own anger hummed through her, building into a pressure that made her unbreakable. "And you know something, Lance? You would've been damn lucky to have me." She started to walk away, but whirled back to him. "You can think about that while you're alone in Vegas," she snapped. Then she hurried to her truck and drove away before her strength crumbled.

Chapter Twenty-Three

Instead of following Jessa like he knew he ought to, Lance hunched over and leaned his elbows on the porch railing, letting his forehead fall to his hands. All this time, he'd thought the forgetfulness, the shaking, the weakening physicality in his father was simply old age. But he'd been wrong. He'd ignored the signs, the symptoms. His own hand trembled some as he kneaded his forehead, trying to force it all to sink in. His father had Parkinson's. A label. A disease that would slowly eat away at him until there was nothing left...

Pain shot through his chest, then traveled down his arms, forcing his hands into fists. He was half-tempted to put one of those fists through the wall.

Before he could, the door banged open and Luis poked out his head.

"Where's Jessa?" he asked, glancing toward the empty spot where her truck had been parked before Lance'd gone and run her off.

He straightened, but his shoulders bore the weight of a new burden. "She went home." Because he'd been an asshole. He'd directed the brunt of his anger and shock at her. He turned to his father, trying to block out the image of her wounded eyes.

"You mean you sent her home," his father corrected.

"I was blindsided," he muttered. All afternoon, the fears and possibilities had stewed somewhere deep inside him while he'd sat on the porch waiting for Luis and Jessa to get home. Then when he saw her, without warning, it'd all boiled over, the venom spilling onto Jessa. He'd let the familiar feeling of betrayal get the best of him.

Luis stepped out onto the porch, his thumbs hooked through his belt loops. "She loves you, ya know. I've never been lucky enough to have a woman look at me the way Jess looks at you."

"I know." But he was completely unworthy of it. This little tantrum only proved he could never give her what she deserved. God, he wanted to try, though.

"I know it was a shock to hear it that way." Luis lumbered over to the old bench he'd made with his own two hands. He sat with a wince. "You don't need all this hoopla right now. I wanted to wait until after Worlds."

Lance sat beside him, letting himself notice the age spots on Luis's hands, the arthritic hunch to his shoulders. Truth is, he didn't want his father to get old. Didn't want him to get sick. He was the only one who'd stuck around, who'd stuck it out with him all these years and he couldn't imagine it. Couldn't let himself picture that day when his dad would take his last breath.

Emotion clogged his throat, but he didn't bother to clear it away. "How long have you known?"

Luis stared out at the mountains. "A while. Doc's been running tests over the past couple months."

"And you kept it to yourself." That hurt more than anything else. The fact that he hadn't trusted Lance with it. Or that he hadn't thought Lance would consider it important enough to put his training on hold. But maybe that was on him. Maybe he'd focused so much on winning that he'd made his father believe he wouldn't care. "You should've told me. I would've helped you. I would've taken you to the appointments." He would've sat by his side today while he heard the news. Instead, Luis had chosen Jessa. Maybe that was it, what had set him off. He'd chosen Jessa and Lance couldn't deny she'd been the better choice.

"I did what I thought was best." Luis turned to him, his expression donning that fatherly disappointment. "And you had no right to take it out on Jessa. She's done nothing but help this family."

"I know." Regret had already pooled in his gut, making him feel full to the gills, even though he hadn't eaten since breakfast. "But maybe it's better we end it now. Jessa deserves more than I can give her." Naomi was right. He was too screwed up to do this. He had one foot in, but kept one foot out, just in case. And when things got hard, he found an excuse to be an asshole to keep distance between them.

"That's a copout," Luis muttered. He'd always been one to call it like it was. "You're a better man than I ever was. You love someone, you gotta make it work. You gotta work hard, face up to the troubles, and get past 'em. Trust me. I wish I would've made the effort."

Before he could ask what Luis meant, Levi's truck rumbled into the driveway.

Right. He'd forgotten he'd called in his brothers. He

turned to his dad. "I should warn you. When I found out you'd gone to Denver with Jessa, I called in backup. Told them to meet me here as soon as they could."

"Swell," his father muttered, rising as though preparing to face the music.

"What's the emergency?" Lucas asked, stomping the mud off his boots as he made his way up the steps.

When Lance had finally gotten ahold of them, he'd learned the two slackers had gone fly-fishing.

"Yeah...who up and died?" Levi asked, obviously annoyed he'd been interrupted before he'd caught the big one.

Lance cringed. "No one died." *Yet.* But his brother was gonna have to grow up for this conversation. It wouldn't be easy for either of them to hear. Especially seeing as how they'd both missed out on the last ten years of their father's life.

Silence ate away at his ears, but he had no idea where to start.

"We ought to go inside, sit down," Luis said, plodding to the door. He held it open, and one by one, they headed to the same kitchen table they'd sat around every night for their meat-and-potatoes dinners growing up. Lance took a chair next to Luis while Levi and Lucas faced off on the other side of the table.

Once they'd all sat, Luis didn't waste any time getting right to it.

"Parkinson's?" Levi's voice had shrunk and he almost sounded like a little kid again.

Lucas said nothing, simply stared at Luis as though he was waiting for him to continue.

But the man was a stubborn old ox. He didn't even want to tell them what the doctor said. So Lance broke the silence.

"What's the treatment?" He steeled himself, but that was all he really wanted to know. *Needed* to know.

"Not sure, yet," Luis said, looking neither worried nor confident. "The doc gave me some information. He wants to have a meeting to discuss treatment options in a couple of weeks."

The color had finally started to come back to Levi's face. "Parkinson's isn't bad, right? It's not fatal."

"Nah." Their father dug into the wood with his fingernail. "Might make it harder for me to get around. Harder to think clear, to remember things." He shot them an ornery grin. "Hell, that's been happening for years."

Not funny. None of this was funny. There was plenty Luis wasn't saying. Lance could tell. He knew a few things about Parkinson's. One of his old high school teachers had been diagnosed a few years after Lance'd graduated. Far as he remembered, the man had suffered complication after complication until he'd passed away.

"What can we do?" Lucas finally spoke. The terrified look in his eyes reminded Lance of the day they'd sentenced him to prison.

"Nothin'. Not right now, anyway." Luis took a minute to look at each one of them. "I'm sorry I kept it from you. But I wanted to be sure. Before I went and got everyone all riled up."

"It's okay, Dad." Levi's eyes steeled with determination. "Truth is, we've been keeping something from you, too."

Tension gripped Lance's neck. This was it. The conversation he'd dreaded for years. But he nodded at his brother. It was time. Long past time. "A lot longer than a couple of months," he added.

Lucas seemed bent on fading into the background, but they had to do this. And now was as good a time as any.

Luis sat straighter, his posture apprehensive. "I don't understand."

"Lucas didn't set the fire that night. I did," Levi said directly.

Their father's head shook. He clearly didn't believe them. "But you were only fourteen. And Lucas confessed."

"Because we worked out a plan," Lance cut in. He was so ready to be done with this. To put the past behind them so they could be family for whatever time they had left. "Levi'd already been in enough trouble. We were afraid of what juvie would do to him. So Lucas said he'd take the blame instead. He had the cleanest record." It had made so much sense at the time.

"Why?" Their father was raking his hand through the tufts of white hair that were already sticking straight up on his head.

Levi's jaw tightened. "You were meeting Maureen Dobbins there. And I was so pissed off." He cut a glance to Lance. They'd all been pissed off. Levi was the one who'd caught Luis kissing Maureen in the stables, but they'd all been angry about his frequent indiscretions. They'd heard the rumors around town. And Maureen was married. To the rodeo commissioner.

Levi wouldn't look at any of them. "I thought Mom would come back. So I wanted to destroy it. The place you met up with Maureen. To make you stop."

Their father stared at the table, hands flat and motionless against the wood. "I'm sorry." His voice cracked, nearly breaking the words. "I'm so sorry, boys." An expression of stunned anguish drew Lance's hand to his father's shoulder.

"I didn't know how to be what you needed," Luis uttered.

"I didn't know how to be what she needed. I couldn't hold it all together."

"Doesn't matter now," Lucas insisted. "Things are different. You're different."

"We're all different," Lance threw in. And maybe that meant things could change now.

Luis seemed to shut everything else out as he gazed at his middle son. "All these years..." It was barely over a whisper. "I was so hard on you..."

Lucas slipped out of his chair and knelt in front of their father. "It's okay. You didn't know. I don't want you to think about it now."

The old man couldn't seem to lift his head.

"You did your best." Lance waited until Luis looked at him. "Things might not've been perfect, but we knew you wanted us. We knew you loved us. We never had to question that." Didn't matter what happened, Luis wouldn't have left them. He never would've walked out on them. And in Lance's book, that made him a saint.

"None of us care about the past." Lucas went back to his chair. "Time to move on, focus on you. Figure out how we can get you the best treatment available."

A breath lifted Lance's chest. Hope. He breathed it in. Six months ago, he would've been on his own with this. But now his brothers were home. They could navigate it together.

"I don't deserve you boys." Luis's eyes were all watery. "But I sure am glad to have you."

"I know a couple of doctors back in Oklahoma," Levi said, pushing back from the table. "I'm gonna call them and see if they have any recommendations for a good neurologist. We need the best."

"And I'm gonna call the McGowens. Let them know I'll

be delayed for a while," Lucas said, already pulling out his cell.

After they'd stepped out, Luis faced Lance. "Why'd you keep the truth from me all these years?"

That was a no brainer. "To protect you."

"Some secrets are meant to protect, son," Luis said with a resolute quietness. "Sometimes that's all you can do for the people you love. Try to protect them. Even if it backfires on you."

Ouch. Nothing like tasting the truth of your own words. He slumped against the chair back. "I had no right to get so angry at her." Jessa had the best intentions. Always. She'd already proven that more than once. "Shit." He rested his forehead on the table, trying to formulate some kind of plan for how to take those words back, how to convince her he wanted her around. To be a part of this family.

A hell of a lot of time passed, but nothing came to him.

"Got a lead," Levi said, coming back to the table.

Lucas joined them, too. "They said to take all the time I need," he said, brushing a hand over Luis's shoulder. "We'll do whatever we have to do. You're not gonna go through this alone."

A long-forgotten sting pricked Lance's eyes.

"I made a lot of mistakes," Luis said, looking around at his sons. "But you boys...you're the only thing I did right."

"Come on." Levi rose from the table. "Let's head downtown. Beer's on me."

They all stood, but Lance hung back. "Actually, I have somewhere else I've gotta be."

A knowing look bounced between the others.

"Good luck, man." Lucas whacked him on the back.

Luis only shook his head. "Trust me. He's gonna need it."

Chapter Twenty-Four

We'll always have Paris.

God, was there a more tragic phrase in the English language?

Jessa blubbered into the wad of Kleenex she'd fisted in her hands. "Isn't this the best movie ever?" she asked, reaching over to pat Ilsa's head.

On the couch next to her, the pig was too busy rooting her mouth around a bowl of fresh salad to actually watch the movie. A few days on antibiotics and the pig couldn't stop eating.

Jessa turned her attention back to the television. On a normal night, *Casablanca* drew a sort of dreamy-eyed teary sadness, but tonight it *moved* her. Lance's words had embedded themselves in her heart. She heard them play over and over. Even one of her favorite movies of all time hadn't drowned them out. And maybe it wasn't so much the words as what hid behind them. He'd wounded her on purpose, and she didn't understand, couldn't fathom, ever doing that to someone.

She wrapped her father's old wool blanket tighter around her shoulders, needing to feel that connection with him. With someone. The past few weeks of her life had been so wonderfully sweet. She'd actually felt like a part of the Cortez family. But that was her fault. She'd let herself read too much into it, let herself hope for something she knew she'd likely never have.

Headlights cut across the windows outside. She paused the movie and popped to her knees on the couch, stomach quaking with that familiar hunger Lance teased out in her. All it took was one thought of seeing him and suddenly her stomach groaned as though she hadn't eaten for two weeks.

Sure enough, his truck parked along the curb in front of her house.

Damn it! She slouched down trying to hide herself from those windows. "Quiet, Ilsa, baby," she hissed. She couldn't face him right now! Her eyes had nearly swollen shut from the tears. How pathetic was that?

The dreaded knock came at the door and Jessa scrunched herself down farther into the couch.

"Jessa?" Lance called.

She didn't move. Didn't even breathe. Maybe he'd take the hint that she didn't want to talk to him. Except she did want to talk to him. She really did. Her heart thrummed and her palms grew warm. But that was why she had to ignore him. If she let things go any further with him, he'd break her. He'd hurt her and she'd never recover.

"Come on," Lance said. "I can see you sitting there. Don't make me break in again," he added.

As if he'd earned the right to be cute.

"Fine." But when he saw her ugly, makeup-smeared eyes, he'd regret the threat. She'd always known makeup was a bad idea. What was the point anyway? A girl had to be able to cry without worrying she'd scare people away.

Keeping the blanket snug around her shoulders, she stood and plodded to the door, sneaking in a fortifying breath as she unlocked the deadbolt and opened it a crack. Just a crack.

"I'm sorry," he blurted. "I shouldn't have said that. I was upset. Surely you can understand that. He's all I have..."

She shuffled out onto the porch so he couldn't step foot in her house. If that happened she wouldn't have the strength to make him leave. And she had to. She deserved more than this. The cycle of him losing his shit and apologizing to her. "I get that," she said, forcing herself to look at him. "I know you love him." Luis may be the only person in the world Lance loved. "But he doesn't have to be all you have. That's what you've chosen." He chose that an hour ago when he took the one shot at her he knew would destroy her.

A look of desperation widened his eyes. "I won't give up. I'm gonna make you forgive me."

"That's the thing, Lance," she murmured through a sigh that admitted defeat. "I've already forgiven you." She'd forgiven him the moment he'd said those words. Because she loved him. Once again she loved someone as hard as her heart knew how, but he didn't love her back. And she couldn't do that to herself. After Cam had walked out on her, she'd thought she needed to give up on men, dating, relationships...but that wasn't true. She didn't have to give up on every man. On every relationship. But she had to choose the ones that built her up. She had to be strong enough to hold out for someone who would love her the way she craved. And let's face it...Lance didn't love her. He loved that she made him feel better about himself. That she believed he could win this competition. But what would happen when there were no more competitions? When he no longer needed her to boost his confidence?

He stepped closer, gazing down into her eyes with so much emotion she had to look away. "Let me come in. Please," he begged, brushing his hand across her arm as though he knew how much weight his touch held.

It did. One light touch from him ignited her. That's why he couldn't come in. She had no self-control when it came to Lance. If she let him in, he'd have her naked and in bed within five minutes, which would only make her love him and want him more. At some point she had to stop doing this to herself. She edged toward the door, gripping it for stability. "Here's the thing," she said, scrubbing the emotion from her voice. "I can't keep loving someone more than they love me. It hurts too much." There was no other way to say it. This whole thing with Lance had been more intense, more powerful, than any relationship she'd ever had. She felt it deeper and she had to protect herself.

He held her shoulders in her hands and forced her to face him. "I *want* to love you."

"But you don't."

He sighed and let his arms fall to his sides. "I'm not sure how to yet."

The admission purged her anger and gave sympathy room to grow. "It's not something I can teach you," she told him softly. "I always thought it was. Every relationship I've ever been in. I've tried." But that wasn't the way it worked. "Turns out, it's not so easy. Turns out that it ends up only hurting me. I don't have the energy for it anymore. I'm tired." Of getting hurt, but maybe even more than that, she was tired of trying so hard.

"You don't have to be the one to teach me," he insisted. "I'll learn it on my own. I'll figure it out."

She stepped backward, underneath the open door. Half inside her house and half outside. "It's not something you figure out like some kind of puzzle." It didn't have to be so complicated. It wasn't like passing a test or forcing yourself to work hard. "Love is something you choose. Every day. In the happy moments. But in the terrible moments, too. In the moments you're so angry you want to hurt someone. You still choose love." And he hadn't.

"God." The word came out through a tortured sigh. He lifted his hand to her face and drew her lips closer to his. "I want you so much it makes me hurt." His lips brushed hers and held on, locking her in a passionate kiss.

A sigh gave her away and she wilted against him, letting him bring her arms around him and pull her close. Just once more.

"Jessa, I will make this up to you," he uttered, kissing her mouth as though desperate to prove his words.

But a kiss wasn't enough. Mind-blowing sex wasn't enough. Him running to her when he needed comfort or confidence was not enough. Not for her.

She pushed him away and held him at arm's length. "You need to go now." Before it got any harder for her. Before she wasn't able to do what she knew was best. "Good night, Lance," she whispered.

Then she turned away and escaped into the house.

* * *

It wasn't like Jessa didn't have *anyone*. Surrounded by the light of her friends, the night didn't seem so dark. Darla, Cassidy, and Naomi all sat around her in the living room, forming what had become their sacred circle. They each still wore expressions that ranged from outrage to shock to indignation based on her explanation of what had transpired with Lance.

She hadn't held anything back—nope, the whole ugly truth was out there in the safest place possible. These women would guard it with their lives. When she'd put out the SOS text, they hadn't asked why, they'd simply come over right away, toting along chocolate and wine and ice cream, even thought it was almost midnight.

Naomi hadn't even bothered to change out of her pajamas. She'd simply gone over and asked Luis to sit at the house with Gracie while she ran an errand. Jessa imagined his eyebrows had gone up, but Naomi said he hadn't asked any questions. Of course he hadn't. That was Luis. He strictly minded his own business.

So they were here. All her best girls. And her amazing little piggy was perched comfortably on her lap. And you know what? That was enough. Who needed boys anyway?

"I can't believe he said something so stupid," Naomi fumed around a mouthful of intense dark.

"Oh, I can," Darla cut in. "Lance has no clue when it comes to women. Or love."

"Seems to run in the Cortez family blood," Cassidy grumbled. Jessa didn't know all of the history between her and Levi, but the woman didn't exactly sing his praises.

"I don't know," Naomi murmured, looking down. "I always felt like Lucas understood me just fine."

Jessa reached over Ilsa's head and patted her friend's hand. Seemed she wasn't the only one hurting. Ever since Lucas had come back, Naomi had been subdued and sullen.

"I hope you told him where he could stuff his sorry-ass apology," Darla muttered, pouring Jessa another glass of the good cab.

"I stayed pretty strong." Much stronger than she'd ever imagined she could be. Of course, the confrontation had been pretty short. One more minute alone with him and she would've totally caved. "But I don't trust myself to *stay* strong."

"Of course you can," Cassidy insisted valiantly. "You kept him out of your house. That was smart."

"You got this," Darla agreed.

Jessa withheld the story about getting in the car twice to go throw herself into his arms before they'd arrived. "The thing is, I don't think I can stay away from him. So Ilsa and I are heading to Denver first thing in the morning. To spend the weekend with Mom."

"You sure that's a good idea?" Naomi asked, wide-eyed.

"Yes." She'd thought it over and she didn't have a choice. "She might say I told you so, but she'll also take me out to dinner, and we can go shopping. Maybe even for a pedi and massage." Her mother still loved to take care of her, no matter how pathetic she was. "She'll love Ilsa," she said, giving her girl a squeeze. "Besides, I don't trust myself." She had to get out of there for a while. At least until Lance left for Worlds. Then she wouldn't have to see him, or accidentally run into him at the grocery store or the bar. She glanced at Cassidy. "Can you cover for me at the shelter tomorrow?"

"Of course. I can take more shifts, too. If you want to stay longer."

"That's okay. I don't want to be gone too long." She didn't plan to put her life on hold this time.

If her many breakups had taught her anything, it was that she couldn't sit and wallow.

Chapter Twenty-Five

He sure wished talking to a woman was as uncomplicated as talking to a bull. Wild Willy didn't care what the hell you said to him as long as you fed him. Lance walked away from the corral. Last day of training before he left tonight and he didn't even feel like being out there.

As he neared the fence, he noticed Levi hanging out waiting for him. Knots of tension pulled tight in his shoulders.

"So how'd things go with Jessa last night?" his brother asked, though he had to have some clue, given the fact that Lance couldn't seem to focus.

Damn. He whipped out his bandanna and mopped his face. Levi would love this, knowing he'd struck out. "She told me to take a hike." Not like he could deny it. Levi would find out soon enough anyway.

"Seriously?" he asked through a laugh. "What the hell did you say to her?"

"I don't know." Wasn't like he'd scripted out anything eloquent. He sucked at talking. "I said sorry."

"That's it?"

Thinking back, his words did seem inadequate. He'd been so desperate, but he had no clue what to say to undo the damage. That was the worst part, that he'd hurt her. He'd caused her pain. It definitely sucked that she'd rejected him, but he could take it. What he couldn't take was the deep sadness in her eyes. "I get why she wouldn't hear me out. It's fine. I just wish I knew how to make her feel better. Even if she never wants to see my face again…"

Levi whistled low. "Good thing I came back when I did." Head shaking, he nailed Lance's shoulder with his fist. "Come on." Without an explanation, he trotted away.

"Where're we going?" he called, jogging to keep up.

"To Jessa's house, idiot. I'm gonna help you get her back."

Oh, sure. Like it'd be that easy. "She seemed pretty serious about not wanting me around." All night he'd stewed on the whole mess, trying to think up a way to fix it, and so far he had jack.

"Trust me." Levi swaggered past his front porch. "Women only need to hear the right words. She'll come around."

As they were climbing into the truck, Lucas rode up on his mountain bike. He leaned it against the garage and sauntered over. "What're you two up to?"

"We're going to win Jessa back for Lance," Levi said, turning the key in the ignition. "Wanna come?"

"Hell, yeah." Lucas ripped off his helmet and tossed it into the yard. "I could use some entertainment today."

"Great," Lance muttered, reaching around to unlock the

door for his brother. If he couldn't even beg for her back when they were alone how was he supposed to do it in front of an audience?

Lucas climbed in and belted up, just in time, as Levi gunned the engine and they were skidding down the driveway. He'd always been a shitty driver. Not surprising, given the fact that Lance was the one who'd taught him.

"So what's the plan?" Lance asked, hoping Levi could come up with something better than he had last night.

"The first thing you gotta do is admit you were wrong," his youngest brother instructed, as if he were some kind of expert.

"Did that." And it'd gotten him nowhere.

"But did you justify it?" Levi revved the truck out onto the highway. "Or did you just tell her you fucked up and you were sorry?"

He tried to think back. "I said, 'I'm sorry, but—'"

"*But?*" Levi and Lucas said in unison.

His middle brother shook his head. "Man, even I know you never say 'but' after the word 'sorry.'"

"Why didn't I know that?"

"Because the women you've tended to surround yourself with don't exactly expect apologies," Levi said. "Jessa's different."

"Yeah. I've figured out that much." As painful as it was to let his youngest brother give him advice, that's the only thing that made this worth it. The fact that Jessa was special.

"Don't worry. We'll get her back. It'll take some finesse, but I can help you out with that."

Lance shared an amused, albeit irritated look with Lucas. "And you know this how?"

"I know women," his brother bragged, in full swagger

mode. "Trust me. When you see her, you take her hand, look into her eyes, and tell her you're sorry. And that you love her."

Wait. Love? "What?"

"Tell her you love her," Levi repeated.

"But…" Did he love her? "I shouldn't say it unless it's true."

"It's true. You're definitely in love with Jessa." Levi glanced at Lucas in the rearview mirror as though searching for confirmation.

"Yep," their brother agreed. "Definitely."

He jerked his head to stare at Levi, the cocky prick. "How do you know I'm in love with her?"

"Because you care more about her than what you're missing out on," his brother pointed out. "You said you didn't care that she'd rejected you. You only care about making her happy. That clearly means you're in love."

"Okay, Dr. Phil," he mumbled.

"Lucas? Back me up?"

"I don't know what he's talking about, but I do see the way you look at Jessa." Lucas stared out the window. "I recognize that look."

Of course he would. He still got it every time he saw Naomi. "You ever sit down with Naomi? Go over any of the numbers?" Maybe have the conversation they both seemed too terrified to have?

"That's difficult when she doesn't want to be in the same room with me."

"Yeah, I guess it would be." The woman had definitely been avoiding him. "I'll talk to her."

"Not a lot of good that'll do either one of us. I don't belong in Topaz Falls anymore." He said it like it was a fact.

Lance would have to keep working on that, too.

The truck bounced down Main Street, but instead of heading to the shelter, Levi took a fast left and parked in front of the KaBloom Flower Shop and Boutique.

Despite living here his whole life, Lance had never stepped foot in that store. "What're we doing?"

Levi uttered a long-suffering sigh. "Getting flowers, dumbass. You can't expect to get her back without flowers."

"Really?" He eyed the shop windows.

"Come on." Lucas put a hand on his shoulder and dragged him to the door.

Ten minutes and one bouquet of colorful wildflowers later, they pulled up at the shelter.

Nerves lit him up the same way they did before he got into the arena. "Her car's not here." Maybe he should come back later. Alone. So his brothers didn't hear him sound like a fool.

"Let's go in and see where she is," Levi said, cutting the engine.

Since when was he the boss? Gathering up the bouquet, Lance got out of the truck and led the way inside.

Cassidy was sitting behind the reception desk. She looked up, but then turned to focus on a computer screen as though determined to ignore him.

"Hey," he said, snagging her attention back to him.

"Can I help you with something?" she asked as though she'd never met him before.

Damn. She'd obviously heard what had happened. He tried not to let her glare ruffle him. "I need to talk to Jessa. Do you know where she is?"

She refused to look at him. "Of course I know where she is."

"But you're not going to tell me." That much was obvious. Jessa must've informed her little group what he'd said to her.

"Why would I tell you?" Cassidy asked with a chilly glance.

"Because I care about her?" Love. He loved her. Why did he find it so hard to say out loud?

"Whatever." She rolled her eyes and went back to the computer screen. "Maybe you should call her," she suggested.

"Right. Okay." He retreated to the doors, ready to hightail it out of there, but Levi blocked him.

"Leave this to me," he whispered, then nudged him out of the way and strode to the counter. "Hey there, Cass. How's your mom?"

Her eyes narrowed into dangerous blue slits. "She's not so good. But you wouldn't know that, would you? You don't exactly check in anymore."

Whoa. Lance winced.

"Ouch," Lucas whispered.

"Oh. Uh. Well…" Levi sputtered. "You know how it is out on the road." The fact that Levi didn't have her swooning under the power of his signature smile seemed to throw off his confidence.

Cassidy glared at him, hands stacked on her hips. "Yeah, I know how it is. No time for the people you knew before. So you'd better get going, Levi. Rush on back to that spotlight before it gets too dim."

Lance hid a chuckle behind a hearty throat clearing. He wondered how long she'd been waiting to say that.

"Can you at least tell us when Jessa will be back?" Levi asked meekly.

"No," she shot back without missing a beat. "I can't." Without another glance in his direction, she stood and stalked into the back room.

Levi turned to them, a stunned expression flattening his normally charismatic eyes.

They stepped out the door single file.

"Smooth," Lucas said, giving their youngest brother a cheerful pat on the shoulder. "Real smooth."

Levi sulked his way to the truck while Lance and Lucas laughed behind him.

"We can swing by the Chocolate Therapist," Lucas suggested.

"Maybe Darla won't be so mean to you," Lance badgered as they all climbed into the truck. But Levi didn't grin. It seemed Cassidy had gotten to him.

After a quick stop at Darla's, where she'd flipped them off from behind the locked glass door, they stood on Naomi's porch.

Lance was almost afraid to knock. "Hell hath no fury like a scorned woman's friends."

"No shit," Levi said, shaking his head. He obviously didn't know *everything* about women. In fact, he seemed as clueless as the rest of them.

"Naomi *will* talk," Lucas said, raising his hand to knock. "She'll know how important this is."

It took a while for the door to open. Lance wondered if she'd seen them through the window and had to prepare herself. She said nothing, simply watched them all walk through her front door. Not surprisingly, her gaze lingered on Lucas, but when he came near her, she retreated to the other side of the small entryway.

Man, she wouldn't even stand next to him...

"What're you doing here, Lance?" she asked as if she already knew. Cassidy and Darla had likely warned her.

Guess that meant he had to level with her. "I need to talk to Jessa. Where is she?"

"Does it matter where she went?" Naomi's cheeks looked rosier than normal and she completely avoided Lucas's gaze. "She left. Because of what you said to her."

"It matters." More than she realized. "I'm leaving and I need to see her before I go." He needed to know she was okay. He needed to see her smile and hear her laugh and he needed to tell her he loved her.

"Jessa doesn't want to be found right now," she said, leaving them behind while she walked into the kitchen.

"Wait. Hold on." Lucas followed her.

The woman's eyes instantly went soft, like she saw some warm glow haloed around him. Man, talk about love.

"I know you're trying to protect her," Lucas said gently. "But I'd hate for her to miss out on something because she's too afraid to hear what he has to say," he murmured.

Naomi's tense shoulders collapsed under a sigh. "She's at her mom's. In Denver."

"Thank you," Lucas almost whispered. Their eyes held for a moment before Naomi turned to the counter and snatched a plate out of the dishpan, drying it with frantic motions. "You didn't hear that from me," she said, her voice shaky.

Lucas shoved his hands into his pockets, leading the way to the front door. "See you later, then." His tone was as subdued as hers.

Lance was tempted to drag Naomi over there and force her to talk to Lucas. They were obviously still hung up on each other. Before he had the chance, Lucas slipped out the front door. Guess that confrontation would have to wait. He could only manage one relationship crisis at a time.

On the porch, Levi turned to face him. "What're you gonna do?" Seemed like his younger brother was all out of good ideas.

But Lance had one more. "I guess I'm going to Denver."

* * *

If Jessa had learned one truth in her life, it was that you are never too old to bake cookies with your mom. There was something so comforting about it—being in the kitchen together, measuring out the ingredients, whipping and stirring while a sweet little pig dozed contentedly in a dog bed at her feet.

Jessa's mother had never been much of a domestic diva, but she'd always baked the best cookies, and somehow she did it in heels and a lovely fitted dress, which she'd covered with an apron, of course. Jessa, however, was still in the *I don't feel like showering* phase of wallowing, so she'd opted for sweats. Elastic waistbands always came in handy after a breakup.

She dumped an extra handful of chocolate chips into the dough and went to work folding them in with a spatula.

"Wow." Her mom peered over her shoulder. "That's some serious chocolate therapy."

"I need it." Though they'd already managed to fit in a lovely breakfast at a local café and pedicures, her heart still drooped with sadness. During the last few hours, she'd filled her mother in on the latest romantic debacle. And, surprisingly, her mom hadn't resorted to any lectures. She'd simply listened and asked her questions about Lance. It made it sort of hard to forget about him while talking about how wonderful he was.

"The oven is all preheated. Here." Carla withdrew a cookie sheet from the cupboard and set it on the counter. "Make them as big as you want."

"Don't mind if I do," Jessa said, pulling out a spoon and scooping up a huge blob of dough. These babies were going to be her lunch. Maybe her dinner, too. She was wearing sweats, after all.

"I thought we could go shopping a little later," her mother suggested. "If you—"

The doorbell twinkled a lovely tune. Good lord. Even Carla's doorbell was elegant and refined.

"I'll be right back," she said, untying her apron and pulling it over her head. God forbid anyone see her looking the least bit frumpy. If only Jessa'd inherited *that* gene. The one that cared what people thought about her appearance.

She glanced down at her attire. Nope. She hadn't. "Trust me, sweats are way more comfortable," she informed Ilsa as she continued scooping huge mounds of dough onto the cookie sheet. She'd already bought too many new clothes, but shoe shopping could be fun. At least it would momentarily distract her. And she always loved to people watch at the mall...

Her mother rushed back into the kitchen and ripped the spoon out of her had. "Lance is at the door," she whispered. "He'd like to talk to you."

"*Lance?*" She shot to the other side of the kitchen—as far away from the front door as possible. "What is he *doing* here?" How the hell did he find her?

"Maybe you should ask him," Carla said, ushering her toward the hallway.

She dug in her heels and stopped, looking down at her clothes again. They seemed to scream *You broke my heart!* and *I'm too pathetic to even get dressed!* "No." She shook her head. "I can't talk to him. I can't see him." Her heart fell to pieces just thinking about it. "Tell him to leave me alone," she said, her voice wavering.

Her mother smoothed a comforting hand down her hair. "Are you sure?"

It was so tempting. He'd driven all the way down from Topaz Falls. Topaz Falls! But this is what she did. She always gave in. She never stood her ground. "Please. I can't." Yes, she was being a coward, but they'd both already said everything there was to say. "Tell him to go."

"All right," Carla said uncertainly before she walked briskly down the hall.

Jessa held her breath, but she couldn't hear anything. After checking on Ilsa, she crept down the hallway and hid around the corner closest to the front door.

"I'm sorry," Carla was saying. "Jessa's tired and not up for company."

"I won't stay long." The sound of Lance's voice struck her. It was polite, but firm, too. "I just need two minutes."

"Well…" Her mother hesitated.

Come on, Mom! Jessa almost yelled. Though she understood how hard it could be to resist Lance Cortez.

"I'm sorry," Carla said again. "She seemed adamant, and—"

The pig chose that moment to come barreling down the hall, squealing like she'd been stuck with a pin, her dainty little hooves skidding on the polished wood floors.

"Ilsa!" Jessa screeched, lunging to catch her as the pig shot by. But she missed and ended up sprawled on the floor in full view of the front door.

Lance bent and somehow captured the pig while holding on to a bouquet of flowers.

Ilsa grunted and thrashed, her little legs trying to run away.

"Simmer down, Pork Chop," Lance said, subduing her in his arms. "Not gonna hurt you."

Jessa lay on the floor looking up at him, and he seemed so broad and powerful that he made the pig look like a stuffed animal.

"Hi," he said, gazing down at her.

"Hello," she managed. Not like she could avoid him now.

"I'll go ahead and take Ilsa," her mother offered, reaching out her hands. "And we'll give you two a minute."

Before Jessa could latch on to her ankle and beg her to stay, Carla hurried down the hall, calmly soothing the poor pig.

"I know you don't want to see me." Lance reached down and took hold of her hand, pulling her up effortlessly.

She glanced at her frumpy attire. "I'm not really dressed to see anyone." Especially Lance. Especially looking like this. God! Why'd she have to eavesdrop?

"You're beautiful," he said, his eyes seeming to take her—and all of her frumpiness—in. He held out the wilted and battered bouquet of wildflowers—daisies and wax flowers and snapdragons.

She took them, focusing on the vivid colors so she didn't have to look into his eyes.

"I just came to tell you I love you," he said quickly, as though afraid she might slam the door in his face. "You might not believe me, and I might not be great at show-ing it, but I do. I know I do." He handed her an envelope that had been tucked in his pocket. "This is everything you need to come to Vegas. If you decide you want to. My flight leaves soon, but if you decide to come, there's a flight and hotel voucher in there. And I put in special passes to the events."

Jessa's hand shook so hard, she could barely grip the flimsy paper. "I can't come." She wouldn't go running back to him. Not this time. She'd be like her mom and guard her-self. She'd be better than the girl who went back for another round of heartache. "Sorry. It's not going to work out." She tried to return the envelope to him, but he backed away.

"Keep it," he said quietly. Hopefully. "Just in case you change your mind." He stared at her a minute more as though storing up the vision of her face, then turned around and left.

Trying to hold it together, Jessa dragged herself back to the kitchen, the flowers and envelope weighting her hands.

Carla smiled brightly. "Is everything better?"

"No." She dumped the gifts he'd given her on the kitchen counter. "He told me he loved me. And I didn't say any-thing."

Her mother's sigh was both disapproving and sympa-thetic. Carla leaned against the counter, arms crossed, eyes so much like Jessa's honed in on her face.

"Why are you looking at me like that?" she demanded. "You of all people should be thrilled that I sent him away." She's the one who always told her she should be more care-ful about who she gave her heart to.

Instead of snapping back, Carla gestured for Jessa to sit on a stool.

"Why do I feel like I'm the one in trouble?" She slumped onto the stool. Wasn't this what Carla wanted for her? To be an independent, strong, unaffected woman?

"I guess I understand where he's coming from," her mother murmured as though the admission embarrassed her.

Where *he* was coming from? "I'm sorry?"

"I loved your father, Jessa."

"What?" She must not have heard that right.

"It took me ten years of therapy to figure it out."

"Therapy?" *Whoa.* Wait a minute. Who was this woman? "You don't do therapy." Or at least she'd never said anything.

"Actually, I do." Her mother's smile appeared almost apologetic. "You never knew your grandparents. That was on purpose. My father...he was the worst kind of bully."

Jessa had suspected as much, but Carla had never been exactly open about her own childhood. "You've never talked about him."

"There weren't many good things to say." She paused as though she had forced herself to say them now. "He wasn't abusive, but he was controlling. And he insulted my mother constantly. He treated her like a child. Wouldn't even let her get her driver's license."

"God. Really?" Well, she was glad she'd never known him, then.

"When I left home, I decided I'd never marry. Never fall in love. I thought it made you weak."

Like her grandmother. Her mom didn't have to say it. Jessa could sense the feelings of resentment.

Carla reached over and gripped her hand firmly. "But you're one of the strongest people I know, Jessa. And your father was, too." Tears glistened in her regal brown eyes, softening them. "He always told me he'd love me forever.

Even if I never loved him back. And he did. He sent me cards and letters and gifts all those years."

The mention of her father sent a wave of grief crashing over her.

"I felt so unworthy," Carla went on. "I pushed him away every chance I had. I told him to move on so many times."

"He never did." Buzz had never gone out on another date. He'd never said why, although Jessa had suspected he hadn't gotten over her mom. The two of them never dragged her into their complicated relationship, though. She'd had no clue he'd sent her mother letters.

"No. He never did move on." She laughed a little. "He was so stubborn, that man."

Jessa smiled, too. Stubborn in the best way possible.

"After you left home, I realized I wasn't healthy," Carla admitted, as though somewhat ashamed. "Emotionally. So I started therapy, and it helped me understand how afraid I'd been." Her lips pursed bravely. "The week before he passed, I wrote him a letter and told him how much I loved him. I was going to go up there to see him as soon as the summer session ended..."

But she hadn't made it in time.

Her mother's obvious pain pinched Jessa's heart. "Why didn't you tell me?"

"I don't know." Her head shook. "I guess I was embarrassed. I wasted all those years. We could've been happy. We could've been a family."

"We were a family." Definitely not conventional, but bonded by love all the same. "And at least he knew. Before. At least you told him you loved him." It changed things, knowing that. Knowing he had everything he'd wanted at the end.

Mom's eyes sought out hers. They were so solemn. "Fear does strange things to people. It makes them lash out." An unmistakable empathy echoed through the words.

"You think Lance is afraid." Yeah, well he wasn't the only one.

Carla held her hands. "I think he loves you and I think it terrifies him."

"I can't help him with that." Not again. Not this time. He'd probably just push her away like he had before.

Her mother lifted Jessa's chin like she had so many times when she was young. But this was different. She understood so much more now. Looking back at Carla, she saw a woman who had been wounded, who had spent her life running from relationships. Kind of like someone else she knew...

"How many times have you almost been attacked by an animal you were trying to rescue?" her mom asked quietly.

"Too many to count."

"Why do they try to attack?"

"Because they're in a vulnerable position. They feel threatened, and..." As she said them, the words struck her with meaning. "Oh."

"What do you usually do when an animal feels vulnerable and frightened?" She already knew, but Carla obviously wanted her to say the words.

"I move slowly," she whispered, tears weakening her throat. "And carefully. I show it I'm not there to hurt it." Sometimes it took a lot of convincing, especially when the animal had been neglected or abused.

"And you never walk away," Carla said through a sad smile.

"No." She'd never given up, even in the most hopeless

of situations. She'd always stuck it out, done whatever it took.

"What are you going to do this time?" Carla asked as though she already knew the answer.

Reaching over, she slid the envelope off the counter. "I guess I'm going to Vegas."

Chapter Twenty-Six

Lance had hardly stepped his spur inside the doorway to the swanky media reception before a curvaceous redhead cornered him. Up against a wall and way too far away from the bar for his comfort.

"Lance Cortez," she said in a flirty tone. "I'm Amber Hart."

He did his best to keep the cringe inside as he returned her dainty handshake. "Nice to meet you," he said politely, sneaking a glance at the media badge that dangled from a lanyard hanging over her fake breasts. He didn't recognize the name of the publication. Probably some small-town newspaper or one of those ad publications. They let just about anyone in here.

"So how are you feeling about the final ride?" she asked, leaning into him slightly.

Shitty. Actually, indifferent would be a better way to describe it. For the first five rounds of competition, he'd tried to maintain his focus, but each day that passed was another day he didn't hear from Jessa. Didn't know how she was doing. Didn't know *what* she was doing. He'd held out hope, and every time he went into the arena, he'd checked the seat number he'd given her. But she hadn't come.

Even with that distraction, he'd managed to maintain a spot as fourth overall in the competition, which meant he'd have to have a damn near perfect ride tomorrow to take the title.

If only he could shake the sinking feeling that maybe he'd really lost Jessa for good...

Not that Red had rights to any of that information. Avoiding eye contact, he shrugged. "Oh, you know. I feel ready."

"You sure look ready," she murmured, stripping him down with her eyes.

Five years ago that little suggestion beaming in her gaze would've invited him to take her arm and lead her to the bar, where he'd buy her drinks and charm her all the way up to his hotel room, but apparently Jessa had ruined him for any uninvolved fun because, despite the slinky dress and the impressive curves, this woman did nothing for him. "Um, will you please excuse me, Miss Hart?" He made a quick sidestep and scanned the restaurant over her shoulder. "I should go find my father." They'd come in together, but in true Luis Cortez form, he seemed to have wandered off. Smart man.

"Oh, sure, okay," she bubbled. "Here's my number." Her hand expertly slipped a card into his jean pocket, patting a little too close to his package. "Maybe we can hang out later."

"Maybe." He gave her a smile even though he had no intention of following up.

After he'd left her behind, he worked his way across the room, saying hello to some of the guys he'd competed against over the years and avoiding eye contact with every woman who seemed to be there to snag herself a stag. Finally, he saw Luis sitting at the end of the bar alone, which was exactly where he wanted to be. Head down, he elbowed his way through the lively crowd and plopped down on the stool next to Luis.

His father looked him over. "You look as miserable as a hog who's had his tail straightened," he said, taking a pull on his beer.

"I am," he admitted, signaling to the bartender to bring him whatever Luis was drinking.

"What're you doing here, son?"

He knew Luis didn't mean at the party. He meant why was he here when things weren't resolved with Jessa. Lance inhaled deeply. "Actually...I have no idea." For months he'd had this clear vision, this laser focus on Worlds. Like the closer he got to losing his career, the tighter he'd held on. Except now he couldn't for the life of him think why. It suddenly seemed a hell of a lot less important.

"This world...it doesn't give back to you." Luis looked at him square in the face, wearing the same expression he had when Lance was a teenage delinquent. "You sacrifice your body—hell, your whole life—and in the end you don't have much to show for it."

"So I guess the joke's on us, huh?" Funny. The only guarantee when you were a professional athlete was that you'd have to retire early. You had to be prepared to walk away and start something new. Walk into a whole new life. No one told you that when you were starting out, though.

"If I hadn't had you boys when I retired, I would've lost

myself." Luis turned the stool to face him. "I did for a while. Took some time to get myself straightened out. I don't want that to happen to you. You're a lot like me. The most like me out of all you boys."

"I'll take that as a compliment." Even though that wasn't how Luis meant it. And he understood. He hid behind his career. Used it as an excuse to block out everything else. He'd learned from watching his old man. He studied his father, still saw that spark of a young cowboy in his eyes, even with all of the lines the years had carved into his skin. "Why couldn't you stop Mom from leaving?" He'd never asked, but now seemed like as good a time as any, seeing as how he was going to have to deal with his issues if he ever wanted to get Jessa back.

Instead of deflecting the question with a gruff shrug of his shoulders like he usually did when Lance brought up something he didn't want to talk about, Luis set down his beer. It clanked against the bar top with the tremor in his hand. "Maybe I could've. Truth is, I didn't try." His solemn eyes lifted and found Lance's. "We got married young, and your mom...she worried an awful lot."

"I know. I remember." She was always fussing over the three of them. Though as they'd gotten older she seemed to detach herself more and more.

"It wasn't normal worry. It consumed her, made her sick." His father's cheeks hollowed. "They'd call it anxiety now. And it was constant."

"I guess I didn't realize it was so bad." But now that he thought about it, she stayed home as often as she could. Didn't have many friends. Tended to keep them home, too. She never hung around the corral, never went to any of their competitions.

"They didn't have medication for it then," Luis said. "No help. And I didn't know what to do for her."

"That's why she left?" Because of anxiety? It seemed like such a simple thing...

"She couldn't handle it. The fact that all you boys were following in my footsteps. Riding bulls. She wasn't sleeping, wasn't eating. She was so afraid something would happen to you."

Something did happen to them. All three of them. The day she left, she broke them. God, just look at them. All around thirty years old and not one healthy positive relationship among them...

"She didn't leave because she didn't love you," Luis said quietly. "I never wanted you to think that."

Remnants of the familiar anger stirred. "She could've chosen to stay." She could've tried to get help. She could've gone to counseling or something.

Luis shook his head. "Anxiety's a hard thing to understand if you've never had it. It's not just in your head. It's physical. I saw it in her. It was killing her." For the first time, Lance noticed a tremor in his father's head. It ticked, making Lance look away. He couldn't stand to see it, the evidence of a disease.

"I should've tried harder. I wish I would've done more. I wish I would've at least taken time off to try and help her before it got so bad."

For the first time, Lance let himself consider the possibility she hadn't wanted to leave. Maybe she didn't feel she had a choice. "You think it would've made a difference?"

"Maybe." Luis sighed. "If I'd fought for her. If she would've had more support." He gave Lance a long, steady glare, the same one he'd used when Lance would mouth off as an angry teen. "I know it cut you deep when she left. But it might be time to stop blaming her, son. As a parent you try to do your best with what you've got. In her way that's what she did. That fear she had...it lied to her. Told her you'd be better off without her. I know it's hard to understand, but that's the truth of it."

"Guess I don't have to understand it." All these years, he'd tried. And even knowing what he knew now, he *couldn't* understand. Luis was right. He hadn't stood where she stood. He had no idea what she struggled with. But he did know one thing. He couldn't let fear rob him of loving someone, of letting her love him. He wanted to do better than his mother had. All these years, he hadn't. When he'd lashed out at Jessa, it wasn't because he was pissed. It was because he was afraid. For his father, sure, but also for himself. "You regret it?" he asked his father. "Sticking with your career instead of walking away to be what she needed?"

A deep inhale seemed to steady Luis's tremors. "More than I can say. I was too busy collecting a whole lot of shiny shit that doesn't mean much." He looked around the party surrounding them. "Thing is, that's not my legacy. That room of buckles and trophies and news clippings. No one here gives a rat's ass who I am now."

"I do," Lance argued. His father had done his best for them. In his imperfect way. But it was enough. He'd earned their loyalty, their love, even if he didn't feel he deserved it.

Hope sparked inside of him, filling that empty coldness that'd hounded him since Jessa had sent him away. Maybe his pathetic, imperfect offering could be enough for her, too.

His father reached over and squeezed his shoulder. "You can leave your mark on this world only in the people you love. Not in the stuff you accomplish. You remember that, son."

If Luis had said that to him six months ago, he would've laughed. But now he was starting to understand.

* * *

"It's gotta be perfect, Cortez," Tucker said, pacing on the outside of the chute. "I mean, one hundred percent flawless. You gotta get your leg off him. You need the extra points."

"You think I don't know that?" Lance tightened the chin-strap on his helmet. He eyed the bull that snorted on the other side of the fence. Loco Motive made Ball Buster and Wild Willy look like kittens. The damn bull had already taken eight riders out of the competition and had sent two to the hospital.

Adrenaline boiled in his gut, shooting his body temperature up about a hundred degrees. Damn all the gear they made 'em wear these days. When he'd started out, he hadn't had to bear half his weight in body armor.

"Stay loose up there," Tucker instructed.

How was that possible when he felt this tense? He glanced around at the television cameras, all starting to swing his way. The announcers were no doubt detailing his story, his last title from six years ago to now, when he'd barely qualified to be here.

Was Jessa watching? Would she be cheering him on? God, he wanted to call her right now, tell her everything he'd wanted to say to her. But she hadn't returned any of his messages. Five days. It had been only five days since he'd seen her and yet it felt like five months.

All week, he'd held on to her words. *You can win.* They'd

kept him going. Jessa thought he could do this, so he'd ride perfect. Not for the cheering fans. Not for Luis or Tucker. Not even for himself. For her. From this moment on, he wanted everything to be about her.

The manager gave him the signal to climb up and get into position.

Here we go. He tried to clear his head the way he'd always been able to do. Took some deep breaths, inhaling that manure-tinged scent of the bull. Took about five guys to hold Loco Motive in place while Lance climbed the fence.

Tucker gave him a final pat on the arm, looking a hell of a lot more nervous than him. He couldn't blame him. Lance hadn't exactly had a stellar ride this week. Solid, but nothing that could put him on top. Not yet at least.

"You're on," the director said.

Lance swung his leg over the fence and slid onto the bull. Instantly agitated, the son of a bitch snorted and bucked.

Lance got his right hand gripped onto the rope and kept his left hand up. Had to keep his left arm raised, no matter what happened. If it came down, if it so much as grazed the bull, he'd lose points.

The chute opened.

Loco Motive shot straight into the corral, bucking and kicking. Pissed off as all hell.

But Lance kept his form. Left arm waving, right hand fisting that rope so damn hard it felt like his knuckles would break. The arena flashed around him, fragmented glimpses of the crowd, the judges, the scoreboard.

One...

The bull's body jackknifed, but he saw it coming. His body whipped forward and he clenched his legs tight around the bull's wide girth, waving his left arm over his head.

Two...

The loud roar of the crowd muted Loco Motive's angry snorts. The bull reared up again launching them both.

Three...

Fuck! Could this get any longer? He curved his back, let his upper body jolt freely with the bull's enraged kicks.

Four...

His right hand burned like someone had stuck it in a fire. Another hard jerk sent a shot straight to his back, the muscles threatening to cave in.

Five...

Loco Motive spun in a rage, kicking up the dirt, tossing his head back like he'd had it. Lance's body thrashed, ribs separating, whiplash starting to weaken his neck.

Six...

Every muscle in Lance's body pinched, sending rivers of pain all through him. Not enough. This ride was not enough.

Seven...

He saw lights. Blurred faces. His leg. He had to get his leg up. Straining his back, he raised his left arm higher over his head and shifted his balance. His back spasmed as he lifted his right leg away from the bull, holding his posture, fighting like hell to keep his grip. The crowd's praise droned in his ears.

Eight!

His grip loosened. The right wrist was giving out. He hugged his knees into the bull's sides and flung his left arm high into the air with a whoop. Loco Motive gave one last bucking kick as though he'd taken personal offense to that, and flung Lance toward the corral fence.

A collective gasp hushed the crowd, but elation drowned out the pain in his body. That was the ride of his life. He knew it, felt it. While the bullfighter lured away Loco Motive, Lance lay flat on his back in the dirt, staring up at the scoreboard. Two medics rushed over but he waved them away. He'd be fine. As soon as he saw the score, he'd be fine. It seemed to take forever while the crowd murmured. He lay there under the lights, taking it all in, wishing he would see Jessa's face in the stands.

"Ninety-four point eight," the announcer called with an excitement that reignited the arena.

He had to blink, had to squint his eyes to make sure that was right.

Sure enough, the red numbers lit up the screen: 94.8. There were three riders left, but no one would beat that. No one *could* beat that. His eyes closed and he breathed out, now feeling every aching muscle, every sore bone.

He flattened his hands against the ground, ready to get up, but Tucker catapulted in and landed right on top of him. "Hell yeah!" his friend yelled. "Hell! Yeah!" He slapped him square in the chest. "You nailed it!"

Wincing, Lance rolled out from underneath Tucker and pushed to his feet. The crowd noise deafened him. He waved and started to limp toward the gate, trying to keep a rowdy smile intact for the cameras. But it wasn't real.

There were thousands of people here. The one person he wanted, though, the one who mattered, wasn't. He looked around, at the crowd, all watching the replay on the Jumbotron in an awed silence. And he felt no different. No better than he had twenty minutes ago. He'd just taken the world title he'd been striving for, and he didn't even feel like celebrating.

The crowd, the fanfare, the cheering…none of it even came close to giving him the same rush he got when he made Jessa smile.

Tucker launched himself into another man hug. "I can't believe it, you son of a bitch! You did it."

Lance pushed him off and backed away. He couldn't stay. All he could think about was pulling Jessa into his arms. He didn't care what she said, she belonged with him. And he belonged with her. "I have to get out of here. Now."

"You can't go!" Tucker tried to block him. "You just won the world title, jackass! They're not gonna let you cut out. You've gotta stay for the hoopla!"

He couldn't. Not without Jessa here. He never would've been able to do this if it hadn't been for her.

And she was all he needed.

Chapter Twenty-Seven

OhmyGod, ohmyGod, ohmyGod!" Jessa sprinted down some steps in the dark arena, trying to find her way out so she could get to him. That image of him flying toward the fence replayed again and again, sending her stomach into a downward spiral. When he'd hit the ground, Lance hadn't moved. And before she knew what she was doing, she'd jumped up in a panic, stepping on toes and purses and drinks until she'd made her way to the end of the row. But where was she now? And where was Lance?

Was he *dead*?

Finally, she saw a door and charged it, jogging out into the concessions area. But the place was so big—so many stairs and food stands and doors...

"How can I get down there?" she asked some poor older man pushing a trash can. "I have to find Lance Cortez! I have to get to him."

He looked down as though embarrassed for her.

"I'm not a groupie!" she shrieked. "He gave me this pass!" She tugged at the lanyard hanging around her neck. "Where's the staging area? Where do they take injured riders?"

He pointed at an escalator and got the hell out of there.

Gripping the handrail, she stumble-jogged down the escalator to the main floor and tore down a corridor, searching for a door that would get her back there.

There! Official-looking steel double doors. She bolted for them, but before she got there, they flew open.

Lance ran out. Ran! He was running!

"What're you doing?" she yelled, floating to him in a stupefied jog. "Oh my God, Lance! I thought you were hurt!"

He caught her in his arms, looking her over, touching her like he had to make sure she was really standing there. "What are *you* doing?" he asked breathlessly. "I thought you didn't come..."

Seeing him whole, strong and upright, brought a fast rush of relief that made her dizzy. "I came." She cupped her hand on his uninjured cheek. "Of course I came." A happy sigh pushed her closer to him and she felt his heartbeat against her chest. "I couldn't get a flight out until this morning. Everything was booked." And she'd had to get coverage at the shelter, and find someone to watch Ilsa, and then Naomi and Darla and Cassidy had all wanted to come, so they'd had to find flights, too...

"But you weren't in your seat," he said, smoothing his hand down her hair. "I looked for you..."

"I got here late, so I just sat in an empty seat." Who knew how long it would've taken her to find the right section?

She ran her hands down his arms, searching for damage.

"And when the bull threw you, I got up and ran." She peered up at him, all teary and pathetic. "I couldn't stand it. I thought—"

"I'm fine. Hardly felt it." He hugged her close, kissing her forehead, her cheek, her lips. "When I won, all I could think about was you. You weren't there…"

"You won?" She gasped. She'd been so panicked she hadn't even realized. She pushed him away. "If you won you have to go back in there!" What the hell was he doing standing out here talking to her?

He gazed down at her and his eyes had the power to kill her and revive her all at once.

"I had to find you so I just…ran out."

"You shouldn't have." She never would've asked him to do that. "This was your dream. You should enjoy all of it. Everything the experience will offer you."

"I guess you could say I have a new dream." He lifted his hand to her face, trailing his fingers down her cheek. "One that matters more."

Jessa pressed her hand against her chest, tears welling. His nearness stirred a craving, a tingling rush that covered her skin and while the rest of her felt weak, her heart beat strongly.

"Fact is, I'm pretty messed up," he said, pressing his hand against hers, stroking her fingers. "What I said about you not being part of the family…" His head shook. "It wasn't you I was mad at. I've blamed my mom for everything. Every bad thing that's happened since she left, I put it on her."

"I can understand that," Jessa whispered.

"But I'm ready to let it go. Get past it. I have to or I'll never have anything that matters." His fingertips brushed hers but he didn't hold on. "You didn't betray me. You've only been good to me. And to my family. I'm sorry I hurt you."

She peered up at him, and with that one simple apology, it seemed he'd let her see so much more of his heart. "Thank you."

"This whole week, all I could think about was how you weren't here." He inched closer, and she closed her eyes, feeling his presence up against her. "Without you, I didn't care anymore. I've won competitions. And it's never made me feel as good as I feel when I'm with you."

"Lance..." There were so many things she wanted to say, but he took her hand, stealing the words along with her breath.

"I want you," he said through an utterly helpless sigh. "I don't have much to offer. But I want to be there for you. I want to make you happy. I want to hold you in my arms and feel you against me. Nothing in my life has ever felt as good as holding you. Nothing."

The quiet conviction in his voice filled her eyes. "I want you, too."

He said nothing more, only pulled her against him and sealed her lips with his, right there in the brightly lit corridor with people walking past them, his mouth devouring hers, hungry and passionate, as if he'd been saving up his whole life to offer her this one kiss.

It carried her away, the feel of his chest heaving against hers, the strength of his hands as they held her. "Lance," she murmured, letting her purse drop to the ground. "My God, Lance."

"Let's get out of here," he groaned.

And she couldn't have said no if she tried.

* * *

"My room is closer." She wrapped her arms around his sturdy back, holding on as he urged her into the elevator.

"Floor ten," she said, against his mouth. As the elevator zoomed up, his tongue teased its way into her mouth, weakening her knees, which made her cling to him tighter. The doors rolled open and they stumbled out, moving clumsily down the hall, unable to let go of each other.

"Key's in my pocket," she breathed, already undoing the buttons on his shirt.

He groped a hand into the pocket of her jeans until he found it.

As he unlocked the door, he caught her waist and pulled her against him again, bringing his lips to hers as he somehow pushed into the hotel room.

Her feet faltered along with his and before they'd made it to the bed, she kicked off her tennis shoes while he stepped out of his boots.

"I don't know how I lived without you so long," he murmured in her ear while his hands tugged up the hem of her shirt. "I don't think I was ever really alive."

She opened her mouth to answer, to tell him that she must've never really been in love before because this all felt new. Her heart pounded her ribs so hard they threatened to fracture. And it was so good. So good it almost hurt.

He pulled her shirt over her head and slipped his fingers into her bra and *ohhhhhh*. What was she going to say again? Nothing. She couldn't speak. She slumped against him while he touched her, teasing her nipples in long strokes while she clumsily undid the rest of the buttons on his shirt until she could push it off his shoulders and run her hands over the hard muscled plane of his abs.

H-ello. Just the sight of him was foreplay...

But looking wasn't enough. She wanted to feel him, to taste him. Threading her fingers between his, she ducked her head and kissed her way down his neck to his chest, sucking and licking and breathing hotly against his skin. When she reached the waist of his pants, she let his hands go and started to work at that rather impressive belt buckle, but before she could get it undone, he hauled her back up to him. "Not yet."

Tearing back the comforter and sheets, he laid her down on the bed, hovering over her, those eyes seeming to note every detail.

"I can't get enough of you," he breathed over her. "I'll never get enough of you." With that, he lowered his lips to her neck, sneaking his hands underneath her back so he could pop the clasp of her bra. Rising, he slowly slid the straps down her shoulders as though he enjoyed the torture.

"Too slow," she breathed, pushing up to her elbows. She tore the bra away and drew his face to her breasts.

His warm tongue traced every inch of her skin, forcing her head to fall back to the pillows. Without taking his lips away from her, his hands hitched up her hips and he took down her pants and sensible cotton underwear in one fluid motion.

"Should've worn my pretty underwear," she said with a gasp.

"I like you better without any." He pulled his body over hers, kissing her lips with a sensual rhythm that charged every part of her. God, no one had ever made her ache like this...

His lips moved down her neck again, covering her chest with warm, wet kisses, then moving lower to her stomach.

Sparks flashed low in her belly, sending flares of heat between her legs. She pressed her lips together so she wouldn't moan. She shouldn't be this close this fast...

He paused and glanced up at her. "You can be as loud as you want," he teased. "No one'll walk in on us this time."

Before she could respond, he took her hips in his hands, kissing and nibbling his way down to the inside of her thigh.

Her legs fell open. She did make noise then—a long groan flowed out of her lungs, deflating them completely.

"I love turning you on," Lance said, all low and hot as his fingers parted her.

She felt his sultry breath against her most sensitive parts first, then the slick wetness of his tongue. Her hands grasped for something to hold on to, finding only fistfuls of the sheets. Cries stammered from her lips as his mouth sucked and nibbled while his fingers slid in and out. A powerful tightening in her abdomen intensified until she broke apart, and it came so fast and so forcefully she may have cried out.

Lance's face appeared in front of hers, sly grin firmly in place. "You might've disturbed the neighbors," he said, playfully kissing her forehead.

"That would be a first," she admitted, her breathing still ragged. She'd never had a reason to be so loud before. She'd never been so overtaken that she lost control that way...

"I liked it." His eyebrows danced enticingly. "Let's do it again."

"Nope." Because it wasn't nearly as fun when she was the only one being so noisy. She squirmed out from underneath him, rising to her knees, which might never stop wobbling. "This belt is coming off now, cowboy." Her hands fumbled with the brass buckle until it released. Locking her eyes on his, she gave him a small smile while she ripped open the button fly on his jeans and shoved them down, taking the boxer briefs with them. "I can turn you on, too, you know." She climbed onto him, wrapping her legs around him and grinding her hips into his.

"I'm turned on just looking at you," he uttered, pulling her so tightly against his body that nothing stood between them. His eyes locked hers in an intimate stare and he brushed some hair away from her forehead. "Seriously, Jessa. I want to give you everything. I want to be the person who loves you."

She cupped his cheeks in her hands and drew his lips to hers. "That's enough." She didn't need him to be perfect. She wasn't looking for the perfect relationship. Only someone who was willing to try every day. That was enough.

Still kissing his mouth, she straddled him and adjusted her hips until she slid onto him, pausing there, feeling him quake beneath her. He filled her so perfectly, so deeply, that her body started that delicious throb again.

His fingers dug into her shoulders, urging her chest lower until he took her breast in his mouth and swirled his tongue around the nipple. Urgency pulsed inside of her, forcing her to move. She lifted her hips and thrust down onto him hard but smooth, again and again until his head fell back to the pillow. "Hell yes, Jessa," he panted. "God, I'm so fucking lost in you."

"I have some tricks, too," she murmured, hoping she could hold on long enough. Before it was too late, she squeezed her thighs together, rocking her hips against his, cradling him as tightly into her as she could.

A cross between a growl and a groan purred against

her skin. Lance's hands went to her backside, bringing her against him faster and harder until she was completely lost in the breathless anticipation of what was coming. She tightened her legs around him even more and his body bucked beneath hers, sending a final thrust so deep into her that she came apart again, shuddering and crying out and delighting in the sound of her name on his lips as he convulsed beneath her.

A happy exhaustion took her over as she draped her body over his. He held her, nestling her head into the crook of his arm while his lips sought hers. She kissed him back somewhat lazily, given the fact that her body was sedated.

"I'll love you the best I can, Jessa Mae Love," he whispered in her ear.

And she knew it was true.

* * *

He'd never woken up with a woman in his arms. Not once in his life. And damn, it seemed he'd been missing out. Jessa lay against him, her silky back against his chest, her soft hair spilling over his arm. He didn't want to move, didn't want to disturb her and end this moment. But he also wanted to see her face.

Slowly, he eased up his head to peek over her shoulder.

Her eyes were wide open in a look of fear.

The feeling of contentment snapped and he sat up straight. "What's wrong?" How long had she been awake? Why didn't she look as calm and content as he felt?

She shifted onto her back, her captivating eyes staring at the ceiling. "I just...things moved so fast last night. We may have gotten a little carried away."

Hell yes, they'd gotten carried away and he hoped they'd do it again. As soon as possible.

"Do you regret it?" she whispered. "Walking away from the celebration? I mean, has anyone ever done that? Will you be disqualified? What'll happen?"

"Everything'll be fine." Easing out a breath of relief, he lay back down, gathering her into his arms to coax out her concerns. He didn't care what happened. "The only regret I have is that I didn't discover you sooner." The rest of his life seemed like such a waste compared to this. Compared to being connected so deeply with someone as good and bright and beautiful as Jessa.

"What about Ilsa?" she asked, suddenly looking worried again.

"The pig?" He laughed. He didn't mean to, but Pork Chop was the last thing on his mind right now.

"Yes." She searched his face. "I know you're not that crazy about her, but I love her. She's such a little sweetheart, and if we ever end up...you know...together someday..." She seemed too embarrassed to finish.

He brought her hand to his lips, kissing her fingers. "Actually, she's growing on me."

"Really?" She didn't look convinced.

"If it weren't for Pork—I mean Ilsa—you might never have talked to me again," he said, stroking her arm. "That makes her a saint in my book."

Smiling happily, Jessa propped herself up, gazing down at him, beauty spilling from her bottomless brown eyes. "I don't want the money, you know."

"You deserve the money." And she needed it for the shelter. "I always keep my word."

Her head shook. "I won't take it. You might need it. For

your dad. For his treatments." A smile plumped her lips. "Besides, some of my old grad school friends are helping me create a social media campaign to build a donor base. I guilted them into doing it for free."

He doubted she had to guilt them. Everyone who knew Jessa seemed to love her. And she would always be one of those people who gave more than she took. "We'll see," he said, not willing to argue about it now. If she refused to take the money he'd promised her, he'd simply find another way to give it to her.

"What did it feel like to win?" she asked, trailing her fingertips over his biceps.

And God she was so sexy, her blond hair trailing over her shoulder, her eyes glistening as if he could tell her anything and it would stay safely locked away in the vault of her heart.

"It felt like the end." He hadn't considered that until he said it, but the truth was, it felt like a relief.

"You're okay with that?"

"I'm ready to start the next phase." A whole new life waited for him. One he'd never thought he'd have. "I don't want to be anywhere but here right now. With you," he murmured, running his fingers over her shoulders, down her breasts. He couldn't resist the temptation of touching her. "Doing what we did last night. As many times as you'll let me."

"Mmmm-hmmm," she hummed, her eyes closing as she shimmied her hand underneath the sheets. "I can see you're up to the task." Her hand clasped the solid length of him.

Yeah, there was that. He'd woken up hard. With her in his bed, that'd most likely be the norm. He slipped his hand under the sheets, too, letting it wander down her hip . . .

Turning, she wrapped her legs around his waist and

brought his body against hers. "No need to bother with all the foreplay."

"I like the foreplay," he said as he sank into her. The power of it stole his breath. He had plenty of ways to draw it out as long as possible, to tease her. "It'll be worth it—"

A knock pounded on the door. "Jessa!" a woman's voice screeched from the hallway.

She froze underneath him, her eyes wide.

"Are you in there?" came from another woman.

Lance lifted his head. "Who the hell—?"

She pushed him off her and started to scramble. "It's Cassidy. And Darla!"

"What're they doing here?" he demanded, trying to pull her back to him.

"They wanted to come to Vegas." She gave him a sheepish smile. "They're staying at the Bellagio. Sorry. I forgot to mention that."

He captured her in a hug, settling her back to the mattress. "It's okay. We don't have to answer the door."

"But I was supposed to meet them for breakfast this morning..." She snatched her phone off the bedside table. "Twenty-three missed calls."

Shit. "Will we ever be able to make love without being interrupted?" he wondered aloud.

"Jessa!" Now that was Naomi. He'd heard her worked up enough times to recognize it.

"What's got them all riled?" he whispered. Maybe if they were real quiet the crazies would go away and let him finish what he'd started.

"I should've called them," she whispered back. "They get worried." Squirming out of his grip, Jessa threw on a bathrobe and unclicked the deadbolt.

"Where've you been?" The door burst open and Cassidy, Naomi, and Darla all charged in, then halted, gaping at the two of them like they'd caught them doing jumping jacks naked.

"We thought you'd been kidnapped!" Naomi squealed.

"Vegas is a huge hub for human trafficking," Cassidy added knowingly.

"Then you wouldn't return our calls!" Darla finished as if the whole thing had been scripted.

"Nope. Not kidnapped." Jessa glanced at Lance, biting her lip as though trying not to laugh. "Sorry. I kind of lost track of time."

Despite the fact that there were three high-drama women staring at him naked in bed, Lance grinned back. They'd lost track of a lot of stuff. Shoes. Clothes...

"Obviously." Darla eyed Lance like he was a big juicy cut of meat.

He pulled the covers up to his chin.

Naomi stared at him, too, but it was more of a glare. And judging from the way her hands sat rigidly on her hips, she didn't like this at all. "So you two figured things out?" she asked suspiciously.

You could say that. He still had some work to do, but he'd do whatever it took. "I realized nothing I did seemed to matter without Jessa," he said, even though there would've been a more appropriate time for this conversation. Later. After he'd had his way with Jessa and was fully clothed.

Beaming a happy, teary smile, Jessa sat on the bed next to him and took his hand.

"Awww," Darla and Cassidy said collectively.

But Naomi simply narrowed her eyes protectively. "What does that mean?"

He turned his face to Jessa's and couldn't help but pull himself up to kiss her lightly on the lips. From the sound of the sniffles in the room, that was a good move. "It means I love her. It means I'm dealing with my shit so I can be with her."

"It means that you three need to get out of my room," Jessa added. "If you couldn't tell, we were kind of in the middle of something."

"Oh! Right! Sorry!" Darla clamped her hands onto Cassidy's and Naomi's shoulders, dragging them backward to the door. "You can give us all the details later."

Lance shot Jessa a look.

"Not *all* of them," she promised.

"OhmyGod, I'm so happy for you two!" Cassidy sighed before she disappeared.

Naomi wriggled free from Darla's grasp.

Lance half-expected another angry glare, seeing as how she didn't exactly think he was worthy of Jessa. But instead, she smiled. "I'm happy for you, too. Really."

"Thanks," Jessa called, shooing her away impatiently with a hand. "Okay. Bye, now. We'll talk later."

When the door *finally* slammed, he gathered Jessa into his arms and rolled her onto his body.

She laughed. "Wow, someone's got energy."

"The pressure's on," he said, showering her shoulders with hot little kisses. "I'd better give you some incredible details to tell your friends."

Epilogue

Not once in the history of Topaz Falls had the Cortez family ever hosted a party. Until Lance started dating Jessa, that was.

Jessa stood on the front porch of Lance's home, admiring how the ranch came to life in the spring. All the aspens had their baby green leaves back. Wildflowers were starting to dot the meadows. Though they'd still likely get a few more snowstorms, the land looked like it was finally emerging from winter, so bright and fresh and new. *Every*thing at the ranch felt new and exciting and hopeful. It didn't hurt that half the town had turned out for the first shindig of the season. The laughter and murmur of gossip seemed to give the place a new life.

All winter she'd drifted in and out of this house, laughing and living and loving with this family while she and Lance got to know each other. Lucas and Levi had both stayed on for the holiday months, helping cart Luis to doctor appointments and therapy treatments. They'd all spent the evenings out by the fire pit, surrounded by drifts of crisp white snow while they roasted marshmallows and laughed as the three brothers relived their childhood antics. When the fire burned low, they'd pour the wine and listen to Lucas play his guitar. That was her favorite, snuggling with Lance and his wandering hands underneath a blanket while the soft notes of strings floated around them.

These days if anyone dared tell her she wasn't a part of this family, she wouldn't believe them. The proof was all around her. The Cortez men had actually let her plan a party at their ranch, and even though they'd grumbled about it, they sure seemed to be having a great time.

She gazed out over the white party tents they'd rented, then over to the prefab stage, where a local bluegrass band played. Okay, so it was possible that she'd gone a bit overboard. She couldn't help herself. A while back, they'd received word that Lance was being inducted into the Pro Rodeo Hall of Fame, just like his father, and right away she'd started planning the celebration of the century.

It had turned out perfectly, if she did say so herself. "Come on, Ilsa," she said, tugging gently on her not-so-little piggy's leash. They ambled down the steps and into the crowds. She almost couldn't believe how many people had turned out to honor him. She smiled at each one as she passed, saying hello, even to Hank Green, though she didn't dare get too close to him.

On the outskirts of the tent, she spotted Evie Starlington standing alone, sipping a glass of Darla's special white sangria. Still being considered a newbie in town, the poor woman wouldn't know many people, so Jessa hurried toward her.

Ilsa grunted. She didn't like hurrying. Over the winter, the pig had fully recovered and was quite a bit wider than she'd been when Jessa had found her. Wider and happier, especially when there was a party and there were plenty of scraps on the ground. "Come on, girl," she prompted. "A little exercise will do you some good." Even with Ilsa's protests, they finally made it to the tent.

"Evie! I'm so happy you could make it. Come with me." She took her hand warmly before the woman could answer, and guided her to the tables she'd happened to see Luis sitting at earlier.

Sure enough, the man was still there, chatting with Deputy Dev Jenkins about the unusually warm weather. She hated to interrupt but this was important.

"Hey there, Luis," she said, pulling out the chair next to him. Ilsa plopped down at her feet and started munching on a stray carrot that had rolled off someone's plate.

Evie took a seat across the table. "You remember Evie, right?" Jessa said, presenting the woman grandly.

"Of course." He tipped his hat to her. "Nice to see you again."

"Evie is an artist," Jessa informed him. "You should see her stained-glass work."

"That so?" The man looked at her with interest. "How'd you get into that?"

It seemed her work here was done. "Oh!" Jessa jumped out of her chair. "I completely forgot. I need to check in with Darla. Make sure she has everything she needs."

Luis squinted at her with a small smile as though he knew exactly what she was doing. But that wouldn't stop her. She waved and tugged Ilsa away to give them some time alone. To keep up appearances, she headed straight for the catering tent, even though Darla clearly had everything under control.

"This is all amazing," Jessa said to her friend as she approached what had become the food and drink control command center.

Her friend straightened her apron proudly. "Everyone seems happy and properly drunk, which means I've done my job."

"Everyone definitely seems happy." Even Cassidy was out on the dance floor letting Levi twirl her around. "She must be *really* tipsy if she's dancing with him."

"I think she lost a bet," Darla answered drily. She looked toward the corral. "Naomi's the only one who doesn't seem exactly thrilled to be here."

Jessa peeked over to where Darla was staring. Both Naomi and Lucas were mingling with a group of their old high school friends. Lucas knelt on the ground and said something that made Gracie laugh, but Naomi simply turned and wandered away alone.

"Is he still leaving tomorrow?" Darla asked, fiddling with the chocolate fountain, then dipping in a plastic spoon.

"Yes." Jessa sighed. She'd done her best to convince him to stay. "He says he has to get back to the McGowen Ranch, that they've given him long enough." He also said he'd be back and forth as much as possible, but who knew how often they'd see him.

Her friend licked the melted chocolate off her spoon and dipped in another one, handing it to Jessa. "Naomi sure avoided him the last couple of months, huh?"

"Avoided him? She pretended he didn't exist." She taste-tested the sample Darla had given her. Their friend had taken Gracie to Florida for a month to visit her parents. When she *had* been at the ranch, she'd kept herself busy with running her daughter to camps and volunteering at the school. The only time Naomi and Lucas seemed to politely chat was when they all had dinner together, but the woman always begged out early. Before they built a fire. Before Lucas played his guitar. As far as Jessa knew, they hadn't spent one second alone all winter.

A wave of panic washed over her, making her feel the heat of the evening more intensely. "I wish I could make him stay."

"Guess it's not up to us," Darla said, turning back to the chocolate fountain to refill the plates of strawberries.

"I know, it's just—"

An arm slid around her waist. "I need you," her sexy cowboy breathed into her ear. "Alone."

Those words were all it took to restart her heart. She swore it beat only for him these days.

"You can have me whenever and wherever you want me." She turned to him, and he pulled her into a scandalous hug.

Behind them, Darla made gagging noises. "Not near the food, you two!" she scolded. "And don't get any ideas about the melted chocolate."

"I already *have* ideas," Lance said, eyeing the fountain.

"He does," Jessa agreed. "He has *a lot* of good ideas."

"Okay. That's it." Her friend shooed them away. "Get out. Out of my tent."

"Fine." Jessa held out Ilsa's leash. "But would you mind holding on to her for a while? And don't give her any chocolate. I have her on a diet."

"Of course. I'd love to babysit your pig while you go off and get some." Darla rolled her eyes, but she smiled as she took the leash.

Laughing, Lance swept Jessa up the hill toward the corral. "I have a surprise for you," he murmured, drawing her close to his side.

"Ohhhh. A surprise for me? But this is supposed to be *your* special day."

Just outside the old barn, he stopped and faced her. "The surprise is for you. But I'm hoping it'll benefit me, too."

"Huh?" That didn't make any sense...

Wearing a mysterious grin, he urged her to the barn's entrance, which as far as she knew, stored their old tractor parts and animal feed.

As they stepped inside, he covered her eyes with his hand. She saw nothing but darkness, but that was okay because she'd blindly follow this man anywhere.

After a couple of steps he stopped, pulling his hand away.

Bright lights lit up the space, and this was no barn. It had been transformed into something else. Something sophisticated and clean. The walls had been dry-walled and were painted a lovely soft green. Ceramic tiles covered the once dusty floor. A long counter and desk sat at the front of the room and kennels lined the back.

Jessa gaped at him.

"Welcome to the new Helping Paws Animal Shelter," he said, spreading out his arms in grand presentation. "And don't worry. We'll get the outside fixed up as nice as the inside."

"What?" She gasped, turning herself in a slow circle, trying to take it in, but the blinding tears made it difficult. He'd thought of everything. *Everything.* From the brand-new computer sitting on the desk to the framed animal posters dressing up the walls. There were kennels and examining tables and supplies...

A happy sob squeaked out.

She turned back to him, ready to throw herself at him in a hug, but he'd taken a knee. And he was holding up a small black velvet box.

"Yes!" she blurted before he'd even said anything. Her whole body trembled with a yes. He didn't have to ask.

His exaggerated expression of shock teased her. "I haven't said anything yet."

"Oh. Right." She did her best to rein in her excitement so she didn't steal this moment from him. Knowing Lance, he'd planned out exactly what he wanted to say down to the syllable.

He took her hand in his. "You taught me how to love, Jessa," he began. "Showed me it was possible."

Tears snuck into her eyes. The man definitely knew how to write a speech...

"I know we haven't been together long," he went on. "But I've never been as sure of anything as I am of us. You brought me to life and now I want a life with you. Always. I hate it when you go home. I want the ranch to be our home now. Together. You and me and a whole bunch of kids."

The words warmed her through. Kids. A family...

"Marry me, beautiful," he uttered, tears filling his eyes, too. "Please marry me." He opened the box, revealing the most delicate ring she'd ever seen. It was a solitaire diamond, inset into a wide band, rose gold to match the necklace her father had given her. The last gift he'd given her before he passed away.

"I can answer now?" she whispered, crying softly.

He grinned and rolled his eyes up to the ceiling as though thinking about it. "Sure," he said. "I'm done."

"In that case..." She tugged him to his feet. "I can't wait to marry you. *Obviously*."

He slipped the ring onto her finger and pulled her close. "I'll make you the happiest woman in the world. I promise you." A wicked gleam lit his eyes. "And not just in bed, either."

"You already make me happy. In bed and in everything else." She embraced him as tightly as she could, holding happiness in her arms. "Oh my God, I'm getting married!" she sang, letting it soak into the deepest parts of her. She gazed up into Lance's tender eyes. Tom Hanks and Meg Ryan had nothing on them.

"I can't believe you did all of this." She looked around the room again, at all of the details, the months and months of work he'd kept secret from her. "It's perfect. The most beautiful thing I've ever seen."

"I'm gonna give you everything." He leaned down to kiss her, and she savored it, the feeling of belonging to someone again. She'd always miss her father, but for the first time since he'd passed away, her heart felt whole.

He danced her to the window and together they peered out. "Look at that. It's all ours. Yours and mine." His palms cradled her stomach. "And someday it'll belong to all of our little buckaroos, too."

She stared out at the snowcapped mountains that sheltered the houses all lined up in a row farther down the hill. "I love this place." It would be their place—a haven for their family and friends, a place where they gathered and celebrated and built a life together. All of them.

Lance drew closer behind her, wrapping her up in his arms. "Let's go out and share the news," he murmured against her neck. "Then we'll kick everyone outta here so I can try to get you pregnant."

Eyeing him seductively, she slipped out of his embrace,

backed to the main door, and clicked the lock into place. "We don't have to kick anyone out. No one'll miss us."

"In that case, come here." Her fiancé made his way to her, those breathtaking bluish eyes focused and intent. He slid his hands down her body, and she loved those big manly hands, loved how they made her feel so petite. "I love you," she whispered, kissing him again and again.

"I love you, too," he said, easing his arms around her. "And I love that you're going to be my wife."

His wife! A burst of happiness could've carried her straight to the clouds.

She'd finally found it, what her heart had so desperately craved. Love. And it was braver and bigger and deeper than she ever knew it could be.

Fall in Love with Forever Romance

NEW YORK TIMES BESTSELLING AUTHOR
CAROLYN
BROWN

LUCKIEST
COWBOY
of ALL

2-in-1
SPECIAL!
Includes a Bonus
Novel by Sara
Richardson

LUCKIEST COWBOY OF ALL
By Carolyn Brown

This special 2-in-1 edition features an all-new book from *USA Today*
bestseller Carolyn Brown plus *Hometown Cowboy* by Sara Richardson!
Carlene Varner's homecoming isn't going to plan. Within days of her
arrival, her house burns down and she and her daughter have no choice
but to move in with Jace Dawson, the father Tilly has never known.
Jace is so not ready to be a dad…Yet the more time he spends with
Carlene and little Tilly, the harder it is to imagine life without them…

ZERO HOUR
By Megan Erickson

The Fast and the Furious meets *Mr. Robot* in *USA Today* bestselling author Megan Erickson's thrilling new romantic suspense series! Hacker extraordinaire Roarke Brennan *will* avenge his brother's murder. His first move: put together a team of the best coders he knows. Only Wren Lee wants in, too. The girl Roarke once knew is all grown-up with a sexy confidence and a dark past...and, when years of longing and chemistry collide, they discover that revenge may be a dish best served blazing hot.

MORE TO LOVE
By Alison Bliss

Max Hager isn't exactly who he says he is. Pretending to be a health inspector is (mostly) an innocent mistake. A mistake made way worse by Max's immediate, electrifying attraction to a sexy, redheaded chef. Throw in a whole lot of lust, and things in Jessa's little kitchen are about to really start heating up. But can Max find a way to come clean with Jessa before his little deception turns into a big, beautiful recipe for disaster?

Fall in Love with Forever Romance

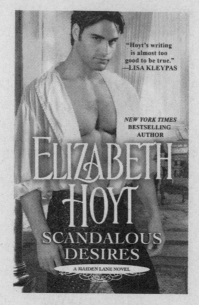

"Hoyt's writing is almost too good to be true."
—LISA KLEYPAS

NEW YORK TIMES BESTSELLING AUTHOR

ELIZABETH HOYT

SCANDALOUS DESIRES

A MAIDEN LANE NOVEL

SCANDALOUS DESIRES
By Elizabeth Hoyt

Rediscover the Maiden Lane Series by *New York Times* bestselling author Elizabeth Hoyt in this beautiful reissue with an all-new cover! River pirate "Charming" Mickey O'Connor gets anything he wants—with one exception. Silence Hollingbrook has finally found peace when Mickey comes storming back into her life with an offer she can't refuse. But when Mickey's past comes back to torment him, the two must face mounting danger, and both will have to surrender to something even more terrifying...true love.